HEART OF STONE TRILOGY

ALSO BY K.M. SCOTT

Ever After (A Heart of Stone Novella)
A Heart of Stone Christmas

The Club X Series
Temptation (Club X #1)
Surrender (Club X #2)
Possession (Club X #3)

COMING SOON FROM K.M. SCOTT

The SILK Serial Volumes 1-4
Satisfaction (Club X #4)
Hold On My Heart (A Heart of Stone Spinoff)

HEART OF STONE TRILOGY

K.M. SCOTT

Published in the United States

First Edition May 2014

Cover Design: Cover Me, Darling

ISBN-13: 9781941594094
ISBN-10: 1941594093

CRASH INTO ME

BOOK ONE

Chapter One

"You're going to be late!" Jordan yelled from the kitchen in her usual bellow.

She didn't have to remind me. As I stood checking out my look in the mirror that hung on the back of my closet door, I cringed at the idea that people were going to actually see me in my outfit in just minutes. I looked more like a waitress than a junior assistant to an art gallery owner. A short black skirt and white button down blouse? I might as well be serving pasta down the street at Mama Leone's. Or serving drinks at some gentleman's club. Why my boss thought this was appropriate for an art gallery was beyond me.

Smoothing my light brown hair that fell to just below my shoulders, I leaned in close to the mirror and saw that the tawny eye shadow and the darkest black mascara did their best to make my blue eyes pop. I stroked a final coat of plum lip gloss over my lips and put on my best supermodel face.

Too bad everything below my neck ruined all my hard work.

I made my way down the hallway, stopping by the kitchen to give my roommate a look at my getup. She'd seen it before, but some things never got old.

"And here she is, Miss America," I sang.

Jordan put her glass down on the counter and brought her hands up to her face to cover her smile. A pretty blonde with knockout green eyes, she was my best friend and the only person who knew just how much I hated the outfit. "Oh, honey. At least you make that look good. Good legs make everything look better, and you have great legs."

"I think I've heard that," I joked. At least Jordan helped make me hate this outfit a little less. That is until I got the first sneer from some overly made up woman dripping with expensive jewelry looking down her plastic surgery perfect nose at me. Then I'd hate it again.

"I'm off to work. What are you doing while I'm moving up in the art world?"

"Justin and I are catching a movie."

"So you're doing Justin," I teased. She'd begun dating him a while back, but recently they'd gotten much closer, much to her delight. Jordan saw him as a possible "Mr. Right" and loved that he wanted to move toward more commitment.

"Don't hate," she said with a smile. "You'll be late, and then that nasty boss of yours will be all over you."

"Enjoy. I'm off to pay my dues again," I joked only slightly as I headed out the door.

I walked toward the subway with Jordan's words rattling around in my head, oblivious to the throngs of people heading out for the night. "Don't hate." In truth, I didn't hate the idea that she had found someone. I actually liked Justin. He wasn't an ass like a lot of guys, and he was pretty tolerant of having a third wheel when Jordan dragged me along with them to save me from a Friday night in. And he was just her type—tall, dark, and lanky. While I wasn't as convinced as she was that he was "The One," simply because I wasn't sure that even existed, I liked that she was happy.

It gave me hope that as she was always claiming good things did, in fact, happen to good people.

The crowd of New York art devotees far less knowledgeable about art than parties milled about the Anderson Gallery, champagne glasses in hand and noses in the air as they feigned appreciation for the work of a new artist that odds were would likely be a has-been by this time next year. The artwork wasn't bad, as far as modern art went, but I didn't have the time to stand around feeling unimpressed. As the lowest rung on the gallery's ladder, I was responsible for ensuring that the patrons were happy, full of alcohol and hors d'oeuvres, and convinced that the artist's work was the "next big thing," as Sheila Anderson, my boss and owner of the gallery that bore her name, had made quite clear in the pre-show meeting just hours before.

Her hand-picked outfit for me fit oddly, which was exactly the purpose. The black skirt was far too short and felt more like a big belt in the chilly, air conditioned room. God, my ass was almost hanging out! And the white, button-down shirt one size too small? My biggest fear that night was that a button would pop, fly from my chest, and take someone's eye out. But since my job was to be a "hostess," as Sheila liked to term my employment as her personal slave, this was what I had to wear. The only thing that made it even bearable was that she'd hired two other women to work that night, so at least I wasn't alone in my outfit of shame.

Four years of school and a degree in art history and I was handing out cocktail weenies. But it was a job that paid the bills. Well, barely paid the bills. No matter. I had bigger plans for my life than this, and I knew I needed to pay my dues before the good things showed up.

On nights like this, though, it just felt like I was paying more than anything else.

A tall, blonde standing near the floor to ceiling window at the front of the gallery lifted her glass to alert me she needed a refill, and away I went scurrying to provide her with the much needed champagne. Unlike most of the other gallery patrons, she was at least pleasant and gave me a nod of thanks. Hopefully, Sheila saw that.

In truth, this wasn't such a bad job. I told myself that all the time, and sometimes I even believed it. The best part about it was that I got to be around the art. That made all the awful jobs I was assigned tolerable. When all the people were gone and it was just me, my broom, and the artwork, I could honestly say I was happy. I'd stand in front of a sculpture from some unknown artist and let my eyes drift over the smooth lines and curves of the piece to imagine what may have been in the artist's heart as he or she lovingly molded their masterpiece. The Anderson Gallery didn't have work from the big names like Monet or Rodin, but it had art and that let me convince myself that years of studying hadn't been for nothing.

A crowd of people gathered near one of the paintings hung on the far wall. It was the best piece in the show, so it wasn't surprising, but from the sound of their voices, it wasn't the painting they were interested in. I moved toward them, curious for a distraction from standing around with trays all night. The group was mostly women, each one more beautiful than the next, and I suddenly felt self-conscious craning my neck to see what they were so intrigued by, as if I didn't belong. A few blondes, brunettes, and a redhead who all looked like supermodels and were dressed in names I only knew from magazines circled around someone, laughing and chattering about things I couldn't understand. Then one woman moved aside and I saw him.

He was stunning, even more gorgeous than the women that surrounded him. Over six feet tall with short dark hair, he wore a dark grey suit and black shirt that hung as if they were made especially for him, accentuating every well-built inch of his body. I edged myself closer, drawn to him, and saw his eyes. Deep chocolate brown, they looked as if they had seen all the things I hadn't in this world. He was wealth, opulence, and excess.

A beautiful brunette hung on his arm, an appropriate accessory for such a man, like fourteen caret gold cufflinks or a stainless steel Rolex. As I stood there gawking at him, I heard one of the women say his name.

Tristan.

In that moment, I wanted more than anything for the whole world to fade away until it was just me and him. I'd heard of love at first sight before and never believed in it, but as I watched him take up all the empty space in the room, I was in love.

No, not love. Lust.

He glanced over at me, and my cheeks flushed with heat. His gaze fixed on mine, brown eyes staring at me as if we knew each other intimately. As if he knew the deepest, darkest parts of me. My brain told me to look away, to break the connection, but the rest of my body rebelled. I wanted to feel those eyes on every part of me.

"Nina, what are you doing? I saw at least three patrons with empty glasses as I crossed the room. Chop, chop!" Sheila barked in my ear, tearing me out of my fantasy.

My boss marched away, and I watched as Tristan and his women moved on to another painting. Everything was as it should be with everyone in their correct place. Him with a group of gorgeous women and me with my tray of cocktail weenies. A few minutes later, I watched him leave, never even knowing his last name or what his voice sounded like.

As the show wound down and the sated art lovers made their way to other fashionable locations in SoHo, I began my post-show duties. Sheila had a look of pure happiness on her gaunt face as she said goodbye to her other help for the night, which could mean that she was high or pleased with how the show had gone. As she was coming my way, I'd know in a minute which it was.

Sheila was a touchy-feely person, so even before she got to me her hand was reaching out for my arm. Raking her long, bony fingers down my shirt sleeve, she purred, "Nina, except for that brief slip with the champagne, I think the show went off wonderfully." Turning to lock the gallery's front door, she waved her hand around the room. "You can leave a lot of this mess for tomorrow, or if you prefer to clean up tonight, you can have Sunday off. Your choice. I know you'll get it done. You're dependable."

She didn't bother to wait for my response before she grabbed her black cashmere wrap and traipsed out the back door. I was nothing if not reliable, so she didn't have to worry about whether I'd clean or not. By the time she returned on Monday, her gallery would be spotless.

As I swept up the last cocktail napkin and put the last champagne glass in the holder for the caterer, I thought about how my boss saw me. Dependable. God, that was an awful way to be seen! Garbage bags were dependable. Wrenches were considered dependable. A good car was dependable.

The only thing worse would be if she'd called me sturdy.

With that cheery thought in mind, I turned off the lights, tied up the garbage bag that shared my dependable nature, and headed toward the back door to drop it off and go home for the night. One last job and I was Brooklyn bound.

I threw the trash in the Dumpster behind the building and locked the gallery's back door. Lost in thought, I heard someone behind me say, "Nice show, huh?"

The sound of his deep voice nearly made me jump out of my skin, and I spun around to see him. The man from earlier. Tristan. He stood leaning against a black sports car, arms folded across his chest, still dressed in that grey suit and looking even more incredible than when I'd first seen him. As I stared at him, drinking in how gorgeous he looked, my brain switched from pure fear back to normal to ask the obvious question.

Why is he here?

"Yeah, it was great. The artist is quite talented," I lied.

"It was shit and you know it. Nice outfit, though."

Instantly, I was once again acutely aware of how silly I looked in my waitress getup. His remark stung, and I snapped back, "It's called working. Now unless I can help you with something, I have to go. Have a good night."

I checked the lock on the gallery door and turned to walk away. I hadn't made it two steps before he quietly said, "I didn't mean anything bad by that. You look nice."

Was that sincerity in his voice? I didn't know. I just knew I didn't want to feel embarrassed by my work anymore that night.

Turning around, I tried to get a feel for this guy, but he just stood there staring at me like I was the most important person in the world at that moment. "Thanks."

"What do you say we go for a ride?"

"A ride?" I was confused, but I probably should have been afraid. I was standing in a back alley with a strange man, no matter how incredibly sexy he was, and there wasn't anyone nearby. How the hell was it possible that in a city of eight million Tristan and I were the only two there at that moment?

"A ride," he repeated in a slow, silky voice that made my stomach flip. "At least I can give you a ride home."

"You don't even know my name."

He stepped away from the car and in two strides was in front of me just inches away. Looking down at me, he smiled. "You're Nina Edwards, you work at this gallery, and unless I'm mistaken, you don't live anywhere near here."

As much as I wished he wasn't right, he was. Sunset Park, Brooklyn was miles away. However, that didn't mean I should forget everything

I'd been taught all my life, even if he was the hottest man I'd ever spoken to. And even if this was one of my fantasies come true.

"I don't even know your name," I lied again.

A slow smile spread across his perfect mouth. "My apologies. I'm Tristan Stone and I'd like it if you'd let me take you home."

He extended his hand and I shook it, noticing how powerful it felt as it enveloped mine. His very expensive suit coat sleeve rode up just enough to show his Rolex, and I smiled at the fact that I'd called it correctly earlier. He probably had gold cufflinks just under those sleeves too. But where was the brunette?

As my mind raced with these ideas, I realized he knew my name. "How do you know my name? We've never met."

Placing his hand on my lower back, he guided me to the passenger side of his car. His touch was light, yet it was thrilling, making my head spin. As he opened the door, he stepped aside and let me sit down before he leaned in close and said, "I asked."

I watched him walk in front of the car while I enjoyed the lingering scent of his delicious cologne, and as he passed through the headlights, I noticed now that he wasn't flirting with me that he seemed to be frowning. He must have sensed I was looking at him because when he stopped and turned to face me, the smile reappeared, almost on cue.

He sat down behind the wheel and revved the engine. "Ready?"

I was nowhere near ready, but there was no turning back now. The sharp click of the car's doors locking signaled it was time to go, and with a deep breath, I pressed a nervous smile onto my lips and nodded. I just hoped this wasn't going to end up being the biggest mistake of my life.

Tristan flew through the streets of SoHo, weaving through traffic at sixty miles an hour as I covered my eyes and silently prayed for my life. Maybe this wasn't a good idea.

"Are you going to keep your eyes closed the whole time?"

I opened my fingers and peeked through just in time to see us swerve around a cab and quickly closed them again. "Yes. The whole time, which will probably be about another minute at this speed."

"C'mon, open them up. You're safe. I won't let anything happen."

Slowly, I lowered my hands to my lap and worked hard not to dig my fingernails into my legs. I wasn't usually this uncool, but then again, I wasn't usually racing through the city at top speeds in a car that likely cost more than Jordan and I combined made in a year.

Tristan's Jaguar rode like it was gliding on air. The body hugging black leather seat may have been more comfortable than any piece of furniture I'd ever sat in. A soothing blue glow emanated from the dash, which was full of knobs and buttons around a center touchscreen. I may not ever have cared much about cars, but even I knew this was top shelf.

"Nice car. Do you always drive it like you plan to wreck it?"

As he swerved to miss a car stopped in front of us, he said, "Drive it like you stole it, right?"

Looking around the inside of the car, I wondered out loud, "You didn't steal it, did you?"

Tristan let out a deep laugh that sounded like it came all the way from his toes. "You're funny, Nina. Nothing like you were back there during the show."

"Back there I was working. My boss pays me to be serious." I stopped and chuckled. "Well, actually, she pays me to be like her personal slave."

"I knew there was something more to you than the pretty girl who served the drinks and disgusting little hot dogs."

God, he was sexy! There was something about the way words slid from his mouth when he spoke that made me want to beg him to stop the car so I could press my lips to his.

I turned to look at him and his strong jaw caught my attention. Even from the side, he was gorgeous. Relaxed for the first time since the car had begun moving, I joked, "I'll have you know those cocktail weenies are a big hit."

He turned his head and smiled a sexy grin. "I bet they are."

While my gaze slid down over his torso and I noticed how perfectly his shirt lay on his body, out of the corner of my eye I noticed a road sign as we sped past it. I-95? "Uh, I think you're going the wrong way. The Cross Bronx Expressway doesn't go anywhere near my house."

He shifted into third gear and hit the gas, pushing me back against the seat. "Guess you should have been paying attention instead of hiding behind your hands."

Fear raced through my body. Was he serious? "Are you kidnapping me? I mean, this feels a little bit like kidnapping since you obviously aren't taking me home."

That I sounded ridiculous and a man like him probably didn't have to kidnap women didn't occur to me in my fear. Women likely pleaded with him to take them anywhere.

"I don't think they'd call this kidnapping," he teased. "Maybe if you were tied up or at least had a gag in your mouth."

"Please take me home, Tristan. We're nowhere near my house and you're scaring me."

My hands began to get sweaty at the real fear that I had made a terrible mistake. I didn't know this man, and no matter how infatuated I'd been with him just hours before, he had total control of me at that moment, something very frightening.

Still speeding toward God knows where, he took his hands off the steering wheel and held them up in front of him. "If you want to go home, take the wheel and turn the car around."

I frantically grabbed the wheel and the car jerked to the right, racing off to the side of the road. I panicked, turned it to the left, overcompensating, and screamed in terror as we began to spin out. Then everything before my eyes went black.

The car rolled to a stop on the shoulder and I heard him say my name in a soft voice. "Nina. Nina, it's okay. We're okay."

I looked around at the car and him and saw he was telling the truth. We hadn't crashed and I was still alive. Adrenaline coursed through my body, and my hands began to shake uncontrollably. Suddenly, I was overcome with emotion and lashed out at him as tears began to roll down my cheeks. "You're crazy! You're fucking crazy! You could have killed me!"

My crying startled him, and for just a moment he didn't possess that cool exterior he'd worn since the first moment I'd seen him. His brows knitted, as if he were in pain, and he leaned in toward me to press his forehead to mine. He cradled my face in his hands, instantly exciting me. Closing my eyes to mask my discomfort, I heard him say, "We only know how precious life is when he come close to death, Nina."

He sat back in his seat, and I turned to look at him, my emotions all a jumble. "Why did you want me to come with you tonight? Why did you come find me? I'm not like those women who were around you at the show. Why me?"

"Those women don't interest me. If they did, I could have any one of dozens right now."

Oddly, that made me jealous. I didn't even know this man, but the idea of him with anyone else bothered me.

Fighting back my insecurities, I said, "Maybe they like it when you nearly kill them, but I don't. Most ordinary women like me don't."

He stared straight ahead into the night and started the car again. "Don't underestimate yourself, Nina. You're anything but ordinary."

In truth, I didn't think I was ordinary, but it was nice to hear from someone other than yourself sometimes. My cheeks warmed at his compliment, making me happy the inside of the car was dim. He didn't need to think I was as infatuated with him as I already was.

Full of fake bravado, I said, "You have no idea what I am. And where the hell are we going?"

"I want to show you something. This is going to take a few, so why don't you enlighten me as to what you are," he said with a smile that made an ache form in the pit of my stomach.

"Isn't it a little presumptuous of you to think I have no plans? It is a Saturday night."

He didn't seem bothered by the idea that I had plans or even had a boyfriend. I had neither, but he couldn't know that.

Turning his head to face me, he looked at me with those soulful brown eyes. "Do you have plans?" he asked with an innocence that made me smile.

I didn't want to admit that I, a young, available, attractive New York woman, had no plans whatsoever on a Saturday night. I mean,

I could have had plans. There were men interested in me. Just not anyone I was interested in being interested in me.

But he didn't need to know that.

"I did have things planned, if you need to know," I lied with enough attitude to hopefully hide my fib.

He chuckled and pushed down on the gas, again throwing me back in my leather seat. He never asked what my plans were and obviously didn't care. Talk about ego! As if I had nothing better to do than speed up the Taconic.

We traveled in silence with the ghostly outline of the trees and the white line on the side of the highway rushing by making me dizzy. The mood felt awkward, but I didn't know what to say. Here I was racing toward some unknown place with a man I barely knew in a car I'd only seen in ads in magazines and movies.

I only hoped I would be alive at the end of whatever this was.

As if he read my mind, he said, "Nina, relax. I don't plan to kill you and leave bits and pieces of you along the side of the road."

Terror raced through my body. I turned in my seat to face him, tugging the seatbelt away from my neck. "Who says that kind of thing? Jesus! Now I'm worried you're actually going to do that. And how do you know what I'm thinking?"

Once again, he laughed at what I said. "Tell me about what you do when you aren't hosting art shows."

Slumping back in my seat, I tried to calm myself. "I guess that's supposed to make me relax?"

He turned to look at me for a moment and then turned back to face the road. "No. It's supposed to tell me what you do when you're not hosting art shows."

"I like to read, hang out with my friends, and paint."

And there it was. The truth of my life in one short sentence. I sounded like some lame teenage girl who really spent her Saturday nights crocheting booties for her cat.

"What do you paint?"

"Whatever I'm feeling."

"Are you a good artist?"

"That's usually in the eye of the beholder."

He arched one dark eyebrow and looked over at me. "Then I'll have to judge your work for myself sometime."

Why was he talking like we were a couple or moving toward being that? We'd spent all of an hour together and now he was making plans to see my artwork. Yet he hadn't made any effort to even hold my hand or kiss me.

What was with this guy?

"Are we almost there?" I asked, uneasy about this entire thing.

"Almost."

As if my question had been a cue, he took the next exit and in minutes we were in the middle of pitch black nowhere. If I was worried before, now I was almost terrified. Scenes from every horror movie I'd ever seen flashed through my mind, all leading to the same ending. Me murdered and in pieces along an isolated country road and my sister devastated because I had forgotten the one thing she'd always told me not to do—get into cars with strangers. Ever since her house was broken into and ransacked, she'd been nearly paranoid about strangers, which I'd thought was a bit of an overreaction, but now I was thinking she had the right idea.

"Can I ask a question and have you answer with more than one word or one sentence that really says nothing?"

He stopped the car at a stop sign and turned to face me with a devastatingly sexy grin on his face. "Yes."

I couldn't help roll my eyes. He was either the most insufferable person I'd ever met or one of the funniest. I couldn't decide which. "Where are we going and can you promise me you're not going to do anything awful to me?"

"That's two questions, Nina."

The car began to roll again, and I let out a heavy sigh, hoping his dry humor was an indication that I wasn't going to be killed anytime soon. "Okay, can I ask you two questions and get straight answers?"

"Of course. You can ask whatever you want and I'll answer."

"I'd like straight answers."

His mouth hitched up at the corners into a sly smile. "As straight as you want."

"Where are we going?"

"To see a house I'm planning to buy."

"Really?"

He turned his head to look at me. "Do you want that to count as your second question?"

And after being scared shitless and almost killed, then confused and finally frustrated by his vague answers, I had to laugh. "No."

"Then what's your second question?"

"Are you going to do something awful to me out here in the middle of nowhere?"

Without a word, he stopped the car and put it into park. Then he leaned over, nearly touching my cheek with his lips, and pointed out my window. "That's the house, and I have no plans to do anything you wouldn't like or even love. What do you think of it?"

He was so close and smelled so delicious that I couldn't think clearly. I turned my head slightly and his lips brushed my skin, sending a jolt of electricity straight to between my legs. Pressing my thighs together, I turned toward the window and pretended to look up at the house on the hill.

"It's nice."

"It's twelve million dollars."

Holy shit! In my mind, I counted the number of zeroes on a check for twelve million dollars. Then I imagined what I could buy for twelve million dollars. And even all that probably wouldn't fill the house I was looking at.

His breath drifted over my neck, and I leaned back slightly, wanting so much for him to kiss me or touch me with his hand. He did neither, though, even as he remained there so close.

In my ear, he whispered in a voice that hit me somewhere deep inside, "See? Nothing bad."

Just when I was sure he would do something, he sat back in his seat and began driving back toward the city. My mind and senses were reeling. Never before had I wanted to feel the touch of a man's lips on me so badly, but he never made a move. The experience left my emotions raw, and I feared saying anything more as I was sure I would embarrass myself, so I sat silently as he drove toward Sunset Park, speaking only when he asked me where I lived.

When he finally pulled the car up to in front of my building, my feelings were all a mishmash. I felt happy about the fact that he hadn't killed me, but it seemed that he never had any plans to do that or anything else, including anything sexual. I couldn't be sure, but it seemed like he just wanted company. I guess I had been that, but my infatuation had secretly made me want so much more.

"Thank you for coming to see the house, Nina."

"Okay. Thank you for not killing me out in the middle of nowhere, I guess," I said with a smile, sad our time together was over, likely forever.

"I'll watch you get in."

"Thanks."

I waited a long moment just in case he wanted to lean in and kiss me, but he simply smiled and stared into my eyes, making me feel intensely insecure. Finally, I blurted out, "Goodbye," and got out.

Crossing in front of the car, I forced myself not to look inside at him. Whatever this had been, it was over, and I needed to get over it. I felt his stare on my back as I stepped onto the sidewalk, but I told myself to not turn around.

Then from behind me I heard the car window lower and he said my name. Turning around, I was struck by how lonely he looked in that car all by himself. I waved and smiled, and he said quietly, "Nina, be careful getting in cars with strange men. You could get hurt, and I wouldn't want anything bad to happen to you."

He drove off, leaving me more confused than before. Frustrated and baffled by my time with Tristan Stone, I hurried into my building.

CHAPTER TWO

Sundays were always the best day of the week, as far as I was concerned. My father had never been a very religious man after my mother died, so my sister and I had never done the Sunday church thing. For us, the last day of the weekend meant sleeping in and then a late breakfast of pancakes and waffles smothered in butter and maple syrup and lovingly made by my father.

I'd continued this tradition as often as possible, even while I was in college, and now that I was out on my own, I loved Sundays even more. Granted, there were no pancakes or waffles usually, but there was sleeping in.

Beautiful, luxurious sleeping in.

Jordan thankfully shared my love of Sunday mornings, so our apartment was like a tomb often until early afternoon. The former best friend of my college roommate, she had been the opposite of Alyssa, who acted like weekends were her own personal version of boot camp. Jordan had joined with me to refuse to rise and shine at the crack of dawn one snowy February Sunday in freshman year, and we'd been friends ever since. We liked to say that it had been in our rebellion against the dawn and Alyssa that we'd become friends.

She hadn't been home when I returned from my bizarre time with Tristan, so I was eager to tell her about it all and get her opinion. But even crazy guy stories didn't warrant waking up before noon on a Sunday.

I rolled over and saw on my alarm clock that it was just about that time, so it was fair game to head down the hall and hope she was awake. Dressed in my usual shorts and a t-shirt I liked to sleep in, I padded barefoot toward her room only to find it empty. She had been getting more serious with Justin lately, so I assumed she'd spent the night at his place. Disappointed, I shuffled back to my room and flopped down on my bed once again.

The discussion of Tristan Stone and his sexiness would have to wait.

That didn't mean he was leaving my mind anytime soon. Even if we hadn't spent any time together, he'd still be rambling around the corners of my brain. I was infatuated, so the memory of his gorgeous face would stick with me for a while.

Clicking on the television, I stared at the show on the screen while I daydreamed about the events of the previous night. Why had he come to find me if all he wanted was someone to drive upstate with? He had many friends, I imagined, so why seek out a stranger who was so unlike him?

Just admitting to myself that I wasn't of his social level made me wince. I hadn't grown up around money, but my father had always made sure my sister and I were taken care of, so money was never a real issue. We weren't wealthy, but we weren't poor. The idea that someone's income would make them better than someone else was foreign to me, but in my time living in New York, it had become very clear that my feelings on money weren't everyone's.

Tristan Stone was very wealthy and far above my place in the world, even if I still counted myself as the middle class person I'd always been before living on my own. This made his actions the night before even less understandable.

I scrubbed my hands over my face in frustration. I wanted him to like me as much as I liked him. I wanted him to be lying in bed thinking of me. Even better would be him lying in bed alone thinking of me. But just thinking of me would be nice.

Who was I kidding? He was likely in bed with the brunette or the group of women he'd attended the show with. A stab of jealousy pinched at me as I imagined what he looked like out of that grey suit and naked in bed…with other women.

Get over it, Nina. It was some kind of game he was playing and it's over.

I silently repeated that a few times trying to convince myself to forget him and the time we'd spent together. I knew I should.

I just couldn't.

He filled my mind, and I loved it. Inhaling deeply, I still could smell his cologne, either as a wonderful memory or because of some fragment remaining inside my olfactory system. Masculine and powerful, it would forever remind me of him. I closed my eyes to imagine his face. The deep brown eyes that spoke volumes even when he didn't. The perfectly shaped mouth and the lips that had lightly brushed my cheek for just a moment, sending my body into overdrive. The masculine jaw of a man who looked like a man, not a boy.

What did he look like when he was just lying around on an early Sunday afternoon? Did he wear boxers or boxer briefs? Or did he sleep naked? I wanted to know what he looked like under his clothes. He had stood at least half a foot taller than I, probably more if I wasn't in those ridiculous three-inch heels Sheila made me wear to shows. He had appeared imposing, but I couldn't say if he was a big man or lean.

All I knew is that I wanted to know.

I let my mind drift back to the house he'd shown me. I fantasized about how he'd look standing in the doorway of one of its enormous rooms dressed in a suit much like the one he'd worn on our ride. In my mind's eye, he looked perfect. He wore a midnight blue shirt and matching tie that he fussed with. I saw myself there with him, straightening that tie as I stood in front of him admiring how truly stunning he was.

The sound of the front door slamming yanked me out of my daydream, and I heard Jordan yell, "Nina! Even I don't think you should be sleeping this late on this gorgeous day!"

Before I could get out of bed, she was standing in my doorway, all smiles. "Good morning, sleepyhead. What are you still doing in bed?"

Her happiness was catching, and I smiled. "Just hanging out. Where were you? Justin's?"

Her smile grew even bigger. "Yes. He and I have moved to me staying over, so you get to have the apartment all to yourself on nights like last night. Tell me you took advantage of that and didn't just come home after slaving away for Shitty Sheila and her crappy art show."

I didn't say anything, but my cheeks grew hot and my blush signaled that I had something to tell her. "Well, there was something. It's probably nothing, but..."

Jordan squealed. "Ooooh! I'm going to get a drink and you need to meet me in the living room to tell me everything. Get up and start talking!"

I loved that she was willing to listen to my silly ramblings about what would likely amount to nothing. Some friends only wanted someone to listen to them but weren't there for you when you had some juicy details, or in this case, wishful juicy details. But that wasn't Jordan.

By the time I made it out to the living room, she was planted in her favorite comfy chair with a glass of diet soda in front of her. "I'm ready, so hit me with the details."

I took a seat across from her and folded my legs under me. For a second, embarrassment rushed through my body. I was twenty-four years old and no stranger to dating. It's not like I was a virgin either. Suddenly, I felt silly about making a big deal out of my time with Tristan.

"Well?" Jordan asked impatiently.

"I met someone, sort of," I said, struggling to describe exactly what had happened.

"Nina, you never like the guys we meet. He must be something pretty damn good."

I screwed my face into a grimace. "I like some of them," I protested half-heartedly, knowing she was probably more right than wrong.

"Uh-huh. Name one."

I couldn't name one. They were all perfectly nice, I guess, but none of them really got me going. It never took long for me to fall out of like with them.

"That's not the point."

"No. The point is that you met someone you actually like. Tell me everything!"

"His name is Tristan. Tristan Stone. He…"

Just as I began to tell my story, Jordan's green eyes grew wide and she leaped out of her chair, nearly knocking over her glass. Marching over to the table by the window, she rifled through the half dozen newspapers she bought every day on her way to work downtown. When she turned around, she held up one in front of her. "You mean him?"

I craned my neck to look at a picture of a couple at some gala event. She walked a few steps closer, and I saw the man in the couple was Tristan. The woman on his arm didn't seem to be any of the women I'd seen surrounding him at the gallery the night before, though.

"What day is this from?"

Searching for the date, Jordan said, "Tuesday. Now tell me what happened with someone so famous that he ends up on Page Six regularly."

Stunned, I sat back in my seat, unsure what to tell her. I didn't know him like that. "What do you know about him?"

"Nina, you're the one who met him. I've only read about him in the gossip page."

God, I felt stupid! He wasn't just some good looking guy with a great car. He was someone famous. Now I was sure last night hadn't meant anything to him.

"I don't know anything about him like that. I saw him at the show and then he showed up at the gallery later on."

Jordan sat down and shook her head. "What do you mean he showed up later on? To buy something? I bet Sheila loved that."

"No, he was waiting outside the gallery in the alley way after I locked up."

"What do you mean? Had you spoken to him during the show?"

I shook my head. "No. He was there with a bevy of hot women and never even spoke to me."

"So what happened? You're killing me here! I swear you tell stories like my students."

To be compared to a group of fourth grade Catholic school kids wasn't helping, no matter how exclusive Jordan's school was. I wrinkled my nose and smirked at her. "Thanks."

"Neen! Give up the details!"

"He was waiting behind the gallery when I was leaving and asked me to go for a ride with him in his Jaguar. He offered to take me home, but instead we ended up driving upstate to see a house he said he was thinking of buying."

"Shut up!" she squealed. "Is he as stunning in person as he is in the papers?"

I reached out my hand to take the newspaper from her. "I don't know. Let me see." She handed me Page Six and there he was, just as gorgeous as he was last night. I secretly wanted to keep this picture so I'd always have him near me.

"So? Is he?"

Tearing my gaze from the newspaper, I nodded. "Yeah. Maybe even more, although I didn't see him dressed in a tux. He wore only a suit to the show."

"Did you sleep with him, Nina?"

"No!"

Jordan knitted her eyebrows. "Stop acting like it's 1952. Sleeping with a hot guy is permissible these days."

"I know all about feminism, Jordan. I just don't choose to jump into bed with every guy I meet."

Pointing to the newspaper I'd stuffed down in between the sofa cushions next to me, she said, "You see the woman in that picture with him? That's the fifth or sixth different one I've seen him with this month. The rumors are that he sleeps with a different woman each night."

I raised my eyebrows more in despair than disgust. "Really? You believe everything you read in the papers?"

"No, but you know how celebrities are. And if the pictures are any indication, he likes tall brunettes who look more like stick figures than humans."

I looked down at my less impressive five foot seven frame and what I liked to call a "healthy" body. I was in pretty good shape, but I was definitely not a stick figure.

"I'm sorry, Nina. I didn't mean to say he wouldn't like someone like you. He'd be damn lucky if he did."

Jordan's sympathetic smile made me feel better and worse at the same time. The reality was that if he was a man who slept with a different woman every night, no matter what type of women he preferred, he hadn't wanted to sleep with me. He hadn't even wanted to kiss me.

"It's okay. I've never had a problem not being a stick figure," I joked.

"So, if you didn't sleep with him, what did you do with Tristan Stone?"

I wasn't sure how to explain it, so I chose to go with the boring truth. "We hung out. Nothing more."

"Nothing?" she asked, her voice sing-song.

"Nothing."

Jordan looked confused. I understood her confusion. I still had no idea why he'd come to find me and then never even really touched me.

"Any plans to see him again?"

I tried to tamp down my disappointment. I didn't want pity now. "Not really. It wasn't much of anything, Jordan, so there's no reason to believe he'd want to hang out again."

"This sounds like a mystery to me. Why would he come find you and then not want to see you again? What was the conversation like while you were heading upstate?"

"Monosyllabic."

"You or him?"

"Him. I spent most of my time worried he was going to kill me and leave me on the side of the road."

Jordan sat back in her seat and chuckled. "Don't be silly, Nina. Wealthy people don't kill people. They hire people to do that."

Rolling my eyes, I mumbled, "Funny. I'll keep that in mind if I ever see anyone who might look like his butler or driver near here."

"Seriously, though. What do you plan to do about him? You obviously like him."

Even though Jordan knew me as well as anyone in the world, I didn't want to admit what I planned to do. It's not like I could coincidentally show up where he spent his time. We lived in two different worlds, and I likely couldn't afford the cover charge to get into that life. What I could do was click around online and find out about him.

Some might call that stalking. She'd likely call it stalking. I liked to think of it as research for my fantasies.

"There's nothing to do about him. We'll stay in our separate areas of the world and that's that."

"Oh, that's so tragic and romantic! It's like that Julie Roberts movie where she's like Cinderella. What's that movie?"

"Holy shit, Jordan! Pretty Woman? I'm not some poor prostitute in fuck-me boots!"

She waved my protests off and walked toward the kitchen with her glass to refill her drink. "You know what I mean. Two people from two different worlds. It's so romantic."

"Like Romeo and Juliet," I yelled toward her.

She peeked her head out of the kitchen doorway. "Now who's being scary? Romeo and Juliet? You do remember from high school that they both die at the end, right?"

Nodding, I chuckled. "Yeah. This is no more like Pretty Woman than Romeo and Juliet. Whatever it was, it isn't anymore."

I ran my fingers over Page Six in the seat next to me. Before Jordan returned, I quickly pulled the newspaper out and stuffed the folded page into my shorts. "I need to get going. Can't spend all Sunday lying around."

Jordan smiled another sympathetic smile as I walked past her. "Okay. Hey, Justin and I are going to be hanging out at The Last Drop Tuesday night. Want to come?"

My spidey senses told me this was a setup. A dating setup in the making. "You and Justin and your third wheel? Or will there be a fourth?"

Her look turned sheepish. "I think you might like him, Nina. Alex is pretty good looking, has a good job, and he doesn't seem like a loser."

"A ringing endorsement if I ever heard one," I joked and continued walking. "I'll think about it."

"At least it'll be a night out. We'll have a few drinks, shoot some pool, and maybe have a few laughs," she yelled as I closed my bedroom door behind me.

I sat down on my bed and opened my laptop, content to spend my afternoon looking up information on Tristan. While my computer turned on, I examined the picture of him with his girl du jour at some gala. His face was expressionless and he seemed more like a statue of himself than the real thing. The woman, however, looked like she was thrilled to be there with him, clinging to his arm and smiling a huge, toothy grin for the camera.

Raising the picture to look at it more closely, I studied it for any sign of the person who'd smiled and laughed as he'd driven to the middle of nowhere the night before. He didn't seem to exist in this person.

Setting the paper aside, I typed my first words into the search bar. "Tristan Stone." I figured I might as well start with the obvious and go from there. It didn't take long to see that Jordan had been right. The pictures I saw showed him with a different woman every time, but he was the same cold figure in each one. The soulful brown eyes that had looked at me were nowhere to be found. Neither was the genuine smile that he'd so freely given, even if it had seemed like he was laughing at me more times than not.

Once I'd looked at enough pictures of him to truly make me feel like a stalker, I began reading and found out the real details on him. He'd inherited his father's luxury hotels along with other businesses that included an internet startup company and some company that had to do with real estate.

I sat transfixed on the words as they stared back at me from the screen. Tristan, the man who'd come to find me just for company, was a millionaire many times over. Maybe even a billionaire. The car was his. The Rolex was his. He was the kind of man women dreamed of, and he'd wanted to spend time with me.

And now I would never see him again.

Closing my laptop, I flopped back on the bed and groaned. I needed to stop thinking about Tristan right now. He was something unattainable, and I needed to accept that. It didn't matter that he had looked happier in the short time with me than he ever looked with all those women at all those fancy parties. None of that meant anything because of the simple fact that even if he'd been happy, he'd made no effort to get my number, kiss me goodnight, or even find out much about me.

I covered my eyes with my arm and tried to push all thoughts of him out of my mind. If I kept this up, I'd end up becoming obsessed over a situation that was doomed never to be. He was where he belonged and I was where I belonged.

Life was as it should be, no matter how disappointing that fact was.

Chapter Three

Tuesday night came, and I chose to accept Jordan's offer to hang out with her, Justin, and Alex at the bar. Monday's work at the gallery had made it difficult to stop thinking about Tristan, but I had done my best to talk myself out of my infatuation. In truth, I probably hadn't really succeeded, but the human mind is an interesting mechanism and very susceptible to delusion. Regardless of whether I was lying to myself or not, I headed out to The Last Drop and promised myself I'd keep an open mind about Alex.

The Last Drop was the one place in Sunset Park that could be picked up and dropped back in my home town in Pennsylvania. It was just a bar, what was traditionally called a "hole-in-the-wall" back home, with a couple pool tables, some dart boards, and a back room with booths and another pool table. Jordan and I had found it soon after moving into our place, and Tuesday night had become our night out each week. It wasn't much, but it was fun.

She'd told me everything she knew about Alex as we waited for him and Justin, and when I say everything, I mean everything. She must have compiled some kind of dossier on him because she knew his height, weight, where he went to school, what he did for a living, how much money he earned, in addition to dozens of other details I probably could have done without. I mean, should a woman really know about a potential boyfriend's favorite sexual position—cowgirl— before she even meets the guy?

As I hadn't heard anything to necessarily turn me off, I figured staying wouldn't do any harm. Worst came to worst, at least I'd occupy my mind with some friends, a few beers, and a few games of pool while I crossed another male off my list of potential boyfriends.

"Nina, I hope you like him," Jordan said as she leaned across the table to talk over the blaring of the music from the jukebox. "We could all go out if you do."

I nodded and smiled my agreement. By the time the song had ended, Justin and Alex had arrived and I got my first good look at the man Jordan had chosen for me. Tall, with dirty blond hair and blue eyes, he was certainly attractive. My suspicious mind immediately went to the question of why he'd be single, but I told myself to give this a chance. I was single and there wasn't anything profoundly wrong with me.

"Hi, Nina. I'm Alex. Nice to meet you."

Good masculine voice, nice looks, seemed intelligent. Maybe Jordan hadn't been wrong.

A few beers and two games of pool later, I had impressed him with the few things that made me stand out amongst the millions of women in New York—my down-to-earth way and ability to shoot a mean game of pool. Why this was so intriguing to men had always baffled me, but I'd learned over the years to make it an asset. I wasn't supermodel gorgeous and I wasn't heiress rich, but I could wield a stick like nobody's business and oddly enough, it was one of the few games men didn't seem to mind losing at.

Crouching down to collect the balls for another game, I looked up to see Jordan's eyes grow as wide as saucers as she looked my way. I hadn't had too much to drink yet, so I figured she wasn't giving me the "Holy Fuck!" look because of something I'd said. Standing up, I gathered all the balls into the wooden rack and positioned the top ball on the break spot. I looked up to see if Alex was ready and saw Jordan still with the wide eyes and pointing slyly in my direction, urging me to look.

I turned around and there was Tristan standing behind me near the entrance of the bar and sticking out like a sore thumb in a suit and tie. Tristan looked around as if he'd never seen the inside of a bar, his expression a mix of curiosity and focus. I watched as he scanned the bar area and then turned his attention toward the back room where I stood stunned to see him.

His gaze met my surprised stare and he smiled that same smile he'd given me nights before as I'd tried to get him to give me a straight answer. Jordan said something behind me about pool or something, but the sound of my heartbeat pounding in my ears drowned much of it out. I stood as if my feet were nailed to the ground and unable to move as I watched him walk toward me in a way that made him look like he was gliding across the floor.

By the time he reached me, I had forgotten there were even other people in the room. He was that mesmerizing.

"Nina."

True to form, he said little but his eyes spoke volumes. As I struggled to form a coherent sentence in my mind, I looked into those gorgeous brown eyes of his and saw a flicker of apprehension. Everything else about him appeared calm and confident, but his eyes hinted at some kind of fear.

Was he afraid I wouldn't talk to him? Why?

"Tristan. What are you doing here?"

"I'm here to see you."

I couldn't help but chuckle. "I figured that. I can't imagine you're acquainted with anyone else in this bar."

His gaze never wavered from me, and he asked quietly, "Can we talk somewhere?"

He wanted to talk more. Okay. Smiling, I found the ability to move my legs again and guided him toward one of the wooden booths on the far side of the room. We sat down across from one another, and I realized I hadn't even said anything to Jordan or Alex. No matter. She'd understand, and I'd apologize to her later.

"How did you know I'd be here?"

He settled his gaze on me. "Do you come here a lot?"

"Every Tuesday. But that doesn't answer the question of how you knew I'd be here."

"There's a billiards tournament in Las Vegas every year that I sometimes play in. You should come with me next time. It's late summer. We could make a week of it."

With every word he spoke, I grew more confused. Why was he talking like we were a couple? Now we were taking trips together? Shouldn't we at least have dinner first? Or maybe sex? God, just the thought of it made me squeeze my thighs together in sweet agony.

"Tristan, what do you want?"

"You."

My stomach dropped and a rush of excitement hit me between my legs. He wanted me.

"You want me for…?"

"You were an art major in college. You'd know a lot about what pieces I should buy, wouldn't you?"

My excitement fizzled back to confusion. "Yes, I majored in art history. I minored in painting. What do you want me for that has to do with that?"

"Why don't you come for a walk with me?" he asked, more as a command than a question as he stood from the booth.

My curiosity was piqued, even if my ego was dinged. I would have likely said yes to anything he asked, so I walked over to where Jordan was standing and quickly whispered, "I'll be back. He wants to go for a walk."

Pulling me aside, she leaned in and asked, "Is everything okay? What does he want?"

"I don't know. I'm thinking maybe he wants someone to help him pick out paintings, maybe for his office or something. Maybe for that house he's buying. I don't know. I have my phone on me, so if anything goes wrong, I'll call."

Jordan hugged me and in my ear whispered, "Be careful. Remember, wealthy people hire people to do their work. I doubt he's here for a decorator."

"I will. And don't worry. I'll tell you all the details when I get home," I teased.

Squeezing my arm as I moved away from her, she said, "You better!"

Jordan and I were breaking the best friend code's first rule: Never let your friend leave with a strange man. He wasn't a strange man, per se, but she couldn't have stopped me even if she thought he was. With each step I took toward Tristan, an excitement began building in me. I hoped he wanted me like I wanted him, but if all he wanted was someone to help him pick out art, maybe he'd pay me enough so I could begin to build up my savings. Whatever it was, at least I'd be spending time doing something with art.

The night air was unseasonably chilly for May, so my little sundress and sweater weren't going to do much to keep me warm. I hadn't planned on walking very far that night, so my shoes weren't really right for what he wanted to do either.

Tristan remained his quiet self as we made our way one block and then two away from the bar. Unable to contain my curiosity, I asked, "What did you want to talk about?"

Glancing at me, he said, "You."

"That's the second time tonight you've answered that way. What about me?"

"What made you decide to live in this section of Brooklyn after college?"

I stopped dead and stared at the back of him as he continued walking. After a few steps more, he noticed I wasn't next to him any longer and stopped to turn around. "Nina?"

"How do you know so much about me, Tristan?"

"I asked."

"Asked who?"

He closed the space between us and stood no more than six inches from me. That gentle smile spread across his lips again. "People who'd know. I like to know about the people I surround myself with."

"What are you talking about? Do I have to ask you to do the straight answer thing again?"

He cocked one eyebrow and then finally said, "You make me smile, Nina. I can't say that about most people."

"That's nice. It's not a straight answer, though."

His hand clasped mine, sending a jolt of electricity straight up my arm. "Let's keep walking so you don't get cold. Your place is near here, isn't it?"

I felt like I was dealing with a madman. It was like we were having two different conversations, neither of which was very satisfying. And now he was holding my hand and appeared to be directing me back to my apartment—a place he'd only been once. I didn't know whether to be flattered he had made the effort to find out about me and remembered where I lived or concerned that he was some kind of scary stalker.

The fact that I had done a little of my own stalking of him didn't escape me either. We made one interesting couple.

"Tristan, please just tell me what you want. I know you're probably used to women who love this mysterious Bruce Wayne-Batman behavior, but I'm just an ordinary soul who likes straight answers."

"Why do you always think you're so ordinary?"

I yanked my hand from his and shook my head. "No more! You show up out of nowhere in the alley behind the gallery, force me to go for a ride, and now you show up at a bar I hang out at. Are you some kind of scary stalker guy or do I owe your company for some kind of bill and you're here to collect? Either way, you're driving me crazy!"

I hadn't meant to sound so emotional, but there it was. The truth. I barely knew this person and already he drove me nuts.

Instead of looking surprised like I thought he would, he just smiled. Not that it wasn't a gorgeous smile, but something about it just sent me over the edge. I stalked away toward home, frustrated enough not to care whether he liked it or not.

I heard his footsteps behind me as he walked quickly to catch up with me. It felt good knowing he wanted to talk to me, even if all he said sounded like damn riddles!

"Nina, I'm sorry. Stop and let me talk for a minute."

Spinning around, I was nearly knocked over as he took a step right into me. His much larger and muscular body crashed into mine, and I went tumbling backwards. Thankfully, he caught me before I landed on my ass.

There I was, in his strong arms, staring up into those dark eyes as he gazed down at me. "You want to talk? All you say are one syllable words and sentences that make no sense. I'd love it if you'd talk, but you don't."

"I'm not usually much of a talker, but you seem to want to hear what I have to say, so let's talk."

He released me and I stood up, smoothing my dress over my thighs. "About what?" I didn't mean to sound so exasperated, but the man had a way of bringing that out in me.

"Art."

More one syllable words. If it wasn't no or yes, it was art with this guy. "Art? What about it?"

"Why do you work at that gallery if you went to school for art history?"

Talking about work wasn't talking about art. Deflated, my shoulders sagged under the disappointment that he seemed once again interested in hearing about my job as personal gopher to Sheila Anderson.

"Because even though I possess more knowledge about the art world in my little pinky finger than my boss does in her entire body, I also only possess a bachelor's degree in art history. To be a curator or someone who deals with exhibitions, you have to have experience in the gallery world, which is what my slave labor job is."

"It's too bad you don't know anyone who owns their own art gallery."

Blowing the hair off my face, I said in frustration, "Yes, it is."

We stood there at that odd point in the conversation looking at each other like neither one of us had understood the other one's language. To be honest, I was beginning to think he was from some other planet by the way he behaved, but since he hadn't grown tentacles or extra heads and was getting more gorgeous by the minute, I still liked him, as bizarre as that seemed to someone like me who prided herself on good judgment.

"You could work at one of mine."

And with those seven words my spirits were buoyed once again.

"You have more than one art gallery?" I asked in stunned amazement, jumping over the obvious first question about him having even one art gallery.

"In some of my hotels. The one here in the city might work, wouldn't it?"

He was sounding decidedly clear, which made me think I must have slipped into some dream dimension or lost my mind. "You have an art gallery in one of your hotels in New York and you want me to work at it? As what?"

If he said anything that even remotely sounded like the job I had at the Anderson Gallery, I was going to punch him right in that beautiful mouth.

"I have a curator, but would assistant curator work?"

I understood the words he was saying, but my brain seemed to have short circuited because I was unable to form an answer. Would assistant curator work? Hell, yes!

He was all smiles, but I wasn't so sure. Putting my hand up, I said, "Wait. This all sounds too good to be true. What hotels do you own?"

With a sense of pride, he answered, "Richmont. I assume you've heard of them."

"And you want to offer me a job as an assistant curator at the Richmont in Manhattan?"

"Yes."

"And what do I have to do for this job?"

"Whatever an assistant curator does."

I looked up into those beautiful eyes and wondered if he was just playing dumb or if it was possible he was really that obtuse. "You know what I mean. What do I have to do to get that job?"

Then I waited for it. There was always a catch. As my father always said, "If it sounds too good to be true, it probably is." Tristan's response certainly wasn't what I expected, though.

"You'll have to pass one test. After that, the job is yours."

"What kind of test?" I asked, wary of where he was going with this. I didn't mind taking tests, but something told me he had something else in mind than a paper and pencil exam.

"I want you to tell me what picture I should put up on the wall in my home."

"The one all the way upstate?" I asked, praying that I didn't have to take that drive again tonight. The buzz from the two beers I'd drunk earlier had worn off, and the thought of speeding to the middle of nowhere again didn't thrill me, even if it was with Tristan Stone.

"No. Come with me," he answered as he took my hand and led me to his car parked at the end of the block.

I went as he ordered and let him take me to the Richmont downtown. I'd seen the hotel from the street once or twice, but seeing it from the owner's point of view was an entirely different experience. A valet parked the car as we were shown into a private elevator lined with mirrors that traveled exclusively to the penthouse. I stared straight ahead at the mirror on the elevator door, my gaze drifting down over the figure standing next to me. I noticed he seemed bigger than I'd thought he'd been the other night, with the top of my head reaching only his broad shoulders. His face was placid, and even now as he stood silently staring at the mirror in front of us, he was beautiful with chiseled features and powerful body. But what made Tristan stunning were those deep, soulful eyes. Warm brown eyes the shade of melted milk chocolate I could have spent the rest of time getting lost in. I looked for any sign that the man from Page Six was there beside me, but the Tristan I got to see was still with me. Quiet, but gentle and drop dead sexy.

The elevator doors opened up to a penthouse unlike anything I'd ever seen. Tristan's home was something right out of a design magazine. I walked around with my mouth agape at the opulence of his place. He seemed almost disinterested in his own home, though, except for the one bare spot on the wall in his bedroom. That seemed of the utmost importance to him.

Pointing at it, he asked, "What do you think should go there?"

I stared at the wall as my mind quickly went as empty as the blank space. "Is this the test?"

"Yes."

"I don't know. I'd have to spend some time examining the rest of the decor. You don't want just anything hanging there. If that were the case, the poker playing dogs picture would work."

He chuckled but wasn't going to be put off. "All you must do is answer the question correctly and the assistant curator job is yours, Nina."

He stood so close that my mind went from blank to muddled. All I could think of was the luxurious feel of his suit as his arm brushed the back of my hand and the sexy smell of his cologne filling my nose. I turned away from looking at the spot to see him staring down at me. I could think of nothing, but I blurted out, "A Cooper," knowing in my heart that wasn't what he wanted to hear.

His expression showed his disapproval—or was it disappointment?—and he turned away, shaking his head. "No."

I had no way of disagreeing, but even now as I knew I'd failed the test and lost out on the dream job of my life, I still couldn't think of an appropriate choice. Dejected, I looked up at him and quietly said, "If you can just take me home, please."

He pulled his phone from his suit coat pocket and spoke into it in a flat tone. "I need a car downstairs to take a young lady to Sunset Park."

Whatever the person on the other end said I had no idea, but in seconds the elevator door opened and Tristan ushered me toward the exit. He said nothing, and I got into the elevator, sad that I'd failed the test and lost my chance but also sad that I'd let him down. It was strange, but although I barely knew him, I was uncomfortable with him being unhappy.

The doors began to close, taking him away, and I pushed back the tears welling up in my eyes. Just before he disappeared from sight, I whispered, "I'm sorry."

And then he was gone.

If I could have called in sick from work on Wednesday, I would have. Just going to the gallery reminded me of him, and even more, it reminded me of how I'd utterly failed at my one chance to really do something in the art world. By the time the day was over, I was committed to spending the night in bed with ice cream and a sad movie so I'd feel justified in crying my eyes out.

Jordan had end of year conferences, so the apartment was all mine to mope around to my heart's content. It was strange, but I felt empty inside after what had happened with Tristan. I knew it should have been over the chance he'd given me, but it was because I'd lost him. But had he ever really been mine to lose? I had no idea. I just knew that as I walked around the apartment aimlessly I was missing him.

By seven o'clock, I had devoured a pint of mint chocolate chip ice cream and was ready for the DVD player to deliver enough sad love stories that I'd cry the memory of Tristan Stone right out of my heart. I needed true love separated by horrible circumstances and life changing romance.

A knock at the door just before the first movie began slowed my mourning, and as I padded barefoot down the hallway to the front door, I hoped it wasn't Alex, who'd called three times since the night before. I didn't have the answer no matter what the question was he wanted to ask.

I opened the door, and instead of Alex, there stood Tristan. My heart leaped in my chest at the sight of him. Dressed impeccably in a suit, as always, he was a sight for sore eyes. I knew I shouldn't be thrilled to see him, but I was.

"Come for a ride with me. I want to talk."

And with that everything that had happened between us came rushing back. All the confusion. All the frustration. And now, all the anger at how he'd toyed with me.

"Go back to your penthouse, Tristan. Find someone else to do your charity work on."

I threw every bit of power I had into slamming the door in his face, but he jammed his foot in the opening. It pushed back against my hands as he tried to stick his face in through the crack to speak.

"I just want us to talk. What can that hurt?"

"Go away. Your brand of talking just confuses me and then I feel bad after," I said as I pushed on the door to no avail.

"Please."

And there it was. The magic word. Please. God, my father's good parenting had come back to haunt me yet again. Something in the word please had a way of making any argument I had melt away.

I stopped pushing on the door and opened it up to see him staring at me with those brown eyes of his. As usual, they told me more than his words had, and now they were pleading with me to go with him one more time.

Even if I wanted to say no, which I didn't, I couldn't have. Whatever power he had over me I just couldn't fight it.

Hanging my head in resignation, I welcomed him in. "Give me a minute to get dressed."

As I walked to my room, I thought about how much I wished I could say no. It was no good that even before a man kissed me that he had this much control over my heart and mind. I couldn't imagine what he'd be able to do if we ever slept together.

He drove out of the city, and I knew where we were going. Back to the middle of nowhere, but this time my fear wasn't that he would kill me and leave me in pieces on the side of the road. No, this time I was afraid he'd already taken the most important piece of me and there was nothing I could do about it.

CHAPTER FOUR

We pulled up to the house he showed me the other night, and he turned off the car. He hadn't said ten words the entire way there, but now he turned to face me and said with a smile, "I didn't want things to end like they did last night."

His voice sounded sincere and made me want to make things better. "I'm sorry I didn't know the right answer."

"That's not important. The test was unfair. I'm the one who should be apologizing."

"Why did you bring me here, Tristan?"

"Let's go in."

As we walked toward the front door, he took my hand in his. His fingers enveloped mine and my hand seemed to disappear into his beneath his jacket. I felt small next to him now.

And then I looked up and what stood in front of me took my breath away. Massive white marble columns held up a front portico a full story high and flanked by the tallest evergreen trees I'd ever seen. A huge center section of the house broke off into a wing on the left and right sides, each the size of a full home itself. A second floor the same size as the main floor sat below a blue-grey color roof forty feet above the ground.

"Wow…your house is…" I stammered out as I stopped walking and craned my neck to take it all in.

Tristan smiled at me and my amazement. "I'm glad you like it. It's got twenty acres too. Come see the inside."

Just like his penthouse, the country house looked like something straight out of a magazine. A massive wrought iron and glass light fixture hung from the twenty foot ceiling in the wide entryway, and the beige marble floor gleamed beneath my feet. The walls were painted a cream color and looked like old world plaster. The entire room was simply stunning, and it was just the foyer!

Room after room unfolded before my eyes, each one unique and gorgeous. By the time he'd finished showing me the main area of the house, I'd seen four fireplaces already. Each room came with an explanation about how he planned to change it or what he wanted to keep, but I couldn't help but wonder what one person would do with all this space. I imagined him wandering through the rooms lonely and looking for someone to talk to.

He led me back to the main entryway where the home branched off into two wings. "Is anyone else here or will you live here alone?" Just asking the question made me sad.

He didn't seem bothered by it, though. "I have a man who handles things, a gardener who moved into the carriage house already, and a few other people who will be working for me here."

"Oh, so you won't be living alone?"

He didn't answer and pointed toward the left side of the house. "I want to show you that wing. I think you'll like it."

"Tristan, how many bedrooms does this house have?"

"Six."

Six bedrooms for one person? "Does that include rooms for the people who work for you?"

Shaking his head, he smiled. "No. They don't count."

He continued to talk about where he was taking me, and I wondered if he meant the bedrooms didn't count in the total or the people who worked for him didn't. After a hallway that left the main part of the house, we entered what looked like an apartment. Well, not an apartment like mine but one that someone like him would live in.

"Do you like it?"

I looked around at the bedroom, which was no less than four times the size of mine and decorated impeccably, and couldn't help but laugh. "I can't imagine anyone not liking it."

His voice turned serious. "I don't care if anyone else likes it. I want to know if you like it, Nina."

I was startled by his tone. What did it matter if I liked a room in his house? "It's very nice."

This was the thing that confused me about Tristan. He never seemed to act the way other people would. He'd taken me for a drive twice, and neither time we'd done much talking, as if sitting next to someone and not saying anything was normal. Now he'd showed me his house and seemed oddly concerned that I like it. Why?

I wanted to ask, but I doubted I'd get a straight answer anyway. That definitely wasn't his way.

He led me back to see the indoor pool, and I fell in love. Even if we only stayed whatever we were at that moment, I hoped I'd get to swim in that pool. It had been designed to look like an enormous Roman bath with a sixty foot pool and sauna. The back wall of the room was an exquisite mosaic tile design that portrayed Neptune riding in his undersea chariot led by a team of sea horses. Artistically, the varied shades of blue and white in the intricate mosaic were stunning. The other three walls of the pool area were filled with floor to ceiling windows along with four sets of double doors that I was sure flooded the area with gorgeous sunlight in the afternoons.

I looked down at the imported Italian tile on the pool's deck and then back up at him. "It's gorgeous, Tristan. Your house is beautiful."

The smile I received in return for my compliment was warm and sweet. "I'm glad you like it. Are you hungry?"

"No."

"Why don't we have a drink then?"

That was an idea I liked. Spending time around him made me nervous and uneasy, so hopefully a drink would calm my nerves. "I'd love a drink. Thanks."

He flashed another warm smile and took my hand to lead me to a large sitting room. Compared to the open and airy feeling of the pool area, this room had a darker vibe. Dark cherry wood moldings and ten foot tall built-in bookcases gave the room a heavier feel. As he poured us drinks, I looked around and noticed examples of fine artwork lined the walls. He had impeccable taste. Art hundreds of years old sat beside contemporary pieces perfectly matched.

So why the test at the penthouse the night before?

This was who Tristan Stone was. Contradictions on top of unanswered questions. And the more I knew about him, the more I wanted to know the answers.

He extended his hand to offer me a seat on the extra deep sofa and handed me my drink. I took a sip from my glass and felt the warmth from the liquor course through my body. Surprised by its almost instant effect, I looked at him and murmured, "Oh. What is this?"

"Scotch."

For the first time since I'd met him in that alley way, his body relaxed as he sat next to me. Maybe it was the double Lagavulin he had in his hand or maybe it was that we were finally getting to know one another. Whatever it was, he wore relaxed well.

By the time my glass was half empty, my drink had definitely relaxed me, and my curiosity got the better of me, along with my inhibitions. I looked at him sitting there in his white dress shirt and dark suit and without thinking, I asked, "Why are you always in a suit and tie?"

His eyes grew slightly wider for just a moment, and then he was that relaxed man again. "You don't like me like this?" he asked in a teasing tone.

"Oh no, I didn't mean that," I answered, afraid that I'd offended him. "I like you very much like that."

Now his smile wasn't that warm grin I'd seen just a few minutes earlier but a mischievous, almost devilish one. He took a sip of his drink and slid his tongue across his lower lip, making it glisten.

"Maybe you're right. It wouldn't hurt for me not to wear a tie," he said as he began to unknot it. Slipping it from around his neck, he let it slide out of his hand onto the table in front of us. "And no tie means I don't need the top button done either."

He opened his shirt and with just one button undone he looked like an entirely different man. His dress shirt sat crisply and the collar framed his strong neck perfectly. I had to fight the urge to lean over and press my lips to the part that had been covered by the shirt and tie and slide my tongue up over his Adam's Apple. What would his skin taste like, I wondered? Would it taste like the soap he used or the cologne he wore or would it have a hint of salt as a man's skin often did?

Nervous and needing a distraction, I leaned forward to take the deep blue silk tie off the table. Running it through my fingers, I asked, "How do you tie a tie? I never learned."

He placed his glass on the table and slid the tie from my hands. "Come. Sit between my legs and I'll show you."

I stood and turned to see him spread his legs wider to accommodate me. Nervous but suddenly desperate to be close to him, I sat down in front of him but on the edge of the couch, unsure of myself.

"Move back."

I did as he commanded and moved back until my shoulders touched his chest. Sitting ramrod straight, I waited for him to begin, anticipating how wonderful it would feel as his hands slid around my neck.

He leaned forward and moved my hair over to one shoulder. "The first thing is to make sure all of this is out of the way."

My neck was exposed, and as he spoke, his warm breath danced across my skin. I closed my eyes and willed my body to relax, hoping he couldn't hear my heart nearly pounding through my chest.

His voice was low and husky in my ear. "Lean back against me, Nina."

I slowly let myself fall back against him, feeling his hard chest against my back. His head was next to mine, his mouth positioned next to my ear so I felt every breath he took in and let out.

"The first thing to know is that there's only one kind of knot you need to master. The Windsor knot."

"Oh. I thought there were others," my voice squeaked out.

"Maybe for boys, but men tie the Windsor knot."

The way he said the word 'men' made my stomach flutter. In truth, I'd probably dated more boys than men, but Tristan Stone was definitely a man.

His arms came over my shoulders until he rested his hands near my collarbone, each one holding an end of the tie. "Now pay attention because I'm going to want you to show me you can do it after this," he whispered in my ear.

Unfortunately, the sensual timbre of his voice combined with the feel of his hands so close to my breasts made paying attention impossible. I thought he said something about the wide end and the narrow end, and he may have said something about looping, but I was lost in the experience and couldn't have cared less about the actual tying of the tie.

"Finally, tighten and you're done."

I opened my eyes and looked down to see his hands so big resting on the tie below a perfectly done Windsor knot, his large stainless steel watch heavy against me. My lower abdomen tightened at the feel of his fingers on my body, and a delicious ache settled into between my legs.

How wonderful it would feel to have those hands gliding over my skin, those fingers touching my body.

He slid the tie from my neck and undid all his work. "Now you show me what you learned."

I attempted to take the tie from his hand, but he pulled it away and whispered, "On me. Turn around and sit toward me."

Nervous fear shot through me as I stood up, and I hoped I'd be able to turn around without my legs giving out. The dress I wore only fell to the middle of my thighs, so when I straddled him, it was likely to ride up so far my panties would show. I didn't care about that so much as him knowing that I was already dripping wet just from sitting there pressed up against him.

Taking a deep breath, I turned around and climbed on top of his lap. He stared into my eyes, unnerving me, but something held me firm in his gaze. His hard cock pressed against the front of his pants and my damp panties. There was no way he didn't know how excited he'd made me.

I took the tie from his hand and slid it around his strong neck, even as my fingers trembled at the feel of him underneath them. Trying to hide my ignorance of my task, I wrapped the wide end of the tie around the narrow end, but it was no use. I didn't know what came next.

Dropping the two ends of silk, I looked down to avoid his gaze. "I'm sorry. I don't know how to do this."

"You didn't listen when I told you how to?" he asked in a voice that was as seductive as it was stern.

Shaking my head, I continued to look down at the untied ends of the blue fabric laying against his shirt. "I couldn't. You were so close, and it was impossible to pay attention to what you were saying."

He slid his hands down my back and cupped my ass to pull me into him, grinding my soaked panties into the thin fabric separating his cock from me. Kneading my flesh through my dress, he whispered near my mouth, "I love how honest you are, Nina. It makes me want to be honest with you."

I wasn't sure how to answer, but it didn't matter. As my head swum from the sensations he'd created in me, he pressed his mouth to mine and kissed me. His lips were soft yet demanding, and I eagerly kissed him back, seeking a release of that sweet ache, but his kiss only increased the feeling, making me want more.

He nudged his hips off the couch, sliding his cock over my sensitive clit, and I couldn't stop myself from moaning into his mouth. I didn't want him to think he had this effect on me so soon, but I was powerless. I wanted him so badly at that moment, I would have done anything to keep his hands on my body.

Unable to stop myself, I began to timidly move my hips to ride him, still fully clothed but needing so much to come. I didn't care that he wasn't inside me or even that I looked too eager. I wanted him to get me off, even if it was just rubbing against his cock through his pants.

He had other ideas, though. Pressing his palms against the tops of my thighs, he stopped me from grinding against him, and I moaned a needy sound into his mouth. God, I wanted him!

His thumbs slid under the bottom of my panties and touched my bare skin, making my thighs quiver in anticipation. Dragging the pads of his thumbs up and down over my pussy, he was careful to avoid my swollen clit, driving me mad with desire.

"Please don't tease me, Tristan," I whispered breathlessly next to the corner of his mouth.

"I want to make you feel good, Nina."

I so desperately wanted that too. Kissing his neck, I moaned my need into his warm skin, so soft beneath my lips.

"Sir, I have completed the task you assigned," a man's voice intoned from somewhere in the room.

Shocked that we weren't alone, I popped upright and looked around. "What was that?"

Leaning his head back, Tristan spoke toward the ceiling. "Rogers, thank you. That will be all for tonight." Facing me again, he smiled. "Maybe we should move this somewhere more private."

Torn out of the mood, I was disoriented. I'd thought this was private.

Tristan kissed me again and I knew instantly Rogers' interruption hadn't dampened his mood any. Lifting me off him, he stood and took my hand. "Follow me."

I did and he led me to one of the bedrooms. It was masculine, with dark woods and deep brick red decor, but I had no idea if it was the one he called his. The room appeared too perfect, as if no one had ever slept there before, but he seemed comfortable as he turned around to face me, still holding my hand.

"We won't be interrupted in here. Come."

He stood looking at me, his eyes tinged with the apprehension I'd seen earlier when he'd walked into The Last Drop. As if I'd deny him or myself the experience that was to come.

I wanted to look away, uneasy at what he might be thinking, but I couldn't. Was he unsure of his choice to bring me here? We were so different and from such different worlds. Maybe it was wrong.

Tristan slipped out of his suit jacket and slowly unbuttoned his shirt, each opening exposing more of his body. I watched wide-eyed, wanting so much to see what each button's absence would reveal. Finally, he tugged the bottom of his shirt out of his pants and released the last button. Beneath were abs so defined I had to hold back from extending my hand to run my fingertips over his skin. A sexy, thin trail of dark brown hair led from his navel and disappeared behind his pants.

"Nina, tell me what you're thinking," he commanded in a deep voice dripping in sensuality.

What I was thinking? I didn't dare tell him the thoughts in my mind at that moment. That I wanted to begin kissing him at his neck and drag my lips over his body until they gave my mind proof of the reality of those abs. That the one true urge coursing through my body at the moment was to then drop to my knees and take the hard cock that had pressed against my clit into my mouth as I looked up at him to see how my worshipping him made him feel.

My mouth was dry and my breath was heavy. I whispered hoarsely, "I can't."

He slid the shirt off his shoulders to reveal a tattoo that began just above his heart and trailed all the way down his left arm to his elbow. It was stunning and accentuated the muscular ridges of his body. My eyes were riveted to the design, two black and grey copperhead snakes that formed an inverted heart shape and blended into a tribal tattoo that covered his shoulder and ran down his arm over his powerful bicep.

Stepping toward me, he brushed a wisp of hair from my face. "Where is that honesty I love, Nina?"

The honesty he loved terrified me almost as much as he did.

His hands undressed me as he tenderly peppered my neck with kisses, sending tendrils of want throughout my body. My dress slipped down over my shoulders and hips to end up in a heap on the floor, leaving me only in my drenched panties and bra, which quickly followed the rest of my clothes.

He moaned my name as he lifted me onto the bed and slid out of his pants as he climbed up to join me. I reached out to pull him to me, but he sat back on his feet and the next thing I felt was the most exquisite sensation I'd ever experienced. I pressed my head into the pillows as his tongue danced over my tender flesh, flicking and lapping so expertly that my body wanted to surrender to him long before it should.

His lips closed around my excited clit, and he sucked gently for just a moment, but it was enough. My orgasm tore through me until it reached the very ends of my body, and I arched my back to feel all of his mouth against me as I exploded into pieces. He pushed my hips down onto the bed and held me tightly as he rode my pussy with his tongue and lips. For a moment I fought against his hold, but soon gave in to his control, begging for more as my skin grew sensitive to the touch.

He groaned my name as he slid his body up mine until he covered me. His mouth pressed against my mouth, and I tasted myself on his tongue as it slipped across my lips. His hands pushed into my hair and tugged, sending a mixture of pain and pleasure skittering over my scalp. My senses threatened overload, but I would have begged for more, if need be. He was power and control, and I loved it.

A quick lean over to the nightstand and the sound of foil tearing and he was back kissing me. Spreading my thighs wider, he settled in between them with a moan and slid the full length of his cock through my wet slit. He was thick and long, nearly making me come again with one thrust over my sensitive clit. As much as that would have been pure pleasure, I wanted to hold back until he was inside me.

I slid my hands down his back and pulled him into me, desperate to have all of him. As he devoured my mouth with kisses, he pushed into my body, inch by delicious inch until every part of our bodies joined together as one.

The feeling was unlike anything else I'd ever experienced. His rhythm met mine and I clung to his shoulders as he thrust up into me, grazing some delicious spot inside me that sent strings of pleasure rippling through my body.

Tristan lifted his head from my neck and looked into my eyes. His gaze was full of need as he retreated from my body and then drove back into me with a deep groan. He was the picture of desire.

I wanted him to feel as wonderful as he made me feel. Wrapping my legs around his waist, I tilted my hips to take him deeper into me. He exhaled heavily into the pillow near my ear, moaning, "Oh, God, Nina," and buried his cock to the hilt.

My nails scratched down his back as our bodies raced toward sweet oblivion. He moved to his knees and rolled his back, his hips thrusting faster as his muscles tightened, signaling his release. In a second, my own orgasm roared through me, and I cried out in ecstasy.

Exhausted, we laid there in each other's arms silently joined together for what seemed like hours. I stroked his hair where it touched his neck, damp from our lovemaking, as his breathing returned to normal next to my ear. Even though he was much bigger than I was, the feel of him on top of me wasn't heavy or oppressive, and I would have been happy to stay like that forever.

When he finally rolled off me, he wrapped his arm around my shoulder and pulled me close. I laid my head on his chest and traced my fingers over his stomach, loving the feel of the taut muscles that rippled just beneath his skin. Beneath my head, his heart beat in my ear as he drew circles with his fingertip on my shoulder. It was sweeter and gentler than anything I'd imagined could happen with Tristan.

I had no idea where we'd go from here, but as I drifted off to sleep in his arms, I knew one thing for sure.

I wanted more.

CHAPTER FIVE

The morning sun streamed in through the bedroom window, forcing me to cover my eyes as I woke. In an instant, I realized I was alone in the bed and Tristan was gone. Running my hand over the sheet where he'd slept, I replayed in my mind our time together, loving the memory and wishing he was still next to me to make love again.

Sitting up, I looked around but saw no evidence of him anywhere. The door to the en suite bathroom was open and I listened for the sound of the shower. Nothing. Scanning the room, I saw my clothes lay neatly folded on a high backed chair near the window, and on top of them was a note.

Immediately, my stomach twisted into one huge knot. A note after a night of sex was never a good sign. A thousand scenarios raced through my mind, almost all involving him saying goodbye in his own way, probably with as few words as possible.

There was no point in putting off the inevitable. Whatever he had to say in that note, I had to deal with, so I threw off the covers and walked my naked self over to where my clothes lay. As I dressed, my knotted stomach did flips and a tiny sense of sadness made me choke up. I liked Tristan and thought we had shared something special.

The paper was folded in half, and I opened it slowly to see a much longer letter than I'd expected. Maybe that was a good sign, I thought, as I began reading.

Nina,

I've enjoyed our time together more than you can ever know. I truly do love your honesty because it makes me want to be honest with you. Toward that end, I offered you a job and it's yours, if you want it. There's only one condition: if you choose to accept the offer, you must agree to be in my employ for six months. After those six months, you may choose to end our arrangement, but you will be contractually obligated to stay for those months.

If you agree to this offer, all you must do is sign the contract I've left with Rogers. Whatever you choose, you must do so before you leave this house today and your choice will be final. To prove I'm sincere, I've also left a $20,000 advance check for you. If you prefer to have it deposited into your bank, simply tell Rogers and it will be done by end of business today.

I believe your talents are far more than ordinary, Nina, and hope you will take me up on my offer. Whatever happens, know that the night we spent together likely meant more than you can imagine.

Always,
Tristan

I stood staring at the sheet of stationary in my hand, stunned at what it said, as the dread unraveled inside me. I could have the job as assistant curator if I wanted it, but I had to agree to work for him for at least six months? What an odd length of time. Would I be sleeping with him during that time? Or was the previous night all there would be to our lovemaking? He'd said our time together had meant something to him, so maybe we would continue dating?

Questions multiplied in my mind the more I thought about his offer. Of course I wanted the job, but he hadn't even mentioned a salary. I quickly dismissed this concern as ridiculous considering how much I was getting paid by Sheila. Tristan hadn't come across as cheap, so he'd likely pay me better. If only all the other questions I had about his offer were so easily put aside.

Why hadn't he spoken to me personally instead of leaving a note and having me deal with his butler, who I knew only as a faceless voice that had interrupted a very hot moment? And why had he included the stipulation that I must sign the contract that day, which meant I wouldn't be able to have anyone else look at it before I committed to everything it entailed?

I'd been worried that a note after a night of sex with him meant goodbye. Now I was worried about what it meant if I decided to stay in his life.

Maybe Rogers had Tristan's cell number so I could talk to him before making my decision. Sure this could help me, I walked down the hall to the main part of the house to find the butler. He was standing in the foyer, almost as if he were told to wait there for me, and nodded as I approached.

Rogers looked like every butler I'd ever seen on television, and as I prepared to speak to him, I had to push down the urge to giggle at how stereotypical he appeared. He wore a dark suit, and his steel grey slicked back hair sat atop a head that showed he was at least in his sixties, I guessed. His face was long, not naturally but from what appeared to be years of frowning, if the lines around his mouth were any indication. However, he didn't look unfriendly. Just unhappy.

"Hi," I began, unsure how to approach this situation with a man who must have known I'd slept with Tristan the night before. I wasn't embarrassed, but I liked to keep my romances a bit more private.

"Miss, the master has left your contract to sign, if you so choose," he said in a deep voice as he handed me a pile of papers followed by a very expensive pen.

I looked down at the contract and pen in my hands and then back up at the butler. "Yes, about that. Would you be able to give me Tristan's cell phone number? I'd like to speak to him before I do anything."

Punctuating my request with a smile, I waited for Rogers to give me the information, only to be turned down.

"I'm sorry, miss, but I do not have that information."

"You must have his phone number. You work for him," I said in disbelief.

"No, miss," he said definitively, making it clear there was no room for discussion.

Well, if I couldn't discuss it with Tristan, I at least could discuss it with Jordan. She'd be able to help. Whipping my cell phone out, I swiped my finger across the screen and saw the No Service message staring back at me.

Terrific. I was on my own for this one.

"Is there somewhere I may sit, Rogers? I need to read the contract before I decide whether to sign it or not."

The butler extended his arm toward the living room off to the right. "Of course, miss. You may take all the time you require. The living room is at your disposal. The master has indicated, however, that whichever way you decide, you must do so before you leave."

"Got it. Thanks."

I took a seat on the very formal sofa and sat back with the contract in hand, determined to read the entire thing from the first to last word. Then I began reading it. I remembered signing the student loan papers when I was in college, and this contract made those look like crayon scribblings. Clause this and part that and on and on it went until by the end of page one I'd read enough.

By that point in the stack of papers, I knew my salary would be $60,000 for the six months and I was obligated to stay in Tristan's employment for no less than those six months. I would be given health, dental, vision, and life insurance and his company, which I found out was called Stone Worldwide, would contribute to a 401K plan, matching my contributions for as long as I was employed by the company.

I knew I should continue reading as the contract went on for six pages more, but as far as I was concerned, I had all the information I needed. I would be paid, have great benefits, and finally, for the first time since graduation, I'd be able to put some money in the bank. All of this and I'd get to work for Tristan in an art gallery. That I wasn't sure what I'd be in his personal life made me wish he and I had talked about it, but I had hope that his note had been evidence of his interest in me. With a deep breath, I prayed I wasn't making a mistake and signed my name on the last page. I looked up and Rogers seemed to have appeared out of nowhere and handed me a second letter from Tristan.

"Miss, do you prefer a check or the money deposited into your account?"

"I think the deposit would work since I assume I'm going to be paid that way. Just give me the papers to fill out," I said with a smile.

"No need, miss." And with that, Rogers turned and walked away. *No need? How was the money to be deposited if I didn't give my account number?* Before I could ask the very same question that was in my mind, the butler was gone. Unsure of what to do, I opened the note and read more from Tristan.

Dear Nina,

I'm happy you chose to accept my offer and look forward to your involvement in Stone Worldwide for the upcoming six months. You're going to need a new wardrobe for your new position, so please allow my driver to take you to Le Ciel. I have spoken to Sheila about your resignation and she's happy to hear you've found another position. I believe she's going to miss you.

Always,
Tristan

I began to think this might be all right and wandered out the front door to find Tristan's driver standing next to a Town Car. He wore a driver's uniform and appeared as stoic as the butler. I approached him and extended my hand. "Hi, I'm Nina. I guess you're supposed to take me to Le Ciel. Where is that?"

He opened the door, bowed slightly, and replied, "Yes, miss. We'll be in Midtown shortly."

An hour later, I was standing inside a Midtown Manhattan boutique and feeling like Tristan in The Last Drop. The only difference was no one at my local bar had looked at him like he was an outsider when he walked in.

Two women walked toward me as I stood in the dress I'd been wearing for far too long, and I so wished I'd changed clothes before going shopping. Feeling self conscious, I avoided meeting their gazes, instead looking out the window at the activity on the sidewalk.

"You must be Nina," the blonder one announced. "Mr. Stone told us to expect you. We have everything picked out and if you follow me, I'll take you to a dressing room."

I did as she asked and found myself in a dressing room almost as big as my entire apartment. A dozen different dresses, outfits, and business suits hung around the room. I looked at the price tag on one of the dresses and my mouth fell open.

My portion of the rent on my apartment was only slightly more. I couldn't afford these clothes.

Immediately, I opened the door and stuck my head out to find the blonde who'd escorted me to the room. She stood with her back to me hanging clothes on satin covered hangers, and I said, "Excuse me. Miss?"

She turned around and flashed me a toothy smile. "Is there something I can help you with?"

I was embarrassed to say I was too poor to afford anything in her store, so I whispered, "I think there's been a mistake. Mr. Stone didn't mention how…" I hesitated and stumbled over my words until I finally blurted out, "He never said they'd be of such high quality."

Thankfully, she seemed to understand what I had so clumsily referred to because she gave me one of her supermodel smiles and nodded. "Oh, that's been taken care of, miss. Mr. Stone will be paying for everything."

She returned to her work, leaving me alone in the dressing room that could house a small family, my head spinning from what she'd said. Not only was I now employed as an assistant curator for Tristan Stone, but now he was buying me an entire wardrobe so I could be ready for my first day at work?

It all seemed too good to be true.

I tried on one outfit and then the next, impressed that the women who worked at Le Ciel knew my size just minutes after I walked through the door. I hadn't stood there for that long, yet the clothes fit me perfectly.

As I twirled around in front of the three way mirror, swinging the black skirt that matched perfectly with the grey see-through blouse, my cell phone rang. I didn't recognize the number, but I was in such a good mood, I broke my usual rule and answered it.

"Hello?" I sang happily to whomever was on the other end.

"Good morning, Nina."

My heart began pounding wildly at the sound of his deep voice. Tristan.

"Hello."

"I'm so happy you agreed to sign the contract," he purred into my ear. "Are you happy with my choices for you?"

I looked down at the clothes I wore and then around the room at all the beautiful outfits hanging there just waiting for me to love them. "You chose these?" I asked, stunned.

"Yes."

"Oh. I don't know what to say."

I didn't. It was all at once exciting and overwhelming to know he'd taken the time to come here and pick out clothes for me.

"What are you wearing, Nina?"

"The black silk skirt and grey see-through blouse. It's very nice."

"I'm sure you look beautiful in it. I want you to take it off," he said in a distinctly commanding tone.

"Do you want me to try a different outfit on and tell you if I like it?"

"No."

Confused, I did as he ordered and stood in my bra and panties, just as I had done in front of him the previous night.

"Okay. I took it off."

"Are you wearing only your pink panties and bra I saw you in last night?"

"Yes," I said with a smile as the memory of our time together flashed through my mind.

"Good. I want you to sit on the large ottoman in the middle of the room."

I did as he desired. "I'm sitting, Tristan."

"Good. Lean back and lie down."

I did as he ordered, loving the sound of his deep voice telling me what to do. "Okay."

"I want you to close your eyes and think about how it felt with my mouth on your pussy."

An involuntary moan escaped from my throat at the sound of his words entering my ears. This was the most he'd ever spoken to me, other than telling me about his plans for his house, and I loved hearing him talk like this.

"I love the taste of your juices on my tongue, Nina. Do you want me to make you come like that again?"

"Yes," I whimpered as I remembered his mouth on my body taking me to such exquisite heights of pleasure.

"Or would you prefer me to fuck you, my cock buried deep in your cunt?"

"God, yes," I answered breathlessly.

"I wish I could be there right now, Nina. I want to fuck you until you cry out in ecstasy, loud enough for the Le Ciel women to know what I've done to you."

I wished he could too. I wanted to feel his hands on me, his lips touching mine as he brought me to the edge of everything my body wanted and held me as I tumbled over that precipice.

"Since I can't, I want you to slide your fingers inside your panties and finger that pretty cunt for me, Nina. Will you do that for me?"

"Yes," I answered quietly as my hand moved down my body and below my panties. My finger slid through my soft folds and easily found its way inside, as he'd commanded.

"Imagine my tongue gently dragging over your clit. I love the feel of it on the tip of my tongue, Nina. It's swollen and eager for me to take it into my mouth and suck on until all those tender nerve endings explode in your orgasm."

As he spoke his sensual words, my finger rubbed in tiny circles over my excited clit, creating soft waves of sensation that felt almost as good as his mouth had on me.

"But I want to feel you surrounding my cock, the soft walls of your cunt gripping me tight as I slide in and out of your willing body. You're sitting on top of me, riding my cock as you've never done with any other man."

"Yes," I whimpered as my fingers moved faster over my pussy. "Yes."

"Bend down and kiss me, Nina. Bring that beautiful mouth to mine and let me feel your kiss while I fuck you. You're getting close, aren't you?" he whispered low into my ear.

"Yes."

"Not yet, Nina. You can't come yet."

I slowed my finger's movement against my clit to stop from coming, loving the feel of holding off until he told me I could.

"I slide my hands over that pretty ass and squeeze as my cock slides into your needy cunt again. Tell me what you want, Nina. Say it."

My finger slid over my clit again, sending a spike of pleasure through my body, and I whispered, "Fuck me."

"Louder, Nina."

"Fuck me," I said in my normal voice.

"I want to hear it louder. Tell me what you want me to do to you, Nina."

In a voice no doubt loud enough for anyone outside the dressing room door to hear, I said on a near sob, "Fuck me! Tristan, I want to come. Please fuck me."

"You feel so fucking good on my cock, Nina. Time for good girls to come. Let me hear you come for me, Nina."

My finger circled tightly on my swollen and needy clit as my thighs began to tremble. I moaned softly as the first curl of pleasure came over my body, opening my legs wider as my orgasm took over.

"Oh, God! Yes, don't stop!" I cried as every inch of me shook from my powerful release.

"I love hearing you like that," he moaned as the final quakes of my orgasm waned. "Thank you, Nina."

Feeling almost boneless, I closed my eyes and took a deep breath in, loving how good he made me feel. "I've never done anything like that before," I quietly confessed as I sat up and looked around to see if anyone was standing outside the door.

"There's that honesty that I love in you. Maybe we'll do something like this again. Would you like that?"

His voice made me want to do something like that again right now. "Yes." Needing to know what this was to him, if anything, I asked, "Tristan, this isn't how you are with all your employees, is it?"

The question sounded silly as soon as I heard the words out loud, but when he chuckled on the other end, I didn't feel so stupid.

"No, I don't have phone sex with anyone else who works for me, Nina. But you're not like my ordinary employees. Now I want you to buy the clothes I picked out and whatever else you like and I'll see you back at the house later."

"I can't go back upstate, Tristan. I don't have any of my things I need if I'm going to be away for more than one night," I protested. "I need to go home to get some stuff."

The phone went silent for a long time and when he finally spoke, his tone was markedly colder than I'd ever heard from him. "Nina, you signed a contract to work for me. For the next six months, if I tell you to do something, you do it. Do you understand?"

His words stung and all the frustration I'd experienced days earlier because of his behavior bubbled up inside me. "Are you saying I have to obey you twenty-four hours a day for six whole months?"

"Nina, everything comes with a price. This was part of the deal clearly spelled out in the contract that you signed."

I sat there stunned. "What are you saying? I'm some prostitute you paid to have for half a year?" Suddenly, all the clothes hanging around the dressing room looked ugly, like everything about this made me feel ugly.

"Nina, you wanted a job where you could show off your skills and love of art. I wanted to give you that. I'm willing to make sure you have the clothes required for the position and many other things that can make you happy, and all I ask is that you agree to a few simple things to make me happy. I have a contract that stipulates you're obliged to do these things, but I'd love to think that you want to make me as happy as I want to make you."

What was I supposed to say to that? I'd been foolish in not reading the entire contract, and now I was going to be forced to pay the price. As I gathered up the clothes to take them to the register, I told myself there were worse ways to spend a few months.

At least I'd be getting paid handsomely to be someone's indentured servant.

Chapter Six

The driver carried the almost $10,000 worth of clothes Tristan had purchased for me into the house and disappeared like Rogers had hours earlier. I stood in the foyer unsure of where I was supposed to go and feeling no better after stewing over the situation all the way home.

"Nina, come. I have dinner waiting for you."

I turned to see Tristan standing in the doorway of the formal dining room. He was dressed in his suit and tie and looking like he had all the times before, except now he was my jailer or my owner. I hadn't decided which title sounded better.

He extended his hand and smiled that warm smile that had never failed to charm me. Even now, it had the desired effect and I walked toward him, almost as if my legs were controlled by him directly.

I attempted to walk past him into the dining room, but he stopped me short with his arm in front of me. Turning to look up at him, I saw a look of hurt in his eyes. As if he had something to feel hurt about!

"Did you enjoy shopping?"

I didn't know how to answer his question. I had enjoyed it and everything we'd done in that dressing room until I found out I had signed my life away, even if it was to someone as gorgeous as him.

He tilted my chin up with his index finger and stared down into my eyes. God, those brown eyes could just melt my heart sometimes. I wondered if he knew that and used them to manipulate me or if they were just the windows to a soul that was as lonely as I suspected it was.

"Nina, I want to make you happy. Will you let me?"

I closed my eyes to avoid looking into his as I spoke. "You don't want me to be happy. You want someone you bought to do as you command. There's a difference."

My eyes still closed, I felt his lips brush mine in a tender kiss. Then he spoke again, and my heart broke. "I can't be anything but what I am. I can give you everything your heart desires, but I can only do it this way."

I opened my eyes and tears slid down my cheeks. He softly swiped the pad of his thumb under my eyes to dry my tears and kissed me again. "I had the cook make a meal I hope you like. Let's eat."

We sat at the end of a long dining table with him at the head and me seated to his left next to him. In front of us were five main courses, all my favorite foods. There was shrimp scampi, roast beef, turkey with stuffing, sausage and peppers, and a cheese pizza. I scanned the heaping plates of food and looked over at Tristan.

"Did you know these are my favorite things to eat?" I asked, unsure I wanted to know the answer.

"Yes," he said in that innocent tone that seeped into his voice every so often.

"How did you know these were my favorites?"

He smiled proudly. "I asked."

For the first time, I asked the follow-up question I had never given voice to before. "Asked who?"

"Jordan. I asked her to tell me what you liked when I went to see her today."

He'd gone to my house while I was shopping? "Why?"

"Why did I ask her to tell me what you like or why did I go to see her today?" he teased.

"Please give me a straight answer, Tristan."

He knew I wasn't happy, and I saw the joy slide from his expression. "I asked her what you liked because I wanted to make sure you were happy. I visited Jordan today to give her the rest of your portion of the rent for this year. Now what would you like to eat?"

There was no point in fighting him on this. Jordan would be helped by what he'd done and I had a hard time finding fault with that. His behavior didn't seem to be intended to be manipulative, and as I accepted that, I accepted him.

"Turkey," I said with a smile.

"Excellent choice," he said as he pulled the platter toward him. He carved a slice of turkey off the breast and placed it on his plate. I waited for him to pass the plate to me, but instead he began cutting the slice into smaller pieces. He stabbed one piece with his fork and held it in front of my mouth.

"Eat, Nina."

The meat was perfectly cooked, juicy and tender with just a hint of seasoning I guessed was rosemary and thyme. He scooped up another forkful of meat and placed it on my tongue. Turkey had never tasted as good. I swallowed my food, and he wiped the corner of my mouth with the pad of his thumb.

"Do you do this all the time with women?" I asked, knowing I probably didn't want to know the answer but needing to ask anyway.

He shook his head slowly. "No."

As he readied another bite for me, I asked, "Aren't you planning to eat?"

He smiled and shook his head again. "No."

I ate another bite of turkey, and all the while he watched me as if my happiness was of the utmost concern to him. When I finished, he pushed the platter of turkey away and pulled the plate of shrimp scampi toward him. Scooping up a forkful of shrimp and rice, he turned toward me and brought another of my favorites to my mouth.

The scampi was just as delicious as the turkey, but all I could think of as I ate it was that my breath would stink of garlic. Looking around the table, I saw a pitcher of water and a bottle of wine. I reached for the water, but before I could grab the pitcher, Tristan was filling my glass.

"You don't have to do that. I mean, it's nice, but I can get it."

Handing me the glass, he said, "I don't have to do anything. I want to."

I drank all the water and placed my glass on the table. "This is very nice of you. Thank you for doing this."

"I just want you to be happy, Nina. Are you happy?"

He stared into my eyes as he waited for the answer to his question, and I didn't know what to say. No one had ever worked to find out exactly what my favorite foods were and as he'd fed me, I was sure it was the most erotic experience I'd ever had in my life. His gaze never left mine, and I felt like I was the most important person in the world—the center of his universe. With each forkful of food, I felt cared for.

"I am happy, Tristan. I guess I'm just not used to anyone being so attentive."

He turned away from me to pull what looked like a silver ice bucket toward him. Taking his spoon, he sunk it into the inside of the bucket and pulled out a spoonful of green ice cream. "Mint chocolate chip is your favorite, I believe?"

He'd even asked Jordan about my favorite ice cream. As I savored the sweet taste of it on my tongue, I couldn't help but smile. "Is there anything you don't think of?"

Shaking his head, he scooped out another helping of ice cream and slid the spoon between my lips. "Not if I can help it."

"Is it just with me that you do this, Tristan?" I asked, only half-joking.

"Is it just with me that you ask so many questions, Nina?" he asked in return, once again not giving me a straight answer.

"I liked the way you spoke to me this afternoon. Not only what you said but how much you said. One of these days, I hope you'll want to say that much to me about other things."

His expression quickly clouded over. "You may not like what you hear."

I reached out and squeezed his hand. "I've always asked lots of questions. I guess you think it's a personal flaw?"

Tristan placed the spoon in my mouth so I could have another bite. "No. It's part of your charm."

His attempt at making me feel good was sweet and I appreciated it. I don't think anyone had ever thought my questions were charming, but he did. By the time I'd finished eating, it wouldn't have mattered what he'd done. I'd have forgiven him.

Reaching out, I touched his hand. "This was wonderful. Thank you, Tristan."

"Nina, I have something to show you. I hope you're happy with it."

He led me from the dining room to a hallway on the opposite side of the house from the room we'd slept in the night before. Stopping, he gently backed me against the wall and kissed me. His lips were tender but insistent, taking from me what he desired and giving me that part of him that I so wanted.

Nervous at what it could be that he wanted to show me, I caressed his cheek with the back of my hand. "I can't wait to see your surprise."

My answer seemed to make him happy and he led me to a bedroom that looked just like his. He opened the door and proudly announced, "I had everything of yours brought here. If you need anything else, just tell me and I'll make sure you get it."

"You had everything from my home brought here?"

"Yes."

"Tristan, I need to know. Am I a prisoner here?" I asked feeling fear for the first time with him since we were racing through the city in his Jag that first night.

His expression hardened and he dropped my hand from his hold. Without a word, he turned and left me standing there feeling terrible for asking a question anyone with a brain in their head would have asked.

I checked the closet and dresser drawers, and all my clothes were in exactly the same spots and the same order as they'd been at my apartment. He'd transferred my life exactly from Sunset Park to his house upstate, the only difference in his mind that I was living with him instead of Jordan.

I couldn't decide if I should be terrified by his behavior or touched by his thoughtfulness.

Lying on the bed in my new room, my mind was a muddle of ideas, one more conflicting than the other. I had the job I'd always dreamed of, yet I seemed to have signed a deal with the devil. Tristan was everything I'd ever wanted in a man. Gorgeous, his face was pure beauty and his eyes were gentle hints at the quiet soul beneath who shone through far too infrequently. He was more successful than any man I'd ever been with and seemed intent on lavishing upon me anything I could desire, no matter the cost, yet I had to leave my home. He was attentive to my every physical need, taking my body to places of pleasure any woman would beg to experience even once, yet there was a distance he forced between us. Above all, he wanted more than anything to make me happy, but it was to be on his terms.

What had I gotten myself into?

I needed to clear my head, so I stripped down, hoping a nice hot shower would help me figure out what to do. As the water steamed up the room, I stepped in and saw every item I kept in the shower at home with Jordan was there, only replaced new. My razor. My soap. My shampoo and conditioner. Each was there brand new. Had he gone shopping too?

What kind of person did this?

Standing under the hot water as it trailed over my head and body, I wondered if I was the one who was wrong. Tristan hadn't done anything to hurt me, and even his attempts to make me feel at home I considered suspect. Why? What kind of person was I to see sinister motives behind everything?

The shower had helped me see things more clearly, so I quickly dressed in one of my new outfits and set off to find him. I wasn't sure what I'd say, but maybe if we could talk a little I'd be able to show him I knew he meant no harm.

But he was nowhere to be found. Either was Rogers or the driver, so I wandered around the house, peeking my head into every room looking for him. By the time I made it to the pool, my spirits were crushed. I'd asked the wrong question and he'd left, likely returning to his penthouse in the city, and I would be left alone here in the country. I began to wonder if I really was a prisoner.

It was a beautiful warm summer night, so I took my search outside to the grounds, knowing he was likely nowhere nearby. The fireflies were putting on their nightly show, one that I hadn't seen since moving from Pennsylvania. I sat down near the front porch and watched as they illuminated the garden, my mind traveling back to simpler times and the nights when my father would watch as I ran around our yard with a glass jar trying to catch fireflies to keep as my own.

Just thinking about his death in my senior year in college still made me cry. After my mother died when I was only five, he raised my sister and me, never having much of a life other than us. I regretted how much he gave up for me, always there to take me to art classes and dance lessons instead of finding someone to share his life with. He died alone before he got the chance to see me as an adult who so wanted him to find love again.

That was the reality of life—loneliness was often a choice. Here I was with the opportunity to have everything I'd ever wished for and all I could do was look for reasons why I shouldn't accept it. Whatever it was that I was letting hold me back—fear, mistrust—I had a chance to share my life with someone. I had a chance to not be lonely.

Now all I had to do was take it.

The sound of footsteps on the porch behind me roused me from my thoughts, and I turned my head to see Rogers. He approached me stiffly, as was his style, and descended the porch stairs to stand in front of me. The man was oddly cryptic, but he seemed to have something to say, so I waited.

"Miss, do you require anything? The master instructed me to ensure you want for nothing."

Shaking my head, I gave him a weak smile. "No, thank you, Rogers." He stood there a moment longer, so I added, "Actually, I do need something. Where is Mr. Stone?"

Whatever warmth the butler had offered disappeared at my question concerning Tristan's whereabouts. If I had ever doubted it before, I knew now that Rogers was more than just a mere butler. He was the protector of his employer's secrets.

"He is gone for the evening, miss."

I nodded, disappointed that Tristan had left me there with just this spooky shell of a human. "Oh. Tell me, Rogers. How do you stand living out here?"

For the first time, Rogers seemed like someone I might be able to relate to, but I doubted he found living in the country as boring as I already did. To my surprise, he answered, "You may avail yourself of the car if you choose, miss. I can have Jenson bring it around, if you'd like."

"Thank you, Rogers, but I have nowhere to go. I had hoped to see Tristan, I mean Mr. Stone."

The butler's expression changed back to its usual stoic look and he merely nodded before he walked back into the house, leaving me wondering where Tristan had gone.

I sat outside watching the fireflies and looking up at the stars for hours. Living in the city included many great perks, but stargazing wasn't one of them, so I found a spot on the grass and watched the night sky as it moved above my head. The night was so dark, with no moon at all, and the stars had the stage all to themselves. They winked at me as I made a wish, hoping it would come true before I grew tired and had to go inside to my lonely bed.

By midnight, my wish hadn't come true, so I laid back in the cool, damp grass, closed my eyes, and painted a picture of my perfect night sky in my mind. I'd always found solace in that ever since I was a child. Whatever was bothering me, I'd close my eyes and imagine a scene I could paint. Then I'd rearrange things exactly the way they'd look if I were painting the picture.

Finally, I gave up waiting for Tristan and walked to my room, tired and disappointed. As much as I tried to push the thought out of my mind, I was sure he was out with another woman at some event much like the one I'd first seen him at less than a week before. Jordan's comment about him sleeping with a different woman every night chased all other thoughts out of my mind until I was convinced he'd never cared anything for me and all of this was some game he played because he could.

I was still tossing and turning when there was a knock on my door at three a.m., and I braced myself for Rogers' face on the other side of the door giving me the message that Tristan wasn't coming back. Anger at what I'd done to make that happen churned in my stomach, but there was nothing I could do now. I didn't even know where he was.

I opened the door and hoped I could at least keep my emotions together. Something told me Rogers wasn't good with tears and seeing me break down and cry would probably make the top of his head explode. But instead of the butler, there was Tristan standing in front of me dressed in a tux and looking even better than he did in a suit, if that was possible.

"Tristan!" I said with no attempt to hide my happiness at seeing him.

He was stunning in the black tux, white formal shirt, and black bow tie. The last time I'd seen a male close up in a tux was at my prom, but poor Bobby Jackson had been out of his league in that. Tristan wore it like other men wore jeans and t-shirts.

"Nina, I have something I want you to do. Come with me," he said as he held out his hand.

I looked down at my shorts and t-shirt I liked to sleep in and felt distinctly underdressed. "Should I change?"

"No. You look beautiful as you are."

Taking my hand, he led me to a sitting room similar to the one we'd sat in before, but this one had an enormous painting of an impressionist country scene on one of the inside walls. I began complimenting him on it and explaining the background of the style, but he continued walking to a door next to the painting, paying no attention to my impromptu art lecture. Opening it, he placed his hand on my lower back and escorted me into a narrow room with no lights.

"Tristan, what is this?" I asked as I turned to take hold of his of his hand and looked around in the darkness.

"Wait."

He spun me around to face the other wall, and I watched as lights began to illuminate the room. Unlike all the other rooms in the house, this one had very few furnishings and little decoration. It was painted white and had a single couch and table. Otherwise, the room was bare.

I reached my hand out to touch the wall and felt cool, smooth glass against my skin. "Are these windows?"

"Yes. I have something I want you to see," he said in a low voice in my ear.

My excitement grew with each second that passed until I saw two people enter the room, one woman and one man. Both were attractive and young, and they acted as if they were a couple.

Confused, I turned toward Tristan. "What's going on?"

"I want you to paint them."

Looking around, I saw an easel, canvas, and paint pots at the far end of the narrow room. "I don't paint portraits. I simply paint what I feel."

He caught my face in his hands. "Exactly. I want you to paint what watching them do makes you feel, Nina."

"What do you mean? Can they see us, Tristan?"

For the first time, a tiny grin formed on his lips. Shaking his head, he answered, "No, but it wouldn't matter. All I care about is what you paint."

Just in case somewhere in the back of my mind I doubted what was going to happen next, the man and woman showed me I was right in my suspicions. As I watched, they began to undress, the man slowly easing the woman's dress off her body to show her wearing nothing underneath.

"Tristan, who are these people? Why are they here?"

"They're here because they like to have people watch. We're here to watch them, and you're here to paint what it makes you feel to watch them fuck."

I wasn't sure if I was embarrassed or excited by his words. It didn't matter, though, because in seconds they were both naked and the show he'd brought home for me had begun.

I stood transfixed at the sight in front of me. The woman knelt down in front of the man and took his cock in her hands, running her tongue the full length of it. The expression on her face was one of pure joy, as if licking his cock gave her a kind of happiness that was only found in the way she made him feel.

Tristan stood next to me and whispered, "Watch her. She loves sucking cock."

His comment instantly made me wonder if he'd been with her. "How do you know?"

As he watched the woman take the man's cock deeper into her mouth, he said, "They love having people watch them. I've seen it at parties."

I liked to think I'd seen a lot, but never had I seen people perform sex at parties. That usually happened behind closed doors at the parties I attended. Jordan was right. Wealthy people were different.

His hand touched mine and I was torn from my thoughts on wealthy people and their wild parties. "You thought I'd been with her, didn't you?"

I looked at the woman sucking her boyfriend's cock and then looked at Tristan. "Yes. Since I know nothing about you before I met you, I did."

He lifted my hand to his mouth and softly kissed my palm. Looking up at me, he smiled. "She's not my type."

"Why? Because she's blonde?"

"No, because she likes to fuck in front of people so she can get off. I tend to like my women a little less attention whore."

I couldn't tell if his tone was sharp because I'd asked if he'd been with her or because he had no respect for her. Either way, I felt better knowing at least he hadn't slept with her.

Tristan pulled a chair out from the corner of the room and sat down, motioning for me to join him. "Come sit on my lap, Nina. I want you to tell me how this makes you feel."

I sat down on his lap and noticed that he wasn't aroused. He pulled my face toward his and kissed me hard, sending a rush of excitement through my body.

"Don't you like watching them?" I asked as I ran my palm over the front of his pants.

His tongue slid over his lip, and he grinned. "It does nothing for me."

"Me neither," I lied. In truth, he did it for me. I couldn't have cared less if the people doing their sex act disappeared and never came back.

Sliding his hand slowly up my leg, he gently stroked the tender skin of my inner thigh. "Nina, watch them. I want you to show me in your painting what it makes you feel."

I leaned in and whispered in his ear, "Watching them fuck doesn't make me feel anything, Tristan. You make me feel."

He closed his eyes and exhaled again. "Then paint what I make you feel, Nina."

I stood and walked to the easel to begin painting how he made me feel. I dipped my paintbrush first into red and then blue, pushing it swiftly across the canvas as I let my emotions come out for him to see. The frustration of always wanting more. The need he created in me to make him as happy as he made me. The fear that our differences were too great and would someday tear us apart. They all came out in the reds and blues that filled the picture.

His stare felt hot on my back, and I turned to see him watching me, intently interested in my work. Could he see how much he affected me and how much I wanted him? Was my painting telling him everything I so wished I could?

I looked up over my easel to see the couple had moved to full out fucking, but Tristan remained focused on me. He gave me a smile that nearly melted my insides. "Feeling the muse?"

"Yes," I answered shyly, timid he might disapprove of my work.

"Can I see?"

"Not yet."

My paintbrush continued its dance through the colors as I blurred the lines and edges to soften the ribbons of feeling he created in me. Finally, I dipped my brush into warm brown paint and began to form the abstract images of his eyes, always on me, watching me. Showing me the tenderness I believed existed deep within him.

Out of the corner of my eye, I saw him stand from his chair and walk toward me. Unsure of how he'd judge my feelings, I raised my arms to hide my work, but he moved around me and slid his arms around my waist.

In my ear, he said low and hoarse, "Tell me what you feel, Nina."

I wanted so much to tell him how he made me feel, but all I could do was let my painting speak for me. Turning my attention to the couple to avoid Tristan's critical eye, I held my breath as he studied the colors and hues of my emotions.

He pulled me to him and softly placed kisses over my neck. "The colors are beautiful, Nina. Tell me what I should see."

"The reds and blues represent my frustration and fear. I try to understand why you keep me at arm's length, but I can't. Then I fear we're too different and at the end of our time together or even before you'll cast me aside with a one-syllable word and whatever we are will be over."

He kissed my cheek and leaned his head against mine. "Why are the colors blurred?"

Shyly, I answered, "Because I can't express myself clearly when you're around."

Tristan turned me in his arms to face him. Looking deep into my eyes, he asked, "And the brown smudges?"

I let myself get lost in his gaze. "Your eyes. They can be so kind and gentle when you look at me before you kiss me or give me one of your gentle smiles. They make me believe there's more to the man who so often seems to hold me at arm's length. But they watch me always, making me ask questions that anger you and make you leave me alone."

He was silent after my confession, and my hands shook in fear that I'd said too much, revealed too much too soon and ruined everything. He cupped my cheek, and I leaned into his strong hand. "So honest all the time, my Nina."

Pulling me to him, Tristan held me close as he stroked my hair and kissed me tenderly on the lips. In the next room, the couple continued to writhe and grind against one another, but we stood silently in each other's arms and I felt more beautiful at that moment than at any other time in my life.

CHAPTER SEVEN

Tristan promised to have my painting framed and hung in his bedroom, thrilling me more than I thought was possible. I wasn't a painter, in truth, but it was a true expression of my feelings for and about him, and that he appreciated that meant the world to me.

That night, after he'd had Rogers send the couple home, he asked me to stay with him in his room and we made love again. When I finally fell asleep with my head on his chest, I was exhausted but happier than I could imagine I'd be with him.

As before, I woke up alone in his bed, already missing him. This time he'd left a note on his pillow, and I groggily focused my eyes to read what it said.

Dear Nina,

I have to go away for a few days, but I've instructed Rogers to get your painting framed so I can see it every morning when I wake. I'm sorry I had to leave before you got up, but I didn't want to disturb you since you looked so sweet all curled up next to me. While I'm gone, my car and driver are at your disposal. Feel free to use them to go wherever you like. When I return, your first official assignment as an assistant curator will begin.

Love,
Tristan

I held the paper in my trembling hands and stared at the last two words he'd written. *Love, Tristan.* Love. Not always, as before. Love.

Was this all a dream?

It had only been about a week since we'd first met. Was it possible there was such a thing as love at first sight and he'd felt that about me? I wanted to believe that more than anything, but something inside me whispered the doubt that anyone could fall in love that quickly, especially someone who could have anyone he wanted.

Times like this required a heart-to-heart girl talk with Jordan. I hurriedly ran to my room and then jumped in the shower to get ready for my trip back to Brooklyn. As I fixed my hair and makeup, I realized I hadn't thought about the trip as going home but going to Jordan's.

I, too, seemed to have become lost in my feelings.

Jenson was as accommodating as he was supposed to be, and by lunchtime I was back at our apartment and looking forward to hashing things out with Jordan. With school's ending, she was on summer vacation, so we had all the time we needed to figure out if I'd somehow won the romantic equivalent of the lottery or was just fooling myself into thinking that my situation with Tristan was good when it was anything but.

I threw my purse on the kitchen table and yelled for Jordan. Her scream from down the hall told me she was home and I found her in the bathroom cleaning smeared streaks of black from her eyelids.

"Jesus, Nina! I look like a damn raccoon now. Who walks into a person's house and screams like that?"

Three tissues later, she was back to finishing her makeup and I said in my best pouty tone, "Sorry. I thought this was still my place too."

Turning to face me, she smiled. "It is. I just got a little freaked out when you yelled. I wasn't expecting you since he came by and paid your part of the rent for the rest of the year."

The look on her face—complete with raised eyebrows of disbelief—told me she was just the person I needed to talk about things with. If there was any tough love I needed to hear, Jordan would give it to me.

"Yeah, well, that doesn't mean I would never come back. I need some friend time pronto and you're the only one I can trust."

Concern clouded her gaze. Reaching out, she squeezed my arm gently. "What happened, Nina? Are you okay?"

Nodding, I smiled. "I'm fine, but I want to stay that way. Can we talk?"

"Yeah, of course. Let's go for a walk. It's a beautiful day, so it'll feel good."

I agreed, happy I wore flats instead of the cute little pumps I had grabbed first. After listening to all the latest news about Justin, I set out with her for our walk and more importantly, our heart-to-heart.

Sunset Park in the summer was a pretty place, not like what people think big cities look like at all. The trees were all in bloom, so there was far more green than one might expect in the concrete jungle. Jordan and I walked our usual route, enjoying the weather as I told her about my new job and all its great benefits.

"So you hit the jackpot? This is great!"

I bit my lower lip. Tilting my head right and left, I said, "Yes and no. That's what I need your keen insight for."

Jordan stopped and raised one eyebrow. "I know that lip thing. Something's gnawing at you. And what's this yes and no? I've seen this man in the flesh, my friend. It's a yes. I nearly fell over dead when he showed up at the apartment. The watch that he wears alone is worth more than anything I've ever driven. And the way he says things…it's like honey dripping out of a jar."

I couldn't help but blush. Tristan was stunning, and when he stood in front of someone dressed in a suit and tie, he made quite an impression. There was no doubt about that. His physical side was a resounding "Yes!" without a doubt. It was the other parts of him that I wasn't sure about.

"He does have a way when he speaks, although I'm thinking he might have said more to you than to me by the way you're talking."

We began to walk again. "Oh, he didn't say much at all, but there's something about how the words come out. You have to tell me, Nina. Does he sound that sexy when you're…alone?"

"Since I have to assume he didn't tell you we're sleeping together, I guess it's that obvious?" I asked, wondering if I was telegraphing the fact that I was actively having sex with him.

Jordan turned her head to look at me for a second and then turned back to face forward, wrinkling her nose a bit. "Actually, it was the way he acted. No man comes to pay a woman's rent for six months and arrange to take everything she owns to his house if he isn't sleeping with her, Nina. You're obviously making him happy."

Happy. Now that was the tricky part. I sighed and blew the air out of my lungs in a heavy breath. "That's the problem I need your help with."

"You aren't going to say he's not happy with you, are you? You've been dating for less than a week and already he's taking care of you like you're a kept woman. Seems pretty happy to me."

"I'm not sure he is happy. I'm not sure about much of anything where Tristan Stone's concerned, Jordan. He had me sign a contract that I thought was for the job as an assistant curator at his hotel downtown, but I haven't done any work in that area yet. He bought me a new wardrobe for the job that literally cost nearly ten thousand dollars, Jordan, but he picked out all the clothes himself."

Pressing her hands to above her heart, she said, "I think I'm in love."

I stopped her and grabbed her arm. "I'm serious. I think I'm being paid to be his sex slave."

Jordan's laugh was so loud the children playing nearby stopped to pay attention to us. I guess it sounded funny now that I'd said it out loud.

"Sex slave? Nina, you're his girlfriend. That's how he's supposed to act. Girlfriends of wealthy men always have honorary titles and things like that. You're not expected to actually work."

I leaned in close to her and whispered, "Then what am I getting paid for?"

Jordan laughed again. "Honey, this is how wealthy men are. Think of it as an allowance. Instead of the kind you got when you were a kid, when you had to clean your room and do the dishes, this is the kind where you make him happy and he makes you happy with his money."

"But that's the problem. I don't think I'm making him happy. He goes to events and never asks me. I seem to be only the woman he keeps around his house."

"Hmmm….well, I don't think you're getting a bad deal. His driver takes you places, he does nice things for you, and you like him, don't you?"

I more than liked him. What had begun as an infatuation quickly had blossomed into something much more for me and I hoped for him too. I wanted to believe he meant what he'd written in that note, but I wasn't sure.

"Jordan, he's not like anyone else I've ever dated. Sometimes I can barely get him to answer me with more than a yes or no. Then he's affectionate sometimes only to be distant at other times. I don't know what to think."

She stopped and grabbed me by the shoulders. "That's your problem, Nina. You're overthinking this. What's wrong with a man giving you everything you want and all you have to do is be what he wants in return? Isn't that what everyone wants?"

When she explained it that way, it all sounded so perfect. He made me happy. I made him happy. Everyone was happy.

Then why were those niggling doubts in my mind still sending up red flags?

"Here's the thing," she said as she began walking back toward the apartment. "The whole relationship is brand new. Give it a while and see what happens. I think you might be pleasantly surprised. Good things do happen to good people. I think you're proof of that."

"I can't just give it a while, Jordan. I signed a contract for the next six months."

"And for that what do you get paid?"

"Sixty."

Jordan smiled. "Honey, you're getting paid sixty grand and you get to live with Tristan Stone. I think you should be more concerned about convincing him to keep you for longer than just six months."

"Maybe that's it. What happens if I fall madly in love with him and he decides to get rid of me after the time is up?"

"If you fall madly in love? I can tell by your face now, Nina, that's already happened. And I wouldn't be surprised to find out that he's crazy about you too. Just enjoy this. It's not everyday that a girl like you or me gets a guy like that. Let it ride and when the time is up, who knows what might happen."

I blushed at her ability to see through my facade, but my talk with her had helped, even if just a little. Looking at her, I saw out of the corner of my eye Jenson standing at the car waiting for me. "I guess it's time to go."

Jordan gave the man the once over and turned back to face me. "He certainly does like to know what you're up to, doesn't he? This poor guy hasn't been more than a few feet from us the whole time."

"What do you mean?" I asked as I looked over at the driver again as he patiently leaned against the car.

"Nina, he followed us the whole time. I didn't say anything because I figured you knew."

"Of course I didn't know! Who does that?"

Jordan leaned in and hugged me tightly. In my ear, she whispered, "I told you. Wealthy people are different. If he can't watch you, he'll have one of his men do it. I wouldn't worry. At least you'll never get mugged."

Her joking didn't make what I was feeling any better. "I'll call you, okay? I'm just glad you have some extra money now. Tell Justin I said hi."

"I will, honey. And I'll tell Alex you're doing fine. He's asked about you at least five times this week."

I smiled. Alex was a decent guy, so it wasn't a bad thing that he was interested. "Tell him I said hi and I'll be looking for a rematch of our pool game sometime."

Jordan's face grew serious. "Remember what I said, Nina. Good things do happen to good people. Don't forget that."

"I won't."

I returned to Tristan's house upstate hoping he'd be back, even though his note had said he'd be gone for a few days. The place was lonely without him, and I missed him already as I wandered around looking for something to occupy my time.

Rogers didn't seem to be anywhere to be found, so I explored without restraint, finding a media room and even a game room with a pool table. An hour or so of shooting pool by myself and I was even lonelier. Even the stoic butler would have been welcome company.

The house had an empty feel to it with just me in it. I'd never been to the attic, so I roamed up to the top floor and after looking around at a bunch of boxes and trunks, found one of those heavy, black old-fashioned telephones. On a whim, I picked up the receiver and heard a dial tone. There wasn't another landline in the entire house, but this one telephone sat up here all alone and worked!

Unsure if I should use it, I looked around and saw I was still alone. My cell phone got no reception out here, so I took the opportunity to dial my sister's number and heard her phone begin to ring. It was a small thing, but a rush of excitement pulsed through me. It felt like I was in one of those old mysteries and had found something no one else knew about.

"Hello?" she said loud and clear.

"Kim?" I whispered. "It's Nina."

"Nina! I tried to call you two days ago. It went directly to voice-mail. Are you okay?"

Looking around, I said, "I'm fine. My phone's been acting up. How are you?"

My sister was married with two beautiful children and lived in a quiet suburban neighborhood outside of Philadelphia. I hadn't seen my two nieces for months and just hearing Kim's voice made me wish I was there to see them.

"We're all good. Jeff's doing well at the firm, and you know the girls. Growing like weeds. They've been asking about their Aunt Nina, about when she's coming to see them again."

A lump formed in my throat. "I know. I've just been really busy. I promise I won't let so much time go by between calls, Kim."

"What's wrong, Nina? Your voice sounds so sad."

Kim's voice reminded me of my father. She had a way of phrasing things that sounded just like him. Neither of them would think what I was doing with Tristan was right, and they'd let me know about it. I didn't want to hear that, but I would have given anything to talk to him again.

"I was thinking about Daddy last night when I saw some fireflies. Remember how he'd sit with me while I ran after them on summer nights?"

"Yeah, I remember. I thought you were so silly, but that was the six years between us. But where did you see fireflies? I don't know where they'd be in Brooklyn."

Damn. I wasn't very good at this lying thing. "Sure. Fireflies go everywhere," I joked in a forced voice. "We have everything in New York, Kim."

I laughed nervously, hoping she'd be satisfied by my joking, and she laughed too. "Next time you're here you can chase fireflies with the girls. They'll love that."

"Okay, it's a date. I better get going. I'll talk to you soon, Kim."

"Okay, baby. Behave yourself out there."

I smiled at the word baby. Ever since our dad died four years earlier, she'd ended every one of our conversations by calling me the name he'd used all my life. As I said goodbye and hung up, tears welled in my eyes. It would likely be a long time before I got to see her girls, unless Tristan's driver didn't mind taking a joyride to the Philly suburbs.

I scanned the attic and saw dozens of boxes and a spooky sewing mannequin standing alone in the corner. Turning to head for the stairs, I ran my left shin into a chest that sat on the floor. As I bent down to rub my leg to ease the stabbing pain, I saw that the chest's lock was open. The ache in my shin abated, and I sat down on the floor. The lid opened easily, allowing me to peer in to see what was stored inside.

Stacks of old photographs and letters tied with a red silk ribbon sat at the bottom of the chest. Leaning up against the side walls of the chest were larger pictures. I lifted one out and held it up to see a portrait of a family of four with a mother, father, and two boys possibly four years old smiling for the camera. The children were identical twins, but I recognized Tristan instantly. He and his brother shared the same features, but I could tell them apart. His eyes gave him away. There was that familiar gentleness I loved in them even when he was just a boy.

Suddenly, I felt like I was intruding on something private. He'd never talked about his family with me, not even to say he had a twin. From the moment I met him, I'd felt like he was all alone in the world, so where were this brother and his parents?

My gaze drifted up to the top of the picture to his mother and father, and I tried to find his eyes in one of them, but couldn't. Everyone else in his family had dark eyes too, but there was something different about his. He resembled his father more than his brother did, if that was possible, and as I stared at the man, I recognized a lot of him in Tristan now.

I'd heard that even identical twins could be told apart easily because of their personalities, and nothing proved that more than this picture. Beaming a smile of a gregarious child, Tristan sat next to his brother, a child who looked far more serious with his tiny downturned mouth. Each boy was positioned in front of a parent, Tristan's twin in front of the father and Tristan in front of his mother. As I stared at all of them, I imagined him being more like his mother. She was beautiful, with long brown hair, high cheekbones, and a lovely smile, the kind of woman everyone admired.

I placed the pictures back inside the chest and hurried downstairs, fearful Rogers would appear out of nowhere like he always seemed to and see me rummaging in Tristan's personal things. Another hour passed before I gave up and slipped into bed, feeling lonely and wishing Tristan was next to me.

Would I ever meet these people or did he plan to keep me a secret out here in the country, never to appear at any of the functions or events he attended or to see the people closest to him? As I tossed and turned in bed that night, I couldn't help but wish that I hadn't gone to the attic. Now I had more questions about Tristan, and he seemed content to exist only in the present with me, never mentioning anything about his past or our future.

Chapter Eight

"I missed you."

Tristan's voice stopped me dead in my tracks as I shuffled into the kitchen to look for my morning coffee. He stood leaning against the massive island in the center of the room, a sly grin on his face as he watched me gawking at him.

"You're back? I thought your note said days."

And love. I hadn't forgotten the love part. Hopefully, he hadn't either.

"I finished what I had to do early and got back a few hours ago. You must have some great boss to let you sleep in on a workday."

I liked this relaxed Tristan and smiled as he teased me. "I'll have you know that it's Friday, which is basically the weekend to many people." Walking around the island, I stopped in front of him, looking up into his beautiful face. "And my boss is the best."

He took my chin between his thumb and forefinger. "Thank you. However, your new job begins today, so you better get ready."

"My new job? The one at the hotel downtown?" I asked excitedly.

Tristan shook his head and grinned. "No."

I lowered my head in disappointment. It had been too good to be true, after all. Now he had me here for the next six months, and the best I'd likely get was the consolation prize of being Tristan's paid love interest. No matter how appealing Jordan had made that sound, it still seemed like second place.

"Don't look so unhappy. You'll love it," he whispered in my ear.

"I guess. Let me go get dressed and you can tell me all about it."

I turned to leave but he held me by the shoulders, forcing me to face him. My expression surely showed my disappointment, and I couldn't hide it. I didn't want to hide it.

"Nina, have faith in me," he said quietly, those brown eyes boring holes into my soul.

When he looked at me like that—like I meant more to him than anything else in the world—I wanted to believe he cared and wanted me to be happy like I wanted to make him happy. "I do," I said, half-believing it myself.

"Meet me in my office in ten," he ordered as he released me.

"I'm here, as commanded," I said with as much bravado as I could muster.

He sat behind his large cherry desk and crooked his finger at me. "Come. I have a surprise for you."

I walked toward the leather Queen Anne wingback chair in front of his desk, but he stopped me as I began sit down. "No, come sit with me. I want to show you what your job is going to be."

So I *was* going to be his sex slave. I knew it. There would be no art, no need for the new wardrobe, no great job. Just fucking for money. I was no better than a prostitute, no matter how he or Jordan phrased it. A whore.

"Should I just sit on your lap or would you prefer me to skip the preliminaries and just get on my knees?" I asked as I rounded the corner of his desk.

He said nothing but turned his laptop and looked up at me. "I love your idea of work, but I had something slightly different in mind."

I looked down at the laptop and there on the screen sat ten small thumbnails of artwork. My face felt red hot as I stood there staring down at the screen while my words echoed in my ears. What an ass I was!

Embarrassed, I looked down at the floor. "I'm so sorry. That was uncalled for. I didn't know."

Tristan chuckled and took my hand in his. "I love how honest you are. I've told you that. Don't ever stop being that way. There aren't enough people in this world who will truly say what they're feeling, Nina."

Biting my lip, I looked up in humiliation, his soothing words not working. "I really am sorry. I feel like such a jackass. I just assumed that…well, all I've done with you so far is…" I really wasn't explaining myself well and was probably making things worse. I definitely felt worse.

All he did was smile and stand from his chair. "Here, sit down and let me tell you what I plan to have you do. Unless you'd rather go down on me first. I'm not going to say no to that."

Oh, he wasn't going to let me live this down any time soon. I deserved it, though. As I sat down in his chair, he dragged one over next to me. "I know you want your job to involve working with art, so that's exactly what you'll be doing. Those pictures are just ideas I have for your job."

I looked at the pictures on the screen again, studying each of them and seeing no common theme or period. "What exactly is my job, Tristan?"

"I want you to choose the artwork for the penthouses and suites in my hotels. You'll have to choose pieces for each one and pitch them to me to convince me to buy them. If you succeed, then I'll buy them and put them in that suite or penthouse. If not, you'll have to choose something else and pitch that to me. I'll have the final say as to the choices, but I'm trusting that you'll show me excellent pieces."

I looked at him, instantly worried. "What happens if you don't like anything I choose?"

That gentle smile he sometimes put on spread across his lips. "Nina, I have faith in you. I'm sure I'll love what you pick out."

There was that word again. Love. Now he was going to love my choices of artwork in addition to me and my penchant for honesty.

"Tristan, this all seems odd. Don't you have curators in your hotels who do this?"

"They deal with the museums that are housed in some of the hotels. This is different. My hotels are the best in luxury resorts and the people who stay in them expect the best in their surroundings. I have people who decorate them, others who do the tile work that make some look like the finest Roman mosaics, and others who design the rooms to be one of a kind at some of my hotels. What I want you to do is choose pieces that will make all of their work come together."

Suddenly, I felt entirely inept. All those times that I'd bragged that I knew about art now seemed foolish, as did I. Tristan actually expected me to choose pieces that the wealthiest people in the world would see when they paid top dollar to stay in his hotels. What if all my big talk about art had been just that?

Just talk.

"Okay. How many will I be doing?" I asked as I folded my hands in my lap to hide their shaking.

"I haven't decided yet. Maybe a goal of one a week would be a nice place to start."

One a week. Maybe I could handle this. Okay. One was entirely doable. "I'm going to need to know everything about each suite or penthouse. Choosing pieces isn't something that can be done without seeing what the rooms look like and what style is prevalent."

"Of course. We won't be visiting every one, but I'll make sure we get to a few."

I collapsed back in his office chair, crashing against the padded leather. "We're visiting some of them? Where are they located?"

"Around the world. Why?"

"I don't have a passport, Tristan." I don't know why, but that sounded so common as the words left my mouth, like he'd see me as someone less than him because I didn't routinely leave the country.

"Then we'll have to get you one. I'll put a rush on that, but in the meantime, we'll stick with domestic properties."

Tristan began tapping away at his keyboard as I mumbled, "I guess that's that." He seemed to be happy with the way things were going, but I was still nervous and unsure of myself. While my insecurities did their best to plague my already unsettled mind, my eyes focused on him as he searched for something online and I was struck by how relaxed he was at that moment. If I didn't know how much he owned or how much money he made, he'd look like any other man working on his laptop.

I wanted to reach out and touch him to make sure he wasn't a dream. This Tristan was so unlike the man I'd seen in the newspaper and even unlike the distant one I'd begun to fall for. Even dressed for work, he looked similar to someone like me.

"How old are you?" I asked impulsively, suddenly realizing I had no idea about that or other details that would have come to light with a boyfriend by now, like where he went to school or what he'd majored in.

He stopped his typing and turned to look at me. "Twenty-nine."

"What did you go to school for?"

With a smile, he answered, "Nothing."

His answer surprised me. "What do you mean? You run an entire company. Didn't you go to school for business?"

"For a year, but it wasn't what I wanted to do. Wharton was a little stiff for me."

"Wharton, as in Penn? As in Ivy League?"

Shrugging, he went back to searching for what he was looking for. "The same."

"And that was a little stiff for you?" I found the idea that anywhere was too stiff for him amusing.

He nodded. "College wasn't what I wanted."

"What did you want?" I asked, curious about the faraway sound in his voice now that hinted at a very different Tristan.

Ignoring my question, he turned the laptop in my direction and smiled that warm smile that could make me give up almost anything. "We'll deal with my penthouse first. The poker playing dogs picture isn't working out at all, so you'll need to come up with a something else."

I couldn't help but laugh, far louder than was likely proper. Just when I thought he was stiff and distant, he made a joke like that and changed the entire way I looked at him. "You didn't take me seriously about that, did you?"

Faking sincerity, he screwed his face into a grimace. "I wasn't supposed to? Those dogs cost me a fortune."

For a second, I thought he was serious, and then he winked at me. "Let's get going. Pick out what clothes you want to take and I'll have Rogers take care of it."

"Just like that?"

He closed his laptop, sat back in his chair, and folded his arms. "Just like that. I'll give you fifteen minutes."

I began walking toward my room and turned around, feeling playful. "And if I'm not done by then?"

Without missing a beat, he answered, "Then you'll spend your time at the penthouse naked, which also works for me."

He smiled again, and I relaxed a little more. "I never know when you're kidding, Tristan."

"I'm not kidding. As far as I'm concerned, you could never wear anything again and I'd be happy."

"But what about all those clothes you bought? That's a lot of money to waste, don't you think?" I asked, enjoying our verbal sparring.

He stood from his chair and walked toward me like a wild cat stalking prey. When he was only inches away from me, he stopped and lifted my chin with his finger and stared down into my eyes. "I'd spend ten times that to make you happy, Nina. Now go get ready or you're spending our time in the city as God made you."

It was nearly impossible to think about work when he was standing there looking like that and talking about me naked at his penthouse. I hurriedly chose a few outfits and laid them out on my bed before finding him waiting at the end of the hallway that led to my room.

"Ready?"

He'd asked me that right after we'd first met and just like then, I wasn't ready. Everything was moving so quickly that I wanted to stop, ask some questions, and get my bearings. But he never let that happen. It wasn't as if he was rushing me, really. It was more that he expected things to go as he had planned and there never was a moment where I wanted to risk asking what we were doing, afraid that if I did I'd ruin everything.

What woman wouldn't want a man like him to whisk her off her feet and take care of every issue that came up in life?

Tristan's penthouse was familiar to me as I stepped out of the elevator, but this time he held my hand in his. A tiny difference, it made everything I laid my eyes on seem changed. Still appearing disinterested in his magnificent home, he led me to his bedroom and sat down on the edge of the bed across from the bare spot on the wall.

I looked at the wall and smiled. "No dogs?"

"No dogs. And if there's some picture that involves cats playing checkers or something like that, I'm going on record as saying no to that too."

"There goes my great idea. Back to the drawing board for me."

My joke got no response, and he sat silently alternating his focus from the spot on the wall to my face. It made me uncomfortable, so I turned my back to him and faced my first task as his employee.

I felt his gaze on my back, but I remained fixated on the job at hand. It was too easy to want to just turn around and climb on top of him, straddling his hips as my skirt rode up and my body slid over his. I wanted to show him that I could do this.

His home was decorated expensively in a style much like other expensive hotel rooms I'd seen in decorating magazines. I walked around looking at the furniture and coverings, but none of them seemed particularly him. They were luxurious but not unique. Certainly, whoever had chosen them knew how to spend money. From the gold and cream stripe sofas that flanked the beige marble fireplace wall in the living room to the wingback Queen Anne chairs and large mahogany coffee table that must have been five feet in diameter in the sitting room, the home had been carefully decorated to apply to no one in particular. Down the hall was a bedroom with a ceiling that showed the decorator had possessed some flair. Hand painted, the view above the bedroom Tristan didn't sleep in was a stunning design that depicted the seventeenth century Dutch settlement of New Amsterdam near the spot the hotel stood on now.

I wandered to the bathroom and stood with my mouth hanging open. The time before I hadn't gotten to see it, and as I looked around with wide eyes, I was in love. Pale shades of marble and granite covered everywhere my gaze fell, but the centerpiece of the room was a toss up. The deep soaker tub in the center of the room competed with the floor to ceiling windows that showed the splendor of the city below, leaving me unsure which was more beautiful.

Walking back to his bedroom, which while attractive was possibly the least appealing room in the entire home, I made up my mind to choose a piece of art that would reflect him, not just look good or expensive. He sat still waiting for me on the bed, looking almost uncomfortable in his own house.

"Tristan, did you have this decorated when you moved in?"

I was almost sure the answer would be no, but I had to know. I don't think I'd ever seen a home so completely unrepresentative of its owner.

Shaking his head, he said, "No. It just comes with the job."

"No wonder nothing here is like you. I mean, it's gorgeous, especially the bathroom, but nothing about this place says you live here."

"So, have you thought about what might work on this wall?"

"No, but I know I want it to be something that says 'Tristan Stone lives here' instead of something so gorgeously common and expensive that it could be in anyone's home."

"And what would this piece say about me?" he asked, his interest obviously piqued.

"The man who lives here is intelligent—a man of few words but those he does speak are meaningful."

"I knew I'd like your choices in this. I look forward to seeing what you have to offer, Nina. I'll leave you to your work and be back at five sharp. My hotel and my home are at your disposal. When you get hungry, simply call the concierge and they'll take care of you."

He stood and I moved to kiss him, as I would any other boyfriend of mine who was leaving for work, but he merely nodded and silently walked by me as I stood watching him leave. All I could guess was that I was truly on the job now.

Chapter Nine

By five o' clock, I'd narrowed the potential choices for Tristan's room to three, and I was surprisingly tired. While I hadn't done any physical work at all, my mind had been working overtime all day about what piece would be perfect for the man who lived in this expensively furnished yet characterless penthouse. I wanted it to be perfect. I wanted to show him that he hadn't made a mistake having faith in me. Most of all, I wanted to give him something that would show what he was in my eyes.

He returned right on time at five sharp looking exactly as he had when he'd left all those hours earlier. Never wrinkled or rumpled, he looked as he always did in his suit, even though that day's was black instead of the variety of shades of grey he tended to wear. The tan dress shirt was different too, but whatever he wore, he looked gorgeous.

"Did you have a good day at work?" Tristan asked in a teasing voice as he walked into the bedroom loosening his tie.

"I did, dear. And how was your day at work?" I asked as I sat on the bed watching him get more comfortable.

"You know how it is. Another day, another dollar."

Opening the closet, he removed his suit coat and tie and turned to face me once again in just pants and a shirt. "What would you like for dinner?"

"Don't you want to know about the choices I have in mind for your blank spot?" I was eager to see what he thought about my ideas.

He shook his head. "No. Once five comes, I don't want to think about work anymore. All I want to think about is you. I don't want you thinking about work anymore either."

Jesus, when he said things like that, my stomach did somersaults. He didn't want to hang out and watch TV. He didn't want to play video games. He didn't want to go to some place with his friends and never consider if I wanted to really go.

He wanted to think about me. Just me.

I was lost. And damn, I didn't want to be found.

He knelt in front of me, running his hands over my thighs and nearly driving me crazy with his touch. "So what should we have to eat? One of your favorites or something new you've never had? Feeling adventurous?"

He looked up at me, his eyes searching mine. The old me, the me before I met Tristan, would have chosen one of my favorites, but as he knelt there looking up at me, I wanted to be someone different than who I'd always been. I wanted to be worthy of feeling sexy and desirable.

"Let's try something adventurous."

"Next question—eat in or out?" he asked as he dipped his head to place a single kiss on the inside of my thigh.

My head was swimming, but I found the ability to squeak out, "In."

He nipped at my skin, sending shivers of pleasure racing up my body. Against my leg, he murmured, "In it is," before he stood and disappeared from the room. A rush of heat covered me and I crashed back onto the bed, barely able to breathe.

The way he was made me crazy. Crazy for him. Crazy because of him. Fucking crazy. He'd left this morning without a word or even a gentle brush of his hand against mine to say goodbye, and he'd returned wanting nothing but me. What was with this guy? How did he do it? I could barely keep my hands off him, and there were times he stood close enough to touch me and never did.

It was maddening. And I loved it. Without force or any restraints, he'd taken over my every thought and feeling, and I was helpless to fight against it. Hell, I didn't want to fight against it. I wanted to let my mind and body give in to everything he offered.

"I ordered seared duck," he whispered as he slid up my body until his lips met mine in a gentle kiss. "I wasn't really in the mood for too much adventure in my food tonight. Do you like duck?"

"I've never had it. What does it taste like?"

"Chicken."

I opened my eyes at his answer. "Really?"

Smiling, he licked his lips and kissed me again. Against the corner of my mouth, he whispered, "No."

"Oh. Will I like it?"

He hovered above me looking down into my eyes. "Yes, I promise you'll love it. My chef makes it with a fig sauce that tastes incredible."

"Are we going down to the restaurant to eat?" I asked, praying to God he'd say no.

He moved his body up mine until his mouth was next to my ear. "We can, if you want. Do you want to leave, Nina?" His voice was a slow whisper that made a delicious ache coil in my belly, and I would have given everything I owned to not leave that spot.

"No," I said quietly as he pushed his hips forward, sliding his hard cock against my panties. "I think here is perfect."

"Good. Have anything in mind for what we should do until dinner comes?" he murmured in my ear as he pushed his hips toward me again.

"You're such a tease."

He lifted his head and smiled that wicked smile I'd only seen once or twice. "Tease? You want me to tease you?"

"No. I hate being teased."

Tristan rolled off me and propped his head up with his hand. He looked down at me, still smiling, and ran his finger over my lips. "You're cute when you pout."

Cute. That was definitely not what I wanted to be thought of. Cute was for puppies, kittens, and little girls. Now I really pouted.

"Oh, more pouting. I must have said something wrong. Let me guess. You don't want me to call you cute."

He was teasing me, and I didn't like it. "I'm glad I'm amusing you, Tristan. Maybe I can dress up like some little girl and you can pick on me like some bully on the playground."

"Someone's touchy tonight."

That was it. I didn't like this Tristan. He reminded me too much of every other guy in the world. That bothered me. He was supposed to be more, better. Now he was nothing but a guy who seemed to have forgotten how to treat me.

I sat up and stood from the bed. "I'm going to take a bath. Let me know when the food gets here."

As I walked toward the bathroom, I felt like crying. I didn't know why either. I knew I was probably overreacting, but something in Tristan seemed less special now, and I hated that. If he was just an ordinary guy with lots of money, then somehow I felt less, like I'd let myself be fooled.

I slid into the tub and let the water run until it nearly overflowed. I wanted to get lost in that water until everything around me disappeared. Behind me through the massive windows the scenes of the city played out, but I didn't want to see them either. I just wanted to close my eyes and pretend nothing had happened.

The water soothed my body, but my head and heart still ached. I sat there with the bath water up to my chin and fought back the recriminations. My insecurities had reared their ugly heads again, and as the water cooled around me, I silently admitted that this wasn't about Tristan.

This was about me. This was about my feeling like I didn't belong here, just like I'd felt that first night when I'd flubbed Tristan's test.

I heard the door open, and he walked silently past me. I didn't want to open my eyes, hoping that if I didn't, I wouldn't have to see the look on his face.

Tristan crouched down behind me and slid his hands over my shoulders. "Nina, I'm sorry. I didn't mean anything by what I said."

That only made it worse. I had caused the problem and now he was apologizing. "Don't. It was all me."

I opened my eyes and looked down at his hands stroking my arms. This situation was desperately in need of some lightening. "This is some bathtub. I think my dorm room was this size."

He chuckled behind me and slipped his hands from my body. "And I bet you shared a room too."

Leaning back to look at him, I watched as he stepped out of his pants and boxers, leaving them in a heap on the floor. I moved forward in the tub to accommodate his body, sending water flowing over the sides, and he slid into the water behind me, taking me into his arms.

Still hoping to lighten the mood, I joked, "I don't remember being this close to my roommate in college. Maybe our dorm room was a little bigger."

Water sloshed against the sides of the tub and more spilled out onto the floor as he wrapped his legs around me. All the times we'd been together, I'd never noticed how long his legs were. They barely fit inside the tub.

"Do you know this is my first time in this bathtub?"

"That makes sense since your legs are almost too long for it."

I ran my palms over his knees and down his shins, feeling the soft hair against my skin. I'd always loved how masculine men's legs looked when there wasn't too much hair so they looked like grizzly bears or too little that I'd wonder if my legs had more when I forgot to shave for a few days. His had the perfect amount in all the right places.

"I think the designer naturally thought we'd sit the other way since the real view is out the window," he said as he moved my hair off my shoulder. "I like this way better."

"Staring at an empty shower?"

He gently pulled my head back to rest on his chest and ran his fingertips across my forehead. "With you."

Two words and he made me want to forget all my insecurities, all my worries about not being enough. He kissed the top of my head, and almost as if he could read my mind, whispered, "I like how you make me feel, Nina."

I said nothing, knowing he probably wanted to hear me say I liked how he made me feel. I wanted to say something—to tell him that I'd never felt anything like how he made me feel—but I couldn't. If he rejected me there, as I sat naked in his arms, or worse, said nothing in return, everything I feared would finally be true. I couldn't handle that.

His arm rested across my collarbone, and I bent my head to place a kiss on his wrist. I hoped he understood how much I loved hearing that I made him feel something good or special. Closing my eyes, I let myself enjoy his body pressed against mine and his strong arms around me. We sat so still the water stopped moving, as if we both wanted to stop time and just revel in this one moment. Finally, he sighed deeply and a tiny ripple slowly moved the water forward until it lapped against the front of the tub and the tops of our feet.

"I could sit here for the rest of time," he whispered in a faraway voice.

I brought his fingers to my mouth and kissed the fingertip of his forefinger, which had begun to wrinkle in the water. "I think you'd get all pruney."

He chuckled and kissed the top of my head again. "Then we'd be pruney together."

No matter how I tried to make the situation light and easy, he always brought it back right to center, right to the core of who he was. Either he said little and indicated less, or he spoke and made me want to forget everything else in the world but him.

He'd been right about the duck. It was delicious, and I did love it. I wondered if things happened the way he wanted them to simply out of his sheer desire to have them happen that way. Some people seemed to be able to manifest their desires like that. In the short time I'd known him, it had merely taken him expressing his wish for something to make it occur. Over and over, I'd seen him get what he wanted, but I couldn't say it was due to power or manipulation.

Life just seemed to give him what he desired.

And what he desired that night was me. We'd barely pushed aside the plates when his mouth was on mine, urging me to meet his passion with my own. My body was thrilled, but my mind found his changeable ways confusing. As we'd eaten, he'd said no more than five words, acting more like my boss than my lover. When I expressed how much I liked the duck, he merely smiled, saying nothing in return and continuing to eat. Then, like someone had turned on a light inside him, he looked over at me and he was that man who couldn't get enough of me again.

He led me over to stand in front of the floor to ceiling windows in the living room, and the view of the city below took my breath away. I stood just inches away from the wall of glass, my usual fear of heights pushed aside by the beauty of what lay before my eyes. High above

Manhattan, the entire city seemed to be laid out in all its glory. "It's gorgeous, Tristan. It must be impossible to get to sleep knowing this is here all for you to see every night."

His arms held me tight, and he looked up from kissing my neck. "I never look at it, to be honest."

Turning in his hold, I said, "How can you not? It's so stunning."

He kissed me on the lips and pushed my hair behind my ear. "I don't have the artistic eye like you do. It just seems like a million little ants scurrying around to me."

I traced a line from his Adam's Apple to the hollow right above his sternum, drawing circles in that place where his skin was so soft. His pulse beat lightly under the skin, and I stared at the gentle throbbing against my fingertip. "Everyone has the ability to see beauty. It's just a matter of letting it in. There's beauty in everything. That's art."

"I doubt that."

I looked up, intent on proving I was right. "Do you see where my finger is? Just under the skin is evidence of your heart beating. It's just a tiny pulsation, but it's beautiful."

"And this is art?" he asked, not convinced.

"What's more beautiful than the beating of the human heart?"

He took my finger from his neck and kissed it. "I knew it from the first time I saw you. There's something special in you, something light and good that drew me to you."

His words made me blush, and I felt my cheeks warm. No one had ever spoken to me like this before, and to have someone who could have anyone in the world as he could say this to me was thrilling and overwhelming at the same time. My emotions became jumbled again, and before I knew it, words were spilling out of my mouth letting him know everything in my heart.

"When you talk like this, I think that you might truly care for me. Do you know that? Then I let myself believe it and you turn off your feelings as quickly as they came on. I'm not like that. My feelings don't turn off, even when I wish they would."

"I love that you don't try to censor how you feel, Nina. It's one of the things that makes you so incredible."

His compliment was genuine, but it didn't help.

"I want to be able to censor them, though. I want to be able to do what you do. I want to be able to stand next to you and not want to touch you, like you can do with me."

A tiny look of sadness crossed his face for just a moment and then it was gone.

"You wouldn't be who you are if you repressed your feelings."

"How do you do it, Tristan? How do you control what your emotions do to you?"

He leaned down and kissed me softly on the lips. "I told you. This is how I must be. It's who I am. Can you live with that?"

"Can you promise me I'll always know what's in your heart, no matter what?" I asked, laying bare my fears for the first time.

Cradling my face in his hands, he pressed his forehead to mine and whispered, "No matter what you see on the outside, no matter what I say, what's in my heart will always be just what's there at this moment. You."

He took me there, in front of those windows—in front of the entire city—my body pressed up against the glass as he thrust into me again and again. I clung to him, first to calm my fears that I'd fall through the glass and plummet to the street below and then for the very happiness only he could give me. His hands held me to him, protecting me as he invaded my body with his cock and my heart with his words so passionate I would have believed them even if they were blatant lies.

We laid on the floor near where we'd made love, his hands worshipping my body as I tried to force my heart to harden over for the next time he shut off his feelings. I'd accepted who he was. Now I needed to accept who I'd have to become to love him.

Chapter Ten

I was sorry to see our time at Tristan's penthouse end. We hadn't done much except make love and eat, and I couldn't remember a weekend I'd enjoyed more. We'd talked about so many things, yet I didn't believe I knew him any better after all those words between us. In truth, he'd gotten me to speak more than he had, but as he'd hung on every word, I felt safe and opened up about my past. My tales of life in a small Pennsylvania town seemed to enchant him, so I'd told him likely more than anyone would like to know about growing up as the younger daughter of a father who was a writer. By Sunday night we were back in the country, me in my part of the house and him in his until night when I once again slept next to him. As always, he was gone when I awoke the next morning, and there was a note waiting for me.

Dear Nina,

Tonight when I return, we'll discuss the piece you've chosen for my bedroom in the penthouse. I look forward to seeing what you believe represents the man I am and have faith that your artistic heart lets you see what no one else can.

Love,
Tristan

I'd made my final decision before even returning to the house, so my day was spent in searching for it. After hours of looking through gallery and art retailer sites, I found exactly what I was looking for. It wasn't priceless or even expensive, but I was sure it was right for him. My heart soared at my success. If I could choose a piece so perfect as to show the man he was, I could do the job he was paying me for and do it well.

Tristan returned shortly before five and found me waiting for him in his office. Like any other employee, I was dressed and ready to impress my boss, sure my first assignment would end in a great success.

Dressed in a pale grey suit and sapphire blue shirt, he sat down behind his desk and straightened his tie. I waited for him to begin, barely able to contain my excitement at my finding. As I watched him attend to paperwork, the thought of how his other female employees saw him crept into my mind. A tiny flicker of jealousy sparked at the idea of someone like me sitting across from him studying his dress and mannerisms like I did. Did she love to watch his mouth as he spoke, wishing to feel his lips on her skin? Did she notice his hands, the long fingers and strong grip of the pen as he wrote a note to himself? Did she find how incredible he looked in his clothes as fascinating as I did, desperately wanting to loosen his tie as she ran her lips over his strong neck?

"I'm eager to see what you've chosen, Nina."

"I'm excited to show you. I think it's you to a T, and it fits with the decor of your bedroom there. Would you like to see the picture of it? I have it ready on my laptop."

He nodded and I made my way around his desk to show him. A few clicks and the image of my choice was sitting on the screen.

He studied it for what seemed like hours and then turned to look up at me. I couldn't tell anything by his placid expression, so I waited for him to say something to let me know what he thought. But he wasn't going to make it that easy for me.

"Tell me why you think this is what I should have taking up that blank spot on my wall in my bedroom. This will be the first thing I see in the morning and the last thing I see at night before I fall asleep, so convince me this is what I should have on my mind at such important times."

I looked down at the picture I'd stared at for an hour before he came home and began. "The frame is a dark wood, but in truth, it could be any frame you prefer and work with what the decor is there. It's the print inside the frame that's perfect. A masculine design with Greek inspired scrollwork, the words 'No legacy is so rich as honesty' speak to everything you've told me about yourself from the first night I met you. You have all the money and wealth you desire, which I'm sure includes the luxuries of fame, others desiring you, and any material possession you could want. Yet you've told me over and over in the short time I've known you that you value my honesty. I have to believe that for all your wealth you don't have people in your life who will give you this one thing you desire."

He waited a long time before he finally spoke. With a smile, he finally said, "Very impressive, Nina. Your talents were sorely under-utilized at the Anderson Gallery. That's more than clear. Do you have anything else you'd like to present in your proposal?"

I knew he was trying to unnerve me, but I wasn't going to be shaken. I believed in my choice and stood by it. Shaking my head, I tilted my chin upward slightly. "No. That's all."

That sexy, slow grin I loved spread across his lips. "It's perfect. I knew you'd be wonderful at this. Give Rogers the details tomorrow and he'll see that it finds its way to that blank spot on the wall."

I couldn't help but beam my satisfaction. My first assignment was a smashing success, and even more, I'd shown him that I understood the kind of man he was. In some ways, that meant more to me than his approval of my choice.

"Are you hungry?" he asked as he stood from behind his desk. "I've got a craving for pizza."

"I'm always in the mood for pizza! Is there a good place around here?"

"There is. It looks like it's straight out of a movie with checkered tablecloths and placemats with pictures of the map of Italy on them, but the people who own it know how to make good pizza."

This felt like a real date! Excited, I said, "I can be ready in minutes, if you can."

Before he answered, I was off like a shot to grab my bag and make sure I looked presentable. A few minutes later I returned to find him standing there in his suit and tie looking particularly unready for slices at a little pizza place. Likely, dressed like that, he'd stick out as badly as he did at The Last Drop. Stepping toward him, I ran my finger down his tie and smiled up at him. "Maybe you could loosen this tie and look like it's not your first time eating pizza."

Tristan arched one dark eyebrow. "Are you insinuating that I look uptight?"

"You've gone to this place before, right? I'm going to guess that nobody spoke a word to you the whole time you were there."

I saw by the slight downturn of his mouth that I was right. They'd probably thought he was some FBI agent coming to town to track down some serial killer. He had that icy, government official vibe sometimes.

As I slid the tie from around his collar, I explained, "They probably got the wrong idea about you. Small town pizza places don't likely get too many customers who look like you do."

"You make it seem like I'm some sultan. It's a suit and tie, Nina."

I stepped back and looked him up and down. "It's a suit that costs more than many people make in a month and a tie that likely cost more than most teenagers pay for a pair of sneakers, Tristan. Ordinary people don't wear that to get a slice of pizza."

He took the tie out of my hands and brought my fingers to his lips for a kiss. Settling his gaze on me, he said quietly, "Neither of us are ordinary, no matter how much you want to be."

His stubborn belief that I was anything but the regular person I'd always been made me smile. "Well, we don't have to flaunt our extraordinariness all the time. Sometimes it's just nice to appear like ordinary people, so off with the tie and jacket."

Tristan narrowed his eyes slightly for a moment, surprised by my order, but the jacket followed the tie and he was ready to go. "Better?"

"The top button can be undone too, if you really want to look relaxed," I teased.

He opened his collar and motioned toward the door. "I hope the car is going to be okay," he said in a mocking tone. "Or do we have to walk or buy some used car?"

As I headed for the front door, I said, "Now you're not taking this seriously at all, are you?"

"On the contrary. I'm up for buying another car. Or maybe a horse and buggy would help with toning down the...what did you call it?"

I turned around at the car and laughed. "Extraordinariness. It's a word."

"It's a mouthful," he joked and lifted my chin to kiss me. "Now get in the car. Pizza's waiting."

He hadn't exaggerated in his description of Tony's Pizza Heaven. Red and white checkered tablecloths covered the old square Formica tables and at each place setting were paper placemats with red, white, and green maps of Italy and cartoon drawings of major tourist attractions, like the Leaning Tower of Pisa and the Coliseum, on them. The wooden chairs were old and hard, but the place was warm and comfortable.

I skimmed over the laminated menu while Tristan seemed to study it, but when the waitress came over to take our order he was quick to tell her we wanted a large pizza and a pitcher of soda. I sat staring at him thinking how surreal this scene was.

He noticed my confused expression. "Something wrong?"

I wasn't sure if something was wrong. Maybe it was how comfortable he seemed at a place I'd been so sure he wouldn't fit in. Shaking my head, I answered, "No. You seem quite at home here."

"Surprised? You think you know me, but you don't know everything about me, Nina."

"I guess I don't. That's okay. You don't know everything about me either."

Smiling, he remained quiet, making me feel like he knew more than I suspected. The silence between us made me feel uneasy, and I shifted in my chair and looked past him at the pictures on the far wall. Black and white photographs of Italian architecture were scattered along the walls of the restaurant and set me at ease. Very much like art, they were beautiful to look at, even in their cheap faux wood frames.

As the silence between us continued, I wanted to ask if he'd been to this place with his family. The images of their faces stayed in my mind, making me wish I could learn more about them. The idea of an exact duplicate of Tristan out there somewhere in the world intrigued me, and the fact that he never mentioned anything about him or his parents made me want to know about them even more.

But if I'd learned anything in the time I'd known Tristan Stone, it was that he spoke only when he wanted to and only about things he wanted to let the world know.

True to his claim, the pizza was terrific and after he'd gotten a slice into him, he became even more relaxed and began talking. This was the man I loved being around, and there he was sitting in that tiny pizza place in the middle of nowhere, of all the unlikely places.

"I think you'll be tackling Dallas next," he said with a wink.

"Talking about work after five? Doesn't that break your rule?"

"Isn't that what rules are for?"

Who was this man? "Are you saying you like to break the rules? Mr. Suit-And-Tie wants to flout convention?"

"Let's take it easy on the flouting," he said with a chuckle. "As for Dallas, let's plan on Wednesday."

"Well, since you want to talk about work, what can you tell me about Dallas?"

There was that devilish grin again. "Let's just say it's going to be a golden opportunity for you to stretch your imagination."

"Sounds pretty cryptic. Care to offer any more details?" I asked as I leaned over toward his side of the table.

He leaned in toward me and smiled. "Just remember I have faith in you."

I waited for him to continue, but he just sat there staring and smiling at me. Finally, I said, "I think you're making me nervous. Are you just trying to psyche me out?"

"Me? Never."

"Well, that's good because I'm a woman on a mission. You'll see. Expect to be impressed."

His mouth grazed mine, and he licked his lips. "I already am."

When we got back to the house, I expected us to get into bed as we had most nights since I began living there, but he disappeared almost as soon as we walked in the door. I waited for him to come to my room, but an hour later he still hadn't and I made up my mind to find him.

I was surprised to see him coming out of his room dressed in a tux. He was leaving again to attend some affair and not taking me. Instantly, it felt like someone had stabbed me in the chest. I was good enough to sleep with or hang out with at some out of the way restaurant, but I wasn't good enough to show off to his fancy friends.

"Nina, I'll be back later if you want to talk."

Choking back tears, I angrily blurted out, "Talk about what? How unworthy I am to be taken anywhere anyone might see you with me?"

"You're being silly," he said as he tried to push past me.

I pushed against him, refusing to let him leave. "Don't treat me like I'm merely your goddamn employee."

"You are my employee, Nina, even if we are more than just that to each other."

His voice was flat and so much colder than it had been just a short time earlier as we ate pizza together. Why did he have to be like this? Was I really that embarrassing to be seen with at his parties?

"If we're more, then why don't you ever ask me to go wherever you go when you're all dressed up like this?" I asked, hating the needy sound of the words coming from my mouth.

"You wouldn't like these kinds of events."

"Don't dismiss me like this. I don't deserve it."

He pushed past me and walked toward the front door. I caught up with him just as he opened the door to leave, and he turned to face me. "I never said you did. I can't take you to many of the places I have to go, but that doesn't mean I don't want you by my side. It just can't be. That's the way it is."

"Why? I'm good enough for you to basically beg me to work for you and good enough to fuck, but I'm not good enough to be seen with you in public? Is that it?"

He stood silently staring at me for a long time before he finally said, "No. That's not it."

"More evasive answers that say nothing! That's what I get after everything we've done together?" I screamed as tears began streaming down over my cheeks.

My outburst made him cringe, and I saw in his eyes my words had affected him. In a low, almost sad voice, he said, "I told you, Nina. I can give you everything your heart desires, but I can only do it this way."

I watched him walk away and knew I had no answer for that. I'd thought that we were getting closer and he'd begun to open up, but all that was just my imagination. We were the same as we'd been since that first night he showed up in my life.

Tristan Stone and Nina Edwards. Two souls worlds apart, no matter if we lived in the same house or not.

CHAPTER ELEVEN

I marched up the stairs to the attic, needing to speak to someone from the life I'd left behind. The black phone sat on a wooden box hidden away in the corner, right where I'd left it, just waiting for me to reach out and touch someone. I slowly dialed Jordan's number and put the receiver up to my ear. It rang four times and then I heard her say, "Hey, this is Jordan. Leave me a message and I'll get back to you A.S.A.P."

My disappointment kept me silent for a few seconds and then I mumbled, "Hey, it's me. Nina. I'd say call me back, but I don't know the number and I don't even know if I should be using this phone. I'm still out at Tristan's house and just wanted to talk to someone. I hope everything's okay."

I put the phone down and slumped on the floor, pressing my back up against the wood slat wall. Sadness settled into me as I replayed the conversation Tristan and I had, and I wanted to cry but there weren't any tears. All I felt was a heaviness in my chest, like someone was pressing down on me trying to crush me.

What was I to him? That was what was crushing me. He treated me like a girlfriend, yet I was never to be seen. But I was his employee too, a fact that he seemed to impress upon me always at times when it hurt the most. I existed in some limbo between being someone he was willing to show off to the world and someone who was merely there to do his bidding.

As I sat there with the hard wall pushing against my back and my hurt feelings pressing down on my heart, a sense of regret slowly spread over me. I'd been such a fool! No matter what Jordan believed, good things didn't always happen to good people. That was even assuming I was good. I'd accepted Tristan's offer hoping for more than a job, but that's all the contract had promised. What did that make me? He'd never promised anything in that contract other than all that he'd already given me. I was being paid to do a job. The hope of something more was never part of the deal.

But hadn't he promised in every kiss and every time he'd made love to me that something more was what he wanted too?

Never before had a man tangled my emotions in such knots. When he touched me with those hands so strong yet so tender, he made me feel like I was the most important thing in the world to him. When he was inside me, moaning my name as he clung to me and his body shook from the feelings I created in him, his every word and movement said he cared.

Fuck! How had I let this happen to me? I wasn't some pathetic little schoolgirl who had no idea how things worked. I knew how men were and what they wanted. I may not be supermodel gorgeous, but I'd been with other men and knew the ways of the world. How had I fallen so quickly for Tristan and not seen what was really happening?

The problem was I didn't know what was really happening. To me, not showing me off as his girlfriend was a huge sign he didn't care, but in every other part of our relationship it was clear he felt something for me. What that was I didn't know, but I wasn't sure what I felt either, so I couldn't fault him for that. We'd moved fast since the beginning, so being unsure was fine.

Being ashamed of being seen with me at his parties and events wasn't fine.

The phone ringing jolted me out of my thoughts, and I scrambled to answer it before anyone heard the noise downstairs. Pressing the heavy receiver to my ear, I whispered, "Hello?" and held my breath as the line stayed silent.

"Hello? Is anyone there?"

"Nina? Are you okay? It's Jordan."

I sighed my relief and my heart began its normal beating again. "Jordan, how did you get this number?"

"It came up on my phone. Are you okay? You sounded like something was wrong on the message. What's going on out there?"

"I don't know. I think I made a mistake."

"Why? Did something happen?" she asked, her voice full of concern.

"For the second time since I've been here, he's gone off to some event he needed to wear a tux to and didn't invite me to go. I don't know what I'm doing here or why he's ashamed to be seen with me."

"Oh, sweetie. I'm sure he's not ashamed of you. Look at you. You're beautiful and smart and he's crazy about you."

Sniffling back the first of my tears, I sobbed, "He's not crazy about me. I'll bet anything he's at whatever affair he had to go to with one of those women he takes to things like that. Tomorrow he'll be in the paper standing next to some gorgeous, rail thin supermodel."

"Honey, don't cry. I'm sure there's a reasonable explanation why he doesn't take you to these things. Maybe they're boring and he doesn't want you to think he's boring."

"Jordan, I saw the picture in the paper. Did those people look like they thought that party was boring?"

She was silent for a few moments and then said, "He didn't look like he was having a good time. I remember you saying he didn't look like that with you. Oh, Nina, don't cry. It's going to be okay."

"How? How is it going to be okay? I'm contractually obligated to be around him for the next six months and even though we're sleeping together and he treats me like his girlfriend in private, he never takes me to places where other people like him will be. How is it okay that I'm basically some concubine?"

Jordan said nothing as I sobbed into the phone. What could she say? I was crying over something I couldn't have and she couldn't give it to me or help me get it.

"I feel so stupid, Jordan. I know it's only been a short time, but I can't help the way I feel. Why is this happening to me?"

Quietly, she said what I already knew. "Because you're trusting and good, Nina, and you think other people are the same. It's that small town upbringing in you."

"So I'm destined to be a fool for the rest of my life."

"Honey, I don't think you're foolish for caring for someone. And I'm not sure he doesn't care for you either. I don't know why he doesn't take you around those upper crusts he hangs out with, but I want to give him the benefit of the doubt. Not every guy makes a point to find a girl's best friend and ask her about your favorite foods. I bet he picked one of those and had that for you that first night, didn't he?"

I wiped my tears and hung my head. "He had all of them made for me," I admitted.

"See? I know it hurts now, but give him time. Maybe there's something you don't know about and he's not trying to be hurtful or cruel."

"Some best friend you are. I think you're supposed to tell me to dump his ass and that I can do better," I joked.

"You want that? I'm on it. You know I think you're one of the best people I've ever known, so if this is something you can't handle, you need to end this thing now."

That was easier said than done. "I have a contract, Jordan. I can't end it."

"You have a contract to work for him. That's it. If you don't want to be anything more than an employee, then I say you stick to your guns and be just that. An employee."

Jordan always knew what to say to make me feel better. Sitting up straight, I took a deep breath in. I could do that. There was nothing in the contract that said I had to sleep with him. Well, at least I hoped there wasn't.

"I could do that, couldn't I?"

"You could. But be careful, Nina. You may just get what you wish for and there will be nothing between you and Tristan but work. Is that what you really want?"

That feeling of something heavy pressing on my chest came back with a vengeance at the thought of Tristan being nothing but my boss. I didn't want that, really, but I didn't want to feel like I was something to be ashamed of anymore either.

"I don't know what I want, but I do know I hate feeling like this. If he can't be proud of being with me among people he socializes with, then we shouldn't be together. Maybe if I stop being his whatever I am, he'll see that."

"I don't know, Nina. I think you need to be very careful. I think there's something you don't know and if you do this, you could lose him."

"I'm not sure I have anything to lose, Jordan."

We sat silently for a long moment before she said, "Just take care of yourself, okay? And call me whenever you need me."

"Okay. I will. Oh, and don't call this number again, though. I'm not sure I'll be around to hear it."

"I won't. Just be careful and don't do anything without thinking it through first. Promise me you'll at least do that."

"I promise. I'll talk to you soon."

I hung up the phone and closed my eyes to calm the nervous energy that was already taking over my emotions. The mere thought of ending things with Tristan made my body shake, but I had to take a stand. I couldn't live like this, hoping that what he felt in private would someday be how he'd act in public.

Armed with a plan, I left the attic without looking for more details about Tristan and his family. My mind was intent on keeping strong and focused on what I could do about this. I may not have been able to control what he did, but I was able to control how I reacted.

I awoke from a good night's sleep ready to tackle my problems and the world. Stretching my arms above my head, I focused my eyes and there on the table near the window stood the biggest bouquet of roses I'd ever seen in my life. There had to be fifty long stem roses in the tall glass vase if there was one. Deep red, they looked like they were made of velvet, and their sweet fragrance filled the room.

They were beautiful and screamed of guilt. A tiny flicker of satisfaction ignited inside me at the thought that Tristan had felt bad about not taking me with him. Smiling to myself, I saw a note tacked to the large red bow around the roses. As always, he'd chosen to say what he needed to in a letter. It was very Tristan.

Rolling out of bed, I padded over to the gorgeous gift he'd left me—with a tiny nagging question in my mind of when he'd put them there—and buried my nose in the flowers. They smelled heavenly. I gently touched one of those blood red petals and felt its silky smoothness between my thumb and forefinger. As with everything else Tristan did, they were extraordinary.

The note was folded and in an envelope. I pulled it out and held it up to see a short message that left me speechless.

Dear Nina,
A great job deserves a great reward. Keep up the terrific work!
Love,
Tristan

I felt like a balloon whose knot had been untied. All the good feelings I'd had about the roses and how things stood with Tristan left my body in a huge whoosh until I felt totally empty. This gift was merely an attaboy, a pat on the back for a job well done.

Disgusted, I wrapped my hand around the thick bunch of stems and yanked the entire bouquet out of the vase, spraying everything including myself with water. Thorns stuck into my palm, making the whole thing even worse. There was no garbage can in my room, so I marched the dripping flowers down the hall to the kitchen and threw them away, feeling as if I had struck some kind of blow for women everywhere.

And then as I rejoiced in my newfound strength I turned around and saw Tristan standing there looking hurt, of all things. Those deep brown eyes stared past me at the garbage can with all those flowers sticking out and then at me. I wanted to say something, but no words came to my brain. What had seemed such a triumph now turned into a weird sense of guilt that poked at my gut.

He said nothing as we both stood there staring at one another, and the need to flee suddenly came over me. With all the bravado I could muster, I stomped past him through the doorway and bolted down the hall, sure that if I didn't go as fast as my legs would take me that they'd begin shaking uncontrollably and give out from underneath me. By the time I reached my room, I was out of breath and so confused I didn't know whether to congratulate myself or feel bad for hurting his feelings.

As I stood there, my back pressed against the closed door, I told myself I was doing the right thing. *Don't forget how you felt when he walked out that door last night.*

And then an idea hit me. If I could just remember that feeling for another twenty-two weeks, everything would be fine. That was easier said than done, though.

I took my time getting dressed, part of me dreading the fact that I had to face him at some point and he might have that wounded puppy look in his eyes. Another part of me worried that I wouldn't be able to keep up my strength when he touched me or did any of the dozens of things that made me crazy about him.

Jesus, if he got close enough for me to smell his delicious cologne, I knew I'd likely be lost. And if he gave me one of his sweet smiles, I didn't know if I'd be able to remember anything, much less how I felt the night before.

It was going to be a long six months.

"Nina, we'll be leaving early tomorrow morning and we'll be gone for two days and nights, so feel free to take today to get anything you need done."

His tone was decidedly cool, which in a strange way made me feel better. Now he got to feel how I did. Plus, if he stayed upset with me, it could make staying away from him much easier. Things were looking up.

How I was going to handle the sleeping arrangements in Dallas was beyond me, but I'd cross that bridge when I came to it.

"Fine. I have some laundry to do. If that's all, I'll see you tomorrow."

I waited for him to say something, but he just stared vacantly at me and proceeded to begin typing on his laptop. If he had any thoughts on what had happened to the flowers, he wasn't saying and I wasn't asking.

Rebuffing Rogers' offer to wash my clothes, I loaded up the machine and returned to my room. While my laundry did its thing in the washer, I checked my email and found a message from Jordan. All she'd typed was a link so I clicked it, looking forward to some cute pictures of kittens or even some lame chain letter. Anything to take my mind off Tristan.

As the page opened, I sat stunned at what appeared on my laptop's screen. There he stood in his tux looking like he was some marble statue of himself, a blonde on his arm, and other beautiful people around him at some event. I read the caption, needing to know what he'd done the night before.

"Stone Worldwide Charity Benefit at the Fairview Grand Hotel"

My heart sank at the sight of him holding the woman's arm. Some gorgeous blond woman's arm. I couldn't take my eyes off the screen, first analyzing every last inch of his date and then fixating on him. Her hair was the pale color blonde that appeared naturally on Scandinavian women and for a price on anyone who could afford a Fifth Avenue salon. I couldn't tell what color her eyes were, but I was sure any description of them would include the word sparkling. Perfect, brilliant white teeth sat in a mouth with bee stung lips that made me think of those bright red wax lips I used to buy at the candy store as a child. Worst of all, she looked genuinely happy and at home on his arm as they posed for the camera.

He looked less comfortable, which at least was one saving grace. In fact, he looked just as he had in the last picture Jordan had shown me of him on the gossip page and the ones I'd seen of him online back at the apartment. His eyes were cold, and that smile that never failed to melt my heart was nowhere to be found. He was just as gorgeous as always, but he seemed like a shell of the person I'd grown to know.

I so wanted that to make me feel better, but it was fleeting and it didn't take long before that horrible feeling like someone had carved out my insides was back. He'd left me behind to go to some charity event with some blonde bombshell, and there was no denying that. The proof was sitting on my laptop screen staring at me, mocking me.

Closing the tab, I hung my head and willed the tears to come. At least if I cried there was a chance I'd feel better eventually. Crying was useful for that. But nothing came. My emotions were telling my eyes that it was time to do the crying thing, but they didn't seem to get the message. They simply continued to stare at the screen, as if something was going to pop up to make all the emptiness I felt go away.

It was no use. I officially felt like shit and had the photographic evidence to prove that the man who I'd thought was my boyfriend was actually someone who didn't care for me enough to take me to his fancy society function so he'd found a gorgeous woman to go in my place.

And it wasn't even noon yet.

I checked my email once more with the hope that maybe Alex had sent me a message. At moments when a girl felt like nobody loved her, it was always nice to hear from a guy who liked her, even if she wasn't crazy about him. I didn't dislike Alex, but I wasn't really interested in him either. For what it was worth, he was beginning to look like a very good prospect after the whole Tristan thing, though. There was something to be said for a man who was straightforward.

Alex hadn't sent anything, but just as I went to close my laptop, I saw an email come in from Tristan with the subject "Hi." Unsure I wanted to know what it said but unable to stop myself, I opened it and began to read.

Dear Nina,

I'm looking forward to our trip to Dallas tomorrow. If you'd like to talk about it, I'll be back at five. Rogers hung your picture up this morning. It's perfect and exactly what I want to see when I open my eyes.

Love,
Tristan

Love, Tristan. It should have read as a command, Love Tristan, since that was what it seemed like. I closed my laptop and decided then and there I wouldn't be available to talk at five or any other time that day.

I'd made the decision to go down this path and I was damned if I was going to be swayed from it by his soulful eyes, sweet words, and every other weapon in his arsenal of seduction. If I wasn't good enough to be seen with in public, then he wasn't going to see much of me in private either.

Chapter Twelve

It's amazing how being stubborn always made situations so much worse. I quickly found that I was playing in a much bigger league with Tristan than I was used to. After avoiding him all the previous day, if I was thinking that a new day would make everything better, I was sadly mistaken. It seemed that Tristan Stone could be very much the personification of his last name at times and quite able to deal out the silent treatment as well as he took it.

Unfortunately for me, I was more big talk than anything else and the plane ride in his private jet nearly broke my resolve. I'd only been on a plane twice before and never anyone's private jet, so my excitement made the words want to come bubbling up out of my mouth. What stopped them was Tristan's icy demeanor as he sat across from me, only rarely acknowledging my presence with a knowing look and never saying a thing to me the entire three and a half hours it took to get from New York to Dallas.

If I hated the feeling I'd had that night when he'd left to go to the charity benefit, I hated this more. It was like torture to be so close to him and know that he could basically ignore me even as I sat less than three feet away.

He even did the silent treatment well. I sat there across from him admiring how good he looked and wondered if there anything this guy wasn't incredible at.

By the time we arrived at the hotel, I was chomping at the bit to say something, anything, but his hard expression made it clear he didn't feel the same urge. So I remained silent.

The Richmont Dallas was every bit as luxurious as Tristan's New York hotel, even if it had a more distinctly western feel to it. I had no idea what suite I'd be working in and followed his lead as we made our way to the rooms on the ninth floor. When he finally stopped at a door at the end of the hallway, I hoped that now I could at least get lost in work.

Two steps in and I understood his joke from the restaurant. Whoever had designed the Presidential Suite at the Richmont Dallas had been in love with the color gold and all its varied golden hues. From the draperies to the upholstery to the carpet, the color gold was everywhere.

"Golden opportunity," I mumbled accidentally. "Funny guy."

I realized I'd broken my silence and turned to see him smiling at me. There was that warm smile that had a way of breaking down the walls I'd tried so hard to build around my heart. It went all the way up to his eyes, making the skin around them crinkle slightly at the corners.

"I have faith in you, Nina. All you have to do is find art that will make this room appear less gold."

Looking around, I wondered if he'd given me an impossible task. "Wouldn't it just be easier to redecorate?"

His smile grew wider. "Probably, but then I wouldn't have had any reason to bring you here to Dallas."

And with that he rendered me speechless again. I didn't want to be a slave to his charms. I just didn't have a choice.

Swallowing hard, I tried to keep myself all business. "Must I keep to any particular style or period?"

He shook his head. "No. Make your choices based on what you believe will complete this suite and take the attention away from all this gold."

"How many pieces can I choose? This suite is four rooms."

Tristan scanned the rooms in front of us. "As many as you like. My faith is entirely in you."

"Will we be staying here? There are two bedrooms, I see."

He moved around me and walked over to the bar. Pouring himself a drink, he lifted his glass in the direction of the two bedrooms. "So we're to continue our living arrangements from the house?"

His voice had an edge to it. He was unhappy about my insistence on making him understand how much he'd hurt me. I imagined he didn't have many people in his life who dared to do that. I also sensed he wasn't a man who liked being made to do anything.

"I better get going. I've got my work cut out for me," I said with a forced smile.

Tristan took a sip of his scotch. "Dinner is at six, Nina. I hope I'll see you there."

Nothing in the way he said that told me he hoped anything. It was a clear command that I join him for dinner. What wasn't clear was if I'd obey.

Just a few hours later, I'd found some great pieces and was hungry, despite my wishing I wasn't. Tristan hadn't bothered me while I'd worked, but now as six o'clock loomed, I heard him in the outside room pouring himself another drink. The aroma of the dinner he'd ordered in wafted through to where I stood looking at myself in the mirror.

I would have known that delicious smell anywhere. He'd ordered roast beef.

A peace offering?

I stared into the mirror at the face that looked back at me and asked her, "What do I do? Do I let him back in?"

My reflection didn't have the answer either, and I walked out to find Tristan standing in the middle of the main room in a tux. My heart sank. He was going to do it again. I'd sit there alone in that room eating my roast beef he'd so graciously given me while he spent the night out on the town in Dallas with another gorgeous blonde or brunette.

Before I could say all the terrible things that were begging to be let out of my mouth, he took my hand and kissed the back of it. "I seem to be a little overdressed. Perhaps you should change so I'm not all alone in this getup."

"Why? So you can go meet up with your blond girlfriend and I can sit here like some teenage girl stood up for the prom?" I snapped.

"Blonde?" he asked, looking genuinely confused as to how I knew who he'd spent his time with the night before.

"I saw your girlfriend. Nice lips. Does she mind that you look like a statue when you're with her? I think I have it all figured out, Tristan.

You want someone who looks like her for in public, but you want someone who makes you smile like I do in private. Well, sorry. Maybe you should figure out how you can make her do the things that make you happy because I won't be some in-house concubine you keep hidden from everyone but your fucking butler and other household help."

My outburst surprised him for a moment, but then he just smiled. "Oh, you mean Janelle. You misunderstand. She's not my girlfriend. She's paid to be with me at those affairs."

"Paid? You pay a hooker to go with you instead of taking me? And this is supposed to make me feel better?"

A look of distaste crossed his features. "No. She's not a hooker. She's a…"

Waving my hand, I cut him off. "Fine. You're too wealthy for a hooker. What do they call them for someone like you? Call girls? Escorts? Either way, it's still you paying someone to be there instead of being seen with me."

"Nina, you've got it all wrong. She's not there to have sex with or even to date. She's there to act."

"Act? What do you mean, act?" I asked, completely baffled.

"Janelle is an actress who's an employee of mine. My company compensates her to appear at functions like the charity event and act like my girlfriend. There are about half a dozen who I pay very well to pretend I'm with them. Their entire job is to be at my beck and call so I don't have to attend those things alone. I can't imagine it's that bad a job, especially since I pay them handsomely."

I sat down on the chair nearby and struggled to process what he was saying. Who hired people to act like their dates? Jordan was right. Wealthy people did hire people to do their work for them.

"Why not just have a real girlfriend and take her? Is it because I'm not stunning like them?" I hadn't meant to sound so pathetic, but the words had come out far sadder than intended.

He knelt down in front of me and took my hands in his. "I don't take real girlfriends to those things because the press is always there and I learned my lesson a long time ago. It doesn't take long before having to be in front of cameras all the time takes its toll on a relationship. The board of directors likes me to present a successful image, and to them that means having a woman on my arm at all official events."

"Oh. So they aren't even ex-girlfriends?"

Smiling, he said, "No. Just actresses who agree to act like my girlfriends for a lot of money." He leaned forward and kissed me softly on the lips before he whispered, "You are stunning, Nina. And unlike those women, I want to be with you."

I couldn't stop the smile that broke out on my face. His words made me want to beam with happiness. "I don't know if you know this, but it's pretty obvious you don't want to be with them in all the pictures. You look like a really miserable boyfriend to those women. I'm not sure anyone's believing that you really like them."

"Maybe I should look happier? I could pretend better, I guess," he said with fake sincerity.

"No, no. You're doing a great job. Leave the acting up to the professionals," I joked.

He kissed me again, making my stomach do flips as his tongue slid across my lower lip. "I couldn't pretend to like them more than I do anyway."

"I think I feel bad for them now, Tristan. I know what it's like to work for you. To not even get a smile would make the job awful."

Looking up at me with his soulful eyes, he said, "I save my smiles for you. I hope what I've ordered for dinner means you'll give me one. It's roast beef, one of your favorites, if I'm not mistaken."

"It is, but you know that."

"Of course. Let's eat and then see what Dallas has to offer," he said as he stood and we walked toward the table.

"I've never been here, so I'm a newbie in the Lone Star state," I joked, trying to sound clever.

"Hmm, a virgin. I promise I'll go easy."

I sat down across from him and giggled. "Was that a joke?"

He leveled his gaze on me, looking sexier than a man ever should. "It happens sometimes."

As I reached for a piece of roast beef, I said, "I like it."

Tristan licked his lips and grinned at me. "I'll keep that in mind."

We visited Fountain Place, a beautiful park with lit fountains and pathways where we walked and talked about the gold rooms and what I thought might work to take the focus off the overwhelming use of the color. Tristan listened to each idea as if he were truly interested, but I had the sense that I could have been talking about any topic and he'd have been happy. Just as when we'd gone for the ride in his car that first night, I had the feeling he simply wanted company.

He stopped and sat on one of the benches near one of the streams, holding his hand out for me to join him. As we watched the water slowly move by and the fountains leap in the air, he put his arm around me and I leaned against him. It was a very common gesture but strangely unique between us. For as long as we sat there, I felt like we were moving toward something familiar I could relate to.

When we returned from our walk, he left to attend to some business calls that had come in while we were enjoying our time together. I sat on the sofa in the living room and stared at the gold all around me, mulling over my ideas for how to fix his art problem. Slowly, my mind drifted to the sleeping arrangements and the two bedrooms in the suite.

Should I go back to the way it had been before, now that I knew he wasn't spending his time with other women at those events? Maybe it was better if we kept sex out of our relationship for a while since it only seemed to muddy the waters between us.

I closed my eyes and thought about Tristan in his tux kneeling in front of me. Who was I kidding? My physical attraction to him had been so intertwined with what I felt for him from the moment I'd first seen him that the mere thought of denying how he affected me was laughable.

The man himself came back and interrupted my deep thoughts about not having sex with him, and I quickly knew it was not going to happen. He sat down next to me and leaned back against the sofa. Loosening his bow tie, he let the two ends hang around his neck and undid his top button.

Closing his eyes, he whispered, "Is it ever possible to atone for the sins of the past?"

I watched his mouth turn down in a scowl that marred his handsome face and wondered what his statement referred to. It sounded far too serious to be about the misunderstanding between the two of us, but I didn't feel comfortable asking any questions.

Reaching out, I lightly ran my fingertips over his closely cut brown hair, loving its softness against my skin. Seeing him like this bothered me, made me want to fix whatever was wrong, but he kept it inside him, locked away from where I could reach it.

His eyes still closed, he pulled me onto his lap and held me close. We sat together, our bodies pressed against one another, without saying a thing. It wasn't sexual but simple closeness. It was sweet solitude, and I wanted to believe for those moments I was able to give him some respite from what troubled him. When he finally spoke again, any trace of what had bothered him was gone, and he was the Tristan who could seduce me with just a few words or a glance from those beautiful eyes.

Cradling my face in his hands, he said in a voice full of emotion, "Nina, I want you in my bed tonight and every night. I don't know if things should be moving so fast or where we'll be in the future, but I don't want to spend another night without you."

I stared into his eyes and saw that flicker of apprehension I'd seen before. Did he actually fear that I'd deny him what I so desperately wanted myself?

I kissed his lips tenderly and sensed his desire grow inside him as he responded to my unspoken answer to be his with a kiss so passionate it nearly took my breath away. Pulling my body to his, he moaned into my mouth a sound so full of need that it sent an ache to the deepest part of me. I wanted to be the one to fulfill that need.

I tilted my hips into his body, and I was sure he knew how excited he got me, but I didn't care. This was who I was and I wanted him to accept me like I'd accepted him. He slid his finger under the cotton fabric and through my drenched slit, making my breath hitch.

"You're so wet," he groaned next to my ear. "I love how fucking wet you get when I touch you."

I tried to ignore his use of the word love again in relation to yet another thing I did, but I couldn't. I hung on every syllable he uttered, thrilled by the words he strung together as he stroked my tender flesh. The deep sound of them as he told me that he loved something about me only excited me more.

His mouth plundered mine, his tongue snaking in and out as he flicked the tip against my lips. I clung to him, my fingernails scraping across his neck as he inched me toward that feeling my body begged for. He knew what he did to me, and I loved it. He was power and control and expertly used them both to make me want him more than I'd ever wanted anyone else.

Sliding one finger and then another into me, he rubbed his fingertips over that one spot deep inside that sent my body into overdrive. I rocked back and forth on his hand, riding it as I desperately searched for relief from the need he created in me.

A vibrating sound jarred me from my ecstasy, and he pulled his phone out of his jacket pocket, never stopping his fingers' movement inside me. A quick look and then he set the phone on the table beside him, still focused on me.

"Do you need to get that?" I half-heartedly asked as I continued to ride those incredible fingers.

His dark gaze fixed on me and he shook his head. "That can wait. I want to see you get off first. Let yourself go, Nina."

I loved when he talked like that, his voice deep and husky telling me he wanted to give me pleasure. Spreading my legs wider, I rubbed my pussy against the heel of his hand, sending waves of bliss rocketing through me. He thrust hard into me, inching me closer and closer to orgasm, and I moaned at the feel of the first delicious contraction of my body around his fingers.

Tristan cradled the back of my head with his other hand, forcing me to meet his stare as I began to come. I wanted to close my eyes, afraid of what I looked like as he took me over that edge, but he sternly ordered me to keep them open.

"Look at me, Nina. I want to watch you come from just my fingers inside you. Don't look away, baby."

My orgasm roared through me and I stared into those gorgeous eyes completely focused on me and my happiness. He watched my every movement, whispering sexy little things as my release rolled on and on.

When my body finally finished and only tiny quakes continued to flutter through me, I collapsed on top of him, panting and weak. In my ear, he whispered, "I love watching you come. I want to see that again when my cock is deep inside you. Choose one of the bedrooms and wait for me. I'll be right back."

Pouting at his leaving, I moaned, "Don't go. Whatever it is, it can't be that important at this time of night."

"I promise I won't be long. And when I get back, I want to see that sexy look in your eyes again."

I slid off his lap onto the sofa and watched as he took his phone and left the suite. Frustrated, I trudged off to the closest bedroom and flopped down on the bed. I'd barely slipped out of my dress and he was back standing in the doorway grinning at me as I lay there in just my panties and bra.

"That was fast," I said with a smile, thankful that he'd gotten rid of whoever had called him so quickly.

He slipped out of his jacket and slowly unbuttoned his shirt as he circled the bed like an animal stalking his prey. "I had to take that. Some things can't be handled by anyone else." He shrugged his shirt off his shoulders and leaned down to kiss my lips. "Like what I'm about to do."

"More work?" I asked with a smile.

He climbed onto the bed and pulled me to him. "No more work. Just pleasure."

"Mmmm, I like that," I cooed as he kissed my neck, his tongue gliding gently over my skin and sending shivers over my body as we began to make love.

We laid there in each other's arms, and I looked up at him to see him staring vacantly off in the distance. "Hey, you look like you're a million miles away."

"Not that far. You're there too," he said quietly, but his eyes still looked so far away from our bed.

Running my finger over his tattoo, I traced the intricate design across his chest and over his shoulder, feeling a raised scar just above his heart. I'd never seen it before, but now it was as obvious as the tattoo.

"What's this from, Tristan?"

He looked down at where my finger touched and frowned. "That's where a piece of metal went through me."

"That close to your heart? What happened?" I asked, horrified at the thought that anything had come so close to killing him.

"I was in a plane crash with my brother and parents. I was impaled by a metal rod which pinned me to the seat. The doctors said it missed my heart and everything else by millimeters."

His voice was full of sadness, and I squeezed him tightly to me. I was afraid to hear any more, but he continued. "I sat in that seat, unable to move, as my family died around me. My twin brother was sitting behind me and was stabbed by the metal rod, but it hit him right in the heart."

"Oh, Tristan. I'm so sorry."

My words felt so inadequate, but he wasn't listening to them. He continued to talk, his voice low and sad. "My mother died instantly, thank God, but I watched as my father lingered in agony, crying out for someone to help us. I couldn't speak, couldn't let him know that I was still there right behind him so he wasn't alone. I don't know how long he lived, but by the time the crews arrived, he was gone too. I didn't know about Taylor until they finally got me out and days later told me the metal rod that had somehow missed my heart had found his."

"When was this?" I asked, thinking about that portrait of a happy family sitting in a dark trunk in the attic.

"It will be four years this December. That's how I ended up as the CEO of Stone Worldwide. I never wanted to be that. That was Taylor's dream. He wanted to take over when my father retired. He'd groomed him since high school. Remember when I told you I attended Wharton? So did my brother, except he graduated. He'd just finished his MBA when the accident happened."

His story broke my heart. I understood all too well what it felt like to lose someone you loved. My mother had died when I was just a little girl, and my father had been murdered just around the time Tristan's family had died. To watch them in agony and not be able to do anything to save them was more than I'd be able to stand.

Tears filled my eyes at the thought of him sitting there, helpless to save the people he loved, injured, and not knowing if he too was going to die. Gently stroking his cheek, I kissed him, wanting to take away the pain he held inside. "I had no idea, Tristan. I'm sorry."

He shrugged and pressed a smile onto his lips. "So I'm all alone, I guess."

I cradled his face in my hands, looking into his sad eyes. "You're never alone. I'm here, and the ones we love never really leave us. As long as they stay in our hearts, they're with us."

His smile softened. "That sounds like something my mother would say. My father and brother would never think that way."

"Are you more like your mother?" I asked, curious about the beautiful woman with the hint of sadness in her face I'd seen in that portrait.

He closed his eyes. "I don't know. I never felt like I was like my father or brother, so if I was like anyone it was my mother."

"I never really got to know my mother. She died when I was five, and from then on, it was just my father, my sister, and me."

Tristan's opened his eyes and turned to me, pushing my hair off my face to kiss my cheek. "I'm sorry about your mother. I guess I was lucky to have twenty-five years with mine."

"I lost my father right around the time you lost yours. Someone gunned him down one night while he was working on his latest exposé of some industrial problem or something. I don't remember. All I know is that one night he was gone, and I felt like I was alone. But then I remembered that he told me when my mother died that the people we love never leave us as long as we keep loving them. It's hard, but I think he was right. It's four years next month, but he's still with me."

Pulling me closer to him, Tristan's body tensed. "I'm sorry, Nina. I guess we've both seen a lot."

CHAPTER THIRTEEN

"So what do you think?" I asked nervously as Tristan stood next to me, his arms folded.

His face was expressionless, something I suspected was intentional, even though the twinkle in his eye made me believe he liked my choices for the Presidential Suite. The series of prints showing hand painted blue and white vases was simple, but just the thumbnails on my laptop screen gave the overly golden room an entirely different and more pleasant feeling.

I knew I was feeling pleased with my choices. Now it was just up to Tristan to give them his seal of approval.

His silence was unnerving, though. While I didn't mind standing there staring at him, I could think of better things to do that involved the two of us together.

"Well?" I asked again, hoping to egg him on.

Tristan turned toward me and smiled. "I don't think so. I'm not in favor of these."

Everything in my body sagged for a moment before my brain clicked into defensive mode. What did he mean he wasn't in favor of them? "What's wrong with them?"

He tilted his head as he looked at the pictures again. "They don't work for the feeling of the place."

"You mean the gold feeling?" I asked sarcastically.

A slow smile spread on his lips as he straightened his head and looked over at me. "I like the colors, but the images aren't right. You'll have to try again."

"Hmmmph."

"What was that you said?" he asked, obviously teasing me.

I stuck my tongue out and pouted. "Nothing. I have work to do. Art doesn't just happen you know, Mr. Stone. When I'm ready, I'll request your approval again."

He flashed me that warm and sexy smile that made me think about him on top of me in bed. "Thank you, Ms. Edwards. When you need me, I'll be in the other room. Dinner is at five."

Grabbing my laptop off the desk, I turned and walked toward the end of the suite as I yelled back, "I'll be hungry by then, so I can see me showing up, Mr. Stone."

I didn't look back to see his expression at my comment because it was too hard to keep my hands off him when he looked so good. How anyone could make a pair of black pants, brown dress shirt and a tie look so incredible was beyond me. Suddenly, an idea jumped into my mind. Who picked them out?

My curiosity quickly took up every inch of my mind, and I returned to the outer room to find him standing and reading the newspaper. "Tristan, do you buy your own clothes?"

He looked up from the Wall Street Journal and raised his eyebrows. "No."

"Oh." That wasn't the answer I wanted to hear. Now I had a vision of one of his actresses trolling upscale men's stores picking out his wardrobe with loving care. Or worse, one of them picking out his clothes and then calling him like Tristan had called me in the dressing room. I was nothing if not ordinary when it came to the green-eyed monster.

"I have a personal shopper handle that. His name is Angelo. Is there something you want me to tell him for the next time he does my shopping?"

For the moment, my ugly jealousy crawled back into the dark recesses of my mind and I rejoiced at the idea that Angelo was the one with the incredible taste. "No. He's doing a great job."

Tristan put the newspaper on the coffee table and came to stand in front of me. Looking down, he ran his finger along my jaw line. "I'm sure Angelo will be happy to know my girlfriend approves of his choices."

Girlfriend. I was his girlfriend.

"Well, at least *he* is successful with his choices," I joked as I turned to go back to my work, pleased with that one word he'd said with such ease.

"Okay, this time you're going to be blown away by my choices. I see what the problem was with the first group, but this will get the Tristan Stone seal of approval. I know it."

To be honest, much of what I'd said was bluster, but I did want him to approve of my art choices. As much as I truly wished to succeed at my job, I wanted more to make Tristan as happy as he made me.

I held my arm out like a hostess on a game show and introduced him to the thumbnails of a series of five watercolors of blue and white Mexican owls. Charming yet sophisticated, they were more in line with a southwestern motif and still helped to diminish the effect of the overwhelming gold found everywhere around me. Now all I had to do was convince Tristan they were as perfect as I thought they were.

"Let me introduce you to the Mexican owls."

He leaned down and rested his palms on the table as he studied the pictures of those sweet birds. I saw his eyes move slowly from left to right across the screen before he turned his head to look at me. "Okay. Tell me why these are perfect."

"These are pictures of owl pottery from Mexico. Containing a number of different shades of blue from navy to royal blue along with pure white, they're examples of Mexican folk art, as can be seen in the floral motif painted on the part of the bird's body below his head. As we're in Texas, which has been heavily influenced by Mexican culture, the pictures of these pieces work with the area, and the blue and white colors are perfect to alleviate the overpowering gold your decorator seemed to fall in love with courtesy of your checkbook."

His gaze never wavered from mine as I spoke, and when I was done, he looked back at the pictures and stood to his full height. "Very nice, Nina. Very nice. Thank you."

As we were in work mode, I suspected that was all I was going to get. Perhaps I'd receive a bouquet of flowers tomorrow, though. That might be nice again, and this time I wouldn't throw them in the trash.

"Thank you, sir," I said playfully. "I'm pleased you like my choices for your suite."

"Sir?" he asked in a stern voice.

My face warmed at his question, which told me I might have taken my teasing too far. "I was just playing around. You know. Lightening the mood a little."

He looked down at the watch on his right wrist for the time and lifted his eyes to me. "It's five, so we're not working anymore. Are you hungry?"

"Not really."

"Good. I've decided we're flying back to New York early, so we'll take off in about an hour. My staff will make sure our bags are taken to the plane, so we best be on our way."

"Tristan, I haven't packed anything. All of my things are all over the bathroom," I said in protest, uncomfortable with the idea of one of his people touching things like my razor and moisturizer.

"I'll buy you replacements when we get back then."

I wrinkled my nose at the thought of wasting money like that. "That's ridiculous. Why can't I just pack my things myself? Why would you spend money when you don't have to?"

He lifted my chin with his fingertip and smiled at me. "I'd spend all I have if it made you happy, Nina."

Wrapping my hand around his finger, I brought it to my mouth in a kiss. "You don't have to spend money on me like that. I mean, I love the clothes, and it was very sweet of you to buy me all that new shampoo and conditioner when I moved in, but you don't have to. I thought that wealthy people had money because they didn't spend it."

"Wealthy people have money because they spend it wisely. I think buying things to make you happy is very wise."

There was no point in fighting him on this. He had decided the issue, and I was expected to be content with it. In truth, I knew there were far worse things than a man buying me whatever made me happy whenever I wanted it.

But the stubborn part of me still thought it foolish.

"I'd be happy if you never bought me a thing again just knowing you love me."

And as soon as the L word left my mouth, I felt like crawling into a hole. He'd never said he loved me—just written it—and the look on his face screamed that he hadn't meant what I'd hoped when he used it in his notes.

That same look of fear I'd seen in his eyes a few times before returned, and he quickly looked away toward the bedroom. "Well, you better get your things packed so the bags can be ready. We're going to be late if we don't get moving."

I'd done it. Ruined everything by using the L word too soon, and now I felt like a fool. I hurried into the bedroom to escape the look of discomfort in his eyes. He was probably thinking of how he could let me down easy. He could be sweet like that. Maybe he'd disappear back to the city, leaving me out in the country. Or maybe he'd suddenly have a lot of work functions to attend with the actresses, again leaving me alone out in the country.

Whatever he would do, I cringed at what I'd done. I knew better than to introduce that word into a relationship so early. Nothing worked better to send a man running for the hills than to start talking about love this soon, and I'd gone and done it. What an ass I was!

I quickly packed my things and returned to the living room. Tristan stood waiting, and as we left, I had the feeling whatever progress we'd made while we'd been in Dallas was gone, blacked out by my silly slip of the tongue.

Men were funny when it came to expressing what they felt, but a woman knew the truth about the man she was with if she cared to pay attention. Tristan was very much the same man he'd been with me all along as we rode on the plane and the drive back to the house. He laughed at my forced jokes, which was nice since I felt like I was walking on eggshells, and even held my hand as we rode from JFK to his house upstate.

But there was something different about him. It was subtle, but it was there.

By the time we got back to the house, all I wanted to do was skulk into my bedroom with my tail between my legs and hope that a little time apart would repair any damage I'd done. I wouldn't have blamed him if he wanted to escape to the city. He seemed as interested as I was in going off on his own and made some excuse about having work to do as we walked through the front door.

A quick shower and I was ready to crawl under the covers. I changed into my t-shirt and shorts and flopped down on the bed, physically and emotionally exhausted. How he travelled like he did baffled me. Just the trip to his penthouse and then to Dallas had worn me out, but I knew what I was feeling was more in my heart than in my bones.

Regret was exhausting. And for two days and two nights it nearly wore me out. I busied myself with researching possible art groupings for future suites and penthouses, just trying to keep my mind off what had happened. Noticeably absent were any flowers in my room when I woke up either morning.

On the third day, I checked my email and saw that Jordan had sent me a message. I stared at my laptop's screen in terror, praying to God that she hadn't sent me anymore links to pictures of Tristan and stunning women. Finally, after a long tug of war between wanting to know what she'd sent and pure, unadulterated dread at the thought of him with someone else, I clicked on the little envelope icon and breathed a tremendous sigh of relief. No Tristan and hot women, thankfully. Just an email to tell me I needed to pay my cell phone bill. Seems I'd forgotten to pay it and the fine people at the phone company had been good enough to send me a reminder that had ended up in her mailbox that morning.

I tapped out a quick thank you email, making sure I let her know that everything was so much better now between Tristan and me. Lying to my best friend made me feel worse, but I didn't know how to explain that I'd actually succeeded in finding out he wasn't with other women only to ruin everything with a rookie dating mistake.

Despite not having even a bar of service out there, I had to keep my cell. I may have been out in the country, but I wasn't back in time. A few clicks and I was at my bank's online site with the hope that I had enough in my account to pay my bill. Poor and I were long time friends since college, but if Tristan had deposited the $20,000 advance in my account, I'd be in better shape than ever before.

I logged in and for the first time in my life, a number took my breath away. My eyes were glued to the page for so long they began to dry out. I rubbed them and opened them again to see my bank account had a balance of $25,085.47.

There must have been some mistake. Over and over I told myself those exact words as I clicked to check the source of the deposits. One for $20,000 had been made the day I'd signed my contract and one the day after we returned from Dallas for $5000. But what was that for? I wasn't due to be paid for my first month for weeks.

A knock on my door that night shook me out of feeling sorry for myself and my lovelife woes, and I opened it to see Tristan standing there in just the silk pajama bottoms I'd seen draped over a chair in his room.

"I'd hoped you'd be in my room," he said with that innocence that sometimes seeped into his voice.

I looked away and bit my lip nervously. "I just figured you'd want to be alone. I mean...well, I thought maybe you'd be back at the penthouse instead of staying here."

"Why?"

His question made me turn to look at him, and he seemed genuinely confused by what I thought. There was a gentleness in his eyes that made me want to say what was on my mind, so I came clean.

"I'm so sorry I said that back in Dallas, Tristan. I didn't mean to put words in your mouth. It's only been a short time that we've known each other. I mean, it feels much longer since we've spent so much time together, but..." I let my sentence trail off and finally said, "I didn't mean that I actually thought you felt that way."

He extended his hand and held it out for me to take it. "Come with me."

I took a deep breath and slowly lifted my hand to place it in his. He closed his fingers around mine and began leading me to his bedroom. We said nothing as we walked, until finally he closed the door behind me and whispered, "You belong here with me. And you don't have to be sorry for anything you said."

For the moment, remaining silent seemed like the best idea. What could I say? That I wished he really felt that way about me so I wouldn't feel ridiculous for falling in love with someone after only two weeks? I knew how that would sound. I mean, I'd been the person who'd told friends time and again that it took months or even years to truly fall in love with someone and here I was full on, head over heels in love with Tristan Stone, no less.

He sat on the edge of the bed and looked over at me like he wondered what I was doing all the way over near the door. The chair near the window was empty, so I sat there, so not wanting to talk about this anymore.

"I think we should talk."

Ugh. There it was. The international signal for what's about to come next is going to rock your world. I said nothing while my stomach dropped and I swallowed hard. I had no idea what he'd say, but as the seconds ticked by and he still hadn't said a word, the room began to feel like it was shrinking around me. The fun house feeling was anything but fun.

"This has been moving pretty fast, Nina. I didn't intend on things getting to where they are so quickly."

It was so much worse than anything I'd imagined. He was dancing around the elephant in the room, but it was no use. He was breaking up with me. This explained the extra five grand. That was my parting gift, like the losers got on game shows.

I wanted to run away and hide. Standing up, I tried to steady my legs and get the hell out of there, but I didn't take three steps toward the door before they gave out and I was in a heap on the floor. All I could think was that was the perfect moment to be struck by lightning and disintegrated into dust.

"Nina, open your eyes. Talk to me."

Tristan's voice was laced with concern, and I opened my eyes to see a matching look on his face. Or maybe it was pity. Either way, I was still there in one piece and he was leaning over me.

I propped myself up on my elbows and plastered a smile on my face. "I'm fine. Just slipped. No big deal."

Scooping me up from the floor, he lifted me in his arms and onto the bed. He was so gentle, but I was even more convinced that he was breaking up with me. Now he probably just felt bad.

"Are you okay?"

Silently, I nodded. I was fine. The same old Nina I'd always been and always would be. It had been fun and the thought of being Tristan Stone's girlfriend had been very seductive, but it was over now.

"Tristan, I think I should go back to my room now. I don't feel so well."

"You should stay here where I can be sure you're okay," he said so sweetly with that tender smile that melted my heart.

I looked up at him and suddenly everything came flowing out of me. "Why? I know what you're going to do. My falling shouldn't stop you. I understand. Guys like you don't need or want just one woman. You can have anyone in the world, so why stick with just one?"

His eyebrows lifted as I spoke and he grimaced. I guess the truth hurt. Well, I understood that.

"What are you talking about?"

"Don't play dumb with me. You're breaking up with me. Don't worry. I'll be fine. It's not like we were together for years. I won't make any trouble for you either."

"Oh. Well, that's good. I wouldn't want to have to sic my lawyers on you."

Before I could tell him that I thought he was acting really shitty, he smiled and smoothed my hair from my face. "I wasn't breaking up with you. I just wanted to talk after the awkward business the other day."

I sat up and stared at him, confused. He wasn't breaking up with me? "What do you mean? I thought I scared you off with the L word."

He sat down next to me and hung his head. "I have to admit I did freak out a little when you said it. Sorry about that."

"I just said it because you kept writing it in your notes. It wasn't like it was a big deal."

Tristan turned to face me. "It is a big deal. I don't say I love you to every woman I date."

"That's good to hear," I mumbled.

"I don't think one word is a reason for two people to stop spending time together, Nina."

"I guess not." Sitting up, I blew the air out of my cheeks. "So what do we do now?"

"We could forget anything like this ever happened and continue like we were," he said in a hopeful voice.

"What were we doing, Tristan? You meet me one night, convince me to work for you, make me move in here, all the while sleeping with me. I haven't dated thousands of men, but I can safely assume most people don't call that dating."

"I'm not most people, Nina." He leaned toward me and pressed his forehead to mine. "I need you to trust me. This is the only way I can do this. Can you trust me?"

I closed my eyes and imagined not having Tristan Stone in my life. Suddenly, my chest felt hollow, like my heart had been drained of every drop of blood and all that was left was an empty, useless part of me. I didn't want to lose Tristan. I wasn't sure what this was we had together, but being with him was so much better than not.

"Yeah. I can."

He kissed me long and deep, making my legs go weak all over again, but for a good reason this time. We may not have been at the place where we said we loved each other, but it felt like it.

And I loved that.

CHAPTER FOURTEEN

The summer went by and every day Tristan and I grew closer and closer. By the time we'd known each other for four months, I could honestly say I loved him. I loved the way he left flowers in my room some mornings and surprised me with jewelry other days. I loved how he slowly withdrew from attending events with the actresses to spend time watching movies with me.

I loved how attentive he was, even if I didn't understand it sometimes. Like why after he shot down one of my choices for a penthouse or suite he always deposited more money in my bank account. Or why he made sure Jenson watched over me when I went back to Brooklyn to see Jordan. I'd asked him about these things once or twice, but he always just smiled and said something about how much he enjoyed taking care of me.

It was a comfortable existence, even if it wasn't the type of life many women would like. I understood not to ask questions about certain things, and I didn't. It was a trade off I was willing to make.

The summer night air grew chillier, signaling autumn's coming in upstate New York. It had been a long, hot summer and I welcomed the change fall would bring. As the leaves began to slowly turn the vibrant golds and reds so typical of the trees in the Northeast, Tristan announced at dinner one evening that we would be leaving to see another suite. It had been over a month since he and I had traveled to San Francisco on what had ended up feeling like the trip of a lifetime, so I couldn't imagine what could top that.

"We'll be gone for at least a week, so be sure to tell Jordan," he said casually as he poured himself a drink.

I couldn't help but smile. "I think it's really great that you don't want me to forget about her."

"Why would I? She's your friend. Plus, I owe her. If it wasn't for her information, I wouldn't have been able to surprise you that night."

How long ago that night seemed now. Then we'd been basically strangers, learning those first things about one another. Now, just months later, we were like an old married couple eating dinner each night at five, laying in bed late on Sunday mornings, and bickering about which movie to watch on Saturday nights.

I stood behind him and wrapped my arms around his waist, pressing my cheek to his back. "Where are we going?"

Covering my hands with his, he turned his head to face me. "Venice."

I moved around him and stood looking up in amazement. "Venice? As in canals, gondola rides, and the Doge's Palace?"

"Yes, yes, and I have no idea."

"I can't believe it. And how can you have no idea what the Doge's Palace is?"

"Just wait until you see it, Nina. The hotel is on the Grand Canal, and although I can't say most of my hotels do much for me, the one in Venice is an exception."

"What am I going to be able to add to one of your suites in Venice?" I asked, feeling immediately incapable to do anything to improve anything in that great city.

He lifted my chin to make me face him. "Don't doubt yourself. I believe in you."

That was easy for him to say. He didn't have to pick art to improve on one of the most artistically beautiful cities in the world. "Is this some sort of final exam or something? My six months are almost up, so is this the big test to see if I can keep my job?"

Tristan winced ever so slightly at the mention of my contract. "No. Think of this as merely a vacation."

"A working vacation," I corrected him. "Will we be able to visit some of the museums?"

"Of course."

Just as I began to chatter on about all the great museums in Venice, his cell phone vibrated in his pants pocket, and as he seemed to do more and more, he apologized for having to take the call and left the dining room. Of all the changes that had occurred over the past months, this one I disliked. Ever since that night in Dallas, it seemed like his phone was always interrupting our time together. It rang almost constantly, and at least once a day, he left to speak to someone, even though with me he claimed that after five was a time he wanted nothing to do with work. I didn't know if he answered only one person's call or if he allowed himself one call each night, but whether it was during dinner, as we relaxed, or just as we fell asleep, he took that one call, always leaving before he answered it.

At first I'd been suspicious and worried that it was another woman, but each night he returned to the house and me and rarely left. Even when he went out to attend some work function, he told me where the event was to be held and which actress he was escorting that night, even joking about his stiffness and being a bad fake boyfriend. And every morning after, I saw him and the girl du jour on Page Six, with Tristan as uncomfortable and rigid as always at just the place he'd said he'd be.

I'd considered asking him about the calls, but something told me I shouldn't. Maybe it was the stressed look on his face every time the phone vibrated, but I didn't want to know what made him unhappy. And I didn't believe he wanted me to know.

When he didn't return for nearly thirty minutes, I began to get worried. Had he left on some emergency he couldn't tell me about? After roaming around the house for ten minutes more, I finally found him down near the indoor pool just sitting on one of the chaise lounges. Leaning back with his eyes closed and a slight frown, he looked very much like he always did after his daily phone call.

"I think people generally take off their shirt and pants in this room," I joked, hoping to cheer him up.

He said nothing, but the tiny beginnings of a smile formed on his lips. They never really got to a full grin, but for a moment he seemed happier.

"Is everything okay, Tristan?"

Opening his eyes, he sighed and sat up. "I need a drink." Before I could say anything in reply, he was up and gone from the pool leaving me standing there alone. When I caught up to him, he'd poured himself another double scotch and was doing his best to get the alcohol into his system as quickly as possible.

I stood in the doorway of the living room and saw the sadness in him. It hit me in the middle of my chest and made me want to take him in my arms and never let him go. His posture screamed that he was dealing with something that weighed on his mind. He sat in a chair in the corner of the room, his shoulders drooped and his head tilted back. He watched me approach him, but I had the sense he was far away and looking right through me.

"You can talk to me, Tristan. I'm more than just your in-house art expert," I said sweetly as I ran my fingertip over his closely cut hair. "I hate to see you so unhappy."

Those deep brown eyes looked up at me and he said, "It's nothing I can't handle, Nina. Don't worry about me."

I was worried, though. The drinking, the frown, the phone calls that seemed to affect him more and more. Bending down, I kissed the top of his head, loving the feel of his soft hair against my lips. "I don't like seeing you like this, Tristan," I whispered.

He caressed my arm and gave me a forced smile. "It'll be fine. Once we're in Venice, everything will be better."

I hoped what he said was true, but I feared there was something slowly coming between us—something that he wanted to keep hidden but was gradually separating him from me. Later that night as he held me in his arms after we'd made love, nearly all traces of whatever was troubling him were gone and he was the sexy and charming man I'd fallen in love with. He played with my hair as he always did when I laid my head on his chest, wrapping it around his finger and then releasing it again and again, while he told me about his first time visiting Venice years ago as a teenage boy, long before he was the owner of Richmont hotels.

"You sound like you had a great time."

"I did. It was one of the best times I had with my father. It was just the two of us that time. Taylor and my mother stayed behind because he got sick at the last minute, so for one of the few times in my life, it was just me and my father."

There was something unsettling, something darker in his voice as he talked about how his father had spent the entire week in meetings as he'd wandered around the city alone. His words were all about how much he enjoyed Venice and the freedom to explore it at the age of sixteen, but beneath them was an emotion I didn't think even he knew was there. I listened as he recounted stories of late nights on the Piazza San Marco with girls he barely knew and his first night of drinking while he laughed at his youthful foolishness, yet all the time his left hand rested on the bed balled into a tight fist.

I kissed over the ridges of his stomach, loving the feel of his body against my lips. "Am I going to have to worry about you and Venetian girls on this trip, Casanova?"

"No, I promise to behave this time," he joked.

Sliding up his body, I kissed him on the lips. "I love it when you smile like that. I like to think that it's a smile you save only for me."

"You've seen pictures of me, haven't you? I don't ever smile for them."

I placed a tiny kiss on the tip of his nose. "Good. I like that."

Tristan cradled my face in his hands. "You're the only person in the world who's allowed to know that I'm nice. Everyone else thinks I'm that cold man who shows up at work and those charity things I have to attend."

"So if I told your other employees how you are with me they'd be surprised?"

"I don't usually talk to the people who work for me. I have managers and assistants for that. In fact, you're the only person who works for me that I speak to."

I wrinkled my nose at his distinctly elitist comment. "I guess little ole' me should feel blessed."

He either didn't pick up on my sarcasm or didn't care to pay attention to it. "I don't know about blessed, but you certainly can consider yourself special."

"Oh, can I?"

Sliding his hands down to cup my ass, he pulled me into him. "Yes. You are the only person I smile for and the only one I sleep with. I think those are two very good reasons to think you're special."

I wanted to say "I love you" at that moment as he smiled up at me and held me close, but I didn't. It wasn't fear of rejection now, but I didn't want to ruin things between us. He probably knew how I felt even though I hadn't said it, and in my heart, I believed he loved me. That we hadn't said it didn't mean a thing. They were just words. We told each other every day with our actions that we loved each other, and I was content with that.

"We should get some sleep. Venice waits for us tomorrow," I whispered as I rolled off him onto the bed.

In my ear, he whispered, "Good night, Nina," as he wrapped his arm around me, pulling me to him.

I brought his hand to my lips and kissed it gently. "Good night, Tristan."

I love you.

I twirled around the living room in our suite at Tristan's hotel in Venice, my eyes straining to open as wide as possible to take everything in. Nearly nine hours on the plane and even though I hadn't slept the whole time, I was keyed up and eager to see as much of Venice as I could that day.

"It's gorgeous! I can't believe I'm here in Venice and this incredible hotel is yours," I gushed. "No wonder you love this place!"

Every wall I set my gaze on was more beautiful than the last. Frescoes and reliefs adorned the walls, evidence of the expert artistic hands of Venetian craftsmen from long ago.

Tristan stopped my turning and stood behind me with his arms around my waist. "I'm glad you like it. It really is nice, isn't it?"

Turning in his hold, I looked up at him and couldn't believe how understated he was about all of the beauty around us. "Nice doesn't do it justice. It's the most beautiful place I've ever seen. I can't believe this is yours."

"Aw, shucks," he teased. "It's nothing."

"Don't get all humble on me now. This is extraordinary. I don't think I have the words to describe how extraordinary this is."

He leaned down and whispered in my ear, "Then get ready to be speechless when I show you the balcony."

I followed him out the enormous glass doors to a balcony that overlooked the Grand Canal of Venice. Gondoliers steered their boats through the water past hundreds year old pink and gold colored gothic buildings. These were the places I'd spent hours fantasizing about as an undergrad art student, and here I was staring across the water at them from my very own balcony.

"Oh my God, Tristan…it's the most incredible view I've ever seen. Thank you."

He said nothing and after a few minutes of staring at the beauty in front of me, I turned to see him watching me. "What? Am I gushing too much?"

Shaking his head, he smiled. "No. I'm happy you love this like you do. And I'm happy I'm the one who could give you this."

He kissed me so tenderly I thought I might cry. There I was standing in a scene straight out of a picture with a man unlike anyone I'd ever met and he was saying he was happy because he'd made me happy. If there was a luckier woman than me, I couldn't imagine how.

"I thought we'd visit the museums tomorrow. Would you like that?" he asked as he nuzzled my neck. "I figure it's about time I see some art in this city."

"I'd love that! Is it too late to go today?"

Tristan lifted his head from kissing my shoulder and cocked one eyebrow. "Aren't you tired from the flight?"

"No way. I'm in Venice, baby. I could probably stay up the whole time we're here."

"Well, I'm exhausted. Plane rides do that to me. I thought we could stay in tonight and have dinner before we spend some more time out here on the balcony."

I knew the flight had been stressful for him. Each time we flew anywhere, he grew quiet. More than once on the flight there, I'd noticed his knuckles were nearly white as his hands tightly gripped the armrests on his seat. It wasn't surprising after what he'd been through.

Standing on my toes, I stretched to kiss him on the cheek. "I think that sounds perfect."

That smile I loved came out and he hugged me tightly. "Good. I'm going to speak to the concierge, but I'll be back in a few minutes. You stay and enjoy the view."

"Yes, sir. I can do that, sir," I joked.

"Sir? Be careful. I hear your boss is a real bastard. Seems he's miserable to his employees. Never smiles, I hear."

"Oh no. He's nothing like that. They just don't know the real man. I'm not worried. He's pretty fantastic, actually."

Tristan turned to leave and stopped as he opened the suite door. "Just pretty fantastic?"

"Okay, he's extraordinary, but he doesn't flaunt his extraordinariness all the time," I said with a wink.

After he left, I turned back to look at the view from our balcony. That's how I thought of things. Our balcony. It had a romantic ring to it. Leaning against the wrought iron railing, I scanned the canal below and saw couples in love on their gondola rides enjoying the beautiful Venice evening. It was the most enchanting thing I'd ever seen in person, and I felt like I needed to pinch myself to be sure I wasn't dreaming.

I didn't know how long I stood there, but when I finally looked up from the romantic scene below, the sky was dark and the stars that twinkled overhead made it look like the perfect painting. The sound of the suite door closing signaled Tristan's return, and I turned around to see not only him but three uniformed waiters with trays full of food.

He opened his arms wide as the men set the table across the room. "A feast fit for a queen, my lady."

I was embarrassed for a moment, but the waiters didn't seem to care who was in the room, so I took Tristan's outstretched hand and let him kiss me in front of them. "It's so much food."

"Enough for my queen." Tristan looked past me. "Thank you, gentlemen."

Turning, I saw the three men bow and leave us with a table full of food. Fruits, vegetables, meats, breads, and desserts covered the five foot round table, leaving no room for either of us to place a plate down to eat. Looking at Tristan, I asked, "Where are we eating? You've gotten enough food for a queen and her entire court."

"I like the idea of dinner in bed. Breakfast shouldn't have all the fun."

At times like this when he was utterly charming and funny, I couldn't help but smile. He really was adorable. "Dinner in bed it is then. What does one wear to such an event?"

Taking my hand, he led me to the bedroom and turned me around so I faced away from him. His fingers tugged the zipper down on the back of my dress, and he whispered in my ear, "Nothing. Dinner in bed is definitely a no-dress affair."

My dress fell to the floor and I turned around to face him to slide his suit coat off his shoulders. "I like how this dinner is shaping up already." A few gentle pulls on his perfect Windsor knotted tie and I tossed it on the bed nearby. As I unbuttoned his black dress shirt to reveal his solid chest and stunning abs, I couldn't help but lick my lips. He was like a Greek god standing there in front of me.

He looked down at me with eyes full of desire as I slid my fingers beneath the waist of his pants. In a needy voice, he groaned, "Maybe we'll have dessert first."

Chapter Fifteen

My fingers grazed the head of his already excited cock, and I heard him take a sharp breath in above me. As I stroked his silky skin, I looked up to watch him close his eyes and tilt his head back. I loved seeing him like this. He was sex incarnate, and I wanted to feel every inch of him on me.

He moaned softly when I unzipped his pants and took his cock in my hand. He'd gone commando, so I slid his pants over his hips and they fell quickly around his ankles. This was what had been in my mind that first night when he'd asked me what I was thinking, and now I wanted to show him exactly what he made me want.

Dropping to my knees, I ran my hand from the base of his cock to the head and back again as I watched his face relax in pleasure. I slid the mushroom-shaped head into my mouth and sucked gently as I eased my lips down over his cock until they touched my hand gripping the base. He tasted incredible on my tongue, like a slightly salty treat I'd waited too long to enjoy.

He buried his hands in my hair and began to move my head at a rhythm both of us liked. Humming against his skin as my mouth slid down over him again, I sent vibrations up and down his cock, making him moan a noise like I'd never heard from him.

"Oh, God, Nina…don't stop. Just like that."

His voice was hoarse and strained from desire, and I loved the sound of it. I made him sound like that. Me. I wanted to hear him tell me how much he loved it again and again. It made me wet just listening to the need in every word. The need for me to give him what he so desperately wanted.

I looked up to watch him as I took him into me, loving the expression on his face as he watched me. Leaning my head back, I slid him out of my mouth, my hand still stroking his hard, silken shaft. He was thick and long, and I licked my lips at the feel of him so heavy in my palm.

"Fuck, don't stop," he moaned. There was almost a painful sound to his voice now.

My tongue slid over the head and I licked around him like a lollypop as my hand cupped his balls. His eyes grew wide with desire before he closed them and a strained look crossed his face. "Baby, you're killing me."

"Time for good boyfriends to get what they want then."

I drew him into my mouth slowly, my tongue darting over the area just below the tip of his cock. His breath left his lips in a hiss, and he whispered deeply, "Faster."

Humming against his skin again, I took as much of him as I could into my mouth and sucked gently as I moved up and down his cock. His grip on my hair tightened as he worked to direct my efforts to exactly where he wanted them, sending a delicious mixture of pleasure and pain shooting across my scalp and down my neck.

His movements grew to short, stabbing motions into me, and I knew he was getting close. My hand slid faster around the base, giving every inch of his cock pleasure. I wanted to feel him lose control, to feel him experience that release that came from letting go.

He sounded like he was on the verge of losing his voice as he whispered in a deep, hoarse rasp, "Nina, much more and I won't be able to hold back anymore."

I stared into his eyes so wild now and prayed he understood how much I wanted him. All of him. *Don't hold back, baby.*

His cock twitched and grew larger, telling me it was time. I relaxed my body to take as much as he offered. He pulled my head down onto him, exciting me more than I'd ever thought possible, and my throat accepted everything he gave as he exploded into me.

When he finally pulled out of my mouth, my legs were weak and shaking and I sat back on my heels to catch my breath. Closing my eyes, I got my bearings as he removed the last of his clothes. His lips brushed mine and I opened my eyes to see him kneeling in front of me.

"See what you do to me? You bring me to my knees."

I smiled at his confession. "Are you happy?"

"Happy isn't the word I'd use," he said as he slipped my bra strap off my right shoulder and then my left. "More like ecstatic."

I looked down as he slid his hands behind me to unhook my bra. "Good."

"And now I plan to do the same for you, so get those panties off before I tear them off with my teeth."

Lying back on the floor, I slithered out of my panties as Tristan moved forward to catch me with his hands, pressing my hips to the floor. I let my legs fall open, and he moaned, sending a shiver of desire straight through me. I wanted his mouth on me, devouring my pussy as that gorgeous tongue of his lapped my tender and needy clit.

He flicked his tongue and grinned a sexy smile. "Don't close your eyes. I want you to watch me, Nina. Watch me give you what you gave me."

Lowering his head between my thighs, he kept his gaze focused on my eyes as he ran his tongue up my dripping wet slit. Those brown eyes looked so sexy staring up at me, nearly making me come at the first touch of his mouth on me. He sucked my delicate skin into his mouth, sending waves of pleasure washing over me.

I squirmed as he moved up to gently suck my clit into his mouth, and he moaned against me, "No fidgeting. Don't make me hold you down."

His command resonated deep inside my excited pussy, thrilling me, and he placed his hands on my hips. "Just in case there's any more wriggling. I want to see you fucking come apart because of my tongue."

I looked at his large hands on my stomach, so powerful as they rested on my tender skin, and I loved it. I squirmed again just to have him take total control, and his reaction was swift. He pressed hard against my hips, pinning me to the floor.

"I told you. No more wriggling."

His tongue plunged into me, making me desperate to buck against him, but I was trapped. Fucking me with his tongue, he stabbed into me as his thumb drew tiny circles on my clit. The sensations were exquisite and better than anything else I'd experienced before. I wanted to lay there open for him to do what he wanted forever.

My orgasm began to uncoil inside me, and my eyelids lowered as my eyes rolled back in my head. Just as they closed, I heard his deep voice order, "Look at me, Nina. I want to see you looking at me when you come."

I did as he commanded and watched as he sucked my clit into his mouth one last time, sending me crashing over that sweet edge. My release roared through me, and I cried out his name while he rode me until the last tiny quake finally subsided. When he sat back from me to place a tiny kiss on my quivering inner thigh, he whispered, "Feel good?"

"Mmmm…ecstatic."

He nipped at my skin and stood up. I took his hand when he held it out, ready for whatever was waiting for me, but I was surprised when he said, "I think it's time for dinner now that we had dessert first."

My expression must have signaled my disappointment because he quickly added, "Don't worry. We'll get back to that after dinner. I need to make sure you're fed so you have enough energy for later."

I stood up and walked with him toward the table full of food. "Enough energy? Whatever could you mean?" I said with a giggle.

He turned around and leveled his gaze at me. "You know what I mean."

I did and I loved how he thought. We loaded up our plates and walked back to the bedroom to have our dinner in bed. As I crawled into the king size bed, Tristan popped a strawberry from his plate into my mouth and followed it with a kiss.

"I guess I should have asked if you liked strawberries."

I put the plate down on the bed and grabbed at my throat. Making my voice hoarse, I croaked out, "Actually, I'm allergic to strawberries. I only have ten minutes before…" I fell to the bed and closed my eyes, doing my best to playact an allergic reaction.

"Jesus, Nina! I didn't know. We'll get you to a hospital!" I peeked out from behind my lashes to see him jump out of bed, knocking over his plate onto the floor. He raced around grabbing his pants and shirt, hobbling on one foot as he struggled to get dressed. "Baby, I'm sorry. Don't worry. Don't worry."

I opened my eyes as he rushed over to my side of the bed. Dropping to his knees, he leaned over and said in a tortured voice that made me feel instantly guilty, "Baby, don't leave me. Talk to me, Nina. Please say something."

His face was the picture of fear, making me feel even worse. "I'm sorry. I was just kidding, Tristan. I'm not allergic. I was just joking around. I didn't think you'd take me seriously. I'm sorry."

He sighed heavily and his shoulders sagged, as if just hearing me say that made every ounce of stress leave his body. Taking me in his arms, he squeezed me tightly to him. "Don't ever do that again. I thought I'd lose you."

"I'm sorry. I didn't mean to ruin everything," I said quietly as he continued to hold me.

When he finally released me, I saw how much my joke had affected him. Those soulful brown eyes were full of sadness and his mouth was turned down in a soft frown even as he told me how happy he was that I was okay. My heart broke at what I'd done—at what my callousness had done to him.

Caressing his cheek, I kissed him softly on the lips. "I'm sorry, Tristan. I didn't mean to be so thoughtless. I didn't think before I did it."

"I'm just happy you're okay."

I felt like shit that I'd ruined everything so wonderful that he'd tried to do. He'd brought me to Venice and his stunning hotel, worshipped me like no man had ever done, and I hadn't even been good enough to consider the idea that maybe someone who'd lost his entire family wouldn't find it funny that he'd mistakenly fed his girlfriend a food poisonous to her.

"Tell me I haven't wrecked our entire trip. Please don't let this spoil our good time."

"You haven't spoiled anything, Nina. Let's have a drink and eat something."

He stood and walked out to the suite's living room to pour himself a scotch while I cursed my stupidity and cleaned up the mess he'd made when he jumped out of bed. Sometimes I could be such a jackass, but rarely had I felt so awful about being one.

I found him sitting naked on the couch with a nearly empty glass in his hand. His face was drawn, and he looked tired as he swallowed the last gulp of alcohol. He stood to pour himself another drink, a sign that no matter what he said things weren't okay.

This was my doing, so I had to fix it. I knelt in front of him as he sat back down and leaned my head on his leg. "Did you eat anything? Do you want me to get you a plate?"

He shook his head. "No. I'm fine with just a drink. You eat, though. The food is impeccable."

I didn't want to eat. My appetite was gone. All I wanted was to fix what I'd done, but I didn't know how. There was something sad between us now. It was nothing obvious, but I felt it as I sat so close to him. Looking up at him, I wished more than anything that I knew the right words to say.

"I'm looking forward to visiting the museums tomorrow," I said quietly. "Are you?"

He smiled sweetly. "Only because you're going to be there."

"We're going to see some great works of art. I think you'll like it."

"I know I will because you like it."

"Love it, actually. Ever since I was a little girl, I've loved art."

He placed his hand on the back of my head and stroked my hair. "Love then."

We sat there saying nothing for a long time until he finally cupped my chin in his hand and said, "Let's go back to bed."

Taking my hand, he led me to the second bedroom past the one we'd been in earlier. He closed the door behind us and leaned down to press a passionate kiss onto my lips. His tongue slipped into my mouth to mingle with mine, making moisture rush to between my legs. I ran my hands over the soft skin of his back and moaned into his mouth.

As I was beginning to think we'd moved past the problem of earlier, he pulled back and stared down at me. My blood ran cold that he was angry or upset, but when he spoke, his words were full of tenderness that touched my heart and brought tears to my eyes.

"Your happiness and safety is all I care about. The thought of losing you terrified me."

"I know. I'm so sorry. I just didn't think," I said, wanting so much to make him feel better.

He kissed me to stop me from talking and shook his head. "Don't apologize. It made me realize I should have said this a long time ago. I love you, Nina, and I don't want to lose you."

Tears streamed down my cheeks at his words. He loved me like I loved him. Smiling through my tears, I sobbed, "I love you, Tristan. I'm the luckiest woman in the world because of you. You've given me everything a girl could dream of."

"I haven't given you anything you don't deserve. Don't ever forget that."

Within just a few minutes, the melancholy that had covered him lifted and he was the Tristan I loved to be around. We made love sweetly and tenderly, and as we lay there in each other's arms, I tried to forgive myself for what I'd done.

The truth was that I sometimes didn't know how to act around him. He was so hard to gauge at times, which made me feel like being myself was inappropriate. In the beginning, I had thought it was the money—the way he spent money on me unnerved me, making me feel as if he believed I was someone I wasn't. I'd never pretended to be anyone but myself, but I found it hard to believe that a man would simply give gifts just because he could. It was never him but me who had the problem. Just because I'd never been fortunate enough to meet someone like him didn't mean I didn't deserve him.

I didn't know if he knew how troubled my mind was over things like that. If he did, he never spoke a word about it. But that was his way. He wasn't a man who spent hours talking about what was on his mind. He decided on matters and they happened.

It was one of the many things about him that I admired.

I absentmindedly ran my hand over his ribs, loving the feel of his body under my touch. Even now after a wonderful lovemaking session, I could spend hours worshipping his body again. He had that effect on me, unlike any other man I'd ever met had.

"Tristan, are you asleep?" He twirled my hair around his finger, a sign that he was still awake. "I'm really looking forward to seeing the museums tomorrow."

"Good. It will be educational for me since I know little about art."

I lifted my head from his chest and looked up at him, confused. "I've seen your house and penthouse. I think you know a great deal about art."

He smiled and pursed his lips. "I know a great deal about hiring people to decorate the places I live in."

I didn't know why, but his remark stung my feelings. The truth was that I was an employee of his, no matter how intimate we were after work hours. But something in his tone signaled a disdain for the people he'd hired to decorate his homes, and I suddenly felt like I was grouped in with them.

Rolling over, I turned my back to him and worked to push these thoughts out of my mind. I was sleeping next to him in our hotel room in Venice where he'd brought me for no other reason than to enjoy a city renowned for something I loved. Whatever slight I'd felt was silly.

His arm snaked around my waist, and he pressed his body against mine. "What happened there? Suddenly tired?"

"It's been a long day," I said as I stared at the wall.

He kissed my neck, nuzzling the space between my shoulder and my ear. "I love you. Get some sleep and we'll head out bright and early so you can teach me all the things I should know about art so I'm not a philistine anymore."

His self-effacing way made me smile, and I turned my body to face him. Kissing him, I said, "You're no philistine, even when it comes to art."

"Well, I'm a cultured philistine then," he joked.

Wrinkling my nose, I said, "I don't think such a thing exists."

He leaned forward and kissed me. "Then maybe I just want to impress the woman I love."

And with just those words, any slight I'd felt melted away. "I can report that the woman you love is already impressed."

Pulling me close, he held me and kissed the top of my head. "She loves me and is impressed. I must be doing something right."

"Definitely."

He fell silent for a long time, never releasing his hold on me. Finally, just as I was about to fall asleep, I heard him say quietly above me, "She loves me."

I did. More than I could ever explain to him.

CHAPTER SIXTEEN

Sunrise in Venice was just as incredible as the sunset the night before had been, and after a light breakfast, I was ready to show Tristan some of the greatest artwork in the world. The idea that I could be better than him at something thrilled me, and I wanted to impress him as much as he wanted to impress me.

Dressed comfortably in a light yellow cotton dress and flats so we could visit as many museums as time allowed, I walked out of our bedroom to see Tristan ending a phone call. His grimace was profound, marring that beautiful face.

"I'm going to have to miss our tour of the museums today, Nina. Something's come up that I need to deal with."

His body language was stiff, telling me he was unhappy about whatever the problem was. I wanted to cry my disappointment was so great. All my fantasies about showing him my knowledge of the art world disappeared in a heartbeat, wrecked by another of his phone calls.

I tried not to pout, but my efforts weren't very successful and I lowered my gaze to look at my shoes so perfect for walking around Venice. He walked toward me and lifted my chin with his forefinger. Looking down into my face, he wore an expression of disappointment mixed with something else. I just couldn't put my finger on what that something else was.

Anger? Disgust?

"I'm sorry. I wanted to go with you, but it's important I take care of this."

I bit my lip and tried to control my tongue so I didn't make his situation even worse. "I know. I just so wanted to show you…" I let my sentence trail off. My desire to impress him sounded silly now.

"I want you to still go. One of my men will escort you, so go wherever you want."

"I don't need an escort. You roamed around Venice all by yourself when you were sixteen. I'm sure I can handle myself."

He shook his head definitively. "No. One of my men will be with you, if you choose to go."

There was no arguing the point, so I didn't. I wouldn't have Tristan, but I'd have a shadow. "I guess one of your guys will be okay," I mumbled.

Placing a kiss on my forehead, he whispered, "I promise I'll make it up to you."

"You better. I'm thinking The Louvre might be the only thing that could make this better."

"It's a date," he said and flashed me a smile that made it next to impossible to be angry with him.

Whatever the problem was, it required him to leave immediately, but within ten minutes my escort arrived. Nearly as tall as Tristan, Jared was much bigger, like bouncer-at-a-club bigger. I guessed he had little appreciation for art. After trying twice to strike up a conversation as we stood there in the living room of the suite, I surmised he had little appreciation for talking too.

"Well, Jared, it's nice to meet you. My name is Nina. I guess you're going with me to visit some museums today."

My giant shadow nodded once and said, "As you wish, ma'am."

Ma'am. Oh, I was sure I wasn't going to enjoy my time with him.

After visiting two museums, I had all but forgotten about Jared and immersed myself in the works of art at the Ca'Rezzonico museum. The landscape painting exhibition on the first floor took my breath away. I stood staring at paintings showing eighteenth century Venice as it truly had been back then, mesmerized at how similar so many things in the city still were. Yet the paintings showed a different Venice in many ways, and I was taken back to those days I'd studied about in school, finally feeling like I was experiencing them for myself as I studied those pictures that hung on the walls.

I moved through the floor wishing Tristan was at my side so I could tell him about all the wonderful history of landscape painting in Venice. A touch of sadness came over me, but I pushed it out of my mind, reminding myself that while Tristan had given me time off from my job for this trip, no one had given him any.

Lost in thought about landscape painting, I didn't see the man next to me until he spoke. Surprised, I jumped and turned to look at the stranger. "Excuse me? I didn't hear what you said."

"I said it's beautiful, isn't it?"

"It is." I continued to look at the man, surprised by his American accent. "You're an American?"

He nodded. "Yes, I am. It's nice to meet another person from back home."

I studied his face as I tried to determine his age. The corners of his eyes were wrinkled slightly, but his face was tanned, giving him a glow that made me think he might be in his thirties. His hair had streaks of grey at the temples, leading me to believe he might be older, though.

"Where are you from?" I asked, thinking I picked up a Midwest accent.

"Minnesota. Land of ten thousand lakes."

"That's a lot of lakes," I joked.

"Beautiful country there. Where are you from?" he asked as he studied my face, likely to ascertain the answers I'd sought a minute earlier.

"Pennsylvania. We don't have that many lakes."

The man extended his hand and introduced himself as Derek. I smiled and said, "It's nice to meet you, Derek. I'm Nina."

"I used to know someone from Pennsylvania with a daughter named Nina. His name was Joseph. I met him on assignment years ago."

"Assignment? What did he do?"

"He was an investigative journalist."

"Do you remember his last name?" I asked excitedly, amazed at the idea that I might be talking to someone who'd known my father.

"Edwards. His name was Joseph Edwards."

"Oh, my God! That was my father!"

"He was a good man. Great writer," Derek said in a solemn voice, using the past tense, which told me he knew about my father's death.

"It's so wonderful to hear that. He loved what he did."

"He did. I remember him talking about you too. You were the apple of his eye. His little artist is what he called you, if I remember correctly."

I beamed at Derek's memory, loving that my father had spoken about me like that. "I haven't heard that in so long. I miss hearing him call me that."

Derek's eyes narrowed. "I think it's a shame they never charged the people responsible."

My heart slammed against my chest at Derek's implication. The police had repeatedly told my sister and me that all the leads had gone cold, but it sounded like he was saying someone knew who'd murdered my father. "Do you know anything about that?"

"Ma'am, it's time we got going."

I turned to see Jared ready to do his best escort impression. "I'll be ready in a minute. I'm talking right now."

My shadow looked around and then back at me. "Ma'am, I think he left."

Jared was right. Derek was nowhere in sight. I took off to find him, but it was like he'd vanished. I searched all four floors, but I never found him. As Jared escorted me back to the hotel, the man's claim echoed in my head.

Someone knew who had murdered my father.

I left Jared behind in the lobby and raced up to the room to get my head together. I needed a cool drink and some time to think about what Derek had said. The idea that the people responsible for my father's death still roamed free while he lay cold in the ground tore at me. I'd never believed what the police told us, but without any proof, all I had was my gut feeling that what they knew about the case was only the tip of the iceberg.

Throwing my purse on one of the chairs in the suite's living room, I stripped nude and ran myself a bath in the soaker tub. I poured myself a glass of red wine and slid into the water, wanting so desperately to calm the craziness that was racing around my brain. The wine quickly dulled my senses, as alcohol always did, and I closed my eyes to silence my thoughts.

At last, my brain calmed and all that was left was the feeling of loss that I'd had since the moment I learned that my father had died of a gunshot wound in an abandoned warehouse in Newark. My father and mother for so many years was gone, taken from me in a moment of hate or passion. I didn't know which. As I sat in the warm water there in the hotel suite I shared with Tristan, all I really knew was that my father was murdered and gone forever.

I'd cried so many tears since that night that I hadn't thought there weren't any left in me. My emotions had traveled from sadness to rage to nothingness. I'd felt so much that where it concerned my father's death, my heart was numb. But Derek's words had pricked at that numbness like a needle in a dead limb and I'd felt it.

"How were the museums?"

I opened my eyes and saw Tristan standing in the bathroom doorway. He smiled, but his expression did a poor job of hiding the fact that whatever the problem was that he had been dealing with all day was still plaguing his thoughts.

"I missed having you there. It was nice, but it would have been better with you by my side."

His smile widened into a warm grin, and he walked over to crouch next to the tub. "I know. I'm sorry. The Louvre, right?"

Chuckling at his recollection of my words from that morning, I flicked a few drops of water at him. "You better believe it. I'm holding you to that, you know."

"I'm counting on it."

He leaned forward and kissed me gently on the forehead, making me feel loved and cared for. Closing my eyes, I sighed. "Thank you."

"For what?"

I looked up into his curious eyes. "For making me feel so loved."

Pushing my hair behind my ear, he whispered, "Always."

His touch was so comforting, and I leaned into his palm to rest my head. "Do you ever find yourself thinking back to before your parents and brother were taken from you? I can't get my father off my mind tonight."

Tristan said nothing for a long time. I worried that I'd said something wrong by asking about his family, but finally he quietly said, "Sometimes it's all I can think of. There are things that happened when they were alive that still haunt me today."

Something in his voice told me he understood what I was feeling. The loss. The regret that not having the chance to say goodbye brought with it.

He kissed my head and leaned his against mine. "Did something happen today?"

I wanted to tell him about Derek, but what did I have to go on? The word of some guy from Minnesota who'd made some vague claim? I didn't want to ruin our vacation, and I could tell him everything when I found out some actual facts.

"No. I just had a lot of time alone today and visiting art galleries reminds me of when I was a little girl and my father would take me to the Philadelphia Museum of Art. It was there that I first fell in love with art."

None of that was a lie. I just hadn't told Tristan about Derek.

"He sounds like a great father, Nina. You were lucky."

Things were getting too serious, so I slid up against the back of the tub and took a drink of wine. Forcing a smile, I said, "I was. So what's on the schedule for tonight? A little dinner in and some TV with the ball and chain?"

He raised his eyebrows in surprise. "I had something a little different in mind, but if you'd rather watch TV…"

"No, no. I can watch TV any night. It's not every night I'm in Venice. What do you have in mind?"

His face turned sheepish. "I know it's pretty clichéd, but I thought we'd take a gondola ride."

I couldn't help but smile. He really was so cute when he was romantic. "That's so cool! Give me a few minutes and I'll get ready. A gondola ride! I get to cross off another thing on my list of things to do before I die."

Nearly leaping out of the tub, I raced to get ready, eager to experience what I'd only seen in movies and paintings. It may have been clichéd, but I didn't care. There was no way I was visiting Venice and not taking a gondola ride, and that I'd be taking it with the man I loved was better than anything.

"Isn't this romantic?" I cooed as the gondolier guided the boat past those great Gothic buildings that lined the Grand Canal, the ones I'd looked out at from our balcony the night before.

Tristan slipped his arm around my shoulders and pulled me close. "It's actually really nice. I'd heard horrible things about the canal water, but this isn't bad."

I rolled my eyes at his understatement. "Nice? Isn't bad? You really know how to seduce a girl."

Nuzzling my neck, he whispered, "You want seduction? I'll give you seduction."

I turned my head to catch his mouth in a kiss. He tasted like scotch, and I liked my lips as I pulled away. "Promises, promises."

Our gondolier eased his craft around another stopped gondola as Tristan whispered, "Did you know that all gondoliers must wear black pants and a striped shirt?"

I looked our guide up and down and saw he was wearing that exact uniform. "I'm impressed."

"Good. But I feel compelled to tell you that the concierge at the hotel gave me that tidbit of information," he admitted in a low, husky voice that hit me deep inside, oddly enough considering what he was saying.

I ran my hand up his thigh and licked my lips. "I love honestly in a man. Now I'm even more impressed."

As the gondola drifted to a stop, Tristan winked at me. "Time for that seduction."

We walked into the Piazza San Marco as the first drops of rain began to fall. Tourists and locals headed for cover in the restaurants and hotels nearby, leaving just a few of us alone in the enormous square. Puddles quickly formed on the stone patio, forcing us to zigzag toward the Moorish style arches that lined the piazza as the skies opened up above us.

Thunder boomed overhead, chasing nearly everyone from the square. Soaked to the bone, we ran for shelter behind the colonnade. My hair was drenched and plastered to my head, and I slicked it off my face just so I could see. I looked up at Tristan, who was scrubbing his face dry with his hands. He looked as incredible as always. Dipping my head, I wiped under my eyes to get rid of any smeared mascara and mumbled, "I must look like a nightmare."

He lifted my chin to force me to look at him and shook his head. "You look beautiful. Come here."

Pulling me close, he kissed me deeply, sending a rush of arousal through my body. His hands fisted my hair as he slid his tongue over mine seductively. His hips pushed forward, brushing his hardening cock between my legs and making me tilt my hips to eagerly meet his thrusts.

"You wanted seduction, didn't you, Nina?" he asked in that deep voice that made me want him more than anything at that moment.

"Yes," I answered breathlessly as he gently pinned me against a column.

"Yes," he repeated as he slid his hand under my dress all the way up to my panties. "Yes." He moaned softly in my ear, "Right here, Nina. Right here."

Were there people nearby? I didn't know and I didn't care. I wanted him inside me now. His mouth plundered mine and mine plundered his in return as I fumbled with his belt, finally pulling it loose. My hand reached into his pants and tugged on his boxer briefs, yanking .them down below his balls so his stiff cock sprang out at attention while the other hand yanked his shirt out of the way, sending buttons flying in all directions. I slid my hand over his smooth cock and drew a sharp breath in as he tore my panties from my body.

He was like a man possessed, his hands grasping at my face and neck as he kissed me. Lifting me onto him, he slid his cock inside me and wrapped my hands around his neck. Those dark eyes stared into mine, wild and full of desire, and he began pumping into my body raggedly. His grunts filled my ears as with each thrust he pushed me back against the marble column, but I was oblivious to pain or anything other than Tristan.

He was everywhere around me—his mouth, his hands, his cock becoming essential to the happiness every part of my body cried out for. I clawed at his scalp, looking for some leverage as he fucked me wildly there behind a column for anyone to see. My legs ached from their hold around his waist, and with each plunge of his cock inside my wet pussy, I pushed my heels against his back, praying this time he'd finally bury himself deep inside me.

"Faster, Tristan. I'm almost there," I cried as the first twinge of my orgasm began. "Harder."

My pleas were met with exactly what I wanted—he pounded into me like a madman, his hands gripping my ass tightly and roughly pulling me into him. His moans and grunts surrounded me, edging me closer to coming as his cock moved like a piston in and out of me.

I cried out, "Yes!" and squeezed his neck as I began to come. Every part of me felt release as my orgasm shuddered through me, and I pushed down to take every inch of his thick cock as my legs quivered against him. He buried his face in my neck and grunted one last time as I felt him explode into me, bathing my insides with his own release.

His legs shook as he moaned my name over and over until there was nothing left for either of us to take from the other's body. I was his completely, and he was mine. Tristan lifted his head and pressed it against mine, his forehead drenched with perspiration.

"God, I love you," he groaned. "I can't fucking live without you, Nina. Promise me no matter what you won't make me. I can't do it."

I caressed his face and kissed his lips as the last word left his mouth. There was nothing in the world that could tear me from him. He was everything to me, as essential as the air I breathed or the food I ate.

"Never. I'm yours like you're mine. Forever."

Chapter Seventeen

Venice had been the turning point I'd hoped and prayed for with Tristan. With every word and every action, he proved he was as devoted to me as I was to him. We'd even made it through a whole night without any phone calls souring his mood. When we fell asleep in each other's arms that night, I was happier than I ever thought a person could be.

My happiness was shattered within minutes of waking up the next morning, however.

Once again, I woke up and Tristan was nowhere to be found. I'd half expected to find a note sitting on his pillow, but reaching out to run my hands over the fine Egyptian cotton pillowcase, there was nothing.

I didn't have to wait long to find out what had taken him from our bed so early. His footsteps pounding against the floor in the next room told me something was wrong, and I slipped into the white dress shirt he'd left slung over a chair the night before and made my way out to see him.

He stood near the glass doors to the balcony with his arms folded across his chest. His profile showed a grimace as I walked toward him. I gently touched his sleeve, saddened when I saw his expression as he turned toward me.

"Hey, what's wrong?"

Tristan leaned down and kissed me softly on the lips. "Work. I'm sorry, but we're going to have to cut our trip short. I wish I didn't have to get back, but you know how it is."

I couldn't hide my disappointment and turned away to look out through the doors at the Grand Canal. "Oh. Okay."

"I'm sorry, Nina. I promise to make it up to you."

Nodding, I looked up at him and forced a smile onto my face. "I know. Such is the life of a bigwig."

My joke made him laugh, and at least for a moment he appeared happy, even if there was a hint of sadness in his words. "Bigwig, huh? Well, this bigwig would take a smaller wig and being able to stay here with you."

I stood on my toes and wrapped my arms around his neck. Those deep brown eyes stared down into mine, almost as if he were begging forgiveness.

"You do know women often don't like men with smaller…wigs," I teased with a giggle.

His smile in return was genuine and warmed my heart. "Well, thank God I've been blessed in the wig department."

Sliding my hand down his torso, I ran my palm over the front of his pants before I turned to head into the bath. "Blessed indeed."

I didn't get far before he pulled me back against him and said in a deep voice, "I won't be able to get any work done if you keep making me think about last night."

His reference to what we'd done behind that pillar in the Piazza San Marco made an ache form between my legs. Finally, I'd seen the man behind the expensive suits and hardly any words—that passionate heart that no one but me saw. I would have given anything for the world to go away and have him all to myself for the rest of time.

Blushing at the memory of the rawest, most erotic moment of my life, I covered his hands with mine and leaned my head back against his shoulder. "You're going to make me so completely crazy about you that I become your love slave, Tristan Stone."

He nuzzled my neck, sending chills down my spine. In a husky voice, he whispered, "You've figured out my diabolical plan."

Turning in his arms, I smiled up at him. "I knew you had an ulterior motive."

"I have to get some work done before we leave, Nina. We need to be ready in little more than an hour."

Even the mere mention of work changed his mood from playful to serious, almost worried. His beautiful face became marred by a deep frown. I wanted to ask what the problem was, but I let it be. For all I knew, it could be the flight we had to take. So I toddled off to take a nice hot bath before having to spend eight hours on a plane, satisfied that even with the abbreviated holiday, it still had been the most incredible few days of my life.

Tristan vanished almost the minute we arrived home, so I headed straight to my room, ready to throw myself into my next assignment with the Miami Richmont hotel. I opened the door to the room that had become my home and instantly knew something had changed. Nothing I'd left on the desk while we were in Venice was there, including my laptop. Frantic, I ran down the hall yelling Tristan's name. Didn't he have security that handled things like this?

Rogers heard my screams and in his usual fashion seemed to appear out of nowhere as I reached the kitchen. Fully convinced my belongings had been stolen, I blurted out, "We've been robbed! My laptop and a bunch of other stuff is gone, Rogers! Did you see anyone?"

"Miss, we haven't been robbed. I think you'll find all your personal belongings have been moved to the master's room, as per his orders. If you'd like, I can escort you there where your things are safe and sound."

I stood stunned at the butler's words. Unsure of what to say, I mumbled a quick thank you and quickly made my way to Tristan's side of the house to find everything as Rogers had claimed. My laptop sat in the exact same position on his desk as it had in my room. Every stitch of clothing I owned, even down to my underwear, had been moved and placed in the enormous walk-in closet just beside his clothes. My hand instinctively reached out to touch his suits and dress shirts hanging perfectly on their hangers, loving the feel of their crisp softness against my fingertips as I ran my hand all the way toward the furthest point of the closet. I checked the bathroom and there were brand new, unopened bottles of everything I used—shampoo, conditioner, facial scrub, moisturizer, and even a tube of my favorite toothpaste.

Tristan had arranged for all of this, but when?

I walked out of the bathroom impressed with his attention to every detail, even the tiniest one. Other women may have loved his money or stunning looks, but for me, his way of noticing what other men didn't was one of the best parts of him.

Grabbing my laptop, I plopped myself down on the bed and opened it to begin searching for information on the Miami hotel. There on the keyboard was an envelope. I opened it and found another of Tristan's letters I'd grown to love.

Dear Nina,

It's only right that the woman I love be in her rightful place next to me. When I get home I'll be eager to see your ideas for Miami. I'll be spending my day fixing problems, but you can be sure that our time in Venice is on my mind.

Love always,
Tristan

I beamed as I reread his letter, loving the sweetness of him writing one at all. I stared at the note, running my finger over the handwritten words. God, I loved him! Folding the heavy stationary back into the envelope, I pressed it to my heart before I slipped the letter into my purse to join the others.

As much as I wanted to lounge around and think about Tristan, I had work to do. Just because he was as crazy about me as I was about him didn't mean I wanted to slack off at my job. In fact, it made me want to be even better at it. Doing a great job would help him in some small way, and that made me feel like I deserved that rightful place next to him.

Before I began searching for the perfect artwork for the Miami Presidential suite, my email lured me in like a siren's song. Jordan had sent me a message just a few hours earlier. Clicking on it, I read her email to find that I had some kind of letter waiting for me. She didn't say much about it, other than that it looked official, which piqued my curiosity, but that would have to wait. She and Justin seemed to be fine and moving toward bigger and better things, and our neighbor Mrs. Phillips on the first floor was just as crazy as she'd always been, but now that madness included a long-lost grandson who Jordan hated because he was one of those people who kept eye contact for too long.

I had to laugh at Jordan's rundown of life back in Brooklyn. She was happy, and things were just as she'd always said they'd be. Good people were having good things happen for them, and this time, we were those people too.

I tapped out a quick email to tell her I'd be dropping by the apartment the next day, and then I was a woman on a mission with her nose to the art world grindstone. The suite in Miami had recently been redecorated to reflect the varied cultures and artistic styles found in that city. The pictures of the suite were breathtaking and intimidating. Tristan's decorators had spared no cost in creating a wonderful suite of rooms showcasing the fusion of Latin American flavors and Caribbean influences so key to Miami. The vibrant blues, yellows, and reds made the suite look like the perfect getaway spot, and I wished we'd visit there just to experience it.

That I now had to find that one perfect piece of art to bring the rooms together felt like a Herculean challenge. Of all the assignments he'd given me, this one threatened to show that I wasn't as good at this as I wanted to be.

I rubbed my temples and rolled my shoulders. *You can do this, Nina. You can do this.*

My pep talk worked a small wonder on my psyche, and I set myself to the task of finding that one piece I had to believe existed. Thankfully, the designer hadn't gone with the obvious choice of art deco for the Miami suite. I could appreciate that. Her choices had made the Richmont unique in a sea of luxury hotels in South Beach.

Rubbing my hands together, ideas began popping in my mind and I had a brainstorm. My fingers set off clicking away on the keyboard, but two hours later, I still hadn't found what I was searching for. What had seemed like such a great idea didn't seem to actually exist. The thought occurred to me that I could create something on my own, but my skill as a painter wasn't great enough to have one of my pieces hang in the Presidential suite.

By late afternoon, I hadn't found anything and Tristan was set to be home any time. I had to find something to show him. Even if he vetoed my idea, it was better than letting him down completely. Another quick inspirational talk with myself and I was determined to find something to show for my day's work.

After another exhaustive search, a purple and gold circle print by a Miami artist that would work perfectly was what I finally came up with. To be honest, I was pretty sure Tristan would give it a thumbs down, but at least it was something.

Satisfied, I bookmarked the page at the gallery and closed my laptop just in time to see him enter the bedroom. Whatever he'd been dealing with had taken a toll on him as I'd never seen his face look so drawn and tired.

"Hey! Somebody stole all my things and then left them in here, oddly enough," I joked as he sat down in the high backed chair near the window.

Tristan loosened his tie and smiled. "That's what I love most about you, you know that? When nothing or no one can make me smile, you can." He leaned his head back against the chair and closed his eyes as he let out heavy sigh.

"Tough day?"

"Too tough."

Walking over to behind him, I leaned forward and slid my hands over his shoulders. They were tight and knotted and almost up near his ears. Slowly, I began kneading his stressed muscles, whispering in his ear, "I thought men like you didn't have to deal with the everyday hassles we ordinary people do."

He groaned low and deep. "No, we have to deal with bigger hassles."

"Want to talk about it?"

Tristan shook his head. "Nope. Tell me about your day." He arched back to look at me. "You liked my surprise?"

I leaned down to kiss his forehead. "Very much. And your note. Would you like to see what I came up with for Miami."

"Later." He held my hands on his shoulders. "Tell me what you did other than work and don't stop the massage. That feels good."

"Jordan emailed me. I'm going to stop over to see her tomorrow. She says someone sent me an official looking envelope."

I felt his shoulders tighten under my hands, even as he sat with his eyes closed. "Are you expecting something official?"

Chuckling, I pressed into his muscles, kneading even more deeply. "No. I can't imagine who would send me anything official. The last time I got anything from the government or a lawyer was years ago after my father's death."

"Maybe the IRS has a bone to pick with you," he joked.

"Don't say that. I've heard horror stories about being audited."

He laughed at me. "Nina, I don't think the IRS is auditing you, but if they are, just let me know and I'll have someone take care of it. It's not something to worry about."

This was that attention to detail thing I loved. An IRS audit would make me shake in my shoes and stress out for weeks, but he just took it all in stride and made me feel like if it happened, he'd handle it. I could get used to that.

I pressed my lips to his ear and kissed him, nuzzling his neck. "I love how you do that."

"Do what?"

"Just take care of things. I do love a man who takes care of business."

He tilted his head to look up at me. "What kind of men have you been dating?"

I returned to massaging his tired muscles and sheepishly admitted the truth. "The wrong kind, obviously."

He groaned softly as I hit a tender spot where his shoulders met his neck. "I'm glad I took care of that then."

"I'm going to see her after school tomorrow. I should be home by the time you get home for dinner."

He sat quietly as I attempted to ease the stress from his body. I loved these moments when it was so clear I made him as happy as he made me. After a few minutes, he spoke up, as if he'd been thinking about my last words. "We can meet at the penthouse so you wouldn't have to take that ride in and out of the city."

I kissed him on the cheek. "No, I'd rather come back here, if it's all the same."

Tristan turned his head to look at me, his eyebrows raised. "You mean you'd rather come back to this out of the way house in the middle of nowhere?"

Leveling my gaze at him, I stopped my hands' work and grinned. Rogers had obviously mentioned my comment from that night we'd chatted outside. "Yes. If you must know, I've grown to appreciate this house, even though it's a bit secluded. I like to think of it as our home."

He took my hands from his shoulders and brought them to his lips for a kiss. "I can't tell you how happy that makes me, Nina."

The unspoken reality that my six-month contract was almost up hung in the air like a heaviness that pressed down on us. I hadn't mentioned it because I feared what he might say. Even now, after all we'd shared together, he was still a mystery to me in many ways. I'd expected him to say something about it ending soon, but as each day passed, he was silent on the matter, as if he'd forgotten.

I'd just as soon have had him forget, to be honest. What if he was able to let me go as easily as firing any other employee? In my heart, I knew he loved me and no longer thought of me as merely someone who worked for him, but in the past few weeks I'd sensed something between us holding him back from me. I wanted to believe it was whatever he was dealing with at work, but a tiny fear sat in the back of my mind whispering that no matter what we'd been to one another, when the six months was up, so was our time together.

Pushing that out of my head, I said, "So it's settled. I'll visit Jordan and then be back so we can have dinner. Maybe tomorrow night can be pizza night?"

"Tony's?" he asked with a smile in his voice.

I stroked the hair near his nape, loving its softness. Bowing my head, I ran my lips over it and whispered, "I like that."

"Okay. Tony's at six. It's a date."

"A date," I said as I kissed along his neck to just below his left ear. "I'll be there."

Chapter Eighteen

The next day went by quickly as I proudly showed off my choices for the Miami hotel, which Tristan vetoed as I suspected he would, saying he liked the artist but not that particular circle piece. So I continued my search. It was more difficult than I'd anticipated, but when I contacted the artist's representative and told her I was looking to purchase one of Delgado's purple and gold series for the Richmont hotel in Miami, she was far nicer than I'd expected, even offering to have him sign the piece we chose.

The old saying really was true. Money did talk.

By mid-afternoon, I was feeling triumphant about my new acquisition and couldn't wait to tell Tristan about it at dinner, even if it meant breaking the "no work after five" rule. It was a breezy early October afternoon, so I dressed in a dark red dress that fell to right above my knees and black pumps, a celebration outfit of sorts and one I was sure Tristan would love for our date. As I looked at myself in the mirror in our bedroom, a decadent idea popped into my mind. Sexy stockings and a garter belt would be even better.

I slipped them on and attached them to the garter, loving the feel of their silkiness against my skin. I'd love it more when they drove him mad with desire as he tried to concentrate on the road in just a few hours.

Pleased with how I looked, I hurriedly checked my bank account to pay my cell phone bill and saw once again that I had more money than I'd anticipated. Despite working for the stated salary of $60,000, after five months I had over four times that amount in my checking account. Even after all this time, I still marveled at the numbers as they sat there on the screen. For the first time in my life, money wasn't a concern.

It also added to my fear that Tristan was going to simply let me go when my six months were up. Why would he make sure I had so much money if he was going to want me to stay? I wanted to believe that this was just one of his ways of showing me how much he loved me, but every time I checked my balance, an emptiness formed in the pit of my stomach.

Jordan's famous words echoed in my head—*Good things happen to good people, Nina.* I wanted to believe that more than anything. Closing my laptop, I hoped she was right.

I stepped out of the black Town Car in front of the apartment and a brisk wind blew my dress up nearly around my waist, a la Marilyn Monroe on the subway grate. A group of men across the street whistled, making me feel right at home back in Brooklyn. I bounded up the steps, dying to see my best friend, as the men yelled my name and compliments on my red dress.

As I reached the door, I turned around and waved, yelling, "Thanks!" Jordan waited in the apartment doorway at the top of the stairs with a huge grin on her face.

"Look at you! I love it! This new life of yours looks good on you."

I reached her and took her in my arms for a big hug. "It looks good?" I asked as she held me out at arm's length to check out my outfit again.

"Oh, honey. You look incredible. Same old Nina in a wonderful new package."

I beamed at her compliment. I felt wonderful and wanted the whole world to know it.

"Well, come in. Tell me everything. I need to know the details," Jordan ordered as she pulled me into the apartment.

Everything looked the same as it had when I'd left months earlier, except now there were some pictures on the living room walls. Turning toward Jordan, I pointed at them. "I leave and now there's artwork on the walls?"

She sat down in her chair across from my seat on the couch and chuckled. "I wouldn't call it artwork. Just some pictures. I had a little more money since your boyfriend paid your portion of the rent and more that day."

"More? How much more?" I asked, suddenly worried he was trying to buy me.

"About two grand. I told him I didn't feel right taking it, but he insisted. I assumed you knew because you asked him to."

I shook my head and frowned. "No. He never told me. And as much as you know I'd give you my last dime, I didn't ask."

"Why the frown? It's okay that you didn't ask."

"It's not that, Jordan. I just worry that he's trying to buy things he shouldn't."

"Like your love?"

"Yeah," I answered quietly.

"Honey, if he was trying to buy your love, wouldn't he have told you he did this?"

"I guess. It's just…" I didn't know how to complain about all the money in my bank account and not sound like a spoiled child. "He's done the same thing with me. Instead of paying me the amount I'm supposed to get, he's paid me nearly five times more."

"And the problem with that is?"

Jordan's expression told me she still thought I was acting silly all these months later. "I know what you're going to say. I should just enjoy this, right? It's just that my six months are almost up. What if he is giving me all this money because he doesn't plan to stay with me and wants to make himself feel good about it?"

"Still overthinking this, I see."

"But what if it's true?"

"Have you asked him?"

Looking down at my hands as they sat folded in my lap, I shook my head. "No. I'm too afraid of what he'd say."

"How much longer is there on your contract?"

"A few weeks."

"And has he been acting weird, like a boyfriend getting ready to break up with you? You know. Not answering calls or texts. Not showing up for dates. Has the sex fallen off?"

As I listened to her laundry list of signs, I couldn't say yes to one. He always answered my texts, never failed to be where he said he would be at exactly the time he said he would, and the sex had continued to be mind blowing.

"No to all," I admitted with a shrug. "He's wonderful, even though things at work seem to be constantly on his mind."

"So, let me get this straight. Your gorgeous, billionaire boyfriend treats you like a queen and makes sure you have piles of money to spend on yourself, and you're worried he's going to leave you? You're a bright girl, Nina. Figure it out."

"I know it sounds stupid, but I can't help it. I'm dreading the day that contract ends."

That was the cold, hard truth. I was sick to death over a date on the calendar. It never left my mind, no matter how much money he put in my account, no matter how many times he told me he loved me.

Jordan leaned forward and touched me on the knee, jarring me out of my thoughts about that day just weeks away. "Enough of this crazy talk. Tell me how he is in bed. And don't leave out the details. I'll know if you do."

A blush spread from the top of my head all the way to the tip of my toes. Even before I said a word, she clapped her hands together and exclaimed, "I knew it! No man who sounds so incredibly sexy when he speaks about something as boring as paying someone's rent could be bad in bed."

"Stop it! You're embarrassing me!" I cried, half joking. "I'm not telling you a thing."

"You don't have to say a word. It's written all over your face. I bet he's hung like a horse, isn't he?"

"Jordan!" The blush intensified at her words, confirming that she'd hit the nail on the head.

"I swear there's not a thing wrong with this man, Nina. If you say you're worried about anything with him one more time, I'm going to kick you out of this apartment and never speak to you again."

"That's harsh."

"I'm not kidding, Nina. I could understand if he lacked in one or two areas, but he's perfect."

"He's not perfect. I think many women wouldn't like how he's so possessive."

She laughed out loud. "The only time any woman dislikes a possessive man is if he keeps her from doing things she likes. Tristan doesn't do that, so I doubt there'd be many women in this world who wouldn't be madly in love with him just as he is."

I must have had a worried look on my face because she added, "And don't start thinking he's cheating on you or you have to be concerned about other women. That's not what I'm saying."

Putting my hands up in surrender, I smiled. "I know. I'm being stupid. You don't have to say it again."

"Good. I don't like telling people I love that they're being stupid, but I will when I have to. Tough love."

"Enough about me. Tell me about Justin, school, everything," I said, giving the subject a much needed change.

Jordan gave chapter and verse about how things had progressed with Justin, how she thought they were moving toward possibly moving in together, her class of third graders and how cute they were, and all the news of the neighborhood, including what she thought of the new weird guy on the first floor.

"Do you think Mrs. Phillips will be okay?" I asked, growing concerned about the elderly lady.

"I hope so. I haven't seen her in a few days, but you know how she is. If she doesn't come out for grocery day on Friday, then I'll be worried."

"I'd hate to see something happen to her, Jordan. She's always so nice when she invites us to her apartment for cookies and that crazy spiked egg nog at Christmastime. I'm going to stop in just to see if everything's okay."

"Well, now you've guilted me, so I'll go with you. I just hope I don't have to see that guy."

As we left, I grabbed the letter I'd come for and stuffed it into my purse to read later. We walked down to the first floor as Jordan explained how creepy Mrs. Phillips' grandson was. Even without seeing him, I was repulsed. Greasy blond hair and crooked, yellow teeth were never a good combination.

The elderly woman's door was open just a crack, but I had a bad vibe about going in. Tugging Jordan back as she pushed the door open, I whispered, "No way. If that creepy guy is there, who knows what he'll do. This has the beginning of every Law and Order episode written all over it."

Nodding, she agreed. "Yeah, let's get the hell out of here. I'll check on her later with Justin."

The two of us hurried out of the building to grab a bite to eat and ran straight into Mrs. Phillips' grandson as he hit the top of the front steps. I scanned his face and saw he was more than just ugly. He was definitely high on something. Gripping Jordan's arm tightly, I whispered, "We need to go. He's not okay."

His bloodshot eyes stared into mine, and I knew he'd heard what I said. Before we could get away, he lunged at us and yanked on the straps of my bag. I tried to pull away from him, but whatever he was on made him superhero strong and he wrenched the bag down my arm to the crook of my elbow, pulling me down with it. Jordan screamed, scaring him, and he gave one last violent tug. The bag ripped down my forearm, and as he grabbed it, his elbow slammed into my head. Pain spiked out across the top of my skull, radiating all the way to my ear, and I fell back into Jordan in agony.

"Nina! Are you okay?" she asked as she cradled me in her arms.

I heard Jenson's voice barking some order at Jordan as I closed my eyes in agony from the pain. A headache instantly tore through my head, making me cry. I don't know how long I laid there with Jordan, but at some point Jenson lifted me from the concrete porch and carried me to the car.

The leather seat felt so cool against my skin as I lay there in the back of the Town Car while Jordan smoothed my hair from my face. Jenson returned a minute later and took off, driving quickly through the streets of Sunset Park.

"Honey, how's your head?" Jordan asked quietly. "Let me see."

I leaned forward, making me feel like my head was swimming, and Jordan lightly rubbed her hand over the back of my hair. "It hurts, Jordan. Am I bleeding?"

Lifting my head, I saw a tiny red splotch on her palm. "I don't know, honey. It doesn't seem like you're bleeding a lot, but you're starting to swell up." She turned around to speak to Jenson. "Hey, are you taking her to the hospital? She might need a doctor."

"Miss, Mr. Stone has been contacted and he wants her back at the house."

Jordan wanted to say something more to the driver, but I grabbed her arm and shook my head slowly. "It's okay. I'm sure if I need something, Tristan will take care of it. But you get to see the house," I said with a smile, but even that made my head hurt even more.

"How long will it take?" she asked as we raced toward the Taconic.

"At the rate he's going, no time. Don't worry. Everything will be fine," I joked, trying to hide how terrified I was as my head began to throb all the way down to the base of my skull.

Jenson held his hand back toward Jordan. "I found this on the steps."

She took what sat in his palm and held it up to show me. "He got your phone, at least."

I laughed a little. Leave it to Jordan. "Yeah. At least he knows what's important. Did he get my bag?"

Leaning forward toward Jenson, she asked, "Did you get Nina's bag?"

"Yes, miss." He held out his hand and passed my purse back to Jordan. "I'm afraid there's nothing left in it, though."

She looked inside and saw Jenson had told the truth. Shrugging, she said, "At least he didn't get the bag. It's a gorgeous bag."

I moaned in a mixture of pain and amusement. "Yeah. But my letter is gone. Now I'll never know if the IRS was going to audit me."

"What?" she asked, confused by my inside joke.

"Never mind. I think I'm just going to close my eyes and relax until we get there."

I felt the car stop and then the door flew open and hands reached in and scooped me up from the seat. They were strong and I knew they were Tristan's. Opening my eyes, I saw his face and those brown eyes so full of concern staring down at me. I was in bad shape if his expression was any indication.

"Tristan…"

"Shhh. Don't talk. I want you to lay down while we wait for the doctor."

I rested my head against his shoulder and closed my eyes again. Just knowing he was taking care of everything put me at ease, and I couldn't imagine feeling safer than in his arms. He placed me gently into our bed and sat beside me, still wearing a look of worry.

"I'll be right back. I need to deal with Jenson," he said sternly.

Reaching out, I grabbed his shirt sleeve as he stood. "Jenson didn't do anything wrong. Please don't do anything to him. If it wasn't for him, I don't know what would have happened to me or Jordan."

Tristan studied me for a moment and then nodded his head. "He's supposed to make sure this doesn't happen, Nina."

"Please. He's not to blame. It all happened so fast. He got to me as soon as he could," I pleaded.

He leaned down and kissed me softly on the lips. "I'll send Jordan in until I get back."

Chapter Nineteen

Jordan sat with me and tried to make me feel better as Tristan reprimanded the driver right outside the door. I couldn't hear everything he said, but as Jordan raved about how beautifully the house was decorated, I heard Tristan say, "I want him taken care of. Now. Do I make myself clear?"

I truly hoped he wasn't talking to Rogers about firing Jenson. It wasn't his fault Mrs. Phillps' crazy grandson was some kind of addict and probably stole my bag for money to buy his drugs. I tuned out much of what Jordan said as I strained to hear more of what Tristan was saying, but his voice was so low I couldn't make anything more out.

When he returned, his expression was softer and he smiled when his gaze met mine. As he sat down next to me, he squeezed my hand. "How are you feeling? The doctor should be here any minute."

"How did you get here before us?" I asked, realizing he couldn't have left the city before Jenson left Sunset Park.

"I drive faster than Jenson," he said with a laugh. "Remember how fast my car is?"

"Yeah." The memory of that first night and us racing up the highway toward this house flashed through my mind, and then I heard Jordan speak.

"I think I need to go home, Nina. You look like you're in good hands here."

All I could think about was her going back to where that asshole was. Who knew what might happen if he caught her alone? I looked over at Tristan and squeezed his hand. "Jordan can't go back there. That guy might be there, Tristan."

"Honey, I have work. I have to go back to the city," Jordan protested.

I silently pleaded with Tristan, hoping he understood the look in my eyes. When he spoke, I fell in love with him all over again.

"Jordan, Nina's right. You can spend a week or two at my hotel downtown while my people find the man who did this."

"Are you sure? That's really nice of you."

I brought Tristan's hand to my mouth and kissed it, mouthing "Thank you."

He looked deep into my eyes as he said to Jordan, "It's my pleasure. I think you'll enjoy one of the suites, and the menu for room service is second to none." Breaking his stare, he turned to face her. "I'll be sure to check in on you to make sure you're comfortable. Jenson will escort you back to Brooklyn and wait until you get your things."

Jordan leaned over the bed and hugged me tightly against her. In my ear, she whispered, "Feel better, sweetie. And if you let this man get away, I'll never let you live it down."

Rogers appeared as he always did, just at the right time, and took Jordan to the car. Alone again with Tristan, I pulled on his tie to bring his mouth to mine. Never before had I wanted to show someone how much I loved them as I wanted to at that moment. He kissed me like he'd missed me for ages, covering my mouth seductively as he caressed the inside of my mouth with his tongue. The feeling was sensual and caring at the same time.

I pulled away and ran my hand over his cheek. "Thank you for what you did for Jordan. I can't tell you how much it means to me."

"I would do anything to make you happy, Nina. I'll find the man who did this and he'll understand what happens when he hurts someone I love."

Something in his eyes told me Mrs. Phillips' grandson was in danger, but before I could ask him what he planned to do about him, Rogers knocked on the bedroom door to announce the doctor had arrived.

"Good. Show him in, Rogers," Tristan said in the butler's direction.

The doctor examined me and pronounced me healthy, other than a tennis ball size goose egg on the back of my head. He assured me there wouldn't be any permanent damage and that I'd be fine. It took all of ten minutes for him to complete the entire examination and prescribe a pain killer, and Tristan thanked him and led him out to meet Rogers, returning to my side not a minute later.

He looked at me oddly, and I realized I still wore my red dress and stockings. I didn't know where my shoes were, though. "I wanted to surprise you for our date. Do you like it?"

He removed his black suit coat and tie and laid down next to me. Taking me in his arms, he slid his hands up and down my leg, feeling the stockings. His touch excited me as the pain killer began to dull my pain.

"I do. Did you wear this just for me?" he asked in a voice heavy with sex.

I ran my hand over his shirt and unbuttoned two buttons so I could touch his skin. It felt cool against my fingers. Lowering my mouth to his neck, I licked just below his earlobe. "I did. I thought it would be sexy."

Tristan groaned and ran his hand further up my thigh to where the garter belt connected to the stockings and then between my legs, where my sensitive skin lay bare. "You went into the city like this?"

His voice had a strange edge to it, and I lifted my head to see his expression had changed from just a minute earlier. His eyes had narrowed into angry slits.

"It's okay. I just went to see Jordan, and you know what happened after that. Nobody else saw me." I didn't mention the guys across the street from the apartment or that the wind had blown my dress so high it was likely that at least a few of them had seen a bit more than I'd wanted to show.

He slid his hand between my legs and stroked his fingers slowly over my tender folds. "I don't want you leaving the house like this without me."

The odd mix of gentleness in his touch and the harsh tone of his voice confused me. "Okay. It's no big deal, though."

One finger slid over my clit and sent a jolt of excitement through me. He stared down at me as my face showed the effect of what his fingers were doing to me. "It is a big deal. You're with me, Nina. No one else sees that part of you."

The possessiveness he was showing me was new between us. Until that moment, I'd never gotten the sense that he was jealous or overprotective when it came to me. There hadn't been a moment since I'd met him when he didn't act as if he were the only man in my life. This change in him baffled me even while it excited me. I liked the idea that he was protective about the woman he loved, although I knew there was no reason for him to be jealous.

I loved him so completely I couldn't imagine even thinking of another man touching me the way he did. Looking up into his eyes so intense, I smiled. "I don't want anyone else but you, Tristan."

He drew circles with his fingertip over my excited clit and kissed me deeply before he pulled away and I watched him slide down my body and settle in between my legs. Lifting my dress around my waist, he lowered his head and whispered against my skin, "No other man, Nina."

The feel of his mouth and tongue on me was exquisite. He slid up and down my moist folds, teasing me with the tip of his tongue when he reached my now swollen clit. His fingers thrust inside me, pushing against the tender spot inside that sent ribbons of pleasure racing through me.

His mouth inched me toward my orgasm, taking me to the edge of oblivion just to ease me back again each time as if he knew the very moment my body would give in to his expert touch. Just as I felt the first tiny tug of my release, he pulled away and stood up from the bed.

"Wha...What's wrong?" I asked trying to catch my breath.

He slowly unbuttoned his shirt and slid out of his pants and boxer briefs, revealing his cock pressed against his belly. I wanted to feel him inside me and held my hand out for his. He sat down next to me and without a word, pulled me onto his lap. I straddled my legs over his hips as he held me above him by the waist.

"Tristan, don't make me wait," I pleaded as I pushed against his hold.

Pushing the thick head of his cock through my wet pussy, he teased me to the point that I could barely hold back, and then stopped, leaving me tense and needy. His gaze fixed on me, watching my reaction, as if all this was a game.

"Don't tease," I cooed as I tried to lean forward to kiss him, stopped abruptly as he pushed me down on his legs. Confused, I attempted to feel some closeness from him, but his hands held me tight in place away from him.

He stared into my eyes until I couldn't stand it anymore. "What's wrong? Why won't you even kiss me?"

"I need to know you're mine, Nina. I've given you everything your heart desires, including enough money to ensure you can have anything I may not have considered. When I see something like this, I get concerned."

His words stunned me. "Why are you saying things like this? I wore the stockings and the garter belt for you—to go to dinner with you."

Tristan's gaze never wavered, telling me he was serious. He thought I'd done something. My mouth dropped open in amazement, and then a rush of defensiveness came over me. "As if I'd be able to do anything with your man hovering over me wherever I go. It's not like I'm ever alone, Tristan. You haven't trusted me from the very beginning of us."

He said nothing for so long I worried he might never speak to me again, but finally, he said in a low, solemn voice, "Jenson is there to protect you. Your safety means everything to me."

"Safety from what? I lived in Brooklyn long before I met you. I can handle myself."

And with that, his part of the conversation was over. He placed me on the bed next to him and left to walk to the bathroom, closing the door behind him. Closing me out.

Leaning back onto the bed, I covered my head with a pillow, angrier than I'd been in ages. I'd gotten all dressed up for him and then that fucked up asshole had mugged me, and all Tristan could think of was that I must be sneaking around behind his back? Hadn't I shown him every day and every night how much in love with him I was?

When he didn't come out after five minutes, something inside me snapped. I loved him, but this jealous bullshit based on nothing wasn't going to work. If we were going to stay together after my contract was up, he had to know that.

I marched to the bathroom, threw open the door, and stormed in to find him in the shower. I was all upset, and he was enjoying a nice shower at the end of the day! I stood there staring through the glass shower doors watching him until I became too impatient to wait any longer for him to notice me.

"So that's what you think of me? That I would take your money and everything else and go with someone else?"

He didn't even turn to face me at the sound of my voice, but I wasn't ready to let this go. Not yet. Opening the shower door, I walked in still fully dressed and stood in front of him, my arms crossed as the water hit me. "What? Now you're just going to ignore me? You basically accuse me of cheating on you and now I don't get to answer those charges?"

"Don't, Nina. I'm not in the mood for this with you."

I poked my finger into his chest. "Then you shouldn't have started it."

He looked down at me, those dark eyes barely hiding his anger, as the water rolled down over the beautiful features of his face, making me want to reach out to touch him. I extended my hand to caress his cheek, but he caught me by the wrist and held my hand away from him. Stunned, I tried to pull away, but he wouldn't allow that either.

"Nina, be careful with what you do now."

Yanking my arm from his grip, I snapped, "How about I do nothing with you now?" I spun on the wet tile and moved to take a step, but his arm shot out and wrapped around my waist before my foot could hit the floor. In a flash, I was up against the wall with him staring wildly down at me.

The man in front of me was different now—more powerful than I'd ever seen him. I knew I should have been frightened, but he looked so sexy, so commanding that I was more turned on than I thought I could be. His dark hair glistened with moisture, and I slid my hand over his head to feel its silky wetness. My touch made something break in him.

"Nina..." he moaned deeply as he lifted me onto his hard cock, pushing into me with one fast thrust.

I wrapped my arms around his neck and laced my fingers tightly as he kissed me hard, his mouth and tongue demanding mine respond with the same level of urgency, nearly taking my breath away. His cock pounded into my body, hard and fast like a piston as it stroked in and out of me, and he moaned and grunted into my mouth the sounds of a man driven by need. Our bodies bounced and slammed against the marble tile—my back, his legs—each in turn smashing against the hard surface, but neither of us cared.

It was like all the frustration he'd endured in the past weeks exploded out of him and now he sought someone to share his pain. I knew he may never tell me what had been on his mind, but as we clung to one another's wet bodies and raced toward our release, I felt him reach out for me like he never had before.

Our sex was primal in a way that both thrilled and frightened me, but at that moment as he filled me and my body reacted as only he could make it, I felt closer to him than any other soul on Earth. His hands left the back of my head and skidded down the wet tiles behind me, making him sag against my body. I held his head to my heart, listening as he panted softly against me and murmured my name.

He silently lowered me to the floor without saying another word. I stood looking up at his face that now wore a tortured expression. He gently wiped the pad of his thumb over my lips and leaned forward to press his forehead against mine.

"Tristan, what's wrong?" I whispered.

"Nothing," he answered quietly and walked out of the shower. His tone told me that was his only word on the subject, so I let it go, hoping that when he needed to tell me, he would.

After I'd washed up, I found him sitting in bed, just staring toward the wall at the picture I'd painted for him. He seemed to be looking right through it.

I crawled into bed and lay there wondering what to say. Instead of speaking, I let my actions say what was in my heart and curled up next to him. Drawing little circles on the hard ridges of muscle just above his hip, I waited to hear any words come out of his mouth, but as the minutes ticked by, there was nothing. Finally, I closed my eyes, content and safe in his strong embrace but so wishing to know what he was thinking.

His words came out like a whoosh of air from his lungs. "Don't leave me like everyone else has. I'll do whatever it takes, but don't leave me, even if I screw this up."

I knew as soon as the first word left his lips that this had been what was on his mind. Work had been bad recently, but this was what had been plaguing his thoughts. That I'd leave him.

Lifting my head from his chest, I looked up and saw the torment in his face, just as I'd heard it in his voice. At that moment, all I wanted to do was make him happy.

"I'm not leaving you. Is that what that back there was all about? Me leaving?"

"Yes." His voice was a mixture of fear and shame.

"Why would I leave someone who adores me?" I asked, hoping to calm his fears. "I've never even thought of going anywhere. If anyone should be afraid, it's me. You made me sign a contract, which is up in just a few weeks, and you seem to have given me enough money to ensure when you break up with me that I'll be fine."

"I gave you that money to show you how much more you're worth than the salary I offered. I'd hoped you'd see that."

"All I saw was that you were throwing a lot of money at me and never mentioning anything about what was going to happen when the six months was up."

"So you think I'm going to leave you then?" he asked wide-eyed.

As I laid there listening to him, my fears sounded foolish. "I guess that sounds silly, but I did. Jordan tried to convince me that I was all wrong, but you've been so distant sometimes recently that I didn't know." I stopped talking and looked down, sheepishly adding, "And all that money."

Tristan pushed the hair out of my eyes. "I wasn't throwing anything at you. I have enough money to last for five lifetimes. What good is it if I can't share it with someone I love?"

I heard the loneliness in his words. Without his brother and parents, there was no one to share his money with, except me. But what about the contract?

"I notice you're not saying anything about what happens after the contract."

"What do you want to happen?"

I knew what I wanted. I wanted him to tell me he loved me without any need of some paper that said I was obligated to be with him. I wanted him to show me that his feelings had nothing to do with a contract or money.

"Tell me, Nina. What do you want?"

"It's not fair answering a question with a question," I said, side-stepping the issue.

"You didn't ask a question, so my question doesn't answer anything."

No kidding.

My potential answers receded into the corners of my mind, each one afraid to step forward and show itself. How was I supposed to tell him that even though he hadn't really told me what he wanted after our contract ended, I wanted what every woman in love wanted?

A husband who loved me. A beautiful life. Maybe kids down the road.

"You know I hate when you do that."

"Do what?" he said with a hint of a smile.

"Whatever this is. I always feel like I'm being talked into a corner."

"All you have to do is answer the question, Nina. What do you want?"

All my answers found great hiding places, except for the smart ass ones, which raced toward my mouth. "You know. What everyone wants. World peace. Cheaper prices at the pump."

He cocked an eyebrow at me and grinned. "Funny."

Climbing up his body, I kissed the tip of his nose. "Well, you put me on the spot. Maybe if you gave me some time, I could come up with something better."

He lifted my chin with his fingertips and gave me that sexy look that never failed to make me melt. "More time it is. I want your answer by five tomorrow afternoon. You can tell me what you want right after you show me your choices for Miami. For now, I think you need some rest. You've had a rough day."

Turning me over onto my back, he kissed me goodnight, told me he loved me, and laid down to sleep, leaving me with a deadline of less than twenty-four hours to figure out how to say all the things in my heart.

Piece of cake. Right.

CHAPTER TWENTY

As the first rays of the sun streamed into our room, I rubbed the sleep out of my eyes and reached for Tristan. I wasn't surprised he was already gone, as it was his usual style, but the envelope on his pillow unnerved me a little. I had hoped to have the day to rummage around my own brain to find a way to tell Tristan what I really wanted, but his letter meant he too would be joining me in my head.

If I didn't know better, I would have sworn he'd left a letter to make sure of that.

I turned the envelope over in my palm and then held it up in front of me to see if I could read what he'd said. Nope. I had to open it, which for some reason filled me with dread. It was just like that first morning I'd woken up and nervously spied his note on the chair.

There was no time like the present.

I slid the letter out of the envelope and unfolded it. My eyes focused on the words as I read them aloud.

Dear Nina,

I missed having our date last night, so after you show me your choices for Miami and answer my question, we'll go to Tony's for pizza. I'm looking forward to it.

> *Love,*
> *Tristan*

I'm looking forward to it. Did he mean my choices, my answer to his question, or Tony's pizza? Jesus. This man was going to drive me mad. Even his letters said little and created more questions in my mind.

There was no point in worrying all day. I knew what I wanted to say. Had to say if I wanted him to know how I truly felt about him. I just had to muster up the courage to say the words.

By four o' clock, I was a nervous wreck. The woman who stared back at me from the mirror in the morning with her bravado had dissolved into a panicky mess. Needing to talk to Jordan but too impatient to wait for email, I snuck up to the attic, evading Rogers' careful eye, and called her for a strong shot of courage.

Every step I took across the attic floor seemed to make the floor creak like it was screaming beneath my feet. If only I hadn't hidden the phone all the way in the corner next to that scary sewing mannequin. I finally reached it and crouched down behind a stack of boxes, just in case my footsteps had been as loud as I thought.

The phone felt heavier in my hand than before, and I quickly dialed Jordan's number, pushing my index finger around in the rotary dialer circle eleven times, all the time questioning how anyone called for help and got it in time before push button phones and 911.

"Hello?"

"Jordan," I whispered into the black receiver. "It's me. I need your help."

"Nina, what's up? Are you okay? How's your head? And can I tell you how great this suite is? That man of yours knows how to live!"

"Jordan!" I whispered as loudly as I could and still be whispering.

"Okay. Sorry. What's up?"

"I need to talk to you about something. Something I need to do with Tristan."

There was silence on the other end of the phone for a long moment. "Nina, what's wrong?"

"He asked me what I wanted after my contract is over. I don't want to make a mistake like I did by saying I love you too early."

"I don't understand. What do you want?"

I said nothing, scared even to say it to her, my best friend. Opening my mouth, I tried, but nothing came out. Finally, I just said, "I don't know."

"Oh, honey. You know."

"You're not helping."

"I know, but I can't help with this one. Think about what you'd tell me if I asked you what I should say to Justin if he asked what I wanted with him."

"I'd like to think I'd be more helpful," I pouted.

"What are you afraid of, Nina?" she asked, cutting straight to the center of the issue. "And don't tell me you don't know."

I let the phone sag onto my shoulder and covered my face with my hands. "I'm afraid that I'm going to let him know exactly how I feel and how much I want to be with him forever and he's going to react just like Cal did."

And there it was. Like a huge cloud of doubt hanging over my head right there in the attic ready to suffocate me.

"Cal was an asshole, Nina. He was a liar and a player and an immature fuckup. You were too good for him from the moment you were born. That he broke up with you after you told him how you felt about him isn't a reflection on you, sweetie. He'd been lying for months. You were just too sweet to see that."

"But what if I'm just not seeing the same thing here?"

"Tristan isn't Cal. I promise you that. I'm not even sure they're both the same species. Tristan has been nothing but incredible, so until he shows you otherwise, I say give him a chance."

"What if he doesn't want as much as I do, Jordan?" I squeaked out.

"Then he's a fool and not the man I think he is. Give him a chance, sweetie. I think you'll be pleasantly surprised."

I wanted to. I really did. But my past and all that hurt felt like it was pressing down on my chest, threatening to crush me.

"Nina, do you remember all those days you stayed in your room crying over Cal and swearing you would never let yourself fall for anyone again? I think if you let this guy go, you're going to be like that forever. I don't want to see you get all hardened over. You're too good a person to be that."

Tears rolled down my cheeks at Jordan's words and the thought of losing Tristan because of my fears from the past. Wiping my face, I sniffled. "I know. I'm just so afraid it's too good to be true."

"You're forgetting my mantra. Remember? Good things happen to good people, and you're the best of the good ones, Nina."

"Okay. Thanks, Jordan."

"Your welcome, sweetie. And don't forget whatever happens, you got this."

I hung up the phone and inhaled a deep breath. *I got this.* Getting up, I walked as quietly as possible across the attic, but I stopped as I passed the trunk with the picture of Tristan and his family. It was silly, but something in me wanted to look at him as a child again. Crouching down, I opened the trunk while I kept my eye on the stairs, just in case Rogers had heard something.

I took out the family portrait and studied the childhood face of the man I loved. He looked so innocent. I wanted to see more—wanted to see what he was truly like as a child—so I sifted through the papers and books to a pile of smaller pictures I hadn't noticed the last time. Together, they catalogued Tristan and his brother's youth and as the pictures clearly showed, the vast differences between the two boys.

Identical in appearance, they were like night and day. All smiles, Tristan seemed to always be so full of life, while his brother stood sullen in the few pictures of him. Tristan was obviously the more athletic, appearing in picture after picture holding trophies, each one bigger than the one before. In the background of one picture his brother stood watching from behind the bleachers as Tristan once again received laurels. Taylor wore the expression I'd seen often in the past weeks on Tristan, a face that told whoever bothered to pay attention that the one wearing it felt the most acute sense of unhappiness. Some pictures showed his mother's pride in her winning son, but none included Tristan's father, except the formal portrait I'd studied earlier. As the boys aged, fewer showed Taylor at all.

I searched the bottom of the trunk to find more images of his brother, but there were none. All I found were papers that appeared to be lists of names and legal documents. Suddenly, a feeling of guilt came over me. It wasn't right that I was snooping up in that attic, even if it was for a silly romantic reason.

Carefully replacing everything as I'd found it, I closed the trunk and quietly made my way back downstairs, tiptoeing each step to avoid being caught by Rogers. It was nearly five o'clock and my time for indecision was over. I grabbed my laptop and headed for Tristan's office, prepared to show off my work on the Miami suite and praying to God I was ready to answer his question.

I sat in his leather office chair behind his desk and closed my eyes to calm my nerves, repeating my newest affirmation. *I got this. I got this.* A few minutes later, the sound of his footsteps coming down the wood floor hallway told me my time was up.

"You look good behind my desk, Nina," he said in a silky voice that slid over me, enveloping me.

Opening my eyes, I saw him casually leaning up against the doorframe as he loosened his tie, the picture of calm. As usual, he looked incredible. The dark charcoal suit he wore was complimented perfectly by his black dress shirt and red and black striped silk tie.

"You don't look too bad yourself, boss," I tried to say just as casually in an attempt to keep the conversation light.

But he wasn't having any of it.

He walked toward me as he unbuttoned his shirt's top button. "It's five o'clock. I'm looking forward to seeing your choices for Miami and then you answering my question."

"I'm pretty hungry. How about we head over to Tony's for pizza and then get to the work?"

Tristan rounded the corner of his desk and stood next to me wearing a sly grin. "I'm happy to leave the work until tomorrow. You know I don't like doing anything after five."

I stood to leave, but he caught me around the waist and pulled me to him. He looked down at me with a look in his dark eyes so intense I shuddered. There would be no putting him off.

"But the answer needs to happen before we eat."

"Okay." I sat back down in his chair and opened up my laptop. "Might as well get Miami out of the way, right?"

I was stalling for time and he knew it. "As you wish."

Steadying my shaky hands, I presented my choices for the Miami suite, which Tristan easily approved and congratulated me on. I doubted he had even paid much attention to my ideas this time, but there was no point in belaboring the issue.

He closed my laptop and folded his arms across his chest. "I'm glad that's finished."

Unsure what to say, I stared at the desk and meekly smiled. "Me too."

Tristan caressed my cheek with his thumb and then cupped my chin, turning my face to look up at him. "So I believe the question stands, Nina. What do you want from me after your contract is over?"

My mouth became as dry as the Sahara desert. I wouldn't have been surprised if when I tried to speak that sand flew out from between my lips. If ever I needed a drink, it was at that moment. I tried to moisten my lips, but it was no use.

Clearing my throat, I croaked out, "I don't want this to end."

"Are you referring to your job with Stone Worldwide or your relationship with me?" he asked sharply, stroking the pad of his thumb against my jaw.

"Both."

"I can assure you that you have a job with Stone Worldwide as long as you'd like."

"This job?"

He dropped his hand to his side and pursed his lips. "Well, at some point I'm going to run out of suites for you to work with, but I can promise that you'll have a job that will take advantage of your artistic talents."

I swallowed hard, knowing that we'd gone as far as we could concerning the job. Now he was going to want my answer to what I wanted with him.

"But you haven't answered my question, Nina. What do you want from me?"

I closed my eyes and took the biggest chance of my life. Inhaling a deep breath, I said, "I want you. All of you."

There was complete silence as the last word left my mouth, and I feared opening my eyes to see his reaction. I couldn't even hear him breathe as he stood next to me. My heart sank as he continued to stay quiet. What was he thinking? Had I jumped the gun? Didn't he want me to want him?

"Open your eyes, Nina," he ordered gently.

I looked up to see him smiling down at me. My emotions were a jumble, making it impossible to figure out what to do next. I wanted to laugh. I wanted to cry. I wanted to run. I didn't know what to do.

When he continued with his silence, I blurted out, "You know, I hate this thing you do. It makes me uncomfortable. It's rude to stare at someone and not say anything. I know you're trying…"

He cut me off in mid-sentence and took me in his arms, kissing me deeply. As his tongue teased mine, his lips pressed tenderly against my mouth, telling me everything I needed to know.

Tristan was happy.

After the longest kiss I'd ever had, he pulled away and took my face in his hands. "I just hope I don't disappoint now that you'll get everything I am."

Shaking my head, I said, "No way you could disappoint me. Thank you for not freaking out when I said I wanted all of you. A lot of guys might have wanted to."

He leaned in to kiss me gently and whispered against my cheek, "I know I've asked you before, but what kind of men have you been dating?"

As I wrapped my arms around his neck, I answered with the honest truth. "All the wrong kinds."

"Well, I'm happy to be able to help you remedy that."

My emotions were ready to overflow, so before I began crying tears of complete and utter happiness, I whispered in his ear, "What do you say to remedying my hunger with some Tony's pizza?"

He stood back from me and looked at his watch for a long moment before he nodded. "I think it's about time."

We walked toward the car and as he opened the door for me, I said, "I probably look like a disaster. That lump on the back of my head doesn't hurt anymore, but it's like I have a stegosaurus ridge back there."

He leaned in and kissed me. "That will sound great on Page Six."

Page Six. My stomach did a funny somersault. This was the first time he'd ever mentioned anything even remotely related to being with me in public, and the idea was at once thrilling and terrifying. This was everything I'd wanted and now that it was happening, all I could think about were my deficiencies.

I wasn't a tall, willowy, supermodel type whose clothes hung perfectly off her. I had a tendency to make silly comments when I was nervous. For God's sake, there were times I couldn't even get my hair to lay right and not look all flyaway.

Tristan got into the driver's seat and started the car, but one look at my expression and he knew something was wrong. "Did I say something? What's going on?"

"I just remember you saying you never took girlfriends to those events that land you on Page Six, but then you just mentioned it. I'm just wondering if I'm the right type to be on the arm of someone like you."

He cradled my face in his hands and shook his head. "Don't say that. You're a beautiful, intelligent, charming woman who makes me smile. That's more than I can say for anyone I've ever met at those things. If you don't want to go to them, I'm fine with that. But it would be nice to have someone to talk to at them."

"You're trying to guilt me into going?" I joked. "But what about the idea of people seeing you smile? What will that do to your reputation?"

He rolled his eyes and turned to drive. "I hadn't thought about that. Well, then. It's settled. I'll remain cold and impersonal in public and nobody will know the real me. Except you."

I knew it was selfish, but I liked the idea of the world thinking he was cold. There was something very special about Tristan only feeling comfortable enough to drop his cool facade with me.

We got to Tony's to find the entire restaurant deserted. Peering in through the front window, I saw no one inside. Disappointed, I turned toward him. "I don't think they're open."

Tristan brushed it off and took my hand to lead me inside to a table in the back. A waitress appeared almost instantly to take our order, and as he told her what we wanted, I wondered where all the other customers were.

She walked away toward the front of the restaurant and I asked, "Don't you think it's weird there's no one here?"

He got a strange grin on his face. "No. Not at all."

The lights dimmed throughout the building except where we sat, making me feel there was definitely something odd going on. "Tristan, they're turning the lights out. I think they might be closing early tonight."

I looked around to see where the waitress had gone to and when I looked back at Tristan, he was on one knee on the wood floor next to me and beside him sat a small robin's egg blue colored box. In the palm of his right hand was a smaller black velvet box. He pulled back the top and there sat a gorgeous diamond ring. I'd never seen anything so stunning, and even in the dim light of Tony's, the stone was brilliant.

"It's…oh, my God, Tristan. I don't know what to say." I covered my mouth with my hands and tears began to roll down my cheeks.

"Say you'll marry me."

At that moment, I was sure there wasn't a happier person on the entire planet. As I looked down into those eyes so full of love for me, my heart felt fuller than it ever had before.

"Yes. Yes! I'll marry you, Tristan."

He slid the ring onto my finger and took me into his arms as I cried tears of joy. This was more than I'd ever dreamed could happen in my life. I kissed him right there in Tony's Pizza Heaven and right in front of the waitress, who was standing there with our tray of pizza and crying herself.

The blonde looked down at Tristan with a look of anticipation. "Did she say yes?"

Looking into my eyes, he smiled. "She said yes."

"She said yes, everybody!" the woman yelled toward the kitchen, where a chorus of whistles and clapping exploded. She placed the large tray of pizza on the table and smiled at me. "Congratulations. You're a lucky girl. It's not every guy who arranges a proposal like this."

She left us alone, and I turned toward him. "How long have you been planning this?"

"Since Venice."

I looked down at the dazzling ring on my hand. I guessed the diamond was at least two carets and was set in a platinum setting and band. To say it was gorgeous was an understatement. It took my breath away.

"And you got the people here at Tony's to help you?"

Tristan took a bite of pizza. "I figured it would be easier to get you to say yes if the restaurant wasn't filled with people."

"So you paid to have the restaurant closed to everyone but us?" I asked in disbelief.

Nodding, he smiled. "You sound surprised. Of all the things I've spent my money on, this is the best one. It's not every day a man gets to propose to the woman he loves, and if it costs a little money, that's okay."

I glanced down at the ring sitting on my left hand and back up at him. "A little? I'm not sure I'm ever going to get used to your idea of a little money."

"I've told you before, Nina. I would spend ten times that amount to make you happy. That's all I want."

Leaning over the table, I kissed him sweetly, tasting sauce and cheese on his lips. "I'm the happiest woman in the world because of you. Don't ever doubt that."

With a wink, he smiled and said, "Good. Now eat your pizza before it gets cold."

Chapter Twenty-One

Later that night as we laid in each other's arms after making love for hours, I heard the all-too-familiar vibration of Tristan's phone on the nightstand near his side of the bed. In seconds, his mood changed from the blissful happiness we'd shared all night after his proposal at Tony's to sullen and brooding. His shoulders grew tense under my fingers, and in seconds he was gone from our bed to answer that phone I'd grown to hate.

I laid there feeling cold without him next to me and wondering if now that we were planning to be husband and wife did I have a right to ask him what was going on with these calls. Whatever it was that he was dealing with each time that phone rang and it dragged him out of our bed, it tore at my heart that he obviously believed he needed to deal with it alone.

Straining to hear any bits and pieces of his conversation right outside in the hallway, I was able to make out only a few garbled words that meant nothing to me. He was only gone for a few minutes, but when he returned to bed he was visible shaken.

He laid down next to me and moved to take me in his arms as I'd been before. Pulling me close, he was silent but I sensed the tension coming from him in waves. I laid my head on his chest, and he began to coil my hair around his index finger over and over.

After a few minutes, I whispered against his skin, "Tristan, what is it?"

"Nothing. Just work. Let's go to sleep. We have a lot to decide tomorrow."

I knew he was referring to our earlier discussion of what kind of wedding we wanted or if we should just elope since neither of us had much family, but as he spoke of all that now, it sounded like something unhappy to him.

Kissing his neck, I whispered, "You can tell me anything. There's nothing you can say that will change how I feel. I hope you know that."

He sighed heavily and squeezed me to him. "Everyone has something they're ashamed of, Nina. All we can hope for is that the one we love can see past it."

His words were so cryptic they worried me. "I can't believe you have anything to be ashamed of. I'll never believe that. No one who has treated me like you have could have done anything so bad he should be ashamed."

Tristan kissed the top of my head and sighed again. "Sometimes we have to do things because others have done wrong. All I can promise is that I would never hurt someone like others in my position."

I heard the sorrow in his voice and wanted to ask about it, but it didn't seem like the right time. On the night that he'd asked me to marry him, I didn't want to fall asleep after talking about things that made him unhappy. I wanted to make him as happy as he made me.

Snuggling close to him, I whispered, "All that matters is that I love you and you love me. Everything else is out there. Always remember that and we can get through anything."

My words didn't ease his mind, and when he kissed me just before we fell asleep, all I could feel was his sadness.

In the middle of the night, I awoke to Tristan thrashing around in his sleep next to me. He was mumbling something over and over as he frantically shook his head. His body writhed as if he were in pain, and his face twisted into a terrible grimace.

"No! No! Don't...don't do this. Stop!"

I gently nudged Tristan's shoulder to wake him, but he shook his head violently as he pleaded for the people in his dream to stop. Pressing harder into his body, I finally was able to wake him. He stared at me in terror for a few moments before he realized it was just me there with him.

"You were having a nightmare," I said as he took a deep breath. He nodded, and I gently stroked his forehead drenched with sweat. "Are you okay?"

"Yeah."

"What was that?"

He shook his head as he sat up to get out of bed. "Nothing. Go back to sleep."

I reached out to touch his back, and he turned to face me. "Tristan, what were you dreaming about?"

His body sagged and he hung his head. "It wasn't a dream. I have nightmares. I have since the accident. That's the reason I never stay after you fall asleep. I thought I could do it tonight, but…"

I listened as his voice sadly trailed off, so wanting to help fight whatever demons he was dealing with. "Come back to bed. It'll be okay."

"Maybe it would be better if I say in the other bedroom like I always do. They can get pretty bad."

Sitting up, I wrapped my arms around him and pressed my cheek to his back. "I wish you wouldn't. I'm not going to be scared off by a few nightmares. If we're going to be married, I have to know about even this kind of thing."

He took another deep breath and quietly said, "Okay."

Easing back onto the bed, he pushed his hands through his damp hair and closed his eyes. I laid my head on his chest and curled up next to him, hoping my presence helped to calm him. As he usually did when we laid in bed together, he twisted my hair around his finger over and over until just before he feel asleep when he stopped and whispered, "I love you, Nina. No matter what, don't ever think I don't love you more than everything else in the world."

I woke up feeling happy and refreshed, and for the first time ever, I was still in his arms. I vaguely remembered him leaving during the night, and as I focused my eyes, I saw why. On the table near the window sat a glass vase containing an enormous bouquet of my favorite flowers, pink roses. They were a soft pink color and there had to be three or four dozen of them. I inhaled their soft scent and smiled at his thoughtfulness.

Tristan roused next to me, waking up much easier than I did. As soon as his eyes were open, he was wide awake, but there didn't seem to be any evidence of his nightmare now. "I remembered they're your favorite."

Propping myself up on my elbow, I wondered aloud, "Where did you get dozens of pink roses in the middle of the night?"

My question made him smile that gentle grin I loved to see. "I ordered them yesterday. They were delivered first thing this morning."

I shook my head in amazement. "Is there anything you don't think of?"

"Not if I can help it. I guess if you'd have said no my plan with the roses might have been for nothing, but a man should be prepared."

Nuzzling his neck, I said, "Did you think I would say no?"

"You can never be sure. If you had, I would have just had to work harder to convince you that you should say yes."

I climbed on top of him and straddled his hips. "I do love a man with a plan."

"Speaking of a plan, we need to decide on what we want to do about the wedding. For me, I'm all for eloping. I can see us getting married on some island and spending day after day in bed for weeks."

"Are you okay after last night?" I wasn't sure how to approach the nightmare he'd had.

Smiling, he casually brushed the topic away. "It's nothing. I'm told it's quite common for survivors to have them for a long time after an accident. I just hope I didn't frighten you. I had hoped I could go one night without them, especially since last night was…"

I pressed my finger to his lips and shook my head. "You didn't frighten me. I'd rather have you next to me, no matter what, than anywhere else." I didn't believe for a second that it was nothing, like he said, but I hoped when he felt he could talk about it that he'd know he could turn to me.

"Now about that plan."

Rolling my body, I slid up and down his quickly hardening cock. "Mmm…my sister would probably like to be at my wedding."

"Then we can fly her and anyone else to whatever island we choose. Jordan, your sister, her entire family. Whoever you want. But I say we don't wait."

He grabbed my ass and squeezed, exciting me. Sitting up straight on him, I slid the sheet down to reveal the swollen head of his cock.

Running my fingers over the soft skin, I said, "Sounds like you're in a hurry. What's the rush? I already live here with you and sleep in your bed."

Licking his lips, he eased his hips off the bed, running his cock through my already excited pussy. "I want you to be my wife. No hurry. I just don't see any reason to wait."

I looked down into his gorgeous face and for the life of me I couldn't find any reason either. Running my fingertips along his hips, I grinned the smile of a woman about to have great sex. "Then I don't either. Name the date and I'll be there."

Tristan focused his gaze as if he were deciding on an appropriate date and said, "December 14. It's a Saturday. All we have to do is pick an island and tell everyone we want there. But first, I can think of something better to spend our time doing."

He pulled me down on top of him and kissed me long and deep as he slid into my body, filling me up. There were better things to do first.

I had the urge for a swim, so I headed to the indoor pool for some relaxing laps before I figured out how I was going to tell Jordan and Kim that in less than two months I wanted them to join me on some island Tristan had in mind for our wedding. I'd loved the pool since that first night he'd brought me here, but I'd only enjoyed it once or twice the entire time I'd lived in the house. A quick swim and then my plan was to have Jenson take me to Jordan's suite by late afternoon.

My hot pink and black striped bikini from two summers ago still fit, thankfully after all the dinners Tristan had treated me to, so I slipped it on in the dressing room adjacent to the pool and got ready to jump in. The crystal blue water felt so refreshing as I descended to the bottom at the deep end. As I swam to the surface, though, I felt something strange on my legs and before I knew it, I had no bikini bottoms on and they were floating six feet away on top of the water.

It was Jimmy Mitchell's pool party in sixth grade all over again, except no one was there to see me, thank God.

I swam my bare ass over to where the fabric bobbed up and down in the water and grabbed my bottoms, happy that the flashback to that summer in middle school was the most embarrassing part of my current mishap.

And then I heard a man's voice and there was a fresh new humiliation. I turned quickly in the water and saw Tristan's gardener before I raced flailing toward the side of the pool to hide myself. I only needed to see his face for a second to know he'd seen all that God had given me. Wriggling into the bikini bottoms, I tried my best to be cool.

"Hi. I didn't realize I wasn't alone. I'm Nina."

He hung back away from the side of the pool and smiled a shy smile. Nearly as tall as Tristan, he was thinner and less built but he looked like he was closer to my age than his employer's. His blue eyes focused on me for a moment before he realized he was staring. Looking away, he stammered an apology and finally said, "I'm Blake."

With my bottoms finally in their rightful place, I relaxed and moved away from the wall slightly. "Hi Blake. I've seen you before in the summer."

He turned his gaze back toward me and nodded. "I'm Mr. Stone's gardener. I didn't know you were in here. I was just cutting through taking a short cut to the back of the house. I'm sorry. I didn't know."

"It's okay. No harm done. Did you work here before Tristan bought the house last spring?"

A look of confusion crossed his face and he looked over my head toward the back wall. "I've worked here for almost two years, miss," he said in a far icier tone than before. "It's nice to meet you, miss."

He walked quickly toward the back door of the pool area before I could say another word. I returned to swimming wondering what I'd done to obviously offend him but with bigger things to think about. Ten laps later, I was ready to begin my day.

I climbed out of the pool and looked up to see Tristan standing on the deck next to the chair where I'd left my things. Dressed in a suit, he didn't look like he was there to swim. "Hey!" I said as I walked toward him to get my towel. "I thought you left for work already. I would have asked you to join me for a swim."

Tristan silently stared at me as I dried off. "I see you met my gardener."

Knotting the towel around me, I nodded. "Yeah. I think I offended him. Sorry about that. I must have said something wrong."

"You should be more worried about offending me."

His tone was cold and matched the look in his eyes. Confused, I shook my head. "What?"

"You heard me."

I couldn't help but feel defensive. He was upset about something, but I had no idea what it was. Trying not to let things get blown out of proportion by either of us, I stood on the tips of my toes and kissed him sweetly on the lips. "I better get going. I have to tell Jordan and my sister the good news."

As I turned to walk away, Tristan caught me by the wrist. "Nina, you can't imagine I appreciate my gardener seeing you swimming half naked, can you?"

"Oh! That's what that sour face is all about." Then I looked around the room realizing what he was saying. "Are you telling me you have cameras in here?"

"You didn't answer my question."

I tugged my wrist from his hold. "You didn't answer mine."

"When you and I began all this, I told you that I'd give you anything to make you happy, but I expect certain things from the woman I'm with. One of them is that other men don't see you like I do."

His words came out like ice cold water dripping from his lips, but I saw beneath his cold facade that he was boiling mad. Part of me was pissed at being recorded doing something so innocent as swimming, and I questioned where else cameras were placed in the house. But another part of me loved seeing him this jealous over another man looking at me.

"Tristan, Blake didn't see anything intentionally."

"Blake?"

My choice of words was unintentional and equally as unfortunate. "It's not what you think. I introduced myself and he told me his name. If it makes things any better, he had no interest in talking to me and left almost immediately."

He cocked one eyebrow. "It doesn't."

Cradling his face in my hands, I smiled up at him. "Tristan, there's no reason for you to be upset. I promise there's no one else but you for me."

His expression remained unchanged, and I saw I wasn't getting through. Without another word, he turned and walked away, leaving me unsure where we stood but sure we could work out whatever it was later.

By three o'clock, I was ready to head out to see Jordan to cruise the bridal magazines and call my sister to tell her the good news too. I searched for Tristan, hoping to tell him I was leaving, but he wasn't in his office or our bedroom. As I walked down the hallway from our room, I heard his voice in the front living room and entered to kiss him goodbye.

One step into the room and I stopped dead at the sight in front of me. Next to the couch we'd sat on that first night, Tristan stood with some woman with gorgeous long, blond hair and legs longer than my whole body. She was standing entirely too close to him and fixing his tie like she'd done it before and felt completely comfortable with her hands on him. I only saw her from the side and hated her.

Then I heard her speak and the hate was purer than anything I'd ever felt.

"Tristan, this tie isn't going to work well. You need something brighter." Her voice was intentionally sultry, like she was affecting a sexy voice instead of using her normal one.

For his part, the man I'd just agreed to marry the night before stood like a statue as she fawned over his collar, but that didn't make it any better to watch. Jealousy coursed through my veins, making my hands ball into fists at my sides.

"Excuse me, am I interrupting?"

Tristan looked around the woman and smiled, but when she turned to look at me, her expression telegraphed loud and clear that, in her mind, I wasn't welcome.

"Nina, let me introduce you to my assistant. Kacey, this is Nina."

I waited for him to explain to Kacey who I was to him, but the words never came out of his mouth. Insecurity mingled with jealousy to create a noxious pain in my gut, and I walked toward them. Holding up my left hand, I said, "I'm his fiancée. Nice to meet you."

She extended her long, skinny arm and shook my hand with her bony hand that had just been fondling Tristan's tie. Her blue eyes slid over me from head to toe and back up again, and I was sure she was judging me.

"My pleasure. We're just getting ready for his interview this afternoon with Executive Homes. They plan to do an entire spread on him and this stunning house of his."

Ours. I wanted to correct her but as she stood looking down at me, I suddenly felt small and insignificant. All I could get out of my mouth was, "That's nice."

Then she asked, "Will you be staying?"

The way she said it made me feel like I was an intruder. I looked at Tristan for some support, but he simply stood behind her looking back at me. His silence was deafening and hurtful. I felt like a visitor in my own home, and suddenly, all I wanted to do was run.

As well as I could, I calmed my anger and said, "I'll leave you to your business. I don't know what time I'll be home, Tristan. Perhaps I'll stay in the city with Jordan. She's been wanting me to go out. I'll let you know."

Kacey looked relieved to see me go and returned to fiddling with Tristan's collar, but I noticed as I turned to leave that Tristan's eyes had narrowed ever so slightly. If he could hang out with his little friend, I could hang out with mine.

I marched out of the living room with my head held high and hoped neither of them saw how shaky my legs were under me. On top of the jealousy and insecurity churning in my stomach, now I was angry. Not only had he never told me his assistant was a female—a stunning one who looked like the actresses who accompanied him to formal events, no less—but he stood there like a statue, never saying a word to let her know how much I supposedly meant to him.

Jenson was nowhere to be found, so I waited outside by the car, preferring to shiver in the late fall weather of upstate New York than stay inside with Tristan and his assistant. It could have been twenty below and I wouldn't have felt the cold I was fuming so badly. The man who had made me the happiest woman in the world less than twenty-four hours earlier now had just let some gorgeous Amazon woman make me feel like an outsider with my own fiancé.

The front door opened and I heard footsteps, but when I turned around I saw it was Tristan. I quickly set off down the drive, but he kept pace with me and overtook me in mere seconds. I so didn't want to have the conversation we were about to have.

"Nina, I think we should talk."

I turned my back on him and stomped off in the other direction. "I don't think so. Go talk to your assistant if you need someone to listen to you."

His hand touched my shoulder and I jerked my body away from him. He wasn't going to get a pass on this one with just a touch or a few sweet words.

"Nina, I'm not going to chase after you," he said as he followed behind me.

"Fine. Don't. It's not like I'm anyone you should be chasing after anyway."

"You're acting ridiculous. You can't be jealous of Kacey. All she did was adjust my tie. It's not like she saw me half naked."

I stopped dead and turned around to see him standing there grinning like some sexy Cheshire cat. So that's what this was all about? Blake and my dropping bikini bottoms?

"Don't even tell me she's not a total bitch who made me feel like I was unwelcome in my own home and you didn't just stand there and let her do it."

"You saw what your jealousy wanted you to see. Sound familiar?"

"So it was just a coincidence that Kacey the blond bombshell was here today after what happened with your gardener? I doubt it. And why didn't you ever tell me your assistant looked like that?"

"I've never told you what any of my employees look like, Nina. They're simply people who do things for me. I don't pay attention to what they look like."

I raised my eyebrows in disbelief. "Is that supposed to make me jealous too?"

Tristan smiled and reached out to caress my cheek. "No. You misunderstood. But perhaps you can see my point from earlier now?"

Sighing heavily, I wilted under the weight of my anger. I hated that I was jealous. I hated that it was so easy for me to feel insecure.

"Tristan, I don't want to do this for the rest of my life. I can't be worrying so much that my husband is having some hot thing with his blond assistant that I go crazy here out in the country and begin to stalk him while he's at work. And I have to be honest. I'm not above the whole stalking thing. It's not my most attractive trait, but I get jealous."

He kissed me and pressed his forehead to mine. "I love you, Nina. Even the jealous you. Maybe we should both remember what happens when we get jealous."

"Okay. I promise no more flashing your gardener," I teased.

He straightened to his full height and laughed. "I wouldn't worry about that. I fired him."

Guilt over Blake's firing made my stomach turn and I stepped back away from Tristan. "Are you kidding? How could you do that? You fired someone for something I did? Do you plan to fire Kacey too since she made me jealous?"

He seemed to consider my idea and reached out to take my hand. "No, but I see your point. I will if you want me to."

I pulled away, horrified at what he was saying. "No fucking way! I won't be responsible for you firing someone twice today, even if it is that snarky bitch. If you fire her, it's because you want to, not because I said to."

"Nina, I want you to be happy. Tell me what would make you happy, and I'll do it."

The petty, jealous me wanted him to fire Kacey, but that was no more right than firing Blake. I understood his jealousy, but we couldn't go on like this. Not if we ever expected to be happy together.

"Don't fire Kacey, but promise me she doesn't ever get close enough to you to touch you again."

With a smile, he took my hand in his and brought it to his lips. "Agreed."

"And give Blake his job back. I can understand you aren't crazy about him working as the gardener since he saw me without my bikini bottoms, but give him another job somewhere else."

Tristan took a deep breath and let it out slowly. "Agreed. Now here's one for you. No staying in the city tonight."

"Agreed." I hadn't planned on staying with Jordan anyway, so it wasn't much of a concession.

"I have to get back to work. That magazine is expecting to tour the house, and I have to be there."

A stab of hurt pushed on my heart and I began walking toward the car. I guess I wasn't allowed to be known as Tristan Stone's live-in girlfriend. "Fine. I guess it's your house, so you should be there."

He grabbed my arm and pulled me back toward him. "Nina, let me explain."

"No need. I understand," I said with a pout.

Spinning me around, he forced me to look at him as he explained, "No, you don't. I didn't think you'd want to announce our engagement to the world this way. I know how private you are, and I love that. I don't need anyone else to know how much I love you as long as you know. But eventually the world is going to find out. I just didn't want it to find out this way."

I couldn't disagree with that. This way, I'd have the chance to tell Kim and Jordan first.

"Okay. I can see your point."

Smiling that warm smile I'd loved since the first night I met him, Tristan pulled me to him and held me tight as he whispered in my ear, "I love you. Tell Jordan I said hi and she's welcome to stay at the hotel for as long as she likes."

God, when he said things like that, I had a hard time remembering that sometimes he really did things that pissed me off. How was I supposed to stay mad at him when he was so sweet and thoughtful to not only me but my best friend?

Hugging him, I said, "One of these days I'm going to figure out how you make me love you so much, Tristan Stone. One of these days."

He pulled away and smiled as he cupped my chin with his palm. "Then that's the day I'll have to figure out a new way."

Chapter Twenty-Two

Jordan and I spent hours poring over thick, glossy bridal magazines, oohing and ahhing over the most gorgeous dresses I'd ever seen. Every few pages we'd find another one that we added to the list of "possibles" and fold over the corner of the page so that by the time we were done, the magazines had grown to twice their original size.

My call to my sister went as I thought it would. She couldn't believe her baby sister was getting married and had at least a dozen reasons why I shouldn't marry someone I'd only known for a few months and why they couldn't just pick up and leave to go on a vacation to some island in the middle of December. After her lengthy lecture on how marriage was a serious step that should be taken only after two people knew each other for much longer than six months, I explained that it was an all-expense paid trip for her and her family and if she didn't want to be there, so be it.

Jordan was much easier to convince. I don't think I had gotten the complete story about our island wedding plans out of my mouth before she was jumping out of her chair and racing around the hotel suite rambling about all the things she had to do at work to be able to go. But most importantly, she promised she'd be there, standing next to me as my maid of honor.

By the time I arrived back at the house, the Executive Home people were nowhere to be found. I threw the mail Jenson had picked up at the apartment on the desk in the bedroom and set out to look for Tristan. I found him sitting at his desk in his office looking particularly tired.

"Hey, you. How did your photo shoot go? Did they love the house?"

He looked up at me standing in the doorway and forced a smile. "It was fine. You know how I hate pictures."

"You look exhausted. Tell me what I can do." I leaned over behind him and nuzzled his neck. "A nice massage?"

He hung his head and cracked his neck. "I'd love that. I have to get ready for one of those goddamn events tonight."

My hands eased the tension from his shoulders and neck, which felt like they were twisted into tight knots. "Just remember it's for charity."

Pinching the bridge of his nose, he grumbled, "Not this time. This time it's pure promotion. The Richmont is hosting the release party for some author's new book."

"Why do you have to be there?"

"The board loves to have me at these things. Any time the hotel is featured in some book or movie, they love to build the whole thing up. It's ridiculous, but as the face of the business, I have to be there."

"You mean the hotel was part of the book's story?"

Blowing air out in a heavy sigh, he nodded. "Yeah. It's the setting for a good portion of the book, I guess. Thank God it's not a murder mystery or my lawyers would be suing the poor author for all she's worth."

"Oh. Well, it won't be so bad. You'll have one of the actresses there and you'll be able to practice your looking-like-a-statue skills," I said with a laugh.

He lifted his head. "I have a better idea. Come with me."

"What?"

He spun around in his chair and faced me. "Come with me. It's only a matter of time before we tell the world about us, and at least we won't be the focus tonight. You'll get to see what you'll be facing from now on. I promise to even smile."

"The press will know for sure there's something going on if you smile, Tristan."

"Then it's settled," he said suddenly looking much happier.

I shook my head as the realization of what he wanted me to do settled into my brain. I had no dress to wear to an event like this. I had no practice dealing with the public or the press. My hair and makeup would need to be done.

Shaking my head, I backed away from him. "No, Tristan. I don't have anything I need to be able to go. I don't have anything to wear."

"No problem. Let me take care of that." Turning around toward his desk, he dialed the phone and said, "Angelo, it's Tristan Stone. I need a gown, red or black, for the same client you handled before and I want to see your choices at my house in Dutchess County in an hour."

Angelo said something that pleased him because he smiled broadly as he hung up the phone. I walked to the side of the desk and folded my arms across my chest. "Same client you handled before? I thought you said you picked out all those clothes that day."

Turning on the charm, he pulled me back to sit on his lap. He traced the outline of my lips with his fingertip and said, "I'm guilty. It was a little white lie. I trust Angelo, so it's like I picked them out myself anyway."

"Actually, I think I'm okay with you not picking out my outfits. It has a weird vibe to it and there's something about you knowing that much about women's clothes that I'm not really feeling."

"That's good because other than wanting to tear them off you at times, I don't know much about them. But Angelo does, so don't worry. He'll make sure you have a dress worthy of you."

Worthy of me? Never before in my life had I thought of clothes in terms of anything being worthy of me. If something fit and I liked it, I bought it. Its worthiness or mine was never an issue. A dress worthy of me sounded like another sign that I wasn't ready for this party.

"Are you sure about this?" I asked quietly as he busied himself with shutting down his laptop.

He looked up with a quizzical expression on his face. "Sure about what?"

"Me going with you tonight. I don't want to ruin anything for you."

"Nina, you could never ruin anything for me. You're the woman I love and intend to marry in a few short weeks. Tonight is more for me than anything else. I don't want to go, but at least if you're with me, I'll be happy."

"It's just that…" I stopped myself and then said what was really on my mind. "No matter what Angelo brings for me to wear, I'm not going to look like the women you usually take to these kinds of affairs."

Tristan stood from his chair and wrapped his arms around me, pulling me close. "I don't have any interest in those women. I've told you that. They're picked because they look like the typical type of woman men like me date."

"But that's the point I'm trying to make. I don't look like that type of woman."

"You don't see many of those relationships lasting very long, do you? What kind of man wants to be with a woman who loves the way she looks more than she loves you?"

I looked down to avoid his stare, no matter how much love I knew was in it. "I just don't want to embarrass you."

He gently forced my head up with his hands on the sides of my face so I had no choice but to look at him. His caring eyes stared intently down into my eyes. "I don't ever want to hear you say that again, Nina. I love you for many reasons, but I won't lie. The way you look is one of those reasons. It may not be the only reason or the main reason, but I think you're beautiful. I don't want a stick woman who doesn't enjoy the food I want to buy her or who thinks spending hours doing her makeup and hair is important. I want you because you aren't like them. I can be myself with you. You don't know how much that means to me. I've spent years around women who I had to pretend with. From the first night we met, I didn't have to be anyone but myself. I love that in you."

His words convinced me. I could be the person I needed to be for these events. "Okay. Let's do this."

"That's my Nina. Now go enjoy a nice bath while I discuss something with Jenson. I'll let you know when Angelo arrives."

The bath helped relax me a little, but the reality was that I was terrified of being compared to those other women he always escorted to events. After spending enough time in the water to get pruney, I dressed in the clothes I'd worn that day and fiddled with my hair to get that upswept look like movie stars wore to award ceremonies. Over and over, I twirled and twisted my light brown hair only to have it fall down in a mess around my face. The problem was that Tristan's bathroom had none of the necessary items required to keep my hair like that.

Sure it was hopeless, I stared into the mirror wondering how I'd ever pull this night off. I could probably do something pretty nice with my makeup, but no hair pins meant my sort of straight in parts and sort of curly in other parts look would be the one I'd be stuck with.

Crestfallen, I tried once more only to have the end result be the same, but then an idea struck me. I tore through the house to find Rogers. If there was a hair pin or anything else that might work, he'd be the one to have it. I found him arranging the silverware in the kitchen and as I tried to catch my breath, pleaded, "Rogers, I need hair pins. Please tell me somewhere in this house there's something that can help me look like the women who go to these affairs Tristan attends."

His expression was blank for a long time, and then his long face lifted into a tiny smile. "I think I might know where one or two are, miss. Give me a moment, please."

Thrilled, I nodded excitedly and watched him walk off toward the area of the house he lived in. I waited impatiently, shifting my weight from side to side as he was gone a minute and then five. Finally, he returned with two silver pins that would definitely work.

He handed them to me with a slight bow. "I think these may do the job, miss."

Grabbing them, I turned to race back to the bathroom but turned back as I hit the hallway outside the kitchen. "Thank you, Rogers! You're the best."

The butler nodded and bowed again, deeper this time. "You're most welcome, miss."

The hair pins did the trick and within fifteen minutes I'd transformed myself into a sexy temptress with a gorgeous upswept hairdo and smoky eyes that were all the rage in magazines. Tugging a small clump of hair near each temple out of the pins' hold, I looked in the mirror, pleased with my efforts. I may not look exactly like those actresses Tristan usually had on his arm, but I was sporting a rather sophisticated look, if I did say so myself.

I heard him call my name and found him and a man who I assumed was Angelo in the foyer near the front door. His shopper was thin, immaculately dressed, and expressive, to say the least. He held five dresses in his hand out to the side and almost above his head—all formal gowns that I was sure would look stunning, even on me.

"Mr. Stone, I have five dresses in exactly the young lady's size. Which do you prefer?" he asked with a flourish of his free hand.

"Angelo, I think it would be better to ask the young lady. I pay you to shop for me for a reason."

The man feigned a bow. "As you wish. Miss, which would you like to begin with?"

I turned toward Tristan. "Do we have time for me to try on more than one?"

My question seemed to amuse him. Smiling, he said, "We have as much time as you need. We'll arrive when you're satisfied with the dress. And if you don't like any of these, I'm sure Angelo has more just outside."

I saw a pained look cross Angelo's face telling me he'd brought no more than what he held in his hand. Stepping toward them, I looked through them quickly and picked a black strapless one with a slight bustle in the back. "Let's try this one, Angelo," I said with a smile, hoping he'd see I didn't want to make this job as difficult as Tristan seemed to.

"Black it is, miss."

I tried to take the dress from him, but Tristan ordered him to follow me back to the bedroom with the dresses. Walking back to our room, I heard him attempt to make small talk with Tristan, with little success. As I entered the bedroom, I turned and took the dress from him.

"We'll be out here waiting, Nina," Tristan said with a wink as I closed the door to the dressing room and bathroom.

I soon found that Angelo was just as good with formal wear as he was with my work clothes. The dress fit flawlessly in all the right spots, accentuating my figure and hiding those areas that I'd always stressed over. My breasts looked perfect, and as I twirled around in front of the mirror, I saw the bustle made my behind look incredible.

Looking down at my bare feet, I suddenly realized I didn't have shoes. I flung open the door and before either man could say a thing, exclaimed, "I have no shoes! I can't go without shoes!"

A pair of gold strap stilettos hung from Angelo's hand as he stared at me with a look that screamed he found me silly. "At your service, miss."

Trudging over to him, I took the shoes and slid them on. Just as he'd succeeded with the dress, the shoes were a perfect fit. I wanted to ask how he knew my size, but I figured it wasn't something worth knowing.

I held my arms out and modeled the dress and shoes for Tristan. "Well? How's it look?"

Tristan's expression was serious, and he folded his arms. "Gorgeous. Simply gorgeous."

I beamed at his compliment, agreeing wholeheartedly with his assessment. Turning toward Angelo, he said, "I'll leave Miss Edwards with you for anything else she may need." He looked over at me and smiled. "I have to get dressed, but I'll be back in a few minutes. Whatever you need, tell Angelo and he'll see to it."

He left and Angelo produced a gold choker necklace with diamonds. It looked dazzling merely sitting in his hand. "If you will allow me, miss."

I turned around and he clasped it closed around my neck. Looking down, I ran my fingertips over the necklace, loving the feel of it against my skin. Spinning around to face him, I said, "I love it, Angelo. You have the most wonderful taste!"

"Thank you, miss."

"And not just with my clothes. I love the way you dress Tristan also."

Angelo's demeanor changed ever so slightly and he gave me a genuine smile that made him look almost friendly. "Thank you, miss. If I do say so myself, you look beautiful."

"She does."

Tristan stood leaning against the doorframe dressed in his black tux and looking so incredible I wasn't able to formulate coherent words for a moment. Somehow, that night his tux looked so much better than it ever had in pictures or all those times he'd gone somewhere in it without me. His dark brown hair just barely hit the collar of his stark white shirt and his jacket fit perfectly. Peaking out from beneath it near his wrists were gold and onyx cuff links that seemed to go with my necklace perfectly.

"Thank you, Angelo. You've done a wonderful job. Have a good night."

Tristan's not-so-subtle dismissal of the man made me feel uncomfortable, but Angelo left without another word, and I got the sense that this was how their relationship worked.

"You look incredible, Nina. I want you to remember this whenever you think that you're anything less than anyone. If I wouldn't catch hell from the board, I'd close this door and make love to you for hours like every ounce of me wants to."

I walked over to him and adjusted his bow tie. "After all the work Angelo and I did to get me looking like this?" I teased.

He cupped my nape and pressed his mouth to mine in a hard, passionate kiss that almost took my breath away. My legs felt weak when he snaked his tongue inside my mouth and teased me with the tip of it. He looked so stunning and smelled so good that if he'd told me to strip and tear the pins out of my hair, I would have done so without even a whimper of protest.

Pulling away, he ran the pad of his thumb over my lower lip. "You're right. But tonight when we get home, I'm going to give your pussy what I just gave your mouth. And that's just for starters."

He took my hand and kissed it as he led me toward the car that waited outside. Instead of the usual Town Car or his Jag, we were taken into the city in a stretch Rolls Royce that made the drive feel like we were floating on a cloud. Settled into the leather seats, we talked about the release party and I found out Blake had been given a new job doing work on the rooftop landscaping at Tristan's hotel in the city. And even though I'd wanted Kacey left where she was, within a few days of the Executive Homes shoot and interview at the house she was to be reassigned to the Miami hotel and put in charge of concierge there. I couldn't say I was unhappy, but when Tristan mentioned that her first assignment in her new job was to oversee the placement of my choice of artwork for the Miami suite, I secretly jumped for joy—on the inside, of course.

The whole Blake-Kacey Incident, as I secretly referred to it, had taught me a good lesson. A little jealousy was fine. A lot and it spilled out all over the place and could ruin even the best relationship.

Tristan's hand traced figure eights on my thigh as we traveled down the highway toward the biggest and most prestigious party I'd ever even been invited to, but I wasn't self-conscious or nervous anymore. With every adoring look he gave me, I felt more confident and beautiful than ever before. By the time we arrived, I felt as good on the inside as I looked on the outside.

Jenson pulled up in front of the Richmont hotel and came around to my side to let us out. Quietly, Tristan whispered in my ear as I stepped my foot out onto the street, "Don't ever forget how much I love you, Nina."

Lights flashed all around me before I even could straighten myself and step onto the sidewalk. Thankfully, Tristan was quick to join me and took my arm to guide me into the hotel, poised and cool as if this was second nature to him. Men and women yelled his name and barked out requests to look this way and that way, but he ignored them and held my arm tightly as we walked the red carpet, a private couple no more.

We entered through the glass front doors and the interior of the Richmont hotel nearly overwhelmed me. An enormous crystal chandelier hung from the three story ceiling, reflecting the hundreds of tiny lights that adorned virtually every surface of the lobby. I looked up to take it all in, and in my awe, almost tripped. Tristan steadied me and leaned in to whisper, "Remember, you're marrying the man who owns this. You belong here."

Crowds of people mingled as a string quartet played gentle music meant to provide a background but not disturb the festivities. As Tristan introduced me to members of Stone Worldwide's board and other people he quietly referred to as "people he found worthy of his time and mine," I relaxed into my role as his date and actually enjoyed myself. The author was a quiet woman who seemed out of place at her own event, but I was able to get her to laugh at a story I told when it was just Tristan and the two of us, and by the time the night had ended, I could honestly say I'd had a good time.

Even more, I could say that Tristan had. As he socialized with the guests, I heard the same whispers over and over. Women and men leaned over to those people next to them and quietly noted, "I've never seen Tristan Stone smile like that." And that was followed by the words, "Is that an engagement ring on her finger?"

That he'd smiled because I was on his arm meant the world to me. I may not have been from his social circle, but I'd been able to make him happy. Me. No one asked if I was his fiancée, but it didn't matter. It was enough to know that for the first time, his picture on Page Six would be of the man I knew with me by his side.

By the time we sat down in the back of the car, I was so wound up I wouldn't have been able to sleep even if I had to. I felt like a girl after her first school dance who wanted to talk about everyone she'd seen and everything she'd done. As I chattered on about dresses and drinks and the best tasting hors d'oeuvres, Tristan merely sat back against the leather seats and listened. We were out of the city by the time I'd realized I'd done nothing but talk for miles.

Shifting in my seat, I played with the end of his undone tie. "I'm sorry. I've been so busy talking, I haven't given you a chance to get a word in edgewise."

"Don't stop. I love listening to you when you're happy like this," he said quietly.

"Well, did you have a good time?" I asked, secretly hoping he did. I wanted this to be something I could believe I made better for him.

He thought about it for a moment and turned his head to look at me. "Yes. For the first time, I can say I did."

Happy to hear those words, I leaned over and kissed him on the cheek. "That means a lot to me that you said that."

Tristan caught my face as I moved to lean back against the seat and kissed me like he had in our bedroom hours earlier. My stomach did a flip and that tiny tug in the pit of my abdomen appeared as he pulled the pins from my hair.

"I want you. Here. Take the dress off," he ordered as he unzipped it and began pushing the fabric from my body.

I protested, if only meekly, "Tristan, Jenson's going to know what we're doing back here."

With my dress in a heap on the floor, he cupped my breast and sucked the nipple hard into his mouth. Looking up at me, he flicked his tongue over the peaked tip and said in a husky voice, "I don't care. He can't see anything, and even if he can, I don't fucking care. I want you now."

He slid my panties off and pulled me onto his lap to straddle him. I felt the hardness between his legs as he lifted his hips off the seat and pushed his cock through my drenched folds. Desperate to feel his body on mine, I undid his pants and zipper and freed his stiff cock. He was so long and thick in my hands, and I stroked the full length of him, loving how my touch affected him.

"God, I want to be inside you," he whispered hoarsely as he slid the head of his cock toward my opening. "I want to feel your tight cunt around my cock as you ride me right here, Nina. Ride me."

He eased into me in one slow push, filling me completely before he began guiding my hips up and down on him. The threat of his driver seeing us thrilled me, and I rode his cock with abandon, loving each time he rammed it inside me. His hands controlled my body's movements, and his mouth sent waves of delight racing through me as his teeth nipped at my breasts. The mixture of the pleasure he gave me with his cock and the pain from his passionate biting was almost more than I could take. I begged him to let me go longer, but that only made him fuck me harder so that I came within minutes of him entering me. Buried balls deep in me, he continued to thrust through my orgasm, wanting release of his own.

My body still quivered from coming, but I wanted him to feel as good as he'd done for me, so I returned to riding his cock quickly. His dark gaze as he stared up at me told me he was getting close, so I rolled my hips with each push down on him, grazing the most sensitive part of his cock with my G spot. He came with a force so powerful I felt like I would drown with each blast inside me. Just then, my own release roared through me for a second time, and I cried out as he pulled my hair sharply to bring my mouth to his as he buried his cock inside my body.

Tristan panted near my cheek as his release slowly subsided, and I looked down to see him touching a reddish mark just above my right breast. He tenderly pressed his lips against my skin where he'd bit me and whispered, "Mine."

"I guess I've been marked," I said as I ran my fingers through his sweat dampened hair.

"I want every man who sees you to know you're mine, Nina. I want them to know even if you were covered head to toe that underneath you bear my mark. That as much as I'm yours, you're mine and mine alone."

Pressing my lips to his forehead, I leaned against him as he held me. "Always."

Chapter Twenty-Three

I'd had one of the best nights of my life, and as much as I didn't want it to end, by the time we returned home, I was exhausted. I was spared the embarrassment of having to face Jenson as we left the car since the driver disappeared almost as soon as he turned off the car. The thought that he'd seen this with Tristan before crossed my mind, but I quickly pushed it away with a gentle reminder to myself that I didn't need to doubt how much he loved me and a not-so-gentle reminder to not screw up the great thing we had with my irrational jealousy.

We'd made a mess of each other in the car, so we took a quick shower. As I toweled myself dry, I heard Tristan's phone vibrate on the nightstand and saw his expression instantly turn serious. As if on cue, he picked it up and walked out of the bedroom to answer it.

Curiosity about who was calling and what they said to him to change his mood so drastically played on my mind, and after five minutes of obsessing over it, I made a conscious choice to get into my shorts and t-shirt and distract myself with the mail I'd gotten from Jordan's that day. Junk mail I quickly tore up and a letter from my university about alumni dues took up a few minutes, thankfully taking my mind off what Tristan could be talking about outside.

At the bottom of the pile I found two letters like the one I'd lost that day when Mrs. Phillips' grandson jumped me. Neither had a return address, but they were both addressed to me at the apartment. The envelope of the first one looked like the mailman had dragged it along the street before delivering it to Jordan's mailbox. It was filthy, stained from dirt and what looked like coffee. As I struggled to make out when it had been mailed, I saw the postmark said July 9 and the letter was sent from a post office on the Lower East Side. Turning it over, I saw the hint of a shoe print on the outer edge too.

This letter has been on quite a trip.

I slid my finger under the flap and ripped open the top of the envelope to find the letter inside was in no better shape. Stained from coffee and dirt, it was unreadable, except for one line at the bottom that read in part, "Don't ignore this warning…" I strained to understand the words that came after, but the abuse the letter had endured made it impossible to figure out its meaning through the smeared ink.

Turning the envelope and letter over, I saw nothing more. Sure it was a debt collection letter for some bill I'd forgotten, I dismissed the piece of mail and threw it all in the garbage, along with the alumni and junk mail.

The last envelope in the pile sat waiting for me. I picked it up and examined it, noticing it had the same handwritten address and post office mark on the front of the envelope, but it had been mailed only the day before. At least the mailman hadn't put this one through the wringer. Tearing it open, I unfolded the letter inside and began reading.

The words swam in front of my eyes. *Your father. They got away with murder. Ask Tristan. He knows who's responsible.* My hands began to tremble violently, and I threw the paper away from me. Shaking my head in disbelief, I struggled to hold back the tears.

It wasn't possible. There was no way Tristan was involved in my father's murder. He couldn't be. He didn't even know him.

As I repeated those words again and again in my head, I realized I couldn't be sure he hadn't known him. I knew very little about Tristan before just a few months ago. What if the person who'd written this letter was right?

My head felt like it was beginning to spin, like everything around me was spiraling out of control. My mind raced to find any sign that the accusation made in the letter was correct. Every word he'd said suddenly became suspect, every action confirmation of his guilt.

My stomach tied itself into knots as every moment we'd spent together played out in my mind. Why had he wanted someone like me in the first place? Why had he pushed for me to live here with him? Did the phone calls he'd begun receiving right around the time I should have received the first letter have anything to do with this? I didn't want to believe I was in danger, but for the first time since I'd met Tristan, I was truly frightened.

"Where were we?"

I looked up and saw him standing in the doorway, a look of concern of his face like he always had after taking one of those phone calls. But now he looked different. Foreign.

"Nina, what's wrong? You look like you've seen a ghost."

Staring at the letter that lay near the edge of the bed, I reached over and picked it up. "Tell me you had nothing to do with my father's death. Tell me whoever wrote this letter is simply being cruel."

Tristan's face grew ashen as he stood staring at me, his eyes wide. "What are you talking about?"

"This letter. Someone says you know who killed my father. Do you?" My voice cracked as I pleaded for his answer.

He walked toward me and tried to take the letter from my hand. "What are you saying?"

Jumping to my feet, I pulled the letter from his hold and pressed it close to my chest. "Do you know who killed my father? Tell me!"

"Nina, calm down. Let me see the letter."

I backed away from him, shaking my head. "No! Just answer the fucking question! Do you know anything about who murdered my father?"

His silence was deafening as he remained staring at me, hurt filling his eyes.

"Oh, my God! You do!" I cried. "How could you? Get away from me!"

He followed me and gently touched my arm. "Nina, it's not what you think. Calm down and take a seat."

Pushing his hand away, I screamed, "I will not calm down! Tell me what you know! Who killed my father?"

"Please sit down. I promise you I had nothing to do with your father's death."

Tears rolled down my cheeks as I let him lead me over to the bed. I wanted so much to believe he hadn't been a part of taking my father away from me. Tristan was the man of my dreams and now it seemed like everything we'd had was tainted by this one letter.

I sat down on the edge of the bed and watched him kneel down in front of me, just like he had days earlier when he'd made me the happiest woman in the world. He looked up at me with those brown eyes that spoke volumes even before the first world left his mouth.

He knew. He knew who'd killed my father.

Holding my hands in his, he brought them to his mouth in a kiss. Quietly, he said, "Nina, I never met your father. I need you to believe me. I didn't harm your father."

"Why did the person who wrote that letter say you'd know?" I asked, praying to hear that he knew nothing about my father's murder.

"I need you to understand. Until my father and brother died in that plane crash, I wasn't part of the business. I hadn't found what I wanted to do, but I knew I didn't want to run hotels or anything else they did. I was your typical wealthy kid in his mid-twenties drinking and jamming whatever I could up my nose. I'm not proud of that, but I need you to know I wasn't part of what went on with them."

The man on the floor in front of me seemed so strange now. I'd never known anything about him like that. "Tristan, I need to know what this is all about."

He squeezed my hands and continued in a shaky voice. "When my father and brother died, I was thrust into everything with the business. I had to be that person I'd never wanted to be on top of learning how to run all the businesses, particularly the Richmonts. I had no idea what either of them had done. For months, I found out things about my father and Taylor that I'd never imagined they could do. Then one day I began sifting through documents related to a real estate deal my father and brother had been involved in." He stopped a moment and then said, "I didn't know why, but your father's name was on one of the documents."

Documents? "Why would my father's name be anywhere in papers of your father's?"

Tristan began to speak but his voice cracked and he stopped. "I didn't know. Then when I began digging, I found a slush fund my father used to pay for things he didn't want some on the board to know about. It wasn't until I dug into the money he spent there that I found out why your father would be involved in anything with my family's company. I swear I wasn't involved in what my father did."

"No, don't tell me your father was part of why my father died. Please don't say that."

"I'm so sorry, Nina. He must have been investigating a real estate deal and my father…" He couldn't finish his sentence, so I did.

With a sob, I said the words that broke my heart. "Your father had my father killed because he was getting too close to something he was doing."

Tristan buried his face in my lap and pleaded, "I swear I didn't know. I wasn't part of the business then. If I was, I wouldn't have let that happen. I couldn't get your father's death out of my mind. I wanted to do something to try to make up for what had happened."

I looked down at his head in my lap and realized what he was saying. "It wasn't a coincidence that we met, was it?"

He said nothing but lifted his head to look up at me, and I knew the answer. "No. I was sickened by what my father had done. I needed to do something, so I researched everything about your father and found out about you and your sister. I knew you lived right in Brooklyn and found out you worked at a gallery in SoHo. I just needed to try to fix what had been done, to see if I could help any."

His sorrow touched my heart, but then all my insecurities blew up inside me. "So you thought you'd just come by and see what the child of the man your father had murdered looked like? Maybe throw some money at her to make yourself feel better."

"Nina, I swear I didn't mean any harm. It's all I had to give and I thought if I could help you, then maybe some part of your life could be better."

I pushed him away in disgust and leaped up off the bed. "So that first night you didn't like me or want to spend time with me? You just wanted to take me for a ride in your expensive car and foist some cash on me to ease your conscience?"

He sat hunched over on the floor with his back against the bed. In a quiet voice, he admitted what I already knew. "It wasn't like that. I didn't set out to look for anything romantic. I swear. But then I talked to you as we drove up here and you were unlike anyone I'd ever met."

"So that's what this whole art curator charade has been about? That's why you've been dumping money into my account all these months? To make you feel better?"

Shaking his head, he said, "No. Money's all I ever had to give anyone, so it's what I fall back on. All I wanted was for you to happy."

My heart hurt hearing all of this, but I needed to know everything. "Why did you make up that whole contract thing if you didn't care for me then? Why make me stay here if you didn't even like me?"

He quickly stood and moved toward me, his eyes filled with pain. "That's not true. I did like you and I fell in love with you. I love you, Nina. I'd never do anything to hurt you intentionally. Please believe me."

"But why, Tristan? Why bring me here?"

Letting out a deep sigh, he said, "When my father died, there were still people in the company who had been part of what happened. I realized right after meeting you that they think you have information your father left you that can implicate them. I couldn't stop them from killing your father, Nina, but I could stop them from hurting you. So I came up with the contract and made it a requirement that you live here so I could always watch out for you, either myself or Jenson and Rogers. I figured if I had six months, I could find a way to make sure they knew you had nothing on them."

"And you figured I'd just jump at the chance to live in this great house with you?" I snapped. "Poor, pathetic girl who loved art. It couldn't be hard to convince her to live in a place like this with someone like you, right?"

He cupped his hands against my cheeks. "It wasn't like that. Please listen to me."

"Your father killed my father and you've known every moment you've been with me. How can I believe anything you say to me?"

"Nina, I'm begging you. Listen to me. It wasn't like that. I fell in love with you like you fell in love with me." Tristan's dark eyes pleaded with me as he tried to make me believe him. "This doesn't change anything. I love you. Please tell me you love me."

That was the problem. I did love him. I adored him. If I didn't, then everything he'd just said wouldn't have hurt so much. My heart felt like he was tearing it out of my chest, and the only one who could make me feel better had done the damage.

"Tell me this wasn't some charity thing, Tristan. Tell me that even though I wasn't of your level that you didn't see me like that."

"Never. I never thought of how much money you had or didn't have. It didn't matter."

"Spoken like someone who's always had money. And the test at your penthouse? Why?"

"I can't help who I am, Nina. The doctors say it's probably because of the accident, but I don't trust easily anymore."

"Then why did you return the next night if I obviously hadn't passed your test?" I asked, afraid to hear his answer.

Quietly, he said, "I found out you were in danger. I couldn't let them hurt you like they'd done to your father."

"Did you even like me, Tristan? We slept together that night," I sobbed, the pain of this whole thing settling into my mind.

He leaned down to kiss me, but I turned away.

"I did like you from the moment I began talking to you that night after the art show. You weren't like anyone I'd ever met. I wanted to try to be someone you would want."

"And what about all the possessive stuff? The feeding me. The bringing that couple here for me to paint for you. All that business about you not wanting other men to see me like you do? Was that all because of some faceless people wanting to hurt me?"

He shook his head slowly. "No. I've always been that way. I won't apologize for that, Nina. You're the woman I love, so it's my responsibility to take care of you. It's who I am."

I looked down at the gorgeous diamond ring on my left hand and then back up at him. "When did you love me, Tristan? When did you stop seeing me as someone you could help or protect and really fall in love with me?"

I let him kiss me tenderly, and he pressed his forehead to mine. "Don't do this to us. I love you. You're everything to me, Nina. Don't do this."

I heard all his words but could only focus on the ones he didn't say. I didn't want to be someone's charity case, even one for someone I loved more than I'd ever thought I could love a man.

Pulling away, I backed up toward the door. "You've lied to me from the moment I met you. How can I believe what you're saying now? How do I know the last six months haven't been about making you feel less guilty for the awful thing your father did to my family?"

In a voice that almost tore me apart, he pleaded, "Nina, don't leave me. I can't lose you."

I couldn't answer him. I needed to get away from all the words he was saying and all the emotions he was causing in me. I heard him call my name as I ran through the house to the garage, unsure of where I was going but knowing that I needed to go.

Four cars sat parked in the garage, but the only choice was the BMW because I didn't know how to drive a stick shift. I'd noticed Tristan kept the keys in the cubby under the dash once and as I climbed into the car, I saw he hadn't changed his habit, thankfully.

I hurriedly started the car, turned the heat up high, and drove away as fast as I could, shivering in the late fall weather in just my shorts and t-shirt. My mind was racing faster than the car was tearing down the deserted dark road that led away from the house. Everything I'd thought I'd found in Tristan had been a lie. I'd let myself believe that a man like him would want to be with someone like me just for being me.

What a fool I'd been!

I looked over at the passenger seat and rummaged through my bag for my cell phone. A swipe of my finger across the screen showed me I still had no service. Tossing the phone back onto the seat, I pressed my foot on the gas, taking the car to sixty and then past seventy.

I didn't know where I was going or how to get there. As much as I wanted to go to Jordan's, it wasn't like there were parking lots or parking spaces all over Brooklyn and I didn't know where I'd park the car. The thought of driving around for hours hoping to find someone going out in the middle of the night was definitely not what I needed at that moment.

The car was equipped with GPS, so at least I was able to find out how to get to my sister's. Kim's house was further away, but I needed somewhere to go and hide out while I tried to figure out what to do about Tristan. How could I ever believe anything he said after what he'd done?

And how could I ever love the son of the man who'd taken my father from me?

The thought of life without him made me feel empty inside, and I finally let out the emotions I'd been holding in. I sobbed uncontrollably as the car flew by the trees and fields near Tristan's home, the tears blurring my vision in the darkness. In one night, all that I'd had and loved had been ruined. My heart felt like it did the night I found out my father had been murdered.

Empty and numb.

I wiped the tears from my eyes as even more continued to flow. A car headed toward me flashed its high beams, startling me, and as I moved my hand from my cheek to the steering wheel, it slipped off. The car jerked into the path of the oncoming car, and I swerved to miss it, sending my car off the right side of the road. Everything flew by so fast and I was airborne before I could do anything to stop it.

And then everything went dark…

EPILOGUE

Tristan

"Jenson, find out where the BMW is headed. Now!" I ordered into the intercom as I dressed to go after Nina.

"Yes, sir. Immediately."

Pressing on the intercom button again, I barked, "And Rogers, I want all her favorites on the table when we get back."

"Should I order flowers also?"

"Pink roses. I want only the best and dozens of them. Do you understand?"

Rogers understood more than he let on with his simple answer of "Yes." I heard the madness in my voice and knew he did too. He'd been with me long enough to know there had never been anyone like Nina in my life. I couldn't lose her. I couldn't let what my father had done ruin the best chance I'd ever had for happiness.

"Sir, she seems to be headed toward Pennsylvania," Jenson intoned over the speaker.

Her sister's outside Philly. "Get my car out and ready for me to leave in less than five minutes."

It wouldn't be difficult to catch up to her. As fast as the BMW was, the Jag was faster.

As I thought about what I'd say to her, Rogers appeared in the hallway outside the bedroom. "Tristan, may I ask what you plan to do once you find her?"

"Bring her back, Rogers. She belongs here. With me."

Running my hands through my hair, I checked out my look in the mirror and turned to see him standing in my doorway with his arms crossed, as if he were silently judging me. "What is the look you're giving me?"

"I just have to wonder if it's not a better idea to let her go for the night. Chasing her down on a dark road out here might not be your best move. Perhaps she needs time to let everything you told her sink in."

I'd known Rogers since I was a child and knew full well the concerned tone in his voice was more for Nina than for me. My surrogate father, he'd warned me many times since this all began that she'd run away when she found out. That she had seemed to make him even more smug than he usually was.

"I know what you're going to say. You're going to tell me that I should have told her the truth in the beginning. Well, that wasn't an option. How exactly does a person inform someone that his father killed her father and certain people in his own company want her dead? I had to do it this way."

Rogers' frown deepened. "The problem is that she didn't realize this wasn't going to last forever."

"Fuck you. You don't know how I feel about her. I intend on this lasting forever, so get out of my way so I can find her and bring her back where she belongs."

Storming past him, I felt his hand grab onto my forearm. I stopped dead and stared him down. "I'm not interested in a lecture right now, Rogers. The woman I love is out there and I need to get her back."

He nodded and released his hold on my arm. "Fine. But keep in mind that no matter how much money you have, Tristan, it's not about that for her. I've tried to tell you this all your life. There are some people you cannot buy. She's not like the other women you've been with."

"Which is exactly why I love her. Why are you making me the monster here? It was my father and Taylor who had her father killed. I can't help it I fell for her."

"Tristan, sometimes it doesn't matter what you want to happen. For some, trust broken cannot be mended."

"That's fucking ridiculous. She loves me as much as I love her. I didn't kill her father and once she realizes that I was only trying to protect her, she'll be able to trust me again. Now stop giving me platitudes and make sure everything's ready for her when she returns."

I quickly got to the car and drove out of there remembering Jenson's details on where she was headed. If she changed direction, he'd call me, so all I had to do was drive like a bat out of hell and catch up with her.

The memory of our first night together in this very car replayed in my mind making me smile even as my gut churned in pure terror that what Rogers had said was true. Never before had I wanted to be with a woman and not simply have it be a fuck-her-and-forget-her thing. There was something about the way she never pulled any punches that I loved from that first night. For the first time in my life, a woman made me want something other than just a one night stand. She made me want the rest of my life with her.

That wasn't something I planned to let go without a fight.

Now all I had to do was convince her that I wasn't the bastard she thought I was.

I got the Jag up to near a hundred, letting the V-8 open up and slowing down only on the dark curves, but for miles I couldn't see her. Somehow, I couldn't picture Nina driving much faster than the speed limit, if her actions that first night were any indication, so I should have been able to catch up to her.

Tapping my Bluetooth to answer a call, I heard Jenson's voice in my ear. "She's on Longtree Road, sir. You should be able to find her easily. I believe she's stopped."

"Good! Thanks, Jenson."

A quick left and then a right and I was racing down Longtree, but I still had no sign of her. I got ready to call Jenson to see if he'd gotten his directions screwed up and my phone rang again.

"Hello? Is this Tristan Stone?" a man's voice asked.

"Yes. Who is this?"

"Sir, my name is Jacob Nestle. I'm from the New York State Police. A car registered to your name was in an accident tonight. A BMW, sir."

I jammed my foot on the brake, and the Jag skidded to a dead stop. My hands were shaking too much to hold onto the steering wheel. My mind went blank with terror and I mumbled, "The woman driving the car…what happened?"

I couldn't bring myself to ask how she was, dreading the words he might say.

"Sir, she's been taken to Roseland Memorial Hospital with severe injuries."

The man continued to say something, but I didn't hear him. Every part of my brain shut off, except for the part that screamed for me to get to that hospital. I had to see her.

I stood in the doorway to Nina's hospital room where I'd remained for hours watching each labored breath she took. Someone touched my arm and I looked down to see Jordan standing there next to me.

"Tristan, thank you for sending your car to get me. What happened?"

"It was a car accident. That's all the police know so far. She rolled the car."

Her gaze moved over to Nina and I felt her hand squeeze my arm as the first sight of her injuries settled into her brain. Both arms were bandaged because of cuts and scrapes, tubes and wires seemed to be attached to everywhere on her body, and her head was bloody from where she'd slammed into the windshield. Even worse were the cuts and bruises on her face. She looked like someone had beaten the hell out of her.

But it was the internal injuries—the ones we couldn't see—that were worse. A bruised spleen and kidney. Three broken ribs. And a head injury they couldn't say how bad yet.

Jordan covered her mouth and made a noise that sounded like she was going to cry or be sick. I knew that noise because I'd heard myself make it hours earlier when I'd first entered Nina's room. And even now, I felt sick at the thought that she was lying there hurt and unconscious.

"Is she going to be okay?"

"The doctor told me she'll recover, but they don't know how long she'll be in the coma. She's hurt badly," I answered robotically, as I'd done on the phone with Nina's sister.

As she stood there looking at her friend, Jordan began to cry. "What was she doing in the car alone? You never let her go anywhere alone, Tristan. Why wasn't your driver there?"

I didn't know how to answer her questions. I'd spent hours beating myself up over the very same ones. Why didn't I stop her before she left? If I had, she wouldn't be lying there in a hospital bed hooked up to machines to keep her alive.

"I'm going to get some coffee. I want to make sure someone's here with her all the time, so I can get you some, if you like. I'll only be a few minutes."

Jordan grabbed my arm as I turned to leave. "Honey, are you going to be okay? You sound exhausted. Get some sleep. You look like you need it."

Shaking my head, I said quietly, "No. I can't sleep. It's better that I stay up. I want to be up when she comes out of it."

"Okay. Take your time and get some coffee." She smiled at me and added, "Don't worry. She's going to be okay. Nina's tough."

I tried to smile but my mouth couldn't do anything but stay in the frown it had been in since hearing the officer say she'd been hurt. My body felt numb as I went in search of a coffee machine or a cafeteria. My brain wasn't much better. Nothing mattered but Nina recovering, but I couldn't do anything to make that happen. No amount of money, nothing I could say would help her.

By the time I returned, her sister had arrived. Shorter than Nina, she looked like an older version of her. Looking at me strangely, she had no idea who I was as I took my position in the doorway.

"Kim, this is Tristan. He's Nina's boyfriend. Fiancé, I mean," Jordan said as she introduced us. "He's been here since right after it happened."

I stuck out my hand to shake Kim's and mumbled my hello. I didn't want to talk or socialize. I wasn't good with this kind of thing, and talking was only going to lead to having to explain to her why I wasn't with her sister when the accident occurred.

Kim studied me like I was something foreign she'd never encountered before. "It's nice to meet you. Nina told me just yesterday," she said flatly, but I clearly heard disapproval in her voice.

The two women talked about something I didn't care about. I didn't want to hear about the last time Nina visited her sister or how Kim had been planning to drive out to Brooklyn over the summer but never got the chance. I just wanted to be left alone with Nina, to hold her hand and hope she heard me when I told her how sorry I was and how I would make it all up to her.

Jordan seemed to read my mind and led Kim out into the hallway. I slowly crept over to the hospital bed and reached out to touch Nina's brown hair that laid against the stark white pillow. She didn't move when I ran my knuckle softly over her jaw.

I took her hand in mine. It seemed so small as my fingers surrounded her entire hand. "Nina, I'm so sorry, baby. If you can hear me, I love you. Don't leave me."

All I wanted was to see those soft blue eyes look up at me and to hear her say she loved me. But she didn't move.

Bringing her hand to my lips, I whispered, "Don't make me go on without you, baby. Open your eyes and tell me you still love me."

Nina laid in that hospital bed unconscious as I watched nurses do their best to keep her comfortable. The doctors visited every day and seemed to feel the need to constantly explain how it was normal for patients with head injuries to stay unconscious and how her body simply needed time to heal. I didn't want to hear any of their explanations. All I wanted to hear was that she'd be okay and awake so I could tell her I loved her.

Jordan came every afternoon after school and sat next to Nina holding her hand and telling her silly stories about their time in college. Kim left after the first day, but I knew Jordan made sure to call her with updates every day.

After eight days, her face showed what I knew she was thinking. I was thinking it too. What if the doctors were wrong? What if she never came out of it?

Exhausted, but afraid if I left Nina might wake up and I wouldn't be there, I sat slumped in the chair next to her bed as Jordan joked with her about the first time they met in college. My eyes slowly fell closed as the sound of her voice faded away.

"Nina? Honey, you're awake!"

My eyes flew open and I saw Jordan leaning over Nina. She was awake! I leaped from the uncomfortable chair I'd spent so many hours in and stood behind her. The sweet eyes I loved were open and she was speaking.

"Jordan, what happened?" she whispered.

"There was an accident, honey. But you're going to be okay now." Jordan began crying. "Oh, honey! We were so worried."

"Where's my dad? You called him, right?"

Jordan turned to face me and shook her head before she turned back. "Nina, what do you mean? Your father…"

I moved around her and touched Nina's hand. "Baby, I'm so happy you're back."

Nina stared up at me with a vacant look and then looked at Jordan. "Where's my father?"

Nurses swarmed around her to check her vital signs and I walked out to wait for the doctor. Jordan joined me a few minutes later and neither of us said a word. We didn't have to. We both knew something was very wrong.

By the time the doctor pulled me aside an hour later to explain what Nina was experiencing, I knew. All he did was confirm it.

"I've examined her and it's good news. She doesn't remember some things, but she's going to be fine. All her injuries are healing well, and I think she just needs some time, Mr. Stone."

I looked past him and saw her smiling and laughing with Jordan. "She seems to remember her friend, but she thinks her father is still alive. He's been dead for four years," I explained to the doctor, hoping he could help me understand what was happening with Nina.

"As far as I can tell, she doesn't remember anything after right before his death. She remembers her friend because she knew her before that."

The doctor saved me from having to hear the painful words telling me she didn't remember me. After everything we'd been through, she didn't even know who I was.

"I think if you give her time, she'll remember everything. Just give her some time."

He walked away leaving me standing in the doorway staring at the woman I loved who saw me only as a complete stranger. I pulled the engagement ring I'd given her out of my pocket and slid it over the tip of my pinky. Would she ever remember what we were so it would mean as much to her as it did to me?

Jordan tapped me on the arm, bringing me out of a daydream about the night at Tony's when I'd asked Nina to marry me. "Tristan, you should talk to her. Tell her about yourself. I know it's hard, but she needs to know who you are."

"I don't know, Jordan. It might be too much for her. I don't know what to say about her father and I won't lie to her now."

"She knows already. When Kim called, she told her. She doesn't remember what happened to him, but she knows he died. Go talk to her. Don't give up on her."

With a gentle squeeze, Jordan prodded me toward the bed. Nina looked up at me and smiled, like she had so many times before, but I saw in her eyes she was just trying to make me feel welcome.

She didn't know me.

"How are feeling?" The question was lame, but it's what a stranger would ask.

"Jordan says that you and I are engaged."

Nodding, I smiled and pulled the ring out of my pocket. "I just proposed a few nights ago."

"Can I see it?" she asked as she held out her hand. "It looks like a beautiful ring."

I placed it in the center of her palm and smiled as she took it from me. "You liked it when I gave it to you."

She studied it for a minute and then looked me up and down. "I bet you proposed at some fancy restaurant or the opera. Not that I know if I like opera, but you look like the type of man who does."

I looked down at my clothes and couldn't help but smile. Dressed in my suit pants and dress shirt, I'd thought I looked casual without my tie and coat. Leave it to Nina to let me know just how wrong I was.

Lifting my head, I said, "Actually, it was a pizza place called Tony's that we like. I got down on one knee, though."

A sweet smile lit up her face. "I like pizza. That's good to know."

"And roast beef, turkey with stuffing, shrimp scampi, and sausage and peppers."

She was silent for a long time and then finally said, "I'm sorry I don't remember you, Tristan. You seem like a great guy."

I wanted to take her in my arms and never let her go. To do everything we'd done together all over again just on the chance that she'd remember how much we loved each other.

But I couldn't. I wasn't the man she loved. I was just some guy who remembered.

"Can I ask you something, Tristan?"

"Anything and I promise to give a straight answer."

A confused expression crossed her face for a brief moment and then she smiled. "Why don't I remember you?"

I sadly shook my head, her question ripping my heart in two. "I don't know."

Was it because of what I'd told her just before the accident? Had she forgotten everything about us because somewhere deep inside her mind she couldn't forgive me for her father's death?

After two and a half weeks, her doctor pulled me aside as Jordan and Kim visited with an almost healed Nina. Guiding me to a secluded room near Nina's room, he closed the door behind us and I took a seat across from him.

"I want you to know that the good news is that her physical injuries are healing well. She'll be able to go home tomorrow. Her memory loss is disconcerting, however. I had expected her to remember something of her life from the past four years, but I see no signs of that, as of yet."

Listening to him speak, I knew what he was about to say and instantly, my chest tightened.

"Mr. Stone, I just can't say she'll ever remember everything. The human mind is a difficult thing to predict. All I can say is that if you continue to show her what her life was like, she very well may come around."

Extending my hand to shake his, I pressed a smile onto my face. "I understand. Thank you for everything."

I returned to find Jordan and Kim standing outside Nina's room as the nurses did their jobs inside. The time had come to let them know my plans for Nina after she left here.

"Ladies, I'd like to speak to you privately for a moment."

Escorting them to the room where I'd just met with Nina's doctor, I stood as they both took their seats. Jordan looked up at me with wide eyes, as if what I had to say interested her, but Kim wore the same suspicious look she always gave me.

"The doctor just told me Nina will be able to go home tomorrow. I've made arrangements for her to come home with me to our home. You, of course, are welcome to come too and stay for as long as you'd like. I have more than enough room."

"With you? Why would she go home with you?" Kim asked sharply. "She should go home with Jordan."

"She's coming home with me because that's where she belongs. As I said, you're welcome to come stay as long as you like."

"She doesn't even remember you."

Jordan looked over at Kim and then back at me. "I think Kim might be worried that Nina would feel like a stranger in your house." Turning back toward Kim, she continued, "But I've been there and Nina was very happy there, Kim. She and Tristan were…are in love, and he can help her remember their time together."

I looked down at Nina's sister. "I can certainly understand your concern, Kim, but she belongs in her own home. With me."

Kim stood and folded her arms across her chest. "You keep saying belongs, like she's something you own. I'm not some small town rube like my sister. She may think you're something special, but I don't think so. She's not going to stay with some strange man. Not if I have anything to say about it."

"Well, you don't," I said as I crossed my arms.

"I'm not just some fool you can boss around. My husband is a lawyer. You don't think I'll just let you take her without having something to say about it, do you?" Kim asked, her eyes blazing her anger.

Stepping toward her, I smiled. "And I have a battalion of lawyers, all paid to be at my beck and call to do my bidding. You can try to fight me on this, Kim, but you'll lose. Nina is coming home with me. There's no more discussion on that."

"Really? Well, how do you plan to handle Nina's depression, which is sure to rear its ugly head any minute now?"

I knew my face showed that I had no idea what Kim was talking about. Thankfully, Jordan interrupted. "Kim, you don't know that. Nina's been really good for a long time. She might not get down this time."

Kim spun around to glare at Jordan. "Get down? Is that what we're calling it now? The last time she 'got down' she spent months crying holed up in her room. And I think when someone threatens to kill themselves, Jordan, it's a little more than feeling down."

Jordan quickly looked at me for my reaction and then back at Kim. "That's not fair and you know it. Cal broke her heart. And saying you want to kill yourself is different than actually trying to. She never tried to."

"Fine. If I have no say in this, then I have no reason to be here anymore."

Kim stormed out of the room, leaving me with Jordan, whose face had settled into a frown. Standing, she began to explain what Kim might be feeling.

"I don't care. I've heard how she talks to Nina. The woman is lying in a hospital bed, and her sister is chastising her for getting into a car accident."

Jordan nodded. "I know. She's always been tough on Nina, especially since their father's death. And that thing she said about Nina wanting to kill herself wasn't true, Tristan. Nina was just really sad one time and said a few things she didn't mean."

Shaking my head, I said, "You don't have to worry about me not caring about Nina because of that. I understand."

I didn't care that she'd felt depressed and said things about killing herself. The only part that bothered me about that whole thing was that she probably remembered that fucking Cal who'd broken her heart but didn't remember me.

Jordan looked up at me, her green eyes intently staring into mine. "I need to know you're doing this because you care about her. I need to know this isn't some kind of power thing or I swear, Tristan, I might not have all the money to pay lawyers, but I'll make sure she comes home with me. Tell me you're doing this because you love her."

"Have I ever given you a reason to doubt that I'm crazy about her? Have I ever not shown in everything I do that her happiness is the only thing I think of?"

"No, but she's doubted your feelings, so I needed to ask."

I couldn't hide the surprise I felt at Jordan's words. Nina had truly doubted that I cared for her?

"Didn't know she doubted you, did you? Well, she did a few times."

Leaning back against the wall, I shook my head. "Why?"

"Because you're everything she could ever want. It all seemed to good to be true. I don't know what happened the night she got into the accident, but I wouldn't be surprised if you told me you had a fight about her not feeling that she was worthy of being with someone like you."

Quietly, I answered, "No, it wasn't that. But every time she ever said anything like that to me, I told her how wrong she was. I don't care about the money or anything else. I care about her and want her to see that we were in love. Still are, as far as I'm concerned."

Touching my arm, Jordan smiled. "Okay. You've convinced me. Now all you have to do is wait for her to figure it out. She will. As I always tell her, good things happen to good people, and I'm including you in our group of good people who deserve those things."

I wasn't sure I deserved to be in Jordan's Good People group, but from that point on, I planned on doing whatever was necessary to be worthy of Nina and all the good things that came with her.

Nina was sitting up in a chair next to her bed when I finally got back to her room. Kim had likely given her opinion on her coming home with me, but the smile Nina gave me as I entered her room didn't indicate she was upset.

I sat down beside her and thought about what to say. Unsure anything would sound right, I just said what I had to and hoped it came out the way I meant it. "Nina, you're going to be released tomorrow. I'm going to take you home."

She nodded and said, "I hear my sister wasn't crazy about that idea, but I trust Jordan with my life and she says that I'd want to go with you. She's told me everything you've done for me since I've been in here. I guess you're a pretty nice boss if you're willing to take care of all my hospital bills."

"I guess." This wasn't going exactly the way I'd hoped it would.

"I just have one question to ask. Did I move in with you after we got engaged or before?"

"Before. You've lived with me since you began working for me as my private curator."

Tears filled her eyes and she brought her hands up to her face. "I'm a curator? I wish my father had gotten to see that."

I hung my head and said quietly, "I do too."

We sat together saying nothing for a long time, but then she touched my arm softly and said, "I don't know if I'll ever remember our time together, but I hope I do."

I knew it wasn't the perfect situation, but I didn't care. Nina would be coming home and even though she didn't remember everything we were, I had the chance to show her why she'd agreed to marry me while we rediscovered each other. The problems that had threatened to tear us apart still lurked out there, and I'd have to deal with them if I ever expected Nina to be mine again.

We'd been given a second chance. Now it was up to me to prove to her I was the man she wanted to spend the rest of her life with.

Fall Into Me

Book Two

CHAPTER ONE

Tristan

"I thought you understood how this had to end."

Looking down the hall at Nina's hospital room, I eyed with suspicion every person who walked in and out. Pressing the phone to my ear, I listened as the man on the other end repeated himself and added, "We've given you more than enough time, Tristan. This has to end."

"I won't do it. I told you that. She's no threat to you, Karl."

"You're not thinking with the right head, son. If anyone finds out about the evidence she has, everything your father worked so hard to attain will be gone. Are you prepared to let that happen? We aren't. Take care of this. Or we will."

"She has nothing. I've checked everything she owns and there's nothing. Let her live in peace."

"With you, happily ever after, like some storybook ending? I told you that we can't afford to have any loose ends. There's proof somewhere. Those of us who supported your father all those years won't be taken down by your schoolboy romantic ideas."

"And I told you there's nothing to prove whatever my father was doing. He's dead and Nina's father is dead. Let whatever happened end with them."

Karl was silent for a long time. "We've told you what we want. You decide how this is going to happen. Or we will."

I pressed End Call and stuffed my phone back into my suit coat pocket, disgusted with Karl but more with myself. How had I let this get so fucking far?

All I had to do was find the papers Karl was sure her father had showing what my father had done. I was still in the dark about what exactly Joseph Edwards thought he'd caught my father doing, but I didn't care anymore. Whether it was some tax scam or real estate deal gone bad, it didn't matter. All I cared about was keeping Nina safe from the likes of Karl and the other board members who thought of nothing but protecting their own hides.

"Mr. Stone?"

I shook off my phone call and saw one of Nina's nurses at my side. "Yes?"

"It's time for her to leave. She's all ready. Her ribs might be a little sore at first when she gets back to her daily activity, but that's to be expected. I've told her to just listen to what her body's telling her and she should be fine. Now we just have to wait for her memory to come back."

Nina appeared in the doorway of the hospital room where she'd spent the last five weeks. Seated in a wheelchair, she wore her black yoga pants and white sweatshirt and had the pink roses I'd given her that morning in her lap. Her blue eyes lit up when I stepped out from behind the wall.

"Hey! The doctor said I'm ready to roll."

Bowing deeply, I looked up at her and smiled. "Your chariot awaits, my lady."

The press was out in full force when I pulled the Jag in through the gate at the bottom of the driveway I'd had installed the week before. Cameras flashed on all sides of us, making Nina bury her head in the space between our seats. Snaking my arm around her to hold her close, I hoped this first introduction to my world hadn't made her wish she'd had anywhere else to go.

I leaned my head down and whispered next to her ear, "Don't worry. We'll be home in a minute and we won't have to deal with them again, Nina."

The gates closed behind us and I raced up the driveway, wanting all that bullshit with the paparazzi left back there in the past. Fucking vultures. Like anyone should want to see pictures splattered all over the gossip pages of a man bringing a woman home from the hospital after a car accident.

Nina lifted her head and sat up straight in her seat to look at the house as I stopped the car. "This is where you live?"

"Where we live," I said, gently correcting her.

She turned her head and the look on her face was a mix of uncertainty and disbelief.

As I shut off the car, I flashed her a smile. "Don't worry. It's cozier than it looks."

"Uh huh." She looked unconvinced.

I grabbed her coat and walked around the car to help her out, watching her crane her neck to take in all of the house as I placed my black leather jacket across her shoulders. Looking up at me with those gentle blue eyes, she asked, "I really live here? With you?"

Nodding, I smiled. "You do. In fact, you like this house more than the other one."

She stopped walking and stared straight ahead. "There's another one?"

I shrugged. "Well, it's a penthouse at the Manhattan property, but you told me you liked this one better."

"Wow. First the car and now more than one house. Jordan wasn't kidding when she said you were loaded." Nina fell silent and grimaced. "Sorry. That sounded worse than I meant it to. She just said you were wealthy."

"Wealthy. Loaded. It's all the same. I just hope you're comfortable here."

With a tiny chuckle, she said, "I can't imagine anyone couldn't be."

Rogers met us at the door and bowed. "Miss, it's wonderful to see you again."

Nina studied him for a moment and then smiled meekly, obviously not remembering him. "Hello."

"Get the bags from the car, Rogers."

As he passed us, she looked up at me and frowned. "I guess I've met him before? I don't remember."

"The doctors said it could take some time. Give it a chance."

Nodding, she tried to put on a brave face, but I saw in her eyes she was disappointed. I stood there staring down at her and wishing I could make things better, wishing I had the power to turn back time to before that night when she ran away and…

I pressed a smile onto my lips and extended my hand toward her old bedroom, my heart heavy from the words I was about to say. "Your room is right down this hall."

Nina looked around the entryway and then at me, her eyes wide. "It's beautiful here, Tristan."

Faking enthusiasm the best I could, I said, "Thanks. Let's get you settled in."

I gently placed my hand on the small of her back, a tiny gesture I did out of habit before I remembered for the first time that day that she and I were basically strangers in her mind. She didn't react as I kept my hand against her and escorted her to her wing of the house, and I wanted to at least believe it hadn't bothered her that I'd done it.

Opening the door, she looked around in amazement at her room, her mouth hanging open, just as she'd looked the first time she saw it all those months ago. "Wow, this is great! I thought maybe you were showing me to the servants' quarters or something, but this is as nice as the other part of the house."

Her words cut like knives. To her, I was just some man who paid her to work for him. She had no idea how much I wanted to take her back to our bedroom on the other side of the house, the one she belonged in. The bed she belonged in right next to me.

"You aren't my servant here. This is your home, Nina."

I tried to disguise the hurt in my voice, but it was no use. She heard it too and turned around from looking out the window to face me. "I'm sorry. I didn't mean to say the wrong thing. I didn't mean to make it sound like you'd treat someone like a servant. This is all so new to me."

"Don't be sorry. I'll leave you to get settled in. If you need anything, I'm just on the other side of the house."

I wanted to reach out to touch her hand, to take her in my arms and tell her how much I loved her, but she wasn't ready. I didn't want to scare her off. I knew I had to be patient and hopefully if I was, when she finally started to remember things, she'd also remember how much I loved her.

My insides felt empty as I walked toward my side of the house, alone again as I'd been for so long. I had work to do, but my heart wasn't in it. I didn't care about reporting to the Board as I had to soon at the quarterly meeting. I didn't care about anything involving Stone Worldwide. What did it matter anyway?

I sat down at the desk in my room and looked out the window at the unseasonably warm December day full of sun. All I could think of was that in just over a week the date I'd chosen for our wedding would pass without mention because she didn't remember the day held any special meaning. Nothing like the biggest day of your life going unnoticed.

"Tristan, I've arranged for dinner at five, as you ordered."

Something in Rogers' voice told me he hadn't come to find me to talk about dinner. Closing my eyes, I leaned my head back. "That's fine, Rogers. Thank you."

My words were met with silence, but he didn't leave. I'd avoided Rogers for weeks, knowing what he thought, but I wasn't going to escape this discussion about Nina. Opening my eyes, I turned to see him standing there staring down at me. "Is there something else, Rogers?" I asked, knowing there was.

"I'm simply wondering what I'm to do regarding Nina."

I hated the way he could refer to a human being in the same tone as he'd use to tell me he believed the gutters needed cleaning. Looking into his dark eyes, I leveled my gaze full of disgust on him. "What you're to do regarding Nina? Speak plainly, Rogers. I'm not in the mood for the butler talk. You've known me since I was five years old, for fuck's sake."

Rogers nodded his head slowly, and when he raised his gaze to meet mine again, it was one of doubt. "Nothing has changed, Tristan. Your father is still the one responsible for her father's death and you're still Victor Stone's son. The son of the man who killed Nina's father. Things are the same as they were the night she drove away from here."

I didn't need Rogers to tell me all of this. None of it had ever left my mind since that day Karl had confirmed what I'd found in my father's secret files. I'd lived with the knowledge that my own father had been the architect of Joseph Edwards' murder just as I'd have to continue living with it for the rest of my life.

"I don't need you to remind me of any of this, Rogers. What the fuck am I supposed to do?"

"About what, Tristan? You can't fix what your father did. No one expects you to."

"I don't care about fixing anything Victor Stone did. I care about taking care of Nina, not because of what happened to her father but because I love her. Why is this so difficult for you to understand?"

Rogers stood there staring at me, his face full of judgment. "Because you haven't loved anything or anyone since the accident."

Looking away, I watched out my window as a porcupine walked slowly across the grass. "I'm not incapable of love because of a plane crash. Are you saying you don't believe I fell in love with her?"

"I have no doubt you love her and she loved you. You've been given a second chance to make things right, Tristan. If you do not, I can't see how your future with her could end any differently than it did before."

"All I need is time," I mumbled as I watched the porcupine continue to make his way across the lawn toward the trees on my side of the house.

"Time for what? You must tell her the truth. If you don't, you'll be making the same mistake again and the outcome will be the same as last time."

Time. If I could find the evidence Karl believed existed, then Nina could be safe and never have to know about my father's heinous crime. Never have to know that I was the son of the man responsible for taking her only parent from her.

Turning back to face Rogers, I stood to get to work. "Thank you, Rogers. That will be all."

I saw the disapproval in his eyes as he turned to leave, but I didn't care. I wasn't going to let Nina find out the truth of her father's death. Her memory loss meant I could spare her that. It was the only good thing to come from her accident, and I intended on protecting it, no matter what.

All I needed was time.

At five o'clock I sat in the dining room waiting for Nina so we could eat dinner together as we had every day we'd been here in this house. I'd had Rogers instruct the cook that tonight's meal was to be duck in the hopes that maybe having that would remind her of the time we spent together at the penthouse. I knew it was probably grasping at straws, but what else did I have?

I waited for twenty minutes, watching the steam slowly fade away from the dishes before I was forced to admit that she wasn't coming. Of course she wasn't. She wasn't coming because she didn't remember that this was something we both looked forward to each day. That too was gone.

Loosening my tie, I leaned my head back and closed my eyes in frustration. I couldn't go on like this. It was like being sent to a country where everyone had forgotten the language except that one lonely soul who kept speaking even though nobody understood him, hoping one day he'd find just one other person to comprehend his words.

I pinched the bridge of my nose and felt the stress ebb away for a moment. Maybe I was just kidding myself. Maybe it was time for me to forget that language too.

If I could forget, I may have tried. But I couldn't. Rogers had been right when he'd said I hadn't loved anything or anyone since the accident. He was only partially correct, though. In truth, I'd never loved anyone before the accident either. Not like I loved Nina.

She was my everything. I needed her like I needed air to breathe. I doubted she'd even known how I truly felt about her before the accident. She was unlike anyone I'd ever encountered. Never before had another human being made me want so much more than the things my money could buy me.

All my life I'd been blessed with everything I could want, and it had made me hard and greedy. Nothing meant anything when you could have it at the drop of a hat. I'd learned that was one of the curses of money, but for a long time didn't care. Cars? I'd gone through dozens with not a thought about why I shouldn't. Homes? They came and went without any feeling or connection to them. Women? I could have who I wanted, when I wanted, and how.

And I did. Victor Stone's money paid for whatever I desired, and it didn't matter how fucked up it was. No worries. Money can make anything happen and then make it go away, if someone chooses. I let my cock lead me to places filled with desire, sex, and whatever else I could want. It was all so easy. How often had I fucked someone merely because I could, not because I felt anything for them?

It always amazed me how eager women were to please when good old Benjamin was sitting in my pocket. All it took was flashing the money clip once or twice.

Running my hand through my hair, I shuddered at how many times it had only taken a few bills for me to get everything I wanted or more, if that was what I craved. It all came so easily. A blonde, maybe her friend or two, and as much blow as I could get my hands on. Then it was just a matter of stuffing the junk up my nose and fucking as many women as I could.

And it had felt so fucking good. Life was mine to enjoy, and enjoy it I did. What's that saying about life and letting the juices run down your chin? I had juices enough to last a lifetime.

Then one day all the good times were gone. I was the lone survivor of a plane crash that killed my family. I'd watched my parents and twin brother die around me, listening to their agonizing cries for help and not being able to help them or myself as I waited to suffer the same fate.

I was allowed to live, and what did I do with that gift? I closed myself off from the world and turned into what I'd never wanted to be. The CEO of Stone Worldwide. Shrink after shrink promised with just a little more therapy that I'd find the answer and realize life was worth living again, as if they feared at any time I was going to kill myself. What they didn't seem to understand was there was something worse than dying.

Living.

Having whatever your heart desired and it never being enough to overcome the emptiness that ate away at you every day and night until you felt hollow inside. Dealing with the guilt that every member of your family had been taken away and you were left like some shining monument to Darwinism, as if being alive was some achievement I'd strived for and attained. All I'd done was sit there in that plane seat. That steel bar that had plowed through my brother's heart hadn't been able to find mine not because I was crafty or clever. It wasn't because I was lucky either.

That steel rod hadn't found my heart because I didn't have one. I'd spent my entire life caring for no one enough to call it love. Why would my heart be anything to pierce, much less damage enough to kill someone like me?

So I lived, a sole survivor with everything he could want. Except the one thing he needed.

That all changed when I met Nina. I hadn't intended on anything happening with her. I'd accepted my life alone as a punishment for all that I'd done for so many years. I didn't expect a reprieve. I didn't deserve one. All I wanted to do was try to make up for what my father had done. That she made some good come alive in me was something I wasn't ready for, but I couldn't let it go. Some small part of me was reborn that night we drove up the Taconic to this house.

So now I had a choice to make. Give up or fight. I let all those times I held Nina in my arms fill me, all those times she made my heart leap with one of her gentle smiles. For someone who had never had to fight for anything, it was strangely easy. Whatever I had to go through for her, I'd endure it.

Chapter Two

Tristan

Nina was sitting on her bed when I gently pushed the bedroom door open. She was doing something on her laptop, and I stood there for a moment to watch her. Her brown hair had grown much longer since she first moved here. It hung halfway down her back in soft, natural waves as she sat cross-legged and hunched over looking at something on her computer's screen. The sweet memory of twirling those waves around my finger as she lay in my arms made an ache form in my chest as I stood there.

Not wanting to scare her, I tapped on the door and quietly said her name, but she nearly jumped off the bed from fear anyway. Wincing at my clumsiness, I put my hands up to calm her.

"I didn't mean to frighten you. I'm sorry. I was just hoping we could talk."

Shaking her head, she made her apologies. "No, no. I'm sorry. I didn't hear you there. What's up?"

"I wanted to talk."

She closed her laptop and pushed it aside. "You can sit down, if you like. Or would you rather talk somewhere else?"

What I rathered was taking her back to our room on the other side of the house and showing her all the ways I was crazy about her. Instead, I merely nodded and sat down beside her.

"This is a great room, Tristan. Thanks for letting me stay with you."

I forced a smile at her statement, which sounded like something a long lost relative would say to someone who wasn't thrilled about having them visit. "You're welcome, but this is your home, Nina. You don't have to thank me."

Lowering her head, she looked away from me. "I'm sorry. I can't imagine how hard this is for you. Jordan's told me how crazy in love I was with you, and I get that." Looking up at me, she blushed. "I mean, look at you. Who wouldn't be crazy in love with you? I just don't remember. But I don't want you to think that I don't want to remember. I do."

Nina looked away again, her cheeks red from embarrassment. Maybe that was a good thing. At least she seemed to be attracted to me. That was something I could work with.

I took her chin between my thumb and forefinger and gently turned her head to look at me. She still looked down at her hands sitting in her lap, though. "Look at me, Nina. Please."

She lifted her beautiful blue eyes to gaze up at me, and I swallowed hard, my mouth suddenly dry and my brain devoid of all thought about what I'd planned to say. Licking my lips, I began, hoping the right words would come to me.

"Nina, I know this is probably a confusing time for you. Whatever I'm dealing with is nothing compared to what you're forced to deal with. I don't want to make this worse for you. If I do that, let me know. You never have to be afraid to tell me if you're uncomfortable."

"Okay."

"The doctors think that if you get back to your life like it used to be, you'll begin to remember what we were. We just have to make sure you take care of those ribs."

Nina nodded and pressed a smile onto her pretty mouth. "My ribs feel good, so no worries. I hope that's true about remembering. I had hoped something would seem familiar here, but so far nothing."

Her admission of what I already knew hurt just the same. I'd hoped coming home would stir some memories for her too. I guess we were both disappointed.

"It's okay. No hurry. We've got time."

Time. If that's what we had, then I had to make the most of it.

Nina put her fingers over mine and moved them from her chin. Her touch on my skin sent a rush of electricity racing up my arm, making me want more.

"I do have a question. Is that okay?"

I couldn't help but smile. Same old Nina always with the questions. That was something. "Ask anything you want."

She turned to grab her laptop and opened it to bring up a picture of me with one of the actresses at an event a few months earlier. As I examined the image, all I could think of was how Nina had said I looked like a statue when I was with them. I'd never truly realized it until that moment, but I did.

"You seem to have a lot of girlfriends, but I can't find any pictures of me with you at these parties. Why?"

I blew the air out of my lungs and struggled for the best way to explain why there were hundreds of pictures of me with other women. "They aren't girlfriends, Nina. They're employees."

"And I'm your employee?"

"Yes."

"So they're all like I am to you?"

A groan escaped from my throat. This wasn't going well at all. "No. They're employees paid specifically to appear at events with me because I didn't have a girlfriend."

Nina's eyes lit up. "Oh. So there are pictures of us together at events once we began dating? I guess I just didn't get to those."

"Sure. I'm sure there are."

Arching one eyebrow, she saw right through my lie. "There aren't any pictures of us, are there? Why?"

"Because we only attended one event. I'm sure there are pictures, though."

Her look of skepticism turned to one of hurt. "I don't understand. We were together for six months and you asked me to marry you, but we only went to one event together?"

I knew what she was thinking. That for some reason I wouldn't want to be seen with her like I had with the actresses. This was not going as I'd hoped.

"It's a bit more complicated than that. Those women aren't in a relationship with me and get paid to deal with the press. I didn't want you to have to deal with that."

Leveling her gaze at me, she asked, "And what did I want?"

This was definitely the Nina I knew and loved. Smiling, I answered with the truth. "You were jealous and thought I was ashamed of you until I told you the truth about the actresses. Then you were afraid to go with me to the event we attended, but you ended up loving it. It was one of the best nights I've ever had."

Her expression softened and a smile spread across her lips. "Oh."

I wanted to tell her that the sex we had in the back of the Rolls had been better than any I'd ever had with any other woman. That just thinking of it was making me hard. It probably wasn't the right time, though.

"I wanted to talk about you getting back to doing things you used to do." *We* used to do. "I think it would be good for you to return to work."

"That sounds good. You said I'm your private curator, right? What does that mean exactly?"

"You handle choosing the artwork for the suites and penthouses in my hotels. I give you the assignments and then you present your choices to me."

A look of apprehension came over her face, and she bit her bottom lip. "Was I good at this?"

I'd seen that look before. It was the same one she'd worn that first day I assigned her my penthouse in the city. I'd wanted to take her in my arms and kiss her that day too.

"Very good."

Nina took a deep breath. "Tristan, I'm confused. I work for you as your private curator but I'm also your girlfriend?"

Fiancée.

"You loved the job, so you never mentioned wanting to stop once we began dating and even when you said yes to my proposal."

"So if I didn't want to work as your private curator anymore, you'd be okay with that?"

"If that would make you happy, then I'd be fine with it."

"What if I wanted a different job?"

"I'm sure there's something in Stone Worldwide that would suit you."

She bit her lip again. "No, I meant what if I wanted to work somewhere other than for you? I just wonder how good an idea it is to mix your business and personal life."

"Don't worry. I'm not," I said as casually as I could, hoping to hide how unhappy I was with where the conversation had gone.

"Well, then I'm not sure it's such a good idea to mix those in my life."

Fuck. I had hoped it would never come to the contract again, but I saw she wasn't going to just accept things. "Nina, you signed a contract obligating you to work for me."

The shock at my callous words was written all over her face. "For how long?"

"The initial period was for six months, but there's a provision that in the event you're unable to complete the six months that the contract is extended when you are able."

"What? How long is the extension for?"

"Two years."

She sat there on her bed staring at me with a stunned look for almost a minute before she finally spoke again. When she did, her words were like a sledgehammer to my chest.

Her eyebrows knitted. "So this is your idea of love, Tristan?"

I knew how this all sounded. I came off like the world's biggest dick, both in the boss and boyfriend departments. I knew that. But if I wanted to keep Nina safe, I'd have to deal with her thinking I was an ass, or worse, growing to hate me. I'd rather her hate me than be hurt by Karl and his buddies on the Board.

Her words hurt, though, so before I said something else that further convinced her of my asshole status, I stood to leave and repeated what I'd told her months earlier. "I can give you whatever your heart desires, Nina, but I can only do it this way."

"What if I can't handle this way, Tristan? What happens then?"

Another sledgehammer to the chest, but this time I couldn't stop myself from saying something in retaliation. "Then I guess you get to live rent free and get paid an astronomical salary for picking out pictures for hotel rooms, Nina."

I stared at her knowing that was a shitty thing to say, but I didn't care. I wanted her to hurt like she'd hurt me. If the look in her eyes was any indication, I'd succeeded.

Good for me. At this rate, I was going to have her speeding away in another of my goddamn cars by the end of the week. As I turned to leave the woman I loved and her new hatred for me, I wondered if maybe that was what was meant to be anyway.

I needed a drink, so I made my way to the room where Nina and I had first kissed to pour myself a scotch before I headed back to my room to begin the emotional pummeling I knew I deserved. In the span of less than a day, I'd screwed things up so completely that the woman I adored was likely making plans with Jordan to leave me before I even had the chance to give her a reason to stay.

I let the alcohol slide down my throat and closed my eyes to enjoy it. At least drinking was working out for me. By the time my second glass was empty, I was calm enough to admit that I didn't have a choice as to whether or not this worked with Nina. Even if she hated me, she had to stay. Karl and the others weren't going to spare her, no matter how much she begged and swore she knew nothing about her father's investigation.

I thought about returning to her room and apologizing, but that would have probably made it worse. No, I needed to think. I headed back to my room and relaxed on the bed. Nina's picture hung on the wall across from me, and as I stared at the blues and reds and those light brown smudges she'd said were my eyes watching her, I saw what I needed to do. I had to go back to the person the shrinks and Rogers had always said would never find true love. The woman who'd painted it wanted me to be that man, no matter how much everyone else didn't. I just had to make her want me like that again.

Easier said than done when the object of my affections was sitting on the other side of the house likely planning her escape.

I dozed off staring at Nina's picture as my mind drifted back to that night at Tony's when she said yes to spending the rest of our lives together. A knock on my door roused me from my nap, and I lifted my right arm to see the time. 9:28. Scrubbing the sleep from my eyes, I walked to the door, expecting Rogers to be standing there all dour-faced with something to report like Nina leaving again. I took a deep breath and braced myself for what he had to say as I opened the door.

"I just want you to know that I think keeping a woman prisoner is against the law in New York."

Nina stood there in the hallway dressed in shorts and a T-shirt and looking incredibly pissed off. But at least she was standing there and not driving away at a hundred miles an hour. That was definitely better than her leaving.

"You're not a prisoner." That was the second time I'd had to say that.

Her right hip shot out and her hand landed on her waist. "Then what do you call this?"

"Would you like to come in and talk?"

"What?" she asked with the same pissed off expression that now mixed with what looked like a flash of fear in her eyes.

"Would you like to come in? You slept in here for months, Nina. I promise. You liked it here."

"Do you plan to answer my question if I come in there?"

"Sure."

I opened the door and held my arm out to welcome her to the room where we'd spent hours falling in love. As always, I couldn't stop myself from hoping that she'd remember some shred of our past together.

"Would you like to sit down?" I asked as I dragged the chair away from the desk near the window.

She squinted her eyes at me and appeared to consider my offer of a seat. "I guess it couldn't hurt."

As she sat down in the chair in front of me, I had to fight the urge to slide my hands over her shoulders and lean down to kiss her like every fiber of my being wanted to. I stood for a few seconds wishing so much to touch her until the heaviness in my heart made it hard to breathe and I forced myself to move away. My feet felt like they were wading through wet cement as I came around to sit on the bed in front of her.

"So you were about to tell me how this isn't me being held prisoner," she said sharply as she folded her arms across her chest.

So much for memories of love.

I turned to point at her painting hanging on the wall. "That's yours. You painted that for me, and I loved it so much I had it hung there so I can see it every night before I fall asleep and every morning when I wake."

She looked at the painting and tears welled in her eyes. "I painted that for you?"

Nodding, I smiled. "You did. Do you want to know what you said the colors represented?"

Nina got up from her chair and walked over to stand in front of the painting. She stared at it for a long moment and looked back at me. "Those are your eyes. I've never seen eyes like yours—that color brown. There's no way I would've painted those two brown areas without wanting them to represent your eyes."

"That's right."

Turning back to face the painting, she asked, "What do the blues and reds symbolize?"

"You said they represented the emotions I made you feel."

She looked at me and a look of pain crossed her face. "Like hot and cold?"

"Sort of. I guess I can be difficult to be around sometimes."

Wiping a tear on her cheek, she shook her head and came back to sit in front of me. "I never paint for anyone I'm dating. The only man I've ever painted for was my father. If I painted this for you, I must have…"

She tried to choke back the tears, but she couldn't stop them and as they began to stream down her face, she ran out before I could do anything to make her feel better. I knew how she felt. The frustration. The loss. I didn't know if I should run after her since the doctors had repeatedly told me to give her time, but I couldn't let her sit over in that room alone crying about us when I was feeling as bad as she was at what we'd lost.

When I got to her room, she was sitting on the edge of her bed with her head in her hands, her body heaving from her sobs. Watching her like this broke my heart, and I couldn't stand there and do nothing. Whatever her doctors thought they knew, they didn't understand what it was like to watch the woman you love fall apart.

I sat down next to her and pulled her close to me. She didn't fight me and buried her head in my chest as she continued to cry. Trailing my fingers over her soft hair, I moved my hands to her back and held her to me, never wanting to let her go. She was my Nina.

"I hate this. You don't know what that painting means, Tristan," she sobbed into my shirt. "I never paint for others. I've always been too afraid to. This means I did feel everything Jordan says I did."

Pressing my lips to the top of her head, I kissed her softly and whispered, "Then that's a good thing, isn't it?"

Leaning back away from me, she shook her head. "No, it isn't! We were in love and now it's gone. I can't remember you or anything about this house or what we felt for each other. It's like it's a dark space where so much good is sitting there waiting for me and I can't find it."

"The doctors said it might take a little while."

"I don't want to wait a while! I had a life and now I have nothing. I sit over in this room and feel like I have nobody and nothing to hold on to."

I cupped her chin and smiled down into that beautiful sad face. "You have me. Hold on to me."

"I'm no fool, Tristan. I may not remember things, but I'm not an idiot. I know who you are. I looked it up. You're a bajillionaire. What would you want with someone like me?"

"Bajillionaire?" I asked, unable to stifle a smile.

"It's a word. It means you have more money than I could ever make in twenty lifetimes and I have no business believing you'd ever want me, a wannabe artist and curator."

"It's not a word, and as for me wanting you, you have every business believing it. People don't fall in love in spite of money, Nina. I can tell you I have absolute proof that money can make people very attractive, even when they aren't."

"You're intentionally twisting my words. You know what I meant."

"So because I have money, I can't fall in love? Is that what you meant?"

Nina wiped her eyes and shot me a look of reproach. "What would you want with someone like me?"

"Yeah. What would I want with a gorgeous woman who makes me crazy every time she's anywhere near me? Who'd want that?"

"Hmmph. Gorgeous. I probably look like a deranged raccoon right now, and even if I didn't, I don't look like any of those women you go to those parties with. I saw them, Tristan. They look like supermodels."

"And they're as boring as that dresser. They think I'm pretty boring too."

"They don't look bored. They look like they adore you."

"Good. At least I know that's money well spent."

She wrinkled her nose at me, letting me know I was going to have to be more convincing. "Nina, I pay those women very nicely to look happy with me. They want to be seen at influential parties and the board of directors of Stone Worldwide thinks a man should have a woman on his arm at all times. So I do. If it means anything, I had basically stopped going to those events before your accident because I didn't want to go with the actresses anymore."

"I don't understand. If you loved me so much, why didn't you take me? Is it because I don't look like those women?" she asked with hurt in her eyes.

Shaking my head, I couldn't help but smile. This was definitely the same old Nina. "I know you don't remember this, but you asked me the same thing once, so I'll tell you again what I told you that night. You're gorgeous, and I'd be happy to be seen anywhere on this Earth with you. But being in the spotlight like that has never been good for relationships. I didn't want that to damage what we had together. In my defense, I did ask you to come with me once and you didn't want to. I had to convince you."

Nina hung her head and sighed. "This is so hard, Tristan. What if I never remember all of that time you remember?"

"Then we make new memories together."

The look she gave me was filled with fear. "Do you still love me? Am I the person you fell in love with?"

I didn't have to think about my answer. I knew it in my heart. "Yes. I love you, even though you don't remember me or feel the same.

And it wouldn't matter if you changed. I'd still love you as much as I did the first time I realized I'd found the person I wanted to spend the rest of my life with."

Wiping the tears from her cheeks, she smiled. "I think I know why I fell in love with you."

Her shy smile made me want to take her in my arms and never let her go. "Yeah? Let me guess. It's the way I wear a suit."

"No, but now that you mention it, you do look good in your clothes."

"My great house and the stoic butler that comes along with it?" I joked.

"No, but the house is great."

For the first time she touched me intentionally, sending a shot of excitement racing up my arm. Every clever comment left my head and I stared down at her wanting to press my lips to hers in a kiss that would take her breath away.

"I bet I fell in love with you because of the way you say what's in your heart."

Nothing could have been further from the truth. Shaking my head, I looked away, unable to face her. I couldn't handle feeling like a fraud at that moment.

"Tristan, did I say something wrong?"

I turned back to look at her and forced a smile. "No. How about we say you'll start work tomorrow morning? Nine sharp sound good?"

"Aren't you the boss? Shouldn't you be telling me instead of asking me?" she asked with a sexy grin that made me want to throw her down on the bed and show her exactly who was boss.

Standing, I looked down at her. "You're right. Be in my office at nine and be ready to work. If you need anything tonight, you know where I am."

I'd been right after all. Whether she knew it or not, she wanted the man I'd been all along. Starting tomorrow, I'd be that man again.

Chapter Three

Nina

Tristan left me sitting on my bed wishing that I'd had the nerve to lean in and kiss him when he told me he loved me. I may not have remembered being with him, but my body reacted every time he was nearby, every inch of me wanting to feel his touch, and just hearing him profess his love for me had made my body launch into overdrive.

Jordan had told me all about him—how much he was worth, how crazy he was about me, how sexy he was—but she'd definitely understated that last part because this guy was off the charts hot. Always dressed in a shirt and tie, he appeared stiff and stuffy, but it hadn't taken me long to fall under his spell, as I guessed many women did. Those milk chocolate brown eyes that always seemed to be watching me made my legs go weak when he stared at me, even if he was looking for something in me that I may never remember.

The thought that he and I had been so in love that we'd planned to get married and now none of that existed anymore made my heart hurt. Every time he was near me I felt his loss. It was like a heaviness that emanated from him. He tried so hard to hide it, but it was no use. It covered every inch of him like a cloak of sadness he couldn't shake.

He was a stranger to me in many ways, but even without a memory of everything we'd been, something inside me yearned to be next to him, to touch him. Maybe there was some memory of him deep in my mind that I hadn't found yet but still knew what he'd meant to me.

I looked around my room and couldn't help admit it was beautiful. Designed with the finest fabrics and furnishings, he'd spared no cost with this room, much the same as with the rest of the house. I'd noticed that my bedroom was nearly a replica of his on the other side of the house. Was this intentional? Had he had this room redone while I was in the hospital or had this room always looked like his?

I padded over to the desk to smell the enormous bouquet of pink roses that filled the room with the most delicious fragrance. Pink flowers had always been my favorite ever since I was a child, and the mere fact that I remembered that made me happy. That I seemed to not be able to remember anything of the last four years was still incredibly depressing, but remembering my love of pink roses was something.

Tristan's remembering made me even happier. I couldn't explain why, but I already felt drawn to him. Was it because I knew he loved me, even though I couldn't say the same? I didn't know, but his thoughtfulness with the flowers made me feel cherished for the first time in a long time.

I hadn't noticed before, but there was a small envelope attached to the white silk bow around the flower stems. Slipping the card out, I read Tristan's note.

All my love,
Tristan

As I stood there holding that card, I had the strongest sense of déjà vu. I closed my eyes and struggled to grasp at a shred of an idea of what it meant, but after a few minutes, I gave up in frustration. It felt like there was something, but I couldn't put my finger on it.

Inhaling the sweet scent of roses one last time, I took the card with me and placed it on the night table, reading it once more before I turned out the light. All my love, Tristan. Rolling onto my back, I stared up in the darkness at the ceiling and thought about how many times I'd wished some great guy would feel just this kind of love for me and nothing had happened. He'd either never noticed I even existed or like others, had taken what they could until they grew tired of me.

Them I remembered. The ones who cared nothing were as clear in my mind as my own name. Tristan left roses and cards professing his love, and he was a total stranger.

Sometimes life sucked.

Reaching over to my night stand, I picked up the card with Tristan's handwritten note and pressed it to my lips. If only I could remember…

Then a thought came to me. Maybe he would know why I'd had that feeling of déjà vu when I'd read his card. I walked over to his side of the house and nervously knocked on his bedroom door. He had said if I needed anything I should find him, so I hoped maybe he wouldn't have a problem with me knocking on his door at night.

Idiot, the man says he loves you. He's not going to mind you coming by.

The door opened and there he stood in nothing but black silk pajama bottoms. I nearly passed out from the sight, and every word I would have wanted to say evaporated from my mind to make room for every sexual thought that could fit. God, he looked incredible!

As my eyes roamed up and down his toned, muscular body, I saw the tribal tattoo that sat above his left pec and traveled down his gorgeous left bicep to his elbow. That someone like him had a tattoo at all surprised me, but with a body like his, he should have had tattoos over every last inch of him.

And then the truth dawned on me: I'd slept with this man. I'd touched that body. There was no way in a just world I'd have forgotten that. No way. God, life really did suck sometimes.

"Nina, is everything okay?" he asked as if he were standing there like he normally did, all dressed and covered and exuding just his normal level of sexy, not the so-sexy-I-wanted-to-jump-him level he had going on at that moment.

My mind was filled with ideas about six-packs, whatever they called that cut near a well-built man's hipbones and how incredible Tristan's pants looked as they sat just under those cuts, and every indecent idea I'd ever had about what I would do with my tongue if I had the chance to touch a body like Tristan's. I couldn't talk. Suddenly, my mouth felt parched, and I licked my lips just to enable me to try to form words. It wasn't going to be easy with him standing there like that.

"I…you…I thought I remembered something," I stammered out.

Smooth. This was why hot guys never wanted me, I suspected.

Through all that super hot sexiness came excitement like a child on Christmas morning. His deep brown eyes lit up at the sound of my words and a genuine smile broke out on his face. "You remembered something?"

Nodding, I lifted up his card. "I think so. When I read your note, I had the clearest case of déjà vu."

He stepped back to let me past, and I walked in to stand in the middle of the room, unsure if I should sit on the bed or on the chair near the window. Tristan stood behind me for a moment, as if he wasn't sure what to do either, and then sat down on the bed in front of me.

"Would you like to sit down?" he asked as he looked up at me with an almost innocent look. Almost.

This wasn't going to be easy. I nodded and sat down beside him, all the while attempting to keep my gaze focused on his face instead of everywhere else on his body. Talk about an impossible task!

"Something in my note made you remember something?" he asked as he took the card from me, his fingers grazing mine and making my skin dance with excitement.

"Yeah. I can't put my finger on it, but I felt like there was something."

Without saying a thing, he stood from the bed and walked over to the dresser to open a drawer. He pulled something out, and I saw as he returned to sit next to me that he had a small stack of papers in his hand.

"These are letters and notes I wrote you."

I took them and opened the one that sat on top of the pile. They weren't in chronological order because the first one talked of my moving into his room. The next one was far more businesslike and talked of my job. Right there on his bed, I sat and read through our past together, not remembering anything more but so wishing I would.

More than anything else, Tristan's notes and letters told me we were happy. Two people in love and happy. His handwritten words touched me. Never as flowery as some women might want, they were very much him telling me he cared.

Finally, when I'd read each letter, some more than once, I looked up and saw him watching me intently. He looked so interested in me and how his letters made me feel. I couldn't figure out if I wanted to smile or cry. They were beautiful and sexy and unlike anything any man had ever given me. So simple yet so personal."

Did I write you any letters, Tristan?"

He grinned a sexy smile. "No. You preferred to speak instead of write."

"And you didn't? Strong silent type, I guess?"

"I prefer to express myself in ways I can control."

His answers intrigued me, so I pressed further. "And you can't control your mouth?"

His eyes darkened, and he slid his tongue over his bottom lip. "It's not my mouth I can't control."

I had no doubt about that. Even more, I had no doubt that I wanted to know more about his mouth. And every other part of him.

"Oh. So what can't you control?"

"Let's just say you do things that make me not have the control I prefer."

His voice was deep and made me want to hear him speak more. "Tell me about what I was like with you."

My words sounded almost like they were begging. Maybe I was. I wanted to know the person he'd fallen in love with—the woman who had made such an incredible man fall for her. Was I still that woman? Or had she been replaced by some cipher who clung to any shred of thought that could attach her to the present in the hopes that it would help her remember the past four years?

"Honest. I never had to guess how you felt."

That was definitely me. I probably told him I loved him before he told me. Honest wasn't terribly sexy, though, usually.

"Did you like that? I can be incredibly difficult with my honesty, if I remember correctly."

He looked away and then back at me with a changed look in his eyes. "I loved it."

"Don't get too many people telling you the truth, huh? Most people don't like hearing it."

"Most people don't tell me anything."

"What do you mean?"

He seemed to think about how he wanted to answer before he finally said, "My work life is one in which very few people speak to me during the day. Most people who want to get to me instead deal with assistants and managers."

"So there's no one above you at your company?"

"Stone Worldwide has a board of directors, which I must deal with, but other than that, no."

God, that sounded lonely. "What about in your personal life? You have to speak to people then."

"I have Rogers to speak to everyone in my personal life. He handles the cook and all the household help, except for Jensen, my driver."

"So you only speak to your butler, your driver, and a few people at work? Why?"

"I speak to you," he said, sidestepping my question and making me feel his life was even lonelier than I'd first thought.

"Yeah, about that. Why would someone who prefers to speak to so few people not only take the time to speak to me but hire me himself instead of making me go through your human resources department?"

"I liked you. I wanted to be around you. I hadn't planned on..."

He abruptly stopped talking and looked away again. What hadn't he planned on?

I reached out and touched his hand as it sat on his thigh. "Don't stop. I like hearing about us then."

"I hadn't planned on meeting anyone that night at the art gallery."

Tristan seemed so reluctant to talk about anything concerning how we met. I'd asked him a few times in the hospital and he'd glossed over our meeting as if it were commonplace, but something in the way he spoke now told me it was very important to him.

"Tell me about what I was like there."

He shrugged and seemed to be at a loss for words.

"Please. I'd love to know about that time in my life. I'd planned on trying to find a gallery position when I was in college, so that I did is pretty important."

He looked at me and shook his head. "I don't know a lot about that part of your life. I only saw you once in your job at the gallery."

"What was I like?"

"Beautiful."

"That's it? Beautiful?"

"That's all I saw. And those little cocktail franks."

"Little cocktail franks?" I couldn't help but giggle. He had the oddest way of describing things. Beautiful and cocktail weenies. "You sure do know how to tell a story. Remind me to begin writing a journal so if one of us loses our memory again at least we have something to look back on," I teased, hoping to see one of his gentle smiles again.

For a second, I worried I had offended him because his expression hardened ever so slightly, but then he gave me one of those smiles that I was sure could melt the iciest heart and quietly said, "I remember the important things."

"Like?" I wanted to know those important things. I wanted to hear him talk about every single thing that meant something to him.

"Like the first time I kissed you. The first time you begged me not to tease you and how much I wanted to be inside you at that moment. What you look like when you sleep, all curled up next to me. How jealous you get. The feel of your hair against my fingers when I wrap it around them while we lay in bed talking."

As he spoke, I watched that beautiful mouth say words that nearly took my breath away. He said so little that when he finally spoke freely, it was like a dam breaking. He never took his eyes off my face, watching for my reaction, I suspected, even as his expression remained calm.

This was the reality of us. He remembered everything and so much of that revolved around me, while I remembered nothing but wanted so much to experience those moments that were so deeply etched in his mind.

My eyes drifted down over his muscular torso, and I saw the outline of his cock through his pajama pants. I couldn't deny I too was excited by his words. I was pretty sure all it would take was one kiss and I'd be more than willing, but I didn't want to make the move on him and he seemed content with just talking.

"I wish I remembered those things, Tristan," I said apologetically.

He leaned in and I waited for him to kiss me. His face was so close to mine I could feel his warm breath on my cheek. Instead, he took a tendril of hair and wrapped it around his middle finger. "There are always new memories, Nina."

I closed my eyes and willed myself not to react to the sound of his husky voice right next to my ear, but it was a lost cause. An involuntary whimper escaped from my mouth as I waited for him to touch me again. God, I wanted him to do something so we could get started on those new memories right then and there!

"Yes, there are," I croaked out as he sat there still as a statue, his breathing the only sound I heard.

He released my hair from around his finger and repeated the action, twirling the strand from the bottom up to next to my ear. When he stopped, he gently tugged on it, sending a twinge over my scalp and making me flinch.

"I didn't hurt you, did I?" he asked, but I had the distinct impression he didn't care if it had hurt.

In truth, it hadn't. The tiny bit of pain he'd caused by pulling my hair was intermingled with the pleasure he was creating in me just by being so close that I almost wished he'd do it again.

"No. Is this how you used to play with my hair?"

He shook his head, sighing heavily near my neck, and his warm breath flowed over my skin. "No," he whispered. "I'd play as you rested your head on my chest while we lay in bed. This bed."

This bed. As in the one I wished he would lay me down on and make love to me on at that very moment.

"Oh." That was all I could muster as a response because if I'd said anymore I'd have sounded like some drunken prom date looking to give it up easier than the town tramp. He was driving me mad with desire, but until he made the move, I planned to do my damnedest to keep it together.

"It's getting late and you have a big day tomorrow."

I sat stunned as he leaned back away from me and smiled. "Take the letters. Maybe they'll help you remember something."

"Yeah. Maybe. Thanks," I muttered as I stood on shaky legs to go back to my room. After all that, he didn't even try to make love to me. I couldn't tell if I was exhausted because of the emotions I'd experienced that day or because of the rollercoaster he'd taken my body on just waiting for him to make a move.

I opened the door and behind me from his place on the bed he said, "Nina, I'm glad you came over."

Turning around, I saw he was rock hard. His cock was nearly peaking out of his pants. Why was he playing with me like this?

"Yeah, it was nice. Thanks." I pressed a smile onto my lips and hoped he didn't see how frustrated he'd made me. "Have a good night, Tristan."

I slid my gaze over his body one last time and made my way back to my room. As I climbed into bed, I couldn't say for sure, but I didn't think I'd ever been so turned on merely by talking in my life.

If this was what life with Tristan Stone was like, it was no wonder I'd fallen in love with him before. I was halfway there already.

Chapter Four

Nina

At nine sharp, I stood in Tristan's office on his side of the house ready to get to work, even if I wasn't entirely sure I could do the job. Being a curator was far more than I ever remembered doing, but if what everyone was telling me was the truth, I'd done this job before and pretty well, so all I had to do was remember that and I'd be fine. I had the education and the experience. That was what I told myself about a hundred times over as I'd made my way to see Tristan.

I wore a green cashmere sweater that felt like heaven against my skin, a black pencil skirt, and a pair of black pumps that made my legs look damn good, if I did say so myself. While I may not have been able to remember anything since college, I was sure I'd never worn anything so luxurious in my life as what I was in as I stood there in front of him.

Tristan sat behind his enormous cherry wood desk looking breathtaking in a dark grey suit, black dress shirt, and a stunning red and black tie. After what had happened the night before, I wasn't sure I could work side-by-side with him, and looking like that only made it more difficult.

Why couldn't he work at home in sweatpants and a T-shirt? Who am I kidding? He'd probably still look stunning.

He looked up from his laptop and smiled. "Good morning, Nina. Come sit next to me."

I approached him on wobbly legs and sat down in a chair he slid next to his. As if it wasn't bad enough that I was unsure about my ability to do the job of curator, now I had to deal with him sitting as close to me as he had the night before.

This was going to be a long day.

"Ready to work?" he asked, his deep brown eyes staring into mine.

"Yes, sir," I joked, hoping to ease my jitters with some workplace humor.

He arched one dark eyebrow. "Sir? You don't have to be so formal, Nina. Remember, we're more than just employer and employee."

His deep voice spoke the words that should have put me at ease, but there was a sensual undertone to it that made me need to squeeze my thighs together to ease a desperate, sweet ache that had formed between them the moment I saw him sitting behind that desk.

"Okay. I was just trying to calm my jitters. I'm a little nervous about this," I confessed.

Smiling, he shook his head. "There's no need to be nervous. You're a natural at this. Trust me."

Trust me. He'd said that day after day since I'd met him in the hospital, and I still wasn't sure I could. In truth, it wasn't a could thing. It was an I-was-afraid-to thing. I'd never had much success with men, as far as I remembered, and the memory of what others had done to me was always uppermost in my mind when my heart felt even the tiniest tug in Tristan's direction.

He turned his laptop toward me and began clicking on pictures. "I thought I'd show you the work you'd done already so you could see just how great you've been at this." There was a moment of silence as I focused on the pictures and then he said something in that silky, deep voice that made that ache between my legs rush back with a vengeance.

"Relax. I promise you're great at this."

If only I could focus on the artwork on the screen instead of how close he was sitting next to me.

I took a deep breath and nodded as I examined my previous work, pretending that I wasn't already excited at shortly after nine in the morning. "Okay. These look pretty good, if I do say so myself."

Leaning in next to me, he pointed at a picture full of the color gold. "This one is especially good. I love those owls. Those were a great choice, Nina."

Love. He seemed so comfortable using that word when it came to anything involving me. It was unnerving. Nobody I'd ever dated before had been so free with that word. If anything, the L word was something I was uncomfortable saying, at best.

"Thanks." As I looked at the picture, I couldn't imagine how any art with a few blue and white owls I'd chosen had improved that room so overdone in gold. "That's a lot of gold, isn't it?"

"You should have seen it before the owls," he said with a smile, leaning in closer to my left shoulder. "It's more impressive in person. Maybe we should return to Dallas so you can see your handiwork."

While he spoke, I got lost in the scent of his cologne. I had no idea which one it was, but it was very possibly the sexiest fragrance I'd ever smelled. Fresh, the scent was woodsy and almost citrusy, making him smell delicious. How was I supposed to work like this? While he talked of hotel rooms, my mind was distracted and wondering the name of the cologne he was wearing. He was driving me crazy!

"That will have to wait until after the holidays. I thought we'd stay home for Christmas."

Christmas. The mention of the holiday made my brain switch gears. I hadn't thought much of the holidays because of my accident, but he was right. Christmas was just weeks away.

I turned to look at him and nearly touched his cheek with my lips. Startled, I leaned back away from him and muttered, "Do you do anything special for the holidays?"

A look of sadness crossed his face before he turned to smile at me. "No. I haven't really celebrated Christmas for a long time. I usually work."

"You can't work on Christmas! If any day of the year should be a day off, that's it."

That warm smile he offered far too infrequently brightened up his face all the way to his eyes. "Then I guess I'll be taking that day off this year."

Overcome with enthusiasm for the holiday, I began to tell him all about how I'd always celebrated, complete with tinsel, egg nog, and homemade ornaments. "We can trim the tree on Christmas Eve and make cookies."

Suddenly, as I spoke of all the ways I'd celebrated the holiday with my father, the reality of his death settled into my mind. There wouldn't be any more Christmases with him at home around the fireplace as we opened our presents on Christmas morning. No more holiday dinners with him and my sister and her family. No more surprise stocking stuffers.

"Nina, what's wrong?" Tristan asked as I looked away so he couldn't see the tears in my eyes.

I shook my head as I wiped my cheek. "Nothing. It's just that this will be the first Christmas without my father." Turning to face Tristan, I said in frustration, "Well, not really since he's been gone for four years, but since I can't remember that or anything else that meant so much to me, it all feels like it just happened."

"I know. My first Christmas without my family was hard. I felt like I was all alone, that everyone I'd cared about was gone now. But you're not alone."

I took a deep breath and pushed the sadness away to a place in my head I'd deal with later. "I'm sorry. I shouldn't be doing this during work. It's not very professional."

He lifted my chin with his fingertip and looked deep into my eyes. "You don't have to worry. That's one of the great things about working from home. It's more relaxed."

Jesus, just the feel of his touch on my skin made my heart race! At this rate, I wouldn't get to lunch before I jumped his bones. Leaning away from him, I caught my breath and checked out his relaxed home office look.

"If this is more relaxed, why are you in a suit and tie?" I joked, hoping to stall for enough time to get my bearings.

"I always wear a suit and tie to work, no matter where it is," he said in a fake serious tone I could tell was slightly defensive.

"So you've always worn a suit and tie? I'm trying to imagine you as a twenty year old guy hanging out looking like this."

His brow furrowed, and he shook his head. "Nina, I haven't always been this man you see in front of you. This is the person I have to be now. A long time ago, I was like every other guy you've ever met."

I looked at him as he busied himself with clicking to the next set of pictures he wanted me to see. From those gorgeous milk chocolate brown eyes, to his perfectly shaped mouth, and his ripped muscular body, there was no way he was ever like any other guy I'd ever met. Add to that the money, the houses, and the cars and there was no chance. No way.

A half hour later, even I was convinced I was the right woman for the job as Tristan's curator. The pictures from the projects I'd completed in his hotels showed I knew what I was doing. The colors, shapes, and textures I'd chosen worked well with the decor in the suites, and I'd even come around to believe that those adorable blue and white Mexican owls had done something for the Dallas suite.

I'd also settled down and could focus on work, instead of on the way Tristan looked, smelled, and sounded. The man was indeed the most delicious brand of sensory overload.

Tristan leaned back in his chair and ran his hand through his short dark hair. He had a pensive look on his face and sat silently for a long moment before he turned toward me. "I'm thinking we'll go to Atlanta after New Year's. You can get a head start on that job beginning today."

"Oh. Okay. For a minute there, I thought you were going to say you wanted to go to Atlanta for New Year's Eve." I'd never been to Atlanta, so enjoying New Year's there sounded fun.

"No, we'll do New Year's Eve at the penthouse."

"In the city?"

He nodded. "Yes. It's not as cozy as here, but the views are better."

"Do you have any pictures of that, or didn't I do any work there?"

His voice softened as he spoke of his home in Manhattan. "The penthouse is my home, so it's not like other penthouses at the other properties I own, but you did choose a piece for there."

"You sound like you really love it, Tristan. I look forward to seeing it."

Shaking his head, he twisted his expression into something that looked like he'd tasted bad food. "I don't care about the penthouse. In fact, I've never liked it. The only thing I like there is the print you picked out to cover the bare spot in the bedroom."

"I must have hit it out of the park with that one then."

"It's just what that room needed," he said quietly.

"Can we invite Jordan and her boyfriend to join us on New Year's Eve? I'd love to see her, and because of my memory loss, I don't feel like I know Justin at all."

He seemed to think about it for a moment. "If that would make you happy, then we'll do it. We can have them over for drinks and dinner."

Left unsaid was what would happen after drinks and dinner and after they left. I felt like some teenage virgin who was both anticipating and dreading having sex for the first time. Thank God I'd had sex before the point in time where my memory stopped. Even the memory of bad sex was better than going into it blind.

Not that I thought we would wait until New Year's.

"Thank you, Tristan. It's nice of you to include them in our plans."

He smiled at me and shook his head. "There's no need to thank me, Nina. All I want is your happiness."

I didn't know what to say to that. Everything he'd done from the moment I'd met him as I lay there in that hospital bed all broken and bruised showed me that whatever else I may not know, I could truly believe he did want me to be happy. It didn't matter that I couldn't completely understand why either.

To him, I was his Nina, and every moment that passed, I found myself growing more comfortable with that role. And to my surprise, with each moment I spent with him, I also found myself wanting to make him happy. He had that effect on me. Maybe it was because he was my strength in those times when I needed it every day in that hospital, or maybe it was because he seemed so single-mindedly focused on me. Whatever it was, I was quickly falling for him and honestly wasn't sure I shouldn't be sublimely happy about it.

"This is the property in Atlanta. It's one of the few properties of mine that I've never visited, so when we travel there, it'll be my first time too."

Tristan pointed to the pictures of the Atlanta hotel as he explained that he'd visited most of his properties since becoming CEO of Stone Worldwide four years ago. I had a hard time imagining him as anything like a CEO. He didn't act like someone who ran a worldwide business. As I sat there watching him talk about suites and hotel rooms, he seemed more like someone I might meet at a club.

Except for the idea that he was drop dead gorgeous and likely preferred clubs I couldn't afford to get into. I didn't know which one would have been a bigger impediment to our ever meeting.

"Tristan, do you ever go to clubs?" I asked impulsively, curious to know if my mental ramblings had been correct.

He stopped talking about what kind of art he thought the Atlanta suite could use and turned his head to look at me. There was a devilish look in his eyes that made them seem to dance in the light of his office.

"No. Why? Would you like to go out tonight?"

"Could we?" I asked excitedly, thrilled at the idea of not only getting out after weeks of being stuck in the hospital but also seeing him in a different setting.

He nodded and stood from his chair. As he passed by me without a glance, he said, "Of course. If you'll excuse me, I have to arrange a few things and deal with some work issues, but I'll meet you in the dining room at seven for dinner and we'll go out after that."

His leaving was so abrupt I wondered if I'd done something wrong. He hadn't smiled or even touched my hand as he left. His tone had been decidedly all business compared to just minutes earlier, but I guessed he had important work to do, so I set about studying the Atlanta suite in the hopes that I could add something unique to it.

After I'd done a few hours of work, I headed to my closet to search for something to wear that night. That morning when I'd reached for my work clothes, I'd been so nervous I hadn't paid attention to all the gorgeous clothes that hung next to them. I had no idea when I'd purchased the wardrobe I stood staring at, but I was sure it cost a fortune. Designer names, cashmere and silk, and dresses unlike anything I'd ever owned before filled my eyes.

I pushed each beautiful outfit past me, vetoing some because they were too long and others because they just didn't feel right for the night ahead, until I found a little black dress hidden all the way in the back. I held it up in front of me and measured it against my body. It was perfect. Hanging to about three inches above my knees, it showed enough skin to entice while still allowing me to look classy.

On the floor sat over a dozen pairs of shoes, each one more beautiful than the last. Black pumps, red stilettos, tan patent leather sling backs, but none of them seemed right for that little black dress. Then I spied a pair of gold stilettos on the far right side of the closet, hidden behind other shoes and knew instantly they were the ones.

I wanted this night to be one I'd remember forever. Tristan had repeatedly said we would make new memories, so tonight would be the first of many, or at least I hoped it would. I still wasn't sure how I felt about him, but between the jealousy that had nearly consumed me as I looked at those pictures with him and the women he called actresses and the desire he'd created in me as I sat in his room the night before and in his office that morning, I knew one thing for sure. I wanted to know more about him than the caring boyfriend and the accommodating boss.

I wanted him.

Five o'clock came and I took one last look at myself in the mirror. Smoldering sable eye shadow and the perfect red lipstick gave me the sex symbol look I was aiming for, and my dress and shoes screamed seduction. I just had to hope that Tristan was on the same page and hadn't fallen out of love with me after my coolness toward him.

By the time I reached the dining room, I was a complete nervous wreck. I didn't know how I'd handled the first time with him before, but this Nina felt like she was going to pass out from anxiety as she walked down the hallway from her room. Seduction had never been my strong suit, and an attempt to seduce a man as stunning as Tristan Stone made me feel like I was totally out of my league.

I only hoped he truly did still love me.

CHAPTER FIVE

Tristan

"**D**inner will be ready in a few minutes, as you ordered," Rogers announced as he walked into the dining room.

I waited for something else to follow his dinner information, but instead he simply stood silently watching me. "Is there anything else, Rogers?"

He shook his head. "No, sir."

My second sir of the day. Another person in my house who wanted to call me something entirely too formal.

"Sir, Rogers? There's no one but the two of us here, and even if Nina was here, she's heard you call me by my given name before."

"As you wish, Tristan."

Why did I have the distinct impression that my butler was giving me the cold shoulder? "Is there something you want to say, Rogers? And if it has anything to do with our conversation the other day, don't bother. I'm not interested in hearing it again."

"Then I have nothing to say," he said as he turned to leave.

"I do. Make sure Jensen is ready to go tonight. I'm taking Nina to the city."

Rogers stopped his movement toward the doorway and stood still as Nina entered the dining room in a dress that was nothing less than stunning. She wore the gold shoes she'd worn the night of the book party at the hotel and the effect was just as incredible as that night. The memory of our time in the back of my car made me want her right then and there.

As I stood from the table to pull her chair out, I couldn't take my eyes off her. I'd never seen her look so beautiful. "Nina, I'm happy you're joining me."

She twirled around to show off her outfit and tripped over her feet, sending her stumbling into my arms. I looked down to see her face red from embarrassment, but to me she looked more gorgeous than ever.

"Thanks. I'm too smooth," she joked in the self-effacing way she always did when she was uncomfortable.

"My pleasure."

As she stood back up on her feet, she added, "Thank God you were there or I would have landed flat on my butt."

"I'll always be there, Nina."

We took our seats and her eyes lit up when Rogers began to bring the platters of food in. "Is that roast beef? I love roast beef!"

"I know. I thought it might be nice to have one of your favorites tonight."

Nina rolled her eyes and smiled. "I swear you don't miss a trick, do you? I better start learning some things about you so I can do nice things like this for you sometime."

I loved the idea of Nina thinking about me enough to surprise me, even if I hated surprises. That I couldn't express that had nothing to do with her and everything to do with me.

I felt Rogers' stern eyes staring at me as she talked of how excited she was about our planned night out. His disapproval filled the room, threatening to ruin all the happiness she felt and I wanted to feel. I couldn't stand his glaring at me as if I'd done something bad by falling in love with her.

Taking my attention away from Nina, I waved my hand in his direction. "Thank you, Rogers. That will be all for tonight."

He glared at me and bowed in a way that was undoubtedly meant to mock me. "Sir."

I stuffed down my anger at him and turned back to see Nina looking at me with reproach. "Are you always so short with your butler? He might smile more if you were nicer."

"I doubt it."

"Have you tried?" Her blue eyes looked like they were staring into my soul, like they were searching for the answer to her question.

Sheepishly, I answered, "No."

"Well, you can't know if you don't try. How long has he worked for you?"

"He's been with my family since I was a child. He's known me longer than anyone else in the world."

"Oh. Have you always been like this with him?"

I thought back to the countless times Rogers had picked up after me, first when I was an insolent child who cared nothing for his belongings and then when I became an adult and cared even less for the effect of my actions on others. How many times had he cleaned up some mess I'd made, making sure some female was driven home and sworn to silence or whisking me away from someone's apartment before I could get arrested for possession of enough coke for a small town?

"Are you hungry?" I asked, changing the subject.

She grimaced, marring that gorgeous face for just a moment. "Guess we're done talking about your cranky butler. That's okay. I am hungry, though."

"Good. We'll eat dinner and then head to the city."

Dinner was fantastic and by the time we left for the city hours later, Nina was laughing and full of smiles. It took every ounce of restraint on my part not to tell Jensen to forget the drive, sweep her into my arms, and take her back to my room to show her how much I loved her. I wanted to believe she'd worn the sexiest dress in her closet for me, but even if that was the case, we were still playing the game all first time lovers play—a light touch here, a sexy glance there, and no one truly sure of the other person's feelings, even though I'd told her I loved her more than once since coming home from the hospital.

I loathed the idea of going to a club, to be honest. After far too many nights spent in supposedly the best places in the city doing things anyone with a conscience should be ashamed of, I'd sworn off the city's nightlife, except for the functions required because of my position as the head of Stone Worldwide. I never even visited the clubs my company owned, but Nina wanted to go out to a club, so I had little choice.

If it made her happy, I'd go.

Jensen dropped us off behind a club called ETA just outside of the West Village, and we snuck in the back door unseen by any of those leeches with cameras. ETA was an enormous club that claimed to afford a person all the privacy he or she desired as they sat amongst hundreds of other like-minded individuals. Its name meant Estimated Time of Arrival, a not-so-clever ploy to get patrons thinking even more about sex. Years ago, I would have been happy to come all over every square inch of the place, but tonight I planned to find as secluded a spot as possible for Nina and me and hopefully she'd enjoy herself.

We were escorted into a semi-private room off the main club and seated in a dark corner in a booth covered in soft purple velvet. Dim lights flickered around the room and provided just enough light to see who you were with but not enough light to notice their imperfections.

It was the perfect place for people who craved privacy and those who didn't want to face the reality of their night's companions. For us, it hopefully would be secluded enough that no one would notice me and interrupt our time together. In any event, I'd prepared for the worst, but I really hoped we could avoid any unwanted attention and just enjoy being with each other.

The beat of the music thrummed inside my head, making it hard to hear anything else, so I pulled Nina close to me. "What do you want to drink?"

She looked around the room as the place began to fill up and turned to smile up at me. "What are you drinking?"

"Scotch."

"Do I like scotch?" she asked with an innocence that made me rethink that idea of not coming at ETA.

"No, I don't think you do," I answered after thinking about that first night we'd spent together. "Maybe something sweeter?"

"Okay," she said and then bit her lip nervously. "Any ideas?"

"I'll have the bartender make something you'll love. Wait here. I'll be right back."

The guy behind the bar seemed to know exactly what Nina would like although I said nothing more than 'make it something sweet', and I returned to the table with a glass of twelve year old scotch and a chocolate martini.

Nina looked down at the martini glass rimmed with sugar and then looked up at me. "What is it?"

Leaning over to whisper in her ear, I said, "Taste it. Lick the rim and then take a taste of the drink. It's sweet."

She tentatively slid her pink tongue over the frosted sugared rim of her glass and took a tiny sip. The liquor slid down her throat, and she turned to face me with a smile. "It's chocolate!"

A tiny sugar crystal hung off her bottom lip, so I slid the pad of my thumb across it to clean it off before I licked the sugar from my finger. "Definitely sweeter than I'm used to," I joked as I reached for my drink to wash the overwhelming sweetness down.

Nina touched where I'd slid my finger across her lip and smiled. "You prefer the harder stuff, don't you?"

"I guess I do."

She licked her lips and reached up with her fingertip to touch mine. When she tasted the drop of scotch from her finger, she made a face like she'd just sucked a lemon. "I think I'll stick with my sweet stuff and leave that to you. That's gross."

"It's an acquired taste, I guess."

"Maybe someday I'll acquire it," she said with a tiny smile.

I shook my head. "You're more the sweet kind."

Two hours later, we'd talked little more because the music had become so loud we could barely hear one another over it. Memories of my time at clubs just like this one washed over me, making me wish for somewhere far quieter. Nina seemed to enjoy watching the sea of humanity that flowed past us, but I didn't get the sense she was having fun.

My suspicions were proven correct when she turned to me and said in my ear, "I wish we could find a place just a little quieter. Can we go somewhere else?"

I was thankful to get away from ETA and had a place in mind that would be a bit quieter, although I wasn't sure I should take Nina there. It was definitely more secluded and out of the city, but was Top the right place to take someone like her, even if I was part owner of the place?

Jensen held the door open for Nina and as she climbed in, I said to him in a low voice, "Take us to Top. Do you remember how to get there?"

As stoic as Rogers, he simply nodded his head and waited for me to get into the back seat of the car.

"Where are we going?" Nina asked as we pulled away from ETA.

"A club I know of. We'll be able to talk there. They have a private room we can use."

"Where is it? Near here?"

I shook my head. "Outside the city. It shouldn't take long to get there."

Nina talked about how she and Jordan had always planned a huge celebration for her twenty-first birthday. The sadness at the time she'd lost was clear as her voice dropped and she said quietly, "I wonder if we ever did that."

I texted Top's owner, Chase Mitchell, that we were coming, and almost a half hour later, we were in the suburbs at the club. The facade of the building gave no indication of what Top truly was. An old warehouse, Chase had converted it into a members only club three years ago, and other than an occasional visit now and then, I'd been a completely silent partner in the business. Chase's fetishes weren't my style, but the club had made a handsome profit for both of us, so who was I to look down my nose at one man's turn-ons?

I held Nina's hand as we walked up to the door and as I knocked on it, quietly said, "This place will be more intimate."

Her blue eyes widened and a look of fear settled into them. "What kind of place is this?"

"A private club that I'm half owner of. Don't worry. It'll be fun."

"Okay. Promise you won't let anything happen to me, Tristan."

I squeezed her hand and brought it to my lips in a kiss. "I would never let anything bad happen to you, Nina. Never. You can trust me."

The door to Top opened, and just inside stood Chase with a stunned look on his face. "Holy fuck! I got your text and thought somebody was pulling my chain. Tristan Stone as I live and breathe!"

Nodding, I pulled Nina close to my side as the doorman shut the door behind us. "Nice to see you, Chase."

"You're just in time. The night's just getting started. But I'm more interested in who your friend is."

Chase turned his focus to Nina and extended his hand to shake hers. "Chase Mitchell, owner—well, half owner of Top. What's your name, darling?"

Before Nina could say a word, I pulled his attention back where it belonged. "Remember your place in this, Chase. We want to find a secluded spot and have a few drinks, so how about you show us to one of the private rooms?"

Nina reached her hand out and introduced herself. "Hi! I'm Nina. What kind of place is this?"

Chase shook her hand and looked at her like she was some kind of morsel, ratcheting my anger up a few more notches. "What kind of place is this? Love, this is the finest private club on the East coast."

"Private club?"

"Members only and high rollers. Whatever they want, we have at Top."

Nina looked up at me with a confused look on her face. There was no point in explaining it. This probably hadn't been my best idea, but now that we were there, that was a moot point. I really didn't want to explain anything in front of Chase, so I merely shook my head.

Chase continued to talk, testing my patience even more. "Tristan, I didn't expect to see you so soon after last time. You looking for the same? What can I interest you two in tonight?"

"Interest us in?" Nina asked in a shaky voice as she stared wide-eyed up at me.

"You look like you could be a walking schoolgirl fantasy, my dear. No wonder he brought you here."

We stood there surrounded by an awkward silence as I struggled not to knock Chase on his mouthy ass. He got the gist of my glaring at him in little time, though, and quickly escorted us to a dimly lit private room. Nina took a seat at one of the tables as I excused myself to speak to Chase alone.

Closing the door behind me, I grabbed him by the collar and pasted him against the wall. The bass from the music in the main room of the club began to vibrate the lights that hung near his head and only served to irritate me more. "You have less than five minutes to get me the finest scotch you have in this place and a chocolate martini. And I'm not talking about that bottom shelf shit you try to pass off on the customers."

Chase opened his mouth to protest his innocence, and I pushed him into the wall again. "And one more fucking word out of you and I'll make sure this place is shut down by tomorrow morning. You'll have nothing and I'll be short one pissant fucking club I care nothing about. Do you understand me?"

Chase looked at me with fear and confusion. "What? She seems nice. I was just teasing. Trying to give her a compliment. Is that the one I saw you with at some party a few weeks back? The one who was in the car accident? She's got a nice, girl-next-door look you haven't gone for in years."

"Now you have four minutes."

"How did that couple work out? The ones you took out of here a while back? I never got a chance to hear how that went."

Pushing Chase away from me in disgust, I turned to join Nina, adding, "And have someone else bring the drinks."

I found Nina sitting at a table watching some sex show on a big screen television on the other side of the room. Chase had obviously gotten the wrong idea when I said secluded. I sat down across from her and waited for the inevitable questions.

"What kind of place is this, Tristan?" she asked in a hurt tone. "Do you bring women here all the time?"

I could barely make out the sadness in her face, but it was there. "Don't listen to him, Nina. I barely know him, and he knows nothing of what I feel for you."

"What did he mean schoolgirl fantasy? What is this place?"

"Don't let him bother you. He's an ass. I just helped him get this place off the ground."

"With money?"

"Yes."

"Is this a nightclub? What did he mean when he said it's a private club?"

This hadn't been my best idea. I'd hoped that we could find a secluded spot to talk, but maybe Top wasn't the right place, even if I was the owner.

"The club is sort of a nightclub meets sex fantasy camp," I said, hoping I wouldn't have to go into it more than that.

"Sex fantasy camp?" she asked with surprise in her eyes.

"Yeah. I guess this isn't a place you'd want to be. We can go."

Nina shook her head and smiled. "No. We can stay a little while. I'm curious about this side of you, Tristan Stone. A fantasy sex club seems distinctly un-Tristan."

"It is. Don't get the wrong idea. I'm just a silent partner here."

A waitress dressed in a tight, white T-shirt that left nothing to the imagination and skin-tight black shorts interrupted our conversation to deliver our drinks, and I saw Nina's eyes grow wide in the dim light as the woman ran her fingertips over my shoulders as she left. Looking up, I saw it was a girl named Brandi who'd worked at the club for the last year.

"Haven't seen you in ages, Tristan. Nice to see you back," she purred in a silky voice.

"Do you know her?" Nina asked as she watched her walk away.

"No."

"Well, she knows you. She called you by name."

I didn't exactly know Brandi. She'd been Chase's girlfriend when he hired her, and more than once I'd had to listen to her as she cried on my shoulder about his inability to remain faithful.

"She's just someone who works here," I said casually as I took a sip of my drink.

"Oh. What's her name?"

"Brandi."

"Of course it is," Nina bit out.

I could tell she was jealous, which in some twisted way made me feel good. Her feelings had been relatively tepid since coming home from the hospital, even though I'd hoped she was beginning to feel something for me. Maybe if she was jealous, that wish was already coming true.

Her eyes kept darting to the screen behind me, and I couldn't tell if she was curious or embarrassed by what was playing out on the television. I didn't want her distracted by one of Chase's kinky flicks, though.

There was a lounge area on the other side of the room with couches and chairs, so I suggested we move there instead, hoping to turn her focus back to us. The couches were the best money could buy. Chase was nothing if not eager to spend his investor's money. As we sat down next to one another, her jealousy and my hope crashed into each other.

"These are very nice," she said as she rubbed her palm over the back of the black leather couch. Then abruptly, she said, "I think you know that woman."

"I told you I didn't."

"Then why would she touch you like that?"

"Maybe she thought she knew me or maybe she got the sense that I was available and we weren't together?" I said half-jokingly.

"Why would she think that? I'm just as dressed up as you are and we're sitting here together."

"I think she might be used to something different here. Maybe the women are more obvious with how they feel about the men they're with."

To be honest, I was more than thankful Chase's girl had made that little gesture that I knew she did with every male in the club. At least it had gotten Nina to show something of how she felt. Her jealousy was flattering, but I didn't want just that.

Nina turned her body to face me. "Are you saying that I should be more obvious?"

"When in Rome…" I teased.

I saw a tiny pout form on her lips and then she looked away and sighed. She was silent for a long moment and then stood from the couch and smiled down at me. "Well, then I guess I better act more like the locals."

Nina hiked up her dress and straddled me as I sat looking up at her stunned. My hands instantly found their way to cup her pretty ass, pulling her closer.

"Is this better? I've never been to a club like this, so I'm not sure. Maybe I need to be wearing what she had on. Would you prefer that?" she said in a teasing voice.

My cock was rock hard in five seconds, and I had to rein in my urge to fuck her right there. Struggling to keep my voice calm, I smiled and said, "You look beautiful just as you are, Nina."

"Am I being obvious enough for you, Tristan?"

Her tone was almost biting, as if she was angry. My guess was that she was nervous, but I liked a challenge.

"Just enough."

Nina's mouth covered mine, and she snaked her tongue past my lips to tease the tip of my tongue. Running my hands over her hips, I slid my thumbs along the crease of her legs, dying to know if she was as ready as I was.

She relaxed just a little and lowered herself until she was fully seated on my lap. In her tender way, she looked down at me shyly and whispered, "I didn't think this out completely. Now that I'm sitting here like this, I'm not sure I want to do this here."

I couldn't help but smile. God, she was the same honest Nina I'd fallen head over heels for months before.

Shaking my head, I leaned in and kissed the tip of her nose. "I don't want to do this here either, so don't worry. It's okay. What do you say we go somewhere nicer and get back in this exact same position there?"

Nina bit her lip in that cute way she always did when she was nervous and nodded. Finally, tonight we'd begin making those memories.

Chapter Six

Tristan

Jensen followed my orders and got us to the penthouse in record time. Even though Nina and I had begun to get comfortable at Top, we kept it together in the car. I don't know what she was feeling, but it took every ounce of self-control I possessed not to try for a repeat of that night in the back seat of the Rolls. By the time we got to the hotel, I wanted her so bad I wasn't sure I'd be able to control myself once we hit the elevator.

We rode up to the penthouse with both of us staring at our reflections in the mirrored walls of the elevator as I slid my arm around her waist to pull her close to me. She melted into my body, and I watched as she closed her eyes and her face relaxed. She was happy, and I planned to make her much happier in just minutes.

The elevator door opened and she stepped out into the penthouse, her head swiveling back and forth as she admired the designer's work that I never cared much for. She turned in my hold and looked up at me with a surprised expression. "This is stunning, Tristan!"

As she ran to look at the view of the city in the living room, I followed, happy that she was impressed. I wanted her to like everything in my world, even the parts of it I didn't give a damn about.

"I've never seen anything like this! How do you live here and not just stare out the window all day?" she asked as she pointed toward the twinkling lights of the city below.

"I don't really pay much attention to it," I said, remembering how she'd asked me that the first time. "Do you want something to drink?"

"Any chance you know how to make that chocolate drink?"

"No, but I could have the concierge bring one up for you," I offered as I made my way to the bar to find my bottle of scotch.

She walked over and stood next to me, smiling. "Looks like I'm going to have to drink the hard stuff. Well, I'm a tough chick. Hit me with that scotch."

I poured her a glass neat and handed it to her. "You sure?"

Raising her glass to clank against mine, she shrugged. "I guess we'll see, right?"

I tapped mine to hers. "To new memories."

"To new memories." She lifted the scotch to her lips and took a sip. Instantly, her face screwed into a grimace. "Oh, I don't know how you drink this. It's so strong. I can feel it racing through my body already, and I only had one taste. A few more and I'll be no good to anyone."

I took the glass out of her hand and placed it on the bar. "Then no more for you. I want you sober."

"Sober for what, Mr. Stone?" she said with a giggle, the scotch already taking effect.

Snaking my arm around her waist, I pulled her close and buried my face in her neck and whispered, "For when I make love to you, Ms. Edwards."

I didn't want to hold back anymore. I wanted her to be mine again, body and soul. Cradling the back of her head, I drew her mouth toward mine and kissed her with all the desire I'd kept bottled up for all those weeks. Her lips were soft but as eager and passionate as I slid my tongue into her mouth to find hers. When she sighed into my mouth, I couldn't wait anymore.

My hands clawed at the zipper down the back of her dress, but it got stuck an inch from the top. Aching to be inside her, I tore the two halves of the dress apart, ruining the zipper and the dress.

"Tristan, my dress!" she cried as I pulled it from her body.

"I don't care. I'll buy you ten dresses just like it," I panted as I unhooked her bra and slid the first strap over her shoulder. "Same thing with the bra. And if these panties don't come off easy, I'm going to rip through them too."

Nina's fingers tore through my shirt buttons until it hung open, and I quickly shrugged out of it. She was as desperate as I was to be out of those damn clothes. In seconds, she had my belt off and my pants and boxer briefs off my legs, and I had her pushed up against the wall.

As I lifted her off the ground to wrap her legs around my waist, I pressed my forehead to hers and rasped, "I hope you weren't expecting something slow and gentle. I can give you that, but tonight I don't want to wait. I need to be inside you, Nina."

Moaning, she pulled me close, but just then I remembered her sore ribs. Pulling back, I said, "I forgot about what the doctor said. Maybe we should go easy this time."

She dug her heels into my lower back and pulled my mouth to hers in a deep kiss. Her voice husky, she groaned, "Please, Tristan. I'm not a china doll. I'll tell you if something hurts."

I gently slid just the head of my cock into her, still worried I might hurt her if I didn't take it slow. My body was in agony wanting to bury myself inside her, but I didn't want to risk bruising those already sore ribs. I could give her gentle, even if every part of me wanted much more.

Nina pushed her palms against my chest and held me away from her. Worried I'd already screwed this up, I opened my mouth to apologize but she touched her finger to my lips to stop me. "Don't make me wait. I don't want gentle now. I want you...all of you."

Her fingers pressed into the back of my neck as I plunged balls deep into her wet and willing cunt. Nothing in the entire world ever felt better than that moment when our bodies joined together as one again. Her body was hot and enveloped me, taking my body to places I thought only existed in my imagination.

She consumed me, but I would have given my last breath for another moment with her. My mouth plundered hers as my cock pounded into her, each searching for that bliss that only she could provide.

I planted my palms against the wall for more leverage and heard her cry out as I began to thrust my hips faster. She clung to me, hanging off my neck and waist, but I felt nothing except the pure ecstasy that came from being inside her.

Time seemed to stand still, but our bodies were drenched with sweat as we edged one another toward that sweetest moment two people could share. Nina's mouth delivered sensations to every part of me it touched, and I was on fire from her need. I wanted to be the only one to fulfill that need—the only soul who could quench the desire that raged inside her.

"Tristan, faster. Don't stop! Give me what I need. I'm almost there."

Her moans spurred my own excitement on, and I slid my hands down to her waist to hold her fast to me as I inched closer to my own release. "Let yourself go, baby. I want to feel you come all over my cock."

"Oh, God! Don't stop...don't..."

Nina's voice trailed off as I felt the first tender squeeze of her cunt around my cock. She buried her head in the crook of my neck and whimpered as her orgasm roared through her, raking her nails across my back and shoulders while she bucked against me.

Her body milking my cock sent my body into overdrive, and I came with a rush inside her. My legs shook under me, nearly buckling from my release. I clung to her as she did me, panting in her ear as I struggled to form coherent thoughts.

I was sure of only one thing. Nina was mine—truly mine—once again, and I was never going let her go.

"Tell me it wasn't always like that, Tristan," Nina whispered as she rested her head on my chest. "Tell me we weren't always so incredible together."

I trailed my fingers over her hair, twirling a strand around my forefinger as we lay in each other's arms on the floor. "Why?"

She wrapped her arm around me and squeezed gently. "Because if that's the case, I'm even sadder that I can't remember our time together."

"I could lie, if it would make you happy."

Nina looked up at me and twisted her face into a scowl. "No, that wouldn't make me happy."

"Then tell me what would and I'll do it," I whispered as I pulled her on top of me.

"Tell me about who I was. Tell me more than just that I was beautiful when you met me."

When she looked at me with those big blue eyes, I wanted to tell her everything. The truth of what my father had done. The truth of how long I'd known and how long it had been eating away at me. The whole horrible story and how something so beautiful had grown out of something so ugly.

I cradled her face in my hands and kissed her tenderly on the lips. "You were just as you are now. Gentle and kind and more honest than anyone I've ever met. You took my breath away the first time I touched you, and it's no different now."

"I bet it was love at first sight for me, Tristan. Tell me the truth. Was it?"

"I doubt it. I was with the actresses that night, so you probably thought I was some Hugh Hefner wannabe."

She giggled and sat up straight on me. Her light brown hair fell in gentle waves around her face and shoulders, making her look like a mermaid or some kind of angel. "I bet you looked incredible dressed in a suit and looking the way you always do."

I ran my hands over her stomach and caressed the tops of her thighs. She let out a tiny moan as my thumbs slid over the insides of her legs.

"I'm sure I was wearing a suit. I do all the time."

Nina wriggled her ass against my thighs and smiled. "Except now. I like the way you look now too. I don't think I've ever met a man more perfect than you. Successful, wealthy, gorgeous, and a body that looks like a Greek god's."

"I guess all those hours at the gym have paid off. The other stuff really isn't in my control, though."

Her fingers slid over my abdomen and up over my chest to my shoulders. "It isn't a good idea that I adore you so much already, Tristan Stone. No one should be this crazy about another person."

"Maybe it's okay since I'm even crazier about you."

She leaned down and kissed me softly on the lips. "I better find something about you I don't like before I become totally lost in you. Hurry up and tell me one of your bad traits."

There were too many to even get into. I knew that. My past. My family. The club I'd taken her to just that night. But I couldn't tell her about those, and even if I could, I didn't want to. I had my Nina back and I wasn't going to let her go.

"Well, I don't talk much. Some women may think that's a bad trait."

"Yeah, but then you do that strong, silent type sexy guy thing and make even the lack of talking a good thing."

I crossed my hands behind my head and smiled. "I guess I could work on being a bad man. Any suggestions?"

The smile she gave me was so sweet I almost pulled her to me and kissed away anything she could have said.

"I think maybe an eye patch could work."

"An eye patch? That would look great with a suit."

"Mmmm…now that's a man I wouldn't be able to say no to. Sort of a pirate meets a tycoon."

"I'm not sure I can pull off pirate. Something about having to say arrrgh all the time might not work in meetings."

Nina ran her fingertips across my hipbones and grazed the head of my cock. Gliding her tongue over her lips, she looked down at me and smiled. "It's too bad. I could definitely be into a pirate."

"Arrrgh."

"I do love a man who can be persuaded."

Both of us stopped our joking, and her eyes grew wide at what she'd just said, as if she'd let something bad slip. I didn't want her saying she loved me if she didn't mean it. I'd wait as long as it took to have her say those words if it meant they came from her heart.

She rolled off me onto the floor and looked up at the ceiling. "I don't know if I'm in love with you, but I've never felt like this in my life. Well, I don't know. Since I was in love with you, maybe I did feel like this." Turning her head, she smiled at me. "I guess I'm not making much sense, am I?"

I propped myself up on my elbow and nodded. I understood what she was trying to say. "I get it. As long as you're happy, that's enough for me. It's only been a few days since you came home from the hospital, so maybe this is good."

"I hear that thing in your voice, though. I know you wish for more."

I knew the thing she was talking about. I wouldn't have been able to hide it even if I wanted to. A mixture of loss, sadness, and regret, it was in everything I said to her.

Twisting a long wave of her hair around my finger, I forced a smile. "I'm happy, Nina. You do that for me. No one else has ever made me happy like you do. So it's not the same as it was. Maybe this time will be even better."

"It breaks my heart to hear you say things like that. You have everything a person could want. I can't imagine not being happy with money, success, power—all the things everyone thinks ensure happiness."

"All they ensure is that you'll have people wanting you for everything but you."

"Like Chase tonight?"

I gave a snort at the sound of my Top partner's name. "Chase is one of the best examples of the people money brings to you. If I didn't have the money to help him get that business going, I'd be invisible to him. Not that being invisible to the likes of Chase Mitchell is a bad thing."

Nina rolled over and propped her head up on her hand. "How did you get involved with him and that club? You two don't seem a thing alike."

"Chase is a remnant of my time before I took over Stone Worldwide. Remember I told you that I wasn't always the man you see?" For a second, I couldn't remember if I told her in the last few days or before the accident.

She gently touched my shoulder with her fingertips. "No, no. I remember. You said when you were twenty that you would have been just like any other guy I've ever met. And I can tell you that I think you're full of it. There's no way you would ever be like anyone else I've ever met."

"Yeah, well, Chase is from those days. He comes from money. Not as much as I came from, but his family's got some. Not that they would have been interested in giving him a dime so he could set up his club in a sleepy town outside New York City. That's where I came in."

"If you're not into that, why did you agree to be his partner?"

"Silent partner."

"Okay. Why did you agree to be his silent partner?"

"Because I know a good investment when I see one. When he came to me with his idea, I knew it would make money. So I agreed to go in on the club with him as long as he agreed that I'd have nothing to do with the day-to-day operations."

"So you just sit back and collect the money?" she asked with a sly grin on her face.

"Exactly. I prefer to stay in the hotel business and keep my involvement with Top silent."

"Why stay silent about it?"

"I don't care what people like, but there are certain segments of society that wouldn't approve of the owner of the Richmont Hotel chain as co-owner of that kind of place, even if he's a silent partner."

"Doesn't the board of your company have a problem with it?"

Shaking my head, I explained, "They don't know. I financed Top with my own money, not Stone Worldwide's money or credit."

Her eyes grew wide as saucers. "Holy shit! You are loaded!" Instantly, she covered her mouth with her hand and mumbled from behind it, "I'm sorry. That's not the way the girlfriend of someone like you should act."

I pulled her hand away from her face. "It's not a problem. I am. I always have been. Money is something I've been blessed with. I'm not one of those people who thinks it isn't important. It is. But it's not the most important thing in life."

"I always hate when you see wealthy people or movie stars talking about their success in interviews and saying things like the money isn't something they think about or it doesn't mean anything to them. That kind of thing just bugs me. For those of us without money, it's a big thing and we always think about it."

Her honesty washed over me like a refreshing summer rain. This was Nina, and I loved her. "And then you find out they give little to nothing to charity and you wonder what they do with that money they say they care nothing about."

"Exactly!" she said as she sat up. "I hate that kind of hypocrisy."

I suspected she hadn't checked her bank account since she'd gotten home from the hospital and didn't know how much money she really had now. Not that it would matter. I had the feeling that she could have millions and still be the same down-to-earth soul she'd always been.

Running my fingertips over the soft skin of her arm, I continued, "By the way, you act perfectly to be my girlfriend. Don't ever think you aren't exactly what my girlfriend should be."

"Yeah. I'm sure the board of directors of Stone Worldwide would be thrilled to find out you are hanging out with some middle class girl instead of those supermodels they like to see on your arm."

Her comment brought the ugly reality of Karl and the other members of the Stone board to the front of my mind. No matter how happy I was with Nina, I had to figure out a way to convince them that she was no threat to them or whatever my father had done.

"I can see by the look on your face that I'm right, aren't I?" she said sadly. "It's okay. I understand if you have to take one of those women to your events instead of me."

Pulling her down to lay on top of me, I kissed her full on the lips. "Not anymore. If you want to go with me, then I go. If not, then those functions can do without me and my silent as a statue act."

She traced the outline of my lips with her forefinger. "How's the Board going to feel about that?"

"I don't care. You're the woman I'm in love with, so if I'm going, so are you. If they don't like it, too bad."

"You'd do that for me?"

I caressed her cheek and spoke the absolute truth. "I'd do anything for you, Nina. Anything."

CHAPTER SEVEN

Nina

Tristan and I fell asleep right there on the floor of the penthouse's living room with the floor to ceiling windows showing the entire world our lovemaking. Naked and in each other's arms, we held each other close as the nightlife of Manhattan slipped away to allow the business of day to take over, but as I stirred awake, I didn't feel his arms around me. Instead, a blanket kept me warm. Wiping the sleep from my eyes, I looked around and saw no Tristan but an envelope near my head.

Smiling to myself, I opened it and slipped the note from inside. As always, his words charmed me.

Good morning, Nina. I hope you slept well. I realized when I woke up that I did quite a number on your dress last night. You can find clothes to wear in the closet in the bedroom at the far end of the penthouse. When you're ready, simply take the elevator to the garage and my driver will be waiting to bring you to me.

I hope you're in the mood for shopping. It's the least I can do to replace the dress I ruined.

Thank you for giving me another wonderful memory.

> *Love,*
> *Tristan*

A man who wanted to take me shopping? I thought such men only existed in fantasies, like unicorns and dragons. Stretching my arms above my head, I thought about the other ways Tristan was the stuff of fantasies. Had a man ever made me want him like he did? Those stunning eyes, that beautiful mouth, those chiseled abs and strong arms...

Just thinking about him excited me. If only he was there with me so I could show him how much I wanted him. I could only guess that making love with him first thing in the morning would be another delicious experience.

The man had a way of making love that made other men seem like schoolboys. My hand slid between my legs to stroke through my soft folds as I remembered the exquisite sensations his cock had given me just hours before. Kicking the blanket off my body, I spread my legs open wide and let my fingers try to replicate the feeling of Tristan's hands and cock on my pussy. A tiny moan escaped my throat as each stroke brought back the wonderful memories of him.

Just then I remembered that I was lying in front of a wall of windows and giving the entire city a show. Opening my eyes, I saw in horror that it was late enough that the office buildings nearby would have people in them!

Quickly, I gathered up the blanket and ran from the living room to the back bedroom where he said I'd be able to find clothes. Embarrassed, I blushed from head to toe at the idea that some poor secretary just sitting down with her morning coffee had nearly seen me masturbate. I rolled my eyes at my stupidity, wondering if Tristan was as modest as I was or if he routinely paraded around nude for nearby office workers to see.

The closet was in the corner of the room, and I opened it up to see an entire wardrobe of women's clothes alongside all of Tristan's suits, shirts, and ties. As I ran my fingers over each outfit, I wondered if I had always kept clothes here or if he'd had them brought there before we arrived the night before.

I'd learned so much about Tristan already, but at every turn he seemed capable of surprising me.

Grabbing a grey jersey mini-dress and a pair of underwear from the dresser that seemed devoted to my clothes, I wrapped the blanket around me and made my way to the bathroom to get ready. I stepped into the room and stopped dead, stunned at how gorgeous it was. The man certainly knew how to live. Marble and granite covered every square inch of the room, except where an enormous soaker tub sat in front of a narrow floor to ceiling window and a large glass shower, which stood nearby the tub.

I draped my clothes over the tub and got into the shower, still uncomfortable about the window but hoping that my paranoia about being seen by the office workers across the street was just that. Of course it was. This was Manhattan. No one saw anything here, even with eight million people around. God, I hoped that was true or I was giving some unsuspecting souls a peep show as I showered.

I'd accepted the fact that I was going au natural, and I hoped that Tristan was into the pale girl look, but after I dressed I took a chance and looked through the vanity in the bathroom, desperate for at least some toothpaste I could rub across my teeth to get rid of my morning breath. I was stunned to find a toothbrush next to duplicates of every stitch of makeup I regularly used right there for me. It was like this was a parallel dimension that contained everything the other one at the house had. My father's joke about loving Spock and his goatee in the old Star Trek episode ran through my head and I smiled.

My father. I had tried so hard not to think about him being gone, but every so often something reminded me of him and forced the sadness I so wanted to forget back into my mind. His quirky humor. His lectures about working hard so I could do better than he had. What would he think of me now as I stood in the gorgeous Manhattan penthouse of Tristan Stone, CEO of Stone Worldwide and madly in love with me?

Of all the things and people I'd forgotten because of my accident, my father's death hurt the most. I couldn't help but feel it was unfair that I had to go through the pain of mourning him a second time. Why was this happening to me? Wasn't it bad enough to lose your father once? Why did I have to lose him again and feel all the pain a second time?

I couldn't keep doing this, so I pushed the thought away until some other time when I was able to deal with it. Looking in the mirror, I fixed the hair around my face and put on my best supermodel face. Well, I wasn't a supermodel, but I could make their face as well as any of them. That would have to do. A change of shoes from the closet in the bedroom since the gold shoes were definitely not a good look with the jersey dress and I was ready for my shopping trip.

Tristan was as good as his word, and when I exited the elevator, his driver stood waiting for me as if he was a permanent fixture right there in the garage. I approached him and saw he wore a serious expression on his fifty-something face, but he smiled like it was part of his job when I stopped in front of him.

"Miss, if you're ready, we can leave."

"Where are we going?"

"Le Ciel, miss. It shouldn't take long at all."

"Do you have to call Tristan or something to let him know we're coming?"

The driver opened the back passenger side door to the black Town Car and stood back so I could enter. His gaze drifted up toward the concrete ceiling above us. "Not to worry, miss. He knows."

If I thought the man would give me a more complete answer, I would have asked how Tristan knew we were leaving, but something told me he would simply plaster another formal grin on his face and repeat his cryptic sentence. It didn't matter. I could just ask Tristan when we arrived at the store.

I climbed into the car and settled in for the ride, not knowing where this Le Ciel was but happy that it wouldn't take long. The idea of a man taking me shopping had my curiosity piqued. Was it possible Tristan Stone was gorgeous, wealthy, sexy as all hell, and loved to shop?

No. Even he was a mere mortal man. But that was okay. I was still crazy about him.

As I pondered all the ways Tristan was far more than just a mere mortal, the Town Car weaved through traffic like the driver owned the road. By the time I'd mentally listed half a dozen things I loved about the man who had given me one of the best nights of my life, we'd arrived at a boutique in Midtown. I stepped out of the car and saw even the window showcase was obviously upscale with mannequins dressed in designer names and wearing smug looks that somehow intimidated me, telling me Le Ciel wasn't anywhere I'd ever shop.

As I entered the store, a thin woman with jet black hair and a love of Botox, if her frozen forehead was any indication, approached me with an eager look on the lower half of her face. I guessed my current outfit made it seem like I may have belonged there, but I felt like I stuck out like a sore thumb.

"Miss Edwards, Mr. Stone is waiting for you. Please let me take you to him," she chirped out from her perfect mouth.

I was afraid to open my own mouth, unsure I wouldn't inadvertently say something that would give away the truth of how much I didn't belong in her store. Instead, I silently followed her, catching the price of a few dresses as we passed and mentally adding them up to a ridiculous total on our way to a room at the back of the boutique. I found Tristan sitting with three blondes who appeared totally engrossed in whatever he was saying, each hanging on every word he spoke.

The back room was even more luxurious than the store. The walls were draped in deep blue satin fabric that reminded me of what I imagined a sheik's harem would look like. Tristan relaxed on a black velvet couch, his arms opened wide across the back and his legs spread slightly. He wore his usual suit, that day's a black pinstripe with a grey shirt, and looked so incredibly right sitting there that I felt like I was intruding. He oozed power, and the three saleswomen lapped it up.

They noticed me immediately and straightened their backs when I stepped into the room. Tristan looked over at me with a warm smile and stood to take my hand. "Good morning, Nina. Are you ready to shop?"

I looked up at him and wished we were alone so I could tell him how happy I was to see him. Quietly, I said, "I guess."

"Did you have something to eat for breakfast? I instructed the concierge to give you whatever you wanted."

I sheepishly admitted that I hadn't eaten yet. "I didn't know I could do that."

Tristan leaned down to kiss my cheek and whispered, "I'm sorry. I forgot that you wouldn't know that. I should have remembered."

His voice sounded sad, making me feel bad for not knowing. "It's okay. My stomach isn't grumbling yet, so I'm good."

He slid his thumb over my bottom lip and turned to face the three women. "Ladies, this is Nina and she hasn't eaten breakfast yet. I'm sure one of you can find her something to eat while we shop."

The blonde who stood in the middle nodded her understanding and scurried away, ostensibly to find my breakfast. I gently tugged on the sleeve of Tristan's suit coat to get his attention, and he turned to face me with a smile on his face. "You didn't have to do that. I would've waited."

"Nina, I'm about to leave a nice chunk of money in this store. The very least they can do is run out to the café down the street and pick up some pastries. I just hope you like what she brings back. If you don't, she can go again."

He turned to face the other two women who remained standing there before I could explain that making a salesgirl run out repeatedly to grab a blueberry muffin for me seemed out of line. Neither of the women seemed put off by his request, though.

"Miss," one of the women said, "we can begin anytime you'd like. Do you have a preference for beginning with day or night?"

Confused, I asked, "Day or night?"

Tristan smiled back at me and answered, "Nina will begin with clothes she can wear at night. We have a few celebrations to attend over the holidays, and she's going to need dresses."

The two women sprung into action and dashed out past me into the store. Tristan took his seat on the couch again and looked up at me, obviously satisfied by how it was all going. I remained unsure of what to do, but there was something reassuring about the fact that he was staying. While I was a master at the art of shopping as any woman in her twenties likely was, he fit right in with the ambiance of Le Ciel, while I felt like a fish out of water.

"Should I sit and wait or stand?"

"Do whatever you feel comfortable with. They'll be back in a few minutes, but I'm always a fan of having you next to me."

I took a seat on the couch. It felt like I was sitting on a cloud, and instantly, I felt more at ease. Leaning over, I gave him a peck on the cheek. "Good morning. It's nice to see you. I would have loved to have seen you when I woke up."

"But you got my note, didn't you?"

"I did." Lowering my voice, I whispered, "But it's hard to have great morning sex with a note."

He slid his tongue across his lower lip and smiled. "Ah, now that's true. I'll have to remedy that oversight." Looking down, he ran his finger across my stomach. "How do your ribs feel?"

I couldn't help but smile at how sweet he was. "They feel great. I'm not so easily broken."

The women returned with their arms full of clothes. They appeared far more excited by the idea of my trying them on than I did, although I had to admit I could get used to this kind of treatment. They hung them on movable racks around the room and then took their places at the ends of one of the racks like fashion sentries.

"We're ready when you are, miss."

"Okay. I need to replace a black dress. Is there a cocktail dress in there?" I asked the left sentry.

"Of course!" she answered as she picked out some similar to the one Tristan had shredded the night before. With her arm extended, she held out three gorgeous black dresses and displayed them like she was a game show model. "I think any one of these would look incredible on you, don't you think, Mr. Stone?"

Tristan studied the three dresses for a few moments and nodded his appreciation. Turning to look at me, he leaned his head toward the saleswoman and mouthed, "You're up."

I walked over to the woman and smiled, unsure of where I was supposed to try them on. There didn't seem to be a dressing room in this area of the store. "Hi, what's your name?"

"Regina, miss."

"Hi, Regina. If you can just direct me to somewhere I can change, that would be great."

"Of course. Follow me."

As I walked away, Tristan said, "I'll be out here waiting to see you in them. When Felicia returns with your breakfast, I'll be sure to have her bring it back."

I tried on each dress and modeled them for Tristan, who loved them all. I honestly couldn't choose which one I liked most and told him that when he asked, figuring he'd choose one and make it easy, so he instructed the saleswoman that we'd take all of them. When I protested, he merely pointed at the pastries Felicia had brought back and told me to eat something.

Arguing would have been pointless, so I enjoyed a cheese Danish and thanked Felicia, who seemed surprised by my politeness.

"Next, I thought we'd try something a little different," Regina said in a happy voice. "Mr. Stone mentioned that you're looking for some lingerie."

I looked over at Tristan, who grinned like a cat who'd just eaten a bird. "Really?"

"I think you'll like what I've picked out. I hung them in the dressing room for you," she continued.

"Okay. Lingerie it is," I said as I flashed a smile at Tristan. "But I'm not coming out here to model these."

The dressing room was a well-lit, large room that reminded me of a movie star's closet I once saw on one of those shows about famous people's homes. There were built-in racks along three walls and a large built-in dresser on the wall next to the door. In the corner of the room stood a tri-fold mirror so customers could see how great they looked in any Le Ciel outfit from every possible angle. Positioned in the middle of the room was a large, red padded ottoman directly in front of the mirrors presumably to allow a person to relax in their new outfit while still checking themselves out.

The lingerie Regina had picked out was sexier than anything I'd ever slept in, and as I held the first one up in front of me, I couldn't help but admit that it was nicer than the shorts and T-shirt I usually wore to bed. I slipped out of my jersey dress and slid the white silk lingerie over my head. It shimmied down my body until the hem just touched the floor, and when I looked at how it hung on me, I silently wondered if those high-heel slippers with feathers on top and a long cigarette holder were requirements to wear it.

It fit, so it went on the rack closest to the door and I turned back to grab a much shorter and lacy babydoll set. This one was black and definitely sexier than my usual bedtime attire. I took off my bra and slipped into the babydoll, leaving my panties on instead of trying on the bottoms of the lingerie. Stepping in front of the mirrors, I checked myself out and had to admit I looked good. The babydoll pushed my breasts up until I had some very sexy cleavage and the silk fabric draped nicely down to the top of my thighs.

I heard the door open and was surprised to see Tristan walk in. Closing the door behind him, he slid out of his suit coat, hung it on a satin covered hanger, and walked over behind me. He cupped my shoulders and dipped his head to kiss my neck as he whispered, "You look gorgeous. Do you like it?"

Blushing, I nodded and stared at the erotic scene in the mirror. I looked ten times sexier with him standing behind me nuzzling just below my ear. "I do. It's very nice."

"I don't think you remember, but you've been here before. The day after we were first together, you came here to shop and I called you while you sat in this very dressing room."

His voice was laced with sensuality, and every word made my body come alive. "What did you say?"

Looking up from my neck, he stared at me in the mirror with eyes full of desire. "I'd rather show you."

I didn't answer as he led me to the overstuffed ottoman and dipped his head to place a full kiss on my lips. Releasing my hand, he gently pressed on my shoulders to lower me to the seat, smiling seductively at me as I looked up at him.

"Lay back, Nina."

I did as he commanded, my legs shaking nervously as he slid his palms over my thighs. Right there, in the dressing room at Le Ciel, Tristan was about to go down on me with the saleswomen not more than a few yards away at most. My body was a mixture of pure fear and uncontrollable excitement.

"Tristan, what if the ladies…"

He cut me off with a quick nip on my inner thigh as he pulled off my panties. "Shhh. Don't worry about them."

That was easier said than done. The fear that Regina or Felicia might barge in with some great outfit for me to try on and see Tristan's head between my legs made my stomach knot. I was no prude, but sex in public wasn't something I'd ever done.

At least I didn't think I'd ever done it.

"Nina, relax and enjoy this. I've wanted to taste you since you walked in here this morning. Did you know that?" As he spoke, his warm breath trailed against my skin, making me want him more.

Before I could even get a word out, he slid his tongue up to my clit and did this flicking thing that nearly sent me straight to the moon. My back arched and a moan that came from deep inside me escaped from my throat, but I didn't care at that moment. Whatever fear I'd had about anyone knowing what Tristan and I were up to evaporated into thin air with the first touch of his tongue to my pussy.

His hands caressed my abdomen as his mouth and tongue danced over my tender skin. Every inch of my sex was treated to the most incredible sensations from that expert tongue of his. I'd imagined that mouth that had delighted me with the most delicious kisses would be just as wonderful between my legs, but this was so much more than I could have dreamed of.

Running my hands through his short hair, I pulled him into me. Taking my swollen clit in his mouth, he sucked gently, making me ache for more when he pulled away. Suddenly, I felt cold and alone. Opening my eyes, I lifted my head to see him kneeling there staring at me.

"Wh…why did you stop?"

"Tell me you want me to continue, Nina."

"Of course, I do," I whispered. "Don't tease me, Tristan."

He winced ever so slightly and then that seductive look was back. As he leaned in to go down on me again, he looked up at me with eyes full of emotion and whispered, "I'd never tease you, Nina. Let me give you what you need."

And then he did just that.

As his tongue sent my body into overdrive, he slid one and then two fingers inside me, touching a spot that made me cover my mouth so the rest of Le Ciel didn't hear my cries of delight. Over and over, he stroked in and out of my body with expert fingers as every inch of me craved more of his touch.

The first ripple of my orgasm began deep inside and slowly weaved through me until one last playful flick of his tongue made me come apart. I cried out without any care for who heard me, moaning, "Don't stop," as I clawed at his head to make the feeling continue.

He rode my pussy with his mouth and tongue until there wasn't a tremor left in my body. I was boneless when he moved away, the picture of satisfaction staring down at me. Taking my hands in his, he pulled me up to kiss him, and I tasted myself on his lips and tongue.

"I've wanted to do that for a while," he whispered in a deep voice as he stroked my cheek.

"I can't believe I just had sex in a Midtown boutique dressing room. This is like the on-the-ground version of the Mile High Club," I said with a giggle.

"That reminds me. We're taking a trip after New Year's."

I lowered my head, shaking no. "I could never have sex on an airplane, Tristan. Where do those people do that, anyway? Aren't the bathrooms too tiny?"

"I don't know. I've never been on a public airplane. We'll be traveling on my private jet, so perhaps that will make your initiation into the Mile High Club easier."

I looked up, shocked. He had a private jet? I should have guessed that, but it still sounded incredible that I knew someone with a private jet. That I was dating someone with a private jet.

"Wow. Is there anything you don't have?"

Those deep brown eyes focused on mine. "Just one thing, but I'm working on that."

The idea that all he lacked in his life was my love made me feel like I was the most important person in his world. With every moment that passed, I knew why I'd fallen in love with him and wanted to spend the rest of my life with Tristan Stone.

I just had to let myself go this time too.

Chapter Eight

Nina

"Oh my God! What are you doing here?"

Jordan opened her arms and pulled me into the apartment with a huge bear hug, crushing my face against her shoulder. As she closed the door behind us, she released me just long enough to decide she needed another hug.

"Come here! I've missed you so much."

"I did too. When Tristan and I went to the penthouse last night, I knew I wanted to stop over and see how you're doing."

She released me again and led the way to the living room. We sat down in our usual seats and as she folded her legs under her, she stared at me. "You look incredible, Nina. I know it's just been a few days since we saw each other, but it feels like months."

"It does. I thought it was just because I don't remember anything of the past four years."

She let out a big sigh. "Anything good happening on that front?"

Shaking my head, I tried to hide my disappointment with a smile. "Not yet, but Tristan keeps reminding me that the doctors said it might take a little while."

"How is that yummy man?"

I felt my face warm and grinned. "He's fine."

"Oh, he's definitely fine," she teased with a wiggle of her eyebrows.

Changing the subject, I asked, "So what's new with you? I came here to find out about your life."

"My life is nowhere as exciting as yours. Between that gorgeous man, your gorgeous house, and all the wonderful things that come with both of those things, I wish I had your life."

She wasn't wrong. My life was perfect. Wonderful. Tristan was everything I'd ever wanted in a man. The house was beyond stunning. A driver took me wherever I wanted to go. And my boyfriend loved to spend money on me.

The only problem was that I'd lost four years of my life and no matter what I did, I missed them. I wanted to live in the present, but that void from my past haunted me every moment of the day.

"I know. It's great," I said as I looked away.

Jordan leaned forward and pressed her hand to my knee. "Oh, honey. I didn't mean to say everything was perfect. I was just trying to be positive."

Her frown told me she hadn't tried to be callous. "I know you didn't mean anything by it. I should be happy with everything I have."

"Bullshit. You're allowed to be unhappy about not remembering one-sixth of your damn life. Just know that whatever you want to ask about the last four years, I'm here as your own personal encyclopedia." Tapping her finger to her forehead, she added, "I've got everything stored right up here."

Biting my lip, I considered what part of my past I wanted to know about the most. There was really no question. My father's death.

"Jordan, what happened to my father?" I asked in a quiet voice, as if no one else knew about his passing.

She inhaled deeply and blew the air out of her lungs in a hard wooosh. "Oh, honey. I was afraid you were going to ask that. It was tough on you. I can tell you that."

"What happened? He was so young."

She shook her head and frowned. "You and Kim never found out what really happened. All I know is this. He was in Newark investigating some story and was found dead in a parking garage."

"Shot?"

Nodding, she answered quietly, "Yeah. The police said he was murdered execution style."

Tears welled in my eyes. "Oh my God! Why would someone do that to him? He was a writer who investigated things like small town politics. Who kills someone over nepotism on the town council?"

I couldn't hold back the tears as I had since my sister had told me about my father's death. They poured down over my cheeks as I buried my face in my hands, and my body heaved with each sob. My father was murdered and I'd forgotten the whole thing!

Jordan sat down beside me and took me in her arms. "Let it out, sweetie. You have to let it out or you'll get like you did then."

Another thing I couldn't remember.

I buried my face in her shoulder and did exactly that. I let all the sadness out until I couldn't cry anymore. Until I felt hollow and empty.

Pulling away from Jordan, I asked, "What do you mean I'll get like I did then? What happened to me then?"

She smoothed the hair from my forehead and wiped her thumb under my eyes. "It was pretty bad. You didn't get out of bed for weeks. Thank God your professors were understanding since it was your senior year because day after day, no matter how I tried, you wouldn't do anything but lay in bed. Sometimes you cried. Other times you just stared up at the ceiling or off in the distance."

"For how long?"

"Honey, it went on for a long time. Even after you came back to life, I was worried you might never be the same old Nina again."

"I wish I knew who that same old Nina was now," I admitted sadly. "I feel like I'm missing so much of me."

"You're still you, Nina. It's all in there. It's just a matter of it coming out."

I sat back against the couch cushions and hung my head. Just thinking about my father's death was exhausting. It was like he'd just died that day and not years before. My heart hurt at Jordan's description of his murder.

Looking up, I asked, "Am I really the same? Of anybody, you'd know. Am I? What was I like when I got into that accident?"

"Blissfully happy. I'd never seen you as happy as when you were with Tristan. I mean, I don't want to say it was perfect. Nothing is. But you were as happy as anyone could want to be."

"Is he as incredible as I think he is?"

"Yeah. He is. When you moved in with him, he paid the rest of your portion of the rent for the year. When that weird guy attacked us on the front steps, he let me stay at his hotel in a gorgeous suite for weeks because you asked him to. You were worried for my safety, and he didn't blink an eye. You wanted something and he made it happen."

"Why don't I remember any of that? Why can't I remember how much in love with him I was? Don't you think I'd remember that? I mean, I can understand not wanting to remember my father's death, but Tristan is wonderful. And the rest of those four years couldn't have been all bad. Were they?"

"No. They weren't all bad. We had some really fun times once you got back to being yourself. Two single girls living in New York. Good times."

Her smile faded as the words trailed off. She was hiding something. It hadn't been all good times.

"What aren't you telling me, Jordan?"

"It's not important. Your life was as good as anyone who's just out of college and trying to make it on their own."

"But?"

"But nothing. You were happy."

Everything in her face said otherwise, though. What had been so bad about my life?

"Tell me, Jordan. I need to know."

She got up from the couch and walked toward the kitchen. "Jordan, tell me!" I called after her.

She stopped dead in the living room doorway and with her back to me asked, "Cal. Do you remember him?"

"Of course. I was crazy about him."

Turning around, she looked at me with pain in her eyes. "Do you remember what happened between the two of you?"

I thought about what I knew about Cal. "We broke it off because he had the chance to study abroad in Spain for a year. He was a junior and it was the chance of a lifetime, so we broke up. But it wasn't anything awful."

"That wasn't the end of it. He came back and you two began seeing each other again, but he wasn't the same guy. Whatever he did in Europe, he came back a real asshole."

"What are you saying?"

She walked away into the kitchen, and I followed her, needing to know what the hell she was talking about. Standing with her back to me, she shook her head. "It was bad, Nina. He was a real shit. You were crazy about him, madly in love, and he…"

She stopped and said nothing for a long time.

"He what?" I finally demanded.

She spun around and I couldn't tell if she was angry or upset. "He fucked you up really bad, Nina. You didn't just break up another time. He broke your heart. You told him you loved him and what did he do? He cheated on you that very fucking night!"

My memory of Cal wasn't of a love meant for the ages, but I had no idea what she was talking about. I'd been disappointed when we broke up so he could go to Spain, but I understood why. The person she was describing wasn't the person I'd cared about, though.

"I can't believe that. Cal and I had been fun together. I never thought it was going to be a forever thing, but we had fun. We cared about each other."

"Well, it wasn't like that when you got back together. He was a real dick. He left you in pieces, Nina. Pieces. It was like it was when your father died all over again. Even worse, if you ask Kim."

"Why? What happened?"

Jordan's body sagged under the weight of what she was saying. "You said some things about wanting to die. I don't think you ever really meant it, but it was a lot to deal with. I was afraid for a long time that you might do something."

"Tell me everything. I need to know."

"Honey, it's in the past, and in my opinion, that bullshit can stay there. Don't do this."

I knew she was trying to protect me, but I needed to fill in the huge blank spots in my memory. I needed to begin to figure out why my mind was keeping me in the dark about so much time.

"Jordan, I need to know what my mind's keeping from me. What happened to make me say I wanted to die?"

"You told him you loved him. For the first time, you actually weren't afraid to take that leap. You remember what you were like when we first started school, right? You were always beautiful and sweet, but you never had the guts to go out on a limb and tell someone you loved them. It was probably because of how you lost your mother. And Cal knew that. He knew how much it meant that you were finally able to open up and say you loved him. And what did he do with that gift? He ripped it to shreds."

I did remember being afraid to tell boyfriends how I felt about them. While every other girl in high school had been dying to tell their boyfriends they loved them, I dreaded it. It terrified me. They might leave and then where would I be? I'd never told Cal I loved him.

At least I didn't remember telling him. Now Jordan was saying that the only time she knew of me saying I love you to anyone other than Tristan had ended in disaster. My stomach felt like it was twisting into knots.

She wrapped her arms around me. "Honey, don't get down about it. Cal was an asshole. He didn't deserve you. He deserved the girl who used him and threw him away three months later."

I pushed her away and shook my head. "I need to know what happened. What did he do?"

"Don't do this. It's not going to make anything better."

"Jordan, this is part of my life I don't remember. I have to know."

Sighing heavily, she nodded. "He'd been cheating on you the whole time. We went out for a drink because you were so happy that you'd finally told him how you felt and we saw him with some cheap blonde. It was terrible. You confronted him all in tears, and she was more than happy to tell you how long they'd been seeing each other. He tried to deny it, but it was no use. The proof was standing there in front of you basically throwing it in your face."

God, had I never had any luck with men? Cal had been the one man I'd remembered in all this as a decent person, and now that was all wrong too.

Jordan smoothed my hair away from my face. Her expression was so sad. "You never meant that you wanted to die, honey. That was just something you said because you were feeling down. I know how it feels. It hurts like hell when you care about someone and they betray you. We've all been through it, and sometimes when we're feeling our worst, we say things we don't mean."

"I don't want to die, Jordan. Even when I've felt like I was totally lost these past few weeks, I never wanted to end it."

"I think Tristan's a big part of that, Nina. He's a good man. And I swear to you on a stack of Bibles that he's crazy about you."

"I know. There's no need to sell him to me. I can see it."

She looked away from me and said quietly, "I'm worried you won't give him a chance now."

"Why?"

Turning to face me, she knitted her brows in concern. "Because of what I told you. I don't want you to think you're just unlucky with men."

It was as if Jordan was reading my mind. The only happy memory I'd had concerning the opposite sex, other than Tristan, was Cal. Now that he had turned out to be just like every other male I'd ever been with that I could remember, all I could think of was that I was jinxed in the realm of love.

"Me unlucky? Look at my life. No worries about luck there," I said with as much bravado I could muster, not even convincing myself. I forced a smile as I looked at my cell phone for the time. "I guess it's time to go."

"Okay, honey. Okay."

I knew Jordan didn't believe me, but like the best friend she was, she didn't say a thing. She knew talking about it wasn't going to help now. "Tristan and I would like you and Justin to join us for New Year's. We'll be at the penthouse and it would mean so much to me if we could all hang out."

The darkness that had covered her features lifted and her genuine smile lit up the room. "That would be great! If his penthouse is anything like that suite he put me up in, it'll be incredible."

I couldn't help but grin. Tristan's penthouse was stunning, and I couldn't wait to show it off to Jordan. Just the view was going to blow her away.

"He'll have his cooks make some late night dinner for us and we'll watch the new year come in high above the city. How does ten o'clock sound?"

"I can't wait! It'll be fun!" she squealed as she enveloped me in a bear hug. As she held me, I felt her grow serious. In my ear, she said quietly, "Take care of yourself. I want you to remember something. I don't know if you know what I always say, but it's true. Good things happen to good people, and you're the best, so that means great things are in store for you."

Releasing me, she smiled. "Now promise me you won't forget that."

"Not unless I have another head injury," I joked.

Jordan screwed her face into a frown. "Not funny. Now you go have an incredible Christmas and I'll see you at the top of the world at ten on New Year's Eve."

"I'll be there in sparkles and bangles."

Chapter Nine

Nina

I couldn't help but think about everything Jordan had told me as the Town Car rolled over the highway on my way back home. By the time Jensen got me back to Tristan's house, my mind was filled with doubts about love. Why had Cal betrayed me like that? We'd been so close. Or at least I'd thought we'd been. Would I ever feel the same love I'd obviously felt for Tristan before? Or was that a remnant of my forgotten past I'd never have the chance to enjoy again?

God, everything was so confusing! I felt like everywhere I turned were those funhouse mirrors that distorted people and I kept seeing myself in them—stretched out and wavy in one, flattened in another. Now Cal had to be added to the distortion.

But not Jordan or Tristan. Neither one of them ever veered away from what they'd said to me that first time I saw them in the hospital. I was lucky to have two people who cared about me. I knew that.

I put away my new clothes and flopped back onto my bed. As I lay there, I couldn't help but wonder why the memory of Cal was all I could think about.

Listen to what Jordan said and don't be stupid, Nina. You have a great guy here who tells you he loves you all the time and means it. Leave Cal where he belongs. In the past.

I knew I should leave him in my forgotten past. I just couldn't.

Tristan and I had dinner promptly at five, as I'd come to find out was our routine. He smiled when he saw me and said he'd had a great day after our rendezvous, but those sexy brown eyes told a different story about his day. Perhaps after taking off so much time to tend to me after my accident, the work he'd neglected had finally caught up to him. Whatever it was that made him look so exhausted, I wished I could make it all go away.

Pushing his plate away from him, he forced a smile. "How was your day after you left Le Ciel?"

I felt a blush race over my cheeks at the mention of our time at the boutique. "It was good. I went to see Jordan. She said she and Justin would come to celebrate New Year's Eve with us. I think she's looking forward to it."

Tristan reached out his hand to cover mine as it sat on the table. "And are you?"

"I am. I think we'll have a great time."

His smile softened, becoming more genuine. "Good. Any idea what we should feed them?"

"Cocktail weenies?" I said with a giggle.

Raising his eyebrows, he smirked. "I think my chef can do better than that. Perhaps I'll let him run with the menu. I promise you'll love it."

"I'm sure I will…love it," I said as I slid my hand out from under his.

He noticed its movement immediately and looked down at the spot where my hand had sat and then up at my face. "Is there something wrong, Nina? I'd thought after last night and this morning, we'd turned a corner. Was I wrong?"

I didn't know if he was wrong. The time we'd spent together at the penthouse the night before had been incredible. And the dressing room at Le Ciel? Mind blowing. There was no doubt in my mind that the sex between us worked. It worked like with no one before. But I had to wonder about the feelings underneath what we did with one another when we were naked.

"No. It was great. There's no denying that."

Tristan's eyebrows knitted in that look of concern that he seemed to wear a lot, mostly because of me. "But something's wrong?"

I couldn't think of a way to say what was on my mind, so I just went with the straightforward truth. "There's no doubt we rock it in bed. No doubt. But is sex all we are? I mean, couples usually do normal couples stuff."

"Like?" he asked with a distinct edge to his voice.

"Like sit around and watch movies," I blurted out, unsure if that's what I meant at all.

"You want to watch a movie tonight? Is that what you're saying?"

I could tell by the look on his face that he was confused by my attitude toward him. I couldn't blame him. We'd made love over and over the night before, and then the Le Ciel thing had happened, so he had every right to think that I was beginning to feel something for him.

I was. I just didn't know how to feel about that.

"Could we? Did we ever do that, or did we only have sex all over the place?"

On those rare occasions when Tristan really smiled, he was the most incredibly stunning man I'd ever seen. At that moment when I asked if all we'd ever done was have sex, one of those true smiles broke out across his face, lighting up even his tired eyes.

"Yes, we've watched movies before. You tend to like ones I don't and vice versa, but I'm sure we can compromise."

"Good."

Loosening his tie, he focused his gaze on me. "But I want to get something straight with you. Just because we're attracted to one another doesn't mean we never cared for each other. The two things are not mutually exclusive."

"I'm sorry. I didn't mean anything by that."

"I think you have some idea that because I want you that I can't be in love with you. Nothing could be further from the truth, Nina."

This was one of those times I was sure he had some mind reading ability he used on me. Even before I'd realized it, he'd nailed down what had been playing on my mind since Jordan had told me about Cal.

I looked down at my hands as they sat in my lap. "I guess I'm just worried that sex was all there was between us." Looking up, I saw him staring at me with what looked like hurt in his eyes. "Not that the sex isn't great, but was there more?"

"The sex was great—is great—because there is more. Your mind may not know it yet, but your heart does. Listen to it, Nina."

When he looked at me with those eyes that seemed to look straight into my soul, I couldn't help but prayed that he was right. I wanted to listen to my heart. It's just that my head kept interrupting with all those doubts about him. About love. About Cal.

I needed to know why Cal had so easily dumped me for some girl after I'd told him I'd loved him. Something inside told me that if I didn't find out what had happened between us, then nothing would ever truly be right between Tristan and me.

He interpreted my silence as rejection and leaned back in his chair. "I'm happy to give you all the time you need, Nina. All I ask is that you not fight feeling something for me."

"That's not it, Tristan. I didn't mean…" I let my sentence trail off into the uncomfortable feeling that had formed around us right there in that dining room. I felt bad, but I was sure once I found out what had happened with Cal, everything between Tristan and me could be right. Maybe it would be even better than it had been before.

He stood from the table and placed his napkin next to his plate. "Let me get changed and we'll haggle over that movie. Sound good?"

"Sure. That sounds great. Give me a few minutes and I'll meet you in…" I stopped because I didn't know where to say to meet him. The media room? His room? Now that we'd slept together, spending the night with him in his room seemed like the next logical step, but I wasn't sure it meant the same thing to him.

"Let's get some use out of that media room. I'll meet you there in say twenty minutes? I have some work I have to take care of, but I'll tell Rogers to make some popcorn."

His desire to watch the movie not in his room but in the media room confused me. Maybe last night hadn't meant what I thought it had. But then again, he was the one always professing love.

As he left the dining room, I worked to clear my muddled head. It was probably better if we kept our living arrangements like they'd been for a little while more anyway. I needed to find out about what had made the only other man I'd ever said I love you to leave me. Once the past was cleared up, the present could begin to be great.

At least I hoped so.

Tristan's media room wasn't like any room normal people watched movies in. More like a movie theater than a room, it had an enormous U-shaped black chenille sectional couch that felt like heaven to sit on.

Extra deep, the seats were almost as big as chaise lounges all around. It faced a TV that was so big it took up almost the entire wall. I felt tiny in this room so full of big things.

Easing back onto the sofa, I let myself enjoy the luxury. He did know how to live.

"Don't get too comfortable," he announced as he entered the room, his arms full with a yellow plastic bowl overflowing with buttery popcorn and a roll of paper towels.

I sat up quickly, unsure what he meant. "Why?"

"We need to have some of this popcorn. Three pans of Jiffy Pop popcorn are here waiting for us to dig in."

He placed the bowl on the coffee table in the center of the sofa and walked back to begin the movie as I took a handful of popcorn. The familiar taste of that buttery and salty snack was delicious, even after our perfectly prepared steak dinner.

Popping another kernel in my mouth, I looked back at him. "I haven't had Jiffy Pop in years! I wouldn't think you'd be a Jiffy Pop guy."

He shook his head. "I'm not. I'd never had it before you asked for it one night when we watched one of your chick flicks."

I twisted my face into a look of fake disgust at his cheap shot at my favorite type of movie. "So when did you run out to get some Jiffy Pop in the last twenty minutes?"

He sat down beside me as the movie began. "I didn't. We have it here all the time since you told me you liked it."

"Oh. Well, that's good to know. You know, just in case I decide I want popcorn at two in the morning."

Tristan's casual statement rocked me. I tried to hide how much it meant to me behind my joking, but I was truly touched by his attentiveness.

"So are you ready for some Iron Man 2?"

"And this is what you call haggling? I'm not getting a chick flick vibe here," I teased.

Putting his arm around me, he pulled me close and grinned. "Yes and no. It's not a chick flick, but it's got great cars and there's a girl."

"Please tell me you at least believe I like this movie."

As the film began and he dimmed the lights, he softly kissed my lips. "You do. Trust me."

I ended up loving the movie, and by the time we fell asleep in each other's arms right there in the media room, I was almost convinced that, in the end, my heart would have the final say instead of my head.

The winter sun warmed my room as it woke me the next morning. I rolled over and focused on the clock. 8:05. Looking around, I saw I was in my bedroom tucked under the covers. I vaguely remembered Tristan carrying me there and putting me to bed after the movie.

As I slowly came back to life, I saw a sheet of white paper on the pillow next to me. As was his habit, Tristan had left me his own version of a good morning kiss. No envelope this time. Just a sheet of stationery.

Dear Nina,

Thank you for the movie date. I'm happy you enjoyed it. I'll be busy all day, but tonight I thought we'd visit one of our favorite restaurants. I'll pick you up at six sharp.

Love,
Tristan

My eyes slid over the words, noting each stroke of his handwriting. I'd grown to love these notes from him, even feeling disappointed when he didn't leave one. As I reread his letter, I wondered what restaurant he meant. I guessed I'd see at six.

After a quick shower, I dressed in a cute navy blue sweater dress and knee-high boots and headed to the kitchen for some much needed coffee. As I sipped the French Vanilla roast blend, I thought about the day ahead of me, nervous about what I'd find out.

"Miss, is there anything you need?"

I looked around and saw Rogers standing in the doorway. His expression was kind, as it had been the day I arrived at this house, but he watched me like a hawk, his dark eyes following every move I made. With his slicked back steel grey hair and long face, he reminded me of a maître d' at one of those exclusive restaurants.

Lifting my mug of coffee, I smiled and shook my head. "Got everything I need. Thanks. I'll pick something up to eat in the city when I go shopping."

As soon as I said the words, I felt guilty, as if going to visit someone from my past was a bad thing. Lying had never been something I was good at. I knew Tristan's butler saw my guilt too. Something in the way his eyes grew wider for just a moment told me he didn't believe me.

He stood silently looking at me, and every second that went by I grew more uncomfortable. I began to fidget and my eyes darted around the room to avoid his stare. Finally, I croaked out, "Well, guess it's time to head out. Have a good one."

Rogers nodded slowly and moved aside to allow me to pass, but I felt his eyes on me the whole time. I couldn't tell if it was my own guilty conscience or his silent judging me about something else, but I felt sick all of a sudden.

"Jensen, I'm meeting Jordan to shop, so feel free to take a break. Get some lunch," I chirped out to Tristan's driver.

He lowered his slightly graying head and smiled. I didn't get any sense that he suspected me of anything as Rogers seemed to have, so I happily marched into Macy's and waited for what seemed like long enough before I ducked out the nearest exit.

Out to Cal's office four blocks away.

I raced up the street, walking as fast as I could in my boots, among the throngs of people headed out on their day's business. As I passed the men and women on their way to wherever they were going, I wondered if any of them was like me—going to talk to a ghost from her past.

Cal's office was on the fifteenth floor of a typical skyscraper in Manhattan. I stepped inside the building and looked for the elevator, eager to speak to him and hopefully find out what about me had made it so easy for him to turn his back on my love. I wasn't sure I wanted to know, to be honest, but I was sure I needed to.

The elevator stopped on his floor, and I stepped out into a greeting area for the firm he worked for as an actuary. I'd found out he worked at Peak International with just a few minutes of online searching, and as I stood behind a gentleman in an overcoat waiting to speak to the receptionist, I began to doubt my initial idea of meeting with Cal.

The reception area was modest, with older chairs and a carpet that reminded me of the cream and burgundy print one my grandmother had in her living room when I was a child. The walls were off white, but I couldn't decide if they'd been painted that shade or aged to that color.

"May I help you?" the attractive Asian woman behind the desk asked.

Torn from my thoughts, I smiled and said, "Yes. I'm hoping to see Cal Johnson. Is he in?"

"Who may I say is here to see him?"

I took a deep breath in and exhaled slowly. "Nina Edwards."

The receptionist nodded. "If you'll take a seat, I'll buzz him, miss."

I sat on one of the upholstered waiting area chairs and smoothed my dress over my thighs in an effort to calm myself and dry my hands drenched with nervous sweat. A hundred recriminations ran through my mind, making me want to bolt out the door, but I remained planted in the chair and tried to focus on the possibility of what Cal could tell me about what happened between us. An elderly couple seated next to me whispered to each other about life insurance as I worked to stay relaxed.

"Nina?"

I looked up at the sound of a man's voice and saw Cal standing at the receptionist's desk. He looked like I remembered—light brown hair, blue eyes that hadn't faded a bit, and an athlete's body visible even under his white shirt and brown dress pants.

"Cal," I said with nervous enthusiasm. "Do you have a few minutes? I was hoping we could talk."

Extending his arm toward me, he smiled and nodded. "Sure. Come with me. We'll talk in my office."

Cal led me to his office halfway down the hallway. A small room, it had a single window that let in some light but was overall quite dim. His glass and metal desk took up a majority of the space, but there was room enough for one chair for me to sit in.

"Excuse my office. I generally don't get visitors. Take a seat and tell me what you've been up to."

His voice telegraphed loud and clear that he was uncomfortable, which only served to make me more uneasy than I'd been just minutes before out in the waiting area. Taking a deep breath, I said, "I wanted to talk about us."

"Us? Uh, what about us?"

My hands fidgeted in my lap, and I planted my feet on the floor to stop my legs from shaking. "Cal, I was in a car accident a few weeks ago. I can't remember anything from right before my father died four years ago. I know we're not together anymore, but I was hoping you could tell me what happened to break us up."

A look of discomfort settled into his features. "Oh, I don't know, Nina. That was a long time ago."

"It's important to me, Cal. Anything you can tell me would help."

He seemed to study me for a moment and then a slow smile spread across his face, reminding me of that person I'd dated all those years ago. "I think it's about time I apologized, Nina. I was a real ass. To be honest, if it weren't for the fact that you can't remember anything, you'd probably never speak to me again, and I'd deserve it."

"What happened to us? I remember us being happy. I mean, I know we weren't ready to make it forever, but I thought we were happy."

Cal shifted in his office chair. "We were young. I was probably more immature than most guys at that age. I didn't…uh…I didn't realize what I had."

I didn't know what to say to that. Jordan had made him sound like the worst of all men, but the man who sat across the desk from me seemed to regret how we'd ended. If anything, he looked sad.

"I guess I just needed to know it wasn't me, Cal."

Shaking his head, he knitted his brows and frowned. "No. I don't want you to think that. It wasn't you. It was me."

"Oh, the old It's-not-you-it's-me thing," I joked.

He reached over and touched my hand resting on the edge of his desk. His eyes told me he didn't think this was a joking matter. "I hate to think that before your accident you thought it was because of anything you did that we broke up."

I didn't know what I'd thought then, but he was right. Ever since Jordan told me what had happened, I'd been convinced Cal had cheated on me because of some lack in me. That whoever he'd chosen over me was prettier, smarter, or better at whatever else he wanted.

"It's okay, Cal. I can't remember that now. It's just nice to know that what happened wasn't because of some deficiency in me."

He grimaced at the word 'deficiency.' "I'm sorry that you thought that. That's not right. You were lacking nothing, Nina. I was the one lacking in maturity."

We sat there quietly for a long moment before a knock on his office door broke the awkward silence. Calling the person in, he quickly shook off the seriousness of his words and put on his professional face again. As he and his coworker spoke, I stood to leave, having gotten what I'd come for.

His colleague left, and Cal stood from behind his desk. "Would you like to have coffee sometime? It would be nice to be friends, if you think we can."

"That would be nice. I can't promise I won't want to ask more questions, though. Everything's such a blank from around that time. But I don't want you to think I blame you for anything. That was a long time ago, and we've both moved on."

"It's the least I could do, Nina. And don't worry about blaming me. I deserve it. I just hope we can be friends."

I extended my hand to shake his. "It's a deal."

"Good." He wrote something on a piece of paper and handed it to me. "Here's my cell number and email. I'd love it if we could grab a coffee before the holidays."

I took the information with a smile and slipped it into my purse. "Me too. I'll email you and let you know when I'm going to be in the city again."

"You still live in Brooklyn? I heard you and Jordan were sharing an apartment in Sunset Park."

His mention of my place in Brooklyn surprised me. I shook my head and said for the first time to anyone since I left the hospital, "No, I live upstate now in Dutchess County."

Cal's expression showed his surprise. "You introduced yourself as Nina Edwards, so I thought you were still single. Did you marry?"

"No. I'm still Nina Edwards, but I live with my boyfriend out there. Tristan. Tristan Stone."

I had the sense that the mere mention of Tristan's name changed everything in the room, and Cal's smile seemed to fade just a little.

"You did well for yourself, Nina. Stone's a big deal."

I nodded, unsure of what exactly Cal meant. Turning to leave, I smiled and said, "We'll do coffee before Christmas. Thanks again, Cal. I appreciate you taking the time to talk to me."

As I opened the door, Cal said quietly, "Take care, Nina. I look forward to seeing you again."

My talk with Cal had buoyed my spirits. I'd been so afraid that he'd left me because of me that I hadn't wanted to give Tristan a chance to do the same thing. Now I felt like I could truly let him in and begin to make those new memories, just as he'd promised.

Chapter Ten

Tristan

Looking down at my phone as it buzzed against the top of my desk, I saw a message from Jensen. *Driving home now.* After waiting for nearly an hour to hear from him after his first message telling me Nina had left Macy's and gone to an office building four blocks away, my stomach was tied up in angry knots. The bodyguards who followed us at all times were little help too. All they seemed to know was that she'd gone to the fifteenth floor to some insurance company to see someone named Cal Johnson.

Just seeing that name come up on my phone made my blood run cold. Three little letters and I could barely contain the rage that exploded inside me. Cal, the guy she remembered while I was a stranger. Cal, the ex-boyfriend who had broken her heart. What the fuck could she want with him?

Swiping away Jensen's message, I dialed another number I knew would help me find out what Nina had been up to. A few rings and finally I heard the raspy voice of Daryl Knight.

"Daryl, I have another job for you."

"Tristan. Just the man I wanted to talk to. I finally got something on that Edwards business. We should meet."

Daryl Knight was the man I used to investigate private matters associated with Stone Worldwide, such as researching the actresses' backgrounds to make sure there was nothing unsavory in their pasts before I was seen with them in public. A big, burly guy, he looked more like a mountain man than a private investigator with his full reddish-brown beard and wild curly hair. At first glance, he hadn't seemed to be someone who could find out much of anything without getting noticed, but he'd proven me wrong enough times that I knew if I wanted the details about someone, Daryl was the man to call.

"Fine. Let's say two days from now. In the meantime, I need you to find out everything you can about a man named Cal Johnson."

"Is Cal his real name?" Daryl asked with a chuckle.

"I have no idea. I just know I want everything you can find on this guy."

"Okay. I'll have it for when we meet. You looking for this for business or personal use? You know I don't care and it's none of my business, but do you want me to focus on the gorier details?"

"Both. I want to know where he lives, what he eats, how he makes his money, who he's fucking and if she likes it. You understand me?"

"Got it. What time are we meeting?"

"Thursday at noon."

I ended the call, pushed my phone away in disgust, and leaned back in my chair. I had to hold myself back from racing home at a hundred miles an hour to ask Nina why she'd lied and snuck off to some office where her old boyfriend spent his days.

Jealousy coursed through my veins, and my stomach turned at the thought of her with any other man. In my mind, I saw her naked body sprawled across his desk as he fucked her next to his low budget sticky notes and dollar store stapler. He wore a cheap suit and feared being found out, so he didn't even take his shirt off. Muffled grunts came from his mouth as he rammed his cock into her, his middle manager features all twisted into an ugly sex face while he hovered over the woman I loved.

Over and over, the awful scene played in my head until I couldn't take it anymore. I couldn't just sit there in my corner office torturing myself all afternoon. Pressing the intercom on the corner of my desk, I called for my assistant.

Michelle opened the door to my office and stood waiting for my instructions. The last showing of the ugly movie of Nina cheating on me played in my mind, and I heard Michelle say, "Mr. Stone? You wanted me?"

I shook away my thoughts and focused on the woman in front of me. In many ways, Michelle reminded me of Nina. Gentle and sweet, she cared about her job and me, always making sure every detail was taken care of for every assignment I gave her. Slightly older than Nina, she had dark brown hair, brown eyes, and was married to some advertising guy whose main claim to fame was the semi-successful campaign for some Greek yogurt made here in the States before every yogurt maker in the business began doing the Greek thing. I vaguely remembered her referring to him once as Jeff or Jess and saying they lived in Queens.

"Yes. I'm leaving, so cancel any meetings I have this afternoon. Message me if anything comes up that I need to know about."

"Yes, Mr. Stone. Should I call a car for you?"

Shaking my head, I stood from my desk and slipped back into my suit coat. "No. I'm taking my car."

"What should I say to Mr. Dreger if he calls?" she asked as I walked toward her to leave.

Karl would surely be calling if he got a sense that I'd left the office. The man had basically taken to stalking me since he'd found out about Nina, which had necessitated the two bodyguards who followed Nina and me around whenever we went out, and Nina whenever she was alone.

"Tell him I chose to work from home today. If he presses you for details, tell him you know nothing more and have him call me directly."

Michelle smiled and stood aside as I opened the door. Remembering Karl's penchant for trying to sneak around behind my back to spy on me, I added, "And lock this door when I leave. Do not let anyone in."

She looked at me with surprise in her eyes, but I knew she understood what I was telling her. "You can trust me, Mr. Stone. No one will get in."

"Thank you, Michelle. I'll message you if I'm not coming into the office tomorrow. If I don't, the same thing applies. No one gets in. No one."

"I understand. Have a good night," she said with a sympathetic smile, likely sensing there was something wrong but never asking since we weren't that close. She wished me a good night anytime I left the office, and rarely had I made the effort to say it back to her.

For some reason, the way she was looking up at me at that moment made me want to say it now, though. "Have a good night, Michelle."

My simple effort was rewarded with a broad smile, which made me feel better until I thought of Nina smiling just like that for Cal as she left his office, her light brown hair and her clothes all disheveled from her time with him. Disgusted, I turned and stormed out to get into my car, eager to take my aggression out on the highway between Manhattan and home.

Jensen was outside the garage when I pulled up to the house. I parked the Jag and saw he wasn't there by coincidence. He was waiting for me.

"Mr. Stone, I want to apologize. I neglected my duties and Miss Edwards could have been harmed."

Jensen's mouth turned down in a frown as he stood waiting for me to respond to his confession. While Nina might not remember anything of the recent past, he did and he knew I did. After the attack on her at the apartment by that guy fucked up on whatever drugs he was on, I'd been clear with Jensen that if she was hurt again, it would mean his job.

But she hadn't been hurt, and now that the bodyguards were always around, I didn't expect Jensen, a man in his fifties, to do the work of younger men.

"She wasn't hurt, so we're fine. In truth, the bodyguards I hired are there to protect her more than you are. I still expect you to keep your eyes open for anything suspicious, however, so letting her give you the slip today is a problem."

He hung his head. "I know. I shouldn't have listened to her when she said she was meeting her friend to go shopping. I'm truly sorry, Mr. Stone."

As furious as I was, it wasn't directed at my driver. He was merely someone caught in the middle, and there was no point reaming him out. Reaching out, I patted him on the shoulder. "It's fine, Jensen. No harm, no foul. Just don't let it happen again. I rely on you."

He looked up at me with tired eyes and nodded as relief began to wash over him. "Thank you."

"Where are West and Varo? I want to talk to them too," I asked as I looked around for any sign of them.

"I believe they're around back. They arrived right after we did."

"Okay, relax, Jensen. If Nina and I go out tonight, I'll be driving, so unless something changes, you have the night off."

I followed the brick pathway around the back of the house and across the property to find the bodyguards and hear what they knew about Nina's afternoon adventure. Both men stood near the carriage house where they stayed after my firing of the gardener. Large and bulky, they were exactly what I wanted in the people protecting Nina. They had a bouncer look to them, but as long as they did their job, I didn't care what they looked like.

They stood talking to one another, and a twinge of embarrassment pinched at me as I thought about what I needed to ask them. I suddenly felt like a goddamned fool.

"Gentlemen, I want a report of what happened today."

I spoke with as little emotion as possible, hoping for a matter-of-fact tone to hide the anger and jealousy that continued to churn in my gut. It was bad enough that I knew Nina had gone to see her ex. Having to hear these two tell me the details of it was nothing short of painful.

West was the more talkative one, so he spoke up first. "Miss Edwards left Macy's by a different door than the one she entered through and walked four blocks to an office building on West 39th. She entered the building and rode up to the fifteenth floor to the Peak International offices, an insurance company. She met with a man named Cal Johnson for about twenty minutes and left, returning to the car to ride home."

Talkative for West meant doing the Joe Friday thing—just the facts and little else. He even had that uptight cop look. I was going to have to ask for details.

"Did she look like she'd been harmed? You better hope the answer is no, gentlemen."

Varo, the younger of the two men, shook his head silently, his piercing dark blue eyes staring at me as if he knew what I was getting at, as West continued his report. "She looked the same as when she entered the building, sir. Hair and dress were exactly the same. In addition, she didn't look upset. She looked just as she always does."

"And the person she met with?" I asked with my heart in my throat.

"Average height and athletic build. Brown hair and neither of us noticed the eye color. He seems to be some kind of insurance salesman."

"Did she see you following her?"

Both men shook their heads, and Varo answered for the first time. "She never sees us. She's not looking for us, so we're not seen."

Nothing in what they'd said should have added to my unhappiness with the whole situation, but their answers hadn't helped me feel better either. I waved them away as I walked toward the house to face the final person in this whole affair.

Unfortunately, Rogers was waiting in the foyer, yet another person I had to deal with before I got to Nina. I was definitely not in the mood for his thoughts on my love life at that moment, but his expression looked almost pleasant.

"What do you want, Rogers? I'm in a hurry."

"Just to ask if dinner was to be served at the usual time."

"No. Nina and I are going out."

Rogers nodded slowly. "As you wish."

Behind him on the table in the center of the foyer lay an envelope. It was the same kind I used for her letters and had my name written on the front of it.

"Where is Nina?"

"In her room, I believe."

My hands shook at the thought of what she may have written in the letter. Was this her way of breaking the news to me that she and Cal were back together? Just the idea made me feel empty, like I'd lost everything important to me. Snatching the note from the table, I left Rogers standing there with his semi-smiling face and hurried to my room.

I sat down on the edge of the bed, the note still in my hand. Every time I'd written to her had been to express something I couldn't say to her face—something that was dear to me but I couldn't get out in person. Was it the same for her this time? She'd never shied away from telling me exactly how she felt, so why begin now?

All these questions raced through my mind as I looked down at that white envelope with her handwriting on it.

I wasn't letting her go. It didn't matter what the letter said. I wasn't giving Nina up. Cal couldn't have her back. He didn't deserve her. I didn't even know what he'd done, but I knew he didn't deserve her. Maybe I didn't deserve her either, but at least I loved her. I loved her and I wasn't going to give up on her.

The envelope wasn't sealed and the flap lifted easily, so I slid the letter out and unfolded it. The paper felt heavy in my hands, as if it was a two ton weight I was holding. My eyes focused on the first words, and I began to read.

Dear Tristan,

I didn't think it was fair that you had no letters from me, so I chose this way to say what I have to say. I realized today that even if I knew nothing about you except what I've come to know in the weeks since meeting you in the hospital, I'd know that I'm the luckiest woman in the world. I can't wait to go to our favorite restaurant tonight!

Yours,
Nina

I threw the letter on the bed and raced to Nina's room, overcome with relief from what she'd written. My heart slammed against my chest with excitement as I marched down the hallway to her room, and I stopped short at her door to calm myself before I charged through it like a mad bull. Taking a deep breath, I knocked and pushed the door open to see her sitting on her bed as if she'd been waiting for me.

"Hey, what's up?" she asked sweetly. "Did you get my letter?"

Her smile lit up the room, and I walked to her bedside to pull her into my arms. All the anger and jealousy that had churned inside me for hours disappeared when I held her, as if she was the lone antidote to all my misery.

I kissed her hard on the mouth, not wanting to hold back anything I was feeling for one of the first times since she'd come home. She was my Nina, and I wanted every part of her for mine.

She pulled away and looked up into my eyes. "Tristan, are you okay? I thought you'd be happy with my letter."

Cradling her face in my hands, I kissed her again, softer this time. "I was. Very happy. I liked that you wrote me something."

"Then what's going on? You have this weird look in your eyes. Is something wrong?"

I wanted to hear her tell me where she went that afternoon and what happened. I wanted to believe that she wouldn't keep that from me, but as I stood looking down at her, she said nothing.

"No. I was happy to read your letter and wanted to see you. What made you write it?"

Looking away, she took a deep breath and looked back at me. "I just realized that maybe I am someone you could love."

"Definitely."

"You're home early. Working from home again, Mr. Casual?" she asked as she tugged playfully on my tie.

"Always about my suit and tie. Maybe it's time I changed it up a bit."

"Sweatpants?" She looked me up and down and giggled. "Yeah, I can see it. Grey sweatpants with a mustard stain down the front of them. Maybe a ripped T-shirt?"

Nina's teasing lifted my spirits and I couldn't help but smile. "I'm going to have to work on how you see me. Sweatpants?"

"Well, maybe shorts? You have nice legs. It's something we have in common."

"I think we have other things in common. Did you have a nice shopping trip with Jordan? Are you ready for a great dinner tonight?"

Nina sat down on the bed with a thump and leaned back on her elbows. Eyes wide, she faked an innocent look and ignored my questions. "I swear to God, Tristan Stone, that you're trying to fatten me up. I don't think I've ever eaten this much in my life."

I looked down at her dress as it rode up her thighs, showing just a hint of the top of her stockings. I wanted to hear her answer about her shopping trip, but my need for her overtook my need to hear why she met with another man behind my back. Leaning down over her, I slid my hand up her leg as I balanced on my other forearm. "You look incredible no matter what I feed you." Looking down at my fingers as they slid under her stocking, I said, "I like the way these look."

Nina moaned softly as my fingers traced up her thigh to where it met her body. Arching her back, she groaned, "Oddly enough, I only seem to have these kind of stockings. Would you know anything about that?"

Smiling, I gently pushed my hand between her legs and felt the damp cotton. I slid my middle finger under it to feel her cunt soaked and willing for me. She closed her eyes and licked her lips as I slowly trailed my fingertip from her excited clit to her wet opening.

I loved the feel of her tender skin under my touch. The way her body opened up to take me into her and give me everything she was.

Then, from somewhere deep in my mind, a tiny spike of jealousy tore through me, ripping every gentle feeling from me until all I could think about was Nina with Cal just hours earlier. I pulled away from her and stood up as the knot in my stomach returned and my hands clenched in rage.

Nina opened her eyes and stared up at me in confusion. "Tristan, what's wrong?"

"I have work I have to do. We'll leave at six. No need to dress up. Wear whatever feels comfortable."

Sitting up, she frowned. "Oh. I thought we were going to our favorite restaurant."

Straightening my tie, I nodded. "We are. I'll see you at six."

And with that I left, needing to escape from everything she made me feel. The ecstasy. The pain. And everything in between.

CHAPTER ELEVEN

Tristan

I couldn't turn off the feelings just thinking of Nina and Cal created in me, so I did what I always did when I couldn't control my emotions. After an hour run and beating the hell out of the speed bag, I could at least say I'd reined in the worst of the ugliness that had threatened to take me over. I stood in the shower with my head hung as the water streamed down my back until it ran cold, unable to wrestle those final shreds of jealousy and hatred that continued to spin inside my mind. Over and over, I told myself that Nina cared for me. That I wasn't reading her signals wrong.

And over and over the truth that I couldn't shake from my soul raised its ugly head and forced me to admit its existence: she'd snuck away to meet another man and hadn't told me when I'd given her the chance.

My chest felt like a weight was pressing down on it. Every breath I took hurt, as if the simple act of taking air in was all wrong. An emptiness made the pit of my stomach ache as I tortured myself with that same scene of Nina with Cal on his cheap desk.

I knew I couldn't show her this side of me. She'd never love me if she knew my demons. How many times had my shrinks lectured me on the need to control my emotions? I'd been more than successful, in my opinion. I kept myself and my heart walled off and life had been good. Well, if not good, at least not painful for me or the rest of the world.

Then Nina came into my life and every emotion she brought out in me seemed magnified. I wanted her. I needed her. She was all I thought about from the moment I found out what Karl and his friends on the Board planned to do. And then I fell in love with her and she became my life.

My brain raced with thoughts about her ex. I hated him, and I didn't even know him. I didn't care. I hated him because he had a place in her mind. She'd let him into her heart once, so why wouldn't she again?

Of all the things I could give her, he had that one priceless thing I couldn't. Her past.

I waited for Nina at the end of her hallway, not knowing what I'd do if she kept her visit to Cal a secret. At six exactly, she opened her door and came toward me in the same dress she'd worn earlier.

When she'd snuck off to meet him.

She stopped dead in front of me and looked me up and down. "You aren't in a suit? I don't think I've ever seen you not in a suit. Well, except when you're not wearing any clothes at all."

A cute blush pinkened her cheeks, making her even more beautiful.

"I don't think jeans and a shirt are anything that different, Nina."

Stepping toward me, she hooked her thumbs in the belt loops near my zipper. "I like this look. Even jeans look incredible on you. You okay now?"

I wasn't okay, but she was too sweet standing there looking up with those beautiful blue eyes for me to shut her out again, so I pushed down my feelings about Cal. "Troubles at work. Nothing to worry about. I'm hungry. I hope you are."

As I turned to walk toward the car, she caught my arm and pulled me back to kiss me. Standing on her toes, she crushed her mouth into mine as she pushed her body against me, exciting me even if I didn't want to want her at that moment. That's what kind of effect she had on me.

When she pulled away for a moment, I asked, "Did you remember something you want to tell me?"

"Yes and no. Let's just say that I'm looking at things between us a little differently now."

I liked this new Nina, but I hoped her change of heart didn't have anything to do with her midday rendezvous. "Really? Anything you want to talk about?"

She kissed me softly and smiled. "First, I want to see our favorite restaurant. After that, who knows?"

I accepted her answer and tried hard to push Cal and all my jealousy away. "Your chariot awaits, my lady."

I'd arranged for Tony's Little Pizza Heaven to be ours exclusively for the night, just in case she remembered something. I didn't want her feeling overwhelmed by a memory and have to deal with the other patrons at the same time.

We walked from the parking lot around to the front of the building, and just as we reached the front door, she took my hand in hers. It was the first time since before the accident, and when I looked down at the sight of her hand so delicate in mine, it seemed so natural, like that's where it belonged.

"I can't wait to see this place!" she said as she looked in the window.

We sat at the same table as the first time we ate there, and I hoped that even that might spur some memory. Nina looked around wide-eyed at the decor as the waitress who'd been there the night I asked her to marry me arrived to take our order. In seconds, I realized I hadn't thought of everything.

Recognizing us, she lowered her order pad and pen, and smiled, her eyes wide with friendly enthusiasm. "I haven't seen you guys in weeks! How are you?"

Nina looked at me, unsure of what to say, and before I could answer, the waitress said to her, "I have to tell you I've told everyone I know about how lucky you are. What he did that night was so sweet. So when's the big day?"

She winced, like she was embarrassed, and I quickly stood from my seat. "Nina, excuse me. I need to speak to the waitress for a moment."

The woman looked even more confused than Nina did as I guided her toward the back room. In a low voice, I whispered, "I'm sorry, but she doesn't know what you're talking about. There was an accident and she suffered a head injury that made her forget a lot of things."

"Oh, sweetie. I'm so sorry. I didn't know. You two were just the nicest couple and what you did that night was so romantic. I just wanted to wish you well."

"It's okay, but she doesn't remember."

The waitress touched my arm in sympathy. "Are you saying she doesn't remember saying yes or she doesn't remember anything at all?"

I looked over at Nina sitting alone and said quietly, "Nothing at all."

"I'm so sorry. I'll get your usual, if that's okay, and leave you two alone. I hope things get better for you real soon."

Taking my seat next to Nina, I saw the sadness in her eyes. Our night out was already a mess.

"I'm sorry about that."

"Tristan, did you make sure we'd be alone here tonight?"

I nodded. "Yeah, but I didn't remember that the waitress who served us before might be here. I'm sorry. I should have thought of that."

She covered my hand with hers and smiled. "That you went to that much trouble is so sweet, but you can't shield me from everyone who may remember more than I do. I appreciate the effort, but you don't have to. I have to accept that people like her remember things I don't."

An uneasy silence settled in between us as Nina slid her hand back to rest in her lap. It felt like we were strangers suddenly, so different from the two people flirting in her hallway just a short while earlier.

The waitress brought our drinks, and we pretended like nothing was wrong, fooling no one. Sitting there drinking semi-flat birch beer, I wondered if we'd ever get past this stage of one step forward and three steps back. Just when I thought we'd turned a corner, we were back to being like strangers again.

"You proposed here?"

"I did. I promise it was more romantic than the time we're having now."

Nina smiled and leaned over toward me to squeeze my forearm. "Don't be so hard on yourself, Tristan. I'm having a great time. I'm here with you and I remember I love pizza, so I'm looking forward to this."

"You're being kind," I said, allowing my disappointment to show.

"Well, you said that was something you liked, right?" she asked with searching eyes.

"I did. Just one of many things."

"Like what? What do you like best about me?"

What I can't give you. Yet.

I brought her hand to my lips and kissed it, looking up at her. "I love your honesty most, Nina. When we grow old and grey and neither one of us looks like we do now, if I have your honesty, that's all I could ask for."

A pained look came over her, and when she turned away, my heart skipped a beat. Something had happened at Cal's office and she just didn't want to tell me. My blood felt like it ran cold in those moments as I waited for her to turn back to face me.

Biting her lip, she looked at me and took a deep breath. "About that. I have something to tell you."

I pasted a smile on my lips as my stomach dropped to the bottom of my body, and I feared that the next words out of her mouth would be to tell me she'd decided that she wanted to be with Cal again. Maybe having a second chance at life had made her want more. Maybe she wanted to rekindle that relationship.

No. I couldn't let her do that.

"You can tell me anything, Nina. Always remember that." Even as the words were leaving my mouth, I silently prayed that she'd never tell me what I feared I'd hear in the next seconds.

"I don't want us to start this relationship again with anything bad between us. I need to tell you about some things."

"Okay."

Nina smiled meekly and began. "I dated a man named Cal long before I met you. When I was with Jordan the other day she told me that he broke my heart by cheating on me the very night I told him I loved him. I guess it sent me into a depression. I didn't know that I ever suffered from depression until she told me."

"Nina, I'd never look down on someone because of that."

"I know. But that's not what I wanted to tell you. I had to know why he could so easily throw me away, Tristan. I had to find out."

I couldn't hold back anymore. "Because he's a fucking idiot. He's not worthy of someone like you, Nina."

Nodding, she continued. "I know. He knows too. I went to meet him at his office today. I didn't tell you because I didn't know how to say I wanted to go see an ex-boyfriend to find out why he didn't love me enough to not cheat on me."

I waited for her to say those next words that would make my world come crashing down around me. That she realized that Cal was the man she wanted, not me. With each second that ticked away, it seemed like an eternity until she finally spoke again.

Her blue eyes filled with tears, and my heart clenched in my chest as she spoke. "Cal was an immature boy back then. He knows that now. It felt so good to hear that, Tristan. All I could think of since Jordan told me what he did was that I was lacking in something that would mean he couldn't love me. But that wasn't the case. It was him, not me. I know that now."

"Nina, it would never be you. You're a beautiful woman with a lot to offer any man," I mumbled as the sound of my heartbeat pounded like a sledgehammer in my ears.

"But I guess I needed to hear Cal say that it wasn't me back then. I needed to hear that so I could believe that someone like you would really ever want me. Do you know what I mean?"

I nodded silently, waiting for her to get to the part where I was supposed to give her up.

"Tristan, you've been so patient with me and I can't thank you enough for that. I know it's been hard on you too. I think it might even be harder on you than on me. Remembering what we were when all I know is what we are now must be so painful. I'm sorry most for that."

Sorry most for that. Her words rang in my ears, like the final shot from a gun right before the bullet slammed into my heart and ripped it to pieces.

Just then, the waitress returned with our pizza, saving me from hearing what else Nina was sorry about. As we ate, I pretended that I was happy to be there and enjoying our time together. Nothing could have been further from the truth. This place that had been the scene of one of the best memories of my life was now just an empty room with us taking up a tiny sad space in it.

Nina enjoyed her return to Tony's, but I barely finished one slice of pizza before I felt too sick to stay. My mind raced with ideas, my demons trying desperately to take over. I could take her away and Cal would never be able to find her. I could make sure Jensen never took her anywhere without me, ensuring she never left. I could work at home from now on so I was always there to make sure she stayed.

"Tristan, you're so quiet. I thought you loved this place, but you only ate one piece of pizza. Are you okay?"

"I'm fine. Let's finish up and get out of here."

She was obviously surprised by my desire to leave what I'd described as our favorite place. Now it was just another place I remembered being in love and she didn't.

I threw a couple twenties on the table and stood to leave, but Nina grabbed my arm and I looked down to see her staring up at me with that look that never failed to make me want to take her in my arms and hold her forever. If this was when she planned to tell me goodbye, I'd let her say it and then deal with her hating me because I had to protect her, even if that meant watching her want another man.

"Tristan, I want to finish what I started to say. I went to see Cal today because I needed to know if there was something wrong with me. Ever since I saw you that first time in the hospital, I've doubted that you could ever feel what you say you do for me. It didn't matter how many times you said you loved me. I still felt like I didn't belong with you—that I wasn't good enough."

"Nina, whatever you thought, I need you to know that I'm not going to just give you up. I love you, and you loved me once. And if you loved me then, you can love me again."

Her eyes lit up with surprise. "Tristan, what are you talking about? I'm telling you that I finally believe everything you said. All this time I'd doubted myself, but now I realize I'm not some defective female no one can love."

Every ounce of stress left my body and I slumped back down into my chair. "Defective female? Baby, you are perfect. I don't know what those assholes you dated in the past were thinking, but you're everything I've ever wanted."

Nina leaned over toward me and kissed me gently. "I hope you aren't mad that I didn't tell you I was going to see Cal."

"I wish you would have told me."

"Would you have been okay with it?"

Shaking my head, I said, "No way. I'm never a fan of the woman I love spending time with another man, especially her ex."

"You couldn't actually think that I'd want anyone but you, could you?"

"I think it's time to go."

I stood and stepped back to let Nina out, and she reached up to put her arms around my neck. Standing on her toes, she slid her tongue over my bottom lip, teasing me. "You thought I was going to say something else, didn't you?"

Chuckling, I shrugged off her question. "No. I had no idea what you wanted to say."

She stared up into my eyes for a moment and a sexy little grin spread across her lips. "You just seem happier now. That's all. Seems suspicious."

I pushed the hair away from her face and pressed my forehead to hers. "Did you have anything else you wanted to say?"

A tiny whimper escaped from her mouth and she closed her eyes. "I think I'll save that for when we get home."

"I wasn't thinking of doing much talking when we get home," I said quietly in her ear.

We walked out to the car as rain began to fall, and my mind flashed back to that night in Venice. Covering Nina's hand with mine, I squeezed it and she looked up at me. "The last time you and I were caught in a rainstorm was in Venice."

She stopped short as the rain began to fall harder. "I've been to Venice?" she asked in a stunned voice.

"Yeah. You loved it." I tucked her hair behind her ears and caressed her damp cheek. "That was where I told you I loved you for the first time."

"We fell in love in Venice? That's so romantic!"

Shaking my head, I smiled down at her. "No, I fell in love with you long before Venice. I just didn't tell you."

Nina wiped the rain from her forehead. "Why?"

"I was afraid to say it because I didn't think I could handle it."

"Did I love you before Venice?"

"I don't know."

Chuckling, she stuck her tongue out. "Now you're just playing dumb. I bet I was crazy in love with you before Venice."

An awkward silence came over us. Even if she had been crazy about me, that was then. Now, she wasn't in love with me. Yet. I had to believe that what we'd had before could be again, though.

"Let's get out of this rain. We can continue this at home," I said as I guided her to the car.

She flashed me a devilish grin. "I thought we weren't going to be doing much talking when we got home."

As I opened her car door, I tilted her chin up and kissed her full on the mouth, loving the feel of her lips on mine. "We aren't."

Chapter Twelve

Nina

After standing in the rain staring into each other's eyes in Tony's parking lot, we were both drenched, but I don't think either of us cared. We made out all the way down my hallway, finally stumbling into my bedroom as he slid his hands under my dress to cup my ass. Lifting me, he held me just above his cock as I wrapped my legs around his waist, desperate to feel him inside me.

Tristan lifted his head from my neck and looked over at my bed where the babydoll he'd bought me was laid out. Turning back toward me, he licked his lips and grinned. "I want to see you in that tonight."

God, he could drive a woman insane! There I was, my body ready and waiting for him, and all he could think of was window dressing.

"Really? You want to stop?" I said with a pout.

"I love that on you. I want to see you in it when I fuck your brains out," he groaned against my neck.

"If I put it on, what do I get?" I teased as I rubbed my achy clit against the front of his pants.

"Other than me fucking you like a man on a quest to make you come more times than you ever have?"

I loved it when he talked like this. His voice was so deep and so filled with need, and something in it traveled straight to my core.

"I do like that, but what else? I should get something for putting up with you stopping right in the middle to make me put on a babydoll."

His eyes flashed his desire—or was it something else? With a firm grasp, he cupped my ass and pulled me to him so I could feel the full length of his stiff cock. "You tell me what you want and it's yours."

I couldn't think of a thing I wanted at that moment more than to feel him inside me. I slid my tongue across his bottom lip. "Surprise me."

Tristan lowered me to the floor and as I turned to grab the lingerie from the bed, yanked me back until I was pressed hard against him. In my ear, he whispered heavily, "Don't make me wait long."

I raced to the bathroom and changed, wanting to make a real entrance for him. I wanted so much to make him happy, to be the woman who drove him mad with desire. He had such power over me that with just a word or a glance, he could make me forget all my fears to be what would please him.

As I dressed, I glanced at the mirror, not entirely happy with what I saw. I pushed up my breasts to look more like the woman who'd served us at his club, but the effect wasn't the same. No matter. I was the woman he lived with, the woman he said he loved, I told myself.

When I came out of the bathroom, he was sitting on the edge of the bed, still fully dressed. Confused, I walked toward him. "Is something wrong? You're still dressed."

His brown eyes seemed to dance as he looked at me. "Not a thing. Turn around for me, Nina."

I did as he commanded, twirling the babydoll so the panties beneath showed. When I faced him again, he was staring at me, his eyes focused on mine. He sat there silently while I waited for him to speak, each moment that ticked by making me uncomfortable as his gaze never wavered.

"Tristan?"

He shook his head. "Shhh. Come here."

Taking my hand, he pulled me onto his lap so I straddled him. I pressed my hands to his chest as he slid his finger under the strap on my right shoulder, teasing my skin with his touch. He leaned in to lightly pepper kisses across my collarbone, and I shivered from a chill that ran down my spine.

I wanted him so badly. How he could be so calm and controlled when I could barely contain my need to have him touch every inch of me drove me wild. It was enthralling, sexy, and maddening all at the same time.

My body ached for him to do anything, yet he seemed content to simply watch me as he lightly traced the outline of my babydoll across the top of my breasts. Breathing became next to impossible as I waited for him to do something to ease my need for him.

His cock pressed hard against my excited pussy, and I began grinding slowly against him, wanting so much to feel a sense of release from everything building up inside me. Leaning forward, I tried to kiss him, but he backed away, leaving me lost and frustrated.

Staring up at me, his brown eyes heavy with desire, he pushed down on my hips until our bodies met. Holding me there, he whispered, "I want nothing to come between us, Nina. When I think of you, you're mine. Every inch of you, mine. I want every man who sees you to know you belong to me."

As he spoke, he lifted his hips ever so slightly off the bed to slide his hard cock over my needy clit. His words created a desperation to have him inside me that I found hard to control.

"Yes," I whispered. "I'm yours. Please…"

"Patience, baby. You'll get what you want soon."

I didn't want to be patient. I wanted him to fuck me hard as I rode him until he made my body shake from my release and my limbs felt boneless.

Tugging his shirt, I tried to pull it over his head, but he stopped me and took my hands in his. Holding them above my head with his right hand, he trailed the fingers of his other hand over my breast, lingering on my excited nipple until he squeezed it hard between his thumb and forefinger. I cried out in a mixture of pain and pleasure, unsure of which I felt more.

"Tell me what you want and it's yours. Jewelry, clothes, trips— name it and it's yours," he said with a sexy smile. "I'll give you anything you want."

I didn't care about any of that. For the first time in my life, things I could buy with money didn't matter. I could have anything my heart desired, and none of it meant a damn thing. All that mattered was him. I loved him. I needed him. I couldn't deny him. In just weeks, he'd become everything to me and I wanted to make him see that.

"I want you. I want to feel you inside me as we make love. I want to taste your lips and feel your tongue in my mouth when you kiss me like you can't live without me. I want to hear you moan when I make you come. I don't care about things. It's you I want."

He closed his eyes and spoke in a voice that sounded strained. "I'd give you anything to make you happy. Just the thought of you visiting your ex-boyfriend makes me crazy, Nina. You live here in my house, just feet away from me each night as I lay in bed alone and wanting you so bad it hurts."

When he stopped talking, he opened his eyes and I saw all the need he hid so often. He yearned for the Nina who'd loved him and I could finally give him that. I loved him. I adored him. His happiness was in my hands, and I wanted to be what he loved.

"No more waiting. I want to be yours. Heart and soul. I love you. You're everything to me, Tristan."

For a moment, he sat there perfectly still, like he was frozen in time, but then those gorgeous brown eyes that had haunted me from the first time I saw him gazing down at me as I lay in that hospital bed softened and in them I saw all the emotion he kept hidden inside. I leaned in and kissed him deeply, wanting him to give me those feelings he so rarely showed.

Releasing his hold on my wrists, he slid his hands over my back and pulled me to him. His voice was ragged as he whispered hoarsely, "I love you, Nina. No more distance between us."

"No more," I promised as he let me slide his shirt over his head.

I filled my eyes with the view of his muscular body as he lifted me off him to take off his jeans. Every inch of his body looked hard, like he was in total control of every muscle's movement. My gaze slipped from his broad shoulders, down over his chest with that unusual double snake tattoo, to his rock hard abs. He stepped out of his clothes and as I stood there enthralled with how beautiful he looked, he knelt before me.

"I want to see you," he rasped as he slid his hands up underneath my babydoll. He made quick work of my panties and then moved to pull the straps of the lingerie down as the entire silk and lace top dropped to the floor around my feet.

Tristan licked his lips and looked up at me as I stood naked before him. His hands caressed my hips, and he placed a tiny kiss just below my navel, making my legs go weak from desire. So good at drawing out our lovemaking, he was always in control while I craved him so much I would have raced to the part where he was deep inside me. He was pure seduction, and he drove me wild.

He knew it too.

He drew his fingertip down through my wet slit until he reached my opening. Quickly, he thrust two fingers inside me, and I almost fell to the floor at how incredible my pussy felt filled with any part of him, even if fingers weren't what I wanted.

"So tight," he groaned. "I love how your cunt feels. So wet for me. Do you hear how wet you are?"

"Yessss…" I mewed as he fucked me with his fingers and the pad of his thumb drew delicious circles on my clit.

"Do you know how sexy you look right now?" he asked while his eyes searched my face for how good he made me feel.

It was all too raw, and I closed my eyes to save some part of me from those eyes staring up at me. But he wouldn't let me escape.

"Keep your eyes open, Nina. I want to see every sensation through them. I want to see your soul through them."

I opened them and looked down his body to see his cock standing thick against his stomach. It touched the bottom of his navel, and I yearned to be filled with it instead of his fingers. To feel him push deep into me and retreat, leaving me empty and wanting more, before he filled me again, taking my breath away in the most sublime way.

"Tristan, don't make me wait," I whimpered as he continued thrusting two fingers in and out of me.

"What does my Nina want?" he asked in a voice laced with sex and just a touch of sharpness.

"You. More than just fingers. All of you."

In one swift movement, he slid them out of me and stood to his full height. "I promised you slow and easy the other night."

I palmed his thick cock, wrapping my fingers around it as far as I could, and looked up at him. "Give me slow and easy the second time. Now I want to feel you inside me fucking my brains out, like you promised."

"That I can do," he said in that deep voice I loved as he took me in his arms and pushed me onto the bed.

He held his body over mine and ran his cock through my wet folds, skimming its full length over the tiny bundle of nerves at the top. The feeling was exquisite, a mixture of aching desire and pure pleasure like nothing else in the world.

I reached up to wrap my arms around his neck as he rammed deep into me, nearly taking my breath away. His cock stretched me, forcing me to accept him, as he fucked me just as I'd asked. I wanted to see him stripped of the control that ruled him. I wanted to see the real Tristan Stone.

He groaned next to my ear as his hips flexed back and forth, pistoning his cock into me as I grasped at him to hold on. Our sex was animalistic, but I loved watching him shed the veneer of civility he wore around everyone, including me.

My body was his to do with as he pleased with no fight from me. Even if I wanted to resist, I couldn't. I craved his touch, the feel of his body invading mine as he made me his completely.

"God, you feel so fucking good," he moaned into my ear as he buried his head in the pillow next to me.

"Don't stop," I cried out when he slid out of me and didn't return. "Please, Tristan."

"Roll over, baby. I want to watch your face as I fuck you this way."

I flipped over onto my stomach and raised myself onto my hands and knees. Looking up, I saw the image of us in the mirror above the dresser—him kneeling behind me in control of our pleasure and me smaller in front of him and his to take as he chose.

He pressed his body against my back and tenderly wrapped his hand around my throat, his lips grazing my earlobe as he spoke. "Don't take your eyes off the mirror, Nina. Watch me as I fuck you."

I waited to feel him enter me again, anticipating how it would feel in this position and wondering if we'd made love like this before. His cock nudged into me slowly, like sweet torture, until he was fully seated inside my body. With his hand still around my neck, he began stabbing into me, creating the most incredible sensations with each thrust in and each pull out.

In the mirror, he watched me watch him, his gaze never wavering as he stroked in and out of me. He was power and desire personified, and I couldn't get enough of him. I pushed against his cock, eager for him to move faster, and he met my silent desire for more, fucking me faster and harder.

His body crashed hard against my ass, pushing me forward on the sheets, but I leaned back, guided by his hand around my neck. The sensual sounds of our lovemaking filled the room—his moans and mine, the slapping of skin as our bodies met each time he entered me. He snaked his arm around my waist and pulled me upright, changing the angle of his cock and sending my body into overdrive as he continued to fuck me.

I watched in the mirror as he slid his finger over my clit, making my thighs quiver as my orgasm began deep inside me. I was so close and only needed just a little more. One more thrust of his cock inside me. One more touch of his finger on my clit. One more delicious moan of my name in my ear.

"Come for me, Nina. Let me feel you surrender to me."

His hand tightened around my throat, and I came so hard I was afraid I might collapse if he wasn't holding me to him. I heard him groan and just as I was sure I couldn't take anymore, he thrust his cock into me one last time and came, sending jets of hot liquid deep inside me.

He held me close until our bodies finally calmed and kissed me softly on the cheek. "I love you, Nina. Thank you."

He slid out of me and eased me down onto the bed, taking me in his arms. I looked down our bodies to see our legs entwined as if we were one. With my head on his chest, I heard his heartbeat slowly return to a normal rhythm. I'd never felt so relaxed and safe in my life.

"Tell me your favorite memory," I whispered against his skin.

"Right now," he said. "I've never been happier than right now."

"Even when we were together before?"

Tristan sweetly pressed a kiss on the top of my head. "Every day is better than the last one. No matter how happy I was then, I'm even happier now."

I lifted my head from his chest and looked up at him. "Why?"

"Because we've been given a second chance. Not everyone gets that in life. I've gotten it twice now."

"What was the first time?"

A look of sadness settled into his face. "When I didn't die and the rest of my family did."

"I'm sorry. I didn't know. Well, you know what I mean."

He nodded and forced a smile. "It's okay. I understand."

I looked down at the tattoo on his chest and traced the outline of the two snakes that formed an inverted heart over his left pec, lingering on the place where they joined at a point. "What's this tattoo mean?"

"I got it after the accident. A metal rod pierced me just above the heart there where the scar is and continued to run through my brother's heart, killing him. It symbolizes our twin hearts joined even in death."

"I'm so sorry, Tristan. Were you identical twins?" I asked, hoping to lighten the mood slightly.

"Yes. We looked the same. Many people couldn't tell us apart, unless they knew us. But we were like night and day otherwise."

I heard something in his voice—a change in tone or a hitch that told me their differences weren't as simple as that. "Who was older?" I asked with a smile, knowing how silly the question was.

Tristan returned my smile with a tiny one of his own. "Taylor was by seven minutes. He never let me forget that he was my older brother either."

"I've always wondered what it would be like to have a sister my same age. Kim is six years older and we've never really been close. Those six years were always between us."

"It's like having any other sibling, just that you look exactly like another person."

His voice trailed off as his sentence ended, and I got the surest sense talking about his brother was painful for him. I didn't want to ruin our time together, so I hastily changed the subject. "Did you get the tattoo on your arm after that one on your chest?"

He looked down at his left arm and shook his head. "No, that one is from those days before I became the man I am now I told you about. My wilder days."

That was a topic I wanted to hear more about. "And about this wilder days guy, was he really different from the Tristan of now?"

He hesitated a moment before he answered. "Yeah, a lot."

I was nothing if not inquisitive, and this sounded like a mystery. "Tell me about him. I can't imagine you were that different than you are now."

"I can barely remember him anymore. He wasn't anyone you'd want."

"I can't believe that, Tristan," I said and kissed him.

His face told me he was uncomfortable. "You should. That man wasn't someone who would deserve someone like you."

"I probably would have been crazy about that man and he wouldn't even have known I existed is more likely."

Turning toward me, he lifted my chin with his forefinger. "Then he'd have been an ass not worthy of your time."

"Tell me about those wilder days, Tristan. I want to imagine you as the type of guy you were then."

Instead of telling me anything about his bad boy days, he rolled me onto my back and pinned my hands above my head. He loomed over me, his deep brown eyes staring down into mine, and said in a low voice, "I've got something far better in mind."

By the time I woke in the morning, Tristan was gone and I saw through the window that snow was falling, covering the grass and making it finally look like winter. My room was still warm, though, and my thought of venturing outside to go to visit Jordan suddenly seemed like something for another day.

Thoughts of the Atlanta suite filled my head, so after lying around enjoying memories of my time with Tristan just hours before, I finally crawled out of bed to face the day. Throwing my robe around me,

I knew he'd be long gone at work, but I walked to the kitchen for my morning coffee with the hope that he'd be there to join me for breakfast.

Disappointment washed over me as I rounded the corner and saw no one there. I understood a man like him had to be a slave to his work, but always waking up alone in bed made me feel as I was something extra in his life, like an addition he didn't need.

I was being silly. I knew Tristan loved me, and the wonderful life he offered didn't come easily for him. Being CEO of Stone Worldwide was a twenty-four hour a day job, if the phone calls and emails he received at all hours of the day and night were any indication. That we got to spend any time alone at all was something I should appreciate instead of whining to myself about waking up alone.

The French Vanilla roast in my mug began to work almost immediately, and I was wide awake in no time. Grabbing a sesame bagel Rogers had brought home from the local bakery, I headed back to my room to get ready for my day of research for Atlanta.

Chapter Thirteen

Tristan

"**M**r. Stone, Mr. Dreger is here."

Ten o'clock. Karl was getting a late start to his daily stalking today. I looked over at the speaker on the edge of my desk and groaned. No day was a good day to deal with him, but after the night I'd just spent with Nina, I didn't want him to ruin how good I felt.

The man himself opened my office door and without even being asked in made himself at home on the leather couch on the side wall. A big man, his scalp showed more of his large bulbous head every day, and he seemed to be gaining weight in exchange for the loss of his hair. The seams of his suit pulled, as if at any moment it was going to give way and cease to hold back the girth it was containing.

I crossed my arms and leaned back in my chair. "Karl, what can I do for you today?"

"You know what I'm here about. It's the same thing every day. Your time is running out. We've been patient, son."

"Don't call me son, Karl. My name is Tristan Stone. My father was Victor Stone, not you. So remember who the fuck you're talking to."

"Fine. And you remember who the fuck you're talking to, Tristan. You aren't all-powerful at Stone Worldwide. The Board has power too."

I knew he was baiting me, but I took it all the same. "Power to do what? This company has never seen better days. Everyone's making money, Karl. Are you saying the Board isn't happy about that?"

"You know what we're unhappy with. If you don't want all this to come to a screeching halt, you have to take care of the loose ends. She can't continue to be a risk to this business."

Ten o'clock in the fucking morning and I already had a splitting headache, thanks to this asshole. Pinching the bridge of my nose, I repeated to him what I'd said so many times it was like the words were tattooed on my tongue. "Karl, she has nothing. She knows nothing.

She would never do anything to hurt me, and that includes anything that would hurt this company."

"And what happens when she finds out the truth? What happens if she finds out that her father died because he couldn't keep his damn nose out of other people's business?"

"She knows her father's dead. Why would she find out anything about how he died? That was years ago. There's no reason for her to go digging about it. It will remain as it always has—an unsolved murder. So you and the Board can rest easy. Nina cares nothing about that."

Karl lurched off the couch and moved to stand in front of my desk. "You don't have any silly romantic plans to tell her yourself, do you? You can't imagine that would be a good idea."

I nonchalantly pushed a pen back and forth across the top of my desk, praying to God my plans to confess everything to Nina weren't written all over my face. After her show of honesty about Cal the night before, I didn't want to go on lying to her anymore. I could make her understand that no matter what my father had done to hers, we could be happy together. I knew I could.

"If you're done with your daily visit, feel free to let yourself out, Karl. And don't feel the need to come back tomorrow. Nothing is going to change. Nina is the woman I love—the woman I intend on marrying—so she's going to stay a part of my life."

"Son, you're not going to win this. We helped your father build this company into the gem you now get to claim as yours, so we won't be cut out."

"Nobody's trying to cut you out, Karl. You and the Board members are safe."

He sneered at my comment, and in a flash, my patience was all used up. Standing from behind my desk, I approached him until we stood toe-to-toe. "I'm going to warn you just once, Karl. If I get the sense that you or any of your friends in this even think about going through with your plans to hurt Nina, I'll kill you myself. I'm not like you old men who won't get their hands dirty. So remember that when you go back to them today. Let what happened with Victor Stone and Joseph Edwards end with their deaths."

Karl chuckled, but I heard the nervousness in his voice when he spoke. "Your father always said you were the one not to cross. Everybody thought Taylor was the piranha, but your father believed otherwise. I guess he wasn't wrong. Fine. You should know, though, that this isn't over."

I turned away from him and waved him off. "Yes, it is."

He stormed out, barking something at Michelle as he passed her desk, while I thought about his comment about my father. Never close to me, my father had always favored Taylor. They'd sit for hours talking about business, sharing his favorite brandy and smoking cigars in his study as they plotted their takeover of some helpless company one of them had spied in distress that day.

That world had never appealed to me. Even now, I remembered the stink of their cigars as I passed that room on my way out at night, never asked to join them and happy for it. They were like strangers I was oddly related to but had nothing in common with. I couldn't imagine sitting around in leather high backed chairs playing like some captain of industry in their private, real life game of Monopoly.

I wasn't a saint, but I wasn't the kind of men they were. Maybe it was because I'd never wanted this. I was happy living a life of excess and good times, hurting no one but myself. Well, that wasn't exactly true, but I certainly wasn't guilty of the things my father and brother were.

"Mr. Stone, Mr. Knight is here to see you," Michelle announced over the speaker, tearing me from my daydreams about the past.

What was Daryl doing here today, a day early? "Send him in, Michelle."

I prepared myself for Daryl's report on Nina's ex and more importantly, what had happened with her father. Daryl came in with a bounce in his step he always had, like the world's biggest leprechaun, and took a seat in one of the chairs in front of my desk.

"Tristan, I know I'm a day early, but I thought you'd want this information ASAP."

My heart pounded against my chest at the thought that Daryl was about to tell me something about Cal and Nina. I took a swig out of my water bottle and sat back in my chair as I worked to calm my nerves. "What did you find out?"

"Which do you want first, loverboy or the father?"

"Give me the information on Cal Johnson first," I answered with a lump in my throat.

Daryl reached into his suit coat and pulled out a notepad. Looking up at me, he smiled. "Loverboy it is. Let's just say your guy has gotten around. I don't know how he does it, but on what amounts to a clerk's salary, this guy has seen more ass than a toilet seat."

Fucking fantastic. This day was just getting better and better. Forcing a smile onto my face, I said, "Love the way you describe things, Daryl. What are we talking about this for?"

"I thought you wanted to know who he was fucking."

Leave it to Daryl to make this amusing. I had said I wanted to know that, but only because I was afraid the answer would be Nina. Chuckling, I said, "Okay, is he fucking anyone interesting?"

"Not in your league, but he does like women who have money. He's piss poor, but the women he sleeps with aren't."

"What is he, some kind of Casanova, Daryl?" I asked, sure my jealousy was obvious.

"Not as far as I can tell. Used to be some kind of college athlete. Rugby or something like that. Now he's just some guy who runs numbers at an insurance company."

"Then I doubt he's piss poor. Actuaries make good money. I think your detective skills are getting rusty, Knight."

Daryl raised his eyebrows at the joking insult. "You didn't let me finish. He used to make good money at the firm he worked at before this one, but he was fired under a cloud of suspicion that he'd stolen from the company. As far as I can tell, he didn't steal money but was sleeping with the boss's wife. He hasn't been able to get a decent job since. This one at Peak International appears to be a favor from one of his college profs."

So Cal was a philandering dick. I wasn't surprised. From what Nina had told me about him, I hadn't expected much better.

"Does he have a girlfriend now?"

"None that I can find, but he's left a long line of girls behind him. Did you know one of them is the daughter of the man whose murder you have me investigating, Nina Edwards?"

"Yes," I answered, adding, "Nina is my fiancée."

"Ah, I get it. Well, from what I can tell, she's not with him now. I can watch him to see if they still speak, assuming you don't think they do."

"I know they've met once recently. I don't think they'll be meeting again."

Daryl grinned and shrugged his shoulders. "Okay, but it's not a big deal to watch him for a little while."

I thought about it and even though I knew I shouldn't, I nodded my silent agreement to watching Cal Johnson.

"Okay, onto bigger fish than our boy Cal. This Edwards thing is going to get ugly, Tristan. I just want to warn you. The daughter's your intended and what I'm finding out is bad. I don't know if you're ready for this."

I leaned forward and planted my elbows on the desktop. "If you're going to tell me you know who murdered Nina's father, let me save you the effort. My father had Joseph Edwards killed. I just don't know why."

Daryl twisted his face into a scowl. "You could've told me that when you set me on this. Christ, I thought I was going to have to tell you that your own father was responsible for the guy's death."

"I know all too well what Victor Stone was capable of, Daryl. Joseph Edwards wasn't the first person he had disposed of, and he might not even have been the last. My father was every bit the monster you're going to tell me he was."

Shaking his head, he frowned. "I don't have all the details yet. All I know is that he was behind it. I haven't found out exactly why yet, but I do have one piece of information I'm planning on acting on."

"And that is?"

"There's a storage facility in Plymouth Meeting, Pennsylvania that Joseph Edwards stored things in a week before his death. It's in his wife's name, though. Seems she's been dead for years and he had her belongings stored there, but it's interesting that he'd visit it right before he died. I think there might be something useful there."

"Has anyone opened the storage unit since then?"

"No," Daryl said, shaking his head. "The guy at the storage facility said that their records show it wasn't opened for years and then one day Edwards came and opened it just once. That was a week before he was murdered. Since then, it hasn't been opened even one time. My guess is that your fiancée doesn't know it's there."

Or she didn't remember it was there, even if she had known about it. I doubted she had since it was simply a place her father had kept her mother's things after her death. There would be no reason to tell her about it since she was so young when she died. But did her sister know about it, I wondered.

"When are you planning to go out there? I want to know what you find."

"I can go anytime you want. I was planning to wait until after the holidays, but if you like, I can go sooner."

"I don't want to wait, Daryl. Get out there tomorrow and find out what's in there."

"Okay, tomorrow I can do. I'll take a nice drive out of the city and do my best Storage Wars impression. Christ, I have to admit I'm never a fan of digging around these storage units. I think it's ever since that scene in Silence of the Lambs. I'm always afraid I'm going to find some head in a jar. Remember that scene?"

"Yeah," I answered absentmindedly as I thought about what he might find in Joseph Edwards' storage unit. Daryl continued to ramble on about dismembered bodies and other grotesque oddities he'd heard about being found in storage facilities, but I wasn't paying attention. He had a tendency to go off on tangents like that, so I'd learned to just wait until he was finished. Ordinarily, I wouldn't give someone that much leeway, but Daryl was a decent guy, even if he was a little weird.

I stood from my desk and held out my hand to shake his, a not-so-subtle sign I was ready for him to leave. Daryl took the hint and stood to go, still mumbling about the things he could imagine uncovering the next day.

"Call me as soon as you get in. I want to know everything you find," I said as I escorted him out toward Michelle.

"You got it. Talk to you then."

Dinner was ready at five when I got home, but Nina was nowhere to be found. I quickly hunted down Jensen, but he hadn't driven her anywhere all day. West reported that she hadn't left, but he did think he'd seen her on the grounds within the hour. The snow that had been falling all day had tapered off, but it was getting colder now that the sun had gone down. I called her cell phone three times, but it went directly to voicemail. Frustrated, I stuffed my phone back in my pocket and set off to find her without even grabbing my coat, scared something might have happened to her.

The doctors had warned me that she may act abnormally at times because of her head injury, so immediately I was concerned about her walking the grounds since she'd never spent any time outside, as far as I knew. I hurriedly walked around the house and then headed out toward the gardens, finally catching a glimpse of her as I rounded the first stand of hedges.

"Nina! Wait up!"

She turned and waved at me, giving me the sense that she wasn't out there for any dangerous reason. I jogged over to her and saw she was dressed for the cold weather, so at least she wasn't wandering around half-clothed unsure of where she was or what her name was.

"It's freezing out here, Tristan. Where's your coat?" she asked in a worried voice.

"I'm looking for you. Why are you out here?"

"I was feeling cabin fever inside after working all day. I was going to go into the city to see Jordan, but I decided not to. When it stopped snowing, I figured I'd take a stroll around and see what the rest of the place looks like. It's nice out here."

She seemed okay and was making sense, so I guessed she wasn't having some episode from her injury like the doctors had described. "It's cold out here. Let's go inside."

Nina held out her hand to take mine, and we walked back to the house together as she described her day researching pieces for the Atlanta property. It was moments like these that erased all the bad of my days—everything with Karl, the job I had Daryl doing for me—and made me feel as if things were going to be okay between Nina and me, no matter what came our way.

I took her coat as we entered the house and felt for her cell. Sitting in her pocket, it showed no calls at all. One of the disadvantages to living out in the country.

"How was your day at work? I was so busy talking about my day I didn't even ask how yours went," she said as we sat down to dinner.

"Same as always. Just another day at work," I answered, knowing it was a half-truth but preferring her to believe that my days were like hers instead of the nightmare that they were.

We ate and then laid in each other's arms after as we watched one of her chick flicks I hadn't wanted to deprive her of again. As if the universe had chosen to give me a sign, Nina picked a film about some woman dealing with the death of her mother. I watched and patiently waited until it was over to ask her about her own mother's death, my conversation with Daryl weighing heavily on my mind.

"Does watching something like this make you think of your mother?"

Shaking her head, she said it didn't, but I saw it did. The woman in the film had died of cancer. Had hers?

"What happened to your mother, Nina?"

Cuddling up next to me, she quietly said, "She died of leukemia. It was fast, I think. I was so young I don't really remember, but my father told me she didn't suffer. They diagnosed her and a few weeks later she was gone."

The sadness in her voice made my breath catch in my throat. I'd always thought that losing my mother the way I did was better than watching her fade away for months or years, but I could tell by what Nina said that it wasn't that way for her. Maybe because she'd had so little time with her mother. At least I'd gotten most of my life with mine.

I kissed the top of her head and hugged her tight. "I'm sorry. I know it hurts."

"Even after all this time, it still does. I sometimes think of what it would be like if she was still here."

"I know. I think the same thing about my mother. What would she think of me now?" I wondered out loud.

Nina lifted her head and smiled. "She'd think you're an incredible success with a great girlfriend."

"At least the second part," I said, unsure if anything I'd done could be considered a success.

"You would have liked my mother. She was sweet and kind. My father used to say I was just like her. Were you more like your mother or your father?"

"My mother, I guess. Taylor was always closer to my father, so I naturally gravitated toward her."

As she curled up closer to me, Nina whispered, "Then I would have liked her."

We laid there silently thinking about the people we'd lost, good and bad, and for the first time in a long time, I missed my mother. I rarely thought of her, something that my shrinks always considered to be a serious problem. They'd always talked about the need for me to mourn her, but I had mourned her. Just not the way they wanted me to.

Nina fell asleep on my chest as I remembered the last time my mother and I talked alone just days before the plane crash. She'd been upset about my unwillingness to do anything but party and sleep around, not that she knew the full extent of either activity in my life. I'd pushed her off with my usual ability to charm her as I always had as her favorite. I saw in her face the worry that I'd never grow up and be the man she believed I could be or find someone to spend my life with.

My mother sat alone at the dining room table with three empty place settings. I had no idea where my father and Taylor were instead of sitting with her for our traditional Sunday afternoon dinner, but I'd just rolled out of bed a half hour before and wanted nothing more than something to bring me back to life after a night of partying till dawn. One thing was for sure. Sunday dinner around the family dining table wasn't it.

She looked up at me as I entered the room, her big brown eyes telegraphing she wanted to talk to me. I knew what she wanted to say. It was always the same.

"Tristan, come sit with me. I want to talk."

"I'm just grabbing a roll and heading out, Mom. Maybe when I get back."

"Tristan Ryder Stone, I want to speak to you."

Anytime my mother used my middle name and said anything in that choppy tone, I knew there was no escaping whatever she wanted. Sighing, I hung my head and pulled out a chair at one of the empty places.

"I'm concerned about you, sweetheart. You're twenty-four now. I realize you're not like your brother, but you can't stay a boy forever."

If she knew what I did with my nights, she wouldn't call me a boy. With a charming smile, I said, "Okay, Mom."

"Tristan, it's time you grew up. Again, I'm not saying you have to be just like Taylor, but your father and I are concerned that you don't seem to have any direction, other than toward parties and girls. I want to see you settled and happy."

"My father's concerned?"

I knew by the look that crossed her face that it was only she who was worried about me and my nightly behavior. I wasn't even sure my father knew I existed most of the time, even though we lived in the same house.

My mother reached out to touch my hand. I looked down at her long manicured nails that screamed opulence and then up at her face to see those big brown eyes once again fixed on me.

Two could play at that game.

"I'll settle down when I meet the perfect woman. You wouldn't want me to settle for anything less, would you?"

Now it was her turn to sigh. My usual answer never satisfied her. "Tristan, I want to believe that you mean that and you aren't just playing on my emotions."

"Who, me? Your favorite son? I wouldn't do that," I said, oozing the charm that never failed to work on her.

I rose from the table and leaned over to kiss her cheek. "Don't wait up. I might spend the night in the city."

She said nothing but simply smiled at me as I turned to leave. I felt her stare on my back as I walked out, but I didn't turn around. There was no point. We both knew that.

I watched as Nina snored lightly on my chest and stroked her soft hair. For whatever it was worth, I'd finally figured out that my mother was right. I just hoped she could see that at least she'd been wrong about me finding someone to love.

Chapter Fourteen

Tristan

I chose a tie and closed my bedroom closet door. "Jensen, I want you at my office at quarter after nine exactly," I instructed him as I fixed my tie. "Michelle will have a package for you. I want you to bring it back here and give it to Rogers. He'll know what to do with it."

"Yes, Mr. Stone."

"Tell Rogers to come here. I need to talk to him."

As Jensen left, I dialed Daryl's number, hoping to catch him before he took off for Pennsylvania. I'd thought about that storage unit all night and didn't want him rummaging around in it, an unfeeling stranger rifling through Nina's mother's things.

"Tristan? How are you this morning?"

"Plans have changed. I want you to keep an eye on Cal instead of heading out to Plymouth Meeting. Text me address of the storage facility."

"You sure you want to do that? You usually have me do the dirty work."

At that moment, Rogers appeared in my bedroom doorway. "Daryl, you stay in the city. And call me if you see anything I might want to know about."

"You got it. Enjoy your day trip."

I put away my phone and turned my attention to Rogers. "Jensen will have a package for Nina. Make sure she gets it as soon as she gets up. I want you to give her this note also."

"Will you be going out of town, Tristan?"

Looking up from my letter, I shot Rogers a glare. "Taking to eavesdropping now?"

"Not in the least. I just happened to hear part of your conversation, sir."

I wasn't in the mood for his attitude this morning, so I ignored his use of sir again and read over my letter to Nina.

Dear Nina,

You looked so cute lying there all curled up in bed that I didn't have the heart to wake you up, but I had to leave on an emergency business trip. I hope you like your new phone. Text me when you get this letter, and I'll call you this afternoon.

Think about me. I'll be thinking about you. Miss you already.

Love,

Tristan

Folding the note in half, I slipped it into an envelope and handed it to Rogers. "Make sure she gets this."

"Are there any other instructions?"

I put on my suit coat and adjusted my tie in the mirror. "I don't know if I'll be home in time for dinner, so make sure Nina gets whatever she wants. I expect to hear that she was happy. Are we clear?"

Rogers' expression showed his hurt at my comment. "I would never do anything to foster Nina's unhappiness, Tristan."

I didn't entirely believe that, but I wasn't going to stand there and debate the issue with him. "Just make sure, Rogers. I'll call you to let you know if I'll be home for dinner."

As I walked past him to leave, he asked, "Is she allowed to leave the grounds?"

Sighing in frustration, I stopped and turned toward him to see that same hurt expression still on his face. "She's not a prisoner here, Rogers. I've had enough of this. I'm doing my best to make things right. Just give me a break."

I didn't give him a chance to respond. I didn't care what he thought. I didn't care what anyone thought but Nina. She was the only one I owed any explanation to.

Daryl had texted me the address of the storage place right before I left, and less than two hours later I pulled up in front of U-Store on Chemical Road in Plymouth Meeting. The clerk behind the counter was barely out of his teens and still working through an acne phase, so he was easy to get by. He also didn't seem to have any knowledge of the law whatsoever, so all I had to do was tell him I was Joseph

Edwards' son and I'd lost my key to my mother's unit and he was happy to oblige.

We walked past a dozen green garage doors until we reached the last one in Row 8. The clerk unlocked the door and turned to me with a smile. "If you need anything else, Mr. Edwards, just let me know."

I looked in and saw the 10 x 10 unit wasn't packed to the ceiling, thankfully. Stacks of boxes four high lined the three walls, but it was organized so someone could walk easily through the middle around a few chests and belongings that weren't in boxes.

Now that I was standing in the middle of Nina's mother's things, I suddenly realized I didn't even know her name. All I knew was that she was the woman who'd given birth to the one person I loved in the world and she'd died when Nina was young. Her life was now only memories and her things stored in a dark storage unit.

A feeling of guilt came over me as I looked at her entire life around me. I was an intruder, a stranger about to search her things for something that had never had anything to do with her. It was like I was ransacking a grave for my own benefit.

I had to remind myself that I wasn't there just for me. If I didn't find the evidence of my father's actions that Karl and his friends were sure Joseph Edwards had hidden somewhere, they'd never leave Nina and me alone.

The first box I chose solved the mystery of what Nina's mother's name was. Written on the box were the words *Diana's Clothes*. That one had nothing but clothes in it, so I moved to a second box filled with pictures. I stood there as the photographs I looked at told the story of her life. Her in a 1960s bikini at the beach. When she was pregnant with Nina's sister and sitting at a picnic table on a beautiful sunny day. Diana at an art show standing next to a sculpture with a blue ribbon on it. Nina's parents kissing under the mistletoe at a Christmas party.

I stared for a long time at the picture of Joseph and Diana Edwards, wondering how they'd met and if they were happy. They looked like two people in love. Her hair was long, much longer than Nina's, and darker brown. She was beautiful like her daughter, and Joseph Edwards was a good looking man. A good six inches taller than his wife, he had dirty blond hair. I noticed these things randomly as my eyes remained riveted to that picture.

My phone vibrated in my coat, and I pulled it out to see a text from Nina. *I love my new phone! I'll finally be able to call out here. Wish you were here to thank. :) Love you. Come back soon.*

Her text made me smile, but as I looked around at where I was, I wondered if she'd still love me if she knew what I was doing. I couldn't think about that, though. If this was what I had to do to keep her safe so we could have a life together like those two people in the picture had, then I'd do it.

I texted back *Miss you. Wish I was there with you right now. I'll try to get back tonight. I love you* and put my phone away to get back to work, wanting more than ever to get back to her.

Within two hours, I'd rummaged through the three walls of boxes and found nothing that appeared to be related to Joseph Edwards' work or his investigation into anything concerning my father or Stone Worldwide. Turning to the middle of the storage unit, I began to look through more boxes, but these were filled with art materials like paintbrushes and sculptor's tools, along with paints, clays, and stone. Diana Edwards had been an artist like her daughter, but I suspected she wasn't a painter but a sculptor. Stainless steel tools and finished clay and stone sculptures of animals, mythological creatures, and people filled a chest that sat next to an artist's easel.

I wondered if Nina knew her mother had been an artist. That she was very much her mother's daughter. Hopefully, someday I'd get to tell her what I knew without sounding like some crazy stalker guy.

Even though I was sure I wasn't going to find anything I was looking for amongst everything in the sculpture boxes and chest, I inspected each tool and piece of sculpture the best I could without harming Diana Edwards' art. Finally, after I'd looked at every item, I saw at the bottom of the chest sat a wooden box with the initials DE carved into the top. Kneeling on the cold ground, I opened the box and found a set of stone carving chisels. Just as with the other tools, they had no identifying marks or symbols on them, other than the name of the company that made them.

I'd looked through every inch of that storage unit and found nothing. Disappointed, I sat down on the ground next to the chest and hung my head. I'd hoped that I'd be able to find some shred of evidence to give to Karl so Nina would finally be safe, but there'd been nothing. I'd failed.

Diana Edwards' chisel set box was still in my hands, and I traced the outline of her initials as I sat there feeling lost as to what I was supposed to do next. Maybe Daryl had another lead. Maybe there really was nothing to show what Nina's father had found out. I sighed from the weight of this entire thing with Karl and his insistence that there was evidence out there that could do them all in. What had begun as disgust at my father's actions had snowballed into a problem that I thought of day and night and still hadn't figured out how to solve.

As I slowly traced her initials over and over, my finger moved the lid of the box to reveal an inset that could be removed. Tipping the box over, I tapped the lid and the center came out, leaving a small compartment open where a key and a slip of paper sat. The key had no name or clue as to what it opened, but the paper had written on it one word: Fidelity.

Quickly, I typed into my phone the words fidelity and Plymouth Meeting, getting two results that might be useful. There was a First Fidelity Bank and a Fidelity Securities in that very town. Looking down at the key, I saw it had no grooves like an ordinary house key or basic lock key. It was a safe deposit box key.

Had Joseph Edwards left a key for his daughters to find something important in a safe deposit box at a nearby bank in the event of his death? I could only hope that was the answer, but since Nina and her sister were his only children, there was no way I was going to convince a bank to allow me access to the box, even if I had the key. A young kid working part time at a storage unit facility was one thing, but a bank manager was going to be harder to fool.

I stuffed the key and the paper into my pocket and called Daryl. If I could find out more information about Kim's husband, I might be able to get the bank to let me see what was in that box.

"Hey, Tristan, how was your trip to Pennsylvania?"

"Daryl, I need the name of Joseph Edwards' son-in-law. He's married to Nina's sister Kim."

"Hang on. I think I have that somewhere. Give me a minute."

As I waited for Daryl to flip through the notebook he carried with him at all times, I walked out into the sunlight, shocking my eyes after all that time in that small room full of the remnants of Diana Edwards' life. Pulling the door down, I turned to walk toward my car and prepared to drive to the closest of the two banks.

"Sorry, I knew I had it written down, but I couldn't find it. His name is Jeff Hopkins."

"Okay, thanks Daryl."

"What's up, Tristan? What are you doing?"

"I'm going to pretend to be Jeff Hopkins. I found a safe deposit key I think might help give me the answers I'm looking for."

"Whoa, before you go off and do whatever the hell you're planning to do, maybe you should know something else about him other than his wife's name. They have two kids—two girls—named Emily and Sarah. You know the guy's a lawyer, right? So if you're planning to say you're him, you need to keep this stuff in mind."

"Right. Kim's the wife, Emily and Sarah are the daughters, and he's a lawyer. How old are the kids?"

Daryl was silent for a moment. "Six and eight, I think."

"You think?" I asked as I got into the car.

"Sorry. I didn't spend a lot of time on anyone but Edwards' daughters."

"Okay, Daryl. I have a hunch I found something here. I'll let you know."

"You sure you want to do this, Tristan? I can be out there in no time and handle things. That's what you pay me for."

"No, I'm here already and I can do it. How hard can it be to pull off being a lawyer?"

Daryl laughed at my attempt at humor. "You might have to convince them not because you don't look like you could be a lawyer but because you're wearing a suit no small town lawyer could afford."

"Point taken. I'll keep it mind, just in case."

"Just remember this. People are more willing to do things for people who sweet talk them. Use some of that charm I know you have and hope you get a woman at the bank to help you. Also, pray you aren't going to a bank where they'd actually know this Jeff guy. If they do, you're probably shit out of luck."

"Thanks for the pep talk," I said sarcastically.

"All you have to remember is charm. Let me know if you need help."

I ended the call and started the car, programming the GPS to give me directions to both locations. Fidelity Securities was closest, so I put the car in gear and drove there first. I was lucky enough to have a female employee in her first month on the job wait on me, but when she saw the key she knew it wasn't from her institution. That left First Fidelity.

I could only hope I'd be lucky enough to run into another young woman like the first one.

First Fidelity Bank was just what I'd hoped it wouldn't be. A small building on the corner of Main Street and Park Avenue, it looked like a bank I had for my miniature train set when I was a boy. I parked across the street and prayed to God there would be more than two tellers and a branch manager who knew everyone in town by their first names and what teachers they'd had in high school.

Two steps into the building and I knew I was going to have to work for this one. Three tellers stood at their stations, each one in their fifties or older. One had teased up hair the color of pewter and smiled when she saw me, so she was my go-to girl. Hopefully, the smile meant she was at least friendly.

In my best schoolboy voice, I said, "Hi, I need to get into a safe deposit box." I looked down next to her stack of envelopes and saw her name. Roberta. As my mother always said, "There's nothing as magical as hearing one's name," so I flashed her a smile and added, "Roberta, I'd so appreciate it if you could help me. It would mean a lot to me."

She looked up at me with faded blue eyes and smiled a grandmotherly smile. "Oh, that's easy. All I need is your name and the key."

I let out a sigh of relief and then she added, "And your identification, of course."

Fuck.

Holding the key up for her to see, I said, "My name is Jeff Hopkins and here's my key, but there's a problem. I don't have my ID. I had my wallet stolen the other day when I had to take my daughter to the specialist in Philadelphia, and that's why I need to get into the safe deposit box. That's where my birth certificate is, and I can't get my ID again without it."

"Oh, well, we can't let you into the box without some form of ID, Mr. Hopkins. You don't have any form of identification?"

I was going to have to lay it on thick if this was going to work. Leaning forward, I settled my gaze on Roberta's pale blue eyes and stared deeply into them as I softened my voice. "I can certainly understand, Roberta, but that man who stole my wallet has made that impossible. Is there no way we can get around this? Without that birth certificate, I can't get my driver's license. I've already gotten one ticket after getting pulled over for driving without a license and I can't afford another one, but I need to drive my little girl to the doctors."

This kind of wheedling had never been my strong suit, and I was sure by the look on her face that she wasn't convinced as she sat there staring silently at me. Breaking the connection, I looked down at a picture on her desk of a little blond girl I guessed was her granddaughter and then back up at Roberta with the best pleading look I had. Just when I was sure our silent standoff would end in my defeat, her shoulders sagged and she said with a sigh, "Oh, one time can't hurt."

"Bless you, Roberta. You've just made my day."

As I suspected, she was a God fearing woman and my words only served to convince her she'd done the right thing for a decent soul in need. As I explained that the box was, in fact, my father-in-law's and told her about Joseph Edwards' wish to keep all his family's most important documents safe, she checked his information and located the box. She escorted me to a back room full of metal filing cabinets and I sat down at a conference table in the center of the room.

Roberta returned with the box and placed it in front of me. "I remember Joseph Edwards coming in with his little girl. She was a cute little thing. Nina I think was her name. How is she?"

I smiled at the mention of Nina's name. How was she? I had to keep up the facade of being not Nina's fiancé but her brother-in-law, so I simply said, "She's doing well. She lives in New York now and works as a curator."

Roberta nodded her happiness. "That's so good to hear. Please let me know if you need any additional help, Jeff."

As she walked out to help other bank customers, I quickly turned my attention to the safe deposit box. I would have loved to spend my time thinking about Nina, but I needed to find what Joseph Edwards may have hidden here and then get the hell out of that bank before someone figured out I wasn't who I said I was.

I lifted the metal lid and saw only a notebook sitting there in the bottom of the box. As much as I wanted to read what Nina's father had written about what my father had done, I simply stuffed the tablet inside my coat and left, thanking Roberta as I made my way outside. I hurried to my car with my heart racing at the knowledge that in minutes I might finally know what had started the chain of events that had led to the death of Joseph Edwards and ultimately, my finding the love of my life.

Chapter Fifteen

Nina

At three o'clock, I looked down at my new phone as it buzzed with a new text. I swiped the screen and saw it was from Tristan. *Probably won't be home for dinner. Make sure Rogers has the cook make you anything you want. Can't wait to see you. Love you.*

Disappointed, I texted back that I missed him and loved him too before I fell back onto the bed in frustration. While I'd loved this house in the good weather, now that winter had finally arrived, I was feeling cabin fever more and more. Being stuck out in the hinterlands in the snow without Tristan was definitely not how I wanted to spend the next few hours.

Well, if I couldn't spend time with the man I loved, then I could spend time with Jordan. We hadn't had a girls' night out since I left the hospital, and one was long overdue. A minute later, her phone was ringing and I was thinking of the perfect place to grab some dinner and drinks.

"Hello?"

"Jordan, it's Nina. This is my new number. Let's get something to eat."

"Are you nearby or out at the house?"

"I'm still at the house, but I can be there in an hour. Sooner, if Jensen is in the mood to drive fast," I joked. "I'd love it if we could get dinner tonight."

Jordan hesitated. "Well, Justin and I were supposed to hang out and watch wrestling tonight, but he won't miss me if I beg off. We better have a good time, though, since I'm missing hot guys beating the hell out of each other."

"Well, I'm not sure I can do better than that. I was just thinking of some good food and drinking these chocolate martinis Tristan introduced me to. They're delicious! You have to try one."

"I'll do dinner, but I'm not a martini girl."

"No matter. It's the company that's important. Can you be ready in two hours? Maybe we can go shopping too."

"I'm just getting out of school now, so two hours will work. Are we being driven around tonight, or is it like old times?"

No matter how much I may have wanted it to be like old times, I'd accepted the fact that Tristan wasn't about to have me driving or taking the subway. All the better, actually, since it was cold and snowy.

"We're going in style, girl. I'll have Jensen honk when we get there," I joked.

"Some date you are," Jordan said with a chuckle. "Okay, I'll be ready in two. See you then!"

I reread Tristan's text to me, focusing on the words *Can't wait to see you. Love you* and wishing he was there next to me as I lay on my bed. I understood now how I'd fallen in love with him the first time. He was like an addiction I never wanted to quit. My spare moments were filled with thoughts of him—how my heart raced when he kissed me, how my stomach did somersaults at the merest touch of his fingers on my body, how his beautiful brown eyes said so much even when he said nothing.

In just this short time, he'd become my everything. I couldn't imagine life without him.

I rolled over to run my hand across where he'd laid the night before, fantasizing about the way we'd made love, his hands so powerful as he held me in place while he thrust into me, so completely in control of every moment of our fucking.

Even now, with him miles away, just the thought our lovemaking caused a need in the pit of my abdomen, and I squeezed my legs together to feel the sweet ache the desire for him created in me.

I grabbed my phone again and texted once more before I got up to get dressed. *Just the thought of you makes me wish you were here in bed with me. When you get home I'm going to show you how much I missed you.*

He didn't text back immediately, so I got into the shower. By the time I finished and had touched up my makeup, he had texted back but only a brief message. *Miss you. You have no idea how much.*

Something in those words sounded so lonely as I read them, so I called him but got no answer. I tried again as I dressed, but still no answer. Hopefully, he'd be home when I got back, but just in case he'd had a terrible day, I wrote him a letter and slipped it under his bedroom door.

I found Rogers in the dining room looking as surly as ever. "I'd like to go to Jordan's. Can you tell Jensen?"

He looked at me as if he were looking through me, and I repeated my question, which only seemed to irritate him. "As you wish, miss," he said sharply as he walked past me out the dining room door.

I stood in that spot unsure of whether I should wait or follow him and wishing Tristan was there to deal with his butler. Maybe there was a good reason he was always so short with him. As I wondered what Rogers had against me, he returned with Jensen, who was always much nicer.

"Miss, I'm ready to go as soon as you are," he said with a nod and a hint of a smile.

Shooting Rogers a nasty look, I thanked Jensen and followed him to the Town Car. "We need to pick up Jordan at her place and then we're going to go out for dinner. We're not going to make it a late night, though, so you won't have to be out too late."

Jensen closed the car door behind me and slid into the driver's seat. "It's fine, miss. I'm available for as long as you need."

"Thank you, Jensen. I appreciate you driving me and Jordan around."

As Jensen pulled through the gate at the bottom of the driveway, he looked back at me in the rearview mirror. "It's my job, miss. Mr. Stone expects me to drive you wherever you need to go."

The mood between us was suddenly awkward, and after I told him what restaurant I'd chosen and we stopped at the ATM, I leaned back against the leather seat to wait silently until we reached Brooklyn. Jensen got us there in no time and as I'd promised, I had him blow the horn, over his polite protests that he'd be happy to escort me to the building's front door to get her.

Jordan popped her head in the back driver's side door and scrunched up her face. "Honking? What am I? Some cheap high school girl?"

"Get in! We're on a mission for great food and chocolate martinis!" I squealed.

She sat down in the seat and as we drove off, she looked at me and smiled. "I never get tired of seeing you this happy. Do you know that?"

"I guess what you always say is right. Good things do happen to good people."

I never got tired of being that happy, to be honest. Everything in my life had changed so much, and at the center of it was the reason for all that happiness. Tristan. I slipped my phone out of my bag and checked for new messages. Nothing.

Jordan leaned against me and stared over my shoulder. "Didn't you just leave Mr. Tall, Dark, and Gorgeous?"

I elbowed her gently in the arm. "He's out of town. I was just hoping he'd text me again."

"So, while the cat's away the mice will play, huh?" she joked sing-song. "Where are we mice heading to tonight?"

Putting my phone away, I turned toward her in my seat. "I thought we could try The Channel. I heard it was great, and it's supposed to be a great club too."

She looked down at her black dress and back up at me. "I'm not sure I'm dressed for that place, Nina. I feel like your poor country cousin."

"That's ridiculous! You look incredible, as always. You've always had much better style than I have, no matter how much you spend or don't spend."

"I just don't want you to look bad," she said quietly. "I mean, now that you're with Tristan…"

I stopped her with my hand on her arm. "Jordan, my being with Tristan has nothing to do with what clothes we should wear. Well, it does for me since he bought most of mine, but we're still the same two girls we've been since we met that day in college."

She laughed at my admission that my clothes were all bought and paid for. "So you're a happily kept woman now? Whatever that's like, it looks good on you."

"How did Justin take you bowing out of this week's wrestling matches?" I asked, eager to change the subject.

Rolling her eyes, she said, "He said he was fine with it, but something in his voice said he wasn't, so I promised him I'd stop by his place before I go home."

"And you tease me about checking for texts? Sounds like someone else is crazy about a guy too."

She jabbed me in the arm with her fingers, tickling me until I giggled. "No more of that. This is a girl's night out, so let's get this party started!"

Jordan and I were like two peas in a pod, as we'd always been, and dinner was a great time. We laughed ourselves to tears as she told me about her third grade students and their very demanding letters to their parents about what gifts they wanted for Christmas.

I took a sip of my chocolate martini as Jordan's laughter ebbed away. She looked at me intently, as if she was studying me. "What? What is it?"

"You look so different tonight drinking that martini and wearing that dress I know cost a fortune, but even though the outside seems to have changed, you're still the same old Nina. I like that even with all the changes you've been through that you're still you."

"Of course I'm still me. Who else would I be?" I asked, unsure of what she meant.

She took a gulp of her beer and shrugged. "Well, you're basically Mrs. Tristan Stone, aren't you? That might change someone." Looking down at my left hand, she got a confused look on her face. "Why aren't you wearing the engagement ring he gave you? Aren't you still planning to marry him?"

I didn't know what to say to that. I wasn't wearing the ring because I wasn't sure he still wanted to marry me. I believed with all my heart that he loved me just as much as he said he did before the accident, but he hadn't mentioned our engagement or any plans to marry me since we'd rekindled our relationship, and I didn't want to pressure him. I was happy with the way things were going between us and didn't want to ruin it.

Instead of telling her this, though, I fibbed and hoped she wouldn't see right through me. "Of course, but since the accident I've lost a little weight so it doesn't fit right."

"Good. I don't want to hear you two are breaking up or anything stupid like that. I know things must be pretty strange since you don't remember him from before yet, but if any two people are supposed to be together, it's you and Tristan."

"No need to worry about us. I promise. What about you and Justin?"

Jordan sighed deeply and smirked. "We're doing fine, but it's not like you two. We're just average people in a regular relationship. No bells and whistles. Just comfortable."

Quickly, she stood from the table and looked around. "I need to find the ladies' room. Be right back."

I knew Jordan well enough to know she was uncomfortable about me asking about Justin. Her tone said boring instead of comfortable, but I didn't think I should press the issue. In my eyes, Jordan was anything but regular and average. She deserved a man who set her heart racing and turned her world upside down in the best ways. My heart was sad at the news that she didn't believe he was that only a few months into the relationship.

She returned in just a few minutes wearing a smile from ear to ear. Grabbing my arm, she squealed, "Oh my God! Nina, I just saw the most gorgeous man, and I swear he was checking me out too. Brown hair, the darkest blue eyes I've ever seen, and a body to die for!"

I looked around for this perfect specimen of man but didn't see anyone. She sat down and while she gushed about her sexy mystery man, I joked, "Um, weren't you just saying you have a boyfriend? I think his name is Justin or something like that."

"I know. I know. Justin is nice and everything, but this guy was stunning. And I think he was into me too. Well, enough of my mystery man. I can't wait to hang out with you and Tristan on New Year's Eve. We're going to have such a good time, especially compared to last year. You don't remember what we did last New Year's Eve, do you?" she asked with a giggle.

I shook my head. "Still nothing. Why? Tell me. What did we do?"

Putting her hands up to cover her face, she groaned. "I'm still trying to forget Paul. He's teaching fifth grade this year. His classroom is right down the hall from mine."

"What happened? Don't keep me in suspense! I'm a woman with a head injury, for God's sake!"

"He tried to have sex with me in the coatroom of the hotel just as it turned midnight. As if I was going to just hike up my dress and bang him right then and there!"

"No way! You have to tell me what my date was like."

"You got off slightly better with his friend, a short accountant who spent the night unsure if he wanted to kiss you or bore you with details about his job. Thankfully, he only tried to maul you once and you didn't have to fend him off like I had to with Creepy Paul. You know, that's what I silently refer to him as every time I see him at school."

"You're terrible! The poor guy was probably in love with you from a distance and just jumped the gun a little that night," I joked.

"I think the best part of that New Year's was laughing ourselves to sleep that night," she said with a smile. "We began the year pretty badly, but we've come pretty far since then, don't you think?"

Her phone buzzed on the table and I saw that it was Justin. As she took the call, I accepted with disappointment that our night out was over. It was okay, though. All the better that I got home early just in case Tristan was there. The sadness of his message stayed in my mind still, and I wanted to be there for him in case his trip had gone badly.

"I have to go, Nina. I have work tomorrow. A few more and I'll never be able to handle the little angels."

She was lying, but it was okay. "I'll have Jensen come around and pick us up," I said as I moved to get up.

"No, that's okay. I'll take a cab. Finish your drink."

"Are you sure? Jensen can take you to Justin's. It's no problem."

Jordan gave me a definite shake of her head. "No need. It's out of your way to take me back to Brooklyn." Opening her arms, she smiled. "Come here and give me a hug before I go."

"I'll see you in a few days, so tell Justin I'm looking forward to spending time with both of you," I said as she hugged me. I released her and stepped away. "I know we usually give our gifts on Christmas morning, but yours won't be in until after that, so get ready to be blown away when it comes in January."

Jordan waved me off. "You don't have to get me anything, Nina. I know you've been dealing with a lot just before the holidays."

"Forget that. I have just the perfect gift for you, so get ready. I know you'll love it!"

Her phone rang again, putting an end to our goodbyes, and as I watched her walk out, I saw my phone light up on the table. Excited to finally talk to Tristan, I swiped the face to see it wasn't a call but an email notification. I tapped the little envelope and saw a message from Cal asking if we could meet. Since I was in the city, I figured it was perfect timing and emailed back for him to stop by The Channel if he was free and able to make it. A minute later, he replied he was nearby, so I ordered another of those candy sweet martinis and sat back to wait for him.

Checking my phone, I saw Tristan hadn't texted again. Disappointed, I quickly texted him the words *I love you* and hoped that would make him reply. Within fifteen minutes Cal had arrived but still no text from Tristan.

"I'm so glad you emailed me, Nina," Cal said as he sat down across the table from me. He settled into his chair and smiled. "You look incredible. Life certainly has treated you well."

"Well, except for that whole car accident and amnesia thing," I joked.

He looked at me as if he were sizing me up and shook his head. "I don't know. Maybe forgetting the past is something we all should do because you look great."

"Happiness does that for a person. You look pretty good after all these years, so you must be doing something right too."

In truth, Cal looked a little haggard. His grey wool coat was old and worn, and I'd noticed when he took off his gloves that the leather was ripped between his right thumb and forefinger. He still had those boyish good looks that had attracted me years ago, but now they were tinged with worry or weariness. I couldn't decide which.

"I have to tell you, Nina, that I was surprised at first that you came to see me, but now I'm so happy we're getting a chance to get reacquainted."

"I am too, Cal. I think bygones should be left as bygones."

I finished my drink and a waiter arrived almost instantly to ask me if I'd like another. I probably shouldn't have, but they tasted so good, so even though I was already feeling a little lightheaded and giddy, I ordered another martini.

"And you, sir?"

Cal shook his head and forced his lips into a thin line. "No, thanks." The waiter moved away from us, and Cal turned to face me. "This is a fancy place. I don't remember you liking places like this."

I couldn't tell if the tone in his voice was condemnation or insecurity. Either way, it made me uneasy to see Cal like this. As if I had to come up with an excuse why I'd want to eat in a nice restaurant, I said, "This place has gotten great reviews. I just thought I'd try it and see if it lives up to all the hype."

The truth was that I enjoyed restaurants like this now. I could afford them and I'd learned quickly from Tristan that I deserved to enjoy myself. I wasn't hurting anyone, so why shouldn't I have a nice meal in a trendy restaurant? As I sat there silently defending myself and my desire to eat good food, no matter how expensive it seemed to Cal, he shifted in his chair and seemed to not know where to put his hands as he moved them from the table to his lap and back again.

"Cal, you seem uncomfortable. Is something wrong? Is there something you didn't tell me the other day that I should know?"

He hung his head and quietly answered, "No, there's nothing more to tell. I was an ass and deserve anything you say to me."

Reaching over, I gently touched his sleeve. "It's okay, Cal. Things happen when you're young. That's why they say people are young and stupid. Nobody ever says someone's young and wise."

He frowned at my attempt to make him feel better. "It's just that I have no right to ask you for anything."

His voice strained as he spoke the words, and I could have sworn I saw him tear up. This wasn't the person I remembered at all. He was suffering right there in front of me, and I couldn't just let that happen.

"What's wrong, Cal? What's happened to you?"

He blew the air out of his cheeks and shook his head. "I've had a bad run of things, Nina. My mother was sick for a long time and passed away just a few months ago. She always liked you, I think because you were a lot like her."

"Oh, Cal. I'm so sorry. Your mother was a terrific lady. I had no idea."

"It's just been one thing after another, and tonight I found out that my girlfriend has been seeing someone else and is moving in with him. I just don't know how I'm going to afford our apartment since I signed the lease thinking we'd both be paying toward the rent."

My heart broke at the sight of this sad man sitting in front of me. The boy who'd broken my heart was now feeling what I'd felt, but it didn't give me any pleasure. I'd been blessed with a great man in Tristan, and I wanted everyone I knew to have the same wonderful luck I'd had. I couldn't help Cal out in the girlfriend department, but I could give him some money to help with his rent. I had it, and it would be a crime not to pay it forward.

I reached into my purse and pulled out all the money I had left after paying for dinner, leaving just enough to pay for my last martinis. Handing him the cash, I pressed it into his palm. "Take this."

"No, I couldn't," he weakly protested.

I understood. He didn't want to be emasculated by an ex-girlfriend he'd recently asked forgiveness from. "Then consider it a loan. You were right when you said life has treated me well. It has, but it means nothing if you can't help out a friend in need. I know it's only a few hundred, but I can give you more tomorrow."

"Nina, no. It's okay. This is more than enough. Thank you."

I squeezed his hand before he moved to pocket the money. "You know how to contact me if you need more."

He began to say thank you again, but we were interrupted by Jensen, who suddenly appeared behind Cal. "Miss, I'm sorry I'm late. The car is waiting just outside."

For a moment, Jensen's words confused me, but I realized as he stood there looking down at my purse as it sat on the table in front of me that he believed he was safeguarding me. Before I could set his mind at ease, Cal stood and thanked me again as he quickly headed toward the door.

Tristan's driver nodded silently at me, and I slipped into my coat to return to the house. I considered asking him if he planned to mention any of this to Tristan, but I knew the answer already. Jensen worked for Tristan Stone, not Nina Edwards, and his employer likely knew all about my friendly loan to my ex.

I followed Jensen to the car and got into the back, half expecting Tristan to be sitting there waiting for me. A stab of disappointment hit me when I saw the car was empty, and as it pulled away from The Channel, I knew I'd have to explain what I'd just done, but I wasn't worried.

I hadn't done anything wrong, and once Tristan heard about the hard times that had befallen Cal, I knew he'd understand. No matter what the rest of the world saw, in my heart I knew Tristan was a kind soul like me.

Chapter Sixteen

Tristan

I'd driven halfway back to the house, but I couldn't wait any longer to read Joseph Edwards' notes. Pulling over at a diner on the side of the road, I bought a cup of coffee and opened up Nina's father's notebook on the table in front of me. I took a sip of the drink that tasted like a cross between dishwater and mud and pushed the cup and saucer away from me. Pressing my phone on again, I brought up Nina's message telling me she loved me and stared at it, silently promising to show her how much she meant to me when I returned home.

As I'd driven here, the need to see what was written in the notebook had been overwhelming, but now that it sat there in front of me with nothing stopping me, I hesitated, unsure I could see the truth he'd uncovered about my father that had gotten him killed. My hand hovered over the tablet, shaking at the thought of what could be contained in those pages.

I was no fool. There was no way I'd be able to read the proof of my father's crime and not tell Nina the entire truth of her father's death, but the memory of how she'd reacted the last time was like a fresh wound still nearly splitting my heart in two. I couldn't lose her again, this time possibly forever.

But I couldn't live in ignorance not knowing what had happened between Victor Stone and Joseph Edwards.

Taking a deep breath in, I swallowed hard and opened the notebook. My eyes flowed over the page, taking in each word and its meaning.

Stone Worldwide—Victor Stone—Taylor Stone

I was surprised to see my brother's name mentioned so prominently at the top of the first page. Taylor had worked closely with my father in Stone Worldwide's business, being groomed to take over when he retired, but he was more an office mate than anything else. At least it had seemed that way.

Atlanta—October 2008

-civil suit—sexual harassment/judge?? Why a problem? Name of judge?

Joseph Edwards' notes made no sense. A sexual harassment case wasn't particularly noteworthy in Stone Worldwide. Thousands of employees across the globe meant at any time someone may feel they had a case, especially considering my father's proclivity for young women who happened to work for him. Sexual harassment cases had become commonplace by the time I was old enough to understand much of anything my father did at work each day.

Had Taylor been involved in one of those cases? I had a hard time believing that. If anything, he was the good son, never getting into trouble with drugs, women, or anything else. He'd graduated with honors from college and gone on to earn an M.B.A. He was the one who rose everyday before dawn to be ready to leave for work at six and stayed until late at night, often putting in fifteen hour workdays.

I'd been the one who'd been arrested twice for drugs, only getting off when the Stone family money had conveniently found its way to that local police chief in northern Jersey. It had been me who'd been carted out of apartments and clubs by Rogers more times than either he or I wanted to remember, usually costing my father money to keep the press quiet and women I liked to call girlfriends pacified so they wouldn't talk about the sex and my all-day coke binges.

As I remembered those days of my past, I shook my head in disbelief that it could be Taylor who had some part in anything unsavory. That was my role in the family—I was the black sheep. He'd always been the golden child, at least as far as my father was concerned.

October 2008. Taylor and I had been twenty-four then. He was still in graduate school being the exemplary student he'd always been.

Edwards' note indicated that something about the judge in the case had been a problem. What had he meant by that? I continued to read down the page, hoping to understand any of this.

-Amanda Cashen—July 1992-May 2008

My mind raced as I tried to find a memory of anyone with that name, but it didn't ring a bell. I'd never heard that name. 1992? Had my father had a child with another woman then and Amanda was the name of the baby? There had always been rumors that my father had other children. More than once I'd walked in on my parents fighting and heard my mother accuse him of fathering children with other women. His response was always the same—a sneer thrown in her direction as he belittled her claims as the rantings of a pathetic woman who didn't understand the way of the world for men like him. He never outright denied her accusations, which I was sure hurt even more than the painful doubts she had about her husband's love for her.

If a child named Amanda did exist and Edwards had found out, perhaps making that public would be reason enough for my father to want him out of the picture. As I sat there staring down at this mystery female's name, I couldn't imagine that could be the case, though. The note about a sexual harassment case made an illegitimate child a non-issue, unless the child was the product of my father doing something illegal.

I turned the page after unsuccessfully trying to read a number of notes that appeared to be simply scribblings and illegible symbols and saw a sentence that stopped me cold.

Atlanta 2008—gas explosion cafe—end of Stone's problems
-sexual harassment case ruled in his favor November 2008

What did some gas explosion have to do with a sexual harassment case that ended up going in Stone Worldwide's favor shortly after? Edwards' notes were too vague for me to understand what he was referring to. I flipped to the next page and saw one word over and over and in all caps at the top of the page.

TAYLOR

What had Joseph Edwards meant by writing my brother's name all over the page? None of this made any sense. I kept going, baffled by what the connection was between my father's illegitimate child, a sexual harassment case against him, and some explosion at an Atlanta cafe.

Folded in half between the next two pages was a newspaper article from the front page of the Atlanta Journal-Constitution dated October 23, 2008. I laid the paper out flat on the table. In the center of the article was a picture of a cafe that looked like it was in the middle of a war zone. The front of the coffee shop was blown out, leaving a gaping hole in the building. Chunks of concrete lay everywhere, exposed wires hung low, and remnants of the store that had once served people their morning coffee lay in pieces inside the building.

Under the picture read the caption *50 Dead In Rush Hour Explosion.*

My hands began to shake as I leaned forward to read the report of the bombing. The words swam in front of my eyes as I struggled to comprehend the horror of what had happened.

50 men, women and children killed at coffee shop blast. Gas explosion thought to be the reason.

Investigators still looking for clues.

Witnesses report the scene was "pure carnage."

7:38 am the explosion rocked the Corner Cafe one block from the courthouse.

Children on their way to school killed. Hundreds injured.

Reports of people smelling gas just before the blast.

Judge Albert Cashen one of the victims.

I flipped back through the pages to where the illegitimate child's name was written. *Amanda Cashen.*

There was no way it was a coincidence that a judge with the same last name as a child who could be my father's was killed in a gas explosion at a coffee shop near where he worked. And that he was a judge was likely no coincidence either.

My mouth tasted like bile as my insides churned at the idea that would explain this all. My father had the judge in a civil suit murdered. My father had been a monster, no doubt. Victor Stone was a man who got what he wanted, and if that required the sacrifice of someone, he wasn't above that. There was a long line of damage trailing behind him for most of his adult life. I didn't want to believe any of this, but it was all too easy. My father was like many powerful men. Any obstacle in his way to what he wanted was overcome or eliminated. If he hadn't been able to overcome Judge Cashen, then he would have eliminated him.

I leaned back against the booth and closed my eyes. The room felt like it was spinning around me. Taking a deep breath, I tried to push out the images of all those people lying dead and maimed because of my own father's actions. Children suffering, their parents devastated, all so Victor Stone could once again slip out of being held responsible for his behavior.

"Are you okay? Can I get you more coffee?" I heard someone ask and I opened my eyes to see the middle-aged waitress standing over me with a look of concern on her plain face.

I shook my head and mumbled, "Just a water, please."

She left me sitting there, my stomach sick as I turned the idea of my father's crime over and over in my mind. I didn't want to know any more. Not only had he killed the judge and Nina's father, but he'd killed innocent men, women, and children who'd never heard of him just going about their daily lives on their way to work and school.

My phone vibrated in my coat pocket, and I reached in to see a text from Daryl. I read it, feeling like the Universe had suddenly decided it was time to pile on. *Need to meet. Got some interesting pics of loverboy you want to see.*

A hollow feeling took over my insides as my mind raced with thoughts of Nina with her ex again. I didn't want to think about that now. *Meet tomorrow at noon in my office.*

The waitress returned with my water, placing it down and patting my shoulder as she walked away. I had to continue reading Joseph Edwards' notes, no matter how sick what he'd found out made me. After downing a big gulp of water that tasted faintly of chlorine, I flipped to the next page of his tablet.

Jessica Cashen—3:30 pm 1/6/09 832 Sturges Way Alpharetta

The rest of that page was filled with my father's and Taylor's names, along with Albert and Amanda Cashen's names linked with arrows showing how Edwards had attempted to figure out the connection between these four people. In the center of this drawing was one word followed by a question mark.

Child?

Was it a simple case of an illegitimate child that had led to the death of so many?

I read over the note about Jessica Cashen again and guessed Edwards had arranged to meet with her. Those were the details that would tell me what I needed to know.

Two empty pages later, I found his notes from his meeting with Jessica. I read the words, but they didn't sink in. I couldn't comprehend them, my mind unwilling to accept the truth of them.

Doubts it was a coincidence

Taylor and Amanda—together for months, according to Jessica

Found out she was pregnant March 2008—told Taylor soon after

Refused to see her or answer her calls—begged to see him but nothing —devastated became depressed

I knew what was coming next. Even so, when I turned the page, the words hit me like I'd crashed into a brick wall at a hundred miles an hour.

Hanged herself May 12, 2008—3 months pregnant

-father found her in the basement

Jessica Cashen's story of how her sister died and how her father blamed Taylor for her suicide went on and on for lines down the page, but I couldn't read anymore. I pushed the tablet away in disgust, my heart sick from what I'd read.

The person described in these pages wasn't someone I knew. Taylor had always been the good son. He'd never even really dated many women, sticking with one shy, rather nondescript girl he met freshman year in college. My mother had always said he'd marry her, have children, and live happily ever after, unlike me, who had no stability in his life and refused to even consider any kind of happily ever after that didn't involve late nights and a different female for each one.

Taylor and I had never been as close as twins were supposed to be, but I thought I had known him, at least. Never in my wildest nightmares could I have imagined he was this person. Amanda Cashen had been a girl—fifteen years old. What the fuck had he been doing with her?

For the first time a horrifying thought settled into my mind. Had Taylor raped her? Jesus Christ! Even if she had agreed to sleeping with him, she was just a child, a minor he had no business touching.

I had to get out of there. The dingy yellow diner walls felt like they were closing in on me, suffocating me. Scooping up the notebook and newspaper article, I threw a twenty on the table and got the hell out. By the time I reached my car, it was all I could do to toss it all onto the front passenger seat before I bent over behind the rear bumper and puked up coffee, water, and whatever the fuck I'd had for lunch. I stood there hunched over in the cold night air until there was nothing left in my stomach and all I had left was dry heaves that made my ribs ache in pain.

Finally, I stood up and wiped my mouth, thankful for the bracing December air against my face. Swallowing hard, I tried to push every terrible word I'd read from my thoughts, but I couldn't. All I saw over and over was the image of my brother on top of some helpless girl and my father standing behind them coldly ordering the death of Albert Cashen.

I floored it, hitting over a hundred and twenty at times as I raced home. I wanted to be as far away from that storage unit and that diner, but it was no use. Everything I'd found out stayed with me, and I feared it would never leave me.

As I drove up to the house I shared with Nina, the realization of what I'd learned hit me. How could I face her after everything I now knew about why her father had died? It was worse than I'd ever imagined. Joseph Edwards hadn't just uncovered some shady land deal or my father's philandering ways. He'd pulled back the protective cover shielding my father and my brother and their unspeakable actions. Nina's father had been murdered to protect Taylor's despicable acts with a teenage girl and my father's callous desire to have the world bend to his orders, no matter how terrible or depraved they were.

I shut off the car and sat back in the seat, drained from my trip. I'd flown halfway around the world at times and not felt this exhausted. I didn't know how I'd face Nina now. She had no idea of the kind of people I came from. How would she ever forgive me for what my family had done to hers?

I sat there staring into the darkness until I knew I couldn't avoid facing her any longer. As I walked through the door, Rogers met me, almost as if he'd been waiting for me. His expression was stony, instantly making my blood run cold. Had something happened and Nina was already gone?

"Tristan, Jensen needs to speak to you. He's waiting in my part of the house."

"What's this about? I'm tired, Rogers. I'll deal with him tomorrow," I said as I brushed past him to see if Nina was still there.

"She's in her room, Tristan. That's what Jensen needs to talk to you about. He's worried you're going to fire him this time."

I spun around to face Rogers, my heart racing wildly in fear. "Did something happen? Is she hurt?"

He slowly shook his head. "No. She's fine. I think it would be better to hear what Jensen has to say before you speak to her."

"Rogers, what the fuck is wrong? If Nina isn't hurt, then what could Jensen be worried about?"

I turned to leave and he caught my arm. Surprised, I turned my head and looked at him and saw a look of concern I hadn't seen on his face since those days when he was rescuing me from my self-destructive behavior.

"You need to speak to him. Take a few minutes before you go to her to hear what Jensen has to tell you."

Something in his voice convinced me and I followed him to his part of the house. I found Jensen a worried wreck pacing the floor of Roger's personal study.

His usually calm expression twisted into one full of fear. "You told me to make sure she was safe, and I know the bodyguards are always there, but I thought I should step in. I meant no harm, Mr. Stone."

"Stop. Tell me what happened."

Jensen took a deep breath as he quit his pacing. Hanging his head, he said, "I took Miss Edwards to pick up her friend Jordan and then took them to a restaurant. When West and Varo told me her friend had left, I pulled the car around to pick her up, but instead another person joined her. A man she obviously knew. I didn't want to intrude, but as I watched, she gave him money. I finally did interrupt them to tell her the car was ready because I was afraid he was going to take even more money. I'm sorry if I was out of line. I was concerned she was giving this strange man so much money."

So this was what Daryl was talking about when he texted that he had interesting pictures of Cal. Nina had met him again, and now he was busy trying to con her out of money, as he had with other women, and doing it quite successfully, it seemed. On top of everything else I'd felt that night, jealousy and rage now burned in my gut.

Struggling to hide my feelings, I patted Jensen on the shoulder, thankful for his attempt to keep Nina safe. He'd done the right thing.

If only Nina had.

CHAPTER SEVENTEEN

Tristan

Instead of going to see Nina after hearing Jensen's report, I went to my room alone, thankful in some ways for having a reason to avoid seeing her. On the floor just inside the room lay an envelope with my name written in her handwriting and a tiny smiley face drawn on the front. As with her other letter, fear flared inside my mind at the thought of what she might have written. Maybe she'd confessed to giving her ex-boyfriend money while they sat at a restaurant earlier that night. Or maybe she'd remembered something and this was the letter in which she finally told me she couldn't forgive me for what my father had done.

Fuck. Not knowing was like torture. If only I could dismiss her as easily as I'd always been able to dismiss the rest of the world, but I couldn't. I loved her to distraction, and even the unknown words she'd written on a sheet of paper inside that envelope could tie me up in knots.

I slid my finger under the flap of the envelope and tore it open, unable to wait any more. Unfolding her letter, I silently prayed for some release from all of this soon.

Dear Tristan,

I like our letter writing back and forth. It feels like we're romantic pen pals separated by some huge distance and someday someone will find our letters and see that no matter what separated us, we ended up together because we loved one another. What can I say? I'm an incurable romantic. ❤ *You didn't answer your phone, so I'll tell you what I wanted to say here. I hope your day was good. I missed having you near me. Come find me when you get home. I'll be waiting up for you.*

I love you.
Nina

I didn't go see her right away. I needed to be able to look at her without feeling guilty, but that wasn't going to happen without at least taking a shower. Maybe if I did that I'd find some way to wash off some of the ugliness and be able to deserve someone like Nina.

Half an hour later I'd stood in the shower until my fingertips wrinkled but it hadn't worked. The reality of what I was—the son of the man who'd done so much to hurt so many—couldn't be washed away, no matter how much I tried.

The story Jensen had told me rattled around in my head as I walked over to her room. I didn't want to be jealous, believing the whole thing had been just another example of Nina's goodness in helping that manipulative fuck of an ex. I couldn't help it, though. Anything that made me feel like it would take her away I hated instinctively.

She was already asleep when I reached her room, but I quietly slipped in and stood beside her bed watching her as she softly breathed in and out, her mouth in that beautiful pout she hated and I loved. I wanted to kiss that mouth and wake her up, my Sleeping Beauty who I could whisk away to another kingdom and take care of forever.

Nothing was stopping us. I had enough money to last for this lifetime and the next. We could run away and never be found again, just the two of us living for love. No more of Karl and the Board. No more Cal. No more anyone but us.

That wasn't right, though. There would always be something we couldn't run away from. Someday she'd remember who I was and what part my family had played in taking her father from her, and then there would be nowhere in the world I could go for forgiveness.

I had to tell her what I knew. I had to tell her why her father had been taken from her. I had to tell her everything.

As I stood there watching her, she stirred awake and smiled up at me. She had no idea the man she was happy to see could very well be the one person she'd never want to lay eyes on again.

"Hey, what are you doing there staring at me as I sleep?" she jokingly asked. Stretching her arms above her head, she pushed away her drowsiness. "I missed you."

"I missed you too. I got your letter."

Nina sat up and rubbed her eyes. "Did you like it?" Looking up at me, she held out her hand. "Sit down. Tell me about your day."

I sat down beside her and ran my fingers through her hair. "I'd rather hear about yours. Jensen tells me you and Jordan had a girl's night out."

"I'm guessing he told you about me seeing Cal too."

"He did," I said flatly, hoping to hide how jealous it made me.

She squeezed my hand. "Don't be angry, Tristan. He's down on his luck and I did him a little favor. That's all."

"I don't think you know your friend Cal very well, Nina. What you call down on his luck is actually his con. He does this to women all the time."

"No, you're wrong. Remember, he didn't come looking for me. I found him after all these years. He's just going through some bad stuff now. You'd help someone like him too. I know you would."

I lifted her chin with my forefinger so her gaze met mine. "You're too nice. I know all about him and I'm telling you he's playing you."

"I don't believe it. No girlfriend cheating on him and leaving him with an expensive apartment to pay for? He told me his mother died too. Was that a lie?"

Shrugging my shoulders, I admitted I knew nothing about either of these things. "But I can find out. Whatever he's claimed, I'm guessing it's a lie. He does this all the time, Nina. You're going to have to be careful now that you have money."

"About that. Why do I have all that money? You can't be paying me that much to be your private art curator."

"I can pay you whatever I want."

Nina pulled me by my T-shirt until my mouth was next to hers. With a smile, she said, "Well, I guess that answers that, now doesn't it?"

I kissed her lips and whispered against them, "Now promise me no more money to Cal."

"If what you say is really true, I won't give him any more."

"You doubt me?" I asked, half-teasing and half bothered that she might not trust me on this.

"You know I like to question everything. I thought you liked that about me."

"I like you questioning other people, not me."

"Cro-magnon much?" she said with a giggle. "Somebody has to keep you on your toes, Mr. Stone."

"On my toes?"

Nina playfully ran her tongue over the seam of my lips. "And all those other fine body parts."

My cock stiffened as she teased me, and for at least a little while I wanted to believe I could forget all the bad I needed to confess and get lost in her. Fisting my hand in her hair, I tugged her head back and covered her mouth with mine, thrusting my tongue into her mouth to find hers. I wanted to escape inside her body.

"I want to be inside you so bad," I groaned as I trailed kisses down her neck.

She arched her back, rubbing her breasts against my chest and cooing as she wrapped her legs around my waist. Looking down at the silk pajamas I wore, she licked her lips and slid her forefinger just under the waistband. "Then get these off."

Not waiting for my answer, she tugged them down over my hips while I pulled her shorts and panties off. I threw them away from me and watched as she did the same with my pants.

"Didn't we buy you something nicer to wear to bed?" I asked as she stripped off my T-shirt.

Nina skimmed her hands over my stomach and looked up at me, her eyes sparkling with desire. "Uh huh, but what's the purpose of wearing them if it's just me?"

I tore her shirt from her and pulled her to me. "It's never just you. I'm always nearby, even if I'm not right next to you."

Her teeth nipped at my collarbone as she mumbled against my skin, "I like it better when you're right next to me."

I loved the feel of her mouth on me, exciting me as she showed how much she wanted me inside her. Slipping my hand down over her stomach, I probed between her legs, loving when I found her dripping wet.

"Tell me what you want, baby," I whispered as I pushed a single finger inside her eager cunt.

She wriggled against my hand, desperate for the pleasure I wanted to give her, and whimpered, "I want you. Inside me. Fucking me until I come and then until I come again."

I loved when she talked like that. There wasn't a man on Earth who didn't want exactly this kind of woman—a lady in public any man could be proud to show off and a whore in the bedroom who knew what she wanted and wasn't afraid to let her man know. That Nina could be both thrilled me and made me love her even more.

Her hand stroked my cock from base to tip, making my control ebb away. Struggling to hold back, I had to give in and pushed her back onto the bed. I wanted to feel her warm and wet cunt surrounding my cock as I thrust into her to reach that place where I could give her what she wanted and find some peace from everything that plagued my mind.

Taking a nipple into my mouth, I sucked it hard and bit down gently until she cried out more in pleasure than pain. Her heels pushed against my lower back, urging me to enter her and leave the foreplay for another time.

"Don't tease, Tristan. You always tease," she whispered in a needy voice as she clawed at my back to pull me close.

"Not teasing, princess. Control," I said low in her ear as I slowly eased my cock inch by inch into her eager body.

She thrust her hips upward to welcome me into her and pressed her fingertips into my back. "I don't want controlled Tristan. Let me see what's inside your heart instead of always being so in control."

"You don't want that, Nina," I said in a strangled voice as I began to slowly make love to her.

Cradling my face, she stared deep into my eyes as I continued to push my cock into her. "I do. Show me that man," she moaned.

I slowed to a languid pace in and out of her body. I wished I could show her that man—the one who didn't need to be in control of everything in fear that if he didn't, his life would spiral down to nothing. Burying my head in the pillow next to hers, I said quietly, "I am who I am, Nina."

She stopped my motion with her heels against my back, keeping me inside her as she threatened to tear away the walls I made sure to protect myself with at all times.

"I love who you are, Tristan, but I know there's someone else inside there. Someone who has nothing to do with control or money. That Tristan wants to say things to me. I wish you'd let him."

"I love you, Nina. I love you with an need that scares me sometimes. I've never loved anyone like this. I spend my days dreading that you're going to wake up one day, realize who I am, and tell me you can't do this anymore. That you can't live with someone who's as fucked up as I am."

She kissed me softly on the lips as tears welled in her eyes. "I don't know what you're talking about. You're not fucked up. Why would you say that?"

Closing my eyes, I took a deep breath. "There's so much about me no one would want."

"That's not true, Tristan. No matter what you think, you're wonderful."

I stayed silent for a long time until I finally admitted the truth at the heart of us. Opening my eyes, I whispered, "One word of rejection from you would kill me, Nina. Please tell me that even if you ever think that you can't take who I am anymore, you won't leave. Give me a chance to show you I love you."

No matter how much I asked for her to make that promise, I knew there was the real risk that she would leave again when she found out what my father had done and how much I'd known about it all this time. This time I'd make sure things turned out different, though. I had to.

"Tristan, I'm not going anywhere. I promise no matter what. I love you. That means no leaving."

We made love sweeter than it had ever been before between us or between me and any other woman. Deep inside, I hoped that Nina would want to live up to the promise she'd made. The time was coming that I'd have to finally confess everything. Each day that passed meant the risk that she'd remember everything grew, but until I knew the whole ugly story, I had to wait.

I just hoped that when the time came, it wouldn't be too late.

As always, I slipped out of Nina's room after she fell asleep and returned to my room. I'd grown used to my nightmares since the plane crash, but I knew tonight would be filled with more than usual. Over and over, I was haunted by the image of Taylor and my father standing over two dead bodies. I got less than an hour's sleep total, tossing and turning until I woke up in a cold sweat twice before I just gave up and got ready for work.

I stood in the kitchen hoping coffee would undo what my lack of sleep was working hard to accomplish, but even the caffeine in the special blend Rogers bought for me wasn't able to do the job. My eyelids drooped heavily as I leaned against the center island, my day ahead and all that I'd learned in Pennsylvania weighing on my mind.

My eyes closed, but I felt a hand touch my arm and I looked around to see Nina standing in front of me, her expression full of concern.

"Hey, are you okay?"

I shook the grogginess from my head and forced a smile. "I'm fine. Good morning." Bending down, I kissed her softly on the lips. "Sleep well?"

She stroked her fingertips down my tie. "Better than you, I'm guessing since I'm not sleeping standing up. I thought only horses did that."

"I'm fine. Long day ahead of me."

Nina wrapped her arms around me and pulled me into her. "I'm worried about you. Why don't you ever stay with me all night?"

I couldn't tell her the truth—that I wasn't sure she was ready to see the real me, the man who suffered through each night with nightmares, sometimes just one but other times dozens. Would she even want me if she knew I was so fucked up?

"I'm one of those workaholic types. My brain never shuts off, so a lot of times I get up and do work when you're sleeping. I don't like to bother you, so I go back to my own room."

She squeezed me in her arms and looked up at me with a smile. "It wouldn't bother me and it would be nice to see you there when I wake up."

I couldn't say no when she looked at me like that, with those blue eyes so sweet. "Okay." I didn't mean it. There was no way I could stay with her all night feeling like I did now.

Nina turned to pour herself a cup of coffee. "I'm going to do some work on the Atlanta suite today. I have some good ideas, I think. How's your day look?"

Atlanta.

"I need to move up our trip there. Be ready to leave this afternoon," I said before I took my last sip of coffee.

Spinning around, she splashed coffee down the front of her shirt and rushed to pat it dry with a towel from the counter. "What? I'm not ready. I need more time."

"I have things I have to take care of there, and they can't wait. I'm sure whatever you choose will be great," I said calmly. "Be ready to go by three. I'll be back in a few."

I left Nina stunned in the kitchen and quickly got away from the house before she could ask any questions. I wasn't ready to explain everything yet.

Michelle was waiting for me when I got to my office, along with Daryl and Karl. While I would have liked to make both of them disappear, I had to deal with them. As I breezed past them on my way in, I decided Karl and his threats would be the first hurdle of the day.

"Karl, how nice to see you. Join me in my office."

He barely let me sit down before he began. "Is there anything you want to tell me, Tristan?"

I looked up and saw him standing in front of my desk. He held his chin high, as if he was looking down on me or had something over me.

"Other than what I told you last time, Karl, no. So if you're here with some bullshit bluster, I'm not in the mood. Go bother someone else."

He stepped forward and placed his palms on the edge of my desk, pushing the platinum nameplate aside. The symbolism wasn't lost on me. His meaty, rough hands with their thick knuckles shoving me out of the way.

Leaning forward, he jutted his face toward me. "Made any trips lately, Tristan?"

I'd been foolish in thinking he hadn't had someone watching me. Faking nonchalance, I leaned back in my chair and laced my fingers behind my head. "None recently, but I'm planning to head to Atlanta right after New Year's. Would you like me to bring you back some peaches, Karl?"

His expression changed as he mentally filed away the nugget of information I'd just given him, and then he grinned. "Speaking of peaches, how is your young lady? Feeling well?"

I bristled at his reference to Nina. "Have you taken to caring about Nina's welfare now, Karl?"

"I'm just here to remind you that if there is anything incriminating, she would be in grave danger."

I couldn't help but chuckle at him. "You been watching A Few Good Men recently? Your threat might work better if you sounded like Nicholson."

Karl didn't seem to understand my joke and continued, "This is almost at its end, son. Remember that."

He turned to leave as the triumphant victor of our lame battle of wits, mumbling something as he flung open the door and stalked past Michelle. This was a hell of a way to start the day. And now I had to deal with Daryl and his pictures, which would require more playacting on my part to avoid looking like a boyfriend who was in the dark as to what his woman was doing.

"Tristan, I have so much I want you to see," he announced as he entered my office and closed the door behind him.

"Take a seat, Daryl. Let's see what you have."

He sat down in front of my desk and pointed toward the door. "Before I begin, I should let you know that I saw him watching your lady while I was watching loverboy."

I couldn't hide my surprise at hearing that Karl himself was watching Nina. Thank God I had two bodyguards on her. But he was beginning to be a real problem. Stalking me was one thing. Stalking Nina was an entirely different thing and one I didn't like.

"I'm guessing by the look on your face that you didn't know. He didn't get close to her, but he was there and watching her."

"Thanks, Daryl. Did you see anyone else there?"

"Just the two giants who are always around her. I'd keep them with her at all times. That guy is no good, Tristan."

"So what do you have for me, Daryl?"

He handed me the pictures he'd taken as he watched Cal. "Pics of him with a handful of women. That boy gets around. Pics of your lady with loverboy. He's a real player and unless I'm reading her entirely wrong, she's way out of her league with him. You need to make her realize he's playing her. Got a decent amount from her the other night."

I sifted through the pictures of Cal Johnson and his catalog of women, stopping when I reached the few of Nina and him at the restaurant she'd told me about. I couldn't help but stare at her expression as she sat listening to the lies he spewed about a girlfriend breaking his heart and whatever other bullshit he told her. She looked so innocent sitting there next to him, her blue eyes intense as she sympathetically listened to his tale of woe, her mouth turning down slightly as the pictures went on and she heard how awful his life was. Did she look like that next to me, I wondered? In many ways, Cal resembled someone like me. I'd been accused of being manipulative many times by women. Had they seen me like I saw him now?

"I'm happy to report that nothing happened between them, you know, sexually. If you ask me, he doesn't seem interested in that from her at all. And she gives off no vibe that she wants him. I think it's a case of she's too nice and he knows it."

I handed the pictures back to Daryl, my gaze still fixed on the last one of Nina smiling warmly at Cal as she gave him money. "I'm wondering if it's time I paid our friend Cal a visit."

"If you're asking me, I say no. Don't bother yourself with this. Deal with your lady. I really don't think she's planning some kind of rendezvous. I think she's just naive and wants to help out an old friend who's down on his luck. She doesn't know this is his game. Let her know what's going on and I guarantee you I won't have any more pics of them together."

I thought about Daryl's suggestion and nodded my agreement. I didn't expect to see anything more from him about Nina and Cal, but it was best to keep an eye on loverboy for a while longer. Standing from my chair, I walked around to lead him out. "Keep on him for a little while. I want to be able to show without a doubt that he's scamming women."

"No problem, Tristan. Want to schedule a time to meet after Christmas? Say, the Friday after?"

Patting him on the back, I escorted him to Michelle's desk so she could mark the date on my calendar. "That's fine. If I don't see you before, have a merry Christmas, Daryl."

"You too, Tristan. Enjoy your holiday with your lady."

When he was out of earshot, I turned to Michelle. "I'm going to be out of the office until after the holidays. The same order as before applies. Do not let Karl in, but I want you to tell him I'll be in Dallas for Christmas when he asks."

"Okay. I will, Mr. Stone," she said quietly, as if her agreement was to be a secret too. "Is everything okay?"

I ignored her question as I spied the gift box at the back of her desk, evidence that Angelo had gotten her the Christmas gift I'd wanted. I'd told him to choose a necklace, something classic but nice, leaving him as much room to choose as he liked.

She blushed and looked back at the box. "You didn't have to go to such trouble, Mr. Stone. It's lovely."

Michelle knew as well as I did that I hadn't gone to any trouble since Angelo had done all the leg work. Smiling, I said, "It's the least I can do to make up for years of not doing enough. I hope he picked something you like."

She turned back toward me with the necklace laid across her palm. A white gold necklace with a diamond and pearl pendant, it was very much her style—classic and understated. Thank God for Angelo because if I had to pick out gifts like that, I'd likely be standing dumbfounded for hours in front of the counter at Saks.

"I love it. Thank you."

"I hope you have a nice holiday, Michelle. Make sure security locks the suite as you're leaving on Monday. I'll see you when I get back."

"Monday? You don't want me here on Christmas Eve, like every other year?"

Suddenly, I felt like Ebenezer Scrooge. I had made her work every other Christmas Eve since I'd started at Stone Worldwide. I was there, so it had never occurred to me that she shouldn't be there working too.

Shaking my head, I smiled at her. "No. Enjoy your holiday, Michelle."

"You too, Mr. Stone. I hope it's a happy one."

I didn't continue the conversation, silently praying that Nina and I would have a happy Christmas. It was our first, and I wanted it to be perfect for her. But first, I needed to find out the rest of the story from Amanda Cashen's sister. After making arrangements to fly out that afternoon, I took care of some business and headed back to the house to find Nina, my stomach in knots about what I'd find in Atlanta.

Chapter Eighteen

Tristan

The flight was thankfully uneventful, even though the smoothest plane ride was still terrifying for me. I spent the entire time sitting like a statue in my seat while Nina talked about what she planned to do for the Atlanta suite, intentionally trying to take my mind off the trip. I hadn't exaggerated about wanting to join the Mile High Club with her when I'd teased her about it, but the minute I stepped onto the plane, it was like every other time I'd flown since the crash. My heart raced and I didn't feel like I was getting enough air in my lungs, as if someone had their hands wrapped around my neck and their fingers were pressing against my throat, slowly strangling me. None of the tricks the doctors had given me worked, but I couldn't help but smile at Nina's attempt to make the flight bearable.

The Atlanta Richmont was all decked out for the Christmas holiday with a twenty-five foot evergreen tree decorated with gold and red ornaments as the focal point in the lobby. It resembled the kind of tree my mother used to love for the holidays.

"Tristan, this hotel is gorgeous! Do all of them look like this?" Nina asked as she swiveled her head left and right to take in all the view.

"Pretty much. Some are better than others. This is my first time here too, but I must say it's not bad."

She jabbed me in the ribs with her finger and grimaced. "Always so understated. This place is great!"

I leaned down to kiss her and whispered, "I'm glad you like it. Let's hope you think the same way when you see the suite."

Located on the top floor of the hotel, the Peachtree Suite was one of two suites that took up the space a penthouse in other hotels would. I'd originally chosen this suite instead of the other Dogwood Suite because I'd hoped it would be a good way to ease Nina back into work.

Unlike in Dallas, with its ugly gold everywhere, the designers my father had hired for Atlanta were top notch, so all she'd have to do was choose a piece or two she loved and she'd have succeeded.

Nina followed me into the suite and whistled behind me. "This is even nicer in person than it was online. I'm still not sure what artwork I could pick to improve on it, though."

I poured myself a drink to calm my nerves from the plane and what I was about to do. "I'm sure whatever you pick will be great, Nina."

Wrapping her arms around me, she pressed her cheek to my back. "Is there something wrong? I know you said you hate flying, but all of a sudden, you seem different."

I put my glass down on the bar and placed my hands over hers on my chest. "Nothing wrong. I'm always like this after a flight."

"You sure? Anything I can do?" she asked sweetly, making me wish I could just tell her what was making my stomach twist in knots. I couldn't. Not yet, anyway. I had to do this alone, but I hoped that once I met with Jessica Cashen that all the secrets I'd kept from Nina could finally come out.

I turned in her hold and cupped her chin. "I need to take care of some business this afternoon, but I hope we can have dinner when I get back. I shouldn't be long."

Nina smiled up at me, blissfully unaware of where I was going. "Okay. I'm going to get working on the artwork for this nearly perfect suite, Mr. Stone. Don't worry. I'm on the job."

I couldn't help but smile. She did that to me. "I'm happy to hear it, Ms. Edwards. I'll expect a full report when I return then."

"Of course." She faked a bow and stood on her toes to kiss me. "Don't work too hard, okay? Tell whoever you're meeting that I'm going to have something to say to them if you come back here all grouchy because of work."

Kissing the tip of her nose, I promised not to work too hard. I couldn't promise I wouldn't be a miserable fuck when I returned, though. I hadn't been able to get all those terrible things Joseph Edwards had detailed in his notes out of my mind and what Judge

Cashen's daughter had to say likely wouldn't make things better. But at least I'd know the full truth.

The concierge had a car service take me to Jessica Cashen's home in Alpharetta, and nearly an hour later I was standing on the front porch of her home with my heart in my throat. A cool breeze chilled me as it began to lightly rain. I rang the doorbell and balled up my shaking hands, bracing myself for what was to come.

The door opened and in front of me stood a woman I guessed wasn't even Nina's age. Maybe twenty-two, she had short blond hair and brown eyes that grew larger by the second as she stared at me. She was petite, but quickly I found out that small package was full of power.

"Who are you? How can you be here?" she asked in a voice seeped in rage.

I raised my hands in front of me in surrender, hoping to put her at ease. "I'm sorry. I didn't mean to upset you. My name is Tristan and I was hoping to speak to you about your father."

"There's no way you can be standing here in front of me. Is this some kind of cruel joke? If so, I don't think it's funny."

She tried to slam the door on me, but I quickly stuffed my right foot next to the doorjamb and said quietly, "Please. I don't know what you're talking about, but it's very important I speak to you."

"Who are you?"

I looked in through the opening and saw a look of horror on her face. "Don't be scared. My name is Tristan Stone. I just want to talk. Please."

The look in her eyes told me she recognized my name. Slowly, she opened the door and her gaze scanned me up and down. Finally, she stopped on my face and narrowed her eyes to angry slits.

"You look just like him."

I didn't have to ask who she meant. Nodding, I said, "He was my twin."

"I heard he died. Is that true?" she asked with venom in her words.

"Yes."

"Good. I hope he suffered." She looked away and then faced me again. "I'm sorry. I just can't feel bad that he's gone."

"May we talk? I need some answers, and I'm hoping you can help me understand some things."

Silently, she welcomed me in and we sat in a small living room off the entryway with a small, unlit Christmas tree in the corner. I studied her for a moment as she did the same with me, and then I said what I guessed no one in my family had ever said to her. "I'm sorry about the deaths of your father and sister."

"I'm having a hard time believing you knew nothing about that, Mr. Stone. Your brother sure did."

"My brother and I were two very different people. I swear to you I knew nothing about what happened to your family. That's what I'm here for tonight."

Jessica Cashen sighed heavily and her mouth turned down into a frown. "You don't understand how hard it was to accept what your brother did. Even today, if I hear the name Taylor, I have a hard time not lashing out. My husband has been through so many nights of me being miserable over this I had to promise him I'd let it go."

"I understand, Jessica, but I need to know things only you can tell me. There's another person hurt by all this, and she'll be helped by what you tell me."

"Are you saying your brother did this to another girl too?"

I shook my head. "No, but there was another person hurt by my brother and father. What you can tell me about what happened may help her deal with the loss of her father."

"I'm sorry to hear someone else went through what my family had to endure. My mother died last year right in this house, never fully recovered from the shock of losing my sister and father just months apart. She just shriveled up."

"I'm so sorry."

She wiped a tear away and took a deep breath. "I'll tell you what I know. You'll have to fill in the blanks."

"Thank you." I sat back on the couch and listened as she began her story.

"My sister was only fifteen when she met your brother, Tristan. Even now as I look at you, I can see him. Those same brown eyes and look of money you both have. How old are you?"

"Twenty-nine."

"Did you like teenage girls when you were twenty-four? Your brother did. I never found out how he met her. I can't imagine why a fifteen year old girl, a freshman in high school, would be anywhere near where a grown man would be. Amanda was sweet and innocent, not in the way people say someone is but in reality they're out every night sleeping with anyone. She was still a virgin when she met him."

My stomach turned at the idea of being with a teenage girl when I was twenty-four.

"Wherever they met, she was crazy about him from the first night. I remember she came up to my room and told me she'd met someone. I thought she meant some boy at the mall. She told me his name was Taylor and he was gorgeous with big brown eyes she was sure were the most beautiful eyes she'd ever seen. I bet you've heard that a lot too."

Jessica stopped for a moment and stared at me. "It's amazing how much you look like him. When I first saw you standing in my doorway, I wanted to lunge at you I was so angry. You're identical down to the shape of your face and even your teeth."

For the first time in my life, I hated the way I looked as she described Taylor through my features. "You met Taylor, I assume?"

"Once. It was then that I realized my sister had gotten into something that was going to be bad for her. I just didn't realize how bad."

"What happened to make things go bad?" I asked, knowing the basic outline of the story. My brother had gotten a teenage girl pregnant and like a coward, had turned his back on her and the baby. What I didn't know was why.

"She found out she was going to have his baby. I tried to convince her to have an abortion. She was only fifteen, for God's sake. I was nearly nineteen at the time and I couldn't have handled a baby. She was too young, but she wouldn't listen to me. She was in love with him and thought they'd get married and live happily after. I tried to explain things to her, but she just said over and over that he could take care of her. I guess she thought since he was wealthy that he'd do just that."

"Did she tell your parents who the father was?"

Jessica shook her head sadly. "Not at first. She told him, but then the calls from him stopped. He wouldn't talk to her. She became depressed and stayed in her room all the time. My mother began to ask questions and finally Amanda told her she was pregnant. But even then, she wouldn't give up his name. She was sure he would come around. She thought he might be scared because of who our father was. Amanda wasn't stupid, even if she was naive. She knew a twenty-four year old man with a fifteen year old girl was considered statutory rape, even if she was madly in love. My father was a judge, and she was worried that Taylor might be afraid to live up to his responsibilities because of the difference in their ages."

I tried to imagine this person Jessica was describing, but I didn't know him. My brother had always been so on the straight and narrow. I couldn't imagine how he'd think sleeping with a teenage girl was okay.

Knowing what I was about to say may upset Jessica, I lowered my voice and quietly said, "Was your sister a willing participant?" I couldn't bring myself to ask if my twin brother had raped a child.

"If you're asking did he force himself on her, the answer is no. He wasn't a rapist, Tristan. He was a son-of-a-bitch who discarded my little sister when things got too real for him. He was fine with her when she was a simple thing to play with, but when real life crashed in on them, he abandoned her, leaving her to deal with a baby on her own."

"Why?" I wondered aloud. "He'd have to pay for the child whether he admitted it or not."

"Because he never cared for her like she cared for him. She was a toy he liked playing with. She adored him and hung on his every word. She'd tell me about meeting him and I never heard her say they talked about her. It was all him. He was a narcissist and she was his adoring fan. As long as she stayed in that role, everything was fine, but once she began to make demands on him, he wanted nothing more to do with her."

"I'm sorry, Jessica. I had no idea. I wasn't part of Taylor's world then. I was busy making my own bad choices. Nothing like he did, but…"

I let my sentence trail off. This wasn't about me and my stupid decisions.

"Something tells me you're not as alike as I would have thought. Do you have children, Tristan?"

Shaking my head, I forced a smile. "No. None yet."

"Your brother's child would have been going to kindergarten this year. I think about that sometimes. A little boy or girl ready to begin school. That never came to be, though."

"What happened?" I asked, my heart heavy at the thought of her sister dealing with having a child at such a young age herself.

"Amanda tried to get him to talk to her, but he wouldn't even answer her phone calls. She didn't know where to find him and when he changed his number, she became depressed. It broke my heart to see her like that. She cried all the time, wouldn't eat, and stopped going out. Finally, she gave up and took her life when she was three months pregnant."

Jessica could no longer hold back her tears, and as they streamed down her cheeks, all I could do was sit there feeling like I was in the middle of a horror story. Taylor's neglect had been the direct cause of Amanda's death, and nothing had ever been said about it by my father or mother. Had they known about it? My father had, if the dots Joseph Edwards had connected were true. My father had known what Taylor did and then made it worse.

I wanted to reach out to touch her hand, but how could I, the identical image of the man whose monstrous behavior had taken her sister away?

She wiped under her eyes and sat quietly for a moment. "She made me promise not to tell our parents who the father was, but when she died, I couldn't lie to my father and mother anymore. I told them about Taylor and who he was. They deserved to know who had done this."

"Do you remember talking to a man named Joseph Edwards after your father's death?"

Shaking her head, she suddenly got a look of recognition in her eyes. "I do, actually. He came to see me because of the bombing. He wanted to know about your father, though, not Taylor. I told him I didn't know anything about him, but then I explained everything that had happened with Amanda and your brother. He seemed to think that they were connected, I think."

"The bombing and what had happened to your sister."

"Yeah. The police never thought that, though. They still believe it was a gas explosion. I don't. I find it too coincidental that after my father tracked down your brother and told him what had happened to my sister and then your father's company is part of a case my father is judging that he suddenly is killed in a gas explosion."

"Do you remember anything about the case?"

"Not much. It was just a basic sexual harassment case, a civil suit. Your father's company was being sued by some woman and my father was the judge in the case."

I thought back to what Joseph Edwards had written in his notes about Stone Worldwide winning the case once Jessica's father wasn't the judge anymore. As much as I wanted to believe my father hadn't been responsible for Albert Cashen's death, there was too much to show me otherwise.

"That man, Joseph Edwards, told me he'd want to talk more with me, but he never returned. How did you find out about him?"

I swallowed hard before I began to tell the events that had brought me to Nina and ultimately, to Jessica and the truth of my family. "Joseph Edwards was murdered shortly after he spoke to you. His daughter is the person I believe may be helped by what you've told me."

Jessica covered her face with her hands. "Oh, my God! He was murdered? They killed him, didn't they? Your father and brother killed him like they killed my father."

Unable to hide from the overwhelming facts anymore, all I could do was nod in agreement. A young girl was dead because my brother had been a manipulative bastard and coward, and my father had had two men killed to protect Taylor and his own despicable actions.

"I don't know anything else, Tristan. That's all I have. I heard your family was killed in a plane crash a few months after my father and sister died."

"They were," I said quietly.

"I'm sorry. I guess you're the CEO of Stone Worldwide now. You know, I fantasized at least a thousand times about what I wanted to do to ruin your family like your brother and father ruined mine. I used to think about exposing everything they did and taking all that money your family has. I wanted to hurt you like they hurt me."

Jessica's voice caught in her throat and she looked away. When she turned back to face me, her expression wasn't one of hate or anger as it had been seconds earlier but sadness. "I think I feel sorry for you, Tristan. We've both lost everyone in our families, but I get to remember my sister and father as good people who never intentionally hurt anyone. You can't do that. Now that I've met you, I'm sorry you have to go through life knowing that."

I felt like I'd just been slammed in the chest with a cinder block. The truth of her statement was almost too much to handle. Here I was in a common suburban home I could buy twenty of with someone who had lost everything in her life, and I was the one being pitied. I, Tristan Stone, was worthy of pity for my family's guilty behavior.

"Please tell Joseph Edwards' daughter that my sympathies are with her. I know what she's going through."

I stood to leave, needing to get out of there as quickly as possible. She followed me to the door as we said our generic goodbyes, and as I left, she grabbed my arm to force me to turn around. I stopped dead and looked at her, not wanting to hear any more.

"I believe you're trying to do the right thing, Tristan. I can't imagine how hard this must be for you. I hope after what I've said you can find some kind peace with all this."

The car waited for me at the end of the sidewalk, and while I watched Jessica's house grow smaller as I drove away, I also hoped someday I'd be able to find some kind of peace after everything I'd learned.

CHAPTER NINETEEN

Nina

I had basically fallen in love with the Peachtree Suite within an hour of being there. This was my first trip to one of Tristan's hotels since my accident, not counting his incredible penthouse, and I loved the idea that I could add my artistic touch to such beautiful places. The colors of the suite were muted neutrals, but the designer had included a splash of color with deep burgundy draperies. I wanted to highlight that accent and really make it pop.

That's not to say I was even sure I could do the job. I hadn't told anyone, not even Jordan, but just thinking about picking out art made my palms sweat. Hours and hours of studying artistic styles and techniques in my room each day since I'd been released from the hospital had given me a small sense of confidence, but the real litmus test would be when I had to choose pieces for my first assignment.

I had a feeling Tristan had picked this suite as a simple job so I could ease myself back into things. As I scanned the over one thousand square foot area surrounding me, I tried not to feel intimidated. How couldn't I, though? The rooms rivaled the country house in beauty. The walls were painted to look like aged cream colored plaster, heavy white crown moldings typical of southern architecture framed the rooms, and the showstopper of the living room was a white cararra marble fireplace flanked by two French doors draped in that stunning burgundy color.

What could I add to all that?

All the ideas I'd had when I was searching at home felt wrong now that I was standing in the middle of this stunning suite. I wondered if maybe I should focus on something that would resonate with the local area instead of choosing something based on a certain style or color palette. I'd always loved the art at the Philly museums in part because it showcased the flavor of the local art scene. If I could find a piece or grouping that was not only beautiful but meaningful to Atlanta area instead of focusing on improving what the decorator had chosen, the room might actually be better because of the art.

At least that's what I tried to convince myself of as I stood there in the center of all that beauty.

I set off to the first bedroom to do some searching. Sitting legs folded on the bed, I tapped away on my laptop for information on artists right there in Atlanta. As I looked through page after page of artwork, none of them seemed right. They were all beautiful, but I was looking for something else—something that spoke to me—even if I wasn't sure what it was.

And then I saw that something. A local artist, Everett Shean, painted scenes of Cumberland Island, a barrier island off the coast of Georgia, and as I studied his oil paintings, I saw a turtle he'd created a series of paintings around. A few clicks to get to the series' page on his website and I found out the turtle was a loggerhead sea turtle that was an endangered species on Cumberland Island.

Déjà vu struck as I stared at that turtle and all of a sudden I realized I was having a memory from the past four years! The turtle looked like the turtle character from Finding Nemo, the one that sounded like a surfer and called everyone "Dude." The memory of watching that movie with one of my nieces hit me and out of the blue I had remembered that entire evening I'd babysat for Kim and Jeff!

I needed to tell someone, and since Tristan wasn't back from his meeting yet, I grabbed my cell phone and called my sister. She'd be so happy to hear my memory was finally coming back.

She answered, and I blurted out, "Kim, I remember that night I babysat and we watched Finding Nemo! Do you remember? You and Jeff went to dinner, and I babysat. Isn't it great?"

"Whoa! Slow down. What are you talking about, Nina? Are you okay? Where are you?"

I jumped off the bed and began to pace, my free arm flailing as I spoke. "I'm great! I'm in Atlanta with Tristan and as I was researching the art I wanted to show him for the suite, I saw this turtle that's endangered on one of the barrier islands off of Georgia. The turtle is the focus of a series by a local artist. He paints in oil, which is always so rich. You should see these paintings, Kim. They're gorgeous!"

"Baby, what turtle are you talking about? You're talking so fast I can't understand what you're saying."

"The one who calls everyone Dude, like he's a surfer."

"What?"

"In the movie," I explained in frustration. "What's the Finding Nemo turtle's name?"

"Nina, I have no idea what you're talking about. Who's Nero?" she asked, sounding almost as frustrated as I was.

"Nemo! You know. The fish. He's lost and his father has to find him. Oh, forget it! The point is that I remembered something from the past four years. My memory is coming back! Isn't that great?"

"It is, but I'm still not comfortable with you staying out at that house with someone you barely know, Nina."

Her voice had that condescending tone it got when she was chastising me for something. I hated that tone of voice. "Kim, Tristan isn't a stranger or someone I barely know. I was engaged to him before the accident. He's a good man, and I love him. Don't ruin this for me. I was so happy when I called you."

"I don't want to ruin anything for you. I just think you're too naive and get yourself into things you don't understand."

My chest tightened as tears welled in my eyes. I couldn't help get emotional. All I'd wanted to do was share my wonderful news and now I had to defend myself once again to my sister, whose opinion of my life I didn't give a damn about.

"Why? Because I don't keep myself all closed off and guarded? Because I give people a chance? I know that people like you think that makes me stupid or idiotic, but it's who I am. I can't change that, and I don't want to. I like being open to new things, and that includes new people. If I was like you, I would have never gotten to know Tristan."

"How would you know, Nina? You can't even remember. For all you know, he manipulated you into this whole thing. You don't know everything about him."

"Thanks, Kim."

I jammed my fingertip onto the screen of my phone and hung up on her. Throwing the phone on the bed, I let the tears come as I stood there with my shoulders hunched from the weight of her negativity.

I should have known better. Why didn't I call Jordan?

A noise behind me made me turn around and I saw Tristan standing there looking as beaten down as I felt. His tie was loosened, his suit looking like it hung from a body exhausted from dealing with the world all day. I wiped the tears from my cheeks and forced a smile.

"Hey, you look as bad as I feel."

"What happened? Did someone come by the room?" he asked in a voice filled with worry.

Shaking my head, I tried not to think of Kim's words, but I couldn't help it. I'd been so happy just minutes earlier and now sadness that my only family member left couldn't find any joy in my news made my heart heavy. "No. I was just on the phone with my sister."

Just as he had in the hospital, Tristan grew stiff at the mere mention of Kim. "What did she say? I hope you aren't listening to her, Nina."

"I'm not. I just called her with good news and she was so negative. All I wanted was to share something that had made me really happy, and she didn't care."

Tristan walked toward me and stopped just inches away. Leaning down, he kissed me and stroked the pad of his thumb over my damp cheek. "I'm here now, so you can tell me."

I leaned into his hand, loving the strength of it beneath my head. Looking up at the concern etched into his features, I smiled, hoping to ease some of his worry. "I remembered something. It's not much, but it's something."

His expression changed to one of surprise, but I sensed his concern wasn't abated. Brown eyes that said so much about how he was feeling looked intently into mine as he spoke. "What did you remember?"

"Babysitting my nieces one night. It's nothing important."

Pulling me close, he held me tight as he kissed the top of my head, whispering low, "Don't say that. It's very important. You're beginning to remember things."

I loved the feel of his arms around me, protecting me from even the unkind words of my sister. I wished I could do the same for him. As strong as he was, I knew whatever he'd been dealing with had worn him down.

"Thank you. That's all I wanted to hear when I called her, but instead she just harped on how stupid she thinks I am. She thinks you're manipulating me into doing things I shouldn't be doing." I looked up at him and smiled. "As if falling in love is something I shouldn't do."

He cradled my face and shook his head. "Don't listen to her. Falling in love with me was exactly what you should do. I should know. I fell in love with you first."

I tapped his chin with my finger. "This time. I'm still convinced when I remember everything that I'm going to find out that I was crazy about you long before you loved me."

A shadow crossed his face and then it was gone and he was smirking at me like I was acting silly. From anyone else in the world, that kind of smirk would have irritated the hell out of me, but from Tristan, it was just too cute.

"So would you like to see the art I think would work here?"

"Sure."

"Righteous, dude," I joked as I headed over to the bed.

"Righteous, dude?" he asked as he raised his eyebrows in disbelief.

I motioned to him to come sit next to me as I browsed through Everett Shean's website. When I finally found the turtle pictures, I turned my laptop toward him. "These are loggerhead sea turtles and they're an endangered species on a barrier island off of Georgia's coast. I know they aren't fancy or the kind of art you would normally see in a hotel suite like this, but I think they'd work. He blends vivid colors on the turtle backs that I think might look nice here against the effect your designer created on the neutral color walls."

"And these are, what did you call them? Righteous?" he asked as he leaned in to examine the paintings.

I couldn't help but giggle. Sometimes he was so serious. "No. I was making a reference to the turtle in Finding Nemo. You know? The one who talks like a surfer?"

"Finding who?"

"Finding Tristan Stone's sense of humor. It was a huge hit," I teased. "I can't believe you never watched that movie."

Before I could explain any more about the cartoon or the turtle paintings, his phone vibrated inside his jacket and all traces of any happiness slid from his face as he rose from the bed. "I have to take this."

Like always, I wanted to ask who it was who could make him instantly miserable every time they called. I didn't, though, silently swearing that one of these days I would find out who the bastard on the phone was who ruined so many nice moments between us. He walked out of the room and I heard the door to the suite close behind him, but something inside told me to follow him this time. I wanted to know now who was haunting him.

I flung open the door to find him standing in the hallway with a man who looked to be about fifty or so. He was thick and reminded me of a police detective from a TV show. He stood too close to Tristan, like he was trying to intimidate him, and although I couldn't hear clearly what he was saying, it sounded ominous.

"Tristan, is everything okay?"

He spun around, his eyes flashing angrily, and for a second I recoiled back into the room, afraid of what I'd interrupted. Stepping toward me, he took my hand and squeezed it tightly. The other man followed him into our suite, and we stood awkwardly for a moment before Tristan finally spoke.

"Nina, this is the Vice President of Operations for Stone Worldwide, Karl Dreger. Karl, I'd like to introduce you to my fiancée, Nina Edwards."

Karl extended his meaty hand and shook mine. "How very nice to finally meet you, Nina. I've heard a lot about you."

Smiling, I pulled my hand away as soon as I could. "It's nice to meet you too."

"I'm so sorry to interrupt your little getaway. I just needed to remind Tristan of a deadline. Now that I have, I'll leave you to your evening. I hope you have a wonderful holiday, Nina."

His voice made my skin crawl. It was smarmy and threatening at the same time. Tristan's hand continued to clutch mine tightly, as if he was afraid to let go. I was glad for the feel of him holding me, protecting me from this person. This man he worked with was only in the room for a few moments, but I was left with the surest sense that he held something dark or evil inside him.

As the door closed, Tristan pulled me close to him, wrapping his arms around me. "Nina, you are never to be alone with him. Please don't ask me to explain. Just promise me that if you ever see him again without me, you'll get away."

My ear pressed against his chest, and I heard his heart race wildly. "Tristan, is he the person who calls and ruins your mood every time? I won't ask you to explain, but tell me if that's him."

He was silent for so long I wondered if he'd heard me over the pounding of his heart, but finally, he said, "Yes. I'm sorry."

I squeezed him tighter. "You don't have to be sorry. I just wish you felt like you could tell me what's wrong."

Tristan stroked my hair and back as his heartbeat settled into its normal, slower rhythm. Kissing the top of my head, he said sadly, "Someday when you have your memories back, I'll tell you."

"Okay." Hoping to change the subject to lighten our mood, I looked up at this face etched with a frown and said, "I liked the way you introduced me. Fiancée. I don't know if you said that for some other reason than wanting me to be that again, but I'd like it to be true."

His eyes sparkled as he smiled broadly, looking more gorgeous than I thought I'd ever seen him look. "I'd like nothing more in this world, Nina, than for you to agree to marry me again."

Even as he smiled and told me he wanted more than anything to hear me say I wanted to marry him, his voice was still weighted down with a sadness that made me wish he would tell me whatever was eating him up inside. I so wished I could make him as happy as he made me.

"I'd like to wear the ring again too."

"You don't remember this, but we were supposed to get married on December 14."

"Are you asking me to run off and elope, Mr. Stone?" I said in a playful voice.

"Yes. Marry me. We can leave tomorrow from here and go wherever we want."

I leaned back away from him, shocked that he was serious. "You're not kidding? Can you do that? Don't you have to run a huge company?"

"Nina, I can do what I want. Part of being the CEO. Marry me."

I couldn't say no. Looking down at me, he was so cute I didn't want to say no. "Okay, let's do it! I need to go back to the house, though. I only need a few things and we can leave right after that."

"I can get you whatever you need so we don't have to go back. We'll leave from here tomorrow morning."

"Tristan, it will only take me a few minutes at the house and then we can go wherever we want. I promise I won't be long."

"Okay, but we'll go back and leave tonight."

I stood on my toes and kissed the tip of his nose. "You drive a hard bargain, sir. You have a deal."

"Good. Pack your things and I'll let the pilot know we're leaving."

Tristan headed into the other room to get things ready for us to fly back to New York, and even though things felt like they were moving a hundred miles a minute, I was ready to do it.

I was ready to marry Tristan and begin our life together.

Chapter Twenty

Nina

My hands shook as I gathered up my makeup and dumped it all into my suitcase. I grabbed a few dresses from my closet, folding them hastily, and stopped to take a deep breath. Tristan and I were eloping in the middle of the night like two kids in love. This was really happening.

It's not that I didn't want to marry him or that I wasn't in love with him. I was crazy about him and nothing had ever felt as right as when I said yes to becoming his wife. But my sister's scolding echoed in my mind, sowing the seeds of doubt like they always had. I didn't want to think like that, though. She wasn't me. She'd never fall for someone like Tristan and elope in the middle of the night. It was far too risky for her.

But I wasn't her.

I wanted to take a chance and be daring. I'd never really done anything wild or crazy. I'd been the good daughter, always getting good grades and doing just as my father told me to. Even that hadn't been enough for Kim, though. My artistic side had always made me "flighty," according to her. She didn't understand viewing the world through eyes that wanted to see beauty. All she wanted to see was the bad—bad people, bad situations, and mostly, bad men.

Whatever she thought she knew about Tristan, I knew in my heart he wasn't a bad man. Did I know everything about him? No. But who knew everything about the man or woman they loved? I accepted the reality of his life, and that meant I might never know more than I did now about him. That was okay.

What I knew, I loved. What I didn't know, I'd have to deal with if and when the time came. That was part of what you did when you loved someone.

Zipping my bag, I took one last look at my single girl face in the mirror. Oh my God! I hadn't told Jordan. I grabbed my cell phone and quickly called her, not caring that it was ridiculously late to be calling anyone with a job.

She answered in a groggy voice. "Hello?"

"Jordan, it's Nina. I'm sorry for calling so late, but I wanted to tell you that Tristan and I are eloping. We're leaving in a few minutes for an island in the Caribbean."

I heard her make a noise like she was sitting up in bed. "What? Who calls someone and says something like that? I thought you were still planning on a big ta-do on the island like before your accident."

"He asked me tonight if I'd elope with him, and I said yes. I didn't call anyone else but you. Please don't tell me not to do this. I already know Kim would say that."

"I would never do that, Nina. Tristan is crazy about you, and you're crazy about him. I'm just bummed that I won't get to do the whole island thing."

"Thanks, Jordan. We'll do the island thing another time, I promise. I'm just glad you aren't trying to talk me out of it."

"Oh, honey, I wouldn't do that, and don't let Kim do that to you anymore. You live your life and know that I'm here in good times and bad. Now go get married, you crazy kids, and call me when the honeymoon haze wears off."

I choked up at Jordan's words and swallowed hard. "I love you, Jordan. I wish you were my sister instead of Kim."

"I am in every way that's important. A sister from another mother, like we always said. Now go enjoy yourself and don't give Kim another thought. Got it?"

"Got it. I'll call you soon."

"I love you, Nina. Tell Tristan I said congratulations."

I hung up and told myself Jordan was right. No more thinking of Kim and all her negativity. This was my life, and I was going to live it the way I wanted to.

Dropping my bag off in the entryway, I looked for Tristan in his office and his room but didn't find him. I'd taken longer than I'd promised, but I'd expected he'd be waiting patiently for me at the end of my hallway. When I didn't find him in the kitchen, I began to wonder where he was and why no one else seemed to be around either. Where was Rogers and his popping up out of thin air trick?

A noise that sounded like angry voices hit me as I turned to make my way down to the pool area. Rogers' area of the house was directly to the left of the stairs to the lower level, and I stopped to listen, straining to hear if the voices were someone in the house or on TV. I couldn't decide which, so I slowly walked down Rogers' hallway, uneasy since I'd never felt welcome enough by Tristan's butler to visit him in his private quarters.

"There's only one way Karl would have known I was in Atlanta. You told him, didn't you?"

The rage in Tristan's voice was unmistakable as he accused someone of betraying him. But was it possible he was talking to Rogers, the man who'd been with him since he was a small child?

I listened outside Rogers' door as he denied telling anyone where we'd gone, but I knew guilt when I heard it. He had told that awful man where Tristan and I were. But why? Why would he betray Tristan?

"I've told you that I don't care what you think of Nina. I don't care if you think we should be together or not. I've tolerated your sideways looks when we're together and your opinion on how I should handle my life. I won't tolerate you getting into bed with the man who wants to ruin my happiness. When you put Nina in danger, then I fucking care what you're doing."

"I would never do anything to cause hurt to come to you, Tristan. You know that," Rogers said in his stiff, official style.

"What I know is that I have a traitor in my house. Are you going to tell me why? I deserve to know at least that."

"I've never done anything but protect you."

"By putting the woman I love in danger? How does that protect me? How does that show your loyalty to me?"

What did he mean by danger? Karl had made me uneasy, but was I truly in danger from him? My mind raced as I jumped to conclusions. Had my car accident been something else and were Karl and Rogers to blame? Bursting into the room, I pointed at Rogers. "He's never liked me, Tristan. Did you cause my accident, Rogers?"

"Nina, wait outside. I don't want you around this," Tristan ordered.

"No. I want to hear from him why he hates me—why he wants me out of your life. And I want to know if he tried to hurt me already."

We stood there staring at each other in Rogers' plain white room, and I saw Tristan consider what I'd just accused his butler of. His expression morphed from one full of rage to one of hurt as he looked over at Rogers.

"Answer her. Was her accident something else?"

"Karl is only looking out for your welfare, Tristan, as I am."

His lack of denial sent a chill up my spine. Was he saying he'd intentionally set out to hurt me or worse, kill me?

"You've been like a father to me. How could you do this to someone I love? I trusted you!"

Rogers tilted his chin up in a gesture of defiance. "I'm proud to say that as much as you're a Stone, Tristan, you've been like a son to me. I've watched over you, protecting you for years. When your father chose Taylor over you, as he always did, I was there to watch your football games and hockey matches. It was I who was there with your mother to cheer you on, to take pictures of you with your trophies. Never your father. When you got into trouble, I cleaned it up for you. I cared for you. I'm doing that now. This is no different."

His mention of Tristan's trophies hit me like a slap to the face. Suddenly, I had a memory of me looking at pictures of him as a child. Everything around me faded away as I struggled to place where and when I'd seen the pictures. I could see in my mind Tristan as a young boy holding a trophy high above his head, smiling as his mother stood nearby gazing at him in adoration for his accomplishment. But none of the pictures in the house were of him as a child, so where had I seen this image?

I was torn from my memories as Tristan's voice grew increasingly louder at Rogers' continued denials of doing anything wrong. "Answer the question Nina asked you. Did you have any part in her accident?"

"I would never physically hurt her, Tristan."

"Did Karl do something to the car with your help?" he barked at the older man. "Tell me!"

"Her accident was not due to anything I had any part in. What Karl did is something you need to ask him."

Tristan lunged at Rogers, grabbing him around the neck as he yelled, "I trusted you! You know how much she means to me! You know!"

Rogers clawed at his forearms to pull him off him, but he was no match for Tristan, who was much younger and stronger. The strangled cries of the butler filled the room as he was slowly being choked to death. As much as I hated Rogers for what he'd done to me and Tristan, I couldn't let the man I love kill someone.

Pulling on his arm, I struggled to tear Tristan away, but I was no match for him either. The more I tore at his arms to make him release him, the more he fought to hurt him. I watched in horror as Rogers' face began to turn blue.

"Tristan, don't! Let him go! Don't do this!"

He stilled, and I was sure that the old man was next to death. Tristan slowly raised his hands up and backed away, his face covered in revulsion at what he'd almost done to the man who'd been closer to him than anyone else in his life.

Rogers fell to the floor clutching his throat and coughing. He sat there with tears streaming down his cheeks as the blood began to flow back to his face. Slowly, the bluish tint faded and he looked like himself again. Unable to talk, he simply looked up in shock at the man he thought of like a son.

"Get out! Take whatever you think you need and get out," Tristan growled down at him.

A gurgling sound came out of Rogers' mouth as he tried to protest the order, but Tristan merely repeated himself with even more viciousness. He was cold and distant, scaring me when he spoke.

"Leave and never come back. You're dead to me now."

Rogers' eyes grew wide at the sound of those words. He stood on shaky legs and slowly walked past us into his bathroom, still hunched over from the attack. I remained there stunned at what I'd just witnessed, unsure what to say. Gently, I touched Tristan's arm, but even that slightest contact made him spin around to face me, his dark eyes flashing the fury that hadn't subsided inside him yet.

"Tristan, it's okay. It's me. Everything's going to be okay."

He seemed to stare right through me for a moment and then his expression calmed as he pulled me tightly to him. No words came, but I felt the tension and rage begin to fade away as he held me in his arms.

"I'm sorry, Nina. I had no idea. I should have known. I would have sent him away if I'd known."

I looked up into his troubled eyes and cradled his face in my hands. "Are you okay? What's going on? Why would he want to hurt me or want me out of your life?"

Tristan looked back toward the bathroom where Rogers still remained. "I want you to go to my room and stay there. Don't come out until I come get you. Do you understand?"

"Why?"

He bent down and kissed me softly on the lips, whispering, "I promise someday I'll be able to tell you everything, Nina, but for now, please, no more questions. All I can say is that I would never let anyone hurt you. I need you to believe me."

Nodding, I hugged him. "I do. Just promise me you won't get hurt."

Above me, he said, "I'll be fine." He pushed me back from him and cupped my chin. "Now go stay in my room and lock the door. Don't come out until I come get you."

I wanted nothing less than to leave him there to deal with the devastating reality of being betrayed by the person he'd known and trusted longer than anyone else in this world, but I was frightened enough not to fight him on this. Quickly, I ran to his room and locked the door behind me, my hands shaking in fear at everything I'd seen and heard.

Looking around, I remembered the first night I'd come over from my side of the house to pronounce my anger at being held against my will. That Nina had been so ignorant of who Tristan really was. Never a jailer, he was my protector. I trusted him, and now more than ever, I needed to rely on him, even though I didn't know what danger surrounded us.

At that moment, my memory was what could help me the most, but all I had was the recollection of watching a cartoon with my nieces and the fleeting images of looking at pictures of Tristan as a child. I sat on the edge of his bed and closed my eyes, trying to piece together the memory Rogers' mention of sports trophies had caused to become so real in my mind.

No matter how hard I tried, I couldn't remember where I'd seen those pictures. Had Tristan shown me them before my accident, maybe as we began to learn things about one another when we were first dating? Something about the images in my mind gave me a sense that I hadn't seen them with him, but then how would I have seen pictures of his childhood?

I opened my eyes and scanned the room around me. Maybe I had seen them in this room. He had said we'd shared this room before my accident, so that would make sense. I knew it might be an invasion of his privacy, but I wanted to know more about why this memory seemed so important, so I began to look through his dresser drawers.

Running my hands over pair after pair of black dress socks and cotton boxer briefs, I found nothing that felt like it would be pictures. I moved through all the drawers and there was nothing but what belonged in them. His desk sat across the room, so I tried there found nothing that made me think I had seen them in this room.

But if not here, where in this house would pictures of Tristan as a child be?

A noise outside in the hallway jarred me out of my thoughts, and I stood frozen in place staring at the bedroom door. I listened for it again, but nothing happened. My fear at a strange noise was replaced with concern for Tristan, so I took a deep breath and opened the door to find him standing there.

"Why did you open the door?"

"I was worried about you. What happened? Are you okay?" I asked as I pulled him into the room.

"I'm fine."

His answer screamed that he was putting up walls to hide how hurt he was. I hated seeing him like this. I wanted to make him smile like he had all those times for me when I laid in that hospital bed all those weeks.

I followed him to the bed and sat down next to him. Taking his hand, I brought it to my mouth and kissed it. "I'm sorry, Tristan. I'm sorry all of this happened because of me."

He shook his head but said nothing.

"I don't know what's going on, but don't shut me out. I don't need to know everything right now, but I need to know we're okay."

Turning to face me, he looked at me with soulful brown eyes full of pain. "Everything I've trusted all my life has been a lie. You're all I have that's honest and true. I need to know we're okay as much as you do, Nina."

I cradled his face in my hands. "I'm here with you. I'm not going anywhere, Tristan. I promise."

"Baby, things are going to get bad. You're going to find out things about me that you're not going to like. I need you to remember when all of it comes out that I love you and never meant any harm."

"You'd never hurt me, Tristan. I'd never believe you could."

He hung his head and said quietly, "I'm sorry we're not going to get to elope. Seems we never can take that last step and finally get married."

Stroking his back, I leaned against him. "Next time we will."

He jumped at the sound of a knock on the door and opened it to find Jensen standing there looking pale. I stood up and hurried to stand behind Tristan as his driver told him the police were at the door and wanted to speak to him.

Tristan grabbed my hand, and we walked out to speak to the police. My heart was racing as I wondered what they could want. Had Rogers reported Tristan's attack on him and the cops were there to arrest him? I couldn't let that happen. I'd tell them everything if that's what they were here for.

I squeezed his hand in mine to let him know I was right there with him as we walked up to meet the two men in uniform standing just inside the entryway. Both were chubby and looked like they'd spent too many breaks at the local donut shop, but they didn't look threatening. In fact, they looked more concerned than anything else.

"Mr. Stone? Tristan Stone?"

Nodding, he answered, "Yes. What can I do for you tonight, officer?"

"Do you have a Jonathan Rogers in your employ?" the policeman on the right asked as the other one waited with a pen and notepad for the answer.

"Yes. Rogers is my butler."

"Sir, when was the last time you saw him?"

"About an hour ago."

Tristan's answers were short, and I watched the officers carefully to see if they found them suspicious. Neither man seemed to, thankfully.

"Mr. Stone, a man with identification showing he was Jonathan Rogers was hit by a car just outside the gate to your property. I'm sorry, but he's dead."

I felt Tristan's body deflate next to me, and I quickly wrapped my arm around his waist to support him. The air left his body in a whoosh as he exhaled heavily.

"What? That…that's impossible. He was just here."

"I'm sorry, sir. Do you know how we can contact his next of kin?"

"He doesn't have any family. He's worked for my family for over twenty years and was never married and never had any children." He stopped for a moment and then said quietly, "We were his family."

Tristan's voice sounded faraway, like in a dream. The officer taking notes began to explain about Rogers' body and burial, but his words all flowed together until they didn't make sense anymore. I watched Tristan nod as if he understood everything, but I saw in his eyes it was all a jumble like it was for me.

After they left, I followed him to Rogers' room. He leaned against the doorframe and stared at the spot where just a short while earlier the last thing he'd said was that the soul he'd known for longer than any other was dead to him. My heart broke as I watched what I knew was guilt wash over him. He had nothing to feel guilty for, but that didn't matter.

For someone who said so little, to have his words come back to haunt him was likely more painful than I could ever imagine. I wanted to make it all go away, to bring a smile to his face like he'd done so many times for me, but the pain he was feeling was too deep for me to reach.

Chapter Twenty-One

Nina

Christmas came, but it had a pall over it that neither of us could deny. Rogers' funeral couldn't take place until after the holiday, so there was no closure to give Tristan any peace. He pretended to be happy for my sake, but I sensed him slipping into a dark place that scared me.

I wanted to call off the New Year's celebration with Jordan and Justin at the penthouse, but Tristan insisted, saying life had to go on. He didn't seem to be going on, though. He spoke even less than usual, and at times he seemed to be lost in his thoughts, staring off in the distance. Still there beside me, he seemed empty and hollow. The gentle smile that made me so happy was almost entirely absent, and his eyes were always full of sadness.

Just as we'd planned, we all met at the penthouse at ten on New Year's Eve. Jordan and Justin didn't know about what had happened to Rogers, but even they could tell something was wrong with Tristan. It wasn't just that he was so quiet. That was nothing new. It was a feeling of sadness that covered him even as he pretended to be interested in celebrating.

Justin and he sat watching some New Year's Eve special after an incredible dinner of filet mignon that Tristan barely touched while Jordan joined me in the kitchen, our first time alone since I'd told her the news that we hadn't gotten married.

Whispering near my ear, she said, "Nina, what's going on? Did you two break up and you didn't want to blow us off for tonight? Tristan looks devastated about something."

I shook my head and let my body sag against the counter, finally able to talk about the whole thing with Rogers with somebody. "No. We couldn't elope because Rogers died. Tristan's not handling it well."

Jordan's eyes grew wide. "Oh, my God! What happened? He wasn't that old."

"He was hit by a car right outside the gate at the house. But that's not all. They had a terrible fight before and Tristan threw him out."

"Why? What's going on?"

I lowered my voice even more and leaned in next to her. "I don't know. Rogers was helping someone in Tristan's company who I think wants to hurt me. When Tristan found out, he went into a rage and nearly strangled him. The last thing he said was that Rogers was dead to him, and then less than an hour later he was dead. I don't think Tristan can forgive himself."

"Oh, honey, I'm so sorry for him, but now I'm worried. Who is this person Rogers was helping? Why would he want to hurt you?"

"I don't know. His name is Karl, and I've only met him once. I can only guess it has something to do with Stone Worldwide, but I don't know why anyone would want to hurt me because of that," I admitted, hoping Jordan could see something I couldn't.

"Does he have security to make sure this Karl creep doesn't get around you?" she asked as she looked out toward the living room.

I thought about her question. "I don't think so. Maybe. I'm not sure. I think he has cameras here at the hotel, so maybe he has them everywhere. He wouldn't let anyone hurt me, Jordan."

"I know. I know," she said as she took my hands in hers and stared into my eyes. "I'm his biggest fan. Trust me, Nina. What did I tell you in the hospital? It doesn't matter what you remember. Just watch how he acts toward you. The man loves you. Of that, I'm certain. I just worry because he's obviously in a funk. I don't want to see either of you hurt."

I nodded, looking out at Tristan as he sat there staring at the TV. I could tell he wasn't even paying attention to what was on the screen. "I'm worried about him, Jordan. He's slipping away right in front of my eyes. He loved Rogers like a father, and now he's really got no family at all."

"He's got you, sweetie."

I squeezed her hand tightly in mine. "I don't know if I'm enough. He keeps telling me he's fucked up. I don't know what he means. What if I'm not enough?"

Jordan lifted my chin with her hand and looked at me with an expression more serious than she had since that first moment I opened my eyes and saw her sitting there in my hospital room. "Nina Edwards, don't you doubt yourself. You're much stronger than your sister or even your father ever thought you were. You love him, so don't you let him fall into something that he may never come out of."

"He doesn't want to talk. He goes out for hours at a time, and I don't know where he goes. I text him to ask and he just texts back that he's clearing his head. Then he comes back home and he smells like he's been drinking. He sleeps in his room, but I swear I hear noises like he's up all night watching horror movies or something. I hear what sounds like someone in pain."

"Maybe if you two got away. I know it's not the time to get married now, but maybe just a vacation to one of his hotels. Get out of town and start fresh?"

"I could try. I don't know what else to do," I admitted sadly. I didn't. I felt helpless to do much of anything. Tristan's walls were so thick, and it seemed like they were getting worse every day.

"Don't give up on him. You were like this after your father died. I didn't know what to do either, but I just stuck with you, telling you that you weren't alone. You came out of it eventually. So will he."

Justin walked toward us and gave Jordan the look boyfriends give when they want to leave. I couldn't blame him. We weren't exactly the host and hostess with the mostess. Ringing in the New Year in such somber surroundings wasn't fun, so after hugs and promises we'd all get together soon, they left.

Tristan sat quietly as the city below exploded in celebration, people toasting a new year and another chance. I curled up next to him, but he didn't move. My heart broke to see him so sad.

"Happy new year."

He said nothing, as if he was thinking about what I'd said, and finally turned his head toward me. "I love you, Nina. Don't ever think I don't."

"I know you do. I can't stand to see you like this. I want to make you feel better like you did for me when I was laid up in that hospital bed, but you keep pushing me away. I'm afraid you're going to push me right out of your life."

Looking away toward the fireworks exploding in the distance, he shook his head. "I'd never willingly let you go."

"Tell me what I can do. Every day, I feel like I'm losing another piece of you."

"You know what my shrinks said after the crash? They kept saying I was supposed to emote. Emote. That's it. As if that was going to make it all go away. Emote. But I didn't have anything to let out."

"Tristan, you can talk to me. Don't forget that. I know what it's like to lose someone. It may have happened four years ago, but it's like I just lost my father."

A look of pain settled into his features, and that hurt I knew he was feeling was right under the surface. If only he could let it out.

By the end of that week, I felt like everyone I knew was in misery. Jordan and Justin broke up on New Year's Day, and even though she claimed she'd seen it coming, I still knew by the sound of her voice that she was hurting. Tristan seemed to spend all his time at work after Rogers' funeral, texting me each afternoon to beg off having dinner together with vague excuses I knew were lies to hide the fact that he was unraveling. Even when he was in bed next to me at night, he was a million miles away.

Each day the distance between us grew, and I didn't know how to stop it.

Then on top of everything, Cal emailed with more of his sad tale. As I read it, something inside me snapped. How dare he play on people's feelings with his phony story about a cheating girlfriend and his dead mother when good people were dealing with real problems. I played the innocent friend, emailing him that I'd be happy to meet him for lunch that afternoon.

He spun the same web of lies he'd done before, but this time, I called him out. I don't think I ever felt better. I couldn't wait to tell Tristan that night, hoping that maybe my triumph in unveiling Cal's fraud right to his face would take his mind off his problems, even if for just a few minutes.

When he finally got home at eight o'clock, I heard him pass by my hallway on the way to his room. I quickly put away my laptop and headed over to his room to share my news. Pushing the door open, I found him standing at his desk with a manila envelope in his hand.

"Hey, you, I have a story to tell you," I said as I peeked my head in.

He turned around with an odd look in his eyes that frightened me. Standing there staring at me, he said, "Did you have a nice day, Nina?"

Even though everything in his body language and voice made me uneasy, I stepped into the room and sat down on the bed. "I did. That's what I wanted to talk to you about."

"Let me help you." He slid something out of the envelope in his hand and held it out toward me. "Is this what you wanted to tell me about?"

I strained to see what he held in his hand. When I didn't answer his question, he walked toward me and threw it on the bed next to me. I looked down and saw a stack of pictures of Cal and me at lunch just a few hours before.

"What are these? Do you have someone spying on me?"

Tristan's eyes flashed with anger. "I told you what he was doing and you still snuck around behind my back to see him. What am I supposed to think, Nina?"

"I'm trying to understand what you're going through Tristan, but I can't believe you'd have someone follow me and take pictures of me."

"And I can't believe you would sneak around and betrayed me with your ex, who is only trying to play you."

His words came out in a hiss. I'd never seen Tristan like this with me. The way he looked reminded me of what he'd been like that night with Rogers.

"So I leave the house once to go to meet Cal and let him know I'm onto his whole scam, and I'm not to be trusted, but you stay away from here day after day and I'm supposed to be fine with that? I'm not the one who's acting like they're doing something sneaky."

Tristan stared down at me with a confused look. "I'm not the one who needed to visit my ex to find out if I could love you."

His words cut like knives across my skin. I'd told him about my insecurities believing he'd understand, and now he was using them against me to indict me on some crime I'd never committed. I threw the pictures at him without saying a word and stormed toward the door before I burst into tears. I didn't want him to think I was sad. I was furious!

He grabbed my arm and spun me around to face him. "Where are you going?"

"I'm not going to stand here taking this!"

"Don't walk away, Nina."

I yanked my arm from his hold. "Why? No matter what I do, you stay away all day and half the night. You're probably cheating on me with whoever you spend all your time with. I bet that's why you're so convinced I'm doing something. Guilty conscience."

"You're being ridiculous. I'm not seeing anyone," he said coldly.

"Nice. Maybe you should practice that a little more in front of the mirror. A little more emotion and I might believe you."

That anger I'd seen just a minute before flashed in his eyes again at the mention of emotion. I hadn't meant to use what he'd told me on New Year's Eve. It just came out. I wanted to reach out and take his hand to show him we could work this out, but something held me back.

"You don't want that, Nina. You don't want me to show that emotion."

"Yes, I do! Finally, show me how you feel instead of pulling away. Let me hear that you still really care instead of making me guess and hope that you do," I cried.

He loosened his tie and walked past me to sit on the bed, avoiding looking at me. Even with me nearly begging him, he couldn't do it. Suddenly, I wanted a fight. After weeks of anger and sadness, there was so much pressure between us I needed to release it.

"So you're going to ignore me? I'm not even worth a few nice words? Everyone in your world wants me out of it. Do you?"

He still said nothing, preferring to close his eyes to block me out. I felt like I was nothing to him.

"You can't even say you want me in your life!" Now my tears couldn't be stopped, and I let them come. I stood there waiting for him to say anything, for him to even look at me as I pleaded for any sign that he still loved me, as everything became blurry from the mixture of tears and makeup clouding my eyes. My mouth was dry at the real fear that he'd never say anything to make me feel like he cared.

Tristan hung his head. "Nina, this isn't going work. I'll have my lawyers draw up a new document saying you're no longer obligated by our contract. I promise you'll never want for anything. I'll make sure that's in there too. I'll make sure you're safe."

His words stunned me. He was breaking up with me over my having lunch of with another man? What was going on?

"Why are you doing this? I don't want anyone else. I just went to lunch with him to tell him I knew what he was doing. I felt so good about it that I couldn't wait to tell you. Now you're sending me away? Don't do this, Tristan. I love you."

"This is best. Just let it happen."

I walked over to where he sat and fell to my knees. I had to see his eyes when he said he didn't want me or us anymore. Looking up, I waited for him to open his eyes so I could see what he was really feeling. No matter what his words said, I knew the truth would be in his eyes.

"At least look at me when you tell me you don't love me. I deserve at least that, Tristan."

He sat silently, his eyes still shut. I laid my head against his thigh and quietly said, "Please tell me what's going on. Maybe I can help. I can't believe you don't love me. I won't believe it. Not unless I see your eyes when you say those words."

I felt his hand gently cradle the top of my head and looked up to see those beautiful brown eyes so full of pain looking down at me. My heart skipped a beat as I waited for him to speak, and I prayed to God that I wouldn't hear him say he didn't love me anymore.

"I'm sorry, Nina. I don't know why I'm like this. I don't know why I make such a mess out of everything. I didn't mean to."

I pulled myself up to my knees and took his face in my hands. "You didn't do anything wrong. It's okay. I get that you're jealous. I felt that way when I saw all those pictures of you and those women at those parties. It's just that I'd never want Cal instead of you. You need to believe that."

"Just the thought of you with him makes me crazy. I'm sorry I'm so fucked up, Nina. I never meant for things to end up this way. I thought I could handle things."

The sadness and pain in his eyes broke my heart. "Things are fine between us. It's everyone else outside of us that aren't okay. We're fine. I love you and you love me. What else is there? I don't know what you mean about handling things, but you can't stop how people feel about things. I don't know why Rogers didn't like me or why that man you work with thinks you shouldn't be with me, but we don't have to listen to them."

"Nina, you should do what I said. Leave here and I promise you'll want for nothing. You'll be taken care of for the rest of your life."

"I don't want that. What do money and things mean to me when the most important part of this life you've given me isn't there anymore?"

Pressing my lips to his, I kissed him tenderly, feeling his sadness. I didn't know why he was so tortured, but it tore me up to watch him like this. Those brown eyes that spoke volumes were crying out in pain, despite his ability to hold back the tears.

"Nina, are we just putting off the inevitable?" he asked in a voice barely above a whisper, as if merely saying the words scared him as much as they did me.

I leaned forward and pressed my forehead to his. "No. I'm not leaving you, no matter how fucked up you say you are. I love you, Tristan Stone. You better just get used to it."

He let out a huge sigh and I wrapped my arms around his neck, wishing that a hug would give him even a little comfort.

"Promise me something?"

"Anything, Tristan."

"Promise me someday when this is all over you'll forget all the bad and just remember I loved you."

Taking me in his arms, he kissed me, pulling me into him like he couldn't get me close enough. There was a desperation in him that I wished I could reach to prove that I loved him and vow that I would never leave, no matter what he tried to do to tear us apart.

When he was like this—so raw and vulnerable—I had a hard time reconciling the man who said so little and could be so cold. As we made love, we clung to each other, Tristan taking the strength I offered, as if nothing and no one could come between us.

I just prayed to God that was true.

Chapter Twenty-Two

Tristan

The low beat of a techno song from a room on the other side of Top reverberated through the building, making the floor beneath me vibrate as I sat staring up at the TV on the wall across from me. Some movie about a mobster played, but I wasn't paying attention.

I'd been at Top for two nights, unable to go home and missing Nina more than I could handle. I couldn't be around her, though. Not now.

Each night I laid in bed afraid to close my eyes, afraid of the nightmares. A new one had taken over my nights since coming back from Atlanta. I saw my face hovering over the body of a naked girl smiling up at me. She reached out for me, and my hands grabbed at her breasts, pinching and tugging until she cried out in pain. Each time, she screamed a single word over and over. Taylor. I knew that wasn't my name, but I couldn't stop myself from wrapping my hands around her throat and slowly squeezing the soft flesh until there was no more life left in her. Gentle brown eyes stared up at me in surprise that I could hurt her as I backed away into a someone who stood behind me.

My father.

He patted me on the back all the while wearing a smile. He said nothing but stared at me like he admired me for what I'd just done to the girl.

Pouring myself another glass of scotch, I leaned back against the leather couch and closed my eyes, letting the alcohol slide down my throat. I didn't know how much more it would take, but I needed it to make me numb. I didn't want to think anymore. I wanted to not care anymore. To not miss Nina like someone had cut out my heart and left a painful, aching hole in my chest.

Karl's announcement that morning that he'd gotten copies of Joseph Edwards' notes from Nina's sister had given me a second's peace and made me believe for a fleeting moment that all the terrible events put in motion by my father would finally end. That we'd finally be free to live without the past haunting our every step.

But Karl wasn't a man to let things go that easily. Kim's copies were just that. Copies. He wanted the actual notes Joseph Edwards took as he dug into the horrible world of Stone Worldwide and knew I had them.

You didn't think I wouldn't have you followed, Tristan? Did you? For God's sake, I had your father and brother followed, and I trusted them. I know where you've been and I know what you have. If you're smart, and I think you are, just give it all up and never tell her what happened and you'll be fine.

Are you threatening me now, Karl?

Son, I'm not the man to play with. This shark doesn't care if your father thought you were a piranha or not.

At least I now knew why Kim hated me from the moment she met me in Nina's hospital room. She'd judged me to be the same kind of man my father and brother had been. Could I blame her? Two Stone men nothing better than lying murderers. Who would want their sister to be involved with a man like that?

Was I truly any better? I'd brought Nina into my world believing I was keeping her safe, but it had been my own selfishness more than anything else. I was no different than I'd ever been. I wanted something and used my money to get it. Typical Stone behavior.

Out of the corner of my eye I saw the door to the private room open. "Get out! I told you I didn't want to be bothered, Chase."

"It's not Chase. It's me, Tristan," a woman's voice said quietly.

I turned to see Brandi standing with her back against the door, frightened by my barking. I wasn't in the mood to hear her sad stories about that asshole ex or current or whatever the fuck type of boyfriend Chase was to her now.

"I want to be alone, Brandi."

"I know. I just wanted to check to see if you needed anything."

She moved cautiously from the door as I turned back to stare at the TV. Taking a seat next to me on the couch, she touched my arm softly. "Are you okay?"

"I'm fine," I lied. "Just want to be alone."

"Sometimes when things are bad it's good to talk to someone. You've done that for me more than once. Maybe if you talk about it you'll feel better."

I drank the final gulp of scotch in my glass, enjoying the warmth as it sat in my mouth for a moment before I swallowed. "There's nothing to talk about."

Brandi shifted herself to face me and took my hand. "I hate to see you like this, Tristan. I can't believe someone who has so much could be so sad."

"Well, believe it."

I felt her squeeze my hand and looked over to see her grinning at me. "I have something that I think might make you feel better, at least for a little while."

"Brandi, don't," I said flatly as I pulled my hand away.

"You know you'd feel better. Just a little. Chase said it could help."

I knew what she meant and I should have told her to leave. I knew that. But as I sat there thinking about Nina and what I knew I had to do, all I wanted was some relief from the pain. A tiny reprieve from my sentence.

Brandi slipped a small box from behind her back and spread out three lines of coke on the coffee table in front of us. She snorted the first line and sniffing, flopped back on the couch and pointed toward the rest of it sitting there waiting for me.

"Your turn."

Leaning forward, I looked down at the white powder that had given me so many nights of good times. Clean since the crash, I hadn't even thought of getting high, but now as it sat there waiting to give me the relief it always had, I could think of nothing but the feeling I'd have in just a few minutes.

Blocking my left nostril, I inhaled a line and closed my eyes. A rush coursed through my head and instantly I remembered why I loved coke all those years ago. In minutes, I was on top of the world—powerful, free, and happy. Truly happy, like the way I felt every time Nina told me she loved me.

One more line and everything that had tortured my mind for weeks was gone, replaced by pure bliss. My heart raced and my body felt like it could run a marathon. Brandi was a novice, so it didn't take more than a line for her to be bouncing off the walls. She seemed to be talking a hundred miles a minute about how she wished Chase was like me, but I wasn't listening. I didn't care about her problems.

All I cared about was that mine had vanished, at least for the moment.

Brandi's hand fastened on my crotch, and she licked her lips in an attempt to be seductive. "Tell me you don't love fucking when you're high, Tristan. Nobody would have to know. You know it would be great."

I didn't want to fuck Brandi. That would only make me feel worse. I had someone I loved already. It didn't matter that I couldn't be with her. I still loved her.

"Get your hand off your boss's cock, Brandi. If Chase doesn't fire you, I will. You're ruining this."

She wasn't going to be that easily convinced. Sliding her palm up and down my zipper, she cooed, "You're not my boss, Tristan. You only own the place. I guess that makes you my owner. Oooh, I like that."

"You know he's got cameras all over this place. Look around. At least smile for your boyfriend as you try to fuck someone else in front of him," I snapped, already hating how this was turning out.

Brandi rubbed her body up against my arm like a cat in heat. "Mmmm, that would be hot. Come on, baby. It will help you forget whatever's making you so sad."

Her lips pressed against mine, and all I could taste was the flavor of her spearmint gum. She jabbed her tongue into my mouth as her hands attempted to pull my shirt out of my pants, but I didn't want any of what she had to offer. I pushed her off me, and she fell back against the arm of the couch, her legs wide open.

"You know you want it, Tristan. Just let it happen. Don't fight it."

The door flung open before I could repeat that I didn't want her, but it was too late. There in the doorway stood Nina watching Brandi rub her pussy through her shorts as she did her best to convince me to fuck her.

"What the fuck is this?" Nina asked, her voice full of hurt.

Brandi leaped off the couch and began explaining how she had just wanted to help me feel better. It only made things worse and made me look guiltier.

Nina turned to face her and put her hand up in front of Brandi's face. "I so don't want to hear another fucking word from your mouth. Get the fuck away from me right now before I totally lose my cool."

Brandi was cheap, but she wasn't stupid. Nina had barely finished speaking and she was running from the room, nearly getting her four inch heels stuck in the door as she slammed it shut behind her.

"Tristan, what is this? Why haven't you been home in two days? What's going on here?" Nina rightfully demanded to know.

I leaned forward to pour myself another drink. "Nina, go home." I couldn't explain to her why I was sitting there with a woman I didn't give a damn about instead of lying in bed with the woman I loved more than anyone or anything in this world.

She wasn't going home, though. That wasn't her style. My mind was still racing as she sat down next to me, but my high was quickly fading, leaving the reality of what I had to do pressing down on me like a weight on my chest.

"I'm not going home. I know we've been dealing with some things, but I can't believe you're just planning on never coming home again. Have you been here every night?"

I looked away, unable to face her when I saw the tears in her eyes. First, I'd been a selfish prick and fallen in love with her, all the while telling myself I'd been keeping her safe. Now, I had to tell her the truth. It didn't matter if she left anymore. Whatever I'd thought I could give her was over now.

"Have you been with her?" she asked quietly.

I shook my head sadly. "No. I wouldn't do that. I never meant to do any of this, Nina."

She took my hand in hers and held it to her heart. "Tristan, what's going on? Why would you stay here instead of coming home to me?"

I couldn't continue like this. I'd kept what I'd found out about her father's death and my family's part in it a secret for weeks, and I couldn't do it anymore. Every day I worried that her memory would finally return and she'd know the ugly truth and leave me again. At least now, I knew that she was safe from Karl and his friends on the Board.

It wasn't her they wanted out of the way. It was me.

"I'm sorry, Nina. I have something to tell you. I can't keep it from you anymore."

She touched my chin with her forefinger and forced me to look at her. "You can tell me anything. I love you, Tristan."

Bowing my head, I kissed her palm. "It's time you knew everything. Come with me."

I led her upstairs to the apartment above the club that I'd been staying at. It was nowhere as nice as our house or the penthouse, but it didn't matter. Telling her the truth as we sat on expensive furniture wasn't going to change what I had to say.

"What's this about, Tristan? Why are we here?" she asked as she looked around at the place where I'd been hiding from her.

"Sit down. I need to get his off my chest before it crushes me."

She sat on the edge of the grey sectional that took up most of the living room and looked up at me with eyes full of worry. I knew what she thought I was about to say—that I'd met someone else and didn't want to be with her anymore. Maybe she thought that I'd lied about Brandi and was actually cheating on her.

At least I wasn't that man.

I took out her father's notebook and held it in my hand as I finally confessed what I'd held in for far too long. "Before I tell you what I need to say, I want you to know that I never meant for things to get to this point. I wanted to tell you every day, but it just never seemed the right time. No matter what you think after this, I need you to know that I've never loved anyone like I do you."

Nina reached out to take my hand and squeezed it in sympathy, not knowing what I had to say would likely turn her away from me forever. Her blue eyes were begging me not to break her heart. "I know you love me. If you're going to tell me you've been with someone else, don't. I'd rather not know. Just let me go on thinking it never happened. I can live with that. I can."

I shook my head and dropped her hand. "I wasn't with anyone else. I wish it was that easy. No, there's no one else. That makes what I have to tell you ten times harder."

"Tristan, what is it? Tell me."

"I thought you'd remember by now, to be honest. I dreaded that every day I might come home and you'd tell me you remember everything and then leave me. Maybe it's better that you didn't. I should have to tell you this. It's the least I can do as the last remaining member of my family."

Her face telegraphed her confusion, and I continued, pacing as I began the story that I knew would be the end of us.

"My father was Victor Stone. I was never close to my father, so I never really knew what he was like. By the time I was an adult, I was too busy stuffing the shit you saw downstairs up my nose to be bothered to find out what Stone Worldwide was all about. My brother was the one my father wanted to take over for him. Taylor was all about business and following in my father's footsteps, so I didn't care about that world. It was for people like them. I was too busy having a good time."

I knew this probably wasn't making much sense, but I needed to get it all out. It was as if saying it out loud might finally exorcise it from my mind and give me some peace. I needed to believe that I wouldn't always be covered in the layers of guilt that covered me now.

"When Taylor was twenty-four, he got a teenage girl pregnant. She was only fifteen. Her name was Amanda. I don't know why, but he abandoned her and the baby she was carrying. He wouldn't take her calls or see her, so she became depressed and when she was three months pregnant, killed herself."

"Oh, my God…I'm so sorry."

Nina's sympathy only made this worse. Shaking my head, I continued on. "The girl's father was a judge who my father's company ended up in front of for a sexual harassment case. It was a common civil suit that Stone Worldwide gets at least half a dozen times each year, but this one wasn't going to be one my father could win because the judge knew what Taylor had done. So my father had him murdered to be sure he'd win the case."

Suddenly, Nina's eyes narrowed to slits and she sat back with a heavy sigh. "Why does this sound so familiar? I swear I've heard something like this before."

My heart began pounding in my chest at the real fear that she was finally remembering. I wanted to stop, to push it all out of my mind and take her in my arms and never let her go. But I couldn't.

Now I had to say the hardest part. "No one would have ever known about all this if an investigative reporter hadn't begun checking into something about my father's company. I imagine he probably thought he was onto some real estate scheme or something like that, but he somehow found out about Taylor and Amanda Cashen, and from there it just snowballed until he had uncovered everything my father had done, including the murder of her father."

"Who was the reporter, Tristan?"

I stopped pacing and looked down into her face. "I never knew what my father and brother were doing. I had no idea, Nina."

"What was his name?" she said again, louder.

"I didn't know, Nina. I need you to believe that."

Her eyes grew wide, and she covered her mouth with her hands. Behind them, she said with a sob, "Oh my, God! I remember. I remember everything. You knew when you met me. You knew who I was and didn't tell me until that night."

I fell to my knees in front of her and stared up into all that pain. It tore my heart out. "Nina, I'm not asking for forgiveness. I know what I did was wrong. I didn't know what to do. If I told you when we met, you wouldn't have come to live with me. Karl and his friends were sure you knew about what your father had uncovered. I couldn't let them hurt you. I wanted to stop the cycle of pain that my father had begun."

"So you lied to me from the minute you met me? I fell in love with you!"

"I fell in love with you. That's the only part that wasn't built on a lie. I love you. I never meant to hurt you."

"This is why you've been avoiding me? You didn't want to face me with the truth," she cried as she recoiled from my touch.

"I'm sorry, Nina. Karl was threatening you, telling me that if you knew anything of what your father had found out that he'd kill you to keep you quiet. I didn't know about any of what Taylor and my father had done to the Cashens until I met with Judge Cashen's daughter in Atlanta. Until then…"

She cut me off as she jumped off the couch to get away from me. "Until then, all you knew was that your father had my father murdered execution style in a parking garage in Newark and you weren't going to tell me."

I slumped against the arm of the couch and hung my head. "I didn't know how to tell you without losing you. I couldn't lose you."

"So you lied to me every day and night."

"I convinced myself that it was okay because I was protecting you. I thought if I could make sure you were safe that someday you'd understand."

"I found out that night when I got into the accident. When were you going to tell me this time?"

I didn't know how to answer that. I'd never gotten that far. I'd been so concerned that Karl would hurt her that telling her the truth had been pushed aside.

"When, Tristan? When?" she screamed.

"I don't know."

"Look at me! At least face me now."

I turned around and looked up at her. "I'm sorry. I thought if I just had enough time I could solve this whole thing and you'd never have to know what my father did. I swear I didn't know about anything he did until right before I met you."

"You aren't to blame for what happened to my father, Tristan. Your crime was lying to me. We built a life together based on a lie. You asked me to marry you. Our entire life is a lie."

Standing, I grabbed her hands, needing to feel her touch on my skin, some small connection I could believe still meant something.

"Don't say that. I know I lied and I know I hurt you, but we love each other. No matter what else happened, we fell in love."

"How could you do this? I wanted to believe we'd be together forever," she said in a sad voice as she looked down at our joined hands.

"I'm sorry, Nina. No matter what else, I need you to believe that I love you."

She yanked her hands from mine and glared up at me. Shaking her head wildly, she sobbed, "I can't listen to this. I can't. I trusted you."

Dropping to my knees, I wrapped my arms around her legs and held her tight. I needed to keep her there. I couldn't let her go. "Come away with me. We can go anywhere. Venice again. Wherever you want. As long as we're together."

Nina stared down into my eyes and I knew. I'd lost her. No amount of begging was going to work.

"I can't do this, Tristan. I can't," she said sadly and then pulled away from me, never looking back.

I watched her run out, knowing that I had to go after her. My feet took the steps downstairs by two, and I caught up with her just as she was reaching the street. Jensen stood next to the car looking over at me for what to do.

"Take me home!" she ordered as she opened the car door, but he stood still as a statue waiting for my orders.

"I want to go home! Take me home, Jensen!" she cried, but still he wouldn't move, his eyes focused on me to know what to do.

Silently, I nodded to let him know he could leave, and he sped away toward the house as I watched everything I loved leave me. I'd told myself over and over that I was willing to lose her if it meant she was safe, but now I couldn't do it. I couldn't let her go. I needed to know she believed I loved her.

I heard her cry as I stood in the hallway outside her bedroom door, knowing I was the only person who couldn't make her feel better. For an hour, I listened to her heartbreaking sobs as my hope that she'd understand why I'd done what I'd done faded away.

Sliding down the wall, I finally leaned against her door and whispered, "I can't do this anymore. I'm sorry. I never meant to hurt you."

I'd lost her. The one soul on Earth that I truly loved and I'd lost her because of who I was. That was the truth at the heart of it all. I was a Stone and because of that—because of what I was deep down—I'd lost Nina's love.

I was no different than my father or Taylor.

Closing my eyes, I pressed my cheek to her door and whispered one last time, "I love you, Nina. I hope someday you can forgive me."

I waited for what seemed like hours for her to say anything, but all I heard was silence.

Chapter Twenty-Three

Nina

My throat hurt because I cried so much, but the tears kept coming. I didn't know which hurt more—knowing what really happened to my father and that Tristan's father had been the one to take him away from me or that everything I loved had been based on a lie. I wanted to run away, like I did before, but I couldn't. Tristan had lied to me from the moment he met me, but I loved him. And he loved me. I just didn't know how we'd go on from here.

I'd heard him outside my door telling me he loved me. His voice was so sad that I couldn't face him. I pressed my ear to the door and heard him whisper that he hoped I'd forgive him.

I knew I shouldn't want to forgive him. He'd lied over and over for months. That should have been enough for me to never want to speak to him again.

If only it was that easy.

Exhausted from crying and thinking for hours, I finally fell asleep just as the first rays of the sun began to stream through my window. Not that I slept well. My body may have wanted to rest, but my mind raced the entire time so that when I opened my eyes at ten I was up and ready to face Tristan and our life together.

I couldn't just let this go. That had been the one thought preoccupying my mind. No matter how many times I told myself I couldn't forgive, it's the only thing I wanted to do. I knew what everyone would say. Kim would tell me I was stupid or being a fool. Once a liar, always a liar. Even Jordan would likely tell me to walk away.

My mind knew that was the smartest thing to do. My heart had an entirely different agenda, though.

For better or worse, my heart had won the tug-of-war, and I got out of bed prepared to tell Tristan how I felt. I could forgive him, but this would be his only chance. The man who'd been there for me when I was broken and hurt deserved at least that.

I spied an envelope sitting on the floor near the door, which was so typical of him. I hurriedly walked over to get it, noticing as I picked it up that it was far thicker than his usual notes. A tiny spike of fear ran through my mind at the possibility of what I'd soon find in those pages. Unfolding them, I began to read his words. As they flowed in front of my eyes, my stomach dropped and an emptiness filled me.

Dear Nina,

I can't say I'm sorry anymore and convince you how much I never meant to hurt you. I was a fool to believe that we could be happy. How could we be when I'm who I am?

You made my days happier than you'll ever know. Before I met you, I had never loved anyone. My life was empty. That was my fate, and I accepted it. I was a Stone, and it was better for me to be alone than to hurt people like my father had.

Then I met you and all that changed. I didn't want to accept my loneliness anymore. I wanted to believe I could make someone happy. I tried, but what I had to give wasn't enough. Money, trips, clothes—none of it made you love me. I didn't know anything else, and for that I'm sorry.

But somehow you made me understand none of that mattered and if I gave my heart I had a chance to have someone like you love me. I gave you my heart, and you gave me love. I know it wasn't easy to be with me. I'm all closed off and I need to have control more than other men. I don't know why I'm so fucked up, but you freely gave me your heart, and your love was the best thing of my life.

I'm sorry I didn't tell you the truth in the beginning. I'm sorry that when I had the chance to make things right when you came home from the hospital that I didn't. I know you may not believe it, but I never wanted to hurt you. That was the last thing I wanted to do.

I will always love you. I can't fix the mistakes I've made. I can only say I'm sorry and hope you'll forgive me someday. You can't accept my love after what I've done, but I hope you'll accept what I promised. Enclosed you'll find a legal document that will ensure you'll want for nothing. This house will be transferred to you, and I've made sure that each month money will be deposited in your account to ensure you have everything you can possibly desire.

I'm sorry that all I am is money and things. For a short time, I was more because of you.

I love you, Nina. Someday, I hope you'll believe me.

Yours always,

Tristan

Tears clouded my eyes so I couldn't read the words anymore, but I'd seen enough. I didn't need to read some legal document to know Tristan was gone. Instantly, I felt alone. I couldn't let him give up on us like this.

I tore down my hallway screaming his name, but I instinctively felt the emptiness of the house now that he'd left. I ran from room to room but found nothing.

"Tristan! No! Tristan!"

All there was in return was silence.

His room looked like it always had, like he hadn't even been there that night. Something in me said to check Rogers' room, and I raced there, stopping dead in the doorway at the sight of the bed. Neatly made the last time I'd been there, now the bedspread and blankets lay crumpled as if someone had spent a restless night there.

I checked the garage to see if Tristan's Jag was still there, but I knew better. He was gone. Jensen stood in the corner ready to take me wherever I desired.

"Where is he?"

"Miss?"

"Where is Tristan, Jensen? Where did he go?"

"He drove on his own, miss."

"Do you know where?"

Jensen stood silent as he stared at me. Tristan had likely told him not to tell me where he'd gone. I didn't care. I needed to find him and let him know I forgave him, even if I didn't understand everything that had happened. I needed to tell him I still loved him.

"I have to find him. Tell me where he went!" I yelled across the garage, shocking the driver.

"He's gone, Nina," a voice behind me said quietly, and I turned around to see a strange man standing there.

"Who are you? Where is Tristan? Tell me! I need to know."

"Come with me. We can talk inside."

I followed the large man with too much red hair and beard to a sitting room. As I took a seat on the couch, I remembered being in that room with Tristan. We'd first kissed right there after he'd taught me how to tie a Windsor knot. I remembered everything. Our first night together. How crazy I was in love with him just days later. Everything was back now.

"My name is Daryl Knight. I work for Tristan. I guess ordinarily Rogers would have had the job of telling you this, but it's fallen on me now."

"I hope you don't hate me like Rogers did because I need you to tell me where Tristan is. I have to see him."

"That can't happen, Nina. All I know is that he's gone. Karl and his friends on the Board want him dead now that your sister gave them her copies of your father's notes. Because Tristan wouldn't give them the original notes, they can't let him stay alive."

"I don't understand. What's so important about my father's notes? Tristan knows what happened with his father and brother. He knows what they did and why my father was murdered. Why doesn't he just give them to Karl and be done with this whole horrible thing?"

"I don't know why. All I know is that he's not done with those notes yet."

"Well, I don't care about that. I just need to see him. Where is he, Daryl?"

He frowned and shook his head. "I don't know. All I know is what he told me when he called. He wanted me to make sure you read the papers he left you."

I angrily waved the envelope Tristan had left me in front of him. "I don't care about the papers. I want Tristan, not things. Please tell me where he is."

"I can't."

Out of the corner of my eye, I saw two huge men who seemed to be hovering just outside the door to the sitting room. Pointing at them, I asked, "Then can they tell me?"

Daryl turned to look at the them and shook his head. "No. They're not here for that."

"Then what the hell are they here for? Who are they?"

He waved them into the room and they took their place in front of us like two giants eying their next victims. The one who stood on the left had very short, cropped dark hair with some streaks of grey, and his face said he was all business. He was enormous, like a bouncer at a club, and he looked as if he could pick me up with two fingers. The man on the right wore his lighter brown hair slightly longer and had no grey in his, but his eyes were the darkest blue I'd ever seen.

"Nina, these men protect you. They've protected you since your accident. When you leave this house, they're always nearby making sure you're safe."

"Do you mean every time I went out they were there?" I asked in astonishment.

I looked at the men as they nodded silently. My bodyguards looked down at me as I worked to process all of this. Two men had been watching me and obviously Tristan had hired them.

"Yes, and they'll be there every time you go out from now on."

"What if I don't want them to be?" I asked, feeling slightly irritated by Daryl's officious tone. It was one thing for Tristan to be all Alpha with me. I loved him. Daryl was just some scruffy guy sitting in what was now my house and bossing me around.

"I'm sorry, but you don't have a choice. They have their job, just as I have mine. Your safety is paramount to Tristan, so you'll just have to get used to having them around."

"I don't understand, Daryl. I thought that Karl and his thugs didn't care about me anymore because my sister gave them what they wanted. Why would I be in danger?"

"If Karl doesn't get what he wants from Tristan, he's not above hurting you. These men will make sure that doesn't happen."

"What? For the rest of my life?"

"I don't know the answer to that. For now, they'll be next to you at all times."

I looked up again at the men. "Since you're going to be my shadows, I should at least know your names."

Mr. All Business nodded. "Nathan West."

The corners of Blue Eye's mouth hitched up slightly, giving him a sort of scary-sexy look. "Gage Varo."

Both men had hollow, deep voices, adding to my anxiety about all of this. Turning to face Daryl, I asked, "How do they know when I'm leaving the house? Does Jensen call them?"

"They stay in the carriage house. When Jensen leaves, they leave."

I sat stunned at what Daryl was saying. These men lived on the same property as I did and I'd never even seen them. And they'd been following me for weeks. How is it I'd missed these two gigantic men near me at all times?

"Why haven't I noticed them all this time?"

The one named Varo answered, "Because you weren't looking for us. Our job is to be invisible. You would have never known we were there if you hadn't been told."

"What if I don't want to live here with bodyguards and a driver?"

Daryl seemed to think about my question and answered, "I think that would make Tristan unhappy. He wants to ensure you're safe, Nina."

"I want to talk to him. I'm tired of all this. Where is he?"

Instead of giving me the answer I so desperately wanted, Daryl simply stood to leave. "I can't help you with that. What I can say is that Tristan has taken care of everything to make sure you're safe."

Jumping up, I screamed, "Why do you keep saying that? I don't care about being safe. All I want is to see Tristan!"

"I'm sorry, Nina. I wish I could say more."

"Then there is more to say. Where is he? Why can't I at least see him?"

My bodyguards walked out, leaving me alone with Daryl. He smiled for the first time and said, "Nina, I can't say more because Tristan hasn't told me more. I don't know where he is. All I know is that in the middle of the night he called me and told me he needed my help to make sure what he wanted to happen happened. That's it."

"Did he sound…" I didn't know how to say it. "Did he sound like he was okay? There was coke and…"

Daryl smiled again. "He sounded tired."

"Would you tell me if you knew anything else, like say, if he said anything about me other than that he wanted to know that I'm safe? Give me something."

"I work for Tristan, but I know how much you mean to him, so yes, I would. He said very little, Nina. All I know is that his first concern was for your safety."

I hung my head in sadness. "Thank you, Daryl. Did he say anything else at about anything I should do?"

"One last thing. Don't try to contact your sister. She and her family are safe from Karl and his friends, but to make sure they stay that way, you can't speak to her for a while."

"Did Tristan do that?"

Daryl nodded. "Yeah. They weren't safe, even after she gave Karl your father's notes."

"When is all this going to end, Daryl?"

Shaking his head, he shrugged. "I don't know, but trust that Tristan won't let Karl and his buddies get what they want."

I wish I knew what that awful man wanted. So much of this was still a mystery to me, and with Tristan gone, I didn't have anyone to help me understand all of it.

Daryl handed me a slip of paper. "This is my number. Call me if you need anything. West and Varo will take care of your safety, and Jensen is here for you like he's always been."

Nodding, I pressed a fake smile on my face. "Thank you, Daryl."

It seemed like I had men everywhere to take care of me except for the one I truly wanted standing next to me. The memory of those pictures of Tristan came back to me as I sat alone, and I found myself in the attic next to the trunk that held those images from so long ago.

I sat down on the wood floor and lifted the lid. Inside were letters and pictures from years before. I recognized the large portrait that sat on the bottom of the trunk. Pulling it out, I propped it against the inside of the lid and studied it in the faint sunlight streaming into the attic. Instantly, my eyes were drawn to the left side of the picture where Tristan's father and brother sat. Hatred coursed through my veins as I stared at their faces. Even though Taylor was just a small child, I hated him. It was almost as if he wasn't Tristan's identical twin. Nothing about him reminded me of the man I loved. All I saw was the man who was to blame for that poor girl's death.

Victor Stone sat behind Taylor smiling and happy. I hated him even more. My hands began to shake as they clutched the sides of the picture containing the two people responsible for my father's death. Not just death. Murder. They'd murdered my father to save themselves. I wanted to scream—to find them and hit them until they felt like I did when I first heard my father was gone.

But I couldn't. Fate had punished them before anyone else could. They were gone, taken from this Earth, and I'd have to learn to live with how much I hated them.

I couldn't look at them anymore. My eyes filled with tears at the hatred inside me. This wasn't who I was, though. I didn't want to hate. I forced my gaze to the right side of the portrait where Tristan sat in front of his mother. Her face was placid, but something in her eyes made her look sad. She was beautiful, her eyes so much like Tristan's now as I stared at them. They seemed to speak from the silence of the image. Had she known what her husband was like? Did she ever find out what Taylor had done, or had she remained blissfully ignorant like many women in her position?

I understood wanting to be ignorant of the painful facts of life. I couldn't blame her if she had chosen to believe her husband and son weren't the monsters they were. I just prayed that she knew how good Tristan was.

Unable to look at the ones responsible for all this heartache anymore, I placed the portrait back in its spot in the trunk next to a stack of letters tied with a red silk ribbon that reminded me of all the notes and letters Tristan had written me. I ran my fingertips over the handwriting as I read the name they were addressed to.

Tressa.

Had they been love letters from Tristan's father to his mother? Tossing them back into the bottom of the trunk, I closed the lid. I couldn't think about Victor Stone being someone good and kind. He was a monster, and that was all there was to it for me.

I walked back to my room, still determined to at least let Tristan know that I forgave him. Grabbing my phone, I laid back on my bed and texted him a message, my fingers saying what my voice couldn't.

I wish you hadn't left. I wanted to tell you this myself, but I'll have to do it this way instead. I forgive you. Please tell me where you are so I can come to you. I don't want this house and the money if you aren't with me. I love you.

For more than an hour I waited for him to text me back and tell me he loved me too. He never answered my text.

EPILOGUE

Tristan

The sun was just setting as I watched the blue sky change to a deep purple shade I hadn't seen since my last time here. I'd only visited this place once when I was a boy. My mother had brought me here with my brother to see a hotel my father was considering buying. She fell in love with its old world charm, but he dismissed it out of hand, knowing full well how much it meant to her to play some part in the business.

The building had fallen into disrepair in the years since, and it was nowhere near as beautiful now. No longer a hotel, it was merely a home under construction. It was the first purchase I made after becoming CEO of Stone Worldwide. I bought it sight unseen and immediately set about reconstructing it. I'd always planned on bringing Nina here once the home was finished. I'd had this fantasy that this could be our summer house and we'd bring our kids here. They'd play in the yard while she and I watched them from the balcony.

As I sat in the livable part of the house admiring the darkening sky, I tried to remember that all those dreams were gone now. Nina had reacted just as I feared when she heard what I'd done. I didn't blame her. How could I? While my crime wasn't the same as my father's or brother's, it was still a betrayal and I'd knowingly committed it, no matter what my intentions had been.

Rogers had been right.

My chest felt like a weight was pushing down on it every time I thought about him. As much my father was Victor Stone, he'd been the one I'd turned to for so long I hadn't seen what he'd become. That he'd chosen Karl and the world I'd sworn to never be a part of over me and had tried to hurt the woman I loved hurt more than I could express.

But his death was as much my fault as the one who'd run him down that night. I wanted to kill him right there in his room in my home, my hands tightening around his neck until there was no more life left in him. I wished him dead for what he'd done—for his disloyalty when I needed him most. For threatening to hurt the one soul on this Earth I'd ever truly loved.

Nina.

My thoughts always came back to her. Thousands of miles separated us, yet I could still smell her perfume each time I inhaled, could still feel the touch of her hand on mine when I closed my eyes.

I wondered how she looked when she read my letter, her gentle blue eyes taking in my words like she had that first night home from the hospital. Had it made her happy when she found out that she owned that house she loved so much, or had she thrown the paper away from her in disgust, unwilling to listen to my apologies even in that form?

Looking around at the almost empty room I sat in now, I accepted how it all had ended up. I was supposed to be alone. I'd told shrink after shrink that, trying to convince them of the reality of who I was while they tried their damnedest to persuade me to believe that no person was meant to be alone, not even someone as fucked up as I was.

That all souls deserved love.

I'd lost my family, Rogers, and now Nina. Whether or not I deserved it, I was alone.

I looked down at my phone, a new one I'd gotten just days before. I knew it was impossible since she didn't know the number, but every so often I checked anyway to see if she'd texted to tell me she'd forgiven me, she loved me, or even that she missed me.

It was better this way. Nina was safe with West and Varo. She had Daryl looking out for her and Jensen at her beck and call. She had as much money as she'd ever need and a home she'd said she'd loved.

Pushing the phone away from me, it slid across the table and I told myself this was how it had to be.

It's better this way.

Even if it wasn't better this way, this was how it was.

I slipped one of the letters she'd written me out of my pocket and ran my fingertips over the words, imagining her hand holding the paper as she wrote the lines that I read and reread every night. I missed her so much my body actually hurt. I missed her voice as she asked me dozens of questions and her smile when she tried to bring me out of my shell. I missed the softness of her lips against mine when she kissed me and the feel of her cuddled up next to me as she drifted off to sleep.

How was I going to live like this for the rest of my life now that I knew what I missed?

I leaned over, pulling my phone toward me, and turned it on. I ran my finger across the screen, but it didn't change the picture. Maybe it was a sign. Staring at it, I tried to talk myself out of what I was about to do.

But it was no use. I had to try.

I lightly dragged my fingertip across the screen, bringing it to life this time, and pressed until the only contact I had saved came up.

Nina.

I miss you.

Pushing the phone away, I watched it, my eyes fixed on it for her text back. I hadn't told her who I was, so she might never reply. Maybe that's what was supposed to be.

I waited for what seemed like hours, although it was likely just a few minutes, before I gave up hope and closed my eyes, silently telling myself this was what I deserved. This was my punishment for my crimes.

Pulling the phone back, I opened my eyes and saw a message come in. *Please come home. Don't leave me here all alone.*

I didn't think it was possible for my heart to break more, but just seeing those words made it feel like someone was tearing it out of my chest. She forgave me, yet I couldn't go home now.

I love you. If I could return, I would.

Texting Nina had been a mistake. Wishing for something that couldn't be was bad enough. Wishing for something that could someday happen was worse.

My phone lit up with another text. *I love you, Tristan. I don't know why you left, but whatever it is, we can handle it together. Please come back to me.*

I didn't answer her. I couldn't tell her I wasn't coming back, as much as I wanted to. I couldn't hurt her again. As I beat myself up for wanting what only she could give me, my phone lit up again with her final message.

I'm not letting you go. I won't let you give up on us, Tristan. If you won't come to me, I'll come to you. Even if no one helps me, I'll find you again.

GIVE IN TO ME

BOOK THREE

Chapter One

Nina

Jordan waited for me at the end of the hallway, ready to head off to school. I was running late, so by the time I reached her, she was tapping her foot and giving me that raised eyebrow look she always did when she was well on her way to lashing out. I saw in her green eyes the anger simmering just below the surface this morning.

"I know this house is huge, but maybe you could remember I have an entire class of third graders and a principal who because of her lack of sex is literally the crankiest woman you'll ever meet. If Sister Fits Nice and Tight reams me out because poor old Jensen can't get me to school on time, you're going to see a whole new Jordan at dinner tonight."

"I'm sorry. I didn't mean to be late. I just got tied up with something," I said in my best "forgive me" voice.

Her face twisted into a scowl. "I bet if I checked your cell phone I'd see what was tying you up. You're still texting him every morning, aren't you?"

"And every night before I go to sleep in his bed as I stare at the painting I made just for him."

Jordan sighed, her shoulders sagging, and a frown settled into her beautiful features. "Oh, honey. It's been months since he answered you. He probably doesn't even have that phone anymore. I'm not saying he's not ever coming back or you shouldn't do that every day and night, but..."

Her words faded away as she stared at me with pity in her eyes. No matter. I didn't care if anyone believed what I believed. I knew in my heart he was receiving every text I sent. I didn't know why he didn't answer, but that didn't change the fact that I wanted him to know that I hadn't given up on us.

Picking up her bag, I handed it to her with a smile. "You're going to be late. Have a good day, and don't be too hard on those little darlings."

"You're not coming today?"

"No. I have a meeting with Daryl, so I can't head into the city today. Maybe tomorrow, though."

Grimacing, she spun on her heels and headed toward the front door. "Daryl? That guy who looks like a mountain man? I'll take the uptight nun and eight year olds, thank you."

"Have a good day, Jordan. What do you say to pizza tonight?"

She stopped and turned to face me. "Are you sure you can handle that?"

"You mean sauce and cheese on crust?" I joked, knowing she saw right through my facade.

"I'm serious, Nina. The last time we tried Tony's you were bummed for days."

"I'll be okay. I've been craving flat birch beer."

Jordan shook her head. "You rich people have weird tastes. I'm off to mold young minds. Later, gator."

I yelled after her, "After while, crocodile!"

As she opened the door, she looked back at me and smirked. "So uncool."

When I knew I was safely alone, I slipped my phone out of my pocket and scrolled through my messages to the one I'd sent Tristan just minutes earlier. My breath caught in my chest as I read the words and prayed for some kind of response.

Good morning. I dreamed about you last night. I miss you so much. Every night I convince myself that you're finally going to come back to me, but every morning I wake up alone. I love you. I haven't given up on us, Tristan.

I hadn't given up, even if Daryl had talked me out of going to look for him. I was sure he knew where Tristan was, but if he did, he wouldn't tell me. He was as close as I could get to the man I loved, though, so when he called and said he wanted to meet, I always agreed, every time hoping that day would be the one when he'd finally tell me what happened to Tristan and when he was coming home.

Scrolling through months of texts, I stood there in the entryway reading what remained of our relationship. Text after text showed the slow progression of my feelings over time from sadness to anger to acceptance. I'd lived through the loss of him from my life in those messages straight from my heart. Some days they'd been the only way I could get out of bed and face the world. Expressions of desperation and hopelessness, they gave me something no person or thing that remained in my life could.

They were a lifeline each morning and night connecting me to Tristan.

Jordan didn't understand why I continued to bother since he'd stopped answering my messages the day after he left. Some days I didn't understand either, but I couldn't stop myself. There was some small relief from my heartache in tapping out my feelings into words, regardless of where they went once I clicked Send.

Some nights I scrolled through every message, terrified that my phone had deleted some of the earlier ones. A sort of mania took over, and I'd have to count each one, reading every single text to make sure they all still existed, as if losing even one meant losing a part of him.

Over the months, I'd gotten better at pretending for everyone around me so they thought I was handling it all pretty well. Jordan knew more than the others, but even she had no idea how much I missed Tristan. Looking down at my phone, I read my newest message to him.

If you see these, you need to know that today's a hard day for me. It's never easy, but today's really hard. I miss you so much.

Send.

I stuffed the phone back into my jeans pocket because if I didn't, I'd stand there texting Tristan all day until Jordan got home. Daryl was scheduled to get there in just minutes, so at least I wouldn't have a lot of time to sit and think. That was the worst. It's why I went into the city most days. At least when I was thinking surrounded by millions of people I didn't feel so alone. The city did that for us lonely folks.

But even visiting art museums couldn't improve my spirits. Lately, I usually ended up at The Cloisters staring at images of death in the Middle Ages, and even in my funk I knew that wasn't a good sign.

A knock at the door told me Daryl was early, so I let him in and we sat in the same room we'd been in when he told me Tristan was gone and he didn't know when he'd return. It was like our ritual. Each time I'd sit on the couch where I'd sat that first night with Tristan, and Daryl would sit opposite me and begin talking about things I pretended to understand. Even now, months later, I had no clear idea about why Karl needed to have my father's notes, and I didn't think Daryl knew either, although he seemed to feel he understood better than I did.

I didn't care about any of that. Karl, my father's notes, and whatever Tristan's father had done meant nothing to me. I just wanted Tristan home and the two of us to live happily ever after. Or at least as much as that was possible with us.

Daryl was looking particularly mountain mannish, as if he'd decided trimming his rusty colored beard wasn't required as long as he wore a dress shirt. He had that chest hair peeking out look that I found gross, and his whole appearance made paying attention to him difficult, especially today.

"How are you doing out here? Any problems? Any security issues?" he asked in his best dad voice.

"West and Varo would have told you if there were any. I don't think they keep much to themselves when it comes to their job."

"True. Those boys do take their job seriously. I'm thinking Tristan must have found them at a military school or something. They're good for what we need them to be, though. I was talking more about Karl or anyone from the Stone Worldwide Board. Have they tried to contact you at all?"

I shook my head and frowned at even the mention of them. "No. Why would they contact me?"

"Because they likely think you know where he is."

"Well, as you well know, I don't, even though I think you do," I said in a voice that reflected my anger and frustration at the whole situation.

Daryl stared at me, and I waited for him to say either he knew or he didn't, but instead he simply continued his train of thought. "If Karl shows up here…"

I cut him off mid-sentence. "I know. Get West and Varo up here lickity split and have them rough him up for me."

"No. Nina, I need you to take this seriously."

"Roughing up Karl sounds pretty serious to me, Daryl."

"Nina, I'm responsible for making sure you're safe. I'm just trying to do my job here."

"Does your job include telling me where Tristan is?" I asked sharply, making the conversation come to a dead stop.

Daryl's expression lacked any emotion at all, and he stared at me, finally answering, "No, it doesn't."

Even his faded brown eyes gave no indication whether he knew where Tristan was or not, so as usual, I gave up and forced a smile. "Fine. What else do we have to talk about?"

"The Karl business is a real concern, Nina. He's gotten the Board to take over Stone Worldwide, but as long as Tristan is somewhere in this world, he can't truly take control of the company."

"I would think if he intended to pump me for information, he would have done it before. It's been four months, Daryl. Karl and the Board think he's never coming back."

My voice caught as I spoke those words. Never coming back. A knot twisted in my stomach as the words echoed in my head. Never coming back.

"We have to be careful," Daryl continued, likely not noticing that I didn't want to talk about this anymore. "Karl is going to be a danger as long as Tristan's gone."

I couldn't do this today. Jumping up from the couch, I threw my hands up. "Then maybe he shouldn't be gone! Maybe he should be here handling things instead of leaving everything up to me!"

Daryl stared up at me, his eyes wide for a moment until his expression calmed once again. I knew this whole situation wasn't his fault, and it wasn't right for me to shoot the messenger. It's just that it all was too much sometimes, and this morning I was really feeling down. I sat again, feeling guilty for my outburst. It wasn't even noon yet and I was exhausted.

"I'm sorry. I know you're just doing your job, Daryl."

"No problem. Everybody has to let off a little steam every so often. I understand."

"Just tell me what you need me to do and I'll do it," I said, resigned to the fact that today was yet another day that I wouldn't hear the words I so desperately wanted him to say.

"I need you to just stay strong. I can't tell you when he's coming back, but he will. You just have to believe."

Nodding, I plastered a smile on my face. "Got it. Believe. I'm on it."

"I also need you to make sure West and Varo know your every move."

I opened my mouth to protest, but he stopped me. "I know you don't like it, but this is the way Tristan wants it. Those two are just doing their jobs too, so how about you give them a break?"

"Got it. Give the big guys a break."

I wanted to scream that I wanted a break, but something about the way Daryl explained things made me feel like an ass for complaining. I lived a life most people would give their right arm for. I had a beautiful home, a cook who made my meals, a driver to take me wherever my heart desired, and bodyguards to ensure my safety. Tristan had made sure my bank account had swelled to a sum more than I could spend in ten years. There wasn't a thing I couldn't buy. What on Earth did I have to complain about?

Tristan may have felt some bond with Daryl, but to me he was merely the bearer of bad tidings. Just once I wished he would show up with a smile on his hairy face and tell me that all this was over and Tristan was coming home.

Daryl took out his small notebook from his jacket and began to flip through the pages searching for some detail he believed I needed to know. I craned my neck in an effort to see what he'd written, but I couldn't read his handwriting upside down. He licked the pad of his thumb and flipped up one last page before he scanned what he'd written and nodded.

Raising his gaze to look at me, he said in a serious voice, "I knew I had one more thing to talk to you about. You're going to have to hire a gardener or caretaker for the grounds now that the weather is getting better."

"This is what you searched for in your little notebook? A gardener? I can't just have West or Varo do it?" Actually, since West was always so abrupt with me, I liked the idea of him stuck on a riding mower for hours a few times a month, but something told me that Jordan would be all about seeing Varo shirtless and weed whacking. She'd tried in vain to get his attention for weeks since she realized the gorgeous man she'd seen at the bar that night months ago lived just yards away from her.

Furrowing his brow, Daryl groaned. "No. They guard you. They don't prune hedges."

Daryl was no fun at all. "Fine. Then I'll get a gardener."

Finished with our meeting, he stood and looked down at me to ask the question he always asked right before he left. "Is there anything you need?"

I took a deep breath in and slowly let it out, letting my shoulders sag. Looking up at him, I said, "Please tell me if you've talked to him. Please."

His face was expressionless but finally he nodded. "I have. He asked about you, and I told him you were holding up."

"Is he okay? Is he hurt?"

A shadow crossed Daryl's face, and I knew his next words would be a lie. "He's fine."

Just the way his voice dropped when he said the word "fine" told me Tristan was anything but that. Fear raced through me at the thought of what condition he was actually in. My heart pounding against my chest, I asked, "Is he hurt? Tell me, please."

"Don't worry. If he's hurting, it's only because he isn't here with you."

Daryl moved to walk away, and I grabbed his arm to stop him. "Would you tell him something for me?"

"Sure."

"Tell him I'll be waiting right here."

I let go of Daryl's arm and he walked away without saying another word. I sat there for a long time thinking about the night Tristan and I had spent together after getting to know each other right there on that couch. God, that seemed like so long ago, even though it wasn't even a year that had passed. So much had changed between then and now.

"Nina, are you ready to go?" Jordan asked as she peeked her head into my room.

I swiped the lip gloss across my bottom lip and threw the case in my bag. One last check of my makeup and I was ready. "Pizza Heaven, here we come!"

Jensen was waiting for us, along with my two giant shadows who were never far behind. The five of us stood in the driveway in front of the garage, an awkward silence hanging around us as we eyed one another with curiosity like usual. Even though I lived with these people, for all intents and purposes, they were barely more than strangers to me, people I knew more by the way they dressed than their personalities. Jensen stood stiffly in his usual dark suit, while West and Varo looked more comfortable in jeans and button down shirts, as they always did. Leaning in next to me, Jordan whispered, "Tony's might be pizza heaven, but I think Varo would be the kind of heaven I want."

I looked at West and Varo, then turned to Jensen. "We're going for pizza. Do you guys want to join us? You're more than welcome."

Out of the corner of my eye, I saw Jordan's eyes grow wide. Maybe I should have told her about my new idea of being nice to my constant companions. It wasn't their fault that Tristan wasn't back yet, so it wasn't right that I took out my unhappiness on them. My change of heart, however, seemed to surprise them as much as it did Jordan, and while Jensen politely begged off, I thought I saw West's eyes light up at the mention of pizza. Varo, as always, stood silently with a smoldering glare that I was convinced was the way his eyes naturally looked.

When neither of them spoke, I shrugged and asked, "Any takers? You guys have to eat, don't you?"

"And we're a pretty good time," Jordan chimed in. "It would be nice to see you guys loosen up for once."

West appeared to rethink his earlier excitement at hearing we were having pizza and said in a low voice, "We're fine. We'll be nearby if you need us."

"Okay. If you change your mind, you know where we are."

Everyone looked around at each other at my statement of the obvious. Jordan chuckled nervously next to me, thankfully breaking the tension for a moment, and we all left for Tony's Pizza Heaven like some sad entourage.

I was glad to see that the waitress who'd been working the night Tristan asked me to marry him wasn't there. I wasn't up for answering questions about him tonight. A short, older woman took our order, and as I sat silently remembering how much this tiny, out-of-the-way restaurant meant to me, Jordan told me about her boss's mini-lecture she gave her for being three minutes late that morning.

Sheepishly, I apologized. "I'm sorry. If it makes you feel better, I had a pretty rotten day."

"Yes. Yes, that makes me feel much better." She rolled her eyes. "Now that I know you think I'm some kind of harpy, why don't you tell me why your day sucked?"

"Same old, same old. I'd rather hear about your class."

"And I'd rather talk about you wearing your engagement ring again. I'm happy to see that, but I'm wondering why now? Was there some news from Grizzly Adams today?"

Jordan's snarkiness always brought out a smile in me. Looking down at the diamond ring on my left hand, I shook my head. "No, no news. I just thought it was right."

She raised her hand to cover her eyes. "It's giving off a glare that's blinding. That man of yours sure does know how to give a gift."

I spread my fingers and moved my hand back and forth. "He does."

"I don't think my eyes can take what he'll be getting you after his little absence."

Now it was my turn to roll my eyes. "Funny. Just drink your flat soda."

"I want you to know that I'm going to miss us sharing a place again, Nina. It was like old times, except in a place ten times the size. With a pool. And a kitchen you could fit a small house in."

"You're just going to miss being so close to my hot bodyguard. Anyway, it's not like you're moving any time soon. Daryl didn't have any news about Tristan or if he'd be coming back," I admitted sadly.

Jordan reached over and covered my hand with hers. "When, honey. When."

Nodding, I smiled at her effort to cheer me up. "I know. When. When he's coming back."

"And as for Varo, I'm not going to deny it. I'll be all over him like white on rice the moment he gives me the chance."

After so much pizza my pants didn't feel like they fit right anymore, we found Jensen waiting outside for us and got in the car for our ride home. West and Varo didn't seem to be anywhere in sight, much to Jordan's disappointment, but I knew that meant nothing. As big as they were, they seemed to know how to blend in so they weren't seen. All the better. I rarely had anything to say to them, and even though I'd pretended all through dinner that Tony's didn't make me sad, the fact was that Jordan had been right.

I still wasn't ready to deal with all the memories.

Climbing into bed, I closed my eyes to remember when Tristan and I were together, happy and in love.

The warm summer air drifted in through the window, lightly billowing the deep green sheers and carrying the sweet scent of honeysuckle across the room to where we sat. Still dressed in his suit and tie, Tristan leaned against the back of the couch and closed his eyes.

I loved these moments together, just the two of us sitting quietly at the end of the day, not saying a thing to ruin the peaceful silence we shared. For me, this was a change. All my life, I'd filled in the gaps with words rather than experience an awkward silence, but with Tristan, I'd learned to appreciate that silence. Sliding my finger down his red silk tie, I watched a sly smile slowly spread across his lips.

"Did I ever tell you how much I love this after a long day?"

He opened his eyes, and I saw how much these moments meant to him. "Yes, but not yet today," I teased.

Tristan sighed and reached out to touch my hand. "All day I look forward to these moments. No more people wanting me for a thousand reasons. No more caring about hotels and the bottom line of the other Stone Worldwide businesses. Just quiet and you."

Even though we hadn't said the words "I love you" yet to each other, it was obvious in every other word and every action. We didn't need to say that to know we loved one another. It was the first time in my life that I truly knew how a man felt about me.

I rested my head on his chest and listened to the steady rhythm of his heartbeat next to my cheek. That steadiness made me feel secure like never before in my life. For all the strangeness that had been a part of our meeting, we'd settled into a sweet space that gave me a sense of stability I'd never known I wanted but now never wanted to be without.

Slowly, his fingers trailed up and down my back. "Tell me about your day," he whispered above me.

"You don't want to hear about my boring day full of art."

I knew how he felt about the artwork I chose for the suites and penthouses. He pretended to be interested, but the man was no art lover. That's what I was in his life for.

"I'd listen just to hear you speak."

Lifting my head, I looked up at him and saw that sexy look in his eyes. "Is that what you really want?" I teased.

"Want to know what I really want?"

I loved this Tristan, the playful, gentle soul who could be so open and sweet and who so infrequently showed himself. Charmed, I would have done anything he asked. He had that effect on me.

"I can guess," I said with a wink. "I thought you were tired, but I like the way you think."

He eased me off him, and standing up, held his hand out to me. "Come."

I joined him and expected to be led to the bedroom we now shared, but instead he smiled and whispered, "Don't move."

Walking over to the opposite side of the room, he dimmed the lights until the room glowed a soft amber color. I watched him do something in the corner before he returned and pulled me close. Kissing the top of my head, he whispered, "May I have this dance?"

I looked around and waited for music, but none came. "Tristan, what are we dancing to?"

"Give it a second."

Very slowly, he began swaying back and forth as he held me to him. At least ten seconds went by and then I heard the first sad notes of a song I hadn't heard in ages. I remembered it instantly.

Nothing Compares 2U by Sinead O'Connor.

While we danced there in the sitting room where we'd first kissed, Tristan whispered the words of the song to me, nearly breaking my heart. He sounded so sad. The song ended and another one I'd never heard began as we continued to slowly sway to the music. Quietly, he said, "When I was a little boy, I heard that song every day. My mother loved it and played it over and over."

Looking up at him, I said, "I never took you for a Sinead O'Connor fan. It's a pretty song, but not one I'd think of for you."

He smiled and shook his head. "I've never heard another song by her. All I know is that song."

"You know all the words."

"It's hard not to after hearing it hundreds of times."

We fell silent for a few moments as we held each other, and I listened to the song playing. "Do you know the words to this one?" I asked him while we danced.

He seemed lost in memory as he looked off in the distance, squeezing me tightly to him. "No. Just that first one."

"Is everything okay, Tristan? You seem a million miles away."

My question was met with a smile, and he looked down at me. "Just thinking. I never did understand why she listened to that song so often. Taylor hated it and would run out of the room every time she put it on. She'd just smile and begin singing the words."

I wanted to ask about his mother. Her beautiful face had stayed in my mind since that first time I'd seen her in their family portrait, but the way Tristan's mouth always turned down slightly whenever his family was mentioned stopped me every time.

"I think it's nice that it reminds you of her."

Tristan stopped dancing and kissed me softly on the lips. "It doesn't anymore. I heard it this afternoon in a store and realized it reminded me of you."

"Me? But isn't the song about how she feels after losing the one she loved?" I asked as a tiny lick of fear took hold of my heart. Was he breaking up with me?

He was silent for so long that I was sure the next words out of his mouth would be to tell me it was over. Bracing myself for the news, I held on to his forearms and waited, each second ticking by making my heart hurt.

I watched as his expression changed to one so serious that my breath caught in my throat, and then he said in a low voice, "No. It reminds me of you because that's how I'd feel if I lost you. Nothing and no one compares to you, Nina."

When he said things like that, my insides felt like molten lava. Never before had any man made me feel so wanted, so desired. His mouth covered mine in a kiss so deep and full of need that my legs buckled. Tristan caught me by the waist and pulled me hard against him, his stiff cock pressing against my body.

"See what you do to me? All the way home all I could think about was relaxing with you and now look. Obviously, my body knows something my brain doesn't."

"I did that, huh?" I asked with a grin as I ran my hand over the front of his suit pants, my body reacting to his excitement.

Leaning over, he nipped my earlobe and whispered, "Yeah, you did that. Turnabout's fair play too."

He lifted the little cotton skirt I wore and cupped my ass. Slipping his finger under my panties, he ran his fingertip up my already wet pussy, just grazing my throbbing clit. So skilled at knowing exactly how to tease me, he lingered there for just a moment before he moved away, making my body ache for his touch.

"Tristan, don't make me wait," I said with a moan as he stepped away from me to unknot his tie and slip it from around his neck.

"Don't move," he commanded, and I stood still watching him remove his black suit coat and begin to unbutton his white dress shirt.

I reached out to help him with the buttons, and he took another step back from me. "I told you not to move, Nina."

Filling my gaze with the sight of his perfectly sculpted body, I watched as he finished with the buttons and slid out of his shirt. "Why won't you let me help?" I asked, eager to feel his skin under my touch.

A look of unhappiness crossed his features for just a moment, like he didn't enjoy me wanting him so much, but before I could ask if anything was wrong, his expression changed and he was that same incredibly sexy Tristan I couldn't get enough of. He extended his hand, and I moved toward him, timidly touching the buckle of his belt as I stared up into his deep brown eyes.

"I so much want you to be happy, Nina," he said in a low voice as I began to undo his belt and pants, his eyes searching for an answer to some unspoken question or doubt he had about us. Did he think I wasn't happy?

His zipper slid open and all that stood between my hand and his cock was the cotton of his boxer briefs. Running my finger over the flat planes of his abdomen, I skimmed the tip of his cock. "I am happy, Tristan. Why wouldn't I be?"

He left my question unanswered and tugged my skirt over my hips, along with my panties as I stroked him from base to tip. Lifting my T-shirt up over my head, he moaned my name, telling me how much he wanted me.

I hurried out of my bra and followed him to the sofa, straddling him as he pulled me down on top of him. With one long thrust, he slid into me until there was nothing separating us. He held me still so he remained deep inside me, pushing on my hips as he kissed me hard. I wanted to move, to ride him until I came so hard my thighs shook, but I couldn't budge. I didn't think I could want him more, but somehow not being able to feel him moving in and out of my body made me almost desperate for him.

"Tristan, don't make me beg," I whispered into his ear. "You're driving me crazy."

"So impatient. If I move my hands, are you going to move?"

I looked into those eyes and saw he wanted me as much as I wanted him. I just couldn't understand why he didn't want to admit it then. "I'm going to ride your cock like it's never been ridden and fuck you like I know you want."

With anyone else, I would've been embarrassed to say those words, but with Tristan, I felt nothing but the desire to make him happy. Maybe that was why he always seemed to be so interested in my happiness—because he wanted to be happy too. I wanted to be the woman who gave him that.

Silently, he stared up at me and moved his hands from my hips, giving me the freedom to do just as I promised. With every tilt of my hips and every thrust of his cock, we raced toward that happiness we gave one another. His hands guided my movement, and mine clutched his broad shoulders until my body exploded into a million pieces, each one sublimely happy and fulfilled. Moments later, he plunged into me one last time and came almost violently, as if some demon inside of him released its control over him to me.

Smoothing the tiny beads of sweat from his forehead, I smiled down into that gorgeous face now so placid as he stared up at me. I loved him, even if I had never said the words, and I knew he loved me. We shared a need for each other that went far beyond what our bodies craved, and I cherished that vulnerable part deep inside him that he showed me in moments like this.

The memory of that night left me longing to hold him and tell him I missed him. Nothing compared to him for me. He was everything to me, and I was lost without him.

Chapter Two

Tristan

Mid-afternoon was the hardest. I could deal with early morning. I felt like shit the moment I opened my eyes, but I could handle it. Nina's texts after I'd been up for hours doing nothing but thinking—that killed me. Every day I had to talk myself out of calling her and hearing her sweet voice tell me she missed me. I knew I shouldn't, but that didn't mean I didn't want to.

I scrolled through months of texts, feeling worse with each passing one. Telling myself what I was doing was for her benefit did little to make me feel like a hero in this. Four months had gone by, and other than feeling like I wanted to die most days because of what I was putting Nina through, I was no closer to finding out what Karl believed was in Joseph Edwards' notebook. I'd read it from cover to cover, dozens of times reliving the horror of what my father and Taylor had done, but still I couldn't find the slightest detail to explain why my possessing those notes meant anything to Karl or the Board.

Each day I spent hours emotionally crucifying myself, only to hear my phone vibrate in front of me with Nina's good morning text that never failed to rip my heart out. I imagined her waking up in our bed alone, all curled up like she always was in the morning, her hair all tousled and that sleepy look on her face.

Fucking hell! How long was I going to have to pay for what my father and brother did?

The first few months I barely remembered. Between the coke and the alcohol, I'd succeeded in losing days at a time, intent on finding some way of blunting my unhappiness. Easier than facing reality, all the self-abuse ended up achieving was making me feel worse.

Hidden in this secret place no one but Daryl knew about, I was more dead than alive, except for those moments when Nina's messages jolted me out of my own personal hell to the one I shared with her. I had all the money I could want in this world, but it was meaningless without her. I wanted for nothing but for the one thing my life with her had given me.

Love. With Nina, I finally understood what it meant to love and be loved. We'd endured her accident and even her learning the truth this time. I'd known by the end of that first day away that she'd forgive me, which made having to stay here even harder. Every ounce of my being wanted to return to her, but I had to find out what Karl was looking for first.

If you see these, you need to know that today's a hard day for me. It's never easy, but today's really hard. I miss you so much.

I wanted to text back and tell her I missed her too. How I would have given anything to hear her ask one of her questions, even the ones that put me on the spot and I didn't want to answer. How just the thought of sharing a pitcher of semi-flat birch beer and a tray of pizza at our favorite restaurant made me more homesick than I'd ever been in my life.

But I couldn't. I didn't want to risk putting her in danger any more than I already had.

Two hours later, my phone vibrated across the tabletop again, and I looked down to see not a message from Nina but one from Daryl. He only texted after he'd seen her or when he had something important about Karl to tell me, so I read his message with a knot forming in the pit of my stomach.

Coming to see you. We need to talk. See you tomorrow afternoon.

I looked around at the mess of my rooms in this place I'd visited first as a child with my mother. The old hotel she'd fallen in love with was now a building under construction, except for this part I'd taken over. Dirty clothes hung over the backs of chairs, unwashed dishes sat on the table and piled high in the kitchen sink, and newspapers lay strewn across the couch I sat on and the floor next to me. Too fucking bad if Daryl had a problem with the way things looked. He'd complained the last time he'd come to see me, not that I cared then either. I didn't need him to act like a parent. I needed him to act like a fucking detective and find out what I couldn't so I could get home to the woman I loved.

A knock at the door nearly fifteen hours later had me face to face with Daryl. Looking exactly like someone who'd flown business class for over half a day, he nearly fell into the recliner across from the couch.

"Remind me again why your damn plane couldn't fly me here?"

"Karl would know where I was if he found out the company jet was flown somewhere."

"I swear I'm going to end up killing that bastard myself after my return flight," Daryl groaned as he arched his back in pain. "Do you have any idea how terrible business class is from New York to Bucharest? Women in labor for days feel better than I do right now. Any chance you know a chiropractor here?"

"Are you here just to complain? You're supposed to be my detective, so please tell me you have something instead of whining about a bad flight."

"And you think I sound cranky? Is this what you get like when you're removed from power?"

I wasn't in the mood for Daryl's bullshit nonsense. It hadn't taken long for Karl and his friends on the Board to move on my position in my absence. I was still technically the CEO, but not for long. Every day I was forced to stay away was more justification for them to officially remove me and then replace me, likely with Karl or one of his handpicked lackeys.

"Just get to why you're here."

"Why aren't you staying at that five star hotel I read about on the plane? The Ambassador or something. I get why you aren't staying at one of your hotels, but why continue living here in this house? I mean, you can still afford it, so why aren't you living in style like usual?"

Looking around at the old building my mother had fallen in love with nearly twenty years ago, I said, "I like this place." Turning my attention back to him, I continued, "Enough with your bitching. Why are you here?"

"Your lady isn't holding up very well."

Leaning forward, I studied his face for any sign of what was going on with Nina. "What's wrong? Is Nina okay?"

"Physically, she's fine. The boys tell me she visits museums a lot. Pretty high brow stuff as far as they're concerned, but she's getting out. I think this whole thing is starting to take its toll on her, though. I'm wondering if you should consider another way of keeping her safe."

"I don't see any other way, Daryl. As long as Karl thinks what I have is a danger to him, I can't be around her. I don't know what he's concerned about. I'd be endangering her for nothing."

"You haven't figured out anything? It's been four months, Tristan. I know you spent the first couple out of your mind in more ways than one, but you've got nothing?"

Shaking my head, I admitted the sad truth. "Nothing. I've been through those notes over and over, and even those pages that are about other investigations. I've got nothing."

"Then maybe it's time to admit what he's afraid of isn't in that notebook. I think you're on the right track, though. Your assistant told me that your penthouse was ransacked twice in the past two months. Michelle said the police think it was an employee each time, but I don't think we're talking about some disgruntled maid or bellboy. Karl wants something he believes you have, so the penthouse would be a logical place to look for it, especially since he can't get at your house."

"West and Varo are still guarding Nina?"

"Of course. And the security system you installed is working fine. No one gets onto the property without them knowing."

"He's going to want to get into the house when he finally figures out that's the only place he hasn't been able to check."

Daryl nodded. "Have any other homes I'm not aware of?"

Chuckling, I shook my head. "No. I only kept the penthouse when I took over as CEO. Well, that's not entirely true. My father kept a place in LA, but I never go there. The house has been empty for years."

"Hmmm. I'll check into whether it's been broken into lately. Any chance what he's looking for is there?"

"I have no fucking idea what he's looking for, Daryl. If I did…" I ended my thought because I honestly couldn't say what I'd do if I had what Karl so desperately wanted. Maybe I wouldn't give it to him. If it just had to do with the terrible things my father and Taylor did to the Cashens and Nina's father, then he could have whatever it was. But was there something more my father had done that I didn't know about?

"I have to ask the question, Tristan. How far are you planning to go with this? Karl's a man who seems to have something important to hide. If we find out what it is, are you going to let it go or is this going to be some kind of crusade for you?"

Daryl's question wasn't an easy one. Karl had always been a dick to me since the day I took over Stone Worldwide, but I'd thought it was just the way he was. Now I had the sneaking suspicion it was something much more. Even worse, if he had his way, he'd have made sure Nina was dead by now. For that, I'd be willing to make it my personal crusade to make Karl's life a living hell.

"It depends on what he's trying to keep hidden. Karl's happiness isn't my concern. If he suffers, I won't be unhappy about that."

The conversation seemed to come to an abrupt halt with my thinly veiled threat, and we sat in silence as I fantasized about Karl Dreger suffering at my hands. My father's closest friend, he'd been in my life from the day I was born. I'd seen him around the table on holidays, a younger, more handsome man then making my mother smile with his jokes and always eager to take my father away immediately after he'd finished eating for private meetings in his study. Taylor had begun joining them in his last year of college, but I'd never been invited into their inner sanctum on holidays or any other time.

I remembered the first time I stood in my office looking at the space where I was supposed to now lead an international business I'd never given a damn about. As I studied my father's degree from Wharton School of Business and commendations from business associations worldwide that still hung on the walls, I felt small and inadequate. I'd never finished college, much less earned an M.B.A. like my father and Taylor.

I saw in Karl's face all I lacked as he stood leaning against the doorframe watching me. The son who'd never amounted to anything. The one who'd never been a part of their meetings. I'd eventually shown him I was more than that, but from the first moment, he'd been an enemy I always knew I'd have to keep an eye on.

"Well, maybe it's time for you to leave Shangri-la here and get back in the game," Daryl said as he looked around at the mess of my home away from home. "We need to find what Karl wants before he does."

"I'm not sure I want to join the world again." I wasn't. I wanted to be with Nina again more than anything else in the world, but the rest of it? I didn't give a damn about that.

"Yeah, well I guess I can see how wallowing in your own self-pity is quite the life, but you don't have the luxury of doing that. We need to get to the bottom of what Karl is looking for. The sooner we solve this, the sooner you and your lady are back together, and that means we need to get you back to the States."

I knew he was right, but I'd let myself enjoy the life of nothingness I'd created for so long that I wasn't sure I could do what I had to for Nina and me.

"And there's something else. It'd probably be better for Nina if it seemed like you weren't coming back for the time being. I'm thinking some kind of subterfuge would be best. You haven't been gone long enough to be declared dead, but I think a good show of her moving on might throw Karl off the scent for at least a little while, which might give us enough time to find out what the hell is going on."

"Declare me dead? What the fuck are you talking about, Daryl? I don't want Nina to think I'm never coming back. This is only temporary."

"Well, her looking like she's moving on will only be temporary too. We'll let the press see her with someone new and…"

Daryl stopped before he completed his thought and raised his hands to calm me as I leaned toward him, my face twisting as I thought about the words that would next come out of his mouth. The idea of someone new in Nina's life made me want to kill someone with my bare hands. Even the mention of it was more than I could deal with.

"I know you might not want to think about it, but it would help if she seemed to be starting a new life. It could take the focus off her.

I'm worried it's only a matter of time before Karl turns his eye toward her. If she looks like she believes you're not coming back, he might leave her alone."

"You just said she wasn't holding up well. Now you want her to act like she's moving on?"

"Well, yeah. Just a few sightings of her with a new man would probably be enough."

Jesus Christ. Every word out of Daryl's mouth was like a punch to the heart. Even though I was more certain than I'd ever been in my life that I didn't want to hear the answer to my next question, I asked anyway. "Since you've obviously given this some thought, who's she moving on with?"

He got a sheepish look on his face, telling me he had thought about this. Quietly, as if saying the man's name in a normal voice might set me off, he said, "I think Varo could work."

Varo. Six foot four inches of brick shithouse Varo. Nina's bodyguard I hired and now lived just feet away from her while I remained here thousands of miles away Varo. If he had said West, I might have been able to handle it. At least I could believe Nina would never want him. But Varo wasn't as easily dismissed.

"No."

"Before you say no, hear me out. He's there already, so it wouldn't be much to just have him move into the house. Once or twice out for dinner for the press and I think that would do it."

"No."

Sitting back in his chair, he let out a frustrated sigh and made a clucking noise with his tongue. "You're not thinking clearly, Tristan. How do you plan to keep her safe? We've been lucky so far, but it's only a matter of time before Karl begins to focus on her. With Varo, we know we can trust him, he can keep her safe, and it could buy us some time to do our own research into what Karl wants."

"She'll never go for it," I mumbled, trying to convince myself as much as convince Daryl.

"She'll go for it if I tell her you need her to. Unless you have a better plan in mind, I say we do it."

I sat there unable to think of anything to replace Daryl's stupid idea. My brain was filled with the thought of Nina and Varo. Even their pretending to be a couple made my gut churn with jealousy.

"Only if we set some ground rules. He doesn't touch her, he remains in the carriage house, and they only pose for the press twice. No more."

Daryl shook his head. "That won't work. He has to move into the house with her if the deception is to be believable. He can stay in another room, but he has to be in the house."

I knew he was right. Karl would never believe Nina had moved on if her new supposed boyfriend still lived in the carriage house with West. Somehow the press would find out, and then the whole thing would be blown. It's just the idea of Varo living in my house, taking my place, acting like the man in her life now nearly drove me out of my mind.

"Tristan, don't you trust her? After all she's done to show you she's devoted to your life together, you can't believe she'll be loyal in this?"

My demons screamed "No!" inside me, threatening to take over my thoughts until I couldn't think straight. I'd never been the master of my jealous nature, and having another man living in my house filling my shoes when I should be there next to Nina wasn't something I was able to handle.

"It has nothing to do with that, Daryl. Can you imagine what it feels like to know that another man will be with the woman you love while you have to stay away from her side? As if it wasn't bad enough I can't go back to her, now I have to agree to being replaced?"

Standing, he looked down at me in sympathy and nodded. "I get it, but it's only for show and not for long. We just have to move fast to find out what there is at the heart of Karl's secrets so Nina's pretend relationship may only have to be those two dinner dates."

Relationship. Dates.

Fuck me.

"Fine. Tell her I think this is for the best," I bit out.

"Good, but that's probably not going to be enough. I think you're going to have to tell her. Oh, and no matter what she does—no matter how many times she calls you or texts you—I need you to keep your distance. This only works if she believes in this. Any sense of how much you hate this and she won't be able to do it."

"Fine, but how am I going to tell her?"

Daryl pointed to the notebook on the table. "Write her something. I'll take it to her."

I found a sheet of paper in an old desk and quickly wrote her a note telling her to pretend to be in love with someone else, my heart feeling like it was being squeezed in a vice the entire time. My notes to Nina always had been to show her how much she meant to me, and each word I wrote added to my betrayal of something I'd only done out of love before. Handing it to him, I silently prayed to God she wouldn't be able to do it. That we'd have to figure something else out that didn't involve her pretending to be another man's date, or worse, girlfriend. Something that didn't involve the woman I loved acting like I was dead.

"I'll be back. It's time you got the hell out of this place. We've got work to do." He headed toward the door as I began to spiral out of control and stopped as he opened it. "Hey, she wanted me to give you a message."

"What?" I asked, my heart pounding against my ribs.

"She said she'll be waiting. Don't worry, Tristan. Your life is waiting for you when you get back."

Daryl left me sitting alone with nothing but my demons to torment me. Each one in turn marched through my mind flying his fucked up flag and goading me to spin out of control until I was sure I couldn't go through with Daryl's plan. I couldn't go on knowing that Nina was with another man, even if it was only for show.

By the time night came, I'd drank enough scotch to drown my misery, but still I wasn't as numb as I needed to be to feel okay with what I had to make Nina do. I wanted to talk to her—I wanted to explain that this was the only way and I hated it more than I hated being away from her. It took everything in my power not to pick up my phone and call her just to hear her gentle voice tell me she missed me or even that she was furious with me for leaving. Anything would have been better than being alone.

I closed my eyes and thought back to the night I first met Nina. I'd barely recognize that man if I met him today. Surrounded by gorgeous, vapid women with little to offer other than their bodies, I'd walked into the Anderson Gallery oblivious to anything but my own desires, intent on finding Joseph Edwards' daughter and assuaging my guilt for my father's crimes. I'd scanned Nina's picture once or twice before leaving the penthouse and believed I knew what kind of person she was.

Simple. Nice. Not my type.

Not that any of that mattered. I wasn't looking for a girlfriend or fuckmate. I was looking to make myself feel better about being the son of the man who'd had her father killed. Maybe I could hand her some money or at least if I could somehow find a way to repay her for what she'd lost, I might have been able to sleep better at night.

The balls I had to think that my throwing money at her would ever be enough to make up for what she'd lost. Even now as I remembered the man I was then, I cringed at my fucking nerve.

"Tristan, what are we doing here? This gallery is filled with nobodies."

I ignored Kamara's comment along with her clinging hold on my bicep and scanned the room. A cluster of people stood oohing and ahhing over artwork that looked like shit, but what did I know? Art had never been my thing. I wasn't there to admire indecipherable pictures anyway.

The girls all grabbed glasses of champagne as the waitress passed by, emptying her tray. Traveling with six women in tow was a hassle on the best of nights, but having to deal with them drunk would likely hamper my efforts to meet Nina Edwards. I shot them all a nasty warning glance and saw they got the message loud and clear. Their job was to stand beside me, behave themselves, and look good, not cause me some bullshit hassle because they couldn't handle their alcohol.

They all chattered about whatever meant something to them as I continued to look for Nina. From behind a column on the far side of the room she peeked her head out as she straightened her waitress uniform. Long brown hair fell down over her shoulders, and she had a pretty look about her in person. I had to admit she looked even better up close than she had in her picture.

I had to play it cool, so I pretended to enjoy myself with the actresses, actually paying only the slightest bit of attention to them. Vanessa beamed up at me, happy to have her turn as the woman on my arm. Out of the corner of my eye, I saw Nina standing with a tray in her hands, waiting to serve the semi-wealthy and society wannabes who were right at home at Sheila Anderson's gallery. She took a step toward me and my entourage and stopped.

"Tristan, are you going to buy this picture?" Vanessa asked in her usual, cloying way. "I think it would look great hanging in one of your hotels."

I wasn't listening to her, though. I was too busy meeting Nina's gaze. She held my stare and didn't look away. She had a fearless vibe to her that impressed me. Standing there dressed like some cheap waitress, Nina looked too good for this place and her ridiculous costume. I wanted to know more about this person, but there was no way I could approach her with the gang surrounding me. I'd have to find another way.

There was a piece of art on the far wall, so I guided the actresses to that part of the room as Sheila Anderson busied herself with barking at Nina. After a few minutes of staring at another picture I didn't give a damn about, I led the girls to the car and instructed Jensen to take me to mine at the hotel and drop the women off wherever they wanted to go. They'd done their job for the night, and I had no further use for them.

A half-hour later I was parked behind the Anderson Gallery unsure of what the hell I was doing there but sure I wanted to meet Nina in person and not only to make amends for what had happened to her father. I hadn't planned on being interested in her. All I wanted to do was see if I could find a way to help her, but something in the way she held her head high as she did the dirty work dumped on her at the gallery impressed me.

I wanted to know more about this woman, and that was something pretty rare for me, so I stood there waiting in that alley next to the Dumpster hoping she'd be the person forced to take out the garbage and not one of the other two women serving drinks and cocktail wieners that night. When the door opened, I saw luck was on my side.

"Nice show, huh?" I asked, willing to lie if it got the ball rolling.

She spun around, obviously frightened, and I realized that a strange man standing in a dark alley waiting for a woman probably wasn't the best move. I was no rapist, but it still didn't look good. I remained cool, standing against the Jag with my arms folded, hoping to give off a non-attacking vibe. I didn't need to begin whatever this was with her screaming for the cops.

Regaining her cool, she answered, "Yeah, it was great. The artist is quite talented."

I didn't know her, but I knew bullshit when I heard it. Whether or not the artwork was as bad as I thought it was, she hadn't liked it. That was clear.

"It was shit and you know it. Nice outfit, though."

I don't know why I took the cheap shot at her clothes. It wasn't like they were anything anyone would willingly wear if they didn't have to. Sometimes I was a real asshole. Instantly, I felt shitty as a frown settled onto her mouth and she snapped at me. I deserved it and tried to fix the damage my stupid comment had already caused to the situation.

I couldn't help but smile at the memory of Nina putting me in my place within a minute of meeting me. She was strong even then, standing there alone with a strange man in an alley way and telling him to basically go fuck himself when he stepped out of line. Looking back, I guessed I should have been happy she even agreed to get into the car with me after my stupid comment.

She'd taken a chance on me that night and trusted me not to be some ax murderer. Now I had to trust her. Whether I liked it or not, I had to give up control of us and hope to God I didn't lose her to someone who could give her the one thing all my money couldn't buy.

A stable life.

Chapter Three

Nina

For the second time in a week, Daryl wanted to speak to me. Just hearing his voice on my phone made my stomach flip with nerves. I still hadn't given up on the idea that one day he'd call and tell me that Tristan was finally coming home. So as I waited for Daryl to arrive, I busied myself with fantasies of Tristan's homecoming and the beginning of our life together as husband and wife. It seemed like we'd been fighting for that life for so long that it was hard to remember when we were just us—Tristan and Nina, happy and in love.

I heard a noise behind me and turned in anticipation to find Jordan standing in the dining room doorway. My disappointment was surely clear in my face, and I saw her react to it with pity. I hated the pity.

"Oh, I thought you might be Daryl," I weakly explained.

"I need to invest in some better makeup if people are beginning to confuse me with that guy," she joked.

I knew she was trying to keep my spirits up and appreciated the effort. "No, he called to let me know he needs to speak to me, so I thought it might be him when I heard footsteps."

Jordan laughed. "I better get back to my Pilates then. Want some company until he arrives?"

Nodding, I smiled at her joke. "Yeah."

Throwing her bag on the table, she sat down and reached out to give me the "sympathetic hand touch" she did when she thought I was sad or depressed. Not that she was wrong. I was feeling bad.

Giving my hand a gentle squeeze, she asked, "Anything I can do to cheer you up? Maybe the tragic story of how I've resorted to doing the most idiotic things to get Varo's attention might bring a real smile out of you."

I'd seen Jordan's attempts to get Varo to notice her and wondered why he never seemed to even give her a second glance. She was knockout pretty with beautiful green eyes and long blond hair. She had a much better body than I'd ever had, probably since she actually exercised regularly and took care of herself. On top of all the outside goodness, she was funny and vivacious. What was there not to like?

Just the day before I'd watched from the sitting room window as she took her daily stroll around the grounds and intentional turn toward the carriage house to try to speak to him. He just stood there leaning against the car, barely smiling in response to whatever she was saying. I knew Jordan well enough to know what she sounded like when she was flirting, and never before had I seen any man just stand there with a stony face like Varo did. It was almost like he was deliberately trying not to like her. West appeared more interested in what she'd been saying and even stood there to talk to her after Varo walked away.

"I think that man must be nuts, but don't feel bad. I can barely get a word from him, and he's supposed to actually work for me," I said in an attempt to make her feel better.

Jordan shrugged. "It's no big deal. I mean, what would I do with someone like that anyway? He's as big as a house. Probably on steroids, and you know what they say about those guys." Measuring out an inch between her thumb and forefinger, she snickered. "Hung like a chipmunk."

I laughed out loud at the thought of such a huge man with such a tiny penis. Leave it to Jordan to make me laugh at her misery and lessen my own at the same time. "You're so bad!"

"His loss. I could have rocked his world, even if he is Needledick the Bug Fucker."

Her words made me choke on my morning coffee, and liquid nearly came shooting out of my nose. Coughing, I croaked out, "Jordan, I'll never be able to look at him the same way again! Jesus, I have to deal with him."

"You're not supposed to deal with his junk. Just his silent as a statue routine. I'm sure you'll forget what I said before you see him again," she said with a wink.

"I doubt I'll ever forget it. Needledick the Bug Fucker is something that sticks with you."

From behind us came the sound of someone clearing their throat, and I slowly turned to see who'd heard us slandering my bodyguard's penis size, hoping that it wasn't Varo himself. Thankfully, it was just Daryl, although the look on his face was pure confusion.

"That's my cue to leave," Jordan said cheerfully as she grabbed her bag. "Call me later, Nina. I'll be in prep time right after lunch."

"Okay. Have a good one filling those kids' minds with knowledge."

As Jordan passed Daryl on her way out, her gaze slipped to below his waist and she chuckled. If he had any idea what she was doing, he didn't show it. Taking the seat she'd just left, he reached into his coat pocket to pull out his little notepad and began flipping through the pages as I sat there stifling my own chuckle.

"We have a few things to deal with today," he pronounced ominously without looking up from his notes.

"Okay. Hit me with them."

He continued to flip through the pages of his pad until he reached one covered in scribbles. I was in no mood to try to decipher what he'd written, so I sat back and watched his lips move as he read over his notes.

Daryl stopped reading and looked up at me. Taking a deep breath, he let the air leave his lungs in a slow sigh. "We think Karl is going to start focusing on you. He's looking for something and we think he's eventually going to run out of places to look other than this house."

"Look for what? What could possibly be here that he wants? I thought the problem was the notebook Tristan has."

"He's looked through that tablet of your father's over and over and can't find anything. If what Karl is looking for is somewhere else, it's not in Tristan's penthouse. It's been ransacked twice already."

"What?" The word ransacked sent shivers down my spine. That Karl and his goons had turned to breaking into Tristan's penthouse scared the hell out of me. It also made me feel violated. While the penthouse wasn't exactly anywhere I'd ever called home, it bothered me that strangers may have gone through our clothes looking for whatever they wanted or trashed the picture I'd picked out for the bedroom.

"It's okay. They didn't do too much damage, but it's obvious that they were looking for something and didn't find it."

"So you think Karl and his people are going to come looking here?"

Daryl gave me one of his rare smiles and shook his head. "Don't worry. The security system Tristan had installed is first rate, and Varo and West are always nearby to make sure you're safe."

"Then why are we talking about this, Daryl? I don't understand what the problem is if I'm safe." He hesitated, making me nervous. "What? You just said Varo and West keep me safe. I'm not?"

"You are. We just think that might not be enough. Tristan thinks you need to make it seem like you're, uh, living your life."

"We think? Tristan thinks? What are you talking about, Daryl? You're freaking me out."

He looked away and then turned back to face me. "Tristan thinks it would be best if you made it seem like you've moved on."

Daryl's words hit my brain and suddenly it felt like the room was swimming around me. Moved on? My hands began to shake at the very thought of moving on without Tristan.

"What the hell does moved on mean?" I asked in a scared voice. "Are you saying Tristan isn't coming back?"

"No, no, no. Nothing like that. Just that you need to pretend that you're with someone else now so Karl can think that Tristan's dead."

My jaw fell open as I stared at Daryl, who acted like he'd just said something entirely reasonable. Was he saying Tristan wanted me to pretend to date another man? Had I heard him correctly?

"I can see by your face that I might have said that wrong. It's just that Tristan doesn't want you to be in danger and if Karl believes you've moved on..."

I didn't let Daryl finish his sentence before I blew up. "I'm not doing it. I don't care what you and Tristan think is best. I'm not pretending to be with someone else. It's just ridiculous! I don't want to be with anyone else, and even if I agreed with this, where would I find someone willing to playact with me? No way. You'll have to tell him I'm not going to do it."

Reaching into his coat pocket again, he mumbled, "I thought you'd say something like that." He handed me an envelope. "This is from Tristan."

I looked down at the first letter I'd received from Tristan since he'd left and felt the tears well up in my eyes. The first time he'd bothered to write anything to me and it was to tell me to be with someone else. My stomach clenched at the thought.

"I'll give you some time to read it and be back in a bit," Daryl said as he stood to leave.

I didn't want to read it. All I wanted all these months was to hear from Tristan, and now that I had, it was just to tell me to show the world that I'd moved on. The envelope had nothing written on the outside, and when I turned it over, I saw the flap was just tucked in, not sealed. It was like nothing of him was there.

Slipping the letter out, I unfolded it and began to read, prepared to remain angry and unwilling to go with his plan. Just two sentences in and any hopes of that disappeared.

Dear Nina,

By now, Daryl has told you what I need you to do. I know you don't want to and God knows I hate the idea of you acting like you care about another man almost as much as I hate being away from you, but I need you to do this for us. I know it won't be easy, but my biggest fear is that it won't be hard for you since I've left you alone for so long. Please know that if there was any other way, I would have done things differently.

Every letter you wrote me, every text you send means more to me than you'll ever know. They're my lifelines—the things that keep me going when I feel like I have nothing of any worth left anymore. I can handle losing everything else but not you. Knowing you're waiting for me is the one thing that makes me go on.

Nina, it tears me up inside to ask you to pretend you've moved on to another. Do this for us and at least I can believe you'll be safe. Think about me and know that I never stop thinking about you. I promise that someday when all of this is over we'll get to live that life we both dream of. Never doubt that we can make it through this.

I love you and wish we were together. Your love is what I live for. Until we're together again, keep me in your heart. What we are is worth fighting for, and trust me, I'm fighting with everything I have.

Love,
Tristan

Just when I was ready to be stubborn, Tristan accomplished what no other man could—instead of being angry at him for what he was asking, I felt sorry for what I had to do. I sensed his heartache in every word he'd written, and it broke my heart.

"Everything okay in here?"

Daryl looked uncomfortable as I wiped a tear away from under my eye. He took his seat again and waited for me to speak, but I could tell he was still feeling uneasy about how emotional Tristan's letter had made me.

Resigned to doing as Tristan asked, I said quietly, "I'm fine, Daryl. Just tell me what you need me to do."

"You won't have to do anything but appear to be with him. Just a few times in public to make the press think you're on a couple dates. He will have to live here with you, though."

"Who? Who is this poor soul you're going to force to pretend to be my new boyfriend?"

"Varo."

"Varo? My bodyguard? No offense to him, but why would I fall for one of my bodyguards?"

Daryl shrugged and smiled meekly. "You know. You were thrown together after Tristan disappeared and one thing lead to another and… well, we can let the press take it from there."

I rolled my eyes at such a ridiculous story. "Nice. So I was able to easily forget Tristan Stone and turned to the comforting arms of a man who barely speaks to me and has never once shown even the slightest interest in me. Yeah, that sounds like a real romance."

More shrugging. "The outside world doesn't know that. All they know is what we show them, and you two will look like true lovebirds when the cameras are flashing."

"I'm a little confused why you think the press would care at all. I'm nobody. They only came out when I was with Tristan."

"They'll care because you're all that's left of Tristan Stone. They can't have him, so they'll take you. Haven't you noticed the press milling about at the end of the driveway?"

I hadn't noticed, but that was because I was too involved in being depressed. The few times I'd left the house recently I'd gone straight to the city, and there I was followed by West and Varo, so they had made sure nobody got close to me.

"So they'll take our picture as we go on our dates and that will make it look like I've left Tristan behind? Isn't that going to make me seem like a heartless bitch? He hasn't even been gone for six months."

"That's another reason why they'll be interested. The press loves showing the worst in people. They'll eat it up."

I already hated this.

"So I get to look like the world's biggest bitch, Varo looks like some kind of gold digger since I'm living in Tristan's house with him, and this helps keep me safe. Is that about right?"

"Yeah. Oh, one more thing. You can't tell anyone about this being a fake. That means your giggly friend there with the fixation on penis size."

I crossed my arms defiantly. "I'm not going to lie to my best friend, Daryl. We tell each other everything. I've never lied to her before, and I'm not starting now."

Daryl stood from the table and leaned down toward me until his furry face was just inches away from mine. "Then you better figure out a way to not tell her and not lie because if you tell her and someone gets to her, all of this will have been for nothing. Remember, your safety is the reason you're doing all of this. Tristan is going to be busy finding out what Karl is up to and he needs to know you're not in danger."

"Does Varo know about this yet? I can't imagine acting like my boyfriend was in the bodyguard work description he agreed to when he was hired."

"Don't worry about him. I'll take care of that. We'll have him moved in here tonight."

Terrific. I suddenly had a new man and somehow I had to find a way to explain to my best friend that he was none other than the one she'd tried to seduce to no avail. Fucking fabulous.

"By the way, how is the gardener search going?" Daryl asked, ripping me from my thoughts.

Confused by the change of topic, I shook my head. "You're all over the place today, aren't you? I hired one yesterday. West and Varo were supposed to check him out today and let me know."

"Good. I'll ask them about it when I talk to him. In the meantime, I'd suggest making plans for where Varo will be staying while he's here. Perhaps the room next to yours? That way he can be close."

"Why does he have to be close? The press can't get onto the property, so why would we have to pretend to that extent?"

"You can never be too careful, Nina."

What the hell did that mean? Was he implying that Jensen, West, or any of the other people who worked for Tristan couldn't be trusted? Did he mean that Jordan couldn't be?

Craning my neck, I turned to look at Daryl as he walked from the room. "Is there something I should know? You and Tristan seem to think that Varo is okay, but everyone else can't be trusted?"

He stopped and seemed to think about my question for a moment. "Varo is okay, but we can't be sure about anyone else. We'd like to think they're safe, but for now, we can't know."

Before I could comment on how much I hated all of this, he was gone and I was left to think about what I had to do. Daryl acted like it would be a piece of cake to just pretend to care for someone else and act like Tristan was never coming back. Nothing was further from the truth. Just the thought of never seeing him again made me feel like curling up into a ball and never getting out of bed again.

I so just wanted all of this to be over. How wrong I'd been all those times I'd wished for a more exciting life. If I'd have known that it would involve all of this, I would have been happy with my boring life of sitting at home and watching TV alone every night.

But then I wouldn't have Tristan. He was worth every bit of craziness our lives were now, although I couldn't lie. A little less crazy would be even better.

Chapter Four

Nina

Unable to figure out a way of telling Jordan what I had to do, I retreated to my room and wished the world would just fix itself by the time I decided to come out. I knew it wouldn't, but that didn't mean I didn't wish for it.

Even though I now knew Tristan received all my texts, I didn't send him a message right away. What was there to say? *Hey, I got your letter and I'm all cool with pretending I'm doing someone else?* Or maybe something like *I miss you. I love you. And now I'm going to be acting like I've forgotten you and moved on just as you said to.*

Over and over, I typed in so many words, only to backspace through them until there was nothing. Finally, I let my fingers spell out what was in my heart, no matter how much it hurt.

I hate what I have to do. I don't want to pretend I care about someone else. I could never just move on like that.

As usual, there was no reply. At least I knew he received it, though.

Where was he? I imagined him sitting on a beach somewhere, his feet in the sand as he sipped some frothy umbrella drink in the sunshine. No, that wasn't right. He was likely somewhere in a hotel fully dressed in a suit and tie with a glass of scotch on the table in front of him. Was he in Venice enjoying the beautiful sunset each night—the same sunset that had been the perfect backdrop to our time together there?

Two light knocks on my door shook me from my daydreaming, and I opened it to see Varo standing there looking distinctly uncomfortable. In fact, I didn't think I'd ever seen him look like that. Instead of looking me directly in the eyes, as he always did, his gaze was fixed on the floor and his hands were hidden behind his back.

"Hi, Varo. What's up?" I wanted to be cool, but my words came out stupid sounding, like I didn't know what was happening.

His gaze met mine, and I saw just how uncomfortable he was. Those dark blue eyes that had reminded me of a snake's more than once seemed bigger, like they were filled with uncertainty and searching for an answer in mine.

"I thought we should talk before we begin doing whatever we're supposed to be doing."

"Okay. Give me a minute and I'll meet you in the living room."

As soon as I walked into that room I knew I couldn't sit there with another man like I had with Tristan. There were just too many memories. It would be wrong. Daryl was one thing, but Varo? No. I couldn't sit there and talk about us being a couple, even if it was all an act. Stopping dead two feet in, I shook my head. "Let's go somewhere else. I could use a drink or something to eat. How about the kitchen?"

Varo had no idea what the problem was and merely nodded as he rose from the couch. I wasn't lying about needing a drink. Even though it wasn't yet dinnertime, I had the strongest urge for anything that would dull my senses and make all this easier to deal with.

He followed me into the kitchen and stood silently near the doorway, as if he was preparing for a quick getaway. I knew how he felt. This whole facade we had to put on made me want to run away too.

As I considered what to say, I truly looked at Gage Varo, possibly for the first time. I'd seen him before, of course, but I had never really looked at him. He was the bodyguard or the guy Jordan liked, but now that he was standing there in my kitchen waiting to talk about how we were going to pretend to be a couple, I felt like I was seeing him in a brand new way.

His dark blue eyes still scared me a little, but I had no fear that he wanted to hurt me. They were just so unlike Tristan's with their warm chocolate color. Varo's were cold in comparison, and they gave me no real sense of what he was feeling.

"So I guess we should talk," I said awkwardly as I stood with my back pressed against the counter, unable to put any more space between us. "Maybe if we got to know each other this might not seem so bizarre."

"This isn't the first time I've done this."

His statement was like an unexploded bomb dropped into the middle of the room. It just sort of sat there for a moment while my brain processed what he'd said. Did he mean he'd been a bodyguard before or that he'd had to pretend to be someone's boyfriend before?

"What?"

"I've done this before. You know, the whole fake boyfriend thing. It's not as hard as you'd think. It's just a matter of acting like you're happy. Once you get that down, it's a breeze."

"Oh, okay," I muttered, still surprised that Varo had committed this same fraud before. "Do you mind me asking who you did this with the last time?"

Shaking his head, he said, "Angela Macaran. She's an actress."

I'd never heard of her, but the fact that he'd been her fake boyfriend made me want to know more about her. "Why did she need you to pretend to be her boyfriend?"

"I have no idea. They never told me, like all I know is what Daryl told me about this. You need me to act like we're together, so that's what I'll do."

This wasn't making it any less weird.

"Did you sleep with her because you won't be doing that with me. We don't have to do that. In fact, I don't think Jordan would ever forgive me if we did, not to mention the fact that I'm in love with Tristan and when he comes back we plan to get married. So there will definitely be no sleeping together." I stopped talking as I realized I was rambling and took a deep breath before I began again. "I'm sorry. I must sound crazy. It's just that this isn't something I have any experience with."

Varo gave me the first smile I may have ever seen from him. It was genuine and lit up his face, making him look so much friendlier than he'd ever been toward me. "It's okay. I know my part. I assume Tristan knew my background when he hired me."

"Oh. Is there anything I should be doing that I'm not?" I asked, feeling supremely stupid at that moment. "I mean, how did that Angela person act?"

Varo's smile grew wider. "She acted like we were sleeping together because we were. I guess that doesn't help, does it?"

"No, not at all. But thanks."

He took a step into the room and then another until he stood next to the huge island in the center of the kitchen. "I think all we have to do is look like we like each other. Hopefully, by the time Daryl parades us out in front of the world, we can pull that off."

"It's not that I don't like you, Varo," I said apologetically.

"Gage. It might be more convincing if you called me by my first name instead of what my Chief Petty Officer used to call me."

"Okay. It's not that I don't like you, Gage. It's just that you've never really been very friendly toward me."

Nodding, he seemed to consider what I'd said. "I'll give you that. It wasn't part of my job, as far as I was concerned. Now that it is, I promise to be friendlier."

I liked this Varo a lot more than the one I was used to. For the first time, I could see what Jordan saw in him. Since I had the chance, I decided I could do some girlfriend recon for her.

"So are you single, Gage?"

"I am. There's not much opportunity to settle down with this job since I have to live in the carriage house with West."

I moved toward the island to grab a handful of grapes from the fruit bowl. Popping one in my mouth, I said, "Well, that's true, but you might have a girlfriend. It's not like you have to work twenty-four-seven."

"Nope. No girlfriend."

"That's good. I mean, you having a girlfriend might make what we have to do a little harder."

In truth, it was good because that meant Jordan had a chance. I was happy to hear that he was single and couldn't wait to tell her all the details about him.

"Are you from around here?"

"No. I grew up in Wyoming, the Cowboy State. That's the nickname for Wyoming."

"You don't look like a cowboy," I said with a smile, hoping he recognized that I wasn't trying to be insulting.

He reached across the island and picked a few grapes off the bunch. "I'm not. I got out of there as soon as I could. Spent some time in the Navy and then spent a few years bouncing around the country before I got into this line of work."

I subtly scanned his muscular frame, imagining him in Navy whites. Jordan was going to melt when she heard he was former Navy. That May we got to experience Fleet Week had made quite an impression on her, and she'd said for months afterward that she'd love to have a sailor. Hell, she might melt when I told her he was from somewhere they call the Cowboy State.

"Ever been married?" I probed.

He smiled broadly. "No. No ex-wife and no kids either."

Check. Single and unfettered. He was looking better and better by the minute. I filed these facts away and popped another grape in my mouth. "Don't you want to know anything about me?"

Varo folded his arms across his chest and shook his head. "Since I'm not scoping you out for a friend, I figured I'd just let you tell me about yourself when you felt comfortable."

Caught red-handed! Damn.

I felt my cheeks grow hot as a blush of embarrassment spread over me. "I…it's just…Jordan's a great…" I stammered out, not having much success in getting my point across.

"It's okay. I'm flattered, even if I can't ask her out."

"Why? She's fantastic. She's a teacher, a wonderful person, and she's a great time. I think you'd like her."

"I already do, but it doesn't change the fact that we can't get together while I'm on this job. It just wouldn't work out."

My shoulders sagged under my disappointment at his words. "Oh. Are you sure?"

"I don't think it's a good idea as long as I'm guarding you. Conflict of interest. Plus, I don't think my boss would like it."

All of a sudden there seemed to be a light at the end of the tunnel. "Then it's all good because I know your boss and he'd be fine with it," I said grinning with satisfaction.

Varo stood silently for a moment and nodded. "You make a convincing argument. Maybe when all this is over I might try to see if we can get together."

A might was better than a no, so I clapped my hands together in triumph. "That's great! I'm not going to say anything to her, though, so I don't ruin it. I don't want to meddle."

"I think they call that matchmaking instead of meddling."

Shrugging, I explained, "I just like to see everyone as happy as Tristan and I are."

Varo looked at me oddly, as if he couldn't believe what I'd just said. I could understand that. It's not like Tristan was anywhere nearby for months now, but I still had hope. "I know that sounds strange, but we are happy. It's just that we're not together now. Soon, though. I have to keep believing it'll be soon."

"I'm all for being happy, but as far as I can tell, very few get that blessing."

Hmmm, the bodyguard is a little jaded.

"Well, as Jordan always says, good things happen to good people. She says that to me, and I'm saying that to you. They do."

"I'll have to take your word on that, Nina. I haven't seen that to be true yet."

"Just you wait and see, Gage. Trust me. I know about these things," I said as I grabbed another handful of grapes and headed out of the kitchen. "Now let's get your stuff moved into your room."

By the time Jordan got home after work, Gage had moved all of his things into his new room next to mine. Not that he had a lot of belongings to his name. A large garbage bag would have held every item he owned. The man certainly traveled light. Even though I'd been uncomfortable about Tristan's idea to make the world think he was never coming back, the part that involved Gage wasn't so bad, after all. I still hated the idea that anyone would believe I'd be able to move on so easily and replace Tristan, but at least I'd found out my partner in the deception was a decent guy. I'd be happy when he and Jordan finally got together.

I met her at the door, thrilled to tell her the small part I could about him moving into the house. Since Daryl had warned me against keeping her in the loop, I had to come up with a story that sounded somewhat believable.

"Hey, you! How was your day with the little darlings?"

She looked up from putting her keys in her purse and frowned. "Awful. Two of my students got into a fight, and now I have to go back at six tonight to meet with the parents. The worst part is that my principal thinks this happened because I can't handle my classroom."

"I'm sorry you had such a bad day. Come into the kitchen and sit down with me so we can talk and eat a little dinner before you have to go back to the city."

Jordan shook her head. "I can't. I'm just going to grab a quick shower and get ready. I hope you don't mind me asking Jensen if he'd take me back."

I took her bag and walked with her down the hallway to her room. "Of course. It's not like you're going to take a bus there. I can come with you, if you like. I didn't get out today, so I can get dressed and be ready to go in no time."

Pushing her bedroom door open, she took the bag from my hand and threw it on the bed. "No, that's okay, Nina. I better do this alone. When I get home, hopefully I'll be in a better mood."

"Okay. Just remember how great a teacher you are. Those kids are lucky to have you, and your principal needs to remember that."

She took a deep breath and forced a smile. "I know. I promise we'll talk when I get back."

"Good because we need an old-fashioned girls' night in, complete with our favorite movies and buckets of popcorn, and tonight looks like the perfect night for that."

Jordan's expression softened. Nodding, she said quietly, "It's a date. I'll see you when I get back."

At a little after seven, she texted me to say everything had worked out and her principal had even apologized for jumping to conclusions before she had all the facts about the fight. I was thrilled and texted back that I was heading to the kitchen to make the popcorn. Girls' night in was on!

We both needed this kind of night. I was feeling a little better since finding out Tristan had been receiving all of my texts, but I couldn't say it wasn't frustrating that he never responded. I was sure Daryl would have some valid reason why he couldn't if I bothered to ask, but it was still aggravating. And with Jordan's job woes, she was dealing with her own frustrations. A few great chick flicks and too much popcorn were definitely what the doctor ordered.

Two Jiffy Pop pans into my popcorn popping, I heard a knock and turned around to see Gage standing there. "Hey, want some popcorn?"

"No. I just wasn't sure who was in here making all that racket," he said with a smile.

"Yeah, it's just me. You have to shake this stuff or it burns," I said as I turned back toward the stove.

He walked in and stood next to me. "Wouldn't microwave popcorn be easier?"

"No way! That stuff is bad for you. Something in the chemicals they use and the heat of the microwave, or something like that. It's Jiffy Pop all the way."

"Health nut, huh?"

I looked up at him and laughed. "Not exactly. I think there's like two hundred grams of fat and carbs in all this popcorn."

He looked down at the giant bowl half filled with Jiffy Pop that sat on the countertop and scooped out a handful for himself. Throwing a piece up in the air, he leaned his head back and caught it in his mouth. "Mmmm....not bad. A little buttery, but not bad."

"Don't tell me you're one of those popcorn eaters who doesn't like butter?" I asked as I continued shaking the pan on the stovetop.

Throwing another piece up above his head, he caught the second one in his mouth and smiled. "Butter's okay, but I don't like my food swimming in it."

I grabbed a kernel and threw it up in the air, but it came nowhere close to my mouth and fell on the floor next to me. I'd never been good at that kind of thing.

Chuckling, Gage looked down at the floor and back up at me. "Looks like you need some practice at that trick. Watch." He stepped behind me and leaned in close so his head was next to mine. "I'll throw it up in the air and just position yourself underneath it."

He tossed the popcorn in the air and moved back away from me so I could catch it. Leaning my head back, I watched as the kernel dropped right toward my face. All I had to do was keep my mouth open and it fell right in. Excited, I stopped shaking the pan of popcorn and turned around to face him.

"I did it! Now with just a little practice, I'll be able to do it without your help."

"Glad to be of assistance. Any time," he said with a smile.

I caught a glimpse of someone standing in the doorway and looked around Gage to see Jordan standing there with a hurt look on her face. Before I could say a word, she turned on her heels and disappeared. Taking the pan of popcorn off the burner, I set it down and asked, "Can you pour this into the bowl when it cools down? I'll be right back."

Jordan had gone to her room, and by the time I got to her, hurt had turned to anger. I knocked on her door only to hear her yell, "Go away!" and knew she misunderstood what she saw in the kitchen between Gage and me. I knocked again and waited a minute for her to let me in, taking her silence as the okay for me to enter.

The look on her face was one of complete betrayal. It stopped me dead in my tracks as I closed the door behind me. "Jordan, I think I know what's wrong, but you're mistaken."

"I don't think I am. What was going on in there, Nina?"

"Nothing. Nothing at all. Gage was just keeping me company while I was making our popcorn, and then he was teaching me how to do that throwing it up and catching it in my mouth trick. That's it."

"Gage? When did he become Gage? What happened to calling him Varo, like you always have? Since when did you two become such close buddies?"

I took another step toward her, but she moved away, her anger coming off her in waves. "He's still Varo. It's just that he told me his name today and I was just trying to be nice."

"You've changed, Nina. I can see it clear as day now as you're standing there. You're different. Maybe it's the money or maybe you're just lonely since Tristan doesn't seem to ever be coming back."

Her words hit me like a fist to my chest. "That's not fair, Jordan. I'm no different than I've ever been. I can't believe you'd bring up Tristan never coming back like that."

"Isn't that what the whole Gage thing is about? You knew I liked him, and still you're acting like that with him? Why would you do that?"

Defensiveness raged inside me, and I lashed out. "That whole Gage thing, as you call it, is just me being the same old Nina I've always been. That I'd never been really nice to him or West wasn't because I didn't think I should be but because I was feeling depressed all these weeks. So now I feel a little better and I get accused of being someone else and not myself? That's bullshit and I don't deserve it."

Tears welled up in her eyes, and she screamed, "You have everything here! Why do you have to go after him too? Isn't it enough to have all the money you've ever wanted? Now you want another guy in addition to Tristan? What happened to waiting for him and being so madly in love?"

Jordan had never yelled at me like that and I stepped back in astonishment for a moment, but I wasn't stunned for long. I barked back, releasing all the months of unhappiness on her. "I have nothing here! What do I care about money when the man I love is absent all this time? You think I stay in my room curled up in a ball so much because I'm fucking happy? I stay there because it's all I have left of him. It's the only place that truly feels like he's there with me. I'm not doing anything with Varo, and if you think I would do that to Tristan or you, the two people I love more than anyone else in this world, then maybe you're the one who's changed, not me."

She looked stunned by my outburst, but I saw the hurt in her eyes too. As I turned to leave, I heard her mumble about West and something he'd said, but I didn't care. I stormed out of her room across the house to my own room, devastated that my best friend had just accused me of trying to steal the man she wanted. Burying my face in the pillow, I let the tears flow from all the frustration and hurt bottled up inside me. How could she think I would ever do that to her?

I wanted to believe she'd lashed out at me because of her problems at work, but her words had hurt. All the money in the world meant nothing without Tristan, and she knew that. She knew how much I loved him, so why would she think I'd ever go after Gage? And that she thought I'd ever break the girlfriend code and chase after someone my best friend wanted, even if there was no Tristan in the picture, was crazy. Since that first day in college, we'd been like sisters. My own sister had never rejoiced in anything that made me happy, but Jordan did. From the moment we met, I'd been able to tell her whatever was in my heart and she supported me, and I'd always been there to do the same for her. I'd never betray her, and it hurt like hell that she could even entertain the idea that I would.

I needed to clear the air with her. No matter what else was going on, she was my best friend. Hurt or not, I had to make her understand there was nothing between Varo and me. How I'd ever explain the two of us being seen as a couple in public was beyond me at that moment, but I'd cross that bridge when I came to it.

Just as I sat up to go back to her room, my phone vibrated with a text. Looking down, I saw the first words scroll across the top of my phone.

I think it might be better if I move

I quickly swiped the phone and read her entire message. *I think it might be better if I move back to the city for a while. Maybe we just need some time apart. I know you'll be safe here with all these people to take care of you.*

My heart sank as her words sat there staring up at me in orange on the screen. What hurt more were the ones she hadn't typed in. That somehow I'd changed and didn't need her anymore. By the time I reached her room, she was gone. She'd cleaned out her dresser and much of her closet, but most of everything she owned was still there. I ran to the garage to catch her, getting there just in time to see Jensen drive through the gate at the bottom of the driveway.

I typed out *I don't want to lose another person in my life* and clicked Send. All I wanted to do was curl up in a ball and close my eyes. I already missed her. When she didn't text back, I walked back to my room and climbed into bed, the smell of buttered popcorn still hanging in the air. It wasn't even nine o'clock at night, but it didn't matter.

Grabbing my phone from the nightstand, I typed out my last message for the day, as I always did before I went to sleep, but unlike usual, it wasn't a profession of love. Losing my best friend had put me in a mood that was anything but loving.

Jordan moved out because she thinks I'm with Varo now and she liked him. I hope this whole plan of yours is worth it. Now it's just me, Varo, West, and Jensen. Maybe it would be better if you got rid of West and Jensen so the world really could see Varo and me as the loving couple we are. Just a thought.

Chapter Five

Tristan

As I lay in bed awake just staring at the ceiling, I heard the phone vibrate on the night table next to me. It was the one Nina messaged me on. Picking it up, I read her text so full of anger—at me, at the entire situation we found ourselves in—and I couldn't blame her. That didn't mean her mention of her and Varo as a loving couple didn't make my insides churn from jealousy. Just the thought of it made me want to race back to the house and remind her how much I loved her.

Except I couldn't. Doing that would put her in as much danger as I was in, and the last thing I wanted to do was get her hurt in all this.

Fuck. I hated this. I'd intentionally avoided the whole business thing with my brother and father for this very reason. All this cloak and dagger shit was what they'd always reveled in. I didn't care. If it weren't for Nina, I would have handed Karl the damn notebook at the beginning of all this and walked away to live on a secluded island somewhere. The problem was that whatever he was looking for didn't seem to be in that notebook.

I'd combed through those pages until I knew their contents by heart. How my brother and father were the monsters I'd never imagined they could be. How the Cashen family had paid more than any should for my family's greed and callousness. Some days, I sat with the tablet in my hands, unable to open the cover because I didn't want to face the ugliness inside. On those days, I hated the name Stone more than I ever thought possible. I wasn't like them, no matter what lies I'd told in my life, but the real fear that what they were wasn't something I could choose but something innate in me terrified me to the bone.

Other days, I did nothing but read those lines over and over, needing for some masochistic reason to be reminded of my family's crimes and the terrible consequences that had resulted. Not that I would ever forget what they'd done. The memory of Taylor's treatment of that young girl and her tragic death, along with Judge Cashen's murder and the killing of all those innocent men, women, and children all for the sake of saving my father from losing some sexual harassment lawsuit would forever be imprinted on my mind and my soul.

I'd be stained by their guilt for the rest of my life.

But what about my mother? Had she known what my father and brother had done? There was no mention of her in any of Joseph Edwards' notes about Amanda Cashen's suicide and her father's murder, but the thought of what she may have known loomed as an unanswered question in my mind every time I thought about what Nina's father had uncovered.

Sleep wouldn't come if my mind continued to race with all these thoughts, but I couldn't stop them. They spun in my brain like some tormented top, slamming into good memories and corrupting even them. Of all my family, my mother had always been an island of kindness in a sea of ruthless behavior, a quiet presence I now understood I never appreciated enough. While my father and brother had worked to rearrange the world to suit their twisted desires, my mother had been the often silent, gentle force behind our family.

Nearly invisible to even me, she'd been an angel among devils who looked on her with distaste and an indulgent son who ignored her in favor of satisfying his hedonistic soul. But as she watched the three men in her life do as they liked with little regard for those they hurt, had she known or even had the tiniest hint of what they truly were?

I slid out of bed and made my way to the living room, lured by Joseph Edwards' notebook like sailors to the sirens' calling. Tonight was one of those nights I couldn't fight the need to read those words once again, filling myself with a loathing for my family and by extension, myself.

My eyes glided over the pages, taking in the words I knew as well as my name. The details never changed, as much as I wished they would. Was it madness to hope that just once that tablet wouldn't contain the horrible truth of who I came from?

I told myself that I continued to read through every page to find that one detail I'd missed so I'd finally know what Karl was looking for, but that wasn't the entire truth. I read these notes written by a man my father had murdered because I couldn't help myself. It was like some kind of penance I felt I needed to pay. Somehow, if I read them just one more time, I'd be able to reconcile who I was with who my father and brother were.

So far, it hadn't turned out that way.

As always, I reached the end of Joseph Edwards' notes on my father and brother's crimes and felt revulsion at every word. My usual next move was to skim over what remained of the notebook and throw it off to the side, discarding it as if it was the reason my life had gone to fucking hell. My first instinct was to do exactly that tonight, but I stopped myself and forced my eyes to focus on the remaining pages in his tablet.

It's not that I hadn't read them before. Separated from the notes about Amanda and Albert Cashen and my family by just one page, there was information about some drug I suspected Edwards had researched concerning another suicide—some drug for heart disease I'd never heard of. It appeared, from what he'd found, that it had received FDA approval but had become a killer drug for those that needed it most. His notes on this only took up a page and ended with the letters TR and a question mark.

I had no idea what that could mean, but as far as I knew, it had nothing to do with the ugliness between the Stone and Cashen families. The next page read like some kind of foreign crossword puzzle, full of clues I couldn't decipher. Edwards had written a series of words repeatedly, the order never changing.

-Cordovex—death?—TR—October

Again, TR. Who or what was TR? Had they committed suicide? Had my family been implicated in their death? TS would make sense because it could refer to Taylor, but TR just sat there on the page meaning nothing to me. Was TR supposed to indicate a name? Someone's initials? Thursday? I had no idea.

A knock on the front door yanked me out of my thoughts, and I cautiously walked over to look through the peep hole to see Daryl standing on the other side. I opened the door, and he pushed past me before I had a chance to welcome him into my temporary home.

"Shit's getting interesting, to say the least, my friend," he said ominously as he plopped down into the chair across from my seat on the couch. "Karl obviously knew about the LA house since it's been turned over three times already."

I sat back down and considered what Daryl had just said. "Not a coincidence since that house hasn't been touched since my father died. What the fuck is he looking for?"

Daryl shook his head, all the while stroking his beard that seemed to grow bushier every time I saw him. "I don't know. I can't decide if he's looking for you or that tablet you have there."

"There's nothing in it. I've looked. Other than the ugly details about my family and the Cashen family, all Edwards seemed to be interested in was some prescription drug for heart disease. Seems it was anything but helpful for some people."

"The girl Taylor was doing died. Any chance she didn't hang herself but instead took the drug?"

I shrugged and shook my head. "No. It wouldn't matter anyway, would it? The problem my father would want to cover up was that she killed herself because of Taylor, not the way she did it."

Daryl silently agreed. He took a deep breath and closed his eyes. "We're missing something here. I say we have to look at the obvious first. Your places are being ransacked for something, but what? Karl's looking for evidence, and he wants that tablet enough to make the copies he got from Nina's sister not good enough."

Leaning forward, I rested my elbows on my thighs. "You're missing the big question. We have no idea if Karl knows what's in this notebook. Maybe he just thinks what Kim gave him wasn't the entire book."

Daryl stared at me with a look of confusion. "But why would he think that?"

"I don't know. I can tell you that he doesn't have everything. I don't know why, but Kim didn't have copies of the pages about the drug investigation her father was pursuing. When Karl showed me what he had, there was nothing about Cordovex or anything like it. He only has the pages about Amanda's and her father's deaths."

Daryl leaned forward toward me, his eyes wide. "Then that's it. Karl worries there's more, and he knows what it's about. What do we know about this Cordovex?"

"Nothing. I've never heard of it. All Edwards says over and over is that he associates it with death."

"Let me see that notebook," he said, reaching out his hand. "I want to see what he's talking about with this Cordovex."

I handed him Joseph Edwards' notebook opened to the page where he had detailed the information he'd uncovered. Daryl's brows knitted as he read it over before he flipped to the last page of the tablet. Running his finger down over the metal coils holding the pages together, he made that clucking nose with his tongue he often did when he was thinking.

Looking up at me, he held the notebook up in front of him. "There's a page missing here. Did you tear any out?"

"No. That's how I found it in Edwards' safe deposit box."

"What about Nina's sister? Any chance she took out a page?"

I shook my head. "No. I saw the copies she had and none were about anything but Taylor and my father."

"Damnit! Why did she give those goddamn copies to Karl in the first place?"

"Because I told her to."

"Why?"

"I didn't want her or her family to get hurt. I knew if Karl found out Joseph Edwards had kept any notes from his investigation of Stone Worldwide, he'd go after her and Nina. I could protect Nina, but not Kim. So I told her to give him everything he asked for. Then I got her and her family to safety as soon as Karl left. If I didn't, they'd probably be dead right now."

Daryl looked unimpressed. "I guess, but she's made this much easier for Karl."

"She did what I told her to do. Not that she didn't fight me tooth and nail. I could barely get her to speak to me at first. It was only when I told her what I'd found out about what Taylor and my father had done that she agreed to even talk to me about all of this. I guess I don't blame her. She probably thought if two Stone men were heartless fucks, why wouldn't the third be?"

I sat back on the couch, tired from trying to convince myself that I wasn't just like them. Kim hadn't made it easy, and by the time I explained everything to her, I still didn't think she believed I wasn't just what she'd always thought I was.

A bad man who shouldn't be anywhere near her sister.

Even when I promised to keep her and her family safe on the island where Nina and I were to be married, protected by guards and catered to twenty-four hours a day, she still looked at me like I was some criminal.

"Well, speaking of that, the last time I checked, they were fine. The guards tell me that they're enjoying a wonderful vacation on St. Vince and the girls love it."

"Good. Speaking of being happy, I'm to understand Nina isn't, if her text is any clue to how she's feeling," I said, leveling my gaze on the one who'd convinced me the whole Nina and Varo plan was a good idea.

"Nah, she seemed fine the last time I saw her. She didn't take to the Varo idea easily, but she seemed okay with it by the time I left. Not that I gave her much of a choice."

"Well, between the time you left and the time I received her last text, things obviously changed. She's anything but okay now."

"Why? What's up? She can't pretend to like Varo? I guess we could have chosen West, but he's got a weird vibe to him."

"It's not the Varo part so much as the problem between her and Jordan. I guess Jordan liked Varo and Nina's charade may have been a little too convincing. She moved out."

Daryl rolled his eyes and sighed. "So? I wasn't feeling great about her friend there anyway. Too many players in the game makes this whole thing more difficult to manage."

I thought about how angry Nina's text sounded. I'd asked a lot of her, but losing her friend was too much to expect. "Jordan's like a sister to Nina. She's upset about her leaving the house. I didn't want that to happen. Maybe you could remember how hard this is on her."

"Tristan, I do understand the hardship of losing her friend, but losing her life or you would be infinitely worse, don't you think? She and her friend can make up when all this is over. They can go shopping or do whatever women do when they make nice."

It wasn't up to Daryl or anyone else to make up for all this. I knew that. I was the one who'd have to make amends for the mess of all this.

"How did Varo take his new assignment?" I asked, trying to mask the jealousy that lingered inside me.

Chuckling, Daryl stroked his beard. "Considering how it's a step up from his regular job, he wisely smiled and happily moved his things into the house. It's not like it's a chore, really. He's just adding devoted suitor to protector. He'll be fine."

Devoted suitor and protector. I hated the way Daryl described Varo with those words. I was supposed to be that for Nina, not some bodyguard I'd only hired because of his size.

"He shouldn't get too comfortable in his new surroundings. I intend on being back in my own house as soon as possible."

My jealousy came through loud and clear, and Daryl knew it. He looked at me as if I were some lovesick puppy to be pitied. I didn't care. He was just some cynical curmudgeon who thought little of love. So be it. I didn't need his approval anyway. All I needed was his help to get back to the woman I loved and the life I'd left behind.

"Not to worry. Varo's not Nina's type. I suspect, if those muscles aren't all from nature, he's not her friend's type either," he said with a chuckle.

"What?" I asked, feeling the smallest relief from his words.

"Nothing. We have more important things to do than gossip about lovesick girls like hens. It's time you returned to the land of the living. Get your stuff, but don't bother shaving." He looked me up and down and added, "You look like you've been sleeping with your head in manure. That's good, though. The longer hair works for what we need."

I hadn't touched a razor to my face more than three times in the past months, even after I'd decided to quit losing myself in coke and alcohol. After the initial itchiness, I'd gotten used to the beard and seen it as yet another thing I didn't have to bother with every day. Not that I had a lot to deal with other than cultivating my self-loathing and missing Nina.

The hair, on the other hand, drove me crazy. I'd kept my hair short since I became CEO of Stone Worldwide, and having it hang in my eyes was a pain in the ass.

"I look almost as bad as you," I joked as I began to gather my things into a duffel bag.

"You wish you looked that good in a beard. You kids today don't appreciate the fine art of the beard," he said proudly as he continued to stroke the shaggy hair around his chin.

"Are you planning to tell me where we're going or do I just get to be in the dark about my immediate future?"

"Sure. We'll be flying coach back to the States so you get to experience the pain and suffering I've had to endure all these times back and forth to visit you here and from there we'll be getting you settled into your new place where you'll have to stay for a while. I've made sure it's close enough for you to keep an eye on the house but far enough away to make sure you're not seen."

I stopped stuffing clothes into the bag and turned to face him standing next to me. "So I get to spy on my own house and Nina is what you're saying."

"Spy is such an ugly word in this case. I just think it would help to have another pair of eyes watching when we can. I don't plan to live out in the middle of nowhere, no offense, so you can."

I thought about all the time I'd spent out at the country house and smiled at Daryl's description of it. After all this time away, it was the only place in the world I thought of as home. Far away from the hustle and bustle of the city, the house was where Nina and I had fallen in love. How many hours had we spent just lying in each other's arms at that house, every second of our time together the most wonderful moments of my life? There was nowhere else I wanted to be, but if all I could have was somewhere close to Nina, then I'd take it and do whatever I had to in order to get back to my life with her.

"Ready to get your life back?"

"I am, and Karl better hope to God he doesn't get in my way. I have too much to fight for to let him get what he wants."

I took one last look around the rooms where I'd spent months hiding out from the rest of the world. I'd lost part of myself in this place, the one part that I couldn't live without. Even though Nina had never given up on me all the while I'd been here, I'd given up. Now it was time to take the chance again to have the life I knew I wanted more than anything else.

Chapter Six

Nina

Jordan's leaving sent me into an emotional tailspin, and for days I didn't get out of bed. Nothing made me feel better, even texting Tristan. How could it? I felt like I was constantly sending out messages in bottles and although I knew he received them, since he never answered it was a one-sided conversation, at best. As the days dragged by, my unhappiness morphed into anger at everything and everyone.

I wanted answers. I wanted Tristan to finally send a message back, even if it just said that he received my texts. I wanted him to hear what my words were saying and come back, even if it wasn't safe for him or me. I didn't care for excuses. I wanted him back.

Our bed became the only place I wanted to be because it reminded me of him. No matter how many times the sheets had been washed, they still held his scent. Not of his cologne but *him*. Closing my eyes, I imagined him next to me, silent as a statue as I chattered on about something. Like he always did, he smiled when I looked up to see if he was paying attention, muttering, "I'm listening" when I gave him that questioning look because he'd said nothing for so long.

God, I missed him.

My phone still held months of messages to him, so I spent my time scrolling through them reading my feelings for him as the time passed. Some were sad, while others made me smile. Each one marked a moment in time without him.

By the third day, it was all I could do to drag my body to the shower and wash my miserable self. While I didn't feel like I had when my father died and when Cal cheated on me, in some ways I felt worse. Those had both been horrible times, but they'd been endings I had to handle. Learning to accept the loss of someone was like having your heart torn out every day, but this was different. Tristan wasn't gone forever. He was just gone.

There was nothing I was allowed to mourn about this situation. Instead, I was supposed to stay in this house haunted with memories of him and act like everything was hunky dory. Well, it wasn't. After months of waiting every day for him to return, all my hunky dories had disappeared, and all I was carrying around was frustration and resentment at what our life had become.

And now Jordan was gone but not gone too. I didn't know how to feel about that. Something had come between us in the time she'd lived here. I really didn't think I'd changed, but had I? Had the world Tristan showed me made me so different that even my best friend didn't recognize me anymore? Even if I had changed, I still didn't know why she'd jumped to all the wrong conclusions with Gage. That wasn't like her at all.

It wasn't like her to not want to talk to me either. I'd tried calling and texting her, but she'd never answered or texted back. I'd apologized for something I really didn't mean to do, if I had done it at all, but still nothing. We'd disagreed before, but never had there been a rift like this between us.

As I stood in the shower remembering all the good times we'd had, I realized for the first time in my life, I was alone. Nobody I'd relied on was there for me anymore. Not my father, Jordan, or Tristan.

Dressed in the clothes that had become my usual outfit for hanging out at the house—yoga pants and a comfy shirt—I made my way to the kitchen, hoping I didn't see a soul since my face didn't have a stitch of makeup on it, my hair was a damp, stringy mess, and I wasn't even wearing a bra.

Maybe I had changed. Or maybe I was just depressed. Whichever it was, I wasn't in any shape to be seeing anyone.

For the first time in days, Maria had brewed the French Roast I loved, like she'd known this morning was the day I'd finally drag my butt out of bed. The only other female with me in the house now, she cooked for me, Jensen, and my giant shadows. She and I rarely spoke since her English was broken on the best of days and my knowledge of Portuguese was non-existent. Maybe if I'd taken Spanish in high school and college I could muddle through a conversation with her, but my three years of German was useless in comprehending what she was saying. Maria was kind, though, with hooded dark eyes that had a motherly feeling to them when she looked at me, and unlike every other person Tristan had working for him here, she seemed to have no interest in what I did with my time. For that reason alone, I liked her.

The coffee was exactly what the doctor ordered, and slowly my body began to come back to life. My spirit was still disheartened, but coffee wasn't going to fix that. The only cure for that wasn't to be found anywhere close, though.

I heard a sound behind me and turned to see Gage standing in the doorway. I couldn't be sure, but I had the sense that a look of surprise crossed his features for a moment. I probably deserved that since I looked like the walking dead.

"Hey, what's up?" I asked in my best pretend chipper voice.

"Daryl called me. It looks like we're doing the dinner thing tonight."

Swell. Daryl had wonderful timing. The day I emerged from my cave of depression looking like shit warmed over was the perfect day for me to pretend I was moving on with my life with my bodyguard. Yeah, this was fantastic.

I put my coffee mug down on the counter and folded my arms across my chest. "I bet right now you're wishing you hadn't agreed to this. I'll see what I can do to look less like a hot mess."

A slow smile spread across Gage's mouth. "No worries. How does six sound?"

"As good a time as any, right? So what does Daryl have planned for us? Casual or black tie formal?"

"He didn't say, but he said I should wear a suit. That's my task today, unless you're planning to leave the house. It seems my usual suits aren't good enough."

I looked down my body and back up at him. "Uh, no, I have no plans, but if you want a woman's help with your shopping, I'd be happy to join you. Sort of kill two birds with one stone."

He thought about my offer and nodded. "It couldn't hurt. Maybe we'll even get some people to see us together shopping. I'm sure Daryl would love that."

"Okay. Give me half an hour and I'll whip my head into shape. Wouldn't want to take out your brand new girlfriend with her looking like a train wreck. What would people think?" I joked.

Thankfully, he said nothing since telling me I looked great in any way would have made him sound like a true boyfriend and simply being supportive would have made him like a girlfriend. Either way, it would have been weird.

"I'll let Jensen know. Daryl was quite clear about that. For some reason, he seems to think that any man who's supposed to be dating you wouldn't drive."

I had to laugh. Daryl had everything planned down to the car we'd be seen in. He was nothing if not thorough. "I'll meet you at the garage in thirty then. I have to tell you, though, that I don't know where Tristan buys his suits. He has a shopper do that for him, so I don't know where to tell Jensen to take us."

"No worries there either. Daryl already told me. You up for Gerard's?"

I'd seen the store mentioned in magazines before, but I'd never been there. "I'm sure they have very nice men's suits there. I wonder why Daryl chose that store? How much do you want to bet he's already arranged for all eyes to be on you today?"

Gage chuckled. "I'd bet on it. No pressure, though, right? All we have to do is convince the entire world that you'd move on from someone like Tristan Stone to someone like me."

I stopped in front of him, struck by how his voice dropped when he basically said that he wasn't the kind of man someone like me would ever be with. Nothing could be further from the truth. In fact, the reality was that Gage was very much the kind of guy someone like me would go with. Tristan was the kind of man girls like me never ended up with.

Well, almost never.

"Don't worry. Just promise me you won't leave me standing in Gerard's while you go off with some salesgirl who doesn't look like a trainwreck."

His mouth turned down in a frown, and I quickly realized I'd offended him by implying he wasn't going to do his job. Touching his sleeve, I lightly squeezed his forearm. "I didn't mean you would really do that. I know you take your job very seriously. I was just trying to say that it's totally believable that the two of us would be together. I mean, you're a good looking guy and I'm sure lots of women are attracted to you."

I was rambling, but I didn't want to chase yet another person away, even if my insult had been entirely unintentional.

He looked down at me, and I saw in those dark blue eyes that I hadn't ruined everything. "It's okay, Nina. No need to apologize. Thanks for the compliment."

"I'm just glad you're not mad. I'll see you in thirty and we'll head out."

Gage stepped out of the dressing room in a dark grey suit and black dress shirt. I'd picked out a few combinations for him and this was by far the nicest looking. Much bigger than Tristan, he still wore a suit well, even if there was a lot more of him to fit inside one.

Standing stoically in front of the tri-fold mirror, he didn't seem to know what to do with his hands suddenly, stuffing them into his pockets and then pulling them out to let them hang at his sides before he fiddled with his shirt collar. The salesperson, a silver-haired older man with a long face who'd introduced himself as Phillip and had an interesting way of slowly buzzing around the periphery while Gage stood admiring himself, made a cooing sound of appreciation behind me. I had to agree. The suit looked good on him.

"Well, how's it feel?" I asked as Phillip swooped in to begin his job.

"It looks fantastic on you," he beamed as he gently tugged on the sleeves near Gage's shoulders. "Fits perfectly."

Gage looked back at me in the mirror with a look of discomfort that made me laugh. Nearly twice the size of the salesman, he looked like he was under attack but didn't know how to fend off the older man.

"Do you like it?"

He looked back at me and nodded. "It's a nice suit."

Phillip looked appalled at Gage's tepid reaction to what was definitely more than a nice suit. Nice suits cost a couple hundred dollars.

The one he wore at that moment came in at over a grand. A little more than just nice.

"I can tell by the look on your lady's face that she likes it," Phillip said in a singsong voice. "Whatever the occasion, this suit will be the right one."

That same look of discomfort crossed Gage's face at the salesman's mention of me as his girlfriend. I merely smiled and played my part in Tristan's charade, convincing enough it seemed for Phillip, who interpreted my smile as approval for the suit and scurried away mumbling about picking out the perfect tie for the occasion. That he didn't know a thing about the so-called occasion didn't seem to matter.

I took my place next to Gage in the mirror and whispered words of support. "The first test wasn't so bad, was it? He seemed to believe we could be a couple."

"He did. If he was paying attention to my face instead of the suit, he might not have, though. I need to work on that."

"I thought you were experienced in this. Looks like you need to work on your gazing longingly technique."

My joke made him laugh, easing the tension, thankfully. Phillip returned a moment later with a stunning black and turquoise swirl pattern tie that truly was the perfect tie for the suit. Placing it in my hand, he watched as I held it up against Gage's chest, all the while staring into the mirror in an attempt to let him know now was the time to practice that gazing skill.

"Doesn't it look great, dear?" I teased. "Perfect indeed."

"Wonderful!" Extending his arm, Phillip pointed toward the register. "I'll take you over here when you're ready. Take your time."

As he walked away, Gage looked at me in the mirror. "Laying it on a little thick there, weren't you?"

"I was just practicing my doting girlfriend bit. Think I should dial it back a little?"

"Yeah. I think if we can find some happy medium between you and me, we might pull this off."

"I don't doubt it for a minute. Go get changed and I'll deal with Phillip."

Gage walked back into the dressing room while I paid for his new look, careful to drop heavy handed hints about how happy we were as a couple as the very nosy salesman hung on every word. Handing me back my credit card, he winked and leaned toward me. "You make a lovely couple."

"Thank you. My fiancé thinks so too."

Assuming I meant Gage was the man I planned to marry, he began to chatter on about how lucky he was to have me as his intended. I smiled, more at my cloaked reference than Phillip's compliments. I had to find the bright spot in all this somehow.

With his new suit in hand, Gage escorted me to the front door of the store, stopping just before we stepped outside. Leaning down, he whispered, "Plans have changed. Daryl's made sure we're seen. He wants us to go to Malone's a few blocks away for lunch instead of dinner. I'm assuming the men standing around outside are here for us, so be ready."

I looked out the glass doors and saw the small crowd of men I recognized as photographers waiting for us. Daryl sure did know how to put on a show. Taking a deep breath, I walked past Gage as he held the door, very much like the boyfriend he was playacting but leaving me wide open for the throng of press to surge toward me. Instantly overwhelmed, I was surrounded by a sea of eager faces pushing toward me as their cameras flashed. I frantically looked around for Gage as I scrambled to make my way to the car, totally unprepared for how close they got to me. From all sides, they yelled for me to look their way, wanting to know how I was holding up with Tristan gone and presumed dead and how long I'd been with my bodyguard. The insinuation was clear—I was a heartless bitch who could forget one man easily and replace him with another even easier.

Something deep inside pushed me to answer that I still loved Tristan, but when I opened my mouth to speak, Gage inserted himself in between me and the men, shielding me from them and quickly getting the two of us into the car. "Jensen, we need to get to Malone's. The quicker the better too," he said calmly as I struggled to stop my hands from shaking.

Turning toward me, he frowned. "Are you okay? I'm sorry about that. I was so wrapped up in acting like a boyfriend that I didn't do my job as your bodyguard. That's always got to be my first concern, no matter what Daryl wants. I need to remember that."

I heard in his voice the anger he was feeling. Trying to help, I rested my palm on his forearm. "It's okay. Nothing bad happened. We're good. I'm Jezebel and the press is eating it up like it's candy."

"Nina, although I'm not entirely clear on what danger you may be in, I do know a slip up like that could let someone close enough to really hurt you. My job is to make sure that never happens. We may be pretending to play house, but Tristan Stone expects me to keep you safe from every kind of danger, even one that only looks like a nuisance like those photographers."

I hung my head, not caring about whatever danger there was around me. Those photographers had gotten to me, their words echoing in my mind. *Who's the new man, Nina? How long have you been together? What do you plan to do if Tristan Stone ever returns?*

The mere thought of Tristan's return as an *if* instead of a *when* hurt. I'd thought with Gage's help I could do this pretending thing, but I didn't realize it would be so hard. I didn't want to be with anyone else, and making people think I did felt wrong.

"You okay?"

I looked over at Gage and forced a smile. "I'm fine. I just wasn't ready for that."

"They're vipers, but that's their job. If you think about it that way, it might be easier."

Looking down at my left hand as it rested on top of my other one in my lap, I regretted ever agreeing to this. The finger where my engagement ring should have been looked like I felt. Empty.

"I guess. I want to go home."

"We need to eat at Malone's before we get to head home," he said, sounding almost apologetic.

"Fine. We'll do that, but then I want to go home."

Chapter Seven

Nina

Malone's was exactly the kind of place I dreaded and exactly the kind of place I knew Daryl would send us to. Small and intimate, it was dark even in the daylight and screamed romantic rendezvous. God, I wished Daryl wasn't so good at this.

The hostess escorted us to a table near a window looking directly out to the street. I quietly protested, but Gage simply showed me his phone and a text from Daryl indicating this was exactly where he'd arranged for us to be seen.

Fucking fabulous.

I held the menu up in front of my face as a small group of photographers began to gather outside. Nothing on it sounded even remotely appetizing, but I tried to convince myself that as long as the bar could whip up a chocolate martini or two, I might make it through our latest performance.

"Nina, I understand you're not happy, but hiding behind the menu isn't really what Daryl wants, I'm guessing."

"I don't care what he wants," I said from behind my menu.

The waiter arrived to take our order, entirely too chipper for my mood. I listened as Gage ordered his meal of a steak cooked medium and roasted red bliss potatoes with steamed asparagus dressed in parmesan. Ordinarily, that would have sounded good, but at that moment, just the thought of it nearly made me sick.

"What will Miss be having?" the waiter asked as he turned and looked down at me.

"Chocolate martini. Make sure the glass is sugared."

He tugged on my menu, forcing it from my hand, and smiled fakely before turning away. I looked across the table at Gage and saw a look of pity on his face. I hated his pity. Self-pity I was all about, but pity from someone who barely knew me just felt wrong.

"Liquid lunch?"

"Yeah."

We sat in silence as the waiter brought Gage's soda and my martini, the crowd outside growing the whole time. What the fuck had Daryl told them? Did they think they would catch us having sex right there in the window of Malone's?

Gage slid his hand across the table to touch mine. "Nina, I know this is hard, but we have to try."

"I don't want to try. I want to drink. I want to forget that I'm sitting here with people watching our every move and waiting for us to act like we care about each other."

"Maybe if I tell you something about me and Angela that might help?"

"Sure," I mumbled as I focused on the taste of my martini as it sat on my tongue, all chocolately goodness.

He didn't move his hand away, keeping it on top of mine and giving the photographers something to snap away at, which they did. Every part of me wanted to take my hand back, but I kept it there as he began to tell the tale of the woman he'd loved.

"I remember the first time we knew we thought more of each other than just bodyguard and client. She was on location in Spain. We'd been pretending to be a couple for months, but one night, it all just came together."

"Was it love at first sight?" I asked as I took a healthy gulp of my drink, enjoying the warming sensation it left in its wake as I swallowed.

Gage shook his head. "No. She was like a spoiled child when I first began guarding her. I don't think we spoke our first words to one another for weeks after I was hired. Well, that's not true. She snapped at me constantly in those weeks. When we finally began talking, I could see she wasn't that diva I'd thought she was."

"Sounds like that Whitney Houston movie, The Bodyguard."

"Not exactly. She wasn't that bad."

I held up my glass to let the waiter know I needed a refill. "Well, it's nice to know there was a happy ending," I said as I looked around the restaurant for the missing waiter.

"Not really. She married someone else last March."

Turning to look at him, for first time I saw emotion in his eyes. God, I was such a bitch! I placed my glass down on the table and rested my other hand on top of his. "I'm sorry. I didn't mean to be so flippant about everything. You obviously cared about her."

"Yeah, well, that whole good things happening to good people thing doesn't always happen to everyone. Sometimes things are bad and that's all there is."

The waiter brought Gage's food and another martini for me, and we sat in silence as he ate and I attempted to drown both our troubles. The press milling about outside had taken lots of pictures when I touched his hand, so I hoped we'd done our job well enough for Daryl to be happy. I didn't want to think Tristan would be happy. I wanted to believe he'd be as jealous as I'd be if I saw him holding hands with another woman.

By the time I'd drunk three martinis, Gage was finished with lunch. In addition to tasting great, my chocolate martinis had the wonderful effect of making me hate the facade we had to keep up a little less, at least for the moment. I was also feeling more talkative.

"It was love at first sight for me with Tristan," I announced as Gage finished the last of his steak and wiped his mouth.

"That's cool. I didn't realize that even existed in real life."

"Well, maybe not first sight, but the first time he kissed me, it was definitely something like love."

"Those drinks sure have an effect on you," Gage joked. "Even your body language has eased up. You look like you did that night at ETA."

"You were there with us that night?" I asked, surprised to know he'd seen Tristan and me then.

Gage nodded. "West and I have been in the shadows with you since you returned home from the hospital, especially when you're alone without Tristan."

He knew that I'd gone to see Cal that time and probably knew I'd secretly met with him those other times. I didn't know why, but I needed to explain that I hadn't cheated on Tristan.

"Then you know about me meeting with Cal Johnson. I didn't do anything wrong, you know. It was all on the up-and-up."

"I know. If you had done anything, we would have had to tell Tristan. I know it's not my place to say so, Nina, but your ex-boyfriend is a scammer."

"I found that out. I guess it's nice to know that you guys were around to make sure nothing bad happened."

"And Jensen too," he said with a smile. "I was surprised he jumped in that night at that bar. You must have made quite an impression on the guy."

Gage's phone dinged, and he lifted it to show me it was Daryl texting him. I didn't have to see the entire text to know what he wanted. All it took was one word I saw scrolling across the top of his phone.

Kiss

His text was longer than that, including where and when to kiss me, and as Gage read it to me, I felt the intense need for another drink. Maybe being entirely hammered would make it possible for me to kiss another man for the cameras.

I lifted my glass, but Gage pushed my wrist down so the glass sat back on the table. "I think we need to go."

"I think I want another drink. You just read the decree from Daryl that I have to kiss you, and what that means is that the man I love told him he's okay with that. I need another fucking drink."

"Let's get you home and then whatever you're feeling you can let out all you want. I just don't want to see you unravel in front of these people."

Turning to look out the window, I saw the photographers and suddenly hated them. I hated this whole thing. I didn't want to do this anymore. As I stared out at them, my phone vibrated and I swiped the face to see Daryl had sent me a text too.

But it was even worse than the one he sent to Gage because this one wasn't from him. It was from Tristan.

Daryl says you won't do what he asked. I know this is hard, but we need the world to think you've moved on. It's just for a short time, princess. Remember that and we'll be okay.

Princess. It was Tristan, after all. All those texts and this was the one he decided was worth responding to? Crushed, I let my fingers fly over the keyboard on my phone. *What happened to the man who was so jealous that I couldn't even have drinks with my ex? Now you're okay with me kissing Gage, the guy the world knows as my incredibly sexy bodyguard who's doing so much more than just guarding my body these days? Thanks for bothering to clear this up for me.*

I waited for another text from Tristan from Daryl's number, but it never came. Whatever he felt about me kissing another man, he couldn't even bother to reply.

The Kiss happened just as Daryl dictated—or maybe it was how Tristan dictated—right outside the restaurant as we walked to Jensen and our waiting car. It meant nothing to me physically, but emotionally, I was devastated that Tristan had actually wanted it to happen. All those months alone and what did I have to show for it? The man I loved and prayed every day and night to see again telling me that I had to kiss another man.

We rode back to the house in silence, my misery stewing inside me as I listened almost hypnotized to the sound of the tires rolling over highway, and I beat a path for my room the moment the car jerked to a stop in the garage. All I wanted was to be alone. No more pretending with Gage. No more orders from Daryl. No more anything. Just me curled up in bed.

Before I did that, though, I had to text Tristan. Even if he didn't answer back, which he never did, I needed to say some things. Slowly, I spelled out how much I hated all of this, ending with the one question I couldn't push out of my mind.

Do you even care about me anymore?

Closing my eyes, I let the tears burning my eyelids slide down my cheeks and prayed to God I could at least suffer in solitude.

Unfortunately, I couldn't even have that. Just minutes after pulling the covers up over my head, I'd barely closed my eyes before I heard a knock on my door. I hadn't told Gage I didn't want to be bothered, assuming he understood that by my behavior all the way home from the city, so I padded over to the door and opened it to find not him but Daryl standing there. His bushy red beard looked like he'd been tugging on it all day, and he looked about as bad as I felt.

"Can we talk?"

"Now? I'm a little busy trying to sleep, Daryl. Come back later."

"Why are you sleeping in the middle of the afternoon?" he pried, irritating me.

"Because I'm goddamned exhausted after my little shopping trip with Gage and the subsequent show you made us put on. So if you don't mind, I'd like to be alone. Why don't you talk to him? Maybe you have some more things you want us to do together. A make out session on Broadway? Or maybe a live sex show right outside the gate so the press can get their pictures and their rocks off? Sort of a kill two birds with one stone kind of thing."

"I can see you're upset, but we need to talk. Tristan wanted me to tell you…"

I pushed my hand in front of his face to cut him off. "Don't. I don't want to hear another thing about what Tristan wants. I know what he wants, so thank you for that. Now leave me alone."

Before I could slam the door in his face, he pushed it back and stuck his hairy face toward me. "We really need to talk."

All the sadness at realizing Tristan was with Daryl but couldn't even contact me, except to tell me to kiss another man, came flowing out of me, and I released the door. I didn't care if my crying made Daryl uncomfortable. I didn't care what he thought at that moment. I was sick and tired of his edicts or Tristan's edicts, or whatever the hell they were.

I just wanted my life with Tristan back.

"Nina, I know this is hard, but it's important."

"I don't care anymore! The only goddamned time Tristan bothers to text me back is to inform me that he wants me to kiss Gage? Are you kidding? I'm supposed to be okay with all of this? Well, I'm not!"

Daryl stepped back as my voice grew louder and louder until it was nothing less than a shrill scream. All the better. After all this time, I wanted to scream. I wanted to hit my fists against something, or better, someone.

"And you can tell my dear fiancé that he should be nervous. I mean, Jordan already thinks that I snuck behind her back to snag Gage from her. Maybe I am. Maybe I'm sick of waiting for Tristan and living here all alone. You had Gage move into the room right next to mine. He's pretty good looking, Daryl. Maybe I'm ready to move on, even though I know Tristan isn't dead. Maybe you should tell Tristan all of that and see how he feels. Tell him I'm all for fucking my hot body-guard, you know, just to make sure the press really believes our story. Maybe then he'll understand how awful I feel."

I'd never seen Daryl surprised before. He usually wore a mainly bland expression with me, but at that moment, I saw that he knew I was serious. Maybe he even believed I did want Gage. Good. Then maybe he'd go back to Tristan and let him know that their stupid plan was tearing me apart.

"Nina, I don't think Tristan meant to upset you."

Rubbing the mascara from underneath my eyes, I snapped, "Well, he did! Let him know that too."

He reached into his coat pocket and pulled out an envelope with my name on it. I recognized the writing instantly. Tristan's. Daryl held out his hand for me to take it, quietly saying, "Maybe this will help you feel better."

This time one of Tristan's love letters wasn't going to do it. In fact, it only served to make me angrier. Shaking my head, I folded my arms across my chest. "Nope. You can take that back to him, wherever he is, and tell him that whatever he wants to say to me he can say in person. And since I'm getting closer and closer to Gage every day, tell him he doesn't have to worry about me being in danger."

I knew my words were harsh, but the ones I left unspoken were even worse. And I knew Daryl. He had no sense of romance whatsoever and little tact, so he'd tell Tristan exactly what I'd said. When he did, Tristan would read into my words, like always, and hear everything I'd said and what I'd left unsaid.

Backing away, Daryl still wore a look of shock on his face as he stood with Tristan's letter in his hand watching the door close in front of him. I walked back to my bed and slipped under the covers again, swearing that I wouldn't come out again until Tristan was the one knocking on my door.

That pledge didn't pan out either, though. As I lay there hearing someone knock on my door once again, I found it stunning that in a house where I was surrounded by mostly men I couldn't be left alone. It was like being in the middle of every woman's dream of having men who wanted to talk. To me, it was more like a nightmare.

I shuffled over to the door, fully prepared to read Daryl the riot act this time. This was my house, and he had it coming. Flinging it open, I saw Gage standing there looking down at me. Reaming someone out would have to wait.

"I just wanted to check to make sure you're okay."

"I'm fine."

"If you want to talk…"

Gage's voice faded to silence, as if he instantly regretted his offer. In truth, I didn't want to talk. I wanted to scream.

"What do you want to talk about? How my fiancé thinks making me kiss other men is a good idea? How I'm devastated over knowing that he's obviously with Daryl and can't be bothered to even fucking text me to tell me he misses me?"

With each syllable, my voice grew louder until by the end, I was yelling at my poor bodyguard-turned-fake boyfriend. At that moment, I didn't care if I was hurting anyone else's feelings. I was just sick of what I was feeling.

I turned away from Gage and walked back to my bed, suddenly exhausted from the weight of my emotions. He cautiously followed me, taking a seat next to me on the bed as I began to sob, and put his arm around my shoulders as they heaved from my crying.

"It's okay, Nina. I know it seems like everything's crazy now, but sometimes that's how it has to be," he said softly as I buried my face in his chest.

"I can't do crazy anymore. This is too hard."

For the first time since that night Tristan and I first made love, the thought that I couldn't handle Tristan's world settled into my mind. I still loved him, but I just didn't know if I was the right person to deal with all that came with him.

Gage let me have a good, long cry, and I sat back from him to wipe the tears from under my eyes. Shaking my head, I apologized for being such a fucked up mess. "I'm sorry you have to see this. I bet right now you're wishing you never said yes to pretending to be my boyfriend, although I'm guessing Daryl didn't give you much choice, did he?"

A gentle smile lit up his face. "Not really, but it's okay. This isn't so bad. I'm used to crying females. I had three sisters all within five years of me, so high school was an almost constant stream of crying and screaming."

"Three sisters so close together? The bathroom arrangement alone must have been a nightmare."

Chuckling, he said, "I don't remember seeing the bathroom much in high school. Thankfully, we had a half bath in the basement or my father and I would have been in real trouble."

"Your family sounds nice."

"My family sounds like a bunch of crazy people. It's okay. You don't have to lie. I know."

Sniffling back the last of my tears, I said, "I don't know what it's like to have a family like that. My mother died when I was little, and my sister's six years older than me. By the time I was old enough to want to hang around with her, she wasn't interested in hanging around with me."

He nodded. "Yeah, siblings can be like that. I never had a brother, but I had three younger sisters, and I can tell you I never wanted to hang with them back then. People change as they get older, so maybe you and your sister could hang out now."

I shook my head, all too sure that would never be the case with Kim. "I doubt it. My sister and I are just two very different people. Do you know that even before she met Tristan she accused him of being a murderer? A murderer! She hadn't even laid eyes on him or ever talked to him for a minute and she was sure he was some ax murderer or something. That's who she is. I just don't think she ever wanted me to be happy."

"I'm hoping he's not an ax murderer because I'm not in the mood to defend myself right now since if he saw us sitting together like this he might want to kill me," Gage said with a smile.

Turning to face him, I folded my legs underneath me and hung my head. "I doubt it. He seemed perfectly fine with me kissing you, so I doubt you sitting here with me would bother him even a little."

Gage shook his head. "I think you're wrong there. Men don't appreciate other men sitting on the same bed with their girlfriends. Sorry, fiancée. I know I wouldn't."

"I would think those men might not order their girlfriends or fiancées to kiss other men then."

Smiling, he shook his head again. "He thinks you're in danger and is trying to keep you safe, Nina."

"Then he should be here taking care of that himself instead of making you and me play house."

"Powerful men have enemies. Dangerous enemies. I don't know Tristan at all, to be honest, but from what I've seen, he cares about you."

I knew Gage was right, but that didn't mean I was feeling any better about Tristan and Daryl's plan. "Sometimes I wonder."

Without any warning, I broke down in tears again. God, I was a mess! Burying my face in my hands, I sobbed at the reality that I wasn't sure if Tristan even cared anymore. Months of wondering where he was and if he was okay had turned into wondering if he still loved me at all.

The bed shifted, and I felt Gage move closer to hug me again. I guess I shouldn't have let him, but being held felt so good. After so long, I didn't feel alone. "It's okay, Nina. Let it out."

Lifting my head to say thank you for him being so understanding, I looked up and time seemed to change into slow motion. Those dark blue eyes gazed down at me so full of concern that for a moment I felt like I should comfort him and let him know I'd be okay. Instead, I just stared up into his face and then it happened.

I didn't know if he kissed me or I kissed him, but we kissed. I hadn't been kissed in months, and for a split second I let myself enjoy the sensation of his soft lips on mine. It was the nicest, most innocent kiss I'd ever had, and instantly, I felt guiltier than ever before in my life.

When time resumed its normal motion, I abruptly pulled away and shook my head over and over. From behind my hand covering my guilty mouth, I mumbled, "I'm so sorry. I don't know why I did that. That should have never happened."

The expression on his face was a mixture of the guilt he shared with me and surprise, which made me believe I'd kissed him. Maybe I had. I didn't know. It all just happened so unexpectedly.

"I better go. I'm just glad you feel better."

He left without another word, and as I sat there with my hand still covering my mouth, all I knew was that I'd never felt so awful in my life.

Chapter Eight

Tristan

While I waited for Daryl to return, I took a look around the apartment he'd rented for me on the edge of the town closest to the house. He'd done a good job getting me as close as possible to Nina. On foot, I was probably only a few minutes away across a field that butted up against the property. All of three rooms and a bathroom, the apartment wasn't even big enough to measure up to the rooms Nina stayed in when she'd first come to live with me, but I didn't plan to stay here long.

I sat on the full sized bed that took up most of the space in the tiny, white bedroom and stared into the mirror across from me. I barely recognized myself. Months of exile had whittled away at my body so I was much leaner. Hair longer than I'd worn in years fell into my eyes, and my beard was practically as long and bushy as Daryl's. Only my eyes still told others I was Tristan Stone, assuming anyone could see them through the hair.

It felt good to be back home, or at least close to home. Soon I'd find out what Karl was up to and finally get to return to Nina and our life together. Until then, I had to hope she'd understand what I had to do to safeguard that life.

A knock on the door told me Daryl was back, and I answered it to find him looking shell-shocked. He pushed past me and walked into the apartment's narrow galley kitchen to rummage through the cabinets.

"I know I stored a bottle up here somewhere. You couldn't have drank it all already, did you?"

I leaned against the doorframe and pointed toward the cabinet on the far end of the wall. "I didn't have any yet, but I'm not sure how I feel about you drinking my Lagavulin. Get your own bottle."

Daryl poured himself a glass neat, never asking me if I wanted one, and sagged against the Formica countertop as he gulped down my expensive scotch. "You owe me, buddy. After what I just went through, I deserve the entire bottle."

Fear that something had happened to Nina raced through my body, settling into my heart. "What happened? Is Nina hurt?"

Downing another mouthful of scotch, he shook his head. "No. The only person injured is me."

I looked him up and down and saw the same old Daryl. "What are you talking about? You look fine enough to drink all my scotch."

He took the envelope I'd given him for Nina out of his coat pocket and threw it on the counter. "She went nuts when I tried to give her this. Told me she didn't want your letter and that you can say what you want to say to her in person. And when I say told, I mean screamed her bloody head off."

Nina had always loved my notes and letters. The fear that I was losing her had haunted me since I'd left and suddenly became very real. Picking up the envelope, I ran my fingers over her name, unsure of what I needed to do.

"That was after she literally balled me out. Her exact words were 'You can tell my dear fiancé that he should be nervous. Maybe I'm sick of waiting for Tristan and living here all alone. Gage is right next door in the room next to me. He's pretty good looking. Maybe I'm ready to move on, even though I know Tristan isn't dead. Maybe you should tell Tristan all of that and see how he feels.' And all of that was done screaming at me!"

"Did you tell her this is only for a short time?"

He mumbled, "Then she mentioned something about fucking her hot bodyguard before she slammed the door in my face."

As he finished his drink and poured himself another glass, I began to spin out of control. I'd expected too much from her. Leaving her alone for months and believing that she'd be fine with it was wrong. Even worse, I'd put another man right in front of her—a man she very well might be attracted to.

"I can't stay away any longer, Daryl. I need to go home."

His eyes bugged out of his head as he threw his hands up in the air in disgust. "Jesus Christ! You can't go home. If Karl knows you're there, you'll put Nina in danger too. You need to just sit tight while we find out what that fucker's up to."

"You figure that out. I need to get back home. I've expected Nina to deal with too much."

"She's fine. Don't worry about her. I'm sure it was just a bad day for her. She's tough. She can handle it."

"I can't handle it."

Unable to admit to Daryl that Nina's hopefully empty threat had made me more jealous than I thought I could be, I just stood there as my mind spiraled trying to figure out how I could go home without putting her in any more danger.

"I know what you're worried about, Tristan, but you can trust her and Varo. He's a good guy."

That made what I was feeling even worse. A good guy sleeping in the room right next to her after they pretended to be in love all day. Fucking perfect. No, I had to go home. Somehow, I had to be able to be near her.

"I don't care. I need to go back. Now. So help me figure it out."

"You're killing me here, Tristan. The two of you lovebirds are just killing me." Stroking his beard to a long point below his chin, he pursed his lips as he thought. "I have an idea, but I need to know. Can you can speak any languages other than English?"

"You mean like French or Spanish? No."

He sighed. "Well, that doesn't help."

"I know sign language, though."

Daryl narrowed his eyes to slits, as if he was considering what I'd just said. "You mean for deaf people?"

"Yeah. I had no interest in learning any language in high school, so they said I could take American Sign Language. I'm still pretty good at it."

I began to fingerspell, quickly remembering the alphabet and some common signs like I'm sorry and thank you.

"Can you do that with gloves on?"

I closed my fist and moved it up and down to sign yes. "As long as my fingers are free, I can sign. Why? What are you thinking?"

Downing the last of his drink, he smiled for the first time since he arrived. "I'm thinking I'm a genius. Hang on."

He took his phone out and tapped in a number before putting it to his ear. In seconds, I understood his plan. "Nina, it's Daryl. You need to fire the gardener. I'll have a new one there tomorrow."

Nina's voice came through the phone loud and clear. "Why? There's nothing wrong with Chip. West and Gage cleared him and he's fine."

"I found out something that makes it appear he might be connected to Karl. I can fire him, if you like."

"Fine, you do it. I don't want to fire him. He's been nothing but nice."

"I'll be right over to take care of it."

Daryl put his phone away and turned toward me with a broad smile. "Okay, now that that's taken care of, you can be the gardener. I'll say you're deaf and dumb and only communicate through signing. We need to get you some sunglasses to hide your eyes, but other than that, you barely look like you after all these months."

"One problem. I can't keep sunglasses on every moment I'm at the house, and one look at my eyes and she'll know it's me in a heartbeat."

Walking past me into the living room, he shook his head. "I'm one step ahead of you. Come with me. It's time to head to Wal-Mart to change those big brown eyes to something even your lady won't recognize."

I followed him, thrilled to know that I'd be close to Nina again and taking pleasure in his amusement at all of this. "You seem almost happy, Daryl. Enjoying yourself?"

"I'll enjoy myself when all this is over and you and Nina are back together so she doesn't ream me out anymore. Ever been to Wally World?"

I followed behind Daryl as he walked the stone path toward the gardens behind the house. Our Wal-Mart trip had been a success, but my color changing contacts wouldn't be in for up to a week, so I questioned whether his whole grand plan was going to fall apart the minute I was introduced to Nina.

Slowing down to walk next to me, he whispered, "No matter what she says, do not take off those glasses. Just let me handle everything. Remember, you're deaf and dumb."

I made the OK sign with my hands, which were hidden inside gloves. That I was already wearing gloves before I began the job seemed even odder than the sunglasses, but I was afraid she'd suspect something if she saw my hands.

"Is that supposed to be something I know?" he asked, staring at my fingers.

"It means OK," I whispered out of the side of my mouth.

"No talking. You want to be able to see her every day or not?"

He knew the answer to that. Just being on the grounds again filled me with anticipation. My stomach flipped when I thought about finally seeing her after all these months. Even if she didn't know who I was, I'd finally be able to be close to her.

Then I saw her. In the distance, she appeared angry as she stormed down the pathway toward us, and I recognized that look of unhappiness on her face. All at once, I knew the story Daryl had told me about her reaming him out was no exaggeration, but even angry she looked beautiful. She wore her long hair up in a ponytail and had no makeup on. But it didn't matter. She was still the most beautiful woman I'd ever seen.

"Nina, how are you today?" Daryl asked as we all met at a bend in the path.

"I'm fine, Daryl. I don't really know why you needed me out here for this, but I'm fine," she said sourly.

"I felt you should meet the new gardener since I had to fire the old one."

"I liked Chip, Daryl. He was a nice guy. I feel bad that you fired him. To be honest, I can't imagine he'd be involved with anyone bad."

"Not to worry. This is Ethan and he's going to be fine."

Nina looked me up and down and then looked back at Daryl. "Ethan?"

"Yeah. He doesn't speak because he's deaf and dumb, but he knows his way around a shrub."

She looked me up and down once more and turned her back toward me to speak to Daryl. "Are you two brothers at the Water Buffalo Lodge or something and you owe him a favor? He looks oddly like you. And deaf and mute? How is he going to do this?"

"He's got a disability, but we can't hold that against him. As for the beard, it's not as nice as mine, but you have to give him points for trying. Don't worry. He's perfect for this."

She turned around, and I saw her expression soften. After studying me for a few moments, she extended her hand. "It's nice to meet you, Ethan. I hope you'll be happy here." I shook her hand, wishing I wasn't wearing gloves so I could feel her skin against mine. I wanted to take her in my arms and fill my nose with the familiar scent of lavender her shampoo left in her hair. I wanted to hold her against me and tell her I was there with her.

Turning toward Daryl, she continued, "I think Chip was working on fixing up the garden so it would be ready for the summer. I'd told him I wanted to plant some vegetables, so have Ethan pick up where Chip left off."

"Got it."

"Anything else, Daryl?"

Smiling, he shook his head. "No. I'm glad to see you're in a better mood today."

"You can thank Gage for that," she said with a chuckle before she turned on her heels and walked away.

In that second, my chest felt like someone hit it with a sledgehammer. I'd never been so jealous in my life and unable to do a thing about it. All I could do was stand there pretending like I hadn't heard her just imply she'd slept with her bodyguard.

Daryl's hand clamped down on my forearm and he whispered, "Relax. She didn't mean anything by it. Remember, they're pretending to be together. I've got an idea on Cordovex to check out, so get to trimming the hedges or whatever and I'll check in with you tonight back at your place."

I barely heard him over the sound of my heartbeat pounding in my ears.

By the time I got back to the apartment that night, I'd nearly gone out of my mind with jealousy. From where I was standing as I raked and hoed to prepare the space Nina wanted to use for her vegetable garden, I was able to watch the inside of the lower level of the house. Varo looked quite at home as he swam in my pool in the middle of the day, joined by Nina at one point who didn't swim but sat and watched for a few minutes as he did.

Sat and watched as his ridiculously muscular body swam back and forth in front of her while she kept her eyes fixed on him.

I spent a half hour filling in the hole I accidentally dug with the spade as I watched the two of them together. He was lucky I was committed to this plan of Daryl's because if I wasn't, I would have used that spade for another far more satisfying purpose that would have required me to dig a much deeper hole.

While one of the bodyguards I hired to protect Nina was busy taking his job far too literally, the other seemed intently interested in me. West watched me pantomime gardening for nearly an hour before he approached me, tapping me on the shoulder none too lightly after I ignored his efforts to say hello three times. When I said nothing in return even after acknowledging his presence, he left frustrated and spent the next hour spying on me, his enormous frame obvious from his hiding spots behind trees and bushes.

Maybe I wasn't fooling anyone. He didn't even make an effort to be sly as he watched me muddle through cleaning out twigs and weeds from the garden area. By the time I finished, I'd decided that once I was back West was gone. If he was this clumsy watching me, I couldn't imagine how bad he was at protecting Nina. Of course, that meant I had to be thankful for Varo's presence around her, which was the last thing I wanted to admit.

I needed a drink.

Sitting down in front of the TV Daryl had been nice enough to include in my new place, I tried to get lost in some sitcom and scotch with little success. There I was, sitting in some hole in the wall apartment while Nina and Varo were enjoying my house, probably my liquor, and…

I couldn't bring myself to think about them enjoying my bed, but somewhere in the back of my mind a tiny, insidious voice whispered again and again, *"They're together."* I'd never been good at handling jealousy, and my paranoia about Nina sleeping with Varo quickly mushroomed in my brain, leaving me with the choice of blowing Daryl's plan by storming over to the house to reunite with the woman I loved and in the process putting her in danger or getting stone drunk.

The half-inch of scotch left in the bottle sitting on the coffee table in front of me made my choice next to impossible. If I was going to get through that night, a trip to the liquor store was in order. All the better. I was already feeling trapped in my new place and looked forward to the half mile or so walk to get more of the only thing that was going to help me forget, at least for a few hours.

I set out on my quest for alcohol and met few people on my way, all of them shying away from me by refusing to make eye contact and one even crossing the street to get away from me. For a moment, I couldn't figure out why until I remembered I didn't look like Tristan Stone with my scruffy hair and overgrown beard. Never before in my life had I experienced people avoiding me because of my appearance. The tiny village of Millbrook, New York must have been used to a better class of person. I used to be that class, but as the gardener Ethan, I definitely stuck out like a sore thumb among Manhattanites visiting their country homes. It was eye-opening, to say the least.

The greasy-haired liquor store clerk gave me a similar reception when I walked into his store, watching me intently as I passed him on my way to the scotch aisle. I stood staring at the various bottles, my mind preoccupied with how differently I was treated looking like I did now. A little longer hair and a bad beard and suddenly I was persona non grata.

I felt a tug on my sleeve and turned to see Nina standing there staring up at me. Immediately, I realized I wasn't wearing my sunglasses.

My hair hung in my eyes, so I squinted at her, hoping to hide my eye color.

She smiled and waved at me, obviously remembering that I couldn't hear or speak. I smiled a closed mouth smile back, afraid if I acted too much like myself that she'd figure out my ruse. She made a motion with her hands that looked like she was trying to ask if I drank, and I nodded. Hoping to deflect her attention from me, I signed *Are you here to buy alcohol?* She had no idea what I was asking and shaking her head, said sweetly, "I'm sorry. I don't know what you mean."

I pointed at the bottles and then pointed at her as I repeated my question with my hands. My distraction seemed to work because she walked away, and for a moment I thought I was safe, but she returned a few seconds later with a bottle of hazelnut liqueur in one hand and a bottle of cheap vodka in the other. I recognized the liqueur bottle instantly as the same one the bartender at ETA had used that night when he made her the chocolate martini.

"I fell in love with this chocolate cake martini a while back and really wanted one tonight," she explained as I smiled down at her and pretended not to understand what she meant, all the while loving the sound of her sweet voice again.

She sensed I didn't understand and put the two bottles she was holding on the shelf next to her so she could take out a pen and paper. She scribbled a few words and held it up so I could read it.

Do you like scotch? My fiancé likes it too. I can't drink it, though. Too hard. :(

God, she was sweet. How much I wanted to hold that beautiful face in my hands and tell her it was me standing in front of her instead of some guy who worked on her garden all day, seething with jealousy as he watched her be friendly to another man.

Thinking it might seem too obvious if Ethan liked scotch too, I shook my head and pointed at the American whiskey further down the aisle away from where I was standing. Then I took the pen from her hand and wrote *I like whiskey instead,* forgetting that I didn't have gloves on. She could clearly see my hands and knew my handwriting from all my notes and letters.

Fearful I'd ruined Daryl's plan, I dropped the pen onto the paper she held in her hand and stuffed my hands into my pockets. Thankfully, she was too busy reading what I'd written to notice that I was hiding my hands. She wrote something else and smiled up at me as I read her message.

It was nice seeing you here. Have a great night!

Before I could nod and hope she understood I wished her the same, I saw Varo come through the front door and march up behind her, his expression filled with protective concern.

"Nina, is everything okay?" he asked.

"I'm fine. I was just talking to Ethan. He's the new gardener."

Varo sized me up and quickly moved to guide Nina out of the store, but I was thrilled to see her fight him. A tiny flicker of joy crept into my heart as she pushed him away to be nice to someone she'd just met that day. She was still my Nina, the same old gentle soul she'd always been.

"Let's go," he insisted, again trying to direct her toward the register.

"Okay, let me say goodbye," Nina answered in a tone I recognized immediately as her impatient voice.

Waving to me as she backed away, she smiled and nearly melted my heart. "See you."

I nodded, remembering not to take my hands out of my pockets and to keep my eyes squinted, watching her walk away with the makings for her chocolate martini and Varo. Even after I couldn't see her anymore, I stood there waiting to hear the jingle of bells on the door when she left, grabbing her note she'd placed on the shelf and a bottle of Lagavulin when the coast was clear and confusing the clerk when I paid with a couple fifties.

By the time I got back to what I was now calling home, I was sick of being judged by everyone I met and in need of a good stiff drink. Two glasses of scotch later, I sat back against my cheap couch and replayed my meeting with Nina at the liquor store, loving that of all the people I'd encountered that day, only she'd been truly kind to me.

As I nodded off to sleep, all I could hope for was that my time away from her wouldn't last much longer. I didn't want to be a stranger anymore.

Chapter Nine

Tristan

Over the next week, my contacts came in but I saw little of Nina. I tried to get a glimpse of her whenever I was close to the house, but she never seemed to be in any of the rooms I could see into. I saw Varo quite often, usually walking back to the carriage house or hanging out with West on the grounds near where he used to live. He paid little attention to me, which could have been attributed to either Daryl telling him about my real identity or his lack of interest in me since I was just a mute gardener.

I didn't care which it was since a ball of hate for him inside me grew larger by the second. It was irrational and it didn't matter. I hated him for being able to come and go in Nina's life as he pleased while I stood there pretending to care about the shape of the fucking hedges on my property or how long the damn grass should be.

One sunny morning, eight days after our chance meeting at the liquor store, she came walking down the pathway to where I stood cleaning up weeds against the fence on the property line. I didn't remember her ever coming out this way when we were together, but I was thrilled all the same. Any time I got to spend with her was better than any without her.

As I watched her make her way toward me, she waved and smiled broadly, looking truly happy to see me. I loved it, but then the fear that she'd found me out raced through my mind, and I stood frozen on the spot waiting to hear what she had to say.

She stopped in front of me and waved again as she said, "Hi!"

I smiled and waved back, putting down the weed whacker.

Then she spoke the sweetest words I'd heard in months. "I don't know much sign language, but I've been reading up on it to learn some." That she coupled that one sentence with an attempt to sign what she meant made me happier than I thought I could be still separated from her.

Even if I wanted to, I couldn't have stopped myself from smiling. Knowing I had to contain my joy at her kindness, I signed back *Thank you* and then finger spelled *M-i-s-s E-d-w-a-r-d-s.*

Her eyes focused on my right hand as I spelled out her name, and she looked up at me with a quizzical look. Shaking her head, she said, "You're too fast. What did you spell?"

I spelled out Miss Edwards slower this time, and she nodded her understanding. "Can you read lips?" she asked staring up at me with a look of hope in her eyes.

Wobbling my right hand to indicate I could read them a little, she finger spelled O-K with two letters, obviously thrilled that she knew how to do at least that correctly. She was too cute, but I still put up the OK sign nearly everyone in the world knew, making her blush at her mistake.

"Oh. I guess I should have known that."

All I could do was smile at how adorable she was. But why did she bother to come all the way out here and why had she taken the time to learn some sign language?

We stood there looking at one another until I signed, *Why did you come here to see me?*

She recognized the why and the see me parts and an uneasy look crossed her face as she shifted her weight from one foot to the other. Signing the words with effort, she answered, *I wanted to say I'm sorry for how I acted that day I met you.*

I touched the tips of my fingers to the center of my forehead and pulled my hand forward and down into the letter Y to sign the question *Why?* as I shook my head to let her know she didn't have to apologize.

Opening her mouth to speak, she shrugged instead. Looking back toward the house, she signed, *How do you get here every day?*

I pointed to my legs and smiled. In truth, I hadn't walked as much in years as I did now. Not that I liked it. I'd have taken the Jag over my feet any day.

Signing, she asked, *Do you live near here?*

Again, I didn't sign but pointed, this time toward the village that sat less than a mile from where we stood.

"Do you live in Millbrook? Have you ever had Tony's pizza?" she asked, forgetting to sign in her excitement.

I pretended not to know what she'd just said, secretly thrilled that the idea of Millbrook immediately made her think of where she'd agreed to marry me. She finger spelled the name of our favorite restaurant and looked up at me in anticipation.

Nodding, I smiled and signed, *Good.*

I love their pizza! she signed with excitement, getting the finger spelling for pizza wrong, but it didn't matter. I was in heaven just listening to her speak.

Unfortunately, Varo made his appearance right at that moment, interrupting what had been the best fifteen minutes in a long time. Just as he had at the liquor store, he marched up behind her, his brows knitted and his expression looking almost too protective as he informed her it was time to go. I enjoyed watching her brush him off with a quick "Okay" and loved that she didn't make any effort to follow him, as he obviously wanted her to.

Needing to know how she felt about him, I probed with the question, *Is that your fiancé?*

She looked back in the direction of Varo and then focused on me. I watched as her eyes welled up with tears, and then she finger spelled, *N-o. M-y f-i-a-n-c-é i-s T-r-i-s-t-a-n.* She stopped signing and looked away to wipe a tear from her cheek, but quietly said, "I hope you get to meet him soon."

I promise it won't be long, Nina. I promise.

Obviously, Daryl hadn't explained to her that she needed to pretend Varo was her man even at home. That she didn't pretend here made me feel better. I still didn't like Daryl's plan, but Nina's willingness to share the identity of her fiancé with me, someone she barely knew and merely worked for her, told me my fears about her with anyone else were based in my stupid jealousy and nothing more.

She looked past me again toward the house and smiled. "This is a lot of property for just one gardener. Do you think I should hire someone to help you?"

As I shook my head to let her know I didn't understand what she'd said, she stared up at me, as if she was studying my face for the real answer. Something told me she wasn't sure about the man she'd hired to handle her gardening.

"Ethan, I just realized other than knowing you're Ethan Cole, I don't know anything else about you."

Her tone possessed a sharp edge, but she didn't sign her words. She was trying to catch me lying. Always my Nina, she hid a great brain behind those innocent blue eyes and gentle smile.

I shook my head and signed *I don't know what you're saying* to indicate I hadn't been able to lip read her words, stifling my smile at her cleverness.

With great effort, she signed what she'd just said, and I signed in return, *Ask me anything.*

She signed *How old are you?* and looked more like Daryl tugging on his beard as he thought about some great question than making the sign to ask how old I was.

Before I could think about my answer, I signed the number 29 and my eyes grew wide at my slip up. I really should have been better at lying by now, but just being around her made all my defenses melt away. My age being the same as her fiancé's didn't seem to register with her, though, and she simply smiled.

Do you like gardening? she asked, fumbling over the sign for gardening and making it look more like a dog scratching for fleas than her fingers raking over her left palm.

I nodded, which was a complete lie. To be honest, I couldn't wait for the moment I wasn't Ethan Cole, mute and deaf gardener. Every night I waited for Daryl to call and let me know that he'd finally figured out the secret of what Karl wanted so I could finally return to my life as Tristan Stone and the woman I loved.

You're doing a nice job, she continued, this time doing much better with her signing.

Thanking her, I added, *And thank you for learning to sign. You're very thoughtful.*

In front of me, Varo stood about twenty yards away impatiently yelling Nina's name. She didn't even bother to turn around to answer him, preferring to stay facing me.

"Time for me to take the stage," she said without signing.

Shaking my head, I shrugged to let her know I didn't understand.

Smiling, she signed, *It's nothing. Just my pretend life.* Nina turned to leave and stopped short to sign one more thing. *Have a good day, E-t-h-a-n.*

It wasn't what she signed but that I got to hear her speak those sweet words, even if her voice was tinged with unhappiness. I hated knowing what I'd convinced her to do was making her miserable, but I had to tell myself that it was what had to be done.

That didn't make it any better, though.

She walked away, her pace a little slower than when she'd approached me, I thought. My mind immediately began to spin out of control thinking about where they were going, what they'd be doing, and how I'd be standing there raking. Taking a deep breath, I told myself I couldn't let that affect me. This was the way it had to be, and that was that.

By six o'clock, I hadn't seen Nina or either of her bodyguards return home, so I left, needing a hot shower and something in my stomach. I had a newfound appreciation for the people who'd worked on my family's properties. I'd always been so spoiled that I never once considered what their lives were like. Where did they live? Where did they eat lunch? What did they do when they weren't landscaping the gardens or cleaning up after my family and me? My stint as Ethan the gardener had made all those people who'd been invisible to me for all those years suddenly come into sharp focus. To say that I didn't like what I saw was an understatement.

It's not that Nina or anyone at the house mistreated me. Quite the opposite, in fact. Nina was welcoming, and although Varo and West weren't altogether friendly, they weren't nasty or rude. I was, however, invisible there, for all practical purposes. Unlike in my life as Tristan Stone, no one wanted to spend time with me for meals or clamored to hear what I had to say about anything.

The change in my status was enlightening, to say the least.

Standing in the shower, I let the water sluice over me, loving the feel of its stinging heat on my skin. Working as a gardener was much harder work than I'd ever believed, and my body already showed the signs of its effects. Muscles that had atrophied for months when I was in exile now grew again, the result of hours of manual labor. I hadn't seen a gym in nearly half a year, but I couldn't remember my body being in better shape. Those muscles didn't come easily, though, and the hot water only did so much to ease the ache of my day job.

Scotch did the rest.

I relaxed on the couch and put my feet up on the coffee table, groaning as I stretched the tired muscles in my legs. A slice of Tony's pizza filled my stomach, and I washed it down with a gulp of scotch. Not exactly the right pairing, but I'd forgotten to ask for soda when I placed the order. It wouldn't have been the same, anyway. Tony's was great not because it was the best pizza in the world but because it symbolized something far better I shared only with Nina.

My phone vibrated across the top of the table, signaling I had a message. It was the one Nina used, and my heart leaped in my chest at the thought of what she might say. Scooping the phone up, I read her message and instantly felt like someone had my heart in a vice, turning the handle until there was nothing but the purest pain I'd ever experienced.

I miss you. I've taken to talking to almost complete strangers because I'm so lonely. Please come back to me.

Fuck. How was I supposed to keep this up? She was tearing me apart. All I wanted to do was text back that I wasn't that far away. That I was as lonely as she was and missed her more than I could say.

Daryl's telltale banging on my door shook me from my misery, and I trudged my aching feet and legs over to let him in, ready for him to add to my shitty moment.

"Nice to see you, Tristan. I hope you saved some of that drink for me," he announced as he brushed past me to take a seat on the old chair that filled out the living room set he'd gotten me.

"Tell me you have something, Daryl. I can't do this for much longer. Nina's texts are killing me. She's miserable, and I'm the reason she's miserable."

Grabbing my bottle of Lagavulin, he looked around for something to pour his drink into. "Get me a glass, would you? I've been working all day. I need this."

I found a glass in the kitchen cabinet and returned to hand it to him. "You're work is nothing like mine, I'm willing to bet. I ache all over."

He poured himself a healthy glass of scotch and sat back in the chair, grinning broadly. "Never did an honest day of work in your life, did you? Now you know how the other half lives."

Seated across from him, I watched him relish my physical pain and admitted he was right. I hadn't worked like this ever before in my life. "Yeah, but can we get to how we're going to get me back to my real life?"

"Right. I spent the last few days working on this Cordovex business. I still don't know what I'm looking at, but I can say without a doubt that whatever it is, it's buried under intentional layers meant to keep prying eyes out."

"Do we know yet if it has anything to do with my family or Stone Worldwide? I'm worried you're chasing shadows and wasting time when we could be much closer to finding out what Karl wants if we focused on something else."

"Like what?"

Shrugging, I silently admitted I didn't know. It just seemed too far-fetched to believe that some heart drug had anything to do with Karl or the reason why he wanted me and Nina out of the picture. "So what did you find out?"

Daryl took another swig of his drink and set the glass down on the table a little too heavily. The man was just clumsy. His lack of grace made me laugh, confusing him.

"Cordovex is a prescription heart drug, but it had a rough time of it after getting FDA approval. Seems it was killing some people. From what I can tell, it shouldn't have gotten approval, but somehow it made it through the process in record time."

"How's it doing today, four years later?"

"That's an interesting question. You know how it's doing, or at least you should know. If you've watched TV at any time in the past few months, you've seen ads for it."

"I haven't seen any commercials for anything called Cordovex."

"Yes, you have."

"No, I haven't. Stop talking in riddles, Daryl."

"All right. Well, from what I can make out, Cordovex has been resurrected as Cardiell now. Ring any bells?"

Not that I had watched much TV in the past few months, but even the little I'd seen had been peppered with advertisements for Cardiell. Smiling middle aged men and women actively pursuing life and all its wonders were the hallmark of every Cardiell ad. They were slick and looked like they'd cost a fortune to produce, easily convincing sick people desperate for help with a heart problem that the drug was the answer to all their concerns.

"Who makes Cardiell?"

"A pharmaceutical company named Rider Pharmaceutical, but there's a problem. I checked out Rider and it's a front—nobody seems to actually work for Rider. There's no physical address for the company. Some other company is the parent, but that's going to take a little more digging."

I grabbed my laptop from the end of the couch and began searching for the company's website. What came up in my search was a site as slick and well-produced as their commercials, complete with success stories and implied promises drug makers always included. At the bottom of the page, Rider Pharmaceutical was given as the maker of the drug, but it was a facade hiding the true business that produced Cardiell.

Daryl leaned over to look at the screen. "Nice site, isn't it? They spared no expense to make it look professional and welcoming, except for the fact that it's meaningless."

"How can a drug that was killing people a few years ago be back on the market with just a new name and some new fancy site?"

Daryl shook his head. "I have no idea. Makes you wonder about the drugs we all take, doesn't it? Give me a few more days and I think I can find what company is behind Cardiell. Then we'll know if it's something or not, but my guess is that we're going to find this is what Karl is worried about."

"Fine, but I can't wait much longer. Every time Nina texts me, I want to run across that field, jump the fence, and march right up to the house to find her. I don't want to do this to her anymore."

Standing from his chair, Daryl gave me his best "I'm working on it" look, but I saw in his eyes he didn't understand what Nina and I were going through. "Give me a couple days. That's all I think I'll need."

"Fine, but no matter what you find out, I'm going home after those couple days. This can't go on."

Rolling his eyes, he left mumbling under his breath about young lovers or something else he didn't understand. At least now I could tell myself there was an end to this whole thing. Whatever happened, Nina and I would be together soon. That's all that mattered.

Chapter Ten

Nina

An afternoon of pretending to have the hots for my bodyguard had left me feeling like a wrung out dishrag. While Gage seemed to be taking on the part of my boyfriend as if it were second nature, I still struggled with our fake relationship. In fact, instead of getting easier to act like he was the man I wanted, it was getting harder each time he and I had to parade in front of the press looking like two young love-birds. Guilt did that to me.

I knew it wasn't his fault, but I took it out on him anyway. In just a short time, what had been a budding friendship between us had morphed into something full of resentment for me. Gage wasn't to blame, but it didn't matter. Every moment I spent with him in front of the world playacting was a moment I betrayed Tristan. Each loving gaze and touch of his hand on mine filled me with guilt and added to my shame over kissing him in my bedroom.

He saw it too. It was in the way I had to stop myself from glaring when we were in public or wouldn't look at him when we were alone in the car after our public displays. I nearly oozed contempt for him.

This was a great plan to Daryl, but to me it was torture. Thankfully, at least it seemed to be working. Karl hadn't made any attempt to reach me, so perhaps it was all worth it, but every night when I laid my head on the pillow next to Tristan's, I hated myself for what the world thought. One mention of Gage and me on Page Six after our first outing called us "Cinderella and Her New Prince." The implication wasn't lost on me—I was nothing but a poor working girl before meeting Tristan and now that he was gone, I'd taken no time at all in replacing him with another man.

Nothing like being seen as a heartless, disloyal bitch by everyone who read Page Six.

Skipping dinner, I headed for my room to curl up in a ball and dream about a time, hopefully in the near future, when Tristan and I were happily married, living in this house without bodyguards, maybe even with a baby. Would that time ever come? On nights like this, as I lay alone missing him like a part of myself was absent, I doubted we'd ever truly be together again. So much had happened since the last time we were in each other's arms. Would we still be the same two people we were then?

I slid out of bed and made my way to his closet. Part of my nightly routine, I slipped one of his dress shirts from its hanger and held it to my nose. Even months after the last time it was against his skin, it smelled like him. Closing the closet doors, I completed the next part of my ritual and took a strong breath of his cologne that still sat next to his sink in the bathroom. Musky, woodsy, and slightly floral, it was all Tristan.

No one on Earth knew I did this every night. I hid each shirt until there were enough for a full wash and ran the load by myself when it was ready instead of letting Maria see my pathetic madness. It was okay. I knew it was crazy to do these things. Maybe I was going mad because I thought it was all right to sniff someone's clothes and cologne, but I'd heard that smell was one of the strongest senses when it came to memories. The vision of something might slip someone's mind, and a voice may be forgotten, but a smell associated with the past could bring it right back, closing the space of time and distance.

Climbing into bed, I leaned back against the headboard and with my phone in hand, completed my nightly ritual with a text to Tristan. *Is it night where you are? I'm in bed, even though it's barely 7. I miss you more every day. New people come into my life but still no you. I've begun learning sign language to speak to the new gardener. I'm sure you know about him from Daryl. I think he's a relative of his. They have similar beards.*

I read over my text and lightly snorted a chuckle. It sounded like a crazy person wrote it. That was okay. It wasn't like I'd get an answer anyway. The texting just made me feel like I still had Tristan's ear, except now he spoke even less than usual.

Clicking Send, I waited as I always did for a message back, but none came. It never surprised me but instead just added a tiny new layer of disappointment to everything else I'd felt for months. As I did occasionally, I added a text to Jordan in the hopes that she'd answer back. She never did anymore, but it was always worth a shot.

Hey you! I hope this finds you doing great. I'd love to hear what you're up to these days. Nina.

When no text came back after twenty minutes, I stopped staring at the phone and covered my head with the sheet, preferring to hide away and hope that tomorrow would be a better day.

Not an hour after waking up, I knew my wish for a better day had been shot to hell. I'd barely gotten out of the shower and Daryl was knocking at my bedroom door like the house was burning down. I quickly tied a towel around me and threw open the door, a combination of irritation and dread coursing through me.

"What? What do you need from me now that requires the damn banging on my door before ten o'clock in the goddamned morning?" I barked at his shocked face.

"I just wanted to remind you about the Stone Foundation groundbreaking today. As the appointed representative of the foundation, you need to be there."

I took a deep breath and adjusted the knot in my towel so I didn't give Daryl a show right there in the hallway. "It doesn't seem like poor form to you to have me attend a Stone Foundation function with Gage right at my elbow?"

I wanted to go to this groundbreaking of the newest Stone Foundation center in Poughkeepsie like I wanted someone to break off my right arm and beat me with it. Tristan's family had established a foundation to help local food banks across the country when he was a small child, and since the plane crash, he'd been the representative of the foundation. With his disappearance, somehow I'd been chosen as the one person to attend functions, even if I stuck out like a sore thumb around all those well-dressed men and women there to ironically celebrate helping starving people each of whom could probably live an entire year on one of their fur coats.

Daryl twisted his face into an expression that told me he was considering what I'd said. "Fair enough. Maybe you should do this without him as the boyfriend, but he and West will still be there as your bodyguards."

At least I didn't have to perform my rendition of the whore of Babylon again. That was something.

"Fine. What time do I have to be ready?"

"The groundbreaking is at eleven, and the luncheon is at noon."

"Do I have to attend both? I'm not really what people want at these kinds of things anyway."

Nodding, Daryl agreed with me for the second time that morning. "No. I think you can leave after the groundbreaking ceremony."

"Thanks. Do me a favor and tell everyone I'll be ready to go in a little while," I said quietly as I closed the door on Daryl and all the responsibilities of the world.

A half hour later, I'd transformed myself into the well-dressed representative of the Stone Foundation, complete with charcoal grey designer suit, black pumps, and hair up in a bun. Whenever I dressed like this, I felt like an actor in a costume. I wasn't a suit kind of woman, especially these days when I spent more time in yoga pants than in anything else. However, this was what was expected, so this was what I wore.

I saw by the looks on my bodyguards' faces that they were surprised by my look too, but unlike when Gage and I pretended to be together, I said nothing, preferring not to discuss the performance I had to give today. It seemed like I was constantly acting these days. If it wasn't trying to convince the world that I'd moved on, it was trying to make everyone around me believe that I wasn't falling apart a little more every day Tristan stayed away.

All this acting was exhausting.

Hiding behind big sunglasses, I smiled for the camera as a group of men in suits symbolically dug gold shovels into the ground for the new center, and then I quickly tried to escape the entire affair. As I stepped back into the shadows behind a tree and away from the throng of people who loved occasions like this mingling on the lawn, I ran into a woman and her son I'd noticed when I arrived. They were obviously out of place, dressed in clean but inexpensive clothes that looked nothing like what any of the other attendees wore, including myself. The mother appeared to be in her thirties, but I couldn't be sure because her face was wrinkled far more than most women's that age. Her dark blonde hair was brushed back into a barrette clipped at her nape, and she wore a navy blue pantsuit and black flats. The little boy couldn't have been more than six or seven, and he wore dress clothes, which looked completely out of place on him.

I apologized for bumping into the woman and saw the hollow look in her pale blue eyes. Instantly, I knew what she was there for. She and her son were to be the day's poster children for the success of the Stone Foundation. Cleaned up from what her life was in reality, she was there to act as much as I was.

Looking down at her son, I smiled. "What's your name, little man?"

"Michael," he said sweetly. "Michael Williams."

"It's nice to meet you, Michael. Are you having a good time?"

"Yeah. We're going to have lunch soon," he said with a grin, proudly showing off the space where his missing front tooth used to be.

I lifted my head and smiled at his mother. "Thank you for coming. The Stone Foundation appreciates it."

She smiled at me and extended her hand to shake mine. "Thank you. I'm Gloria Williams. My son and I are thankful for all the help your foundation has given us. We're getting back on our feet now, and it's the help of the people with the Stone Foundation that's made that possible."

I didn't know why, but I felt the need to tell her the truth about how much the foundation wasn't mine. "It's actually my fiancé's family's foundation. I'm sure he'd be happy to see that it was doing the work it was meant to."

"Please tell him thank you for us."

I smiled at the thought of telling Tristan anything. "I promise I will."

A hand gently touched my shoulder, and I turned to tell Gage that I was fine and didn't need to be rescued from this woman and her son.

I knew he was just doing his job, but neither of these kind souls were a danger to me in any way. Ready to chase him away, I saw instead Karl Dreger standing there looking down at me, one eyebrow arched and making his expression sinister looking. His snakelike eyes peering out of his large head instantly terrified me.

"It's lovely to see you again, Nina. When do you think you'll be able to tell your fiancé about the good work the foundation is doing?"

Swallowing hard, I struggled to form any real answer to Karl's question, my mouth suddenly too dry to allow my tongue to work. Everything we'd done—all the playacting and being seen by the press that had made me feel like a traitor to the man I loved—all of it had been for nothing.

Gage swooped in to whisk me away seconds later, acting more like a lover than a bodyguard and saying something about looking forward to when we got home, but it was too late. I'd ruined everything with my stupid slip up.

By the time we reached the car, I could barely hold back the tears. Gage tried to follow me into the back seat as Jensen started the engine, but I pushed him away.

"Nina, I should be seen leaving with you so people keep believing we're together."

"No!" I cried as I tried to close the door. "It doesn't matter now. I've fucked it all up. Karl knows I'm not with you and Tristan isn't gone for good."

"It doesn't matter what he thinks. We need to keep up the act," Gage protested as I continued to tug on the car door.

"Let me go! It's over now!" I screamed, forcing him to back away enough to allow me to grab the door from him and slam it shut. Slumping back against the seat, I closed my eyes as the tears began to roll down over my cheeks and sobbed, "Jensen, please take me home. I want to go home."

As he raced over the roads of Dutchess County, I texted Tristan the bad news. *I'm sorry I messed up. I didn't mean to. Wherever you are, please know I love you and never meant to ruin everything. I'm sorry.*

For the first time in all of this, I was scared.

I expected to see Daryl waiting for me when I got back to the house, but there was no one except Ethan who stood trimming the shrubs on the side of the house near my bedroom. Even though I had no idea why, I was drawn to where he was, needing to talk to someone about all the emotions tearing through me after my encounter with Karl. I knew it was ridiculous. He couldn't even hear me, but it didn't matter. Maybe it was better he couldn't hear what I had to say.

He watched me as I walked toward where he stood, putting down his clippers when I stopped in front of him. For a moment, he looked confused, but then he just smiled and I could have sworn he reminded me of Tristan.

God, I was losing my fucking mind.

Signing, I asked, *Do you mind if I sit here with you while you work?*

He shook his head and smiled again. Very slowly, he finger spelled, *T-h-i-s i-s y-o-u-r h-o-u-s-e.*

It was. Actually, without Tristan, it felt more like my prison than my house. I still loved it for the memories we'd made here, but now it felt empty without him.

Like me.

Ethan signed *Do you want to talk?* and I shook my head. I did want to talk, but the one person I wanted to talk to was nowhere to be found.

He didn't seem to know what to do, so he just stared down at me until he signed, *How was the g-r-o-u-n-d-b-r-e-a-k-i-n-g?*

All of a sudden, the real fear that I was standing in front of someone spying for Karl exploded into my brain. That would explain how he'd known I'd be at the groundbreaking that morning. I hadn't attended any Stone Foundation functions in months. Why would he think I'd be at the one today?

"How did you know where I was?" I asked, forgetting to sign until I saw the confused look on his face. I asked him again through sign language and watched as he signed, *One of your bodyguards told me.*

There was something wrong now that I stood there with Ethan. Daryl might believe he was okay, but I didn't. Signing, I said, *Take off your glasses, please. I want to see your eyes.* I needed to see exactly who this person was who seemed to know things about me.

He seemed reluctant to do as I ordered, so I told him again what I wanted. Slowly, he slid them off his face and squinted as his eyes adjusted to the sun. I studied them for a long moment, sure I'd seen eyes like his before but unable to remember where. They were a deep blue color, but not dark like Gage's. If he didn't have such a scruffy beard, I imagined Ethan would be quite attractive, even though his hair was much longer than I liked.

That didn't mean I felt any less uncomfortable about him, though. I couldn't put my finger on it, but there was something about him now that made me question why Daryl had made such a point of my firing Chip in favor of this guy.

All sorts of terrible thoughts swirled in my mind. Was Daryl the one who'd told Karl I'd be at the groundbreaking? Had he been keeping Tristan and me apart all this time? Was Tristan even safe, wherever he was, as Daryl had continually claimed all these months?

Ethan signed something, but I couldn't understand any of what he said and left to find Daryl to get some answers. I found him waiting for me in the dining room, looking like he always did as I stormed in, ready to demand he tell me exactly what the hell was going on.

"Nina, I heard what happened. You should have let Gage come with you."

Pointing my finger at him, I barked, "You better start explaining what the fuck is up, Daryl. How would Karl know I'd be there? Something's pretty fishy about all of this. I want to know where Tristan is right now!"

"You know I can't do that, Nina. I have no idea how Karl knew, but I'd never put you or Tristan in danger."

He wasn't going to tell me anything more than that, so I left to go back to Ethan and see if he was easier to crack than his friend. I found the hedge clippers on the ground next to the shrubs, but he was gone. Looking around, I spied him walking quickly across the lawn toward the property's edge.

Where the hell was he going?

I took off after him, hampered by three inch heels and the ridiculous suit I still wore. His much longer stride made catching him impossible, but at least I was able to see him. I thanked God we hadn't seen much rain recently as my heels barely sank into the still solid ground that in late April hadn't forgotten the cold of winter quite yet.

He walked right off the property through a hole in the fence, and I followed him into a field full of much higher grass and weeds. His pace never slowed down, so by the time I found myself in Millbrook, my stockings were torn and my suit was covered in thorns and pickers.

Why he was going home in the middle of the day I had no idea, but I fully intended on finding out. I watched as he entered an old building, presumably his apartment building, breaking into a full run so I didn't lose him. Following him up the wood stairs, I saw him enter a door at the end of the hallway and stopped to catch my breath.

When I finally could breathe normally again, I brushed off my clothes and marched myself down to his apartment. I stood at his door, my hand ready to knock, when I realized he wouldn't be able to hear me. Reaching into my purse, I found one of Tristan's letters to me and tore off a piece of the envelope. But what was I supposed to write? Hi Ethan, I followed you and would really like you to open the door and I promise I'm not a crazy stalker seemed wrong.

Finally, after lurking in front of his door for almost five minutes, I wrote what I hoped wouldn't make me seem like a crazy woman. *Please open the door. It's Nina. I need to talk to you, Ethan.* Crouching down on the old wood floor in his hallway, I slid the torn piece of envelope under his door and waited, hoping he didn't call the police.

He didn't wait long to open the door, and I saw immediately that he looked nervous. Signing, I tried to assure him that I didn't want to bother him. I just wanted to talk. He let me in and quickly pushed by me to clean up the things on his coffee table and a laptop on his couch. Taking a seat on an old chair, I signed, *Please forgive me for following you to your house. I need to ask you a question.*

Nodding, he smiled, so I asked, *How did Daryl find you to be my gardener?*

Ethan finger spelled that Daryl knew he was looking for a job and thought he'd be perfect. That told me nothing, so I asked, *But how do you know him?*

He gave me a tiny smile and signed, *That's two questions.*

In a flash, the memory of when Tristan said that same thing to me that first night on our ride out to the house flooded through my mind and before I could stop myself, I was sitting there in my gardener's apartment crying like a baby. I couldn't do this anymore. Being without Tristan was breaking my heart and I was falling apart.

When I finally stopped crying, I tried to explain what the hell was wrong with me, but all I did was ramble on about missing the man I loved, not that it mattered since I was talking and didn't even bother to try to sign all the messed up shit that was coming out of my mouth.

"I'm sorry. You must think I'm crazy. I'm not. Or maybe I am. I must be since I'm sitting here in your living room bawling my eyes out over something you said that probably shouldn't mean anything to me, but it does."

I wiped the tears from my cheeks and continued to explain my bizarre behavior. "You see, my fiancé said something like you just said the first night I met him, and I miss him so much. I don't know where he is or even if he's okay. He hasn't contacted me in months, except for the other day to tell me to do something that broke my heart to do. I'd hoped he'd message me after I did what he wanted, but there was nothing. I just don't think I can do this anymore."

The tears began flowing again, and before I knew it, I was sobbing with my head in my hands as poor Ethan stood there probably thinking he should run away or at least call the authorities to have me committed. I couldn't stop crying once I started this time, even when I thought I heard someone say my name. I was losing my mind, after all.

"Nina, honey, stop crying."

I had heard someone say my name. Dropping my hands from my face, I looked up to see my gardener standing over me speaking instead of signing. He looked like he always did wearing jeans, a long sleeve T-shirt, and work boots, but his eyes weren't the blue they'd always been. Now they were that unmistakable color of melted milk chocolate I'd only ever seen in one person.

Tristan.

Staring up at the man who stood in front of me, I sobbed, "Please tell me it's you. Tell me I'm not losing my mind. I don't think I can handle it if you're a dream or some kind of mirage."

"It's me, Nina."

I drank in the vision of the man I adored finally standing in front of me again after so long. "Oh, my God! Tristan, it's you!"

Hyperventilating, I was unable to control my emotions any longer. His voice washed over me like a refreshing rain, quenching my heart and soul so long mired in drought from his absence. He knelt down in front of me and looked up into my eyes with those beautiful brown eyes I'd missed so much, whispering, "I'm sorry, Nina. I didn't mean to hurt you."

"Oh, Tristan, I've missed you so much," I cried as I wrapped my arms around his neck and drew him to me.

"Don't cry," he whispered in my ear. "It's okay. No more being apart. I promise."

After all those months without him, just the feel of his arms around me, holding me tight, made all sadness fade away and for the first time in so long, I was happy.

Chapter Eleven

Tristan

Nina sat trembling in my arms, quietly sobbing as she clung to me. Every so often, she'd try to pull back away from me to say something, but I didn't want to let go. It had been so long since I'd held her in my arms that I was afraid if I let her go again, I might never get her back. I'd made that mistake once. I wouldn't make it again.

Quietly, she whispered against my chest, "Tristan, I came here because I blew it today. Everything we worked all this time for is ruined. I'm sorry. I didn't mean to screw up. I had no idea Karl was standing behind me at the groundbreaking. He heard me say I'd tell you something. He knows you're not gone for good."

I lifted her chin and kissed her tenderly on the lips. Pressing my forehead to hers, I tried to reassure her. "It's okay. We'll handle Karl. I'm just glad that's what you meant in your text."

She leaned back and studied me for a minute. "What did you think I meant?"

It tore me up to admit what had crossed my mind when I read her message. "I thought you meant something happened between you and Varo."

Nina hung her head for a moment, making me think my paranoid worrying about her with another man hadn't been so paranoid, after all. Lifting her head to look at me, she cupped my cheeks and smiled. "I would never do that. Not with Varo. Not with Cal. Not with anyone. You're the only man for me, even if I don't like this beard one bit."

"No love for the beard?"

"Yeah, it needs to go," she said with a chuckle. "You remind me too much of Daryl this way."

"Then it definitely needs to go."

Her smile faded, and before I could ask what was wrong, she slapped my face so hard tears came to my eyes. "That's for leaving me here all alone for months. You asked me to promise I'd never run, and then you did."

"Jesus, Nina!" After a minute, the shock wore off. "You're right," I admitted sheepishly as I rubbed the sting out of my cheek.

Nina narrowed her eyes to slits and pointed her finger at me. "You're lucky I love you, Tristan Stone. Other women would have taken all that you gave me and when you didn't come back after a few days would have jumped on the nearest good looking guy around, which incidentally is the man you and Daryl have had me pretending to play house with."

"Don't remind me. You should know I never liked the idea anyway."

"That makes two of us. I'm not sure I can forgive you for making me kiss Gage in front of all those photographers."

"Gage?" I asked, my jealousy quickly ratcheting up.

"Well, you didn't expect me to stay on a last name basis with the man I'm supposedly having great sex with and quickly falling madly in love with, did you?"

I sighed, angry with every part of the situation Daryl's grand plan had created. Not at Nina, though. I was to blame if she had any feelings for the bodyguard. That didn't make it any easier, though. "So you and Gage are close?"

"We're as close as you wanted us to be, Tristan."

"What does that mean?"

A gentle smile spread across her lips, and her eyes grew wide. "I think you're jealous, Mr. Stone."

"You're playing with me, aren't you? Fine. I have it coming. You know how I get, though. Varo will be lucky to have a job tomorrow if you keep this up."

Nina sat back in her seat. "So now you're jealous? Not when you had me kiss him so everyone in the world could see?"

"Are you done yet?" I asked, tempering my anger.

"Will you promise never to leave me again like you did?"

"Absolutely."

She leaned forward to kiss me sweetly. "Then I'm done." Nina sat silently for a long moment, staring into my eyes, before she said,

"Hmmm. What do you think about me running out for some razors, shaving cream, Tony's pizza, and the flattest birch beer in the world?"

"I think this is exactly the reason I'm so madly in love with you. Call for the pizza and I'll wash off the grime from my half-day as a gardener."

I stood to head into the shower, but she pulled me back down, smiling a wicked grin. "In a minute. First, I think it's about time my soon-to-be husband gave me a proper hello after months of being away."

Leaning in, I kissed her for the first time in so long it felt like our first kiss that night after I'd taught her how to tie a Windsor knot. Every inch of my body felt alive like it hadn't in so long. I'd let myself get used to being alone and forgotten how much I truly needed Nina.

Far too soon, she pulled away and shook her head. "That beard has to go. It's picky."

"So much for our reunion," I joked. "A slap across the face and not even a decent kiss for your long lost man."

"Back to Plan A. You get in the shower, and I'll order the pizza. While I'm out, I'll get some razors and we'll get that gorgeous face of yours back to how it's supposed to look."

"Not without someone going with you, and that someone is me."

Raising her eyebrows, she gave me a look of disbelief. "Is that really necessary?"

"Karl came close enough to speak to you today, Nina. It's absolutely necessary."

"Fine. I'll tolerate the protective boyfriend thing for now."

I stood and smiled down at her. "You'll tolerate it until I become the protective husband. Are we clear?"

Grinning, she asked, "Where did the mild mannered gardener go to? I barely remember this man."

"Get used to him," I said as I walked toward the bathroom to clean up before we headed out. "He's back to claim his life and all that he's missed, and that includes you, Miss Edwards."

"Oooh, I do love it when you go all alpha on me," she said with a chuckle as I closed the door.

After an entire pizza and a two liter of birch beer that was strangely flat even though we weren't at Tony's, I sat back on the couch, more satisfied than I ever thought I could be there in my cheap apartment eating fast food. Nina leaned on me, softly humming some song, and I wished we'd never have to leave this spot that had become the most precious place on Earth since she arrived.

"What are you singing?"

Raising her head, she looked up at me. "A song my mother used to sing to me." She looked away and shook her head. "I think so, at least. Maybe it's just something I've dreamed up because I know so little about her."

The memories of the hours I'd spent in her father's storage unit surrounded by the only things left of Diana Edwards' life flooded back as I watched Nina's wistful expression. It was time I told her that I'd found some good in that ten by ten room.

Gently, I pushed her up until she sat next to me and I began. "I think I need to tell you some things. We've spent enough time with me hiding the past from you. I don't want to do that anymore." I saw the concern in her eyes and softly touched her shoulder. "For once, it's not bad."

"Oh? Well, I'm all ears then. I just don't think I could have handled hearing you say you had a wife you hadn't told me about or something like that," she said with a forced smile.

"No, it's nothing like that." I took a deep breath and continued. "I found your father's notebook in a safe deposit box, but he has a storage unit right outside Philly that I searched. I'm sorry I didn't tell you, but I was hoping that I could find out why my father had done what he did and bury that in the past and then someday take you to see the storage unit."

"A storage facility? I know nothing about this. Did Kim know?"

"I don't know. Your father stored your mother's things there after she died and visited it the last time just before his death. I think it might be nice if you took a look at what's there."

There was pain in her eyes as she smiled at me. "I've always wished I could know my mother better. My father never really wanted to talk about her after she died. I don't blame him. Losing the one you love is like losing a part of yourself. It hurts so much that you just want to curl up into a ball and push the world away."

I heard in her words that she wasn't just talking about losing her mother or father. She was talking about losing me all those months. Pulling her toward me, I wrapped my arms around her and whispered what I'd wanted to say since the first day away from her. "I'm sorry I left. I didn't think there was any other way. I didn't mean to hurt you, Nina. I thought you'd be safer without me around."

She sniffled once and then again, signaling she was crying. "I might have been safer, but I needed you and you weren't there. Then when Jordan left, for the first time in my life, I was alone. Every night I'd scroll through my messages to you, forcing myself to believe that you got every one and wanted to respond, even though you didn't."

I tilted her head back, cradling her face in my hands. "I did get every one and every time my phone vibrated, another piece of my heart was cut out knowing that you were unhappy. I know I fucked up, but I promise if you give me the chance, I'll be the man you deserve. Maybe not right now, but I won't give up until I've become that man."

Nodding, she smiled. "Okay."

"But you need to accept that life with me is going to be hard for a while. I stayed away because I'm a target. I don't know why yet, but Karl is playing some deadly game and I'm the prize. That means you're in danger too. We may have to leave home and hide out in places that are nothing like the hotels I own until Daryl and I figure out what's going on."

"I don't care how hard life is with you. All I know is it's impossible without you. You're the one I want to spend the rest of my life with, Tristan. So what if that means we have some rough times? Every couple faces those."

"Not every couple has to deal with someone wanting to kill them, Nina. I need you to understand that things could get rough. I've made sure that if anything happens to me, you're taken care of for the rest of your life. I promise you don't have to worry about that."

A look of horror crossed her face. Jumping to her feet, she cried, "Don't say that! I just got you back. I can't think of you being gone again."

Taking her hand, I looked up into those eyes so sad and worked to fix my blunder. "Baby, I wasn't saying I was going anywhere. I never want to leave you again. It's just that I need you to know I've taken care of everything."

"Well, now I need you to take care of me. Money and everything else you have don't mean a thing to me, Tristan. All I want—all I ever wanted—was you."

I stood and took her into my arms, nuzzling her neck. "I'm all yours, princess."

Squirming out of my hold, she pointed her finger at my face. "Good. Now that we got that straightened out, that beard has got to go. It's time to bring the real Tristan Stone back and put this Daryl twin in the past.

She pointed toward the bathroom, and I nodded. "Your wish is my command."

Thanks to a pair of scissors, after nearly a half hour, I was just about back to myself. All that was needed was a good shave and the real Tristan Stone would return. Nina sat on the edge of the bathtub watching me do my best gardener act on my beard and stood when I finished lathering my face with shaving cream.

Wrapping her arms around me, she whispered, "I've always had this fantasy of shaving a man. You up for making this one come true?"

She was so sexy standing there with one eyebrow arched and a cute twinkle in her eye that I couldn't say no. I followed her arm as she pointed to the toilet and sat down on the lid. "Have you at least watched someone do this? I don't want to bleed to death here in this tiny hole-in-the-wall apartment."

Razor in hand, she smiled down at me and winked. "You're talking to a woman who's shaved three-quarters of her body for years. Have faith. You're in good hands."

If there was anyone I could trust with a razor next to my throat it was Nina, so I angled my head up toward her. "I think this could be much sexier if you were doing this in that babydoll I bought you."

She gave me a sexy grin and licked her lips. "How about bra and panties? Does that work for you, Mr. Stone?"

"Ms. Edwards, I like the way you think."

She placed the disposable razor on the sink and turned her back to me as she slid her suit jacket off, flinging it out into the living room. Turning her head to look over her shoulder, she smiled. "I think this would be better with music."

Her skirt fell to the floor and I sang my best stripper song. "Ba-da-da-da, da-da-da-da." I ducked as her clothes flew toward my head, thrilled to see her standing there in just her bra and panties. And ripped stockings.

"You planning to leave those on? I mean, they might be sexy since they look like they go with a garter belt, but now they just look like some wild chipmunks attacked you."

Nina spun around and put her hand on her hip. "Well, maybe if my gardener hadn't led me through a jungle of picker bushes, I wouldn't look like this." Shaking her head, she looked at me sweetly and asked, "Not sexy enough?"

I left my perch and took her into my arms. "Baby, you're always sexy enough."

"Yeah, yeah. Now get back on the toilet so I can finish this shaving a hot guy fantasy of mine."

Taking my seat on the lid again, I muttered, "That's some sexy talk there. And I think you've become bossy in my absence, Ms. Edwards."

Nina smiled down at me as she ran the razor up my neck in a single long stroke. "Then maybe somebody needs to show me who the real boss is, Mr. Stone."

That was exactly what I fully intended on doing just as soon as she finished cleaning off months of hair from my face. I couldn't keep my hands off her she looked so hot standing there, the same Nina as she was that first night in mismatched bra and panties. Cupping her full ass, I struggled to control myself as she worked diligently to get rid of the rest of my beard.

"Tilt back," she ordered sweetly as she pushed my head back to shave over my Adam's Apple and under my chin. "When was the last time you shaved, Tristan? This beard is like wire."

"I had no reason to shave."

The simple truth that without her in my life I had no reason to care for myself enough to even shave stopped her hand's movement, and she gave me one of those gentle smiles that never failed to melt my heart.

"I love you, Tristan."

"Well, finish this and I'll show you how much I love you."

With a wink, she made quick work of the rest of my beard, only cutting me once or twice in her haste to get done, and in just minutes I was back to looking like myself again. I rinsed what remained of the shaving cream from my face and stared into the mirror to see the man I hadn't been since the night I left Nina.

"I missed this face," she said sweetly as she wrapped her arms around me from behind.

"This face missed you." Turning toward her, I kissed her deeply for the first time in what felt like forever. Her soft lips yielded to my eager mouth, desperate to taste her after being away for so long.

Fisting my hand in her hair, I tugged her head back, unable to wait any longer. I wanted her, right there in that tiny apartment bathroom. It wasn't lavish and it wasn't the type of reunion I'd dreamed of all those months, but it didn't matter. Nina was back in my arms.

That's all that mattered.

My hands slid over her petal soft shoulders and down her back to unclasp her bra. I threw it off to the side and lowered my head to take one deep pink nipple between my lips. Sucking it gently into my mouth, I reveled in the feel of its pebbled softness against my tongue. Nina moaned gently, and I bit down gently at the base of her nipple, remembering how excited it made her.

My gesture was rewarded with a gentle tug of my hair, and my cock throbbed at the sound of her sexy moan. Pulling away, I wrapped by arms around her hips and looked up at her to see her biting her lower lip. She was ready.

"Nina, I want you so fucking bad. Every night I was gone, I thought about this. I wanted this to be everything for us, but I don't think I can wait until we return to the house or one of the hotels."

Shaking her head, she smiled that sweet smile that never failed to do me in. "Tristan, it wouldn't matter where we were. Tiny apartment, grand hotel, our room at home—it doesn't matter as long as you're back with me."

She held out her hand, and I stood up and placed my hand in hers. "Tell me we can be what we used to be, Nina. It's the only fear I have—that I can't make up for the mistakes I made. Nothing else in this world terrifies me more than not being able to have you back. Truly back in every way."

Without a word, she walked out of the bathroom to the bedroom. When she finally turned around, I saw the answer in her eyes. She wasn't sure about us anymore.

"Tristan, I love you. I think I have since the first moment I saw you. It's just been so hard between us. And your leaving me alone for so long hurt more than you can ever understand. I want so much to trust that you won't go again. You say you want me back in your life, really back, but what does that mean?"

I pulled her close and held her to me as I opened my heart. "It means I want all of you. I want you to still walk down that aisle and be my wife. I want you by my side, no matter what. I want to be the man who makes the world a better place for you. I want to be the man who protects you." I stopped and looked deep into those blue eyes so full of uncertainty. "I want us to finally be happy in that house that meant nothing to me until the night you stepped foot in it."

"I can handle the not talking thing you do, Tristan. I get that you don't share what's inside you a lot. That's not what makes me doubt you love me. It's the hidden things, though. Not emotions or how you feel about me, but the secrets. I can't handle those."

"Nina, you know everything about me. That I don't like to talk a lot. The drugs. What my father and brother were. It's all out there—the bad and the ugly. I swear there's nothing else to know."

Frowning, she slowly shook her head. "That's not true, Tristan. There's more to you than that."

"I promise. There's nothing more, Nina."

Cupping my face, she looked up at me and shook her head again. "There's so much more to you than those things, and I'm not talking about the beautiful outside. You're good and kind, no matter what you want to think, and I love you. That's why it breaks my heart to even think of you leaving again."

I covered her hands with mine. "No more leaving. I can't promise it's always going to be perfect, but no more leaving."

None of what I said was a lie. I didn't want to leave her side ever again. Months away had made me realize I was nothing without her. I didn't want to hide anything from her anymore either. All the bad inside that had convinced me I'd never find anyone was exposed now, and she'd accepted me, even after she found out about what my family had done. Now I wanted to deserve her.

Nina pulled my face toward hers and kissed me softly. "Together, no matter what. That's all I needed to hear."

Pressing my forehead to hers, I whispered, "Together."

Her acceptance of who I was made me need her more than I'd ever believed I could need another person. Moaning her name, I lifted her onto the bed and gazed down at the perfect creature who'd agreed to be mine. Her legs opened slightly to allow me to slide her panties off her, leaving that beautiful cunt for my eyes to feast upon. I wanted to taste her, to slide my tongue over the tender skin between her legs and savor her juices as she came for me.

I nipped at her inner thigh, aching to be inside her but wanting to prolong our reunion. My cock pressed full against my belly, but now wasn't the time to plunge into her but to take my time and show her how much I adored her.

She moaned softly as with every kiss I inched closer to my goal. Her hands entwined in my hair, and she urged me to give her what she wanted. I softly placed a kiss where her leg met her body and whispered, "We have forever. No need to rush."

"But you're driving me crazy. Please don't make me wait," she begged in such a sexy voice that I nearly gave in.

I ran my tongue over the spot I'd just kissed. Looking up at her, my gaze met hers. "I never want this to end. I know it has to, so I'm going to make this last as long as possible. I want you to never forget this night."

She tilted her hips off the bed, tempting me to move faster, and I was lost. I covered her with my mouth, my tongue lapping against her clit as her hands pulled me into her. Her pussy, wet and needy, tasted so good on my tongue. Sliding one finger inside her, I reveled in how slick her cunt already was, ready and waiting for me to fill her.

Easing another finger into her, I pressed my fingertips against her tender walls, knowing the effect this caused in her. I wanted her to explode from my touch, drenching my fingers until my tongue replaced them to lick her tender folds until her body shook in ecstasy.

"Oh, God…please don't stop…" she groaned above me, her pleas making me want her even more. Her fingernails dug into my neck as her cunt tightened around my fingers, and in seconds, her release raged through her. Bucking and grinding against my mouth, she rode my tongue as if she depended on it for her very happiness.

Against her trembling pussy, I moaned, "Let yourself go, baby. Don't hold back."

She wrapped her legs around my neck, crushing my head between them until all I breathed was her. But I didn't care. If I died right there at that moment, I would have died a happy man. Her pleasure was everything.

When her body finally stopped shaking from her orgasm, I eased back onto my heels to look at her sated expression. Licking her lips, she smiled. "God, I've fantasized about that for months. I love that tongue of yours. You know that?"

I ran my finger up her moist slit to her swollen nub and grinned. "Then that must mean we're meant for each other because I love going down on you. See? A perfect match."

Crooking her finger, she said, "Come up here, and you should be naked already."

I slid up her body and kissed her hard on the mouth, my tongue snaking in and out to tease the tip of her tongue. Her fingers fumbled with my zipper, tearing at it as my cock ached to feel her touch. Finally past the last barrier between us, she tugged my pants down my thighs and wrapped her fingers around my stiff cock.

"No more waiting. I want you inside me," she whimpered as I ran the swollen head of my cock over her needy clit. "Please…Tristan, give me what I need."

Denying her was impossible, even if I wanted to, which I didn't. I wanted to devour her, to take everything she was into me so if I ever had to be without her again, I wouldn't suffer like I had for months. She silenced my demons and created new ones to take their place— new ones ten times as powerful that threatened to take me over now.

I needed her. I wanted her. I couldn't do without her.

I felt my control slipping away. With each touch of her hands on my body, she seared herself into me, stripping every defense I'd worked years to perfect from my mind until all that was left was her everywhere in my thoughts.

My mouth covered hers seeking the feel of her tongue against mine. I loved that mouth—that mouth that had questioned me so often with words that held me responsible for my actions. Those lips and tongue that brought my body pleasure greater than anything I'd ever thought possible. I wanted to possess that mouth that I'd made her kiss another man with and claim it as only for me.

Nina slid her hands over my back until they came to rest just below my hips, and she pulled me into her, tilting her hips to take all of me. I slid into her hot body so willing and eager for me and thrust hard until there was no space between us. She moaned a tiny noise as the base of my cock touched her slick pussy, her body arching to accommodate all of me.

I buried my face in softness of her neck and reared my hips back to plunge into her again. The demons she'd created spurred me on, screaming in my brain to claim her so no other man could ever see her and not know every beautiful and gentle inch of her was mine. I struggled to hold them back, but they controlled me, and I pushed into her over and over, harder and harder each time trying to force out all the pain I caused her.

My hands slid up her arms and pinning them above her head, I weaved our fingers together, needing as much to have her hold me as I wanted to hold her. Wrapping her legs around my waist, she stared up into my eyes as her body matched each plunge of my cock into her with a desire for more.

The intensity of her need surprised me, and I slowed my pace, not wanting to rush toward the moment each of us craved but to savor the journey we shared. Her heels dug into my spine and she groaned, "I don't want it slow and easy. Show me you were desperate without me like I was without you."

Her words set my mind and body on fire, and I released my hold on her to flip her over onto her stomach. Pulling her by her hips, I set her on her knees in front of me and thrust my cock into her cunt. There was no more me or her. Just us starved for one another.

Our need spurred our fucking to a place it had never been before. I slid in and out of her faster and faster, pistoning into her as she moaned into the pillow. The gentle squeezing of my cock told me she was close, but I wasn't ready to let this moment go yet. Slowing down, I eased out of her and leaned down to gently wrap my hand around her neck. In her ear, I whispered, "I want this night to last forever. I want to fuck you until you know how much I can't live without you."

In a tender voice that hit me deep inside, she said the only word that could undo me. "Yes."

No other words came between us now.

Pushing back against me, she silently begged for me to fulfill my promise. In seconds, I was balls-deep inside her again, thrusting and retreating from her cunt until neither of us could hold back anymore. She came first, her body milking my cock with its sweet tightening as her orgasm tore through her. Before she was finished, I felt my own release begin and pulled her up against me as I came inside her, the sweet sound of her cries of pleasure mingling with my panting until we collapsed onto the bed together.

When we finally were able to speak, she wiped my sweat drenched hair from my forehead and whispered against my cheek, "I missed you so much."

I pulled her close to me and held her in my arms, loving the feel of her next to me. Her body fit against mine perfectly, meant for me and me alone. She nuzzled my neck, her warm breath tickling my skin, and I spoke the words I'd held in all those months as I read her texts full of love and anger.

"Don't make me live without you. I can't do it, Nina."

She looked up at me with a gentle gaze, and I saw my life in her eyes. "I promise."

Chapter Twelve

Nina

Opening my eyes, I squinted from the morning light and rolled over in Tristan's full size bed, crashing into him and waking him up. Looking down at me, he gave me a sleepy grin. "I forgot how sleeping with you is like bumper cars."

Propping my head up, I rolled my eyes. "Says the man who rarely spends the whole night next to me. Are you saying I move around a lot when I sleep?"

He smirked and looked left and right to prove his point. "Well, not usually this bad, but then again, we're usually in a much bigger bed."

"Yeah, yeah. Aren't you Mr. Romance this morning?"

Tristan pulled me close and nuzzled my neck. "Even with you taking up all the room and stealing the covers, I'd rather be here than anywhere else on Earth." Looking up at me, he smiled. "Better?"

I gently pressed my lips to his and whispered, "Much."

We laid there for a long time, silent except for the sound of the two of us breathing, but my mind raced with questions and confessions I knew I couldn't keep inside me for much longer. Our reunion reinforced in me how much I loved him, but this was a fresh start for us and I didn't want it based on lies or misunderstandings.

I had to know he wasn't the Tristan I'd seen that night at Top, and I had to tell him about Gage.

Tracing my fingertip over the tattoo above his heart, I cleared my throat and took a deep breath. Forcing a smile onto my lips, I sat up and began. "Tristan, I want us to be completely honest with one another. I need to know a few things and have some things to tell you. It's important to me that this time we're truthful with everything."

He knitted his brows as he always did when he was concerned and turned to face me. "Things to tell me? Like what?"

"I'd rather begin with what I need to know from you. Like, for example, I need to know that whatever was going on with you at Top that night I found you there isn't going to be a part of our life together. I can handle a lot of things, Tristan, but being in love with a cokehead isn't one of them. I need to know that isn't going to be part of us from now on."

His expression softened, but his eyes filled with pain. "I'm sorry about that, Nina. That's not who I am or want to be. Coke was a way for me to lose myself for a long time. I'm not going to lie. I got lost in that again when I was away from you, but I made a choice to not be that person."

"Okay. Now I need you to promise me you'll tell me the truth, no matter how awful it is. I know you like to handle things on your own and think you have to protect me, but we won't work if you lie to me."

Shaking his head, he grimaced. "I can't promise all of that. I love you, Nina, and to me that means I'm supposed to protect you. The world you're in now is full of people who would think nothing about hurting someone to get ahead. I'm going to shield you from that as much as I can, but if I can't, then I'll protect you from it, and that might mean not telling you everything."

His insistence on protecting me like I was some unknowing child filled me with frustration. I just didn't know if I could be that kind of girlfriend and someday, wife. Sighing, I shook my head. "Why do you think I always need protecting? I'm not a little girl, Tristan. I'm a grown woman who knows the man I love. Do you think I don't understand people at your level?"

"It's not like that and you know it. This has nothing to do with social class. It has to do with me protecting the woman I love, Nina. Why is that so bad?"

"Because it gives you carte blanche to lie to me! We just spent all those months apart and now you're telling me you can't promise you won't continue to lie. How can we be together like that?"

He sat up and leaned against the headboard, pushing the hair out of his eyes. "Nina, I can't change who I am in this. I'm not the bad guy because I won't dump all the shit in my world on you. Most women want a man to protect them."

"From bad guys and people wanting to kill them. Not from everything else. I just want you to say to me that you'll treat me like a full partner in this relationship and not some second class citizen who's forced to react when you make decisions and I have to deal with them."

"This is about me leaving you alone for months."

My mouth fell open. "Of course it's about that! You left me here, all alone, and never once answered any of my messages. All those times when I was missing you so much all I wanted to do was curl up in bed with one of your shirts, I texted you and waited for you to answer but you never did."

"I couldn't answer, Nina. I was trying to protect you."

"Again with the protecting me! Would it have been any less protection for me if I was with you, wherever you were, so you could keep me safe and not break my heart?"

I tried to stop the tears from coming, but it was no use. After the sweetness of our reunion the night before, the reality of how much he'd hurt me was right there in front of us in the harsh light of day. I couldn't go on with Tristan if our life together was going to be like this.

He took my hand and squeezed it gently. "I know I keep making these mistakes. That you've stayed with me this long still amazes me. I hate that what I do makes you sad. I just don't know any other way to be."

Wiping the tears away, I looked at him sitting there, his beautiful eyes so full of sadness. There had to be some way to make him see what I meant. "I love that you want to protect me. If there's ever a time that someone's trying to mug me or kidnap me, I want you to jump in and rescue me. But you're not keeping me safe when you leave me in the dark. I sat in that house surrounded by people and barely alive because I missed you so much. You left me and I didn't know why. Was it me? I didn't know. It doesn't matter if I have bodyguards if you're the one who keeps hurting me by breaking my heart."

"I'm sorry. I never meant to do that. I did what I thought would keep you safe, but now I see that I'm the one who was hurting you the most. I'm sorry, Nina."

He looked away, but I gently tugged his face back toward me. "I just need you to promise you'll protect me from the bad guys but still tell me about things. I want to be your wife, not some childish girl you keep around."

Closing his eyes, he said quietly, "I promise. No more keeping things from you." He opened them and stared into mine with a gaze so direct I feared what he might say next. "I lied and hid things out of fear that if you knew about them, you'd never stay with me. I just want you to know that I come with a lot of fucked up shit. I didn't know if you'd want to be my wife knowing all of it."

I cradled his face and pressed my forehead to his. "I know what you are, Tristan Stone. No matter what bad things you think you have inside you, I know the man you are is good and kind. I love you, and that means all of you. The good, the bad, and the ugly."

He nodded and for the first time in our conversation, smiled. "I love you. I always have, Nina. From that first night we drove up the Taconic, you've been the one person I knew I couldn't deal with losing."

"You're not going to lose me, Tristan. I promise."

He leaned back away from me, and I saw the icy veil he wore so often descend over his features. "So what things do you have to tell me?"

"What's that face for?" I teased, nervous about what I had to tell him.

"I'm just wondering what else you have to say."

He wasn't stupid. He knew I had something to confess in addition to everything else we'd already talked about. It was probably written all over my face. Swallowing hard, I said, "Just one more thing. About that kiss with Gage..."

"What about it?" he asked flatly, his eyes boring holes in me with their accusatory stare.

"Don't look at me like that. You're the one who made me do it."

"I really don't want to talk about that, Nina. The idea of another man kissing you isn't something I ever want to think about again."

"Fine. I can certainly understand. I don't like thinking about you kissing that cheap waitress at Top that night either."

I was messing this up big time. Instead of simply telling him I'd kissed Gage and it meant nothing, I'd ventured into the jealous waters of "you did this and I did that." Never a good place to stumble into.

Tristan simply continued to stare at me as he waited for me to continue, very wisely saying nothing about the Brandi kiss. "I just want to clear the air so we never have to talk about this again. You kissed her, which bothers me, and I kissed him, which obviously upsets you."

"Then we never have to speak of it again. It was only once, and I didn't even kiss her back. Gage was only once, and it was just acting, so that's that."

I nervously bit my bottom lip and struggled to work up the courage to tell the man I loved that I'd kissed another man and it had nothing to do with acting. "It happened another time. Neither one of us meant it. I was upset about you finally texting me back only to tell me to kiss him. It meant nothing, but I don't want this to be between us."

When all the words had finally left my mouth, I held my breath and waited for their meaning to sink in. Tristan said nothing, but stared straight ahead, his face emotionless. I knew he'd heard me, but his lack of response confused me.

Finally, after what seemed like hours of waiting for him to say anything, he turned toward me and took a deep breath. Letting it out slowly, he shook his head. "I know I put you in that position and I know I have no right to be angry, but I am. I can't stand the idea of you with him. I need to know just one thing. Did you sleep with him?"

"No. I swear, Tristan. It was one kiss. That's it."

"Then I don't want to hear about it again."

Never before in my life had any words sounded so final. His expression hardened for just a moment, as if he were working it out in his mind, and then he was back to being that same man I'd fallen in love with.

So ready to move on, I asked, "So, what should we do today?"

Tristan brought my hand up to his lips and kissed the back of it. "I think it's time for my resurrection, don't you?"

I followed him through the front door of the house, noticing he stopped for just a moment to look around the enormous entryway. Quickly, I headed to our room to change into some fresh clothes. Tristan changed into his usual suit and tie and waited for me. When I was ready, he grasped my hand, clutching it as if for support, and guided me to his office where Daryl, Jensen, West, and Varo sat waiting for us. Tristan took his place behind his desk, and I stood beside him as each of the men in front of us waited for him to begin. Pulling me close so I sat on the arm of his chair, he rested his hand across the top of my thigh. "Surprised to see me, gentlemen?"

I scanned each of their faces, and except for Daryl, all of them looked stunned to see Tristan sitting there before them. Daryl must not have let them in on the secret.

"We didn't realize you were back," Varo said quietly.

Smiling, Tristan directed his attention to the man I'd explained less than an hour earlier was the one I'd kissed. "Well, I am back, so you can go back to being merely the bodyguard. Thanks for your service, though. I'm sure Nina appreciates your diligence."

And with that, I knew Tristan wasn't quite as comfortable with my confession as I'd hoped. Varo understood his meaning instantly, if the look of shock all over his face was any indication. I felt bad about that. He'd been a good guy about everything. He hadn't even been the one who did the kissing. It had been all my fault. I gave him a weak smile, hoping it made up for Tristan's sharp words.

"And West, I'm concerned with how you guard Nina. I've told both of you I want you to stay in the background."

West looked to Varo on his left and then back at Tristan. "We always are. If she hadn't been told that we were guarding her, she still wouldn't know."

"Really? I watched you and your giant form spy on me behind trees half your size one afternoon recently. Didn't realize I was Ethan, the gardener, did you? If that's any indication of how you stay out of sight, I'm not impressed."

West grimaced as if in pain as Tristan dressed him down. I considered coming to his defense since I'd never noticed either him or Varo around me any time I went out, but the sharpness of the rebuke told me to not get involved. Tristan continued to explain how clumsy West had been one day as he'd attempted to spy on the new gardener, delineating each problem he'd seen as the bodyguard's embarrassment and anger simmered.

"From now on, gentlemen, you are to be neither seen nor heard as you guard the most important person in my world. Am I clear?"

Both Varo and West nodded their understanding of Tristan's decree and quickly rose to leave when he waved his hand to signal they were dismissed. As they reached the door, he snapped, "And make sure the hole in the fence at the back of the property is fixed. You're supposed to be our security here."

Leaning down near his ear, I whispered, "Was it necessary to be like that with them? They're supposed to want to save me, if I ever need it. I'm not sure after that little pep talk they'd want to get me drink of water if I was in the middle of the desert."

Turning his face toward me, he smiled. "Don't worry. They just hate me right now. They'll get over it."

I leaned away from him and studied this new Tristan. "Are you always like this with the people who work for you, Mr. Stone?"

Arching one dark eyebrow, he grinned. "Only with the ones who don't understand my orders and those who've kissed my fiancée without my permission, Ms. Edwards."

"Tristan…"

He angled his head toward Daryl and whispered, "Nina, we still need to talk to Daryl and Jensen."

"Then we'll discuss the whole situation with West and Varo later?"

"We can discuss my issue with West later, princess. Right now, we have two people waiting."

Usually when Tristan called me that nickname, I took it as a term of affection, but now the edge in his tone said princess was just his way of expressing his jealousy over Varo. Getting the hint, I looked over at Daryl and pasted a smile on my face.

Grinning back at me, he asked, "So how are the happy couple doing today?"

Directing his attention to the driver, Tristan softened his voice from how it had sounded with my bodyguards and smiled. "Jensen, as always, I'm nothing but pleased with your service. I want to thank you for handling your job admirably, especially with what I'm sure was a stressful drive from the groundbreaking yesterday. I'll be heading into the city soon, so I'll let you know when I'm ready."

Nodding his head, Jensen smiled meekly. "If I may say so, it's nice to have you back, Mr. Stone."

For the first time since he sat down, Tristan's smile was genuine as he listened to Jensen. "It's good to be back. Thank you."

The driver was dismissed with another thank you, and we were left alone with Daryl, who seemed to be practically bubbling over with eagerness that morning. I hoped he had some information to help us figure out what the hell was going on and how we could stop Karl.

"Let's get down to business. What have you found out about Cardiell?" Tristan asked, immediately confusing me.

"What's Cardiell?"

Tristan looked up at me and smiled another genuine smile. "I forgot you haven't been with us with all this." Turning to face Daryl, he said, "For Nina's sake, give us the Cliff Notes version of Cordovex and Cardiell."

"Got it. Cordovex was a heart drug approved by the FDA a few years ago, and it seems that it wasn't as good at keeping heart patients healthy as it was at killing them. Eventually, Cordovex was pulled from the market, but the company which produced it, Rider Pharmaceutical, still held the patent to it. Fast forward to earlier this year and now Rider has a drug named Cardiell out. The problem is they're the same drug. Chemically, they're the exact same, which means a drug which was killing people before is back on the market."

"What does this have to do with Karl and why he wants to hurt either of us?"

Daryl nodded. "Good question. Your father mentioned Cordovex in his notebook Tristan has, so I began digging and found out what I told you. We think Karl is behind the break-ins at Tristan's homes, all except here, and he's looking for that notebook. Your sister gave him copies of the notes he had on Victor and Taylor's wrongdoings, but she didn't give him anything on those notes that come after in your father's notebook."

"Why?"

Tristan squeezed me gently. "Because your father didn't make copies of those pages. Karl doesn't know that, though, or doesn't believe it, which is why I made sure Kim and her family are hidden away so he can't find them."

"Are they okay?"

Daryl chimed in. "They're fine. The girls love playing on the beach and your sister and brother-in-law are enjoying a much needed vacation. By the way, I found out that their house has been broken into in the past few months too."

Tristan started to say something, but my phone vibrated in the pocket of my yoga pants. Taking it out, I saw Jordan's name flashed across the screen. Showing it to Tristan, I whispered, "I have to take this. I hope you understand. I haven't heard from her since she left."

Smiling, he slid his arm from around me. "We'll wait for you. Tell Jordan I said hello."

I jogged out into the hallway, eager to hear Jordan's voice again. "Hello?"

"Hey you. What's up?" she said with hesitation in her voice.

"Tristan's back. We just got home."

"Oh, that's great, Nina!" The phone fell silent, and after a long pause, she said, "I'm so sorry. I don't know why I said what I said that night. I was so out of line, sweetie."

I couldn't stay angry at Jordan. I just couldn't. She was closer to me than anyone but Tristan. "It's okay. I understand."

"When I finally pulled my head out of my ass, I knew I was wrong. I just didn't know how to fix it. We've never fought over a guy, and I had no right to accuse you of something with Varo, especially since he never even gave a damn about me."

"That's not true. In fact, I think he does like you. I have to get back into a meeting with our favorite mountain man, but what do you say to meeting me later this week? We can catch up and put all this in the past."

"I'd like that a lot. Thanks for being so cool with me since I was the world's biggest asshole to her best friend."

I chuckled at her attempt at being self-effacing. "Don't say that. Anyway, I guess we were due for a big fight. Most friends don't go years and years without one, so it was time. Let me call you later and we'll set up a time to get together."

"Okay. I love you, Nina. Life just wasn't the same without you."

"Ditto. I missed you, Jordan."

As I hung up, my heart swelled from the return of the other person so important to me. My mind raced with all the details I had to tell her, especially about Gage, who I hoped would now have the chance to ask her out. First, though, I had to be at Tristan's side as we figured out what the hell Karl was up to and how to stop him.

Chapter Thirteen

Tristan

Daryl pointed at me and shook his head. "No more beard. What a shame." His frown deepened and he continued, "You planning to keep the hair?"

"No," I said as I smoothed my hair back off my face. "There's no way I can speak to the board looking like this."

A deep laugh exploded out of his face. "No Bieber hair for you? So how's the homecoming? All better now?"

"I'll be all better when Karl is out of our lives for good. I'm hoping you have something to tell us today because I'm ready to get on with my life and that doesn't include this bullshit with him."

Nina returned to stand next to me, and I wrapped my arm around her again to pull her close. This time it wasn't to make a point like it had been earlier but because I wanted her with me in this. When she'd asked to be treated like an equal partner, I'd immediately dismissed the idea, even if I hadn't told her that. Equal partner with me meant she was going to have to deal with the vipers and sharks that made up my world. I didn't want her around them.

The problem was that she was going to be around them as long as she was by my side. The people who would see me out of power at Stone Worldwide would use anything and anyone to achieve their aims, and that included the one person who meant more to me than anyone else in the world. So if she was going to be my wife, I had to let her in and make her my equal.

Looking up at her as she sat on the arm of my office chair, I watched her sweet expression as she talked with Daryl like they were old friends. As closed off and cold as I was, she was open and kind— the type of person the bastards I dealt with every day loved to devour, using her gentle nature against her. Even the thought of that happening to her made my blood nearly boil, and I instinctively squeezed her closer to me.

She looked down at me and smiled. "I guess Tristan is ready to go, Daryl." Leaning down, she whispered, "And I think you look more like Johnny Depp than the Biebs with your hair like that."

"What?"

"You know. In that movie Chocolat. He wore his hair like yours is now."

I had no idea what she was talking about, but she looked so sweet that I didn't have the heart to tell her. "Daryl, let's get back to what you found out."

"You bet. So the two drugs are the same from the same company. Rider Pharmaceutical. The problem is that Rider is just a front. It's a company in name only. I knew there had to be a much bigger company behind it, so I set about looking for what that could be. Take a guess what the name of the company controlling Rider is."

"One of the major pharma companies?" I guessed.

Daryl shook his head. "No. Much closer to home."

"Don't tell me I own Rider Pharmaceutical."

He made a smacking noise with his lips and grinned. "Yep. I'm looking at the proud owner of Rider right now. Seems your little business was a gift to none other than Karl himself."

"Who gave him a company?" Nina asked.

I could have told her. As soon as I heard it was a gift, I knew my father had given it to Karl. Why I could only imagine. I let Daryl continue his story, though.

"Courtesy of Victor Stone, the former CEO of Stone Worldwide and the father of your intended, Nina."

"So what's the big deal? Karl runs Rider, which Tristan owns. All he has to do is fire Karl, right?"

Nina's eyes searched mine for the answer. "It's not that easy. Since legally, my father made him the director of Rider, which is what he must be if he's been given the company to run, I can't simply get rid of him. The board of directors will have to get involved."

"And Karl's likely been hard at work on them in your absence. They're unlikely to just let you make that huge change and once they get involved, Karl's going to have the upper hand, " Daryl added.

"I don't understand. Why would he have the upper hand?" she asked.

Daryl stroked his beard, pulling it to a point. "Because we have no proof that he's doing anything wrong with the company. Without that, there's no legal basis for getting rid of him."

"What I need to know is what's happening with Cardiell."

"Nothing yet. Hopefully, we can find out what's going on and stop Karl before anything bad starts again," Daryl said more seriously than I'd ever heard him before.

"I don't care what's going on. If Cardiell hurts one person and I could have stopped it, I won't be able to forgive myself."

Nina slipped her fingers through mine and squeezed my hand. "Then we just have to figure out what he's up to and stop him."

Daryl nodded his agreement. "It's my guess he's looking for that notebook because he thinks there's something in there that might cause him a problem. Now we know that's not the case, but that means that we need to find that missing sheet of paper someone tore out of your father's notebook."

That was easier said than done. If ever there was a case of trying to find a needle in a haystack, this was it. We had no idea where to even start looking. "Daryl, we need to eliminate any place we can if we ever want to find this piece of paper, assuming it even exists at all."

"I agree, so let's tick them off one by one. Your offices. Any chance it's there?"

Shaking my head, I dismissed this idea quickly. "No. The only files in my office are ones that I've been through hundreds of times before. I can promise you it's not there."

"Okay. Your penthouse. Any chance his goons have missed it there?"

"No. I had the place cleaned out before I moved in. Until I met Nina, there wasn't anything but a few suits, shirts, and ties."

Daryl took out a pencil and began crossing things off in his little notebook. "Miami and LA are out. The places are basically empty. No files there."

"What if we aren't supposed to be looking for files? What if that sheet of paper is in an envelope or something?" Nina asked.

Looking up from his notes, Daryl cocked one eyebrow. "What do you mean?"

Nina stood and walked over to the painting hanging on the far wall. Lifting it, she held it up for Daryl and me to see. "What if the paper was hidden someplace like this, like you see in mysteries? Not a file cabinet or anything like that but just someplace it could be hidden where no one could find it."

As she ran her hand across the back of the picture frame, Daryl nodded. "She might have something there. Can we still cross off the penthouse, the other houses, and your office if we think about things that way?"

I ran through each place in my mind, mentally scanning each room of each location. My office had no artwork or anything hanging on the walls. I had no diploma or commendations to replace my father's, so once I took his down, the spots they'd once covered remained bare. Only the art Nina had chosen hung in the penthouse, and there was nothing left in the other houses.

That only left this house.

"I don't think there's anything in those places, Daryl. I think if it exists, it could be here."

Nina walked back to stand next to me. Sitting on the arm of the chair again, she said, "Then we need to check every room in this house. Just that one room alone with the secret room next to it has at least half a dozen pieces that could be hiding what we're looking for. And don't forget the attic."

I shook my head. "There's nothing in the attic. Trust me. Just some old things that were my mother's."

"No, Tristan, that's not right. There are all sorts of letters and pictures up there. And that's just in one trunk. I bet there are tons of places we can look."

Nina and Daryl began to draw up a plan of attack for searching the house as I wondered why she knew so much about the attic. I hadn't been up there since I'd moved in. Rogers had been responsible for storing things, so I'd had no reason to even think about it.

"Let's head upstairs," Nina said in a chipper voice as she pulled me from my chair. "I feel like Sherlock Holmes."

"Does that make me Dr. Watson?"

Standing on her toes, she kissed me and smiled. "A very sexy Dr. Watson. Now let's go find this evidence so you can nail that bastard to the wall."

Her blue eyes were ablaze with determination. I'd missed her presence in every part of my life. Even when she tried to be tough, she was still my Nina—sweet and gentle, no matter what.

The attic was very much like every other attic in the world. Stacks of boxes, some reaching nearly to the beams that transected the ceiling, and trunks ranging in size from small to enormous lined virtually every square inch of space. A seamstress's mannequin stood silently watching guard in the corner near the south window, giving that area an eerie feeling despite the rays of light that brightened up that section of the space.

Nina lowered herself to the wood floor in front of a large trunk and looked up at me. "I think we should start here."

Looking down, I watched as she lifted the lid and began rummaging through stacks of papers and pictures. "How did you know these were here?"

A sheepish look crossed her face, and she held her hand out. "Sit with me. I want you to tell me about these pictures. I hope you're not mad at me for coming up here."

I lowered myself to the floor next to her. "When were you up here?"

She stopped looking through the trunk and sighed. "Right after I moved here last year. I swear I wasn't snooping. It was just that I was lonely out here all alone with no one but Rogers and Jensen to talk to and I went exploring."

The mention of Rogers' name made a flood of memories rush back into my brain, and I saw by the look on Nina's face that my expression had changed. Taking her hand in mine, I brought it to my lips in a kiss. "I don't think you were snooping. It's okay."

My forced smile didn't fool her, and she took my hand to kiss it in return. "You're still hurting over him, aren't you?"

I shook my head, trying to lie. "It's okay."

She kissed the back of my hand again and gave it a gentle squeeze. "I'm looking forward to hearing about these pictures. I want to know if the stories I made up were anywhere close to the truth."

Taking the largest photo out, she held it up and looked over at me. "How old were you when this was taken?"

I studied the portrait of my parents, Taylor, and me posing when I was no older than four or five. As with every picture ever taken with the four of us, I sat in front of my mother and Taylor sat in front of my father. Dressed identically, I grinned for the camera while Taylor sat looking so serious, as he always did, and our parents' expressions told the story of their marriage. Self-satisfied and smug looking, my father's presence in the picture bordered on overwhelming, too much strength and not enough kindness. My mother's expression was the one she wore nearly every waking moment of her days. Her mouth appeared to form a smile, but on closer inspection, anyone who knew her could see the sadness in her face.

"I think we were five then," I answered, struggling to remember anything of that day.

"Your mother was beautiful. You have her eyes, but your brother doesn't."

I turned to look at Nina and chuckled at her comment. "Taylor and I were identical twins. I think if I had eyes like hers, then he did too."

She shook her head and smiled. "Nope. Look closely. See your mother's eyes? They're brown, like yours and Taylor's, but they're softer than his. Yours are like that. His eyes look a little harsher. Not yours, though."

For a long moment, I stared at that picture and finally saw what Nina had seen. So many people had always told Taylor and me that they couldn't tell us apart, but now I saw that it was a simple matter of looking into our eyes. "You're right. How did you see that?"

Nina stroked her palm over my cheek. "How could I not? It's impossible to miss. You look like your mother, at least in your eyes. The rest of your face may look much more like your father's side, but those eyes are all her."

Propping the portrait up against the back wall of the trunk, she looked for another picture while I kept my gaze on the four of us. I didn't remember the day we sat for that picture, but the fact that my father even appeared in it was noteworthy. Only formal portraits included him. Any other time a picture might be taken, he was absent, at work or on a business trip that was likely anything but.

"I have a confession to make, though. I didn't notice how much like your mother you were until now. The first time I saw this picture, I thought you looked like your father."

"I did," I admitted, knowing Nina had every right to hate that in me after what my father had done. I didn't like that truth any more than she likely did, but it was the truth. Taylor and I both looked more like Stones than my mother's family.

"It's expected that you'd look like your parents, Tristan. It's okay."

Happy to avoid the comparison between the man who had her father murdered and myself, I reached inside the trunk to lift out a stack of photographs I recognized as pictures from when I played sports as a child. Each one showed me smiling and happy, a winner every time.

"You looked so cute with all your trophies. It's hard to imagine this guy who wears a suit all the time playing anything."

"Then I'll have to take these pictures when we leave so I can remind you from time to time," I joked. "Right now, we need to look through the rest of this trunk."

Nina picked up a pile of letters wrapped in a red ribbon. Holding them up to show me, she read the name on the top envelope. "Tressa. Were these your mother's? I'm guessing from your father. At least you're like him in that."

I shook my head, unable to believe my father had ever written my mother anything. He couldn't even be bothered to call her on most days, so the thought of him writing love letters seemed unlikely. "My father wasn't the type of man to write anything down, unless it made him money."

Handing them to me, she smiled. "Well, just in case, I don't feel right looking through them. It's more appropriate you do it. But why are they here?"

"I took a lot of their things after the crash. Rogers must have brought them here." I looked down at the letters sitting in my palm and wondered if they'd been from an old boyfriend before my mother and father married. The idea of my mother happily in love with someone made me happy. All those years with my father had been so filled with misery for her. The neglect. The rumors of infidelity. The coldness he seemed to enjoy showing only her. That she might have been in love with someone who cared enough for her to write his feelings down so she could forever look back and remember their time together gave me hope that at some point she'd truly been happy.

I unwrapped the bow and slid the first envelope from the top of the pile. Turning it over, I slipped my finger under the flap and easily opened it to find a single sheet of paper inside. Unfolding it, I scanned the page and found the words of a lover. Had it been my father, after all? Maybe before they'd married he'd been the kind of man she deserved.

I hated having to leave you last night, Tressa. I know it's not forever, but it's away from you all the same. Write me and let me know when we can see each other again.

The letter was unsigned and gave no indication who the author was. Turning it over, I saw nothing on the back to solve the mystery of who had written it.

"Who's it from?" Nina asked as she leaned over to take a glance.

"I don't know. There's no signature."

"Try another one. They're probably all from the same person."

Placing the letter back in its envelope, I opened another one and read words similar to the first. Whoever the letter writer was, he'd met my mother and missed her when she was gone. I read two more letters that sounded almost identical to the first ones and wondered if any of them in this stack would be signed.

"Do they have a date on them?" Nina asked as she took the last one I'd read from my grasp.

I opened up another and searched first for a date. None was written anywhere on the paper. Shaking my head, I shrugged. "Looks like another mystery for us."

"Do you think they're from your father?"

"I have a hard time believing that, Nina. My father and mother weren't in love that I remember. He wasn't the type to love anyone."

Looking down, I read an entirely different letter that left me sure it wasn't my father who'd written any of them.

I can't stand even the thought of you with him anymore, Tressa. He isn't worthy of your love. Leave him and come away with me. I may not have his money, but I can give you what he can't or won't. I love you and don't want to live without you another day.

Nina reread the words to me and studied my face for my reaction. "Is this from your father?"

"I don't think so, but if not, my mother was having an affair."

"Maybe it was before she married your father."

Nina's attempt to help me think better of my mother was unnecessary. If she had cheated on my father, as far as I was concerned, all the better for her. At least she'd found love with someone.

"While you read the next one, I'm going to look for her letters to this mystery man. Maybe she had them hidden away too."

The next letter was another plea for her to run away with the letter writer, but it did provide me with a general time period when the letter may have been written. A mention of my brother and me meant that it was definitely an affair. Closing my eyes, I silently thanked whoever this mystery man had been for at least giving her love and the chance for happiness. But had she not taken that chance because of Taylor and me?

I became convinced the name of the man my mother had fallen in love with would forever remain a secret. That wasn't a bad thing, though. Some things should remain hidden.

The next letter's tone was distinctly different than the others. Near the bottom of the pile, it signaled a change between him and her.

I won't let you go. If all I can have is stolen moments with you, then I'll take them for now. I won't let you leave me, Tressa. We make each other happy. Just hearing you say we should end what this is nearly drove me mad last night. I won't let you do it.

I tapped Nina on the shoulder and showed her the letter. "She wanted to leave him. Any luck finding any letters from her to him?"

"Not yet. Just pictures of you all over the place. I swear your brother must have been camera shy, Tristan."

Folding the letter, I slid it into the envelope. "He wasn't much for pictures. Or sports, for that matter."

"Who took all these pictures of you and your mother? Your father?"

The memory of the one time my father attended any of my games for a mere fifteen minutes passed through my mind. "No. Rogers always took the pictures. It was him who came to see every one of my games and matches."

Nina rested her hand on my arm. "I'm sorry, honey. At least you know Rogers cared about you. I think he did."

"I thought so too."

She returned to searching for my mother's letters to her mystery lover without a word, and I focused on the next to last letter in the pile next to me. My eyes scanned the lines that told of their impending break up.

Nothing is more important than love. No matter what excuse you give, I'll give a better one to show we should be together. I won't let you go, Tressa. I can't. Why won't you give in to what you know makes you happy? Come away with me. Leave him and be mine forever.

He was losing her. I sensed it in every word. He knew it too. She probably had told him their affair had to end, and he was just holding on to what used to be.

"I think I might have found something." Nina leaned over the front of the trunk and groaned as she buried her head inside. When she straightened up, she was holding a silver tin in one hand and its lid in the other. Inside the tin were more letters but no envelopes.

She set the box between us and lifted one out for me to read. Opening it, I read one of my mother's letters to the man she loved. Her words were tender and kind, and if my father had ever seen them, he would have made her life a living hell. Suddenly the thought that he had learned of her affair occurred to me.

I sit here alone as the boys play with the nanny and wish there was a way we could all be together, but he'll never let me go with them and I can't leave without them. I'm their mother. They need me. My love for you may be what keeps me going each day, but I can't give in to that and sacrifice them.

"She stayed because of us," I said quietly as I placed the letter back in the tin.

"That's a good thing, Tristan. She loved you. You're lucky to have a mother like that."

"But she was unhappy, Nina. It's all over these letters. She was stuck in a loveless marriage. I knew that from the moment I was old enough to compare my parents with other people's. They never kissed or hugged or held hands. She could have had happiness if she ran away with this person."

"You don't know that. She was breaking it off with him. She had to have a reason, and I doubt it was you and your brother. His letters make it sound like she wanted out for another reason."

I read through more of my mother's letters, hoping to find what Nina said was in fact the truth. I hated thinking she'd given up a chance at real happiness for us. Each one read like the first, some telling him she couldn't leave because of her children and others simply declarations of love.

"Tristan, did you read this last one of his letters? He wasn't going to let her go. Do you remember her acting differently or saying anything to indicate she was frightened? He was threatening her. Listen to this."

He knows, so what's the point of hiding anymore? I know you still love me. After all these years, I know you do. It can be like it was in the beginning. The boys are older now. They don't need you like I do. I won't let you leave me. Not now—not ever.

Nina looked up from the letter. "Do you have any idea when this could have been?"

"No. I never knew about any of this."

The truth was I had never been the kind of son she deserved. I knew she was unhappy, but I never bothered to consider that something other than my father had caused that sadness in her.

"Can I read the letters in the tin to see if we can figure out what happened?"

I shook the cobwebs of memories from my head. "Sure." I didn't want to read any more of the past. The letters had only served to confirm what I'd always believed and shown me it was even worse.

Watching as Nina read letter after letter, I saw her expression change when she reached the last one. "What's wrong? Is there something in that one?"

Turning to look at me, she shook her head. "I'm not sure. Listen to this."

It's over. Take what he's given you and be thankful. He means it to be symbolic. That's why he named it Rider. He's giving you a company he doesn't care about to show you that you'll never have me. Only a company he named after me. Take it and make it yours. I can't see you again. Accept his gift and know he'll never forget this. Be careful.

"What does she mean 'that's why he named it Rider'? What does that have to do with this?"

My mother's words hung heavy in the air as I attempted to process what Nina had just read. My mother hadn't just had an affair. She'd had an affair with my father's best friend.

Karl.

Nina gently shook me by the shoulder. "Tristan, what does this mean? Who is Rider?"

"Ryder with a y. It was my mother's maiden name. Tressa Ryder. My father must have changed it to Rider Pharmaceutical when he bought the company before he found out she cheated on him. That he'd give Karl a company with the same name as my mother's is exactly what she thought. It was supposed to be symbolic. My father would do something like that. Karl could have some company that meant nothing to him, but he couldn't have the woman that my father didn't give a damn about."

"Are you saying your mother was in love with Karl, the guy who wants you and me out of the way?"

I'd been as surprised as Nina was at first, but it all made sense. The holiday dinners when I was a child when Karl would be all smiles as he teased my mother or told her stupid jokes. How sweetly she'd always acted toward him. In my mind's eye, I could see him then, the far more charming younger man he was instead of the odious bastard he was now.

"I guess so. That's the only answer since it involved Rider Pharmaceutical."

"I don't understand. If he was so in love with your mother, why would he do this to you?"

As Nina returned to searching the trunk for what we were looking for, I tried to reconcile Karl Dreger's hatred for me with how much he'd loved my mother. It made no sense, no matter how much I wanted to pretend it did.

Chapter Fourteen

Nina

I rummaged through more pictures and mementos as Tristan sat silently next to me, obviously rocked by the news that the man who was busy doing everything possible to make his life a living hell was also the man his mother had loved, even to the point of endangering her own welfare. I found another portrait the family had sat for years later that showed the life Tressa Stone had accepted. In her expression was etched the sadness of a woman who'd chosen to sacrifice her own happiness. Those brown eyes so similar to Tristan's looked out blankly, even as she smiled for the camera.

Lifting the picture out of the trunk, I propped it up against the lid. "When was this taken? You look like a teenager here."

Tristan focused on the image and nodded. "I remember that day. Taylor and my father barely made it in time for the photographer to get the photo. Not that I was much better. My mother had reminded us every day for a week, but her need to have a family picture meant little to us."

"You were a teenage boy. They never care about things like that. Don't beat yourself up over it."

"Look at her, Nina. She was married to a man who didn't give a damn about her and actually gave the man she was cheating with a company, even though I don't think he gave her one present after they were married. Even if he hated Karl, he treated her worse. And my brother and I weren't much better."

"Don't do this to yourself, Tristan. You were a kid. I'm sure your mother understood that."

He faked a tiny smile and nodded. "Anything else in there?"

Pushing pictures and frames across the bottom of the trunk, I lifted my head and turned toward him. "Not that I can see. I think we should move to some of the boxes and trunks around us."

"Okay. I'll check the boxes. Take a look at that trunk near the wall."

Tristan silently moved toward the floor-to-ceiling stack of boxes nearby still wearing a frown from the news he'd read in his mother's letters. I could understand. It's as if he'd lived all his life thinking one thing, and now he had to grapple with the fact that what he'd believed wasn't true at all.

The image of Tressa Stone's sad eyes stayed in my mind as I searched through the second trunk. I admired her, even though I'd never met her. Whatever her life had been, she'd stayed for her sons, and to me, that made whatever else she did unimportant. That one son turned out to be a monster wasn't her fault. The blame for that belonged on her husband, not her. And Tristan was proof that she'd done something right. That thoughtless teenager had grown into a wonderful man. Her influence was obvious, even if he couldn't see it.

The trunk contained blankets and clothes, but as I pushed my hands through them to see if any papers were hidden there, I realized I was searching through baby things. Holding a newborn onesie up in front of me, I sat amazed at how tiny the little blue outfit was. Had Tristan worn this as a baby?

"You don't look like you're doing much searching over there," he joked from behind me.

Turning around, I displayed the onesie for him. "Was this yours? It's so cute!"

For the first time in nearly an hour, he looked happy. Reaching over, he took the clothing and held it up to examine it. "No, this must have been Taylor's. See? His name is sewn into it just under the tag."

I looked and there was the name Taylor sewn in on a tiny piece of fabric near the collar. "Is that how your mother told your clothes apart?"

Tristan chuckled. "Yeah. And it was more like that's how the nanny knew whose clothes were whose."

"A nanny, huh? I want you to know that I don't plan to have a nanny for our kids. I hope you're okay with that."

He threw the onesie back into the trunk and leaned down to place a tiny kiss on the tip of my nose. "Our kids?"

"Yeah. I thought we should have some after we get married. You know, like lots of people often do."

Twisting a strand of my hair around his finger, he leaned down and kissed me, this time on the lips. Smiling, he said, "Kids it is, but I can't promise normal."

I looked up into his face and for a moment thought I saw a trace of fear in his eyes. "No problem. I've got perfectly normal and average covered, so our kids will be fine."

"Do you remember what I said to you that first night in the car?"

I thought back to that night for a moment. "No. What?"

He tucked my hair behind my ear and gave me that look that always made me feel like lava was pooling in my abdomen. "You said you were ordinary, and I told you you're anything but."

"Yeah, but you knew nothing about me then."

"And I still saw it in you. So forget about this average business. You're anything but, Nina Edwards."

"Well, Tristan Stone, I'll have to keep that in mind."

"Don't worry. I won't let you forget."

I loved seeing him like this. These moments when he was relaxed and playful were so infrequent, but when they happened, they made me realize all over again why I was so crazy about him.

"Did you find anything in those boxes?"

He shook his head and frowned as all the playfulness disappeared. "Not yet. We better get back to it."

Something in the way his shoulders sagged when he turned back to begin searching the boxes again showed how much this was affecting him. I wanted to take him into my arms and tell him everything was going to be okay, but until we figured out how to stop Karl, nothing was going to be okay.

Except us. We would be okay. I knew that in all my heart.

I focused on a trunk next to the one I'd just finished searching and prayed to God that we'd find something soon. Smaller than the previous two, this one contained what appeared to be old Christmas and birthday cards, some from as far back as before Tristan and his brother were born. Although I knew Tristan wouldn't mind me reading them, I felt oddly like an intruder on the private notes and cards from his family.

One handmade card of a wreath made out of silver and gold foil sat on the bottom of the trunk, reflecting the little light that reached it. Lifting it out, I ran my fingertip over the edges of the wreath, impressed with how beautiful it still was after years hidden away. The card's creator had taken care to make folds in each piece of foil to simulate movement in the wreath. Tilting the card up and down, I watched as the light from the window danced over it.

I turned it over but saw no writing or name. Carefully, I pulled the edge of the card and found it opened to reveal a barely legible handwritten Christmas greeting.

May the blessings of the season fill your days with joy.

There was an initial just below that line I couldn't make out. Smudged, it looked like a K or a D. K would make sense if it was from Karl to Tressa, but something about the card seemed distinctly unlike one a man would give to a woman. Setting it aside, I sifted through anniversary cards and birthday cards belonging to Tristan's mother. All store bought, unlike the Christmas card, they were from Victor Stone to his wife. None showed much thought on his part, and none even contained the word love. Tristan's assessment of his parents' marriage seemed to be correct.

Inside one of the cards were three small, white envelopes addressed to her in what looked like a man's handwriting. I couldn't be sure, but it didn't appear to be either Victor Stone's writing or Karl Dreger's. Had there been another affair?

I quietly slipped the letter out of the first envelope, not wanting Tristan to hear the rustle of paper. Not that I disapproved, but I wasn't sure how he'd handle finding out his mother had cheated on his father with yet another man. Some things didn't need to be known.

Looking over toward Tristan, I saw he was busy beginning his search of the next box, so I turned my back toward him and began to read Tressa's letter. I knew from the first sentence I'd been wrong. This was no love letter.

Dear Tressa,

I know it's been years since we last spoke. I've never forgotten how wonderful you were to my girls when their mother died. It's because of that kindness that I'm writing you today in the hopes that by doing so I can lessen the pain of what I must now do.

An investigation into what I thought was merely a simple case of a workplace lawsuit at Stone Worldwide has unearthed a story I have to believe you know nothing about. It's with a heavy heart that I must tell you that I cannot keep this information secret much longer. Please know that if I could spare you the pain I know this will cause you, I would.

Your husband is at the center of my investigation that shows he was responsible for a bombing at a coffee shop in Atlanta that killed innocent men, women, and children. The intended victim was the judge in a sexual harassment case against Stone Worldwide, but the story goes far deeper. The judge's daughter, a fifteen year old, had become pregnant with your son Taylor's child and when he abandoned her, she committed suicide. The judge knew what your son had done and would have made sure the case went against Stone, so your husband made sure that never happened.

Tressa, I wish there was another way to tell you this, but I didn't want to put you in harm's way. I'm sorry. Be careful and if you need to reply, do so only to the address on this letter. Your husband and the men surrounding him are dangerous.

Take care.

Joe

I sat stunned at what I'd just read, unsure of how it was possible that my father had written Tristan's mother. Thinking back to when my mother died, I couldn't remember her coming to see us. How had she known my family then?

Nothing seemed to make any sense. Had my father and Tressa Stone had an affair before my mother died? Just the thought of my father cheating seemed wrong. If not, how had they known one another?

Looking up from the letter in my hands, I saw Tristan finishing with a box and motioned for him to come over. I held the letter up and shook my head.

"What's wrong? Did you find something?" he asked, his voice full of concern.

"I don't know. I…I don't understand this letter. You read it and tell me what's going on."

My hands shook as his eyes moved across the page reading the words my father had written. When he finished, he looked up, his expression telling me he was as confused as I was.

"What does this mean? Your father knew my mother?"

"I don't know."

"Are there any other letters from him?"

I handed him the other two letters I found inside the card. "I found three letters. They're addressed to your mother at somewhere in Pennsylvania. Did she ever live there?"

Tristan nodded as he silently read the address. "My mother was from Gladwyne, right outside of Philadelphia. The address this was sent to was my grandparents' house there. It was left to her when they died."

"How would my father know to send her a letter there?"

"I don't know. Maybe we'll find something out in the other letters."

I watched as he read the next letter, silently hoping it would tell us that my father hadn't been unfaithful to my mother. Lifting his head, Tristan smiled. "I think I know what you were thinking, but it's not like that. Listen to what he wrote."

Dear Tressa,

Diana would never forgive me if I didn't tell you first, and I hope you understand what I must do. We're a long way from the nights when you and she would sneak out of your dorm at Bryn Mawr to come see me at the News Gleaner, aren't we?

You asked me if there was anything you could say or do to convince me to keep what I've found to myself. I wish I could. My investigation has uncovered many secrets around your family. I promise you that the only details that will come out will be those related to my investigation. Please know that I would never intentionally hurt you or your family. You're the reason I met Diana, and I've never forgotten that wonderful favor.

Take care to keep yourself safe. Do whatever you must to protect yourself and your family, but know that I have no choice now.

Joe

The news that my mother had been Tressa Stone's friend and had met my father because of her touched my heart. To me, my parents had always been older. To think of them younger seemed odd, but as Tristan read my father's letter, I imagined the three of them as college friends. The idea left me with more questions than answers, though. Had they remained close after college? How had Tristan's mother met my father and later introduced him to my mother? Sadly, none of them were around to answer any of my questions.

"It seems that your father knew far more than just what my father and Taylor did," Tristan said with a smile.

"They were college friends. My mother and your mother. Do you think we met as kids? My father mentioned that she was wonderful to Kim and me when my mother died. Maybe she brought you along."

"Maybe. Maybe I fell in love with you all the way back then," he said with a grin.

"Now you're just making fun of me. You're terrible! I don't care what you say. I like the idea of us meeting when we were kids and falling in love years later."

"I know what you were thinking, though. You were worried that my mother and your father had been together."

"I was. That's sort of creepy, don't you think? A little too close for comfort for me."

Tristan shrugged and shook his head. "People love who they love, Nina. If my mother was in love with your father, I don't see anything bad in it, especially if he was anything like you. She deserved someone good in her life since she sure as hell didn't have that with my father."

"Then why was she with Karl, of all people?" I asked, still puzzled at how someone so good could be with someone who wanted to kill us.

"I have no idea."

I pointed at the third envelope. "There's one more letter we need to read."

He slipped the letter out and began reading it aloud.

Dear Tressa,

I've found evidence that Stone Worldwide is the maker of the heart medicine Cordovex. The company that produces the drug, Rider Pharmaceutical, is a subsidiary company of Stone run by a man named Karl Dreger. I don't know if anyone in your family knows what Rider is guilty of, but people are dying because of it.

I can't wait with this part of the story. I'm sorry if your family is innocently tied up in this. As I've promised, only what I must reveal will come out.

Joe

"My father tried to warn her. What do you think she did with this information?"

"I don't know, but there are other sheets of paper in the envelope." He pulled the pages out and showed me the first one. On it, Karl's name was written over and over, along with references to Cordovex. "I think we found what he's been looking for."

"That's it. That's what he thinks is in my father's notebook. He had no idea he'd sent the information to your mother instead. But why would he send it to her?"

Tristan shook his head as he read the second note.

"What's that one say?" I asked as he stuffed it back inside the envelope.

"Just more about the Cordovex business. We better find Daryl."

Suddenly, Tristan seemed uneasy. I couldn't put my finger on it, but his expression had changed. Standing up, I took his hand in mine. "You okay?"

"I'm fine. Just a lot to take in."

"I don't think you should judge your mother too harshly, if that's what you're thinking. I don't think she knew about any of what your father or Taylor were doing, and I certainly can't imagine she knew what Karl was doing."

Tristan lifted my hand to his lips and kissed the back of it. "I don't blame her. Of all the people involved in this, only she and your father were innocent. I guess some people would argue that she was responsible even in some small way since she benefited from what Stone Worldwide did..."

His words trailed off, but I quickly tried to ease his mind. "That's bullshit. Your father was responsible for what happened with his company. From what you've told me, she wasn't involved at all. None of the blame is hers, Tristan."

"I know. I do. It's just hard to find out that the woman you thought you knew had all these secrets."

We walked hand-in-hand downstairs and found Daryl peeking behind pictures in the game room. He'd found nothing, but at hearing the news of what we found, his burly face twisted into a clownish grin.

"Good. At least now we know what we have. Any idea how all of that got up there?"

Tristan sat down on a barstool and pushed his hair out of his eyes. "I imagine Rogers took it up there. He was responsible for all of that."

"Well, thank you, Rogers. Now we need to decide what you should do next. You can't get the authorities involved in the whole Cordovex-Cardiell thing until Karl's out of power with Rider," Daryl said.

"Then it's time for Karl to be out of a job. Call Michelle and tell her to schedule a board meeting for three this afternoon."

"Got it."

I watched as the sadness at the mention of Rogers' name slipped from Tristan's face. Stepping close to him, I ran my hands through his hair and kissed his cheek. "Three gives you a little time. Any plans?"

Turning toward me, he winked. "A few things, but first this hair has to go. Time for the Tristan Stone Karl knows all too well to finally be back in full force."

Chapter Fifteen

Tristan

After I'd run a few errands and gotten rid of the boy band angst hair, I was finally back to being myself again, and it was time to return to the building I hadn't seen in over four months. The lobby looked the same with its white marble floors and dark wood walls, and as I passed through security I saw the guards' eyes widen just a little as they recognized me. The oldest one, a man named Bill who'd worked for the company since before I was born, gave me a tiny smile, as if to let me know that he was glad to see me back where I belonged.

Not that I necessarily believed being back at the helm of Stone Worldwide was where I belonged. As I waited for the elevator doors to open to take me to the twenty-fifth floor and my office, I looked at the reflection of myself in the metal panels. The same old Tristan Stone I'd been every day of my time in that building looked back at me wearing my usual suit and tie, but I didn't feel like that man anymore. My time in exile had given me a lot of time to think about my life, and the thought of spending the rest of my adult years in this building no longer seemed right. After the coke and the booze, I finally found out who I was in that old home my mother had loved, and it wasn't the man in front of me now.

That didn't mean I was ready to hand over the company to the likes of Karl, though.

I exited the elevator on the floor that housed my office suite and saw Michelle's face light up as she realized her prodigal boss had finally returned. I could only hope that the reception I received from the Stone Worldwide Board of Directors was half as terrific.

Michelle stood from her desk, obviously excited and with a big smile said, "Mr. Stone! Your office is just as you left it. No one has stepped foot inside, not even security or maintenance. Just as you instructed."

I stopped at her desk and responded to her welcome with a smile of my own. "Good afternoon, Michelle. Thank you for holding down the fort. I'm sure it wasn't easy."

"Mr. Dreger was an almost constant visitor, but I never let him in. He certainly was persistent, though."

"Thank you for taking such care to make sure of that." I turned to head into my office and noticed that there was something different about my assistant. My eyes traveled down her body to a slightly noticeable baby bump. Michelle was pregnant.

"I've been gone a long time, haven't I?" I asked as I pointed to her stomach. "When's the happy day?"

She rubbed her hands over her belly and smiled. "I didn't know the last time we talked. I found out in January. We're due in early August."

"Congratulations, Michelle. Does this mean I'm going to lose you?"

"For a little while, at least. I'm hoping to return after my six week leave, but we're going to have to find care for the baby. It's a big change. We need to find a new apartment first, though."

Michelle paused and a blush came over her cheeks. "I'm sorry. Here I am chattering on about me while you have a big meeting ahead of you. I did as Daryl said and notified all the members of the Stone board that you wanted a meeting at three today. The ones who are out of town will be teleconferencing, but they all said they'd be there."

Chuckling, I said, "I'd rather talk about you than the meeting with the Board, but thank you for handling it. I have a few minutes before I have to head down, so I'm going to gather my thoughts so I'm ready."

"Yes, Mr. Stone."

Michelle sat down and got back to whatever work she had after months of me being absent. Before I walked into my office, I stopped and thought about what she'd just said. Never once had she called me anything but Mr. Stone, but now, it felt wrong. Mr. Stone was my father. I was Tristan.

"Michelle, do me a favor, would you?"

She spun slowly in her chair to face me and nodded. "Of course, Mr. Stone."

"Call me Tristan. We've known each other long enough that you should call me by my first name."

A broad smile spread across her face. "Thank you, Tristan." Hesitating, she added, "That's going to take some getting used to."

"Well, let's hope you have the time to. We'll see after the meeting today," I said as I headed into my office for the first time in months.

The fact was there was a real chance the Board of Directors would inform me that I was no longer able to handle the CEO position, in their opinion. My absence might just have been too much, and if they did move to replace me, I honestly didn't know if I wanted to fight it. I should have wanted to, but as I stood there in my gorgeous corner office looking out the windows at the city below, I wasn't sure. I had enough money to take Nina anywhere her heart desired every day for the rest of our lives.

Why would I stay working in that corner office for another of those days?

Michelle's voice interrupted my thoughts to let me know the time had come. "It's nearly three, Tristan."

Without answering her, I took one last look around my office, just in case that was the last time I could call it mine. As much as I wanted to run off with Nina and never look back at this office and everything about the company, something inside me wasn't quite ready to give up yet. I'd never been meant for this, but after taking the responsibility on, it had become part of me, part of who I truly was.

Michelle was waiting for me with a supportive smile, and as I walked by, I heard her say under her breath, "Knock 'em dead." That's exactly what I intended on doing.

The conference room teemed with board members all ready to discuss the future of Stone Worldwide. The sea of faces turned toward me as I took my seat at the head of the long polished wood table. Never before had I looked at these people and seen them as strangers like I did at that moment. They looked like me in their expensive suits and silk ties, older than I but sitting there like me in comfortable leather chairs discussing topics that until today I actually tried to care about, but now I felt like we had nothing in common.

Noticeably absent was Karl, however.

Lawrence Meister, the chairman of the Stone Worldwide board, sat to my right halfway down the table and nodded silently at me to give the signal it was time to begin. "Tristan, we're happy to see you're back. We look forward to hearing what you have to say."

I took a deep breath and began. "I've never felt close to anyone on this board, unfortunately. If I had, my time away may have been different. That being what it is, I'm here today to let you know that if this board is planning on removing me from my place here, you're going to have a fight on your hands. I am Stone Worldwide. When the world thinks of this company, it thinks of me, just as it thought of my father before me. Each of you may think you can take my place and do a better job, but the fact is, you can't and you won't have the chance."

"Tristan, I'm not sure what you thought, but no one here wants that," Lawrence said as he scanned the surprised expressions on the faces of the men around him. "We're here to find out what you plan to do now that you're back."

"First, I'm curious where Karl is. He's got some supporters on this board and his actions need to be discussed."

A few of the board members whispered to one another at my mention of Karl, but no one volunteered any information to explain his absence. Lawrence's expression showed he knew nothing of what I suspected were Karl's plans to take my place at the head of the company.

"Karl contacted me when this meeting was called and informed me that he would be late. What's going on here?"

I opened the folder Daryl had given me containing all the information concerning Rider Pharmaceutical, Cordovex, and Cardiell. Taking the first packet off the top of the pile, I passed the rest to my right for each member to have for their own. As each man scanned the facts surrounding Rider and its heart drugs, their eyes grew wide in horror. Even the members I'd suspected of backing Karl looked shocked at the information Daryl had gathered.

"What you're looking at is the information the Feds will have concerning a subsidiary of Stone Worldwide. My father gave Rider Pharmaceutical to Karl Dreger to run, and for years he handled the company without a misstep. However, just after my father died, leaving his position to me, Rider found itself in trouble with Cordovex. As you can see on page two, the drug was deadly. The FDA knew, and Rider pulled it voluntarily, but it still held the patent."

James Sheridan, one of the members I'd believed supported Karl in his takeover plans cleared his throat and asked in a shaky voice, "Is this company responsible for Rider's actions?"

I knew what he was afraid of. As a Stone Worldwide stockholder, Sheridan worried more about his portfolio than helping Karl climb over me on his way up the corporate ladder. Nodding, I spoke the truth that no one in that room wanted to hear. "Of course. This board will have to answer for its actions in this matter also, especially considering how accommodating you've been to Karl Dreger's ambitions over the years."

Whatever support he'd had evaporated as they read page after page of his malfeasance as the head of Rider. While the members of the board began to mutter their disbelief, Karl himself came through the conference room doors full of confidence and oblivious to the shitstorm he'd just stumbled into.

He stopped next to my chair and looked down at me, his beady eyes telegraphing his smugness. "Nice to see you again, Tristan. A few days more and you may not have had that seat."

Leaning back, I stared up at him and smiled. "We were just talking about you, Karl. Sit down. I think you'll be very interested in this. Perhaps you'd like to give us a rundown of how Rider Pharmaceutical is doing."

He pulled up a chair and sat down as I slid one last copy of Daryl's report toward him. He hadn't read more than a few words before his hands began shaking.

"Rider? I think you'll find it's doing just fine," he sputtered out. Looking up from the stack of papers with enough proof to cost him everything he'd earned, Karl scowled. "What the hell is this? You all aren't believing this, are you?"

"Yes, they are, Karl, and so are the Feds. Killing people is not only bad business. It's wrong. When it comes out that you knew what Cordovex did and still brought it back as Cardiell, you're going to be the one to pay."

His eyes darted around the room, searching for an ally that no longer existed. Looking like a trapped animal, he swallowed hard. Sweat beaded on his brow, even as the fight inside him struggled to overcome his fear. Thrusting his chair away from the table, he stood upright and shook his head violently.

"This is fucking bullshit! I'm not going to stand here and take this. That company was nothing when I took over. It was nothing!"

Lawrence shot me a glance and calmly spoke up. "Karl, I think it would be better if you got your things in order and spoke to counsel. What we're seeing in this report means you'll have to go."

As if the chairman's words set something off inside him, Karl turned toward me and spat out, "You don't know who you're fucking with, son. You're not going to take me down. No fucking way."

"Time's up, Karl. And don't call me son. I'm Tristan Stone, son of Victor and Tressa Stone."

I watched as the mention of my mother's name made his eyes flash with rage, and he stormed out of the room, slamming the doors behind him. While the members of the board sat in stunned silence at what they'd seen, I stood and leaned down to place my hands on the table. "Gentlemen, if you'll excuse me, I have a mess to clean up."

"Before you go, can you tell us if anyone died this time? There were no details in the report about Cardiell," James Sheridan asked, obviously concerned.

Shaking my head, I said, "Not that we know of. Hopefully, we've caught this early enough."

Sheridan slumped back in his seat, his expression one of disbelief. "My mother takes Cardiell. To think that bastard knew what it could do and still let it be sold to people."

"If you'll excuse me gentlemen." Even though I understood his horror, I had to deal with Karl and the repercussions that would inevitably fall in my lap. Returning to my office, I asked Michelle as I passed her desk, "Can you get Harvey on the phone? Tell him I'm going to need him on this Rider thing."

Dialing the phone, she said, "Daryl had me call him earlier. He made sure to send what he'd found over to his office so he'd be ready when you called."

"Good. Let me know when you get him."

I opened the door to my office and heard her say behind me, "Is everything going to be okay, Tristan? They're not going to blame you for this, are they?"

With a shrug, I tried to downplay how concerned I truly was. "What's that saying—the buck stops here? As CEO, I needed to know what Karl was up to. I didn't. I don't know what they'll do."

The truth was I really didn't know what they'd do, but whatever happened, at least Cardiell would be off the market and Karl wouldn't be hurting anyone anymore.

"I have Harvey on the line," she yelled in as I sat down at my desk.

Raising the receiver to my ear, I pressed the blinking button on the phone. "Harvey, you got the information Daryl sent over?"

"I did. This firm will take care of it. Don't worry."

"I'm not. You never let me down before, Harvey. I know things are going to get ugly before this is over, but I'm prepared for whatever happens. I have something else I need you to take care of too."

"What's that?"

"I want to sell my share in a business I'm part owner of. This isn't part of Stone Worldwide, though. This is a private business arrangement. Can you handle it?"

"Sure. We can talk after our meeting with the Feds."

"Sounds good. I'll see you in a little while."

I hung up the phone and sat back in my chair to look around my office, noticing the bare white walls that surrounded me. After all of this business with Rider was over and Nina and I were back from our honeymoon, I wanted to have her pick out some artwork for this office. It was about time I made this place my own.

Chapter Sixteen

Tristan

Hours later, I arrived home to find Nina pacing the floor in our bedroom. I hadn't made it two feet into the room before she was peppering me with questions about what happened. I'd hoped Daryl wouldn't tell her about the possibility that I'd be held responsible along with Karl for the Rider mess, but I wasn't that lucky. Leave it to that hairy son of a bitch to pick that day for true confessions.

"I've been a nervous wreck for hours. You weren't answering your phone, and Daryl was no help at all. What happened? Can your lawyers get you out of this?"

Loosening my tie, I slipped it from under my collar and threw it on the bed. "One question at a time. It's been a long afternoon."

Nina slid my jacket off, draping it across the desk chair. "I'm sorry. I'm just a mess from worrying. Why didn't you tell me about this?"

I smiled and began unbuttoning my shirt. "Because I knew you'd be like this."

She let out a heavy sigh and sat down on the bed near me. Tugging on my shirttails, she twisted her face into a fake scowl. "What happened to me being an equal and you not keeping secrets from me anymore?"

Lying hadn't been what I'd intended, but she was right. Looking down at her, I hoped if I flashed a smile I could lessen her justifiable anger. "I figured one last time I could spare you. I didn't realize Daryl would suddenly need to bare his soul."

"Don't think you're going to get out of this with that famous Tristan grin. I'm angry at you, Mr. Stone."

I shrugged off my shirt and flashed her another smile. "Then I'm going to have to figure out a way to make sure you're happy again, Ms. Edwards. Give me ten minutes and I'll tell you everything. Then I'll see what I can do to bring back that beautiful smile I love so much."

Nina ran her finger along the top of my pants, her nail grazing the skin beneath my boxers. "Ten minutes. That's it. I'll be waiting."

"You could join me."

Chuckling, she pressed her palm to the front of my pants. "That would only make you think I forgive you already. You're going to have to do a little more than that to make up for this."

Her touch thrilled me, making my cock spring to life. Wanting her more than a shower, I pushed my hips forward, causing her hand to slide down the length of me. "Forget the shower. I've got a better idea."

She pushed me away and shook her head. "No way. Now get in there and wash the day off you. I'll be back in ten minutes so you can tell me everything about what happened."

"I like my idea better."

Standing, she kissed me softly and smiled. "Don't try to charm me. I won't let you this time."

"Can't blame a guy for trying. Get ready for a great night. We're celebrating being back in our own bed and together."

"It's a deal. See you in ten."

After a quick shower, I dressed in pajama pants and prepared to tell Nina everything as quickly as possible so we could get to celebrating. I had a surprise for her I knew she'd love, but she was nowhere to be found by the time I got out to the bedroom. Thinking she may have gone to the kitchen for a snack, I made my way there only to hear her talking to someone in the entryway. When I turned the corner, I saw her standing with Varo, and suddenly all that jealousy I thought I'd conquered rushed back, filling me with rage.

What the fuck was he doing in my house?

Struggling to get a handle on my emotions, I crossed my arms and leaned against the wall to wait for one of them to realize they were being watched. Nina was talking about something concerning her garden, but it didn't matter. Varo worked for me guarding Nina. He had no business standing there talking to her about anything.

He saw me first and instantly his body language became defensive. Crossing his arms, he took a step back away from her. "Mr. Stone, we were just talking about the gardener Nina's looking for."

Nina turned around and quickly the smile she wore faded. "Hey, that was less than ten minutes."

"Be in my office at nine sharp, Varo. Good night."

With a quick nod, he got out of there before I had to say another word, leaving Nina standing in the middle of the room staring daggers at me. "What was that about?"

"What was he doing here?"

Knitting her brows, she frowned and shook her head. "Exactly what he said. I'm hiring a new gardener."

"Then I'll take care of it."

Her disgust came out in a huff, and she stormed past me down the hall. I followed her, knowing what was coming next and wanting it far too much. I found her in our bedroom pacing the floor just as I'd found her a short time earlier. Folding my arms again, I leaned against the doorframe and waited. It didn't take long.

She spun around and pointed her finger at me. "You aren't seriously going to be jealous after making me kiss him, are you? I mean, you wanted me to do that and now I have to deal with this nonsense?"

"Nonsense?"

"That's exactly what it is. You're jealous and it's nonsense. Or maybe you'd rather me call it bullshit. Whatever we call it, I can't believe you're acting like this."

"Like a man who doesn't want his soon-to-be wife hanging out with other men?"

"You're acting ridiculous, Tristan. So now there's a problem with me talking to one of my bodyguards?"

"Maybe you wouldn't mind if I had a conversation with Brandi?"

Her pacing stopped dead, and in her face I saw what I felt. Rage. Jealousy.

"What the fuck are you doing? I did nothing wrong out there and now you're acting like a jackass. A jealous jackass!"

I knew she was right, but it was like I was standing outside my body and couldn't stop the words from coming out of my mouth. My heart told me I had nothing to worry about with her and Varo, but my brain so filled with those old demons egged me on. "I'm not in the mood to discuss this, Nina. I'm replacing Varo tomorrow."

Her mouth dropped open. "What are you doing? Why? He did nothing wrong. If anyone should be fired, it's West. Varo's been nothing but an obedient employee, even when you made him pretend to be my boyfriend," she screamed. "Don't do this."

"I didn't realize you cared so much about what happened to him."

She came at me like she wanted to hit me but stopped short just inches away to stare up into my eyes, as if the answer to my madness could be found in them. Taking my hands in hers, she pleaded, "Tristan, what is going on? Stop acting like this and tell me what's wrong. Whatever it is, we can handle it. Just tell me."

Lowering my head, I shook it, unable to explain why I was acting so stupid. "I don't know. It was just something exploded inside me when I saw you together."

She caressed my cheek with her hand and said quietly, "Baby, I don't know how to convince you that you're the only man I want. I can tell you a million times, but you don't seem to believe me."

I caught her hand and lowered it between us. Looking down at it, I said, "You're not wearing your engagement ring. Why? Have you changed your mind?"

"Is that what this is about? Look at me and tell me. Is that it?"

I let my gaze travel up to hers and shook my head. "No. I'm fucked up. That's it. I don't know why."

"Well, fucked up or not, you have nothing to worry about. Remember you left me for months? I don't want anyone else, so let poor Varo have his job and stop thinking I want anyone else on Earth because I don't."

"I have a surprise for you."

Sighing, she asked, "A good one?"

"A good one. Sit down and close your eyes." She did as I said and I grabbed the box I'd picked up earlier that day. Kneeling on one knee, I opened it and held it in my palm. "Okay. Open them."

I saw in her eyes the surprise I'd hoped for. In my palm sat a robin's egg blue Tiffany's box with a new ring. It was meant as a new start, even though I'd nearly fucked it up with my jealousy just minutes earlier.

"Another ring? Why? I loved the first one," she said as she lifted the box up to examine it. "It's beautiful, Tristan. But why?"

"Maybe we had bad luck the last time. And the time before that. I want this time to go right, so I bought this ring hoping that maybe this can change our luck. Marry me."

"Of course I'll marry you. You didn't have to buy me another ring, though. I'd marry you even without one." Leaning down, she kissed me sweetly on the lips and whispered, "You do this proposal thing pretty well, Mr. Stone."

I pressed my forehead to hers as a sense of relief flooded over me. "Third time's a charm. Isn't that what they say? Put it on."

Holding her hand up, she wiggled her fingers to show me how perfect it looked on her and grinned broadly. "Is it me?"

"It's all you."

"What are we going to do with the other ring?"

"I don't know. Donate it to a charity. Get it reset in a necklace. Save it for our kids."

Nina stroked her fingertips over my shoulder and down my arm. "I like this proposal best. You're already half naked and on your knees."

"Mmm….is that a proposition from you?" I teased as my hands slowly made their way over her thighs. Making quick work of the button at the top of her jeans, I tugged them and her panties off her body in one pull, leaving her wide open for what I planned to do.

"I like the way you think," she said with a moan as I slid my finger through the folds of her wet and ready pussy.

"Lean back," I ordered. She whimpered a tiny noise at the first touch of my tongue to her clit. Sucking it gently, I eased my middle finger inside her tight cunt. Her body clung to me as I slowly added a second finger.

I stared up into her face and watched a look of pleasure settle into her features as I finger fucked her, loving the moans that flooded my ears as I inched her toward release. I wanted to make her forget my stupid mistake from before so all tonight would be in her mind was the night I showed her how much I wanted to spend the rest of my life with her.

"God, Tristan…don't stop. That feels incredible. God, don't stop!"

Arching her back, she angled her pussy toward my mouth and I obliged, running my tongue up to her swollen clit. She moaned my name, and I thrust my fingers into her hard as I flicked my tongue over her tender skin, wanting her to come apart under my mouth. Her cunt tightened around my fingers, and I quickly pulled out, replacing them with my tongue thrusting inside her.

"Yes…yes! Oh, God…yes!" she cried, pulling on the back of my head to hold me as she rode the tremors of her orgasm.

When she finally finished, her thighs quivered uncontrollably against my jaw. Turning my head, I placed a light kiss on her left leg, loving the feel of her soft skin against my lips and the knowledge that I'd made her tremble.

She lay there, eyes closed and biting her lip as she waited for me to get rid of my pants and rejoin her on the bed. I hovered over her and rolled my hips forward to slide the full length of my cock through her drenched pussy, loving how her eyes rolled back in her head when it skimmed her clit.

"Mmmm…you just love to tease me, don't you?" she said with a sexy grin.

"I love watching you come. You are so fucking sexy when I'm between your legs lapping your pussy."

Nina giggled, and a blush covered her cheeks. "Mr. Stone, you have a dirty mouth!"

I placed a light kiss just below her ear and slowly pushed my hips forward again. "You love it."

Nodding, she said whimpered. "I do."

"Good. Now be a good girl and open those legs for me. I'm not anywhere close to done with you."

"Are you going down on me again?" she asked with an innocence that made my cock stiffen to rock solid.

Sitting up next to her on the bed, I dragged my finger slowly down her swollen slit. She bit her lower lip again and moaned as I lingered there watching her. "I might. Then again, I might pin you to the bed and fuck you long and hard, or maybe slow and easy. I don't know."

She opened her legs wider, but I lifted my hand away, receiving one of her all-too-sexy pouts in return. "You are so mean. You make me wait for hours and then you tease me like this. Downright cruel is what you are."

I bent my head down and captured a nipple in my mouth, flicking my tongue over the pebbled flesh. Nina's fingers pressed into the back of my head, urging me on, but I pulled away and sat up.

"What's that wicked grin for?" she said with an edge to her voice that told me my teasing was working.

"I was just thinking about how much I want to bury my cock in your wet cunt and fuck you until you can't walk."

Stretching her arm to touch my thigh, she stroked my cock from the base and smacked her lips. "Put up or shut up, Mr. Stone. The time for teasing is over."

"Ms. Edwards, I'll take that challenge. Get up here on my lap."

Nina stood and straddled my hips, and I positioned her perfectly so all I had to do was lift my hips from the bed and ease into her. She didn't give me the chance, though, and slid down my cock until I was fully seated inside her. Tracing her tongue around the shell of my ear, she whispered, "I didn't want to wait anymore."

"Always so impatient."

I pushed hard into her and stopped, holding her hips tightly in my hands. She cried out, her fingernails digging into my shoulders, her voice filled with aching need. "Don't stop. Please don't stop. I'll beg if that's what you want. Just don't stop."

"You want me to fuck you? To slide in and out of your tight cunt filling you until you can barely breathe? To empty my cock inside you until there's nothing left of me?"

She stared down at me and knitted her eyebrows like she was in pain. "Yes. Tristan, yes."

I wanted her as much as she wanted me, and as she buried her face in my neck, I pumped into her. She met my thrusts with her own, riding me with abandon until the two of us were close to coming apart.

Pulling her head down, I kissed her long and hard, wanting to eliminate any trace of every other man her lips had touched. The thought of Varo's mouth on hers tormented me, even as I tried to push it from my thoughts, and as if she read my mind, Nina broke off the kiss and said quietly as her body closed in around mine, "There's no other man I want. Only you. All I want is you."

Wrapping my arms around her, I held her tight as her release and mine exhausted us both. She was so small in my hold, a precious soul I needed to take better care of now that I was back. I couldn't let my jealousy ruin her love.

I lay there with Nina in my arms and silently thanked God for everything I'd been blessed with. I'd avoided jail time from the debacle with Rider, and as the new director of the company I'd have a chance to make sure nothing like that ever happened again under my watch. Maybe we'd even be able to truly create a drug to help heart disease patients. My business life was going to be rocky for the foreseeable future with Federal investigators combing through every last inch of Rider Pharmaceutical's actions since Karl's takeover of it more than a decade ago, but that was the price I had to pay for turning a blind eye to even the smallest part of the Stone Worldwide empire. From now on, I'd have to accept the fact that being the CEO meant I couldn't do it halfway anymore. I just hoped Nina would understand.

Our lives would have to change. For the first time in my life, I had to devote myself to the business of making money. It wouldn't be enough to playact the role of CEO of Stone Worldwide as I had for the last five years. Now, I'd actually have to be that man.

Nina's finger traced a line across my stomach, telling me she had something on her mind. It was one of the cute things she did when she wanted to talk about something but didn't know how to bring it up.

"Tristan, we need to discuss what we want to do about the wedding."

Lifting her head to face me, she looked at me intently and I knew she'd already thought about it. I pushed a stray strand of hair out of her eyes and smiled up at her. "We'll do whatever you want."

She sat up and grinned mischievously. "Whatever I want? Like if I want us to take our vows at the top of the Empire State Building you'd be okay with that?"

I knew she was teasing me, but I really hoped her plans didn't involve anything in the city. Something small at one of my hotels, maybe in Italy or Greece, was more along the lines of what I had in mind. "Whatever you want. Your wish is my command."

Her smile changed to that special kind she gave me when she was genuinely happy. "I think something small right here at the house would be great. Just a few close friends and us. We could do it sooner that way."

I thought about her idea for a moment. "How does a honeymoon in Europe sound then?"

Nina nodded her head. "I was thinking we could go back to Venice. I'd love it if we could get that same room we had last time. Do you think we can?"

I couldn't help but chuckle. "I know the owner, so I think so."

She rolled her eyes and jabbed me sharply in the side. "I'll never get used to that. Maybe it only seems normal if you're born into it."

Pulling her down on top of me, I kissed her full on the mouth. "Then that's something I need to work on. Once you're Mrs. Tristan Stone, you'll officially have everything I have."

"I still don't think I'll get used to having whatever I want, whenever I want."

"You'd be surprised how easy it is to get used to it."

"Do you have any idea about who you want to invite? I thought maybe just a few close friends."

I thought about who I'd invite and realized there wasn't a soul I'd remained close to after the plane crash. Everyone I'd surrounded myself with before had been people who wouldn't fit into the life I'd created with Nina. Maybe Michelle and her husband. "I don't know."

"Well, I'm thinking Jordan and Varo, at least. Maybe he can be your best man?"

"Maybe I'll let him keep his job and we'll leave it at that, Nina."

She rolled off me and sat up. "Then who will be your best man?"

As much as I didn't want to admit it, there was only one person who I even considered a friend. "Daryl."

Laughter exploded from her, and she covered her face as she continued to giggle. "Oh, Jordan's going to love that. I think I'll make her walk down the aisle with mountain man."

"She likes Varo. Set her up with him. He can be her date for the wedding. That should make up for having to hang out with Daryl for a few minutes."

"Then it's set. Jordan will be my maid of honor, and Daryl will be your best man. When should we do it?"

"We both have birthdays coming up. Which one works better, yours or mine?"

Nina sat silently, and I realized she didn't know when my birthday was. To be honest, I only knew her birthday because I'd had her checked out even before meeting her.

"Well, mine's on a Thursday this year, so that wouldn't work. I think we should get married on a weekend. Your birthday is on the weekend, isn't it?"

"You tell me," I said with a smile.

Tilting her head, she arched one eyebrow. "You think I don't know when your birthday is, don't you?"

"When is it?"

"Well, I'm going to guess May or early June since I met you last May after Memorial Day and starting living with you in mid-June and we've never celebrated it. I don't really know when it is, though. Does that make me a bad girlfriend?"

"No. You're still a great fiancée. It's June 2. And since yours is May 15, we're not able to do it on either day if you want to keep it on a weekend."

Nina twisted her face into a scowl and bit her lower lip. "Then what about next weekend. We're not planning to do anything big, so as long as everyone we want can be here, we're good."

Lifting her left hand to my lips, I kissed her engagement ring. "Next weekend it is. You ready to be Mrs. Stone, Ms. Edwards?"

"I am. And are you ready to tell me everything that happened with Karl today?"

"I guess I'm not going to escape explaining that to you, so yes, I'll tell you everything."

Nina crossed her legs and settled in next to me. "Good. See how nice it feels to not keep secrets?"

"We'll see how you feel after you hear everything. Things are going to change for me at work."

"I'm all ears, Tristan, and don't worry. As long as you don't change what's inside you, we'll be A-OK."

CHAPTER SEVENTEEN

Nina

I listened as Tristan explained how he would have to devote more time to Stone Worldwide business from now on, knowing that he feared I wouldn't want to be with a man like that. He was wrong, though. It didn't matter if he was a CEO or a doorman. All that mattered to me was that he was the Tristan I loved.

By the time he was finished, he looked like a weight had been lifted from him. Even though he'd decided to be more hands on with the company, the fact that he could shape Stone Worldwide into a business he could be proud of was important.

"So it looks like I'm going to become what I never thought I'd want to be—a real CEO. How do you feel about that? This wasn't who I was when you said yes to marrying me."

Lifting his chin with my fingertip, I looked him straight in the eyes. "Tristan, you have to do what's right for you. If that means taking on more responsibility, how could I have a problem with that? You're still the same man I fell in love with. It's not like you've decided to give up everything you've ever been and live in the wilderness without running water. That I'd have a problem with."

He kissed my hand and smiled. "I'm not much of a wilderness type of guy. I couldn't even handle the beard and long hair, and I'm pretty attached to running water myself. I just don't want you to think that I'm turning into my father. I promise I'm not."

Who Victor Stone had been was basically a mystery to me, except for what my father had believed about him. I knew nothing about him other than that he was the man I blamed for taking my only parent from me. But never once had I feared Tristan would turn into that man. I saw in the slight frown he wore as he spoke about becoming like his father that he did fear that, though.

"Tristan, you're not your father. I don't worry about you turning into him."

"I swear I never will. I won't let that happen to me or to us."

"Speaking of us, I've got a million and one things to do before next weekend. One week isn't a lot of time to plan a wedding."

"That's the good part about being the groom. All we have to do is put on the tux and be there on time."

"I thought the good part was getting married to the woman you love."

"Well, yeah, of course," he said with a chuckle. "But not having to do all that wedding stuff is pretty good too."

I jabbed him in the side. "For that comment, I hope I take up all the bed tonight and leave you with just a sliver of mattress."

Pulling me close to him, he gave me one of those truly rare Tristan smiles that told me he was truly happy. "As long as you're next to me, I don't care how much I have. All that matters is I have you."

I hit the last step to Jordan's building and struggled to catch my breath as the door flew open. Jordan stood there grinning from ear to ear, arms wide open to envelope me with a hug. "I am so ready to check out some wedding dresses. We can have lunch, gossip about all the things we need to catch up on, and, of course, find you the perfect gown to marry that man of yours in."

"Let me catch my breath! I think you might be more excited than I am about this shopping trip."

Grabbing me, she hugged me close and then held me at arm's length to take a look at me. "This is going to happen this time. I swear to God, if I have to chain you and Tristan down, it's happening."

"I promise no more false starts. This time we're doing this. You ready to go?"

Jordan looked past me at Jensen and the car waiting for us. "I've missed that old guy." Looking around left and then right, she giggled. "And where would your bodyguards be today?"

"They're somewhere. Tristan told them to make themselves scarce, so we may not see them. Don't worry, though. You'll see Gage at the wedding."

We nearly bounced down the stairs to the car, and Jordan turned toward me, her expression suddenly serious. "By the way, what other females will be there? I need to know who my competition is for the bouquet."

I opened the car door and held it for her. "It's going to be a small affair. I promise to make sure you catch the bouquet."

"Make it look good, though. We don't want people thinking the fix was in," she joked as she climbed into the back seat.

I sat down next to her and tapped on the back of the driver's seat. "We're ready, Jensen."

"Yes, miss. We should be there shortly."

Jordan turned toward me. "So tell me what's going on with that ring. If my eyes don't deceive me, that's not the diamond he gave you when he first proposed."

I couldn't help but grin. "It is a new one. He had it for me when he asked me again last night. I didn't ask for it or anything. I was perfectly happy with the first one."

Taking my hand in hers, she studied my ring like a jeweler. "This ring looks even bigger. What is this, like almost two carets? I'm surprised you're not dragging your knuckles on the ground when you walk."

I pulled my hand away and shook my head. "Don't tease. It's not that big, and I like it. Tristan's got good taste. He knows what I like."

"Yes, he does. Simple round cut but stunning. So what are the plans? You mentioned on the phone it was going to be intimate, so I'm not going to have to mess up other women there if they hit on Gage?"

Laughing, I said, "It will be intimate. Just a few of us. You'll have all the chances you want to get to know him. I tried to get Tristan to have him as the best man, but he wasn't going for it. I'm planning to make sure there's a chance for just the four of us to spend a little time together too."

"Okay. As long as we have a plan. As for today, we're getting your gown and mine. I'm trusting that you won't put me in one of those awful bridesmaid's gowns, right? No horrible pastels like mint green or peach. That would just be cruel, sweetie."

I grabbed her hand and threaded my fingers through hers. "I wouldn't do that to you. You're my best friend in the world, so no mint or any other horrible color dress. I was thinking a nice black gown would look incredible on you with your blonde hair and green eyes."

"Perfect! I knew you wouldn't dress me in something awful. But what about Kim? What is she wearing?"

"I don't know. I didn't ask her to be a bridesmaid. I haven't even told her we're getting married."

Jordan made a clucking sound with her tongue. "I don't blame you. That girl is a drag. Do you plan to let her know?"

Sighing, I shrugged. "I don't know. Kim is never supportive of anything with me, and I don't want her to ruin this. Then I think that my father would never forgive me if he knew I didn't invite her to my wedding. I don't know what to do."

The car rolled to a stop in front of a Brooklyn boutique where I knew I could find a dress on such short notice. As Jensen got out, Jordan gave me a sympathetic smile. "Well, we don't have to think about her today. We just have to find you the world's most incredible wedding gown and me the hottest bridesmaid's gown so Gage sees that I clean up nice and sweeps me off my feet."

"I see you've thought about this a bit," I joked as my car door opened.

"Just a little. Now let's get in there and find that dress!"

My dress wasn't hard to find. I knew exactly what I wanted when I walked into the store, so it was just a matter of finding a dress that didn't look like I was stepping out of a Disney princess parade. Thankfully, I only had to try on three before I found my perfect dress. A white satin gown with a beautiful draped neckline and cut-out back, it hung like it was made just for me. I knew as soon as I looked in the dressing room mirror that it was the dress I'd marry Tristan in.

Jordan's squeals of delight when I walked out to model it for her told me I'd been right. Stepping up onto the carpeted dais, I twirled around in front of the tri-fold mirror. The coolness of the silk against my legs felt luxurious, and the back had just enough sexiness for my style.

"I love it! Is that the one you're going to get?" Jordan asked as she fluttered around behind me checking out the dress from every angle.

Stopping, I smoothed the fabric over my thighs and nodded. "I think so. It's not incredibly fancy, but it's me. I love the way it hangs on me and makes me look taller. Not poofy or prom-like. Now for the veil. What do you think would work?"

"Elbow length would be perfect," Jordan suggested as she skipped over to the rack of veils on the far wall. She choose one and held it out to me. Iridescent and lined with beads, it fit perfectly with the dress.

I placed it on my head and held my hands out as if to model the finished product. "Ta-da!"

In the mirror, I saw Jordan tear up behind me. Covering her mouth, she whispered, "Oh, honey. You're gorgeous."

I looked at the woman I was standing there in that bridal boutique, and for one of the few times in my life I thought I looked beautiful. That awkward art geek who never seemed to get the quarterback or dream boyfriend in high school was nowhere to be found, replaced by the most glamorous version of me there'd ever been.

Jordan sniffled behind me, making the moment so serious I almost cried, so I quickly turned around and changed the subject. Stepping down off the dais, I said, "Now we have to find you a dress. It's your turn now."

"I found a couple while you were in the dressing room. I don't think the saleswoman thinks much of your idea of having me in black, though. She kept trying to foist pink gowns on me, and the last one she showed me was aquamarine. Can you believe it? Aquamarine! I had to stop myself from asking how her trip back to 1987 was."

As I headed into the dressing room again, I carefully slid the dress from my shoulders. "Pink might work, if you want, but aquamarine is definitely out of the question. You sure you want black?"

I closed the door behind me just as the saleswoman came into the room with her arms full of pink, fluffy bridesmaids dresses—exactly the kind I'd promised Jordan she wouldn't get stuck wearing. From inside the dressing room, I heard her announce to the woman, "There's no way I'm going to be caught dead in those prom dresses."

I hurried out of the dress and veil before she offended the woman and got out to her just in time to stop her from explaining just how dreadful the color aquamarine was. As the saleswoman turned on her heels and left, Jordan and I burst into laughter and it was like old times again.

Thankfully, the woman wasn't too offended to bring back four black bridesmaids dresses, and after trying on each one, we couldn't decide. They were all stunning on her. Not willing to take no for an answer, the saleswoman returned with one last dress in a soft peacock blue and before we knew it, we had to admit she had something there.

Jordan hurried into the dressing room and emerged in less than a minute in the dress that made me forget the idea of black in a heartbeat. Next to her long blond hair, the blue satin was stunning. Strapless, with a cuff neckline, it showed off her toned shoulders, and in the back it laced up like a corset, a very sexy touch. Standing on the dais, she turned around to face me and shook her head. "I have to admit. That lady knows her business. She's delusional about the aquamarine, but this dress is fantastic. Are you okay with it instead of a black one?"

"As long as you're happy, I'm happy. And by the way, I think any man would bow at your feet in that dress."

"Oh, I'm happy then. Bring on the bodyguard. He doesn't know what he's up against with me in this dress," she said flashing a gorgeous smile.

"Good. Let's go grab a bite to eat. I'm starving after all this dress stuff. Hurry and get that dress off and we'll hit that little restaurant near your place."

While Jordan changed back into her clothes, I made nice with the saleswoman and paid for the dresses. I also saw Varo and West outside, and channeling my inner Cupid, approached them as they stood near the front door to the boutique. West looked surprised, so I used what I was sure was his concern about Tristan being unhappy once again with their lack of invisibility to my advantage.

"Gentlemen, we're going to head to a restaurant near Jordan's apartment. I'd like you to join us."

Varo looked at me and raised his eyebrows. I had a feeling the expression wasn't one of surprise but amusement. "I'm not sure Mr. Stone would be pleased with that. I distinctly remember him saying he wanted us out of sight."

"Well, that went by the wayside already, so let's move on to lunch and everyone can be happy."

West grimaced and turned to face Varo, who simply smiled and shrugged. "Looks like we're eating lunch today, buddy."

Jordan joined us, and as she explained that the dresses would be delivered to the house by the middle of next week, I saw Varo sneak a look at her. My inner matchmaker had hope!

Brickfire was quaint and relatively quiet, considering it was in the middle of one of the busiest parts of the neighborhood. Long and narrow, the restaurant's central feature was a deep red brick fireplace that in the winter made the place one of the coziest in Brooklyn. Since it was springtime, it was merely the restaurant's inspiration but it was no matter since the food was supposed to be some of the best in the city.

The hostess sat the four of us at a table in the back, and even though the photographers seemed to have far less interest in me now that Tristan had returned, I was thankful for the little privacy the location afforded us. Unfortunately, it took me only a few minutes to see that West intended on making our lunch like some awkward double date he'd been forced into. It was like the man knew nothing of how two people got together. Every time I attempted to introduce a topic of conversation I knew would help Jordan and Varo really get to know one another, West insisted on inserting some comment about what they were supposed to be doing instead of enjoying a nice meal with us.

The server took our order, and I tried for the third time to talk about something that could help my two intended lovebirds get acquainted. "Gage was in the Navy before he began working as a body-guard, Jordan. Remember when we went to Fleet Week?"

Her green eyes grew as wide as saucers with surprise, and for a moment I thought she might be angry with me for bringing up the topic, but before she could say anything, West angrily excused himself from the table and stomped away.

As I watched him leave the restaurant, I wondered aloud, "What's up with him?"

Rolling her eyes, Jordan joked, "Maybe he's an Army guy."

Out of the corner of my eye, I saw Varo smile and knew instantly it was one unlike any he'd ever given me. It went all the way up to his eyes. He really did like her. Thrilled my plan was unfolding exactly as I'd hoped, I sat back and let things happen.

Just as I'd believed, he was charmed by Jordan's humor and occasional snarkiness, and if she liked him before, the mention of him in the Navy made her practically crazy about him. I saw it in her eyes. Only a few times before had I seen them sparkle like they did as the two of them sat there getting to know one another in the back of Brickfire. By the time West returned, I was convinced my matchmaking work had succeeded beyond my wildest dreams.

As we climbed into the back of the car to head to her place, I couldn't help but smile from ear to ear. Jordan was less expressive, but I knew inside she was bouncing off the walls. "Don't tell me you didn't have a great time. I know you did."

"Sure. The food was great. I really liked that fireplace. I bet in the winter it's great to have dinner there."

I smacked her arm hard. "Don't tell me you didn't love getting to know him. I know you did."

She giggled like a schoolgirl and blushed bright red. "I did. He's even better than I thought. I'm trying not to get too excited by things just in case it ends up being nothing."

"Nothing? When he sees you in that peacock blue dress, he's going to want to sweep you off your feet right there in my garden."

Jordan's expression turned serious, and she squeezed my hand tightly. "I just don't want to be let down, Nina. He's gorgeous and hot and everything any girl would want. I don't want to get my hopes up just yet."

I understood her cautiousness. Letting someone into your heart was risky business, and as we both knew from experience, it rarely worked out. I still believed she could be happy like I was, so wary or not, I had hope for her and Gage.

Jensen stopped the car in front of her apartment and with a heavy heart I had to accept my time with her was over too soon. She saw my sadness and hugged me tightly to her. "Just a couple more days and we'll be standing there in our awesome dresses and you'll be marrying the man of your dreams. No sad faces, okay?"

"Okay. See you in a few days. The wedding is set for six next Saturday, so I'll have Jensen come for you around two."

"Two it is. I love you, Nina. Thanks for being such a great friend."

I watched as she climbed the stairs to her place, already missing her. I wasn't sad so much as understanding for the first time that everything was going to change. Living with someone was one thing, but becoming a wife meant something far more serious. I knew I'd see her whenever we wanted, but my life was about to change.

By the time we arrived back at the house, Varo and the still miserable West were there waiting for us, and as I got out of the car I saw Tristan pull Varo aside near the garage to speak to him. Both wore very serious expressions, but I didn't get the sense he was reprimanding my bodyguard. After a minute or so, Varo left and I approached Tristan, happy to see him but curious about what the conversation had been about.

"Hey you! I found a wedding gown and Jordan found her bridesmaid gown, so we're all set on the dresses."

He took my hand in his and smiled. "Good. I can't wait to see it."

Looking up into his eyes, I tried to discern the meaning of his chat with Varo. "Everything okay? I saw you pull Varo aside as I drove up."

"Everything's fine. I have to head into the city, but I'll be back in a few hours. I'd love it if you'd be waiting for me," he said with a wink.

"You know I will be," I said as I stood on my toes to kiss him, missing the feel of his lips on mine after hours away. "Maybe I'll have a surprise for you."

"I like that. You're making it hard to leave, though."

"Good, but I know you have things to do, so just remember I'll be waiting when you get back."

Whispering "I love you," he kissed me again and turned toward the garage. As I watched him walk away, I thought about how I might surprise him. Maybe a nice dinner? Or me in sexy lingerie? Or a nice bubble bath for two?

I'd think of something good.

Chapter Eighteen

Nina

A few minutes after Tristan left, my phone rang. Thinking it was him calling me to say he loved me, I didn't pay attention to the number that flashed across the screen and simply answered the call.

"Hello," I said in a happy, singsong voice.

"Nina? It's Kim."

Just hearing my sister's name made my mood change from blissfully happy to completely miserable. She must have had some kind of happiness radar that beeped as soon as I began to feel good in life, but this time, I wasn't going to let her ruin my great day.

"What do you want, Kim? I'm a little busy."

The phone was silent for a long moment, and then when she spoke again, her voice sounded different, almost contrite, for the first time ever. "I thought maybe we could meet."

"I've got a lot to do this week. I'm getting married, so it's not really a good time. Maybe after I get back."

I knew I was being a bitch, but after years of her being just that, I figured she had it coming. No matter how sorry she felt for our relationship, or lack of, I didn't want to hear it.

"Baby, you're getting married? I thought you and Tristan already had the wedding. You weren't going to tell me, were you?"

Just the word baby made guilt rush over me. My father would be heartbroken to know on the biggest day of my life that Kim wouldn't be there to share it with me. I heard his words echo in my mind at that moment.

"No matter what else you two are, Nina, you're family. Always remember that, baby."

"Kim, what do you want to meet about? I'm not interested in hearing you tell me I'm making a mistake. Considering the man I'm about to marry saved you and your family from being killed, I'd think all you'd have to say to me would be glowing praise for Tristan."

"Please, can we meet? I'm in Manhattan for the night."

Every fiber of my being told me not to go to her, except for that tiny part of my brain whispering that no matter what else Kim was, she'd always be my sister and I owed it to my father to give her another chance. We didn't have to be the best of friends, but I'd always wanted us to be closer. Maybe now we could be.

"Okay. Meet me at a restaurant called Malone's. I can be there in an hour."

As I gave her the address, a sense of satisfaction came over me. Perhaps this was finally the time we could be the kind of sisters I'd always wanted us to be. I felt strong enough to handle her now.

I tracked down Jensen near the carriage house to let him know we'd be hitting the road again, and as I made my way back to the house, I saw Varo. I didn't need a bodyguard to meet my sister, but if I tried to leave without letting him and West know, the hassle wouldn't be worth it.

"Since you're only seeing your sister and Karl's been taken care of, I can probably handle this without West. He seems to be feeling under the weather anyway. He's been scarce since we returned from our little lunch get-together."

I couldn't help but smile. No matter how snide he sounded, I knew he had a good time. "Yeah, don't act like you didn't enjoy it."

He smiled and I saw a sparkle in his dark blue eyes. "Always the matchmaker, Nina. I hope Jordan and I don't disappoint you. We're mere humans, after all."

"All I want is you and her to be as happy as Tristan and I am. That's all."

He chuckled at my statement, and as he walked away toward the car he and West used, he turned around. "I don't know about that, but maybe Jordan's right about that good things happening to good people thing. I guess we'll have to see."

"Just give it a chance," I yelled as I walked back to the house.

The hostess led me to where Kim sat, and I saw that her time in the islands had been good to her. Tanner than she'd been since she was a teenager, she practically glowed. I sat down and was greeted with a smile that looked so different on her. Optimism surged in me, and I was ready to begin what I hoped would be a new future with my only sister.

"Nina! You look wonderful."

"You too. You wear the tropics well."

"You should see the girls. They'd never seen so much sand. It's going to be hard for them to get used to Pennsylvania weather again," she said with a smile.

"I'm glad you enjoyed the resort Tristan arranged for you."

A sharpness crept into my voice that I hadn't intended, but I couldn't deny what lived in my heart. I wanted to repair my relationship with Kim, but that wasn't going to happen with just one dinner and it wasn't going to happen with me forgetting everything she'd done.

The mention of Tristan's name elicited a forced smile from her, and I instantly knew she was still struggling like I was. Maybe that wasn't such a bad thing. Whatever we were going to end up being to one another, I wanted it based on truth.

"It was very nice. I just wish there hadn't been a reason for us being there in the first place."

I knew what she was saying—that Tristan was to blame for a fucking madman being in our lives. Instinctively, I defended the man I loved. "Karl wasn't interested in you because of Tristan, Kim. He thought you had something he wanted because of Daddy. It had nothing to do with Tristan, in fact, so I don't appreciate your insinuation that he was to blame for any of this."

A waiter interrupted our conversation, and I quietly ordered the first dish I saw on the menu, not even sure I was in the mood for a roasted vegetable panini. Not that it mattered. I had a feeling I wasn't going to have much of an appetite tonight.

When we were alone again, a heavy silence settled in between us. I had to admit once again that she hadn't contacted me because she wanted to wish me well or to see if I was happy. As always, Kim had sought me out to be a damper on my life. I felt sad that once again our relationship wasn't going to change.

Unlike every other time I'd accepted that reality, this time I wanted to know why. Why was my happiness a thing she always had to crush?

"Nina, when Daddy died, I promised myself that I'd watch out for you. I know I haven't done a wonderful job, but I tried."

Kim sat there across the table from me wearing some kind of martyr expression, as if she'd struggled so long with me only to be disappointed in the results of her efforts. I wanted to smack that look off her face. How dare she! I'd never been the one who sabotaged her happiness. Never once had I been a hassle asking her for money or to bail me out of trouble. I'd lived my life my way and respected her for living hers the way she wanted to. Why was she acting like I'd been some kind of cross for her to bear?

"What are you talking about, Kim? I didn't need anyone to watch out for me. Why do you make it sound like I've been one problem after another for you?" I asked, feeling the defensiveness rising inside me.

She took a sip of her water and swallowed hard. "Daddy always spoiled you. I told him not to, that it was going to make things harder for you when you became an adult, but he never listened. I think he felt guilty about not finding another woman to help as you were growing up, so he gave you whatever you wanted. It would have been better if he had remarried."

"What the hell does that mean? I had nothing to do with him not marrying again. And Daddy didn't spoil me, unless you call making sure we had a warm place to live and I had clothes on my back spoiling someone."

"That's not the type of spoiling I mean. What I'm talking about is the way he took care of everything for you. You think that's the way it's supposed to be because that's the way you always had it with him."

I wasn't sure where Kim was going with all this, but I wasn't liking any of it. And I wasn't liking the way she was dancing around her true intentions. "Just say what you want to say, Kim. Don't blame Daddy if you're jealous of whatever the hell you're jealous of."

Gritting her teeth, she said, "This isn't about me being jealous, Nina. It's about our father not preparing you for the world and allowing you to be naïve for too long."

That was it. I was done. Leaning across the table, I pointed my finger at her face. "I'm not going to take this anymore from you. You're jealous because I'm not a miserable bitch full of mistrust. I'm sorry you're like that, Kim. I really am. But I didn't make you that way and nothing I do can change who you are. That's on you. I simply won't be the person you dump all your shit on anymore. Don't bother calling me again. I met you tonight because I knew it was what Daddy would want. To be honest, I hoped that we could finally change the vicious cycle our relationship has always been in, but it's obvious that's not going to happen, so don't contact me again."

As I stood to leave, she grabbed my arm to hold me back. "Don't leave. I need to tell you something. Whatever happens after that, at least I can know that I tried and didn't let Daddy down."

I glared down at her, not believing a word coming from her spiteful mouth. "Whatever you need to say, don't bother. I don't want to hear about it."

Reaching into her purse, she pulled out a sheet of paper with tattered edges that looked like someone had ripped it from a notebook. It was folded in half, and she placed in on the bread plate in front of her and looked up at me. "Just hear me out."

As if everything was happening in slow motion, I sat down again and stared at the piece of paper. It looked just like the kind of paper in my father's notebook. "What's this about?"

"Do you remember when you first told me about Tristan? I told you I'd heard horrible things about him—that he'd been responsible for someone's death?"

I raised my eyes from the sheet of paper to look at her. "Yes, and I remember telling you I thought you were crazy. I still do. Tristan couldn't kill anyone. You don't know him."

"No, I don't. I'm afraid you don't either."

Shaking my head, I took a deep breath. "You're wrong. Whatever you think that says, you're wrong. It was Tristan's brother who was responsible for that girl's death. Taylor did that, not Tristan."

She opened the folded sheet of paper and scanned what was written there. "This says Tristan. There's no mention of his brother being implicated in that girl's death. Daddy found all this out when he was investigating Stone Worldwide."

"You're mistaken. I've seen Daddy's notebook, and he knew it was Taylor who got that girl pregnant. He wrote it down himself. I can't believe you'd accuse the man I love of being a murderer again. What is wrong with you, Kim? What did I ever do to you to make you do this to me?"

"I've seen that notebook too, but before Daddy died. He ripped this page out because it wasn't part of his investigation of Tristan's father's company and filed it away. I found it when I cleaned out his house after the funeral. You know, when you were busy spending hour after hour in bed while I had to deal with everything that comes when your father dies and no one else is there to help you."

Her attack stung, and I sat there speechless as my mind attempted to process through the hurt and anger to the meaning of what she'd said. "I'm sorry I wasn't there when you needed me, Kim. I can't help how I reacted to when he died. Daddy and I were very close. His death devastated me."

"I was heartbroken too, Nina. That didn't mean I got to stay in bed, though. I had to be responsible for taking care of all the business that comes with death."

My chest tightened as I watched her expression harden. She couldn't forgive me for not being there because I was falling apart. How could we ever hope to have any kind of healthy relationship while she still harbored these feelings? "Kim, why are you telling me all of this? What does this have to do with why you wanted to see me?"

"When Daddy died, I had to go through every inch of that house, reliving all the memories of Mommy's death. I wanted to break down too, but every day I had to return to those rooms so full of the past. I had to sift through every piece of paper he kept. Do you remember how he'd always write on scraps of envelopes and cocktail napkins when he had an idea or found some fact he needed to remember? That house of his was full of them. Some I threw away, but most I kept, mainly because I couldn't let go and those were all I had left of him. So I stuck the ones I saved in a box, even though I wasn't sure what I'd ever do with them. Copies of that notebook of his you've seen were some of what was in that box, along with this sheet of paper."

"I'm so sorry, Kim. I'm sorry I wasn't there and didn't realize what you had to go through," I said quietly, hoping to at least show her we didn't have to continue like we'd been.

Her hand shook as she lifted the paper in front of me. "When you told me about Tristan, I knew something about him sounded familiar. I couldn't place it at first, but then it all came back to me. I'd seen his name on one of Daddy's scraps of paper. When I searched through that box, I found everything Daddy had discovered about Tristan and his family. How they'd done horrible things and never gotten caught or been punished, and now one of them had tricked the only family I had left into falling in love with him."

Reaching out, I stilled her trembling hand. "Kim, I know all about what Victor and Taylor Stone did. I know they weren't good people, but Tristan isn't like them. He's like his mother. Did you know Daddy and Mommy knew Tressa Stone? She and Mommy were friends in college. It was Tressa Stone who introduced Mommy to Daddy."

My sister stared at me with a look of coldness I'd never seen before in her eyes. "He's not good, Nina. He's a Stone just like his father and brother. His father had Daddy killed and he found you to make himself feel better."

I shook my head violently. "No, that's not true, Kim. I know he felt bad at first and that's why he came to find me, but then we fell in love. He's a good man. I know he is."

Without breaking her icy stare, she slid the paper across the table to me and pulled her hand back. "Then how do you explain your good man doing that?"

My heart pounded so hard that my chest began to ache. I didn't want to look down at what was written on that sheet of paper. I believed deep in my soul that Tristan was a good man and loved me as much as I loved him, and I didn't want to know that I could be wrong. I didn't want to see an indictment of who he was written in my own father's handwriting.

Holding back the tears that threatened to pour down my cheeks, I shook my head. "I won't do this with you. Whatever you think you know, you're wrong. Tristan is the man I love, and I'm going to marry him. I won't let you ruin this for me."

"Look at the paper, Nina. Look at what Daddy found out about your fiancé."

My heart ached at the thought of what I'd find, but I couldn't stop myself. I had to read it, if only to prove that Kim had it all wrong. I unfolded the sheet and there at the top of the page was his name.

Tristan Stone—August 2006—Hoboken

My eyes slowly scanned the next line, but I didn't understand my father's notes. All it seemed to be was an address with a bunch of numbers after it.

99 Garden Street NJ #0002675-2006

I looked up at Kim, confused as to what I was supposed to know from these notes. "What is this? I don't understand."

"Daddy's notes are at the top. He found out about a girl's death in 2006—a girl's death your future husband was responsible for. The notes below are Jeff's. I had him check into this when I realized who Tristan really was."

I read my father's notes about Tristan again, still not understanding them, and then moved on to Jeff's. As my eyes slid over each word, the horrifying truth became clear.

Arrest record #0002675-2006 Tristan Stone arrested for the murder of Melissa Raynard on August 13, 2006. Case dismissed after death ruled an accident.

As I stared at the words swimming before me over the lined notebook paper, I heard Kim speak. "He killed a girl, Nina. He gave her the drugs. She was only twenty-one years old and he killed her. Oh, his father's money kept him out of jail and from what Jeff says the coroner said the death looked like an accident, but if he didn't kill her, he sure as hell was responsible for her death. He was a coke addict and that girl paid the price for knowing him. I couldn't let you go on thinking he was the person he claims he is. He's bad, Nina, and you're going to get hurt or worse if you stay with him."

Opening my hands, I let the paper drop to the table and shook my head in disbelief. "No, this can't be. He wouldn't do that."

"Did you know he used cocaine back then? Did he tell you that?"

I wanted to scream, to run away from every word she uttered. Instead, I continued to shake my head, not wanting to believe Tristan could hurt anyone like that. I couldn't think of him like that person described in my father's notes.

But I couldn't help it. Maybe if I hadn't seen him sitting in front of the coke with my own eyes that night at Top, I could believe it was all a mistake or some awful, cruel ploy of Kim's to hurt me, but I had and now those notes of my father's and Jeff's seemed entirely possible.

"Nina, you've seen him do coke, haven't you? I can tell by the look on your face that you know what Daddy and Jeff found out is the truth."

My head pounded and it felt like someone was strangling the air out of me. I stood up, still shaking my head, and croaked out, "I can't do this. I can't stay here."

I ran out of Malone's into the street desperate to find Jensen. Frantically, I searched up and down the sidewalk for him, but he was nowhere to be found. Where was Varo? Why wasn't Jensen nearby like he always was? God, I just wanted to see a familiar face, someone to get me out of there and take me home.

Home where I lived with Tristan.

My feet were moving, but I didn't know where I was going. My mind spun like a top, making me dizzy and lightheaded. Nausea choked me, making me want to throw up, and I reached out to steady myself on a pole. I couldn't breathe. All I could think of were those words on that paper describing a man I thought I knew. Did I even know him at all if he could keep this from me, even after promising to tell me the truth?

"Miss, are you okay?"

I turned to see Jensen standing next to me. "I'm fine. I need to go home, though. Please take me home."

"Of course, miss. The car is just over here."

He helped me to the car, and as we drove away toward the house, I asked, "Where was Varo? He's supposed to be nearby at all times."

"He's stuck in traffic, miss. I'm sure he'll be home right after we arrive. I'll let him know we're on our way now."

"No, that's okay, Jensen. He has enough to deal with right now. Just get me home as fast as possible."

As Jensen did his best to conquer the very beginning of rush hour traffic, I called Tristan. I had no idea what I'd say, but I needed to speak to him. I needed to hear his side of the story. I tried three times, but his phone went to voicemail every time and I never left a message. There was too much to say.

By the time we reached the house, I'd made up my mind. Of all the secrets surrounding Tristan and the rest of the Stone family, this was the one I couldn't live with.

Chapter Nineteen

Tristan

Hours of questions by Federal investigators had left me exhausted, but just the thought of Nina waiting for me with a surprise was enough to make me top a hundred miles an hour as I drove up the Taconic. Tapping my phone's screen, I saw she'd called three times but left no voicemail. That was nothing new. She never liked leaving voicemails.

Now that Karl was out of the picture, there was no reason to worry. Varo and West made sure she was safe, so she'd probably called just to tell me she loved me. I loved those calls and hated that I missed them, but stopping the Feds to answer a phone call wasn't an option.

Fifteen minutes away from the house, I called her to let her know I was almost home. Two rings and then to voicemail. That was odd. Maybe she was in the shower. A sense of anxiousness settled into my mind, but I quickly dismissed it. The investigators had assured me that Karl would be in custody within the hour, so there was no reason to be uneasy.

I turned onto the driveway and punched in the security code on the keypad. The gates opened, and I raced up to the house, dying to see the woman I loved. The garage door was up, but I could park the Jag later. I didn't want to waste another minute on anything but Nina.

The sun was just setting as I walked to the front door, wondering what my surprise would be. A nice dinner and the rest of the night in bed together would have been good enough for me, but if she preferred something a little wilder, I was up for that too. After all those months without her next to me, I didn't care if we simply laid in each other's arms and watched movies all night, stuffing our faces with Jiffy Pop.

As long as she was by my side, everything was better.

I threw my keys on the table in the center of the entryway and listened for any sign of what she'd planned. The house seemed strangely quiet. As I walked down the hallway to our bedroom, I peeked into the kitchen and sitting room, but both were empty. Convinced she was waiting for me in the bedroom, I prepared myself to act surprised when I opened the door and saw her lying there in her sexy lingerie, or even better, naked and ready for me.

But she wasn't there.

Taking out my phone, I typed out a text telling her I was home and pressed Send. I slid my tie from around my neck and unbuttoned my shirt, relaxing for the first time since leaving the house. My phone remained silent, so I checked it for Nina's text back to me, but there was nothing.

Fifteen minutes went by without any message from her. Had she gone out? If she did, I knew Jensen could tell me. I made my way to his part of the house, but he was nowhere to be found. Where the hell was everyone?

"Mr. Stone? Can I help you?"

I turned to see Jensen standing behind me with a look of concern on his face. I rarely intruded on his personal life or space, so his expression didn't alarm me. The poor guy probably thought I was there to ream him out about something small.

"I was looking for you to find out if Nina went out."

"She did, but we returned over an hour ago."

I clapped him on the shoulder to let him know we were good. "Okay. Thanks, Jensen."

After a look around the entire house, I headed to the carriage house to see if Varo and West had any idea where she could be. The place was dark, and jiggling the handle, I found the front door locked. As I turned to walk back to the house, the car they used when they guarded Nina drove up with only Varo inside.

Opening the door, he looked calm. "You looking for me?"

"I came back to look for you and West, but the house is dark and the door is locked. Where's West?"

Varo shook his head. "I don't know. He said he wasn't feeling well, so I went alone when Ms. Edwards went out."

"Why are you just getting back now if Jensen and Nina returned more than an hour ago?"

"Traffic. Is there something wrong?"

I shook my head and tried to piece together what was going on. "I can't find Nina. Jensen said he brought her back an hour ago, but she's nowhere to be found."

"Did you check the entire house?"

"Yes, and now West is nowhere to be found too?"

"I'll check the grounds. See if you can find anything inside to give us a clue where she could be," Varo said as he took off into the darkness.

I hurried back into the house and went straight to our bedroom. All her clothes still hung in the closets, and there didn't seem to be anything missing in the drawers. Even her toothbrush still stood in the holder on the back of the vanity. As I checked each room again, I saw nothing in the house to indicate she'd been taken against her will either.

But something was very wrong.

Calling Jordan, I prayed Nina just decided to meet her in the city and this all was a misunderstanding. When she answered, I knew just by the tone of her voice Nina wasn't with her.

"Jordan, this is Tristan. Is Nina there with you?"

"No. She and I went dress shopping earlier today, and she dropped me off after we had lunch. Is something wrong?"

"I'm sure there's nothing wrong. I just came home expecting her here and she's not."

"Did you try her cell?" Jordan asked, trying to hide the worry in her voice.

"Yeah. She didn't answer. I sent her a text too, but nothing."

"Let me try. I'll call you right back, okay?"

I pressed End and began pacing across the width of the entryway, suddenly worried I'd let my guard down too soon and Karl had finally found a way to get to Nina. After what felt like hours, Jordan called back and I instantly knew something was wrong.

"Tristan, she answered, but I couldn't figure out what she was talking about. Her phone kept going in and out, but she said something about Kim and some girl. I couldn't make out the name, but it sounded like Alyssa or Marissa. I don't know anyone with those names. She was sobbing. Something happened. I know it. Kim did something, Tristan. I don't know where Nina is, but wherever it is, she's falling apart. You have to find her."

My stomach sank as I listened to Jordan tell me what I'd feared ever since reading Joseph Edwards' note to my mother explaining what he'd uncovered about me. Kim had finally found out about Melissa and told Nina, no doubt to hurt her intentionally. That fucking bitch!

"I'll find her, Jordan. First, I have to find her sister to figure out what damage she's done this time."

"I don't know what this is about, Tristan, but Kim is no good. Whatever she did, I'd bet a hundred bucks she did it on purpose."

"Did she tell you where she was or say anything else?"

"No. I heard something in the background that sounded like a loudspeaker, though. Her phone went out and I couldn't get her again."

"Okay. Thanks, Jordan."

"Whatever happened, you need to bring her home, Tristan."

"I will. I promise."

I stuffed my phone in my inside pocket, my hands shaking from the rage coursing through my body. If I didn't get myself under control before I saw Nina's sister, I might do just what she thought I was guilty of.

Varo knocked on the front door and walked in to explain he hadn't found any evidence of anything wrong but he hadn't found Nina either. "You won't," I said as I grabbed my keys. "She's not here."

"Are you going to get her now?" he asked, confused by my angry tone.

"I don't know where she is. All I know is that her goddamned sister had something to do with this. I'm going to see her to find out if she knows where Nina went. Call Daryl and tell him I want you two to search everywhere, including the penthouse, her old job at the gallery, and anywhere else you two can think of. I want her found before Karl or his people find her. Do you understand me?"

Varo nodded, obviously shaken by the anger I no longer even tried to hide. As I pushed past him, I added, "And find out where the fuck West is!"

I stood on Kim's front porch after making the three hour trip in less than two hours, my hatred for Kim fueling my driving with each mile. Not that it was entirely her fault. I knew that. I knew that I should have told Nina about Melissa, especially after I promised her I wouldn't keep anything from her anymore, but how the fuck do you tell the woman you love about the woman who died as a result of your actions? I never found the right moment to explain that I'd been arrested and charged with the murder of Melissa, even though I'd been innocent.

Banging on the front door, I didn't know what I planned to say. At every turn, Kim had fought me about Nina, but I'd thought that when I'd done everything I could to keep her and her family safe from Karl that she'd finally seen I wasn't a bad guy. Obviously, she'd been saving the information about Melissa for when it would do the most damage.

Kim opened the door and immediately tried to slam it shut, but she was no match for me in my mood. I threw it open and brushed past her with little effort, intent on finding out how much damage she'd done. "Don't bother trying to make me leave. I'm not going anywhere until you tell me what you did to make Nina run away."

Closing the door, she scowled at me. "You can't change things with your money this time. The truth can't be stifled by any amount."

"You just couldn't leave well enough alone, could you?"

"And let my sister marry a murderer? No way. People like you get away with things every day. I hear my husband talk about getting people off all the time, and with your money, your father no doubt had to just flash a few big bills in front of some underpaid D.A. and that was it. No more problems for his baby boy."

I shook my head at how in the dark she was. "You have no idea what you're talking about. I didn't kill Melissa. She overdosed."

"I'm sure. How much does it cost to get a coroner to say that?" she spit out at me.

"I swear to God if Nina is hurt because of you, I'll make your life a living fucking hell. You think I can buy whatever I want with my money? If one gentle hair on Nina's head suffers because of what you've done, I'll devote every last cent of what I have to making you pay. You have no idea what you might have done this time."

Kim shrugged and shot me a sneer. "I told her the truth about you. If that causes you a problem, so be it."

Balling my fists in rage, I tried to keep myself from hitting a woman for the first time in my life. "That man I made sure you and your family were safe from might have her right now. I don't know where she is, and I can only hope that the Feds have him in custody or he hasn't made bail, because if he has, he's going straight for her. All of this because you couldn't let her be happy."

"I was just doing what I promised my father I'd always do for Nina—watching out for her. Your father made sure I had to do that."

Suddenly, everything I'd been holding in exploded from me. "I'm not my fucking father or brother! I've done everything in my power to show you I'm not like my family. If I hadn't made sure you were safe all that time, Karl would have killed you and your family. I'm not a murderer. All you had to do is have your husband do a little searching and you'd know that. Melissa overdosed. I'm not saying I wasn't there or don't still feel responsible in some way still to this day, but I didn't kill her."

Kim's stood there in her living room shifting her weight from foot to foot just like Nina did when she was uncomfortable. She knew I hadn't killed anyone and still she'd told Nina about Melissa. Slowly, she moved toward the table behind the sofa and pulled a sheet of paper out of her purse.

"My father believed you were a murderer. Just because Jeff found out otherwise doesn't mean I have to believe him instead. All that lawyer talk just meant that they didn't have enough evidence to overcome your family's money."

I took the paper from her hand and recognized it as the same kind as in her father's notebook. He'd told my mother the truth. He hadn't revealed everything he'd found about our family, just as he'd promised her. He'd intended on it never seeing the light of day. That's why he'd sent her the information with that last letter he'd written.

Looking down at the sheet of paper in my hand, I read what Nina had learned about me. "Your father had decided not to disclose this information. Why did you think you had to do that now?"

"My father was a sentimental man who didn't always think clearly. He was likely impressed with your mother, probably because of her money, and didn't realize that the person he was friends with wasn't that girl he knew in college but just the matriarch of a family of murderers."

Never before in my life had I wanted to hurt someone like I wanted to hurt Kim at that moment. How anyone so petty and nasty could be related to Nina and her father baffled me, but I didn't have time to ponder what had happened to make her so vicious and jealous. I stuffed Joseph Edwards' notes into my pocket and left Kim to her misery, unsure of where I'd find Nina but sure that I wasn't going to get any help there. I just had to hope I found her before Karl did.

On the way to my car, I felt my phone vibrate and quickly yanked it from my coat, hoping to see Nina's name. It was only Daryl, though. Sliding my finger across the screen, I answered it and prayed he had some good news. "Tell me you found something," I said as I opened the driver's side door.

"Nothing yet," Daryl said in a somber voice. "Do you have any idea why she left? Varo said you went to see her sister."

I started the car and breathed a sigh of disgust, not only at Kim but at myself too. "Yeah. She found out about Melissa. Kim told her."

Daryl said nothing for a long time, and then in his indomitable way, summarized my current problem succinctly. "Well, that was pretty stupid of you not to tell her, especially since you did nothing wrong."

"Thanks. Just what I need. I know it was stupid, Daryl, but since I still think I was to blame, I just never found a way to tell her."

"Water under the bridge now. We need to find your lady ASAP. So where would she go?"

Places raced through my mind, but none stuck out as the place I thought she'd go when she was upset. "I have no idea."

Daryl made that clucking noise with his tongue he made when he was thinking and then said, "I'd suggest getting the word out to your hotels. She might go to one of them. I already checked the penthouse and no one has seen her there tonight."

I headed out of Kim's development toward home, wondering how much time I had. "What do we know about Karl?"

"What do you mean? I thought the Washington guys had him."

"I have no idea if he'll be held. If he's not, how do I know he won't find Nina before we do? And do you have any idea where the hell West is? Varo didn't know where he was, and I'm worried he has something to do with Nina's disappearance."

"Whoa! I don't think she's disappeared, and what the fuck would West have to do with that?"

Putting my foot to the floor, I gassed it and began weaving through traffic. "I have no idea, Daryl. It just seems suspicious that Nina's gone and West is nowhere to be found. I don't care where he is if he isn't with Nina, but if he is, he better fucking hope I don't find him when I finally get to her, or I'm going to fucking kill him."

"Alright, alright. Let's not get crazy here. I'm heading out to the house now. Maybe Varo found something there or Jensen remembered something about the ride home that can help us. I'll see you there in a little while, right?"

"Yeah. If you find out anything before I get there, call me. Do you understand?"

"I get it. Don't worry. We'll find her safe and sound."

Chapter Twenty

Tristan

I drove like a demon over the roads and highways that led to the house I shared with Nina, my mind drifting back to the events that now made her run from me. Even though they'd occurred seven years before, the memory of them still ached like a fresh wound.

A haze of smoke hung heavy over the spacious room, a telltale sign of how long we'd been ignoring the outside world. Melissa giggled as she lay sprawled out across the bed while Sam smacked her on the bare ass. I guessed I should have been jealous since I was sleeping with her, but it wasn't anything exclusive between us and I didn't care if she liked to fuck him too.

Sex wasn't what kept us together. Coke was.

Well, coke was what kept me there. Melissa didn't like what coke did to her, preferring the more mellow high of pot or pills. But she was always good for what I wanted, knowing I liked it and eager to please me, no matter the cost.

I had no idea what the fuck Sam saw in any of this. True, he liked to smoke every so often, but nothing like how often Melissa did. I wasn't even sure I'd ever seen her straight. Not that I cared.

"Tristan, come over here. I'm all alone and Sam won't talk to me," she whined in a voice that I found cute at times other than this. She knew it and used it anytime she wanted something from me.

Sam stood from the bed and pushed her away. "I won't talk to her because she doesn't make any fucking sense. Maybe if you'd get your head out of the clouds one in a while, Lissa, I'd be able to understand what the fuck you're talking about."

This was their usual routine when Sam felt like a third wheel. To everyone but Melissa, it was obvious he was in love with her. I had a feeling he hated me and wished I'd just disappear so he could walk off into the sunset with her, happy and high as a fucking kite. I would have been okay with that, as long as it didn't interfere with what she and I had.

What that was exactly was hard to say, however.

I liked her well enough. I liked her even better when she spread lines out in front of me in an effort to make me happy. I didn't love her, though, and she knew it.

That fact never stopped her from wishing it wasn't true.

"Melissa, I don't feel like talking. I leave that up to Sam," I said with my usual curtness.

Lying there naked, she looked up at me with a stare that was supposed to make me want to fuck her. "Tristan, why are you so mean?" she cooed. "You're always so mean to me."

"You don't want to see mean," I said, hoping to put an end to her attempts to seduce me. Turning to look at Sam, I nodded my head toward her. "Talk to her. That's all she wants."

"I don't want your fucking scraps, Stone," Sam snapped before storming out to Melissa's living room to sulk as he always did.

I let my gaze travel to the bed where Melissa lay pouting. I understood why Sam would want her. Perfect body, at least as perfect as money and a plastic surgeon could buy, lots of laughs, and not a lot of frustration. For many, she'd be the perfect girlfriend.

"Tristan, he's gone. You don't have to sit over there all by yourself anymore. Come over here on the bed with me."

Leaning forward, I snorted the last line on the tray and shook my head trying to handle the sensation of the coke teasing the inside of my nose. "You should be nicer to Sam, Melissa. When I go, he'll still be here."

"Don't say that! You're not going anywhere," she cried as she rolled off the bed onto her feet to come toward me. "I won't let you."

She knelt between my legs and gazed up at me with bloodshot blue eyes. I knew what she wanted, and if I hadn't been so fucked up, I might have wanted it too. "Get up off your knees," I ordered only to have her respond by shaking her head.

"Tell me what you want and I'll give it to you. Whatever you want, Tristan. Tell me." As she spoke, her hands slid up my thighs to the crease of my legs. "I could make you happy if you'd let me."

I pushed her hands away, and she careened back into the table. "I have everything I need to make me happy."

She looked up at me and frowned. "Then why aren't you happy, baby?"

Reaching toward her, I smoothed her platinum blond hair from her eyes. "Don't try to use what you learned in Psych class last semester on me, Melissa. It's not going to work."

"When I become a psychologist, you'll see. I can be your therapist and solve all your problems."

"That'll be the day you're a therapist," I said casually without care for her feelings.

Her face fell as her eyes filled with tears. Why I was such an asshole to her I didn't know. Even if I believed what I said, I didn't have to say it. She'd never been anything other than completely devoted to me and I couldn't even muster up enough feelings to be kind to her.

Closing my eyes, I tried to shut out the truth of how much a fuck I really was.

"This isn't happy, Tristan," she whispered as she lay her head against my knee. "This isn't happy."

"Well, it's all we have. If you want happy, I'm not the person to be with. Stick with Sam."

"Someday, Sam and I will be together. I know it. He'll be in love with me still and I won't be in love with you anymore, so we'll finally be together. But then you'll be all alone, my Tristan without a soul in this world."

"Jesus, Melissa. Stop being so fucking maudlin. I have women all the time. I'm not alone."

Standing, she sat on my lap and straddled me. She cradled my face in her hands and shook her head. "You're more alone than anyone I've ever met, baby. I could change that. I want to change that for you."

My hands slid over her perfect ass and pulled her into me. "I like the way we are. You like the way we are, don't you?"

She didn't dare say she didn't and risk my rejection, and I took advantage of that fear. I saw it in her eyes, though. She loved me, or felt what she thought was love. Fuck, I didn't know what she felt at that moment.

Her hand pressed against my heart, a gentle touch that should have meant something to me. "Your heart is beating so fast."

"That's because I don't spend my time smoking that shit. You wouldn't be such a downer if you gave up the smoke and tried coke."

My vision blurred as that moment of my past came crashing full on into my present. Over and over, I had to tell myself I wasn't the murderer Kim thought I was. If only I could convince myself.

"I'd do that if I thought it would make you happy," she whispered next to the corner of my mouth. "Would it make you happy?"

I turned my head away from her. "You're too fixated on happiness, Melissa."

"Would it make sex better?" she asked before snaking her tongue over the shell of my ear.

"Yeah, maybe," I answered without any thought as to whether my answer was true and not caring.

"Then maybe I should do it," she said with a smile as she scooted up my lap, exciting me.

I stilled her movement before she got me too hot. "Then you're going to have to get more. I finished all of it."

Melissa leapt off my lap and skipped over to the nightstand next to her bed. Pulling out a vial, she showed it off and threw it to me. "You underestimate me, Tristan."

She dropped down next to the table in front of me and spread four lines out. Before I could even have one, she'd snorted two and was moving for a third. I pulled her back by the hair and pushed her hard onto the floor. "Don't be so greedy."

I saw in her eyes as they filled with tears that her feelings were hurt. She'd done exactly what she believed would make me happy and still I didn't come across with anything but nastiness. As she began to cry, something inside me softened toward her, and I pulled her up onto my lap, still unsure I wanted anything physical from her that night but hoping I could stop her tears.

Covering my mouth with hers, she teased the inside with her tongue, exciting me. Pressed against me, she moved her hips back and forth, giving me a preview of what she wanted. Her wet pussy slid over the front of my jeans, drenching them, and for a moment, I wanted her.

But she came with far too much baggage for me at that moment, and Sam was bound to return at any time. The scene he'd create alone was enough to make my cock go soft. I pushed her away and shook my head. "Maybe later, Melissa."

Stung by my rejection, she slid off me, smacking me across the face as she left. "Fuck you, Tristan!"

She kicked the tray of coke as she stormed out, sending the powder into a white cloud that slowly fell in puffs to the floor. I watched in disgust as the rest of my night was ruined in mere seconds, content to ignore both Melissa and Sam in favor of sitting alone until I figured out where I'd be able to find more coke and hopefully salvage the night.

I had no idea how long I'd sat there consumed by my own thoughts when I heard the first siren. It seemed to come out of nowhere and suddenly be so loud it drowned out everything in my head. Another and then another followed, and my instincts kicked in. Quickly, I dialed Rogers to get me the hell out of there. I didn't need another arrest for possession.

I'd barely gotten to my feet when the cops stormed through the door. There was no escaping. My guilt was obvious by the coke all around me. Pushing my hands through my hair, I tried to make myself look less fucked up, but it was no use. What was the term—caught red-handed? That was me. Again.

As they led me out, I saw the paramedics working on Melissa as she lay motionless on the floor next to the living room sofa. Sam paced back and forth, wringing his hands and praying aloud for her to be okay while a cop tried to get him to answer his questions about what she'd taken and when. For a moment, his answers, no matter how disjointed they were, scared the hell out of me, but I'd get out of it. Melissa would be okay too, assuming they pumped her stomach to get rid of any pills she'd taken.

Everything would be okay. My father's money would see to that.

I pulled off the side of the road and leaned back to close my eyes as the memory of what happened next flooded into my brain. Melissa never made it out of that apartment that night. The mixture of prescription drugs and cocaine sent her into cardiac arrest, and she died there on that floor surrounded by strangers as they took Sam and me away.

Arrested and charged with murder for giving her the drugs, I spent the night in jail before my father's attorney got me released. I didn't find out she'd died until two days after she was gone when I was finally home safe and sound in my parents' house.

I sat silently listening to my father explain in detail what would happen to me as he paced from one side of the room to the other, stopping only to glare at me and shake his head.

"What is wrong with you? You've had everything a boy could want. A good education. The best of tutors. Yet still you act like some street kid who doesn't know better. That girl died. Did you know that? You're charged with her murder."

The news of Melissa's death hit me like a brick to the face. Whatever he expected me to say, I couldn't speak. It was like all the air had been sucked out of my lungs.

"Did you hear me?" he bellowed, leaning his face down in front of mine, so close I saw the gold flecks in his brown eyes as they flashed his anger at me.

"Victor, don't do this to him. His friend is dead. He needs time to mourn her. You can talk about the rest of it later."

I looked at my mother as she spoke to defend me, knowing I didn't deserve her kindness. My father stormed out, leaving her alone with me. I didn't deserve that either.

Cradling my face in her hands, she smiled that gentle smile she always gave when she thought I needed saving. "Tristan, I don't know how to reach you. What is it that makes you like this?"

What she meant by 'like this' was a mystery to me. Like what? Any normal American twenty-two year old male? Every other person my age I knew? But I understood my role in this drama and acted accordingly. "I don't know."

"Honey, if you have a problem, we can get you help. There are places where you can get help."

I couldn't give her the answer I knew she needed to hear. She needed me to say I'd accept her help and stop living my life. I couldn't tell her that, so I just nodded, letting her think she'd saved me, at least for now. My father was right, but I didn't care. Someday, my mother would realize that too.

I shook my head to push away the memory of that Tristan. That me had been selfish and careless, thinking I was the only one whose wants and needs mattered. God, I couldn't help but cringe at who I'd been all those years ago.

Now all those terrible acts had finally caught up with me, as I always knew they would. The problem was that now when the most important part of my life was torn from me because of what I did, all I could do was hope that when I caught up with Nina that she'd see that Tristan didn't exist anymore.

I checked my phone for any message or text from Nina. Nothing. Where was she? Was she alone? Images of West or worse, Karl, holding her marched through my mind. No! I couldn't believe that. She was safe. She had to be.

My fingers tapped out a message I prayed to God she saw. *I know what Kim told you, but I swear she's wrong. Tell me where you are and I'll come to you. Don't do this. Don't let everything we have mean nothing.*

After ten minutes, I knew she wouldn't be answering my text. I didn't expect a few words to fix everything. The damage my past had inflicted on us would require far more than that. I didn't expect anything, in fact. Nina had accepted all my demons, even if she'd done so unknowingly at times, but I'd made the biggest mistake of my life by not coming clean just days before as she and I lay in bed that morning for the first time in months. She'd practically begged me to tell her everything, and I hadn't. I didn't know why. Maybe I'd hoped I wouldn't have to tell the woman I loved that I was a thoughtless, callous dick to someone who only wanted love from me, and my carelessness with her had led to her death.

Before I put the car in gear, I tried one more time, hoping at the very least she was receiving my messages and at best she was reading them. *I know I promised to tell you everything, but sometimes a man wants to have the woman he loves see him as more than he actually is. I wasn't trying to hide what happened then. Please believe me.*

I got no response.

Daryl and Varo were waiting for me outside the house when I pulled up, their faces telling the story I didn't want to know. Stepping out of the car, I asked, "Nothing? You've got no clue where she is?"

"Nothing yet," Daryl said nonchalantly as he tugged on his beard, betraying how worried he really was. "What took you so long? I figured you'd be driving at the speed of light."

Varo said nothing, but I could tell he had something on his mind. "You seem to want to say something. Speak up," I ordered.

"I think you might have been right about West. I've been thinking about how he acted today at lunch. He was angry about having lunch with Nina and Jordan. She was playing matchmaker, so I figured he was annoyed about that, but now that he's vanished, maybe it was more."

Daryl spoke up before I could. "What do you mean more? Did he have something against Nina?"

Shaking his head, Varo frowned. "Not so much something against her but something's been bothering him for weeks. I can't put my finger on it, but something's different."

"Something's bothering him? Something's different? What the fuck does that mean? Are you saying he wants to hurt Nina?" I bellowed as fear tore through my body. West may have been the older of the two bodyguards, but she was no match against him. He could subdue her in seconds and she'd be gone.

"No, no. I just mean he seemed more resentful of things once I moved into the house. Even though it was only for a short time, I think he had a problem with that. I just can't imagine he'd hurt her, though. If anything, I got the feeling his problem was with you, Mr. Stone."

"Have you tried calling her?" Daryl asked, easing the tension around us only slightly.

"No," I answered, shaking my head. "Only texts."

"What the fuck is with your generation? A phone is for talking. You know, with your voice? You think she wants to hear from you through misspelled words? She wants to hear you, man. Call her."

Maybe he was right. I took my phone out and pressed 1. Her phone rang, which was a good sign. At least I could still believe it was turned on and still with her. By the fourth ring, I'd all but given up on her answering, but then I heard her voice so full of sadness say my name.

"Tristan."

I turned away from Daryl and Varo and walked behind the car. "Nina, I'm sorry. Please tell me where you are so I can come to you."

"No, not this time, Tristan. I needed you to tell me the truth and you broke your promise. I can't do this anymore."

Her voice was barely more than a whisper. I pressed the phone hard to my ear to hear her, even as I dreaded her next words. "I know I messed up. I know. But you don't know the truth. I need you to know that."

With tears in her words, she spoke the worst thing I'd ever heard. "You've made sure I can live a comfortable life. Not happy, but secure. I just can't do this with you anymore. Maybe if I'd been brought up in your world, but I wasn't. I'm still that middle class girl, no matter how much the clothes I wear or the house I live in costs."

"Nina, don't hang up! Tell me where you are. Let me explain. Don't let everything we've been through mean nothing," I pleaded, knowing I had only the slightest chance of changing her mind.

"I can't. I love you, but we're just no good together. Goodbye, Tristan."

"Nina! Nina!" I screamed into the phone, but it was no use. She was gone.

Hanging my head, I struggled to know what to do next. I had no idea where she was, and she didn't want to see me anymore. To her, we were over.

"Tristan, what did she say?" Daryl asked behind me, but I couldn't tell him. I couldn't admit I'd finally lost her. "Tristan, did she tell you where she was?"

I shook my head and turned to face him and Varo. "No."

"Then we can use the GPS tracking software to find out."

"What? I don't have that on our phones."

Daryl smiled and for the first time since I returned, stopped pulling on his damn beard. "I'd hoped she would willingly tell you where she was, but when love doesn't do the job, technology can. I had it installed on her phone right after you left. I figured that way if she was ever in trouble, we could find her."

I couldn't stop myself from smiling. "You're not kidding? Then show me how the hell I find out."

Slipping his phone out of his pocket, Daryl tapped his finger on the screen a dozen times and turned the screen to face me. "Time for a little trip. Better get that plane of yours revved up."

I leaned forward to read the words in front of me.

Venice, Italy.

Daryl grinned like a Cheshire cat. "Don't you love technology?"

"Damnit, Daryl. I should have you put that on my phone."

Chapter Twenty-One

Tristan

I left Varo at the hotel and set out to find Nina, unable to track her down to any specific place in Venice after she turned off her phone. Unsure of where to begin, I let my feet take me back to the one place in the city other than our hotel room that meant anything to me.

The Piazza San Marco.

It was midday by the time I reached the square. Tourists milled about snapping pictures from every vantage point possible as artisans and vendors hawked their wares to eager buyers. I paced every inch of the piazza, my eyes scanning every arch and hidden corner, but I saw no sight of her.

This place was haunted with memories of a time when Nina and I were happy. I wanted to believe we were happy then. Maybe we'd never truly been happy because I'd never been completely honest with her. If so, I was to blame for any sadness she'd felt because she'd been with me.

I could change that, though. I had to believe that or my being there in that place where I'd finally realized I could tell her how much I loved her was all for nothing.

Hours passed as I sat watching families move through the square, parents chasing after young children who hopped and skipped on their way over the stone pavers oblivious to the flocks of birds they disturbed as they played. The sun traveled in its natural path across the sky until I'd sat there long enough to see the last rays of its light as it began to set behind the Museo Civico Correr. Nina had told me about the museum's paintings, in particular one that even though it had been painted centuries ago showed the city as nearly the same as it stood today.

As I replayed her sweet attempt to educate me on Venice's art treasures, I caught a glimpse of her through an archway walking down the arcade. She wore her hair pinned up in a bun, but I'd know the shape of her beautiful face anywhere. I bolted from my seat and ran toward her, losing her when a crowd of school children paraded hand-in-hand in front of me. By the time I'd navigated around them, she was gone.

Frustrated, I scanned the area for any sight of her, finally accepting I might not see her that day. I could wait, but if Karl knew she was alone in Venice, every second she wasn't with me meant she was in danger. I needed to find her.

The final minutes of daylight highlighted the colorful mosaics on the Basilica di San Marco, and I stared in newfound awe at them, seeing for the first time what Nina had explained about them. The arches and columns of the basilica stood as they had for centuries, tributes to the Gothic style of the Middle Ages. I'd known none of this until Nina.

The crowds began to thin as people left the square for dinner and other parts of the city. I hadn't given up hope, though. If I had to search every square inch of Venice all night, then I would.

"You can't do this, Tristan."

I turned to see her standing behind me, looking more beautiful than I'd ever seen her, even in jeans and a T-shirt with her hair pulled up. "I can't do anything else. If you won't come with me because you love me, then come with me so I can keep you safe."

Sadly, she shook her head. "I have to learn to live on my own, Tristan. I can't do that if I go with you."

"I don't know if Karl knows you're here. West is missing, so I don't know if he's a danger to you."

"It doesn't matter. I have to go."

She turned to walk away, but I grabbed her forearm to stop her. "Don't do this. Let me explain, at least. Give me the chance to show you how much I love you."

Tears filled her eyes, and she looked away. "I know you love me, Tristan. I've never doubted that, strangely enough. I just can't be with someone who won't be truthful with me, no matter how difficult it is for him."

"Look at me, Nina." She shook her head, but I gently pulled her by the chin so she was forced to face me. "Look at me. I know I was wrong, but I never meant to deceive you about Melissa's death. I know that doesn't make what I did right. I know."

"Do you ever wonder why we can't just seem to be happy? Why there always seems to be something that ruins what we have?"

Quietly, I admitted the truth. "No. I know why. It's me. I'm fucked up. That doesn't mean I don't love you more than even you believe, though."

Cradling my face in her hands, she looked up at me with love in her eyes. "What am I supposed to do? We keep messing this up. Maybe we're just not meant to be, no matter how much both of us want to be together."

"I can't believe that. I've never loved anyone before I met you. I can't believe you'd be sent to me just to show me I don't deserve to be loved. I won't believe that."

Her hands slid from my cheeks as she hung her head. "Sometimes it's just not meant to be, Tristan. It's not that I don't love you. I'll always love you. We just can't seem to get it right."

I clutched her wrists gently, afraid if I didn't keep hold of some part of her she'd run away and I'd lose her forever. "I know, but give me another chance. Let me show you I can be the man you deserve." Nina tried to back away from me, shaking her head, but I saw something in her eyes that told me there was a chance. I couldn't let that chance slip away. "Hear me out. Listen to what I have to say and then listen to your heart."

Nina stood silently staring at me and finally gave me a tiny nod. "Okay. I want to know everything."

"Everything. I promise. Just as soon as we return to the hotel, I'll tell you all of it."

Nina slipped her hands from my hold and shook her head. "No. Right here. I believe you bared your soul to me the last time we were here. I want you to do that now. Tell me everything about the worst I believe about you here near that very spot you told me you loved me and couldn't live without me."

"Fine. I'll tell you everything."

We found a bench and I took a deep breath. "Her name was Melissa and she died because I didn't take care of her. But Kim was wrong. I'm not a murderer. Melissa died from an overdose of prescription drugs and cocaine. That's why the charges were dropped and I never went to trial."

Nina grimaced like she was in pain. "Did you love her?"

I thought about her question and hesitated. I wasn't in love with Melissa that night or any other night, but did that mean I didn't have a responsibility to her? I had to tell Nina the truth, no matter how it made me look.

"I don't think I was capable of love when I knew Melissa. That man thought only of his wants and desires without any care for what others needed. I wasn't even a man then. I looked like one, but I didn't act like one. A man would have taken more care with her."

"Were you with her?" Nina asked sharply, her voice full of condemnation.

"Yeah," I said, nodding.

"But you didn't care for her?"

"I cared for her enough to sleep with her and use the drugs she got me, but no, I didn't care for her like I care for you. I was a selfish boy who took what he wanted and didn't give a damn about what she wanted."

Nina's eyes searched mine. "What did she want, Tristan? Did she want you?"

"She wanted me to love her like she loved me."

There in that one statement was the indictment I deserved. A confused girl who only wanted me to love her got nothing but my callousness in return for all she gave me. And now I risked losing the woman I loved because of how I acted then.

"I think I know what she felt. You don't understand what you do, Tristan. You say so little that someone who loves you has to fill in the blanks, so of course, we fill them in with what we hope you feel. Only she was wrong. She hoped you'd love her, but you didn't. I want to believe you love me, but how do I know? You kept secrets from me. You left me alone for months and never answered my messages. You don't know how painful that was."

I took her hand in mine and brought it to my lips in a kiss. "I know. I'm sorry. I thought that was the only way to keep you safe.

I never meant to hurt you. The man I am now is sickened by how I treated Melissa. But I can't change that. All I can tell you is that I wasn't guilty of murdering her. If I was guilty of anything, it was carelessness with her. That's all."

"You say that like it's some small thing. Like being careless with someone's heart is a minor offense. That girl loved you, Tristan, and what did she get in return? Nothing. No, well, she got to spend time with you. That's something, I guess."

Nina's eyes flashed her anger at me as her words cut me down to size. If she wanted me humbled, she was doing a damn good job at it. "I can't change that, Nina. All I can promise is that I'm not that person anymore. I love you—completely and more than even I thought I could."

"You know what? I'm tired of hearing that you can't change that. Someone loved you and she died because you didn't care. That's the truth of it. You didn't care enough for her and she died. Maybe it wasn't your fault, but the way you treated her was. I'm just not sure I want to risk my heart on you anymore."

Angrier than I'd ever seen her, she stood to leave—leave me, leave us. I couldn't let her. I had to make her see what we had was worth fighting for. Forcing her back down onto the bench, I dropped to my knees in front of her, knowing this was my last chance to convince her to listen to her heart.

"You promised me you'd never leave. You promised you were mine forever. Stay with me. Don't be like the person I was. Do what your heart tells you instead of what your head says. I love you. I always have. I can't do this without you."

"I'm sorry. I am. I just don't know."

Her words were like knives to my heart, each one plunging in and carving me up. "No! I can't believe that. I won't believe that. You love me like I love you. You take up every inch of brain, pushing out everything else. I can't live without you. I know I should have said these things every day, but I'm saying them now. I love you so much it hurts sometimes. The months away nearly killed me. We promised each other no more leaving. Stay. Let me show you the kind of man I am because of you."

Her hand slowly caressed my cheek as a tear rolled down hers. "How can I know you won't hurt me like you did her?"

I leaned into her palm and looked up into that beautiful, sad face. "I love you. If I ever do hurt you, it won't be because I don't care. Don't let everything we've gone through be for nothing. I swear to cherish you like you deserve, and someday I promise you'll see I'll be the kind of man who deserves you."

Nina closed her eyes for a moment and when she opened them, I saw my last chance had passed. As I waited to hear her answer, I held my breath, my heartbeat pounding in my ears. When she shook her head, I thought all was lost, but then she spoke and I heard the sweetest words in the English language.

"For a guy who doesn't say a lot, you sure do know how to say exactly what a girl needs to hear. I love you. I don't want to imagine my world without you, Tristan. I thought I could live without you, but I don't want to."

Rising to my feet, I took the woman I loved in my arms and kissed her in front of the whole world to show everyone she was mine and I was hers. As I held her in my arms, I whispered, "No more secrets, no more time apart. From this point on, I'm making it my job to make sure you're the happiest woman in the world."

Nina smiled up at me and held my chin between her thumb and forefinger. "You better."

Taking her left hand in mine, I turned it over and saw the engagement ring I'd given her. "I see you didn't take the ring off."

She let out a deep sigh and shrugged. "I guess I just wasn't ready to really be done with you, after all."

I'd made sure when I checked into the hotel that I'd gotten the same room Nina and I had the last time we traveled to Venice. She needed to know that time had meant everything to me. I might not be able to say the right words, but maybe I could show her I truly couldn't live without her.

Candles flickered in glass containers placed around the room, giving the suite a magical feeling. Nina looked around the rooms like she had the first time, her eyes full of wonder as she admired what I owned. "It's just as beautiful now as it was the last time we were here, Tristan."

Sliding my hands over her shoulders, I whispered, "All for you. Everything I own is yours."

She turned in my hold and shook her head. "I don't want things, Tristan. What I need you can't put a price on or buy. As long as I have the truth from you, I'll be happy. Just the truth."

"I can't live without you, Nina. If truth is what it takes to make you happy, then it's yours. I just hope the real me is what you want."

She wrapped her arms around my neck and stood on her toes to kiss me softly on the lips. "I'm madly in love with the real you, Tristan Stone. I know you're not perfect. I just need you to promise no more secrets. I can't live like that."

I cupped her nape and looked into those gentle blue eyes. "No more secrets. But right now, I don't want to talk about secrets or anything else. I don't want to think about anything but you and me and reliving our last time here."

Her body melted into mine as my lips covered hers in a kiss full of need. She was perfect in my arms, right where she was meant to be. I slid her shirt over her head and her jeans from her legs to reveal mismatched bra and panties. I couldn't help but smile. All the money in the world, and she still was that wonderfully unspoiled Nina who stole my heart all those months ago.

"You're laughing at me, aren't you?" she said with a sexy smile.

I slowly lowered myself to my knees and looked up at her. "No. Not laughing. Charmed."

A delightful blush colored her cheeks. Biting her lip, she rolled her eyes. "Charmed, huh?"

Hooking my thumbs under her panties, I gave them a slight tug as she wiggled her ass to help me remove them. They easily slid down her gorgeous legs, and stepping one foot out of them, she kicked them away, leaving her standing there open to me.

I licked my lips in anticipation of tasting her sweetness on my tongue, dying to feel her slick pussy grind against my face as I slowly and methodically inched her toward release. She looked down at me, so sexy yet innocent, and I couldn't wait anymore. With my hands on her ass, I pulled her to me and slid my tongue the full length of her wet slit. Her body trembled when I touched her swollen clit, and I flicked the tip of my tongue once more as she whimpered my name.

Her hands skimmed over my scalp, gently pulling me closer to give her what she desperately wanted. My mouth devoured her, loving every moment of pleasure her pussy gave me. I wanted to give her that pleasure back. I wanted to be the only man who made her body sing.

"Tristan, my legs can't hold me up when you do that," she whined sweetly above me as I sucked her clit between my lips. "I'm going to fall…"

Lifting my head, I smiled and licked my lips to taste her. "I won't let you fall. Just hold on to my shoulders. This was all I could think of the whole flight here."

I wasn't lying. To ward off the anxiety that always came with flying, I'd spent the entire time fantasizing about making love to her. It had been the best flight I'd ever had.

"You were pretty confident I'd take you back, weren't you?"

I slid my middle finger through her wet folds and sucked the taste from the tip into my mouth. "I had to hope."

Her expression softened as one finger slid slowly inside her. "I do love a confident…ohhhh…man." Another finger made her eyes roll back. "And a man who knows how to…oh God…work with his hands."

"Hang on." While my fingers fucked her, my mouth fastened on her clit and I sucked softly, bringing her to the edge before easing back. I wanted this to last.

Nina's fingers pressed hard into my shoulders just as she was about to come, but by the fourth time, I was ready to give her what she wanted. One last thrust into her made her cunt contract, and her legs buckled. I held her there as waves of pleasure rolled through her, my fingers and mouth unrelenting as she begged me to never stop.

Finally, when her legs stopped trembling and I knew she could stand on her own, I sat back on my heels and smiled up at her. "Welcome home, Ms. Edwards."

She dropped to her knees and kissed me full on the mouth. "That's one hell of a welcome. If I didn't hate being away from you so much, I'd leave more often."

I fisted my hands in her hair, pulling it loose from the bun. "No more leaving."

CHAPTER TWENTY-TWO

Nina

The room was the same as last time we'd been in Venice, but we were different. The Tristan and Nina who'd found each other then hadn't been the real us. They'd been pretending. I'd thought I'd known him, but I'd only scratched the surface. Now I knew the man I loved more than anyone in the world was so much more than a gorgeous billionaire crazy about me. When all the money and possessions were pushed aside and it was just him and me, I saw how deep his emotions ran. The rest of the world could go on believing they knew him, but I knew the truth.

I knew the real Tristan Stone was the man who sat in front of me now. Imperfect, troubled, and bound to fuck up again, he'd bared his soul to show me the man he'd been and now had changed to be. That honesty was worth more than any amount of money.

And who was I on this second visit to Venice? I'd been pretending too—pretending that the fantasies of a teenage girl were reality. When I met Tristan, he appeared to be everything any woman could want. Gorgeous, wealthy, and confident, he was perfect. I'd never allowed the idea that he could be human with flaws like any regular man to get in the way of my fantasy of who I believed he was. Then, when I found out he wasn't perfect, I'd run.

Months without him had shown me I didn't want to run anymore, or so I'd thought. Then Kim's poisonous words flooded my ears and I lazily slid back into my teenage fantasies, condemning him for a past I'd never even given him a chance to explain.

Now it was time for me to grow up, to accept the fact of who Tristan truly was. The man who would fly around the world to impress me and protect me, even though flying terrified him. The man who agreed to bare his soul in the Piazza San Marco not once but twice. The man who'd promised to give me whatever my heart desired, and never once failed.

The man who even with his flaws had proven himself time and again. Now it was time for me to prove myself.

Tristan stared down into my eyes with a look that told me he had other ideas than a discussion of how I'd been a goddamned fool. As he tenderly stroked my jaw line, a look of need sparked in his eyes. "Come with me, Nina. I want to show you something."

His hand grasped mine, but I pulled him back. "Not yet. I want to say something first."

Those beautiful chocolate brown eyes filled with worry, and I watched as he knitted his eyebrows. "Okay. Say whatever you need to. We're all about truth."

I reached up and cradled his face in my hands. "It's nothing bad. I just need to tell you that I've been a childish fool. I expected you to be some perfect specimen of men, but that's not fair. I gave you a hard time when you returned to me last week, but it's been me who's run away all the time. And every time I ran, you followed me. You followed me, and I believe you'd follow me if I left again."

Smiling, he turned his head to kiss my right palm. "A good man knows when to drop the Alpha shit and chase after the woman he loves."

"I acted like an ass, and I'm sorry. I preach about telling the truth and then I don't give you chance to do just that."

"Thankfully, I have a plane that allows me to fly wherever I want to find you," he joked.

"I'm serious, Tristan. What kind of fiancée am I? I know you hate flying and I run away to a place where you have to fly to get to me. I've been such a terrible person. I'm so sorry."

"I told you. I fantasized about making love to you the whole time, so not another word about it. No more apologies. From now on, we follow the truth policy. Right now, to be honest, I'm more interested in less talking and more doing. Come with me."

He took my hand and I followed him to the first bedroom. On the nightstand sat a bottle of champagne in a silver ice bucket and two glasses. A tray of fruit sat next to them filled with every fruit I'd ever heard of, except strawberries.

"Are we eating first or drinking?"

Tristan pointed toward the bed and smiled. "Sit. I'm overdressed for what I have in mind."

As I laid back on the bed, he shrugged out of his shirt. Still leaner than before he left for all those months, his body was tight and sinewy. My gaze slid over his abs, as defined as they'd always been, and I rolled off the bed wanting more than just to watch him undress.

"Let me help," I said as I pushed his hands away from his pants.

He lifted them, as if in surrender, and looked down as I knelt in front of him. "Help is good. This is even better."

I lowered his zipper and reached my hand in to palm his stiff cock. "There's one thing I want the same as last time. Remember?"

A sexy smile spread across his lips and he nodded. I eased his pants and boxer briefs down over his hips until his cock sprang free. Positioned perfectly, I merely had to open my mouth and take him into me. Gripping it near the base, I slipped the swollen head between my lips, playfully flicking my tongue over the silky soft skin.

"Toying with me may be a dangerous choice right now, Nina," he whispered hoarsely as I eased only the head in and out of my mouth.

Staring up into his eyes full of desire, I slid my tongue up the length of him. "Turnabout is fair play."

He ran his hands through my hair and pulled me down onto his cock. "Then let's play."

I moved up and down his shaft, teasing the spot just under the head where he was most sensitive with my tongue and fingertip. Taking the full length of him into my mouth, I crushed my nose against the hardness of his muscles just below his navel and inhaled his fragrance, a combination of a musky sex smell and soap, as I swirled my tongue around the base of his cock.

"God, Nina, you're killing me, baby."

There was nothing better than hearing him groan raggedly while I sucked his cock, totally in control of his pleasure. In those moments, his walls came down and he showed me a side of him so intimate and personal the world never saw in the man so restrained all the time.

Tonight, though, I could tell as his hands guided my head up and down that he wanted to control our lovemaking.

He pumped into my mouth, his long, thick cock stretching my lips to take all of him. I followed his pace, loving the sound of his moaning and panting as I brought him closer to the final edge. His hands fisted in my hair, gently at first but then sending tendrils of pain across my scalp as his body began to surrender to my mouth.

In a voice hoarse with desire, he groaned, "Oh, fuck…right there, baby."

I closed my eyes and felt the first spurt of cum hit the back of my tongue. My left hand clawed at his abs as my right hand milked the base of his cock and gently squeezed his balls. I wanted to taste every drop of him. He filled my mouth, and I swallowed as I opened my eyes to watch him staring down at me, those gorgeous brown eyes watching me give him pleasure.

When he was done, I sat back on my heels and smiled up at him. He stepped out of his clothes and led me to the bed. Easing me onto my back, Tristan slid up over my body until our faces met. His dark eyes stared into mine, holding me with his gaze. "I want you, Nina. When I thought I might never get you back, something changed inside me. You make me want to be the man I see in your eyes. You do that to me."

He pressed my legs apart with his hand and slid the length of his cock over my clit, nearly driving me out of my mind. His hand slid over my breast, cupping it as his thumb and forefinger squeezed my nipple to a sharp peak. Arching my back, I urged him to ease my need, but he was in control, not me.

"Don't tease, Tristan," I moaned as he hovered over me, grinning and licking his lips.

Leaning down to flick the tip of his tongue over my nipple, he looked up at me and whispered, "No teasing. Just pleasure." His lips closed around the needy peak, and he sucked it sharply into his mouth, sending ribbons of desire through my body.

Expert at building my need, he bit down gently, making my pussy run wet. Much more and I'd come without even having his cock inside me. I dragged my nails down his back, urging him to give me what I want.

He lifted his head, a look of pleasure on his face. "Tell me what you want." His voice was ragged, signaling any control he possessed was slipping away.

"I want you inside me. Don't make me wait."

Slowly, he plunged into my body, filling me so completely that he nearly took my breath away and ridding me of all the emptiness inside. My fingers dug into his biceps as he thrust in and out of me, his body moving over mine as he made my body his once again. I adored him. Needed him. Wanted him.

When he finally let me come, my body ached from need, able to cling to him but little else. For hours we lost ourselves in one another, him giving me delicious orgasm after orgasm and filling me as often as I came for him. We'd worshipped each other as we should have, making up for lost time.

Taking me in his arms, he held me and tenderly stroked my skin as he whispered how much he loved me. I believed him. As scary as it was to take that chance, it was even scarier to think of my life without him.

After a long while, he gently rolled me onto my back and placed a kiss on the tip of my nose. "Are you hungry?"

"I could eat. Are you?"

Smiling, he said, "I can eat. Making love for hours should always be followed by a meal in bed."

Tristan poured us champagne and lifted his glass to make a toast. I couldn't help but smile. There I was in Venice, in a gorgeous hotel suite my fiancé owned, drinking champagne in bed. Was this really my life?

"What's the smile for?"

"I just can't believe this is my life. I mean, look at us. In bed drinking champagne. Do people really do this?"

He kissed me tenderly on the lips. "They do, and from now on, we do."

When he said that, it seemed so natural. What was a girl to do with a man like this? "Then let's toast to our life of champagne in bed."

"I have a better toast. Here's to us finally accepting the happiness we've been running away from for so long."

Raising my glass, I met his with a clank. "And more time in bed."

Tristan dangled a bunch of grapes just above my mouth. I craned my neck to grab one with my teeth but only ended up biting the air. Taking one grape off the vine, he held it between his teeth and smiled. "Do you remember that first night I fed you?"

Nodding, I said, "Yes. It was the most erotic thing I'd ever experienced." Plucking the grape from his mouth, I popped it into my own. "I think it's time I fed you."

He swallowed the last of his champagne and leaned back against the headboard. "Mmmm, I like that."

Climbing on top of him, I took the glass and grapes out of his hands. "Then this is perfect. I'll be the last woman to do that for you."

He gave me a devilish grin and looked up at me as I straddled his hips. "I really like that."

I grabbed a chunk of pineapple and placed it on his tongue. "Here's to us being the first and last of many things for each other."

His face grew serious, and he stroked his thumb over my cheek. "I love you, Nina. Don't ever doubt that, no matter how I screw things up. I love you."

Leaning down, I kissed him lightly on the lips and slipped another grape into his mouth. "No more talk about messing up. We're in Venice, in love, and in bed eating fruit and champagne. And when we get up tomorrow morning, I'm holding you to a promise you made the last time we were here. That means museums, Mr. Stone. It's time you see Venice for what it really is."

He smiled and I knew he remembered his promise. "It's isn't the Louvre, but it's a deal. First, though, I have all night with you before we head out to the museums. I plan to make the most of it."

Some problem at the hotel forced the concierge to interrupt us just as we planned to leave for our museum tour, and I was forced to wait in the suite for hours while Tristan cleared up the mess. Just when I believed we'd miss the chance yet again for me to show him the art wonders of Venice, he returned, ready to learn all about what he'd been missing in the art world.

As we walked hand-in-hand to the Piazza San Marco, I explained my plans for the rest of the day. "I first want to take you to Ca' Rezzonico. There's an entire floor dedicated to paintings that show what the city was like in the eighteenth century. Then we can visit the museum you found me at yesterday, Museo Civico Correr."

"We can go wherever you want. I told you it's about time I get some culture."

Climbing the massive marble staircase to the first floor of Ca' Rezzonico, I asked, "Did you know this was a palace before it became a museum?"

He shook his head and smiled. "No, I didn't."

"It was. In 1936 they opened it as a museum, but it was first built in the mid-1600s. Wait until you see the way they arranged it. The entire place looks like it would if it was still a palace. It's really quite beautiful. Oh, and the Triumph of Zephyr and Flora…"

My words trailed off as I watched a man hurry away from the top of the stairs and through the first floor. I hadn't assumed we were alone, but something about him seemed odd, as if he hadn't wanted us to see him.

We reached the first floor and I couldn't see him anywhere. Tristan squeezed my hand, and I turned to face him. "Nina, what's wrong? You look like you've seen a ghost."

I forced a smile, not wanting to ruin our museum tour. "It's nothing. I thought I saw someone."

"The man in front of us a second ago?" he asked as he looked left and right for the man.

"It's nothing. It's just that last time I was here—remember you were supposed to come with me and I had to go with that giant bodyguard instead? Well, I met a man here who said he knew my father. That man we just saw looked like him."

Tristan took me by the shoulders and stared down into my eyes with an intense look that frightened me. "Nina, I need you to think about this. What did that man say to you?"

I hesitated for a moment and he repeated his question. I didn't want to say what that man had told me and bring up all the terrible things from the past, but finally, I said, "He told me he thought it was a shame the people responsible for my father's death were never charged."

"And you think that man was the same person as the one who just nearly ran away when he saw us?"

I didn't know. It could have been him. He did look similar to him, especially his tanned skin. I wasn't sure, though. "You're scaring me, Tristan. I don't know if it's the same man. It could be. I just don't know."

"I'm not trying to scare you, but I think we need to get out of here. Something's wrong. I feel it."

We hurried back down the stairs and out the museum doors. Tristan didn't say anything, but I knew he was far more worried than he wanted me to believe. We walked along the Grand Canal for as long as we could with him looking behind us every few feet. Finally, I realized that we weren't going back to the hotel.

"Where are we going? The hotel is back there."

"Just keep walking," Tristan said, his tone serious.

"What's going on?"

He pulled me into a dark corner and shook his head. "I thought they had him. I thought we'd be safe. Nina, no matter what happens, I won't let anything hurt you. Trust me."

His words were meant to calm me, but I saw fear in his eyes. "You're scaring me. What's going on?"

The sound of footsteps on the stone walkway told me someone was coming. Tristan's hand tensed on my arm as they came closer, and he pushed me behind him. A large man came around the corner and for a moment I held my breath until I heard a familiar voice.

I peeked around Tristan and saw Varo standing there. "I've been looking for you. You lost me at the museum. We need to get you out of here. The plane's ready to go."

Tristan held my hand tightly. "What's happened?"

"Daryl called me. He's worried about Karl. He's been released."

"Released?" I asked as I moved to Tristan's side. "Is he here?"

Varo looked around and shook his head. "I don't know. We need to leave here."

Tristan didn't question my bodyguard's order, which told me he believed we were in danger. If I had any doubt, the gun in Varo's hand put any uncertainty to rest. As Tristan asked him if he remembered something or another, I began to get scared.

Chapter Twenty-Three

Tristan

Varo followed us as I led Nina and him along the streets of the city looking for a water taxi to take us to Marco Polo. As long as we got to the airport, we'd be safe, at least until we got back to the States. There I knew I could protect Nina much better than in Venice.

As we walked quickly back toward the Grand Canal, we ran into crowds of people flocking out into the night, making it harder to look out for Karl and whoever he had with him. I hadn't seen his face yet, but I knew he was there. I'd taken everything that mattered to him, and now he planned to do the same to me.

My heart raced as we weaved through tourists and Venetians, all out to enjoy a beautiful night. They had no idea that among them was a man who wouldn't think twice about killing two people just like them.

Nina held my hand like she was afraid I would let go, squeezing it harder when she heard a loud noise or when someone pushed against her as they passed by. My eyes scanned the crowds as we wound through them, every person appearing guilty as the minutes ticked by.

"We should try to find a water taxi," Varo said behind us. "The sooner we get to the plane, the better."

I saw a taxi coming in our direction, but it was on the other side of the canal. To catch it, we'd have to cross one of the bridges. Pointing toward the nearest one, I tried to make Nina believe everything was going to be okay. "What's the name of this bridge? You know all about Venice."

Her eyes grew wide, and I knew she wasn't buying my act. "It's the Accademia Bridge, not that it matters. Why are you acting like everything's okay?"

"Because it's going to be. Now tell me all about this bridge so we can at least pretend our tour of Venice was successful."

As Nina gave me chapter and verse about the history of the Accademia Bridge, we began crossing over to the other side of the canal and I saw my first glimpse of Karl. We were too late.

Before she could realize what was happening, I stopped and turned toward Varo, who had seen him too. "I need you to do what you said you would."

Varo simply nodded, and I turned to face Nina. "I need you to go with Varo now. He'll get you to the plane and keep you safe. I'll be there in a little while."

Her eyes flashed panic, and she looked around to see what was making me send her away. When she settled back on me, I saw tears in her eyes. "No, don't do this! Don't send me away. You promised no more running. Don't do this, Tristan!"

I cradled her face in my hands as the tears rolled down onto my skin. "Baby, I won't let them hurt you because of me. Go with Varo so at least I can know you're safe."

"No! He's going to hurt you or worse, and then I'll never see you again. Please don't send me away."

I leaned in and kissed her as Varo moved around me to take hold of her arm. "I'll see you soon. Don't worry."

She fought him off, but it was no use. He knew what he had to do. I'd made him promise that if she was ever in danger and I couldn't protect her that he would. I needed to believe he'd live up to that pledge now.

Nina's eyes pled with me not to send her away, nearly breaking my heart, but I had no choice. For one of the first times in my life, I was doing the right thing, no matter how much it was killing me to watch her as Varo took her away.

Karl stood on the other side waiting for me. Dozens of people separated us, each in danger if I didn't find some way to get off that bridge. I took off in the direction Varo and Nina had gone, hoping to at least reach the walkway, but one of Karl's henchmen was waiting. Terrified they'd already gotten Nina, I frantically searched for any sight of her, finally seeing Varo leading her into a building and hopefully to safety.

From behind me, I heard a familiar voice. "Son, I told you not to fuck with me. Like father, like son." I turned and saw Karl's face twisted into an angry smug expression as a man grabbed me from behind to hold me. "Take him to the room."

"Planning to kill me in one of these hotels? Is that supposed to be ironic, Karl?" I asked, hoping to gain some time for Varo to get Nina out of Venice.

"I'm going to do even better, Tristan. I'm going to kill you in one of your hotels. Or maybe I could do it on your plane. I like the symbolism of that too."

"Way to keep it classy, Karl. You always were new money. Never did understand your level, did you?" His answer to my question was a hard right to my face. After a few moments, I could see straight again, if not a little blurry. I knew I had to keep him there as long as possible. A couple more insults might give Varo the time he needed to get Nina to the plane. "No wonder my father only gave you a nothing company. He knew your true worth, didn't he?"

But Karl didn't take the bait. "Always the clever one, Tristan. Take him to the room, and West, find your buddy and that girl now!"

I turned to see West standing behind me. How long had he been working for Karl and living just yards away from Nina? I watched him take off to hunt down Varo and Nina and prayed to God I'd given them enough time to find their way out of the city. I heard two men start to say where to search for them and then all I felt was pain in the back of my head before everything went black.

"Wakey, wakey. Time to rise and shine."

I opened my eyes and saw the familiar gold and burgundy décor of a Richmont Venice room. Karl sat in front of me with a cigar between his teeth, like some kind of evil villain character from an old cartoon. My hands were tied behind me, so I had to blink the sleep from my eyes. "Tie any women to train tracks recently?"

"Still clever, even just minutes before I finally get rid of you once and for all. I have to say, Tristan, you are one tough foe to eliminate."

Shaking my head, I wasn't sure I wanted to have this be my last conversation of my life, but he left me with little choice. The guy was a homicidal madman but even more, a colossal asshole. "It didn't have to be like this, Karl. You were my father's friend."

He blew cigar smoke in my direction and let out a deep laugh. "Friend? You don't know much at all, son. I would have figured that by now you would have found out I was never your father's friend."

"Then you were my mother's lover. One would think that would count for something. I can't imagine she'd want her son killed by the man she loved."

The smug expression slid from his face, replaced by a hint of sadness for only a moment. But then the nasty fuck was back again. "Oh, so you know about that?"

"I know she loved you and you seemed to love her."

"I adored her. I may not have had the money your father had, but I could have made her happy."

"It would have been nice if someone did," I said quietly, unsure how I felt about agreeing with the man about to kill me.

"But she left me. For him! I couldn't have that. I couldn't," he said with venom in his voice.

"She had no choice. Once Taylor and I came along, she had to stay. She's been dead for five years. Maybe it's time to forgive."

Karl stood from his seat and walked over to the bar to pour himself a drink. When he turned around with the glass in his hand, I was struck at how much he reminded me of my father. The few times I'd watched Victor Stone conduct business, he'd had a glass of scotch in his hand each time. That's what this was to Karl now. Business. But it had a lot of the personal involved too.

He walked back and took a seat in front of me again, the ice cubes in the amber liquid clanking against the side of the glass. "Sometimes there can be no forgiveness, son. Sometimes all you're left with is hatred as pure as the blood that courses through your veins."

"So you won't forgive my father or mother and decided to kill me instead? Seems pretty fucked up. You have nothing left, Karl. Can you possibly hate me so much that you have to kill me? Does the fact that you loved my mother mean nothing now?"

He drank a gulp of scotch and took a deep breath before he exhaled slowly, as if some weight had been removed from him. "If only she'd met me first. You know, I used to wish that you and your brother were my sons. Twins ran in her family, so maybe we could have had twins. I never liked your brother, Tristan. Presumptuous fuck that he was, he thought he was too important to deal with the likes of me, even as a teenager. You were different, though. More like me. He was all books and studying, but not you. I could have liked you. I did like you. You're a lot like her. I see her in your eyes, even now."

"You mean the one that's nearly swollen shut or the other one your men haven't started on yet?"

"Your one flaw—do you know what that is?"

He took another drink of scotch while I shook my head, not interested in helping him in whatever the fuck this was. "Boyish charm?"

"Smart ass. Your one flaw is that you get attached to things, people. The drugs when you were younger. This girl now. She's the reason I have to do all this."

I chafed at his mention of Nina, tugging at the ropes that held my wrists behind me. "Don't blame Nina for your being crazy, Karl. At least be truthful with yourself. You're killing me because I found out about Cordovex and how Rider's drugs were killing people. Nina had nothing to do with that."

"But that's not true, Tristan. If only you'd left things well enough alone. You couldn't, though. That's your mother in you. You found out about Joseph Edwards and then you saw his daughter. That getting attached thing, remember? Your weakness. All you had to do was throw some money at her. It wouldn't have taken much. A middle class girl probably would have been happy if you paid off her fucking student loans. But no, you had to ride in on the white horse and save her. You did this."

"My father had Joseph Edwards killed. Once I was CEO of Stone Worldwide, it was the least I could do to try to make up for that." Why I felt the need to explain my actions to this psychotic madman was beyond me, but I did.

A laugh exploded from Karl's face, startling me. "Your father never had a damn soul killed. He couldn't be bothered. You think he was some kind of shark, but the truth was he was just a workaholic. Nothing more. Well, work and those goddamned secretaries he liked to sleep with. It was the work he loved more than the people around him, though. Hell, he loved work more than he loved Tressa. He made it easy for me to get to her."

"The least you can do now is tell the truth, Karl. I know my father ordered Nina's father to be killed. He'd gotten too close to exposing the story of Judge Cashen and his daughter's deaths and Taylor's part in that. I know all about the sexual harassment case and the Judge's part in that."

Slowly, Karl shook his head. "Right puzzle, wrong pieces, son. It's true that Taylor got that girl pregnant. That smarmy fuck thought he could do a teenage girl, but he wasn't smart enough to wear a fucking condom. That he didn't want her was no surprise. She was a fucking child. A throwaway lay. But your father had nothing to do with her father's death. That was me. I ordered his death and Edwards'."

The realization that my family hadn't directly ruined Nina's family stunned me for a moment. All this time the guilt I'd shouldered had been wrong. My father hadn't been a saint, but at least he hadn't killed Nina's father. "Why? Was it because Edwards was getting to close to the dirty laundry my father wanted hidden? Did he tell you to get rid of Cashen and Nina's father?"

Chuckling, Karl lifted his glass and swallowed the last gulp of alcohol. "You have a misguided view of who Victor Stone was. A semi-talented businessman, his real skill was as a worker. He knew more about business than most men because he spent hours learning about it, but he would never have a threat eliminated. He preferred to fight it out. The competition is what he liked."

As he stood to refill his glass, I asked, "Then why were they killed if my father wasn't worried about losing the case or what Nina's father had?"

With his back to me, he answered. "Rider Pharmaceutical."

"What?"

He turned around and smiled, repeating his answer. "Rider Pharmaceutical. The success of Cordovex wasn't going to be ruined by some nosy journalist or your father's inability to keep his dick in his pants. So they had to go."

"All of this over Rider and Cordovex?"

"That competitive streak in your father extended to your mother too. When he found out, he gave me that tiny, pissant company named for her maiden name. I knew what that meant. That was his way of saying I couldn't have the woman I loved but I could have some useless company to remind me every day that he'd won. Over the years, I'd been able to make it into something and then Cordovex came. We got it through the FDA with an acceptable level of problems, but no amount of hope changed the fact that it wasn't what we wished it would be. Your father found out and fired me. He was nice enough to give me some time to come up with a way to save face when I left Stone. That's where his mistake was."

I wracked my brain to remember any evidence of Karl ever being fired, but if there had been any proof, I'd never seen or heard about it. Whatever he was going on about was fiction to feed his demented ego. "My father never fired you. This is all just to make you feel like you weren't some low level operative in a company run by a bigger man."

"So I found a way to make sure I didn't have to leave. I couldn't be forced out if the man doing it wasn't around anymore."

Karl's words slowly sunk into my brain and I suddenly realized I wasn't breathing. It couldn't be true. He must have been lying.

"I see by the look on your face you don't believe what I said. Believe it. I needed to find a way to get rid of your father and Taylor, since he'd take over the minute your father was gone. That your mother would have to suffer for staying with him was poetic justice, but I knew I'd have to find some way to get rid of you too. I figured I could deal with that later. Tressa had secretly told me that Victor planned to fire me over the Cordovex thing your girlfriend's father had found out about and thought convincing him to take a few days off would give me the chance to leave the company quietly. She told me you didn't want to go. Something about some party you didn't want to miss."

As he spoke, I remembered that time like it was yesterday. I'd told my mother I had no interest in going away with them but at the last minute,

I'd given in to her constant asking me to change my mind, thinking a few days in the islands would at least offer a chance to party there with much better drugs. My mother had been so happy when I finally relented.

Rage coursed through my veins as the truth became clear. Karl had killed my family over his petty ambitions and now planned to kill me and Nina because he was a megalomaniacal fuck. "You bastard! You killed them over a fucking job?"

"I deserved that job! I made Rider Pharmaceutical a company worthy of respect and he wanted to shut me out of everything! I deserved everything he was taking away."

"You killed my entire family over some bullshit company the Feds would have ruined anyway. Cordovex would have been the end of Rider," I said quietly, still unable to process the actions of the monster in front of me.

"Not true. Rider only had to pull the drug voluntarily. The FDA is nice like that. Then it was just a matter of playing the waiting game for a few years and reintroducing it onto the market. I just had to make sure that reporter was handled. But then you didn't die in the crash."

A look of disappointment crossed his face and he shrugged nonchalantly. My living through the plane crash had put a damper on his big plans. At least I could know that even though I didn't know about it at the time, I'd been a thorn in this fucker's side.

"But then you disappeared a few months ago and all my plans could be set in motion once again. It was like God was smiling down on me from Heaven. So Cardiell was born, and I had it all, but once again, one of you fucking Stones ruined it."

Karl's face turned bright red, and he jumped up from his chair to begin pacing as he rambled on about how he'd been treated unfairly, first by my father and then by me. With every word, he sounded more and more like a madman out of his mind.

It didn't matter, though. None of his men had returned to report their success in finding Nina and Varo, which meant they'd found a way to escape. As long as she was safe, I could handle anything Karl did.

As long as I believed I'd protected her, I could die with some sense of peace.

Chapter Twenty-Four

Nina

No matter how hard I tugged my arm, I couldn't break Varo's hold on me. I had no idea where he was taking me, and with each step away from Tristan, I feared I'd never see the man I loved again. I tried once more unsuccessfully to yank my arm free from his hand around my wrist, but he pulled me harder down walkway, hurrying me to some unknown place.

"Varo, you're hurting me! Let me go! We need to go back to help Tristan."

"We're going to the plane. He'll meet us there," he said coldly.

I stopped walking, forcing him to drag me. "No! I won't go without Tristan."

For the first time since we left Accademia Bridge, Varo stopped walking and turned to face me. "Nina, I gave him my word that I'd keep you safe. That's what I'm doing."

"I don't care what he made you sign when he hired you. That means nothing to me. We need to go back to help him."

"I can't let you do that. This has nothing to do with anything I signed for a job. He asked me before you left to come here to promise that I'd protect you if he couldn't. I made that promise, Nina. You just have to trust that he'll be okay."

I hung my head in frustration. "He's not going to be okay. Karl's going to kill him. Why don't you see that?"

"I can't help that. I have a job to do, so let's go."

There had to be a way to get through to him. I knew he wasn't the heartless bastard he seemed to be at that moment. That sweet guy who'd helped me when I didn't think I could pretend to move on had to be in there somewhere.

"Gage, I know this is more than a job to you. You're a good guy. I believe that in my heart. Please help me save Tristan. He needs us."

"Nina, I can't. Tristan needed to be sure you'd be safe. Just trust that he'll be okay."

I couldn't fight him like this. "Do you understand what it's like to be so in love with someone that you don't feel like you can go on without them?"

He looked away and said in a low voice, "Don't."

"It's like if they're not in the world anymore, you don't want to be either. Like if you lose that part of you, you'll never be whole again."

I saw by the look in those dark blue eyes that I was getting to him. He knew what it felt like to lose someone from when he lost Angela. It was a shitty thing to do, but I needed to manipulate that soft spot in his heart if I ever expected to get him to help me.

"Tell me you wouldn't have given anything to save Angela if someone was trying to kill her. I know you would."

"Nina, it's not the same thing."

"Yes, it is! You loved her, and if she was ever in danger, you would have given your life to save hers. How is that different from this? I'm not asking you to sacrifice yourself, but don't tell me it's wrong for me to do. I love Tristan more than I ever thought I could love anyone. Just help me find him. Please."

He let out a heavy sigh and shook his head. "I can't let you get hurt, and I have no idea how we can help him. I don't even know where they took him."

The thought of Tristan already dead and floating face down in a side canal somewhere made my chest hurt. He might be dead already, but I had to try to find him. I had to save him, if I could. "There has to be a way for us to find him, Gage. He needs us. Please. There's got to be a way."

Gage was silent for a long time before he shook his head once again. "I can't think of anything, Nina. They could be anywhere in Venice."

His grip loosened, and I tore my arm from his hold. "I can't give up on him. He needs me now, and I won't just leave him. Don't worry. Your conscience is clear. You did what you could, but I won't go with you."

Turning, I set off running toward the bridge, unsure of where to find Tristan but sure I'd never give up until I did. I heard Gage yell my name and then I felt his hand on my arm again. "No! Let me go!"

"I remembered something, Nina. There might be a way to find out where he is. Just stop so we can check."

He held me tightly, giving me little chance to run, so I stopped trying to escape. "Tell me what it is and how we do it."

Gage reached into his pocket and in seconds he was on the phone. "Daryl, they got him. We need to know where he is."

Daryl said something that sounded like it was about me and Gage nodded. "Yeah. I know. Can you find out?"

As he waited for Daryl to answer his question, I looked around, worried we might be caught before we ever found out where Tristan was. "Gage, we don't have time for this. We have to go."

He nodded again and smiled. "Thanks, Daryl. You might be right about technology. I'll tell Tristan you said hi." Gage stuck his phone back into his pocket and pointed down the sidewalk toward The Richmont Venice. "They have him at the hotel."

"How do you know?"

"I don't, but if his phone is still on him, that's where he is. Did he have it when he left the hotel earlier?"

I nodded, unsure of how Gage knew Tristan's phone was there but thrilled at the hope that he could still be alive. "Yes, he had it. He showed me a picture on it as we walked toward the museum."

Taking my hand in his, Gage smiled. "Then let's hope it's still on him. Now we just have to figure out where in the hotel he is and how we get in without Karl's thugs grabbing us."

A tour group of what looked to be at least thirty people milled about the Richmont Venice lobby waiting to check in, so we attempted to blend in with them as we figured out where Karl could be holding Tristan. Unsure if the hotel staff were helping Karl and his men, I pulled Gage behind a marble pillar farthest away from the concierge desk to plan what to do next.

"There are any number of places he could be," I whispered into his ear as I peered over his shoulder to make sure nobody had spotted us.

"The suite you two are in is on the fifth floor. There's only one other suite on that floor, so I think we should start there and eliminate that possibility. The problem is how are we going to get up there without being seen? The main staircase is in the center of the building, and there's no way we can get upstairs and not be noticed, even with all these tourists."

My mind flashed back to something Tristan had told me the first time we visited the hotel. I closed my eyes and replayed the conversation that night after we'd made love and spent hours in each other's arms. Suddenly, I remembered. "There's a back staircase that's only used by staff. It used to be a secret staircase back when this was a palace."

Two women I recognized from the concierge staff walked past us trying to herd all the tourists toward the check-in desk, but one seemed too interested in Gage and me as we stood huddled behind the column. Her stare lingered just a second too long on us, making me worry. Did she recognize me from when Tristan and I returned to the hotel?

I turned my back to the crowd and whispered, "Gage, we need to get to that back staircase, but I don't know where it is. All I know is that Tristan told me it existed."

Gage moved to shield me and nodded his head toward a hallway that transected the lobby. "If this is the front stairway, then maybe the back one is down that hallway."

"I think that could be right. We just need to get past the concierge, who I think might have recognized me from last night."

An elderly female tourist backed into a large ornamental vase and knocked it from one of the lobby's tables with her oversized purse at that very moment, and with its crash to the floor, we had a perfect diversion. She screamed in surprise, and the crowd formed in around her to see the results of her clumsiness, including the two hotel employees. Quickly, I yanked on Gage's arm to lead him away from the scene. "Let's go!"

We raced down the hallway until we reached a door that looked like a closet. Opening it, he found our back staircase. "Come on. We've got four flights of stairs to climb."

Compared to the front staircase with its gorgeous caramel colored marble walls, ornate cut outs, and candle sconces lighting the way, this staircase was sorely in need of repair. Old plaster peeled from the walls and except for a few small windows, the staircase was dark.

Perfect for someone trying to sneak around Tristan's hotel.

We reached the top floor and quietly entered the hallway connecting the two suites. Listening near the door to the one Tristan and I shared, we heard no noises. I pointed to the room and shook my head to let Gage know I didn't think that's where they were holding him.

He whispered, "Did you see the people who were staying in the other suite?"

I shook my head again. "No. How are we going to find out who's in there?"

Gage pointed to an alcove behind two columns on the left side of the hallway. I followed him there and watched as he moved toward the suite's door. "What are you doing?"

He raised his hand to knock on the door. "Ding dong ditch."

I hid behind the column and peeked my head around just enough to see him knock on the door and run behind the column across from me. After a few moments, a young blonde wearing very little opened the door and looked around to see who'd knocked. From inside the suite, I heard a man with a voice that sounded much older than she looked ask who it was.

"Nobody. I guess they were looking for the suite down the hall, honey," she answered in squeaky voice and closed the door, leaving us standing there at least knowing Tristan wasn't being held on that floor.

"I guess we can rule that out," Gage said with a smile.

"Onto the fourth floor," I said as we hurriedly crossed the hall and entered the back staircase again.

The floor below wasn't going to be as easy to search. Unlike the top floor, this one had twenty rooms instead of two suites. Thankfully, it had alcoves too where we could hide as we searched, but ding dong ditching twenty rooms seemed like a poor way to find out what we needed.

Gage held the door as we exited the staircase in the middle of the floor and hurried to the nearest alcove. Five middle aged hotel patrons stood outside a room at the end of the hall as one man fumbled with the room key. They left immediately, so at least we could guess that room wasn't where Tristan was.

"How are we going to find out if he's in one of these rooms? This is going to take forever, and we don't have that kind of time," I said in frustration as we watched them walk by us.

Before Gage could answer, I saw his eyes grow wide as saucers and followed his gaze to someone getting off the elevator. I recognized him immediately. West. He walked quickly to a room at the opposite end of the hallway and knocked.

I leaned in close to Gage and whispered, "He's in there! We need to get in there!"

Nodding, he held up his hand to calm me. "Give me a second to figure this out."

The door closed and tears began to well in my eyes. Hanging my head, I leaned against the pillar, devastated. "We missed our chance, Gage."

"You didn't think we'd just barge in there, did you?" He put his hand on my shoulder to comfort me and quietly said, "Don't worry. I'll think of something."

"No need, buddy. I'll get you in there right now."

Terror raced through me, and I looked up to see West standing there with a gun to the back of Gage's head. We were lost. Tristan would be killed and then they'd do the same to us. I'd blown it.

West led us down the hall into the room, and my first sight of Tristan nearly took my breath away. His left eye was black and blue and practically swollen shut from a beating. Blood trickled down his chin from a deep cut in his bottom lip. Even with all that, he was immediately worried about me.

"Nina, why are you here? Why didn't you just leave with Gage?" he asked as he groaned in pain.

The man I recognized as the one from the museum grabbed my arms tightly, and when I moved to help Tristan, he roughly pulled me back, hurting me. I opened my mouth to answer, but Karl spoke up before I could say a word. "She didn't leave because she loves you, Tristan. Now she'll pay for that love with her life."

"Why are you doing this?" I cried, finally needing to know what the hell I'd ever done to make this person hate me so much.

Karl turned to face me, his snake-like eyes scanning me from head to toe. "Why am I doing this? Because you're the reason why everything fell apart. Just like your father and his fucking investigation. Because all Tristan had to do was throw some money at you to ease his guilt over your father and you would never have ended up here. He'd still have to die, but you wouldn't be here. You'd be back in your little life serving the art world in your inconsequential way. But he didn't do that. He fell in love with you and now we're here at the end of the road."

Tristan hung his head and said quietly, "I'm sorry, Nina. I'm sorry I ever waited for you that night in the alley behind the Anderson Gallery. If I hadn't..."

His voice trailed off and he closed his eyes. I couldn't let him think that I regretted one moment of our time together. He deserved better than that. "If you hadn't, I wouldn't have met you and fallen in love with the most incredible man in the world."

"How touching. Now if we're done with the staging of Romeo and Juliet, it's time for this to end. You'll be dead, and in a few years, I'll be the head of Stone Worldwide. In the meantime, one of my friends on the board will make sure my company thrives in my absence."

A large, bald man who looked nearly the size of Gage stood behind Tristan and violently yanked his head up, and Karl aimed his gun directly at him. I scrambled for anything to delay—to give Gage time to stop him—and blurted out, "Wait! Tell us how you got Rogers to turn on Tristan. He loved him like a son. He wouldn't hurt him unless you did something horrible to him."

Karl smiled, his gun still aimed at Tristan. "Ah, Rogers. I have to tell you, son, you certainly do have some very loyal people around you. Your girlfriend's right. Rogers didn't come easily. You were his world.

He loved you more than your father did. It took me forever to figure out the angle to take with him. Nothing worked. Money didn't matter. Threats didn't work. But you know what did? When you fell in love with her, Rogers couldn't take it. He was jealous. Go figure. Out of all the emotions to manipulate, I only had to wait for jealousy to rear its ugly head. Once it was obvious that you were going to marry her and wouldn't need him anymore, he was putty in my hands."

Tristan's frown deepened as Karl detailed why the one person he'd always trusted betrayed him. It tore my heart apart to know I'd been the reason he'd lost Rogers.

"And then you killed him. Why, if he was helping you?" I asked.

"It seems those paternal feelings he'd always had never left after all. He was weak, and when you told him to get out of your life, I knew I couldn't trust him to handle things anymore."

I watched as Tristan hung his head and said sadly, barely above a whisper, "You made sure you took everyone from me."

Karl smirked. "Not yet, son. Not yet."

Just when I was sure he'd given up, Tristan looked over at West and said, "Obviously not everyone around me is loyal."

Karl turned to look at West and smiled. "Oh, West? He was easy. Right, West? Not everyone thinks a man your age should have everything his heart desires."

West mumbled something about Tristan being a spoiled rich boy, and then out of the corner of my eye, I saw Gage's arm move. In a flash, I heard a gun go off and the man behind me released my arms. I dropped to the floor and covered my head as two more shots rang out. It all happened so fast. Somebody yelled "Get him!" and I heard the most terrifying sound I'd ever heard in my life. A body fell to the floor and a man's voice moaned until another shot exploded and everything fell silent.

I opened my eyes and saw Karl and West on the floor in front of me and blood everywhere. Gage stood over another man in the corner of the room who looked like he'd only been grazed by a bullet. Frantically, I searched the room for Tristan and saw him slumped over in the chair he'd been tied up in. Blood covered the side of his face, and he looked unconscious.

Running over, I knelt in front of him and looked up to see a bullet had hit his right shoulder and his left eye was bleeding. "Gage! Tristan's been shot! He needs help!"

Behind me, Gage called for help while I gently lifted Tristan's head. He didn't respond to my touch, and the real fear that I'd lost him settled into my brain. Shaking my head, I let the tears roll down my cheeks as I pleaded for him to stay with me. "Tristan, don't leave me. I can't do this without you. Don't leave me here all alone. Please, Tristan! Open your eyes. Open your eyes and let me know you're going to be okay."

His eyes remained closed as I sat there praying he'd survive. I heard the ambulance in the distance as it raced up the canal toward us, piercing the night with its shrill emergency cry. "The paramedics are coming. Just hang on for me, Tristan. Don't leave me. Don't leave me, baby."

Gage pulled me away as the paramedics entered the room, and I watched as they took him away, barking out directions about how to get to the hospital. In mere minutes, he was gone and I was left standing there sobbing, hoping against hope that I hadn't lost him this time.

CHAPTER TWENTY-FIVE

Nina

I sat alone in the bedroom Tristan and I shared, my hands shaking as I thought about what I must do in mere minutes. Muffled voices from outside the door signaled it was nearly time. Inhaling deeply, I closed my eyes and tried to calm my nerves.

The door opened and Jordan peeked her head in. "It's time, sweetie."

I pressed my hands to my thighs and took another deep breath. "Okay. I'm ready."

She came to my side and held my hand as I stood from the bed on wobbly legs. "Just wait until you see the flowers. They're really beautiful."

"The flowers?"

Jordan smiled weakly. "That's what they say at times like this, don't they?"

I saw how hard she was trying to be mature at that moment and appreciated it. "I feel like I'm in an episode of some TV melodrama. I know you want to say something snarky or crude, so go for it."

Her shoulders relaxed, and she smiled broadly. "Thank God! I've been tiptoeing around for hours, unsure I should be myself. You've been so quiet since returning from Venice, so I wasn't sure you were up for the full version of me."

I smoothed the back of my dress and rolled my eyes. "You don't have to pretend ever, Jordan. Venice was tough, but I got through it. I'm tougher than I look."

She raised her eyebrows in faux surprise. "Tough, huh? Wait until you get out there and melt into a puddle of girliness when you see your soon-to-be husband."

Jordan wasn't wrong. On normal days, seeing Tristan in a suit he wore to work made my knees weak. Seeing him in a tux waiting for me at the altar might make me fall over. "Tell me. How's he look?"

"Totally badass with that eye patch. Leave it to him to get a black leather one."

"I meant in the tux, Jordan. How's he look in the tux?"

As she buzzed around me tugging and fixing my wedding gown, she chuckled. "Like he was born to wear one. The guy looks more comfortable in a tux than other guys do in jeans and a T-shirt."

Her words took me back to the first time I saw Tristan dressed in a tux and then to that night of the book signing at his hotel. She was right. He wore formality so well, but I knew who the man beneath the clothes was. I knew his passions and his fears, his darkness and his light.

I finally could say I knew Tristan Stone.

Jordan stood back from me and smiled at what she saw. "But when he sees you in this dress, oh, he is going to fall apart. You look stunning, honey."

I looked down at the gown I'd marry my dream man in and nodded. "I hope so. That's the point, right? It won't be much of a honeymoon if the groom doesn't like how the bride looks."

My gown felt more incredible than anything I'd ever worn. White satin that hung like it had been created just for me, it was classy and gorgeous and everything I'd always dreamed I'd be. Now, as I stood in the bedroom I shared with the only man I'd ever truly loved, I finally was that woman in my dreams.

After smoothing my veil over the back of my head, she pulled the ends out near my elbows and let them fall against my arms. One last tuck of a stray hair behind my ear and she was done. "All set. You ready to become Mrs. Tristan Stone?"

I didn't know why, but I began to tear up at those words. Mrs. Tristan Stone. They said the third time was a charm, didn't they? Looking away, I said, "I don't know what's wrong with me. I'm crying like a crazy woman."

"It's okay, Nina. This is a big deal. Just think of it this way, though. After all you and Tristan have been through, getting married is going to be like a walk in the park. Or more like a walk in the garden on a beautiful summer night."

Jordan laughed at her joke about where the wedding was to be held, and I rolled my eyes. "Funny. And by the way, not to make you nervous or anything, but you look pretty incredible yourself in that dress. Maybe tonight's the night Gage asks you out."

She smoothed her hands down over her hips and slinked toward the door. "Oh, by the way, I can report that those muscles are real and there's no sex with bugs."

I thought about what she just said and laughed. "You're terrible!"

Turning her head, she peered over her shoulder at me. "Nothing terrible about it."

"How? Jordan, did you…?"

She winked and then shook her head. "Not yet, but he stopped by my apartment one night last week. We had a nice time together."

"Take it easy on my bodyguard, okay? He saved my life."

Jordan dropped the sexy act and nodded. "I would never do anything to hurt him, sweetie. It's not everyday I have a chance with a hero."

"Okay. Then you have my blessing."

A knock at the door ended our serious moment, and she opened it to Gage standing there. With a smile, he asked, "Did someone order a hero?"

A blush raced up her cheeks, and Jordan turned to look at me with a silly grin. "Mental note to self. Hearing and skulking—expert level."

"Nina, it's time. You ready?" Gage asked, sneaking a look at Jordan.

"I am. Jordan, you ready?"

She nodded and held out her hand to take mine. Squeezing it, she whispered, "I love you, Nina. Now go marry that sexy man so we can have champagne and cake."

"And dancing," I added. Looking past her at Gage, I asked, "Do you dance?"

Flashing us a charming smile, he winked and said, "A little. Enough to get by."

I couldn't help myself and joked, "Saves damsels in distress, has superhero hearing, and he dances?"

Jordan shook her head and walked out mumbling, "Let's go, Cupid. Tristan's waiting."

Gage laughed as she passed, and when she was out of earshot, said, "She's a handful. I'm wondering what you've gotten me into."

"Nothing you can't handle."

From the back of the house the sound of the harpist playing the wedding march filtered through the open windows of the bedroom signaling it was time to go. Gage held out his hand for mine and gave me a gentle smile. "You're on. If we don't get out there, Tristan's going to think you're not showing up."

I took his hand and laughed. "We've had enough of that. I'm ready."

The stone pathway to the garden lay before me, the final walk to Tristan and our new life together. In my hand, I held my bouquet of pink and white roses straight from our garden. Tied with a baby pink ribbon, it was simple and just what I wanted for my big day. With Gage's arm linked in mine, I gazed down the pathway at Tristan as he waited for me stunning in his black tux, his expression a mix of anticipation and love.

We slowly made our way, passing boughs of baby's breath hanging by deep pink ribbons from shepherd's hooks above tea light lanterns to guide us on our way down the stone pathway. Jordan stood to the left of the minister in her gorgeous peacock blue gown holding her own bouquet of baby's breath she chose herself, and candles of all sizes stood flickering soft light behind the altar

Jensen, Maria, and Tristan's assistant Michelle and her husband sat watching Gage and me as we moved closer to the moment he'd give me away. His strong arm held me stable, even as my knees shook from nerves, and then I saw Daryl. Dressed in a black tux similar to Tristan's, he stood at his side as his best man, an odd but understandable choice. Still sporting his mountain man style, he looked like he'd gotten that bushy red hair of his cut and even taken an inch or two off his prized beard for the occasion. He smiled one of those rare Daryl smiles that lit up his features and made me want to giggle.

We were quite a group.

Finally, we reached the end of the pathway and Gage leaned down to kiss me on the cheek. With a simple smile, he handed me to Tristan, and he took my hand in his, giving it a small squeeze. In that moment, nothing else in the world mattered but us and the life we were about to embark on. I looked up at him and saw in his face everything would be all right.

We faced the minister in front of us and listened as he began the ceremony. "We're gathered here together to celebrate the joining of Tristan and Nina. We rejoice in the love of this man and this woman and wish them happiness. Marriage symbolizes the joining of two hearts, each person retaining their own individualism as both travel their path together."

Tristan squeezed my hand as the minister announced we'd written our own vows, and we turned to face each other. I pulled the sheet of paper I'd written mine on from the silk satchel around my wrist, and when I looked back at him, I saw he had nothing in his hand.

Searching his face, I tried to understand what was happening. Had he changed his mind? Fear tore through me, but he simply smiled at me and began speaking.

"Nina, I tried over and over to write my vows last night, but I never found the right words. I woke up this morning and tried again, but still nothing came. I decided I'd just say what was in my heart when it was time, so I hope this comes out right. All my life, I've had whatever my heart desired, and I thought I was happy. Then I lost everything and happiness became something I believed I'd never be lucky enough to have again. I lived like that until one day I was convinced I was meant to be alone. Then one night I met you, and from that moment I've been happier than any man could hope to be."

He stopped for a moment as I struggled to hold back the tears. This man who said so little most times was standing there in front of our friends confessing his love in a way only he could. My heart swelled at how tender and sweet his vows truly were. Straight from his heart, they were him.

"I promise to be the one who makes your days brighter. When the rest of the world can't or won't see who you are, I will. I can't promise I won't make mistakes, but I can promise that you'll never doubt I love you more than my clumsy words can ever say. I love you, Nina."

I covered my mouth with my hand, whispering, "Oh, Tristan" as the tears I'd held back finally began rolling down my cheeks. "That was beautiful."

He silently nodded and gave me a tender smile. I looked at my vows I'd written the night before and suddenly wanted to give him the honesty he'd given me. Stuffing the paper back into my satchel, I held his hand and said what was in my heart.

"Tristan, I love you. You've shown me a world more incredible than anything I'd ever dreamed of. And I'd give it all up as long as I had you by my side. If tomorrow all we had were the clothes on our backs and each other, I'd still be the happiest woman on Earth because I'd be with you. I wouldn't trade a moment we've shared for anything in the world. I promise no matter what you'll always be my knight in shining armor. And someday, when we're old and gray, I'll look back on our life together and know the night I met you was the luckiest night of my life."

With a small smile, Tristan showed me my words touched him like his had mine. We stood there silently, looking at one another like there was no one else in the world at that moment but the two us.

The minister looked at Daryl and Jordan and asked, "The rings?"

We turned and took the rings from them and the minister said, "Repeat after me. I pledge to you my love and my life."

Tristan and I said those words together and gave each other the rings that symbolized our union. All that remained were the minister's final words.

"May you keep the vows you made here today. May you comfort each other, share each other's joys, and support each other in times of trouble. By the power vested in me by the State of New York, I pronounce you Husband and Wife. Tristan, you may kiss your bride."

Cradling my face in his hands, Tristan pressed his lips to mine in a gentle kiss and whispered in my ear, "I love you, Mrs. Stone."

"It's about time. I thought you two would never get here," Daryl joked.

I leaned around my new husband and shot his best man a dirty look. "I'll take that as your congratulations."

Jordan piped up with a comment that put him in his place, and I saw Gage smile at her, probably wishing he had said it. As everyone around us hugged and kissed me and shook Tristan's hand, I thought for a moment how much I wished my father had been there to share this with us.

Performing her maid of honor duties perfectly, Jordan corralled the guests to the table in the garden where the reception was to be held. When they had all moved away, Tristan still stood there, looking down at me in that special way that told me he had something on his mind.

"What's wrong? I see that tiny pout you make when something's wrong."

"It's nothing. I was just thinking about my father and how much I wished he could have been here."

Tristan pulled me close in his arms, and I knew he felt the same. After all that had happened, our love had finally helped us put our families' pasts behind us.

"Somewhere, our mothers are smiling," he said with a wink. "You know how mothers are."

I reached up and gently ran my fingertip over the edge of his eye patch. "I guess I got my pirate after all."

"I guess you did, at least until the doctors say my eye's better. What do you say about letting this pirate escort you to the reception and maybe later I'll make you walk the plank."

"Was that a joke, Mr. Stone?" I asked with a smile, knowing he was working hard to make me forget my sadness over my father missing the biggest day of my life.

He shrugged and said, "It happens sometimes. I don't know what kind of pirate that makes me, though."

Holding his face in my hands, I kissed him long and deep. "It makes you my pirate, and that's the best kind there is."

"I have a surprise for you," he said quietly. "Close your eyes."

I shut them tight and let him lead me ten steps before we stopped. I heard our guests whispering and Tristan said, "You can open them now."

Slowly, I opened my eyes and saw everyone sitting around a long table lit with a line of lanterns and candles down the center. Jordan stood smiling and poked Tristan in the arm. "I wasn't ready yet." Turning to speak to me, she said, "Wait till you see this."

She flipped a switch in her hand and above us what looked like hundreds of little white lights lit up. Strung along grapevines that created a canopy above the table, they twinkled like the night sky. I gazed up at the incredible work Tristan had done to make our reception so beautiful and turned to see him smiling at me. "It's so gorgeous! Thank you."

"I can't take the credit. Jordan is the architect of all this."

I looked over at her and saw her nod. "Your husband here called me as soon as he got home from the hospital and asked for my help. I told him I knew exactly what you'd like. Remember that day we spent looking through all those wedding magazines? You saw that picture of the nighttime garden wedding and loved it. So I told him just leave it to me."

Looking around at all the beautiful decorations and lights, my eyes began to fill with tears at how wonderful the people in my life were. "It's perfect. Thank you. And thank you everyone for being here to celebrate this with us."

"No crying allowed," Jordan joked. "Tonight is a celebration. So let's get to eating and drinking. The best caterer in the city has made us a meal to put all other meals to shame."

Tristan and I sat down at the head of the table as uniformed waiters filled the table with baskets of sliced baguettes and tomato basic garlic crostini. As everyone talked and laughed, a gorgeous summer greens salad was served, and then we all enjoyed our meals of peppered beef and lemon herb chicken home style, sharing our meal together, like it should be.

I watched as the people closest to us enjoyed a night that had been a long time coming. Under the table, Tristan squeezed my hand,

and I turned to see him looking at me. I squeezed his in return and whispered, "You did good here, Mr. Stone."

"You haven't had any cake yet."

"I'm not sure I can fit cake in after all of this," I joked. Of course I would eat a piece of our wedding cake.

His expression grew serious, and he lowered his voice to the merest of whispers. "Are you happy?"

"Crazy, blissfully, in love happy. What about you?"

"Happier than I ever thought I could be. I love you, Nina."

Before I could tell him I couldn't wait until everyone had left so I could show him exactly how much I loved him, a waiter wheeled a cart toward us with a towering pink icing wedding cake made from individual cupcakes decorated to look like pink roses. They were exactly like the picture I'd shown the caterer, even more perfect, if that was possible.

"I made them promise me they'd match your bouquet, Nina," Jordan said with a smile as the cart stopped next to me.

"They're gorgeous!" I said as I took one from the waiter and passed it to Tristan. Turning toward him, I said with a smile, "And if you try to push that cupcake into my face, we're going to have our first married fight, Mr. Stone."

"And ruin a piece of art like this? Never," he said with a chuckle.

"Gorgeous and intelligent. I love that in a husband."

Jordan stood and cleared her throat as the waiter poured champagne into everyone's glasses. When we all had ours, she began her wedding toast.

"Congratulations to Tristan and Nina on their marriage. This day has been a long time coming. I've known Nina for years and always told her that good things happen to good people. I believe that. These two people are the perfect example of that. So now, after all they've been through, this good thing has happened to these good people. Tristan and Nina, here's to great things in your future. You deserve them."

We all raised our glasses, and Tristan clanked ours together as we and our guests said in unison, "To great things!"

I slid my hand over Tristan's and weaved my fingers through his. He turned his head and looked at me with an expression that told me he wished we were alone. I knew how he felt. I did too.

"I think they're going to expect a dance from us at least before they let us sneak off to begin our honeymoon," I said quietly as music began playing behind us.

"Then let's give them what they want," he said with a sexy grin.

He lead me to the center of the garden as the harpist played a love song, and there, for the first time, we danced as husband and wife. Later, after all the guests had gone and we were alone in the house, he took my hand and led me to the sitting room where we'd sat together that first night. As I stood in the middle of the room, he turned on the music and we danced to our song as he whispered the words to Nothing Compares To U by Sinead O'Connor just like he had that summer night a year before.

The music ended and cradling my face in his hands, Tristan whispered, "I love you, Nina. You make happier than I likely deserve."

"You deserve everything good. Remember, good things happen to good people, and you're one of the best people I've ever met, Tristan Stone. So no more talk about not deserving things."

He kissed me and whispered in my ear, "Then let's get this honeymoon started."

Epilogue

Tristan

"Daddy, tell us the story about when you became a pirate!" Tressa squeals as she jumps onto the bed. "Dee wants to hear the princess story, but I want the pirate one."

Diana, her twin sister, struggles to lift her leg to pull herself up onto the bed, so I reach over and take her into my arms. My reward is one of her adorable smiles, a better payment than anything I could ask for.

With a pout, she says in her tiny voice, "Daddy, Tressa pushed me out of the way. I want to hear the princess story. Tell the princess story, pleeeeeease."

Two pairs of brown eyes stare up at me, begging for their favorite stories and making the word no an impossibility. Both girls bounce on their knees as they wait for my decision on which story would be the one for the night.

"Diana! Tressa! Where are you?" Nina calls from the hall. "Are you bothering your father? He just got home from work."

She appears in the doorway, her arms folded across her chest and her best "Mom" face on to let the girls know she isn't happy they've done exactly what she told them not to. I'm more to blame than they are, though, since they know I love to see them after a long day away.

"Girls, your father's tired and it's time for you to go to bed."

Diana turns to face her and quickly answers, "Daddy said he'd tell us a story. He's going to tell us about the princess."

Her sister isn't going to be beaten on this, though. "No, he's going to tell us about when he became a pirate. That's my favorite story ever."

"It's okay, Nina. I like this part of my day best, so I think I'll tell both stories tonight."

In unison, my daughters throw their arms up in the air and yell, "Yay!" They take their seats next to me and wait for me to begin. Which story to choose, though? I prefer the princess story, to be honest.

Nina walks over to the bed and sits down on the edge, taking Tressa's long brown hair in her hands to braid it. "You know what story I like."

I smile at her playful jab. She prefers the pirate story, like Tressa, so now we have a standoff. After pretending to consider my choices, I announce my verdict. "I think the pirate story is the one I'll tell first."

Diana's mouth turns down into an adorable pout much like the one her mother puts on when she's disappointed, so I pull her onto my lap and whisper near her cheek, "But I promise to tell the princess story just for you, honey."

Her pout turns into another of her gentle smiles, and she wraps her little arms around my neck. Kissing me on the cheek, she whispers, "Okay, Daddy."

"One night, your mother and I were at the hotel in the city and she told me that she wished I was a pirate. I told her that I didn't think saying 'Aarrgh' all day during meetings would work, but she insisted that she'd love me even more if I were a pirate."

Tressa reaches out and points at the patch covering my left eye. "And that's why you got an eye patch—because Mommy wanted you to be a pirate."

"Exactly. So now, Mommy gets to say she's married to a pirate."

"Daddy, do the pirate voice!" Tressa squeals. "Please?"

In my deepest voice, I do my best pirate imitation. "Aarrgh, matey! Shiver me timbers!"

The 'shiver me timbers' part always makes her giggle, and she bounces on the bed again, excited her story has been the first one told. Nina just smiles, like she always does when I tell the story to explain why I wear an eyepatch. It's far more interesting and less traumatic than saying I got beaten to a pulp when Karl tried to kill us. Five year old girls demand a far more romantic story than that.

"And that's why you have your pictures on your arms," Tressa says, motioning on her own body where my tattoos are.

"Yes," I say with a smile, amused by the way she refers to them.

Diana touches just above my heart and says, "The snakes are for you and your brother, right?"

I nod. "My brother and I were twins like you and Tressa, so I got the snake tattoo to show we were forever together, no matter what, just like you two."

"Let me see the one about us, Daddy," Tressa pleads as she tries to push up the sleeve on my right arm to show the tattoo I had done right after the girls' birth.

I unbutton my shirt at my wrist and slide the fabric up my arm to show the bottom of a tattoo that depicts an intricate pattern symbolizing both Diana and Tressa. Like the one on my left bicep, it's a tribal design but this extends from my right shoulder down my arm to just above my wrist.

As Tressa runs her fingers over my arm, tracing the tattoo from the crook of my elbow to my wrist bone, Diana whispers in my ear, "Now the princess story, Daddy. Tell the princess story."

"Once upon a time, there was a beautiful princess. She had long brown hair and the prettiest blue eyes. When the prince saw her for the first time, he saw nothing but those blue eyes staring at him. He took her for a ride in his carriage and got to talk to the princess, and he felt like he'd never felt before. She was sweet and gentle and just the kind of princess he wanted."

Nina rolls her eyes and smiles. Diana whispers near my cheek, "Say her name, Daddy."

"And then he found out the princess's name was Nina."

"The same as Mommy's name," Tressa says as she looks back at her mother.

"Yes, it was. So the prince asked the princess to come live with him and help him make his castle more beautiful. Thankfully, she said yes and she became the princess at his castle."

Diana whispers again, "And then she painted the prince a picture, right, Daddy?"

"She did. And she made the prince very happy. Then one day the prince and princess had two little princesses."

"Tressa and Diana!" Tressa screams, throwing her arms up in the air. "No fair, Daddy. That story's about you and Mommy. That's why the pirate story's better."

"Time for bed, girls. Say goodnight to your father."

Nina picks Tressa up and carries her out of the room to the bedroom she shares with her sister. "Goodnight, Daddy!"

Diana remains silent on my lap, staring up at me. Looking down into her soft brown eyes, I ask, "Ready for bed, sweetheart?" as I lift her off my lap and place her feet on the floor.

"Are we princesses, Daddy?" she asks in the cutest little voice.

I look down at her beautiful face and see so much of her mother in her, far more than I ever do when I look at her sister. Tressa is a true Stone—much stronger than Diana, who is gentle and kind, like her mother. She's also very much like Nina with her questions. Tweaking her on the tip of her nose, I nod. "Yes, you're my princesses."

"Will I be a pirate like you when I grow up?" she asks, her eyes wide with curiosity.

Picking her up, I hold her in my arms and kiss her cheek. "No, you won't be a pirate, honey."

She presses her forehead to mine and studies me before she says quietly, "That's because I'm a girl, right?"

I have to laugh at her logic. "No, it's just because there can only be one pirate in the family and I'm already one."

Diana tightens her hold on my neck as I begin walking toward her room. "I love your stories, Daddy. Do the prince and princess live happily ever after?"

We reach her room and I gently place her on the floor in the doorway. Her little face turned up toward me, she waits for the answer to the question she asks me every night. With a smile, I nod. "Yes, they live happily ever after, honey. Night, night."

I opened my eyes to see Nina next to me curled up like she always was in the morning. Rubbing the sleep away, I marveled at how real my dream had been. I almost wanted to walk down the hall to see if we were the parents of two little girls. As I struggled to remember the fine details that were already beginning to slip away, I shook my head as if to answer my own doubts.

Nina snuggled next to my side. I wrapped her in my arms and kissed the top of her head, still thinking about the children in my dream. Twins, just like my brother and me, they were as different as night and day.

"Hey, what's up? You've been tossing and turning all night," Nina said quietly. "You okay?"

Looking down, I saw her smiling up at me as she laid her head on my chest. "I'm fine. Just had a wild dream."

"What about?"

"Well, we had twin daughters named Diana and Tressa, for one thing."

Nina smiled a big grin. "Two little girls? I've always dreamed of having a little girl, but two would be even better. And twins? Wow!"

"Not feeling too rushed, are you? We're still on our honeymoon and I'm already talking about kids. Or at least my dreams are."

"Wait until I tell Jordan. Twins she can be an aunt to. She's going to love it."

"How do you feel about it? That's the important part."

She thought about it for a moment and smiled slyly. "I like it. I guess only time will tell."

Rolling her over, I slid over her body and kissed her on the lips. "Time may tell, but I think for now, we should see what we can do to help it along."

As she looked up at me with love in her eyes, she nodded. "I like the way you think, Mr. Stone."

For now, it was just the two of us, but maybe someday we'd be blessed with those little girls I dreamed about. Until then, Nina was my princess and I was her pirate.

And we'd finally found our happily ever after.

THE END

Club X—A private club where all your fantasies can come true
Meet the gorgeous men of Club X…

Cassian March, the face of Club X, the most exclusive nightspot in Tampa. One of the most eligible men in town, he can have any woman he chooses—and he does as often as he likes. Beneath his cool facade lies a desire for something more, but will his new assistant Olivia have what it takes to fulfill his darkest fantasies?

Stefan March, the manager of Club X, loves the single life. Women are his playground, and this man lives to have fun. Committed to never settling down, he may have met his match in Shay, a bartender at Club X who seems immune to his charms. Stefan loves nothing more than a challenge, though, so let the games begin!

Kane Jackson, half-brother to Cassian and Stefan, he handles the members' fantasies at Club X. Big, bad, and dangerous, his style is hard, like the life he's led. But you know what they say—the bigger they are, the harder they fall and Kane might just fall for Abbi, the one woman able to get beyond his hard exterior to the heart he hides from the world.

LOOK FOR THE CLUB X SERIES TODAY!

Love sexy paranormal romance? K.M. writes under the name Gabrielle Bisset too! Visit Gabrielle's Facebook page and her website at http://www.gabriellebisset.com/ to find out about her books.

Books by Gabrielle Bisset:

Vampire Dreams Revamped (A Sons of Navarus Prequel)
Blood Avenged (Sons of Navarus #1)
Blood Betrayed (Sons of Navarus #2)
Longing (A Sons of Navarus Short Story)
Blood Spirit (Sons of Navarus #3)
The Deepest Cut (A Sons of Navarus Short Story)
Blood Prophecy (Sons of Navarus #4)
Blood & Dreams Sons of Navarus Box Set

Stolen Destiny
Destiny Redeemed

Love's Master
Masquerade
The Victorian Erotic Romance Trilogy